About the Author

Kevin J. Anderson has over 16 million books in print in 29 languages worldwide. He is the author of the X-FILES novels GROUND ZERO (number 1 bestseller in THE TIMES and voted Best SF Novel of the Year by SFX magazine), RUINS, and ANTIBODIES, as well as the JEDI ACADEMY trilogy of STAR WARS novels – the best-selling SF novels of 1994. He is also writing the prequels to Frank Herbert's monumental DUNE series, with Frank's son, Brian Herbert – the US deal for this was the largest contract in SF publishing history. He has won, or been nominated for, the Nebula Award, Bram Stoker Award, Reader's Choice Award from the Science Fiction Book Club, and many others. He is currently writing the fifth volume of the SAGA OF SEVEN SUNS.

Kevin Anderson lives in Colorado.
www.wordfire.com

HORIZON STORMS

the saga of seven suns

BOOK THREE

KEVIN J. ANDERSON

POCKET BOOKS

LONDON • SYDNEY • NEW YORK • TORONTO

First published in Great Britain by Simon & Schuster UK Ltd, 2004
This edition first published by Pocket Books, 2005
An imprint of Simon & Schuster UK Ltd
A Viacom Company

1 3 5 7 9 10 8 6 4 2

Simon & Schuster UK Ltd
Africa House
64–78 Kingsway
London WC2B 6AH

www.simonsays.co.uk

Simon & Schuster Australia
Sydney

A CIP catalogue record for this book is available from the British Library

ISBN 0-7434-3067-0
EAN 9780743430678

Typeset in Weiss by SX Composing DTP, Rayleigh, Essex
Printed and bound in Great Britain by
Cox & Wyman Ltd, Reading, Berkshire

ACKNOWLEDGEMENTS

v

As this series gets longer and more complex, I have had to rely on the assistance of more and more people. Jaime Levine and Devi Pillai at Warner Aspect have helped to shape this series with their editorial suggestions, both large-scale and subtle; John Jarrold, Darren Nash, and Melissa Weatherill have done the same for the UK editions of these books.

Geoffrey Girard jumped into the series with both feet and sharp eyes (to use an anatomically impossible mixed metaphor) to help me minimize contradictions in the details across the volumes.

Catherine Sidor and Diane Jones at WordFire, Inc. offered many opinions and ideas in our brainstorming sessions; Catherine nearly wore the tips off of her fingers by typing the chapters as fast as I could hand her my microcassettes.

Many of the places and events were inspired by the 'Seven Suns' artwork of Rob Teranishi and Igor Kordey, who created the visual universe for *Veiled Alliances*, the 'Seven Suns' graphic novel. I am also indebted to the vision of my fabulous cover artists, Stephen Youll and Chris Moore.

My agents John Silbersack, Robert Gottlieb, and Kim Whalen at Trident Media Group have helped greatly to make this series a success both in the US and in many languages around the world.

And, most of all, my wife Rebecca Moesta spent a great deal of time and mental energy to work with me on *Horizon Storms* from the outline, through drafts, all the way to the final manuscript. Her insight, as well as her patience and her love, have made this the best book possible.

To DEAN KOONTZ,

who has offered his advice, ideas, and encouragement since the very beginning of my career. A long time ago, he told me to 'think big' with my stories; now, with *The Saga of Seven Suns* already longer than Tolstoy's *War and Peace*, I hope this is what he meant!

THE STORY SO FAR

For the first test of the Klikiss Torch – a device discovered in the ruins of the ancient alien Klikiss civilization – the Terran Hanseatic League (the Hansa) ignited a gas-giant planet, creating a small sun. The Hansa's suave Chairman BASIL WENCESLAS intended to terraform the gas giant's frozen moons into new colonies. Humanity had spread across many available worlds under the benevolent but reticent watch of the alien Ildiran Empire and its godlike leader, the MAGE-IMPERATOR. The Ildirans, represented by their Solar Navy commander, ADAR KORI'NH, were sceptical about the Torch project, but came to observe the test.

When the gas planet was ignited, instant reports were transmitted around the galaxy by BENETO, a 'green priest' from the forested planet *Theroc* who had a symbiosis with semi-sentient 'worldtrees'. Like living telegraph stations, green priests provide the only form of instant communication across vast distances through the forest network. Back on Earth, OLD KING FREDERICK, a glamorous figurehead ruler, led a celebration of the successful test.

Unknown to anyone, though, this and many gas planets were inhabited by a powerful alien species, the HYDROGUES. The Hansa had just destroyed one of their populous worlds and unwittingly declared war on an entire hidden empire.

On *Ildira*, the Mage-Imperator's first-born son, PRIME DESIGNATE JORA'H, welcomed the human REYNALD, Beneto's brother and heir to the throne of Theroc. As a token of friendship, Jora'h invited Reynald to send two green priests to study the grand Ildiran epic, the *Saga of Seven Suns*. On his way home, Reynald met in space with the Roamers, fiercely independent space gypsies led by old SPEAKER JHY OKIAH and her beautiful protégée CESCA PERONI. Since both Roamers and Theroc were technically independent of the Terran Hanseatic League, Reynald discussed a possible alliance, even suggesting marriage with Cesca, but she was already betrothed to a skyminer, ROSS TAMBLYN (while secretly in love with his brother JESS).

The merchant woman RLINDA KETT came to Theroc in the *Voracious Curiosity*, hoping to open trade between Theroc and the Hansa. She was supported by ambitious SAREIN, sister to Reynald and Beneto, but MOTHER ALEXA and FATHER IDRISS were happy with their isolation on Theroc. Rlinda agreed to deliver two green priests – old OTEMA and bright-eyed young NIRA – to Ildira at the invitation of Prime Designate Jora'h.

On Earth, Chairman Wenceslas secretly began searching for a replacement for King Frederick. Basil's henchmen kidnapped a scamp, RAYMOND AGUERRA, then staged a terrible fire in his dwelling, killing his mother and three brothers, leaving no evidence. The Hansa then altered the young man's appearance, told him he was now 'Prince Peter', and began brainwashing him, using the Teacher 'compy' (a companion robot) OX to instruct him in his new role.

After the success of the Klikiss Torch, the archaeologists who had discovered the technology, MARGARET and LOUIS COLICOS, began a new excavation on the desert planet of *Rheindic Co*, where ancient Klikiss cities remained untouched. The only functional remnants of the alien civilization, their hulking beetle-like robots, explained that their memories had been erased long ago. To learn more about their own past, three of these antique robots accompanied the Colicoses to the excavation site. The archaeology team also included a compy, DD, and a green priest. While Louis studied the ruins, Margaret worked to decipher Klikiss hieroglyphics in the hope of finding answers.

Meanwhile, angered by their near genocide, the hydrogues began to attack human facilities around gas giants. One of their first targets was a 'skymine' – a huge cloudtop facility that skimmed gas giants for *ekti*, vital stardrive fuel – owned by Cesca's fiancé Ross Tamblyn. Roamers and their skymines were the main suppliers of ekti to the Hansa and the Ildiran Empire. The hydrogues also destroyed the space station left to observe the new sun at the Klikiss Torch site – never demanding terms, never showing mercy. These unexpected attacks stunned both the Hansa and the Roamers. Chairman Wenceslas met with the commander of the Earth Defence Forces (EDF), gruff GENERAL KURT LANYAN, to discuss the threat. Old King Frederick worked to rally the populace, recruiting new volunteers for the EDF.

Vowing revenge for her brother Ross, spunky Roamer TASIA TAMBLYN heard the call and ran off to join the military, taking her compy EA and leaving her brother Jess in charge of the family water mines. Although Ross's death left Jess Tamblyn and Cesca Peroni free to confess their love, they couldn't bring themselves to take advantage of the tragic situation for personal gain.

Meanwhile, Raymond Aguerra continued training to become the next King, watched over by OX. At first he enjoyed the change from the rough streets to the opulent palace, but soon he began to resent the rigid control imposed upon him. To his horror, he discovered that the Hansa had arranged the deaths of his family.

On Ildira, the green priest Nira spent a great deal of time with Prime Designate Jora'h, who was destined to become the next Ildiran leader. Though he had many assigned mates, he genuinely fell in love with Nira. Another son of the Mage-Imperator, the grim and intense DOBRO DESIGNATE UDRU'H, interrogated Nira about her telepathic potential as a green priest, then reported to the Mage-Imperator about secret Ildiran breeding experiments on the planet *Dobro*. Udru'h suggested that Nira might have the DNA potential they needed for the breeding project.

Digging through supposedly perfect and indisputable records of their past, an Ildiran historian uncovered documents proving that the hydrogues had appeared long ago in a previous war, but that all mention of the conflict had been *censored* from the *Saga of Seven Suns*. Before he could reveal his shocking discovery, the Mage-Imperator killed him, saying 'I *wanted* it kept secret.'

Solar Navy commander Adar Kori'nh promoted ZAN'NH, the first-born son of Prime Designate Jora'h, and took the fleet to the gas giant *Qronha 3*, the site of an old Ildiran skymining facility. When hydrogue warglobes rose from the clouds to destroy the ekti facility, the Solar Navy engaged in a furious battle. Although hydrogue weaponry proved far superior, one Ildiran subcommander crashed his battleship into the nearest sphere, destroying it and giving the Solar Navy time to retreat with the rescued skyminers. In the thousands of years chronicled in the *Saga of Seven Suns*, no Ildiran had ever experienced such a terrible and humiliating defeat.

On Earth, the EDF built new ships and commandeered civilian spacecraft to mount a defence against further hydrogue attacks. Rlinda Kett was forced to surrender all of her merchant ships to the war effort, except for the *Voracious Curiosity*. Newly enlisted Tasia Tamblyn excelled in military training, besting spoiled-brat Earth recruits. Her particular bane was PATRICK FITZPATRICK III; her closest friend was fellow trainee, ROBB BRINDLE.

In an uproar after the repeated hydrogue attacks, many Roamers ceased all skymining, but Jess Tamblyn decided to strike the enemy aliens himself. He gathered loyal workers and went to where the hydrogues had destroyed his brother Ross's skymine. They sent giant comets plummeting down to batter the gas planet with the force of atomic warheads.

Upon learning that the Ildirans had also been attacked by hydrogues, Chairman Wenceslas went to meet with the Mage-Imperator to propose an alliance. The hydrogues had neither acknowledged nor responded to requests for negotiation. While Basil was away on Ildira, however, a giant warglobe appeared at Earth and a hydrogue emissary demanded to speak with flustered and incompetent King Frederick. Contained within a pressure vessel, the alien emissary informed the King that the Klikiss Torch had annihilated a hydrogue planet, slaughtering millions of their people. Frederick apologized for the inadvertent genocide, but the hydrogue demanded that all skymining cease. This would mean no ekti fuel for the Ildiran stardrive, the only viable method of space travel. As Frederick pleaded with him, the hydrogue emissary detonated his containment tank, killing the King and all observers in the throne hall.

Basil rushed back to Earth and told royal trainee Raymond that 'King Peter' must take the throne immediately. Peter gave a carefully scripted speech, defying the hydrogue ultimatum and declaring that humans would take the fuel necessary for their survival. He dispatched a battle group, including Tasia Tamblyn and Robb Brindle, along with commercial ekti harvesters to Jupiter. For several days all was quiet, but then warglobes engaged the EDF in a terrible battle. Tasia and Robb survived, although the battered human ships limped away, beaten . . .

Before anyone learned of the humiliating defeat, Basil presided over King Peter's coronation, designed as a show of hope and confidence. Peter, hiding his hatred for Basil, was drugged into cooperation. Feigning paternal pride, Basil promised the new King that if he behaved, they would find him a Queen . . .

On Ildira, Nira discovered that she was pregnant with Jora'h's child, but before she could tell him, the Mage-Imperator dispatched Jora'h on a diplomatic mission. Then, in the stillness of a sleep period, brutal Ildiran guards captured Nira and stabbed to death her mentor, Otema, who was too old for the breeding pens. Nira was turned over to the evil Dobro Designate for genetic experimentation . . .

At the Roamer capital of *Rendezvous*, Speaker Okiah challenged the resourceful clans to find alternatives to skymining, then abdicated her position in favour of Cesca. Jess watched the woman he loved take her place as a strong leader, realizing she was farther away from him now than ever before.

On distant Rheindic Co, the Colicos team discovered an arcane transportation system, a dimensional doorway controlled by complex machinery. Though the Klikiss robots insisted they remembered nothing, Margaret was able to translate archaic records. Apparently the robots themselves had been responsible for the disappearance of their parent race and were also involved in an ancient war with the hydrogues! Surprised by this news, Margaret and Louis rushed back to their camp, only to find that their green priest had been murdered and all communication cut off.

Working with their faithful compy DD, Margaret and Louis barricaded themselves in the cliff-city, but the sinister Klikiss robots broke through. Although DD attempted to defend his masters, the robots captured him, taking care not to hurt a fellow intelligent machine. At the last moment, Louis got the 'transportal' functioning, opening a doorway to an unknown alien world. He urged Margaret through. Then, before he could join her, the gate closed – and the robots were upon him.

For five years, the hydrogue war continued; the human race and the Ildiran Empire struggled to cope with the loss of stardrive fuel. King Peter announced strict rationing schemes, taking public blame for the act while Basil Wenceslas made all the real decisions. Roamer daredevils led by Jess Tamblyn and DEL KELLUM – a clan head who ran shipbuilding operations in the rings of the gas planet *Osquivel* – made hit-and-run sweeps on gas giants, grabbing ekti before the hydrogues could strike them; many missions ended in tragedy.

Prime Designate Jora'h was told that his beloved Nira had been killed in a fire; the Mage-Imperator kept the Dobro breeding scheme secret from him, along with the fact that Nira was alive and well, being used as a test subject. After bearing OSIRA'H, Jora'h's own daughter, Nira gave birth to several more half-breed children. She had no choice but to perform the slave labour imposed on her and other human captives taken generations ago from a lost colony ship, the *Burton*. To ensure that no one from the Hansa discovered the breeding camp, the Dobro Designate ordered the destruction of the derelict *Burton*. Adar Kori'nh reluctantly followed his orders, but was disturbed to get rid of such a historic relic. The breeding programme had to remain secret.

On Nira's home planet of Theroc, Reynald searched for a suitable wife, accompanied by his younger sister ESTARRA, since he would soon replace his parents as the leader of his people. Their grandparents urged them both to choose a good match, since Reynald and Estarra had plenty of responsibility on their shoulders.

Cut off from the traditional business of skymining, the Roamers developed new schemes for obtaining fuel – from breaking down cometary ice, to flying huge nebula sails. Eccentric engineer

KOTTO OKIAH established a risky metals-processing colony on the extremely hot planet of *Isperos*. At the shipyards in the rings of Osquivel, Del Kellum showed Jess all he had done; his daughter ZHETT was clearly interested in Jess, but he was still in love with Cesca.

Jess's sister Tasia was sent with a group of battleships to the rebellious Hansa colony of *Yreka*, where settlers were hoarding ekti. The EDF cracked down hard, first isolating and then raiding Yreka, confiscating all stardrive fuel for military uses; Tasia was uneasy that the EDF chose to turn their might against their own struggling colonies, instead of the real hydrogue enemy.

Chairman Wenceslas, who had been hoping that Margaret and Louis Colicos might unearth another weapon as useful as the Klikiss Torch, discovered that the archaeologists had vanished without a trace. Although their scholar son, ANTON COLICOS, had sent repeated inquiries about his missing parents, his letters vanished into Hansa bureaucracy. Before Anton could learn anything, he received a surprise invitation from an Ildiran historian, REMEMBERER VAO'SH, to study the *Saga of Seven Suns* on Ildira. He eagerly accepted.

Chairman Wenceslas sent the merchant woman Rlinda Kett to *Crenna* to pick up an undercover spy, DAVLIN LOTZE, and take him to Rheindic Co in order to discover what had happened to the Colicos team. While on Crenna, Rlinda also met with her favourite ex-husband BRANSON 'BeBob' ROBERTS, who had been drafted to fly EDF recon missions against the hydrogues but chose to go AWOL instead. Leaving BeBob behind, Rlinda took Davlin to Rheindic Co, where they found the bodies of Louis Colicos and the green priest, but no sign at all of Margaret or their compy DD.

Hapless, kidnapped DD watched the evil Klikiss robots perform horrific tests on captured compies to 'free' them from the programming that forced them to obey humans. DD also discovered that thousands of Klikiss robots, buried in a sort of hibernation, were being reawakened as part of their insidious schemes. The robots took little DD into a gas giant to the bizarre high-pressure cities of the hydrogues. There, DD learned that the Klikiss robots were forming a deadly alliance with the hydrogues against humans, but the little compy was helpless to stop their plans.

On Earth, King Peter and Basil Wenceslas were surprised when a Klikiss robot, JORAX, unexpectedly volunteered to let himself be dismantled for science. Jorax claimed that the Klikiss robots wanted to assist humans in the hydrogue war, and that the robotic technology could be used to create highly proficient Soldier compies. Peter was suspicious of the offer, but Basil saw too many possible benefits to turn it down. The robot was dissected, and many of the Klikiss robot programming modules were immediately copied, adapted, and put into production.

While sleeping with Sarein, Basil complained that the aloof green priests would be extremely valuable as communication tools in the war, but they refused to help. Sarein suggested a plan to strengthen ties between Theroc and the Hansa: her sister Estarra should marry King Peter. When they attended Reynald's coronation ceremony on the forested world, Basil and Sarein offered this plan to the new leader of Theroc, and he accepted. When Estarra learned the news, she was at first surprised and alarmed – she had never met Peter – but her friend, the eccentric green priest ROSSIA, encouraged her to give the alliance a chance. Estarra communicated with her brother Beneto, serving as green priest on *Corvus Landing*, and he wished her well. Sarein then spoke to the gathered green priests and convinced nineteen of them, including her uncle YARROD, to volunteer to help the EDF.

After his little sister's engagement to the King, Reynald sent a marriage proposal to Cesca Peroni. Though she was in love with

Jess and continued to meet him for secret assignations, they had never formalized their plans. Now, for the good of her people, she considered the proposed alliance with the Therons. Jess urged Cesca to accept the offer, regardless of her feelings for him. To make the choice easier for her, Jess signed up for a long and lonely voyage to collect ekti in one of Del Kellum's nebula skimmers; he launched from the Osquivel shipyards and flew off alone into space, leaving Cesca to do what she must.

On Ildira, the Mage-Imperator revealed to Prime Designate Jora'h that he was dying and that Jora'h would soon have to take the throne. Adar Kori'nh escorted Jora'h to the pleasure planet of *Hyrillka* to retrieve his oldest noble-born son THOR'H, who was destined to replace him as the next Prime Designate. Thor'h resented his change of status from his soft life and pouted when his father told him he must prepare for his new duties. The Adar's warliners put on a spectacular performance for hedonistic DESIGNATE RUSA'H.

Before they could depart, a group of hydrogue warglobes swept in to destroy Hyrillka. Designate Rusa'h was seriously injured as the citadel palace collapsed around him. Although Adar Kori'nh and his warliners were resoundingly trounced, he managed to escape with Jora'h, Thor'h, and the unconscious Rusa'h.

When they returned to Ildira, the dying Mage-Imperator instructed Kori'nh to abandon weaker colonies in the Ildiran Empire to consolidate their strengths. Kori'nh saw this as a devastating blow: for the first time in millennia, the Empire was shrinking – and under his watch! While Rusa'h remained in his coma, the Mage-Imperator revealed to Jora'h details of an ancient hidden war, in which the hydrogues had been allied with fiery beings known as FAEROS against watery entities called WENTALS and a forest mind called the VERDANI. Jora'h realized that the sentient worldtrees on Theroc must be the verdani, and he began to suspect that his beloved Nira might not have died in the convenient way his father described.

In the Ildiran breeding barracks on Dobro, Nira told the prisoners stories about what life was like for free humanity. Unfortunately, they had been experimental subjects for so many generations they could not imagine freedom. Designate Udru'h trained Nira's daughter Osira'h to enhance her mental powers. Udru'h brainwashed the little girl to believe she was the saviour of the Ildiran race in the struggle against the hydrogues. When Nira and other prisoners were put to work fighting a brush fire in the hills, Nira tried to escape, rushing to scrub trees and attempting to use her green priest abilities to call for help. But the trees were silent, and she was captured, beaten, and dragged back to the camps.

General Lanyan went on a survey cruise with Tasia Tamblyn's old nemesis, Patrick Fitzpatrick III. They encountered a lone Roamer cargo ship; after confiscating his load of ekti, Fitzpatrick quietly destroyed the ship and its captain, careful to leave no witnesses. Later, the EDF battle group responded to a distress call from a planet under attack by hydrogue warglobes. Aided by an innovative idea from Tasia, they rescued many of the colonists, but they could not fight the hydrogues. Tasia's lover Robb Brindle chased after the departing enemy, tracking them to the ringed gas planet Osquivel, the site of Del Kellum's secret Roamer shipyards. When Robb reported his find to the EDF commanders, General Lanyan decided to make an all-out attack on Osquivel. Knowing that the hidden Roamer facility would surely be found, Tasia sent her loyal compy EA off to warn Speaker Peroni. Meeting with the EDF commanders, Robb proposed a risky scheme to go down in an encounter vessel in a last attempt to communicate with the hydrogues before the EDF attacked; it was almost certainly a suicide mission.

When EA delivered her warning, the Roamers at Osquivel scrambled to hide their shipyard before the EDF could arrive. By the time Tasia and her fleet came to the ringed planet, the Roamers had completed their work just in time. Robb descended in his diving bell, offering a last chance for negotiation, but his transmissions cut off abruptly. When hydrogue warglobes opened fire, Robb was presumed dead, and General Lanyan ordered a full-scale attack, using the new Soldier compies. The battle was a massacre of human ships. Zhett Kellum and her father watched the disaster from their hiding places in the planet's rings. Ship after ship was destroyed, and the scattered EDF finally declared a retreat, leaving fallen comrades behind. Tasia barely managed to drag her cruiser away; Patrick Fitzpatrick's ship was destroyed. Utterly defeated, the remnants of the fleet limped home . . .

Cesca travelled with celebratory Roamer ships to formally accept Reynald's offer of marriage. Jess was far away, alone, on his nebula skimmer, collecting hydrogen, gases, and water molecules. Gradually sensing that he was no longer alone, Jess realized that the water was somehow alive and began to communicate with it. He had gathered one of the supernatural beings, a wental, which told him about the ancient war against the hydrogues. Jess now had a new mission: if he dispersed this wental to other water planets, helped it grow strong again, then humanity could have a powerful ally against the hydrogues. He took the wental to an empty ocean world, where the entity miraculously spread; then Jess departed to find another candidate planet.

On Rheindic Co searching for information about Margaret Colicos, the spy Davlin Lotze accidentally discovered how to activate the Klikiss transportals and was whisked to another planet, while Rlinda Kett could only watch helplessly. Through experimentation, Davlin activated the transportation system again and spent days hopping from planet to planet, until he finally found his way back to Rlinda, who had nearly given up on him. Though exhausted and near starvation, Davlin was also exhilarated – he had discovered a new means of interplanetary travel that did not require the embargoed stardrive fuel ekti!

Still without word of his missing parents, Anton Colicos travelled to meet with the historian Vao'sh at the Prism Palace where he learned about Ildiran tales and culture. After spending time on the main world, he and Vao'sh were assigned to the resort planet of *Maratha*, which was in constant sunlight for half the year and full darkness the other half. Klikiss robots were constructing a second city on the opposite side of the world, but the buildings were not finished. Eager to show the dark-fearing Ildirans the thrill of a 'haunted house', Anton convinced a group to visit the dark-side construction site, where the black robots diligently worked. Later, as the day season ended, all tourists left Maratha, and only a small skeleton crew remained behind during the long night. Anton and Vao'sh also stayed, waiting as the darkness fell . . .

At the Roamer base on the near-molten world of Isperos, Kotto Okiah's systems began to break down. Though he struggled to hold the base together, too many components failed, and he knew they were doomed. Kotto sent an urgent call to the Roamers, who responded with rescue ships. But the solar flares increased and the hellish environment was so harsh that the ships began to overload as they tried to take the refugees to safety. Before they fell to the punishing storm, however, fiery ellipsoidal ships emerged from the sun itself. At first the panicked Roamers feared they were under attack, but the fireballs – the faeros – actually protected them until they could get away . . .

Back at the space battlefield at Osquivel, Roamers inspected the EDF wrecks to see what they could salvage. Zhett found a drifting lifetube that contained a weak Patrick Fitzpatrick.

Although she nursed him to health, she could never let him return to his former life, because he knew too many Roamer secrets.

Destined to be the next Queen, Estarra arrived on Earth. When she finally met Peter, she felt a connection with him, but Basil kept them carefully apart. As the wedding preparations proceeded swiftly after the EDF defeat at Osquivel, she had little chance to get to know the man who would become her husband, but her sister Sarein arranged for them to have time together. During the spectacular wedding, Peter pointedly snubbed the Chairman, making Basil very angry. On their wedding night, the King and Queen felt they could be much stronger together, and perhaps even learn to fall in love with each other . . .

Prime Designate Jora'h sent resentful Thor'h back to Hyrillka to supervise the reconstruction activities after the hydrogue attack. Jora'h followed his suspicions, eventually discovering that Nira was indeed alive and held hostage on Dobro – and that her daughter by him, Osira'h, was being trained as a new Ildiran weapon. Feeling betrayed, Jora'h confronted his father and the Dobro Designate, neither of whom denied the accusations, insisting only that Jora'h must accept the truth for the good of the Empire. For days, Jora'h tried to commandeer a ship to Dobro so that he could see Nira again. When the ailing Mage-Imperator realized that the Prime Designate would never understand, he took his only course of action: a Mage-Imperator knows everything in the Ildiran racial mind through his connection with the telepathic force of *thism*. Jora'h would know his place once he became the next godlike leader. Therefore the Mage-Imperator poisoned himself, leaving his son no choice but to do his duty.

The death of the Mage-Imperator severed the telepathic bond holding the Ildiran race together, sending a mental shockwave across the galaxy. Jora'h collapsed, then dragged himself to his father's deathbed. All around the Empire, Ildiran men cut off their hair and nearly went insane.

On patrol with the Solar Navy, Adar Kori'nh had felt helpless and resentful, his hands tied by clear orders that he must never engage the hydrogues. After the shocking death of the Mage-Imperator, though, he realized that, for once, he could act entirely on his own, without the leader observing his every action. He called forty-nine of his battleships and went to Qronha 3, the site of the first major Ildiran defeat by the hydrogues. Kori'nh remembered how one of his officers had destroyed an enemy warglobe by crashing his ship headlong into it. Now, when the hydrogues rose up to meet them, Kori'nh gave his orders – and all forty-nine of his battleships slammed into enemy vessels, reaping a great but costly victory, and earning himself a place in the *Saga of Seven Suns* for ever.

Prowling hydrogues encountered Jess Tamblyn on his journey to disperse the wentals, ancient enemies of the hydrogues. The water entities told Jess that he had to survive. On their instructions, he drank a vial of the energized wentals just as the hydrogues destroyed his ship over a cloudy and uncharted planet. Jess later woke up, floating in an alien sea – charged with superhuman powers, but marooned and completely cut off from everything he knew, including his beloved Cesca . . .

The hydrogues next attacked Corvus Landing, where Estarra's brother Beneto made his home. The aliens sent a small ship to Beneto's worldtree grove, demanding to know the location of the main worldforest. The trees came alive and destroyed the emissary, but the larger warglobes obliterated the colony and all the worldtrees. Beneto remained connected through the forest, reporting what was happening up until the last minute . . .

Friction continued between King Peter and the Chairman, especially after Basil made Peter issue an abortion decree to reduce the populations of struggling colonies. The King wanted to think and rule for himself – which did not sit well with Basil, especially since Peter did not agree with all of Basil's actions and decisions. The Hansa even announced the existence of 'Prince Daniel', a replacement in training for Peter, should he continue to be intractable. Peter christened and dispatched a survey group of EDF battleships, crewed primarily by Soldier compies, with only a few token humans aboard; the ships went to observe a hydrogue planet . . . and vanished without a trace.

While studying the Soldier compies, the Teacher compy OX discovered enough troubling details to make the King's suspicions stronger. Peter issued a royal order to shut down the compy factories until the copied Klikiss technology was better understood. Basil angrily countermanded the order, since the Hansa desperately needed Soldier compies for the war. This was the last straw for him; the Chairman put into motion an assassination plot that would remove King Peter and Queen Estarra, while implicating the annoyingly independent Roamers in the crime. With the help of OX and Estarra, Peter foiled the plot, but now the King and Chairman knew they had to watch each other every moment.

Finally learning the location of the worldforest, a massive fleet of hydrogue warglobes arrived and immediately began to destroy Theroc. Led by Reynald, the Therons tried to fight back against the hydrogues. Mother Alexa and Father Idriss evacuated the people to the lower levels, but even that was no use. The towering trees retaliated, crushing some of the enemy warglobes, but they quickly faltered. Unexpectedly, faero fireballs arrived, joining the forest in its fight against the hydrogues. The titanic battle obliterated many hydrogues and faeros, and the collateral destruction set great portions of the worldforest on fire. Reynald's youngest sister CELLI was caught high in a burning tree, only to be rescued by a young green priest. Reynald himself died in the treetops when a duelling fireball and warglobe crashed into the canopy. Eventually, the faeros drove off the hydrogues. The enemies departed, leaving the worldforest in burning ruins.

When Tasia's compy EA returned from secretly warning the Roamers about the Osquivel offensive, Basil intercepted the compy and tried to interrogate her. But EA's automated systems wiped her memory core, shutting her down. Suspicious, Basil ordered scientists to study EA; as far as Tasia knew, her compy had never arrived back from her mission. Meanwhile, Tasia went to inspect the site of the original Klikiss Torch test, where she was surprised to discover the hydrogues and faeros engaged in a giant struggle in the burning star itself. Eventually the hydrogues extinguished the sun, killing the faeros . . .

Receiving good news at last, Basil listened as Davlin and Rlinda described the new Klikiss transportal system they had discovered on Rheindic Co. The dimensional gateways required no rare ekti. Basil seized the opportunity and announced a new colonization scheme to send people to abandoned Klikiss worlds through the transportals – essentially establishing a new network that bypassed the fuel shortages.

On Ildira, Jora'h ascended to become the new Mage-Imperator and endured a castration ceremony that gave him access to all *thism* and the entire truth. He suddenly understood the terrible plots his predecessors had arranged; he didn't know how he could endure it, but he had to continue the distasteful work. On Dobro, while Designate Udru'h was away attending Jora'h's ascension, Nira escaped from the breeding barracks long enough to meet with her daughter Osira'h, to whom she was mentally linked. Joined together for just a moment, Nira telepathically revealed her past and everything she knew about the awful things that were being done there. As Osira'h reeled from the knowledge she had been given, Nira was dragged off by Udru'h's guards and clubbed. No longer able to sense her mother, Osira'h began to turn her thoughts against Designate Udru'h and his schemes . . .

King Peter and Queen Estarra, still fearful for their lives because of Basil's machinations, looked into the sky at the stars, knowing that out there the war between hydrogues and faeros continued, and that sun after sun was winking out . . .

ONE

CELLI

Though blackened by flames, the surviving worldtrees on Theroc remained defiant in the aftermath of the nightmare that had befallen them. Skeletal branches twisted upwards, frozen in agony, as if warding off an unexpected blow from the skies. Damaged bark had sloughed away like leprous scabs. Many of the trees had been mortally wounded. The forest itself was a morass of dead branches and half-fallen trees.

Celli, the youngest child of Mother Alexa and Father Idriss, could not look at the painful ruins without blinking back tears that came too readily to her large brown eyes. At eighteen, she was skinny, tomboyish, with a dusting of light freckles on her mocha skin. She had a shag of short, corkscrewy auburn hair that she cut only when it got in her way. Soot and ash scuffed her cropped, fitted top that left her midriff bare and her short flutter skirt that added a splash of colour. Normally, she had a bright smile beneath her upturned nose, but of late there had been few occasions to smile.

After the hydrogues had been driven back, it had taken all the remaining energy of the worldforest, a herculean effort from the

Therons, and the assistance of a delayed rescue fleet from the Earth Defence Forces, to bring the wildfires mostly under control.

Even so, whole continents lay wasted. Some patches still burned, and smoke rose into the blue sky like stains drawn by bloody fingers. Each day green priests and Theron labourers gathered at central meeting places to face the endless task of recovery.

Each day, Celli joined them. With every breath as she ran along, the sour stench of burned pulpy foliage caught in her throat, and she knew that she would find the smell of roasting meat and burning wood nauseating for the rest of her life.

When she arrived at what remained of the fungus-reef city, an enormous shelf mushroom that had coalesced over the centuries, she gazed up at it with a fresh sense of shock. The host tree had been badly burned and the fungus reef half destroyed, the carved-out pocket rooms unsuitable for habitation.

In a trampled clearing beneath the damaged fungus reef, her parents – though overwhelmed by the enormity of the task – did their best to organize the weary, red-eyed workers. Idriss and Alexa had officially retired from their leadership role and made Celli's oldest brother, Reynald, their king. But he had been killed in the hydrogue attack. She remembered her last vision of him, standing defiantly atop the worldforest canopy as the hydrogues and faeros battled overhead . . .

Today, though, as on every other day since the hydrogue attack, no one would stop to mourn, or dwell on thoughts of all those who had died. To pause right now in their labours, even out of pure grief, would have been too self-indulgent. There were countless trees and people that could yet be saved, if only there were hands enough to do the necessary work. That was why all Therons who were not too severely injured returned without complaint to the tasks that must be done. Celli, like every other Theron, grieved while on the move.

Her brother was lost along with so many others, including three of Celli's close friends and her other brother, Beneto, a green priest killed when the hydrogues attacked Corvus Landing. Every day, moment by moment, Celli worked to the point of exhaustion, trying to avoid the worst of the pain. She didn't dare think too long about Lica, Kari or Ren for fear that the grief might immobilize her.

Before the hydrogue attack, Celli and her friends had spent their days amusing themselves in the forest, never thinking much beyond the next day or two. She would practise treedancing moves, and Ren was particularly good at catching condorflies. Lica and Kari both liked the same boy, but he hadn't noticed either one of them. How they had all laughed and played together, never expecting anything to change . . .

None of them had ever guessed that enemies might lie beyond the sky.

Celli, the baby of the family, was now the only one of her siblings left on Theroc, since her sisters, Sarein and Estarra, both lived in the Whisper Palace on Earth. In the past, her sisters had often accused her of complaining too much; now, the worries and discomforts of her youth seemed petty and meaningless. For the first time in her life, Celli felt both a spark of independence and the weight of real responsibility. And she was determined to help her people get through this tragedy. The problem seemed impossibly large, but Celli lifted her chin and gritted her teeth.

Like Celli, the Theron survivors possessed a new determination that formed a tough veneer over their despair. The people had been unprepared for such a holocaust, but this desperate time had revealed an inner resolve, as they simultaneously shored up the worldforest and drew comfort from it.

'We are not alone. We care for the trees, and they care for us. We will never abandon each other. *This* is the source of our strength, and together we will all get through our ordeal,' Father

Idriss had pronounced when, shortly after the attack, he called the survivors together.

Now, support ladders and pulleys, makeshift ramps and walkways were erected against the main fungus-reef tree as crews salvaged what they could. Adults worked to clear debris and charred mushroom flesh from the lower levels, while cautious younger children crawled onto precarious perches, marking safe routes for the heavier adult workers. Celli remembered when she and Estarra had climbed to the top levels of the giant mushroom to harvest the tender whitish meat Beneto loved so well . . .

Fortunately, since their initial attack here, the hydrogues had been preoccupied with a new conflict against the faeros and had not returned to crush the worldforest. But Celli took little heart from that. There was too much death and destruction around her.

From above, Celli heard a shout of surprise, then moans of grief. In one of the fungus-reef chambers, a child explorer had just found an asphyxiated woman. Others made their way across the hardened fringes to where they could drag the victim out. Celli had known the woman, a family friend who made delicious treats from forest berries. Her heart sank, but her grief had no further to go; each fresh drop of cold tragedy ran like water off an already-saturated cloak. Reynald, Beneto, Lica, Kari, Ren – the names rolled through her conscience, one after another. She was terrified she might forget somebody – and that didn't seem fair. They deserved to be remembered. Each one of them.

Not wanting to be at the base camp when the workers brought down the woman's body, Celli went to her grandparents. 'I want to go where I'm needed most, Grandmother. Send me out.'

'I know you're impatient, dear.' Old Lia's watery eyes seemed extremely tired. 'We're all trying to decide which work is most important.'

Her grandfather scratched his seamed cheek. 'Every day we've been doing triage for the forest.'

Uthair and Lia were busily keeping track of scouting teams, scribing notes and keeping records that only they could decipher. Normally, the green priests could connect to the worldtrees to see the whole scope of the forest, but the magnitude of the destruction was so overwhelming, many of them could not sort through the visual information to make sense of it all.

The old couple spread out detailed satellite images taken by EDF ships, showing the extent of burned and frozen areas like a blight across the landscape. Reeling green priests had already shared this information with the trees through telink, but the forest already felt its enormous injuries, which made direct and clear communication difficult. Her grandmother pointed to an unmarked spot where hundreds of acres of broken and toppled trees lay flattened as if they had been no more than stalks of grain in the path of a hurricane. 'No one has gone into this area yet.'

'I'll go take a look.' Celli was glad to have a useful assignment she could do by herself. She welcomed the responsibility. After all, she was now as old as Estarra had been when she'd married King Peter. Everyone on Theroc, down to the youngest child, was being forced to grow up too quickly.

She sprinted off, picking her way through the haunted forest. The fast blaze had scoured away the underbrush, but the hydrogues' icewave had been like dynamite, blasting trees into kindling, shattering them into tangles of fibrous pulp.

Celli moved lightly on graceful legs that were muscular from climbing, running, and dancing. She imagined she was practising to be a treedancer again, a profession she'd aspired to for many years. She had trained diligently, seeing herself as half ballerina and half marathon runner.

As she ran, she encountered more human bodies – broken statues killed by the hydrogues' icewave or horribly burned cadavers drawn into a mummified fetal position as muscles and sinews tightened in the heat. Far too many had died, both trees and humans.

But Celli forged on, her feet sending up puffs of ash. Each living tree she could report would be one little victory for Theroc. Each such triumph would gradually tip the scales against the despair the hydrogues had brought.

As she explored in slow, broad zigzags through the devastation, the surviving trees were few and far between, but she touched each one briefly, murmuring words of encouragement and hope. Scrambling on her hands and knees, Celli climbed through a tangle of toppled trees as wide as a house. Though the jagged branches scratched her, she pressed forward and reached an artificial clearing in which all the trees had been knocked down in a circular pattern, as if something huge had exploded there, leaving an open area at the centre.

Celli caught her breath. In the middle of the circle of destruction, she saw a curved shell of smoke-blackened crystal and the shattered fragments of what had been an alien warglobe. Pyramid-shaped protrusions thrust like claws through the spherical edges.

A hydrogue ship.

She had seen these awful things before, though this warglobe was nothing more than a fractured shell, half of it strewn around the clearing. Celli couldn't help but clench her fists while her lips curled in an angry but triumphant snarl.

Thus far, the EDF – for all their sophisticated weapons – had achieved little success against the hydrogues' diamond armour. Celli was sure the Earth military would be interested in having a specimen of an enemy warship that they could analyse up close –

and she intended to give it to them, if there was any chance it might help in the fight.

Flushed with her discovery, Celli raced back towards the fungus-reef city, happy to have good news to share at last.

T W O

MAGE-IMPERATOR JORA'H

M ere days after his ascension, Mage-Imperator Jora'h went to watch the handlers prepare his father's corpulent body for its dazzling incineration.

He had never expected to become Mage-Imperator under such circumstances, but the Ildiran Empire was his to rule now. Jora'h wanted to make changes, to improve life for his people, to make amends to those who had suffered . . . but he was bound by obligations and commitments, forced to continue schemes he had not previously known about. He felt trapped in a web woven from a myriad sticky strands – unless he could find a way around them.

But first, before he could face those tangled responsibilities, Jora'h had to preside over the funeral of his poisoned father.

Attender kithmen carried his chrysalis chair into the chamber where the dead Mage-Imperator had been laid out for his final preparations. Jora'h sat silently in the spacious levitating throne, looking down at the slack features of his father. Resenting him.

Treacheries, schemes, lies – how could he endure everything he knew? Jora'h was now the mind, soul, and figurehead of the Ildiran race. It was not appropriate for him to curse his father's memory, but that didn't stop him . . .

The previous Mage-Imperator had killed himself, seeing his own death as the only way to force his son to inherit the Empire's cruel secrets. Jora'h was still reeling from the revelations. Much as he disliked what he had learned, he understood the rationale for those hateful deeds. He had never suspected the hidden danger to the Ildiran Empire or the slim, desperate hope of salvation, which could be achieved only if he continued the experiments on Dobro.

Jora'h was handsome, smooth featured, with golden hair bound back into a braid that would eventually grow long, like his father's. Over time, his classical features might change, too, as he evolved into his sedentary, supposedly benevolent role. His sheltered life as Prime Designate had not prepared him to imagine the awful things that were happening where he couldn't see them. But now, through the *thism*, he knew everything. It was exactly as his father had intended, both a gift and a curse.

And now he was compelled to continue the same acts, when all he wanted was to see his beloved and imprisoned Nira again. If nothing else, he would free *her*. That, at least, he could do – as soon as he finished the transition of leadership and found a way to leave the Prism Palace.

Now, exercising extreme care, gaunt handlers washed the former leader's heavy body, preparing it. Cyroc'h's ample flesh sagged on his bones like a rubbery fabric that would easily peel away from his skeleton.

Diminutive servants, gibbering with despair, pushed forward frenetically to assist, but they had no place here during this ceremony, and Jora'h sternly sent them away. Some of them would no doubt throw themselves from a turret of the Prism Palace in their grief and misery. But their misery could not compare to his own dismay at all he had learned. No one could help him decide how best to rule, or what to do at Dobro . . .

'How long will it be?' he asked the handlers.

The stony-faced men looked up from their work. Their leader said in a grim voice, 'For an event of such magnitude, Liege, this must be our best work. It is the most important duty we will ever perform.'

'Of course.' Jora'h continued to observe in silence.

Wearing armoured gloves, the handlers reached into pots and withdrew handfuls of silvery-grey paste, which they spread thickly and lovingly over the dead Mage-Imperator. They made certain to cover every speck of exposed skin.

Even in the dimness of the preparation room, the paste simmered and began to smoke. The handlers increased their pace, but did not grow sloppy under Jora'h's watchful gaze. When the Mage-Imperator was completely slathered, they wrapped his body with an opaque cloth, then announced their readiness.

'To the roof,' Jora'h said from his chrysalis chair. 'And call all of the Designates.'

The dead Mage-Imperator's sons, along with Jora'h's own children, assembled on the highest transparent platform atop the spherical domes of the Prism Palace. The dazzling light of multiple suns washed down on them.

As Jora'h waited in the bright sun, ready to fulfil his role in the ceremony, he scanned the faces of his brothers, the former Designates, who had come from splinter colonies around the Empire, regardless of the shortage of stardrive fuel. Jora'h's own group of sons – the next generation of Designates – stood grim and respectful beside their oldest noble brother, Thor'h, who was now the new Prime Designate. Pery'h, the Designate-in-waiting for the planet Hyrillka, stood next to his brother Daro'h, the Dobro

Designate-in-waiting, others clustered in ranks next to their uncles, whom they would soon replace.

Their awareness that the Hyrillka Designate could not attend and still lay unconscious in the Prism Palace's infirmary cast a deeper pall over the ceremony. Though his bruises and contusions had healed, Rusa'h remained lost and unresponsive in a deep sub-*thism* sleep, probably having nightmares of the hydrogue attack on his citadel palace on Hyrillka. It was doubtful the Designate would ever awaken, and his planet would soon need a new leader. Though not yet prepared, Pery'h would have to take his place without Rusa'h as his mentor . . .

Handler kithmen delivered Cyroc'h's wrapped body to a raised platform and adjusted magnifiers and mirrors. Everything proceeded in sombre silence. Silently respectful carriers brought the chrysalis chair adjacent to the indistinct form of Cyroc'h, still shrouded in its opaque cloth.

Jora'h lifted his gaze to his brothers and sons as he grasped the thick cloth with his left hand. 'My father served as Mage-Imperator during a century of peace and also in recent times of crisis. His soul has already followed the threads of *thism* to the realm of the Lightsource. Now, here, his physical form will join the light as well.'

In a single abrupt motion, Jora'h yanked away the cloth to expose the soft form of the dead Mage-Imperator. The intense light of seven suns pounded down, activating the shimmering metallic paste that covered the dead leader's skin. Piercing white flames instantly engulfed the smothered, sagging body. The photothermal paste did not burn the body so much as dissolve it, making the skin and muscle and fat dissociate into the air, glowing, sparkling . . .

The fallen Mage-Imperator vanished in a cloud of writhing steam and smoke. The air cleared. All that remained were Cyroc'h's glowing bones, impregnated with bioluminescent compounds. His clean, empty skull was only a symbol of the great things that he had been . . . and the dreadful things he had done in the name of preserving the Ildiran Empire.

As Mage-Imperator, Jora'h's immediate obligation was to dispatch his Designates-in-waiting to seal the process of governmental transition. Then he could finally find a way to free Nira. He turned to his sons and his brothers. 'And now the Empire must move on.'

THREE

BASIL WENCESLAS

King Peter was in fine form as he stood on the Whisper Palace balcony to address the great crowds. It would be one of his most important speeches in recent years.

Watching the young King from his observation window, Chairman Basil Wenceslas straightened his expensive suit, touched his steel-grey hair. Hidden cameras around the Whisper Palace gave him alternate views that allowed him to study Peter's body language, the barely readable expressions on his smooth young face, the intensity of his darting blue eyes. *Good . . . so far.*

At least this time when he'd read the scripted words, the King had not objected to them. Instead, Peter had looked directly into the dapper Chairman's grey eyes and visibly swallowed. 'You're certain this is what we need to do, Basil?' There was no sarcasm in his voice, no taunt in his words. His dyed blond hair was perfect, his artificially coloured blue eyes bright and sincere.

'We have studied every alternative. The people must be made to understand that there is no choice.'

With a sigh, Peter had set down the display pad, having

memorized the script in his first reading. He ran his hands through his blond hair, messing it without a care for who might see him; assistants would make it perfect again before he made his public appearance. 'I will make them understand.'

Now, waiting for the speech to start, Basil tapped an appraising fingertip against his lips. At the moment, the King looked particularly regal. Only a month earlier, however, the Chairman had been goaded by Peter's mulish insubordination to set in motion plans to assassinate the King and Queen. Basil had arranged to make it look like a Roamer plot, so that the EDF could forcibly bring the space gypsies – and all of their resources and capabilities – under direct Hansa control. Layers and layers of schemes. It would have been advantageous all around.

But Peter and Estarra had somehow foiled his assassination attempt. There was no denying the King hated him with a deep coldness that was never likely to fade, but at least Peter now understood the lengths to which Basil would go to ensure that his orders were followed. If Peter had genuinely learned his lesson, then the Chairman and his fellow Hansa officials would heave sighs of relief . . . and the King and his lovely bride would be permitted to keep their heads on their shoulders. There was a government to run and a war to fight, and if everyone would just cooperate . . .

At the appointed time, King Peter stepped out into the bright daylight where everyone could see him and raised his hands. Basil narrowed his eyes and leaned forward, resting his chin on his knuckles. The crowd greeted Peter with cheers that quickly gave way to a hushed, expectant murmur. Sometimes the King's speeches were no more than pep talks; at other times he delivered dire news of fallen heroes or slaughtered colonies.

The King's voice was rich, well practised. 'Eight years ago, the hydrogues began to prey upon us. Eight years of blood and unprovoked outrage and murder! And how do we stop it? How can anyone end this conflict against an enemy we cannot possibly understand? Finally, we have a way!'

He had their full attention now. 'In this terrible struggle, we have no recourse but to use every possible tool, every weapon at our disposal – regardless of how reprehensible it may be to our moral character. Now is not the time to be reluctant. Now is the time for action.' Peter smiled: a true leader's smile. Basil was surprised to feel his own emotions stirring.

'Therefore, in close consultation with the Hansa Chairman and the commander of the Earth Defence Forces, I have concluded that we must employ our final option. After witnessing the heinous destruction of peaceful Theroc, the home of my Queen Estarra—'

He shuddered. Basil flicked his gaze to different views on the screens. Were those actual *tears* in his eyes? Excellent.

'After sustaining unprovoked depredations on Hansa colonies such as Corvus Landing and Boone's Crossing . . . after enduring the untenable interdiction on gas-giant planets that prevents us from harvesting the stardrive fuel we vitally need . . . indeed, after suffering the murder of my predecessor King Frederick' – he drew a deep breath, then raised his voice, shouting at the crowd and igniting their pride and defiance – 'the time for mere reaction and defence is at an end. We must begin waging an *offensive* war.'

The roar of raucous approval was so loud that the sound drove Peter back a step. Basil turned to the two uniformed military advisers beside him, General Kurt Lanyan and Admiral Lev Stromo; both men nodded. Eldred Cain, the pale-skinned Hansa deputy who was under consideration to become Basil's successor, made detailed annotations to his copy of Peter's speech. Everyone seemed satisfied with the King's announcement.

So far.

Peter continued, lowering his voice and making them listen again, playing the mood of the crowd. 'I have done a great deal of soul-searching, and I can come to no other conclusion.' He paused, letting the crowd wait, letting the silence build. When he spoke again it was like a slap. 'We must deploy the *Klikiss Torch* again. Intentionally.'

There was a gasp, followed by mutters, then a swell of applause.

'We will utterly annihilate hydrogue planets, one after another, until our enemy capitulates. It's time for them to endure their own losses!'

Peter bowed, and the audience continued to cheer without pausing to consider the consequences. Perhaps it was just as well that they didn't, since the Klikiss Torch seemed to be humanity's only option, the only effective weapon they had found so far. This decision would dramatically turn up the heat in the war. He looked stoic and determined, a man who had wrestled with a difficult decision and had come to the only possible conclusion.

Basil considered it one of the best-delivered speeches the King had ever given. Perhaps the young man was salvageable after all.

FOUR

TASIA TAMBLYN

The Grid 7 battle group had returned to the shipyards between Jupiter and Mars for refurbishment and refitting and to take on new personnel. They would also incorporate fifteen recently completed Juggernauts and Mantas, but that didn't begin to replace all the ships the battle group had lost during the debacle in the rings of Osquivel. In the month since that disaster, the Earth Defence Forces had jumped at every shadow.

Tasia Tamblyn herself had gone to the new star of Oncier, site of the first test firing of the Klikiss Torch, and had watched the titanic battle between hydrogues and faeros, which had resulted in the complete snuffing of the artificial sun created from a gas-giant planet. Seeing a war in which whole worlds and stars were casualties, Tasia didn't know how tiny humans could hope to cause any damage to the enemy . . .

But it wouldn't stop her from trying. The drogues had killed her brother Ross on his skymine, and her lover Robb Brindle when he'd gone down into the clouds under a white flag of truce. If vengeance was at all in her power, Tasia didn't intend to let the deep-core bastards get away with that. A stern expression had once looked out of place on her heart-shaped face, but not anymore.

She had pale skin from growing up under the icy ceiling of her clan's water mines on Plumas, and had never got much colour from serving in the EDF aboard ships all the time. Her light-blue eyes reminded her of the frozen walls of the family settlement beneath the glacial surface of the isolated moon.

While her Manta was in dock at the asteroid belt shipyards, some of her crew had been rotated either to Mars or the Moon base for a week of downtime. For herself, Tasia had no use for furloughs and did not wish to visit Earth. The only time she'd gone there, in fact, was to contact Robb's parents and tell them how their son had died.

The optimistic and kind-hearted young man had been more than her lover, he had been her best friend. Of all the recruits in the EDF – many of whom were painfully bigoted – Robb alone had taken Tasia at her word, given her a chance to be herself, and had loved her for it. In the dark days of the war, she still missed him very much. He'd thought he was doing something important and meaningful by volunteering to bring a message deep into a gas giant's clouds, but in the end it had proved a foolish waste of his life. Now a talented young man was gone, leaving a small void in the Earth Defence Forces and an aching hole in Tasia's heart.

It didn't help matters that her compy EA had also disappeared shortly after delivering a warning to the Roamers at Osquivel. Tasia had been unable to find any clues to where the Listener compy had gone. Not only was EA a valuable piece of 'equipment', she was also a friend who had been owned by clan Tamblyn for many years. Tasia still held out hope that the compy would eventually find her way back to EDF headquarters, even if she had to take a lengthy, roundabout route.

Though it no doubt added to her feelings of isolation, Tasia preferred to spend the week aboard her ship, watching entertainment loops or playing games. She had a medium build, was fit and strong but didn't show it. She'd become adept at ping-pong, thanks to practising with Robb – so adept, in fact, that most of her crew made excuses whenever she challenged them to a match. She couldn't wait until all repairs, upgrades, and inspections were finished, so she could be on her way again, to go head to head with the inhuman enemy.

Unexpectedly, Tasia received a summons to go to the Grid 7 flagship. She shuttled over to the *Jupiter* to meet with Admiral Sheila Willis, adjusting her clean uniform, making sure her shoulder-length light-brown hair was bound in regulation-fashion under her cap.

When Tasia presented herself in the Admiral's lounge, she was surprised to see the brawny, dark-haired EDF commander, General Kurt Lanyan, sitting in a visitor's chair. Tasia snapped to attention. 'General Lanyan, sir. And Admiral Willis. You called me, sirs?'

She had met the swarthy General in a strategy session before the Osquivel offensive, when Robb had volunteered to attempt to communicate with the drogues.

'Commander Tamblyn, we have noted your exemplary service.' The General had a gruff voice. 'Your solution of creating instant artificial rafts at Boone's Crossing saved thousands of colonists. After reviewing your ship's internal log, I have concluded that your performance during the Osquivel battle was exceptional. Furthermore, at Oncier you recently obtained vital information about the faeros and their struggle with the hydrogues.'

'Yes, sir.' Tasia didn't know what else he wanted to hear. Her heart pounded. Was she somehow in line for another promotion? True, the Battle of Osquivel had killed a great many officers, and the EDF would need to replace them . . .

Admiral Willis folded her hands together. Willis was a thin, folksy woman who spoke in obscure platitudes, yet she had a wit as sharp as a monofilament wire. 'Commander Tamblyn, would you be at all interested in having your ship carry a nasty little present to the drogues? King Peter has finally yanked off the leash and let us run loose.'

'What sort of nasty present, Ma'am?'

The grandmotherly woman smiled. 'How'd you like to drop a Klikiss Torch down their throats and blow the crap out of a whole hydrogue planet?'

Tasia responded instantly. 'Admiral, General, I would welcome any opportunity for a little payback. We all have plenty of personal reasons for carrying a grudge.'

Lanyan chuckled. 'I like your attitude, Commander Tamblyn.' He handed her documents and maps pinpointing the chosen target for the Klikiss Torch, an obscure gas giant named Ptoro.

Tasia couldn't hide her surprised response. The Roamer clan Tylar had operated a large old skymine on Ptoro, but the facility was withdrawn after the hydrogue ultimatum. As far as she knew, no one had gone to chilly Ptoro in years. 'Ptoro? Why would you want to—' She caught herself, and the General frowned at her.

'You've actually heard of it? It seems to be a fairly insignificant planet.'

'You're right, sir. It's just . . . in the middle of nowhere, isn't it?'

'We've detected drogue activity there. That's what counts.'

Admiral Willis added, 'We'll be sending a whole battle group along to keep you company, but your Manta will carry the big surprise.'

'As soon as we're out of space dock, my crew and I are completely at your disposal, sirs.' Tasia had practically danced her way back to the shuttle.

*

Roamers didn't judge maturity by age, but by capabilities. The clans considered a person to be a functional adult once he or she could strip down, break apart, and reassemble virtually any piece of mechanical apparatus and could successfully navigate using stars and the old Ildiran databases. After being coached by her two brothers, Tasia had been particularly proud when she'd demonstrated that she could don a spacesuit and correctly match all the seals, ten times out of ten. She had been twelve the first time she'd done it.

Now Tasia felt the same measure of pride as she stood in her Manta's cargo bay. Swarms of engineers and technicians worked to install the racks, monitors, and peripheral equipment needed for deploying the Klikiss Torch. Oh, how she was going to enjoy seeing a bloated hydrogue planet turn into a bright new sun.

The green priest, Rossia, Tasia's communications link with the rest of the Spiral Arm, came up beside her, walking with a pronounced limp due to an injury he had suffered on Theroc many years before. His eyes were bulging and oversized like stray ping-pong balls from the rec room.

'Turmoil . . . always turmoil,' he said. 'The EDF seems to relish banging and pounding and reconfiguring things.'

Together, they watched engineers load blunt-nosed torpedoes, part of the Klikiss Torch apparatus. The crew had already brought aboard a fast cargo ship that would be used to deliver the other end of the wormhole-generating machinery to a neutron star that would be transferred like a stellar bomb into Ptoro's core.

'Gotta crack a few shells if you want to scramble the drogues,' she said. 'After what they did to Theroc, you want to see them stopped, don't you?'

The pop-eyed priest bobbed his head. 'Oh, certainly the worldforest wishes the hydrogues to be defeated – or at least neutralized. But more than anything else, I want to go back home.

The worldforest has been terribly injured and, like all green priests, I can hear it calling. I should be there helping to replant and rebuild.'

'But you volunteered to help the EDF, and you're a vital link in our communications,' Tasia said. 'We need you.'

He scratched his green cheek. 'When everyone needs you, Commander, you're forced to choose who has the greater need.'

'Well, it isn't really your choice to make, once you've joined up with the military and given your word.' Many times, Tasia herself had wanted to return home to her clan's water mines on Plumas, but she didn't have that option – and neither did Rossia.

'I should tell you, Commander,' Rossia said, 'that other green priests have been grumbling across telink, on other worlds, on other ships. They all feel the call of the worldforest. Not all of them can resist. We simply volunteered our services, remember. We did not formally join the Earth Defence Forces.'

She frowned at him as the work of installing the Klikiss Torch continued. 'I would rather be someplace else, too, but we all have to keep up the fight. We each need to follow our Guiding Star, not be distracted by other flickers of light.'

Rossia gave his jerky nod. 'A true green priest sets down roots of conviction, and is not blown about like a featherseed in the breeze.'

'Pick whatever metaphor you prefer. But you know the drogues are not going to stop attacking. In all probability they'll go back to Theroc to finish the job they started.'

'All the more reason for the green priests to come home and help protect the worldforest.'

Tasia frowned at him. 'On the contrary – all the more reason to stay with the EDF and hope we kick the stuffing out of them. How can you possibly protect the trees if you're standing beside them on a planet that's under attack? The full-blown military has a better chance than a handful of green priests does.'

Rossia touched the potted treeling he always kept with him, reticent and deep in thought. 'Perhaps. I do not intend to leave, Commander Tamblyn. Many green priests have forgotten that the forest itself asked us to assist you in the struggle. We have all suffered losses in this war.' He shook his head slowly. 'And we all make sacrifices.'

FIVE

DD

Though his memory core was already filled with service modules, specialized task programming, and decades' worth of experiences, DD still had the unfortunate capacity to keep holding memory after unpleasant memory. He wished he could erase them all, but the experiences were burned irrevocably into his computer brain.

The Friendly compy had been held hostage for years by the evil Klikiss robots, and now they had taken him below the sky oceans of a hydrogue gas giant called Ptoro. The little compy endured day after day within the alien cityspheres, which were hundreds of times more immense than even the largest hydrogue warglobes.

Continuing their quiet treachery against humans, the Klikiss robots engaged in incomprehensible vibrational discussions with the liquid-crystal beings, a sophisticated and unusual form of communication that was part music, part lyrical visual pattern disruption, part something that was beyond DD's ability to understand. It was far too complex for him.

When he'd been with the Colicos xeno-archaeology team, DD

had known his place, known his duties, but the ancient robots had insisted on 'freeing' all competent computerized companions from their servitude. With their unnecessary vendetta, the Klikiss robots meant to exterminate all humans. An alliance with the hydrogues extended their power and abilities far beyond what they could have achieved on their own.

Inside the shimmering walls of the fantastic citysphere, DD stood surrounded by unusual conglomerations of exotic geometric shapes that grew in the extreme high-pressure environment. Sensor perceptions were distorted by the laws of physics pushed to their extremes. Entire structures were fabricated from elements that DD normally knew as gases. Quantum effects took hold. Solid materials moved unpredictably, with strange side effects.

DD wanted to depart from Ptoro and find a place where he could be safe again. When he had learned about the group of desperate human captives who were held in special chambers of the citysphere, he asked Sirix for more information. The Klikiss robot pondered the question, then answered in a buzzing signal, 'Disorientation and fear make for interesting responses. There is little of value to be learned from human beings, but the hydrogues do not concur with us. That is why they keep test subjects.'

DD felt sad for the helpless prisoners the hydrogues had seized over the past several years. 'I would like to see these human captives, Sirix. Would that be possible?'

'There is no purpose to your interacting with the prisoners.'

DD pondered a set of responses and selected an answer that might sway his captor. 'If I observe these humans in their most unpleasant condition, full of fear and hopelessness, then I may be convinced of the failings you ascribe to their entire race.'

Sirix twitched his segmented insect-like legs and folded his hemispherical carapace back together. 'An acceptable analysis. Follow me.'

The black machine led DD up and down dizzying ramps that defied gravity until they arrived at a shimmering wall that led to an array of jewel-like pressurized chambers, like faceted soap bubbles clustered together. Hydrogues flowed around them, incomprehensible creatures that could turn into gases or fluids, occasionally taking human shape.

Sirix emitted a series of chiming notes, his sensors and indicator lights glowing. The shimmering film wall became transparent. 'You may enter.'

'Is it safe to breach the barrier? Those environment cages appear fragile.'

'Pressurized chambers protect the specimens from the hostile surroundings. The captives are safe, for now. If the hydrogues wished to kill them, they would have done so without delay.'

Sirix sent a time signal explaining when he would return. DD stepped forward, glad for the opportunity to be away from the oppressive scrutiny of the Klikiss robot. He pressed against the resistance of the protective wall, then passed through. As he readjusted his systems to the new environment, he felt a response akin to great relief at the sensation of being in 'normal' air pressure again.

The watery light filled with swirls of unusual colours. His body steamed and crackled as he reached equilibrium with a human-compatible environment. DD swivelled his head to observe the sixteen captives huddled in their self-contained shell of relative safety.

'Good Lord, it's a compy!' said one of the humans, a coffee-skinned young man who wore the wrinkled uniform of an EDF soldier. Consulting his database, DD determined he was a wing commander.

'Great. Our own compies are betraying us now,' said a second prisoner, a female captive with a pinched face and a bitter expression. An ID tag on the tattered pocket of her grey crewman's uniform gave her last name as 'Telton'.

'Not necessarily. Maybe he can help us get out of here! We can't stop looking for opportunities, no matter how crazy,' said the first prisoner.

'Crazy is right.'

'I am here against my will, just as you are,' DD confessed. 'The Klikiss robots wish to convert me to their cause. Thus far, they have been unsuccessful.'

'What's going on? What do the drogues want from us?' said a third prisoner.

'Be careful not to believe anything that compy says,' grumbled the dour female captive. 'Could be a trick.'

'Hey, give him a chance, Anjea,' said the black EDF officer. 'We'd like you to tell us what you know, compy. I'm Robb Brindle. What's your name, so we can have a real conversation?'

'My shortened serial number is DD. I would prefer that you call me that.'

Brindle rubbed his hands together. 'A friend of mine in the EDF was always close to her compy. I'm sure we can be friends. Right?'

'I would like that, Robb Brindle.'

Brindle's honey-brown eyes brightened. 'We're pretty out of it here, DD. Several of us have already died, and we haven't even come close to creating a workable escape plan.'

'We're stuck in the middle of a gas giant!' Anjea Telton snapped at him. 'Do you expect to just walk away?'

'No,' Brindle said, frowning at the other prisoner. 'But I expect some cooperation in seizing an opportunity if one presents itself. Like DD, here. Hey, pal, can you help us get out of this place?'

'I have no means by which to effect a rescue. My body was modified to withstand the pressures outside, but your organic forms could never survive any attempt to depart. I believe that these environment bubbles are the only safe places for you within a gas-giant core.'

For just a moment, Brindle's shoulders slumped, but then he straightened himself, as if unwilling to show disappointment in front of the other prisoners. 'We figured as much, but we had to ask.'

'I am sorry. If I encounter new possibilities, I will attempt to help.' DD took another step forward. 'Perhaps you could each describe how you came to be captives. I am as lacking in information as you say you are. Did the Klikiss robots seize you, or were you each taken in hydrogue attacks?'

'Damned black bug robots are worse than the drogues! They pretended to be our friends.'

'Can't trust robots.'

'No kidding.'

'But we can trust you, DD, right?' Brindle explained how he had been captured during a diplomatic mission while descending in an environment chamber to the hydrogues. Other captives had been stolen from lifepods in the battle of Osquivel or kidnapped in ships flying between star systems. One, Charles Gomez, had even been snatched from the forested colony of Boone's Crossing.

DD assessed all of the stories, seeing few common denominators. 'I will ponder your situation. Perhaps I can determine a solution.'

'Why bother? We're all dead anyway,' said sullen and distraught Gomez. 'The drogues already killed five of us in their experiments. It's only a matter of time.'

'We can't let ourselves think like that,' Brindle said, putting a hand on the man's shoulder.

DD looked around at the human prisoners. 'You have survived so far. My master, Louis Colicos, always instructed me to be optimistic, while my other master, Margaret Colicos, insisted that I be practical. I will try to synthesize both.'

'You do that. And we'll try to do the same.' Brindle gave him a hopeful smile. 'We appreciate whatever you can do, DD. And thanks for visiting us. It's given me the most hope I've had since I got here, especially considering everybody probably thinks I'm already dead.'

DD's time signal showed that his brief visit was nearly over and Sirix would soon be coming back for him. 'Perhaps we can prove them wrong.'

SIX

JESS TAMBLYN

'Everybody probably thinks I'm dead.' Jess sat alone on the shore of a windswept alien sea, naked and clean, but not cold. He had never felt so isolated – or so . . . different – from other human beings in his life. His skin tingled with unnatural and explosive energy, as if ready to spark and jump. The light dusting of hair on his bare chest looked normal – and completely out of place – on his altered body.

He remained alive even though his ship had been destroyed by marauding hydrogues. After the attack, Jess barely remembered falling through the clouds, striking the ocean . . . and then emerging again, reborn, bobbing with the tides as he studied the flat, grey horizon. He was naked, all his garments burned away, but unharmed. He found himself afloat with no land in sight, no food, no way to survive, and gradually came to realize that his new existence required none of those things. The wentals kept him alive, gave him energy. He could have drifted there for ever.

His altered body swelled with incalculable power – abilities and thoughts and surging energies he had never imagined. Yet he was stuck in this empty place, unable to get home to the Roamer clans, to any part of the human race. An eerie watery lifeforce pulsed through him and through the ocean of this uncharted world.

The hydrogues had left him for dead – and the wentals had saved him.

That first day, while Jess had drifted, he sensed enormous swimming things beneath the currents, heavy shapes like plesiosaurs or sea serpents from a legendary Earth past. When one of the hungry monsters came up from the depths, Jess saw an immense maw, long teeth, spined tentacles reaching out – but the wentals protected him, sending a message through the water that this man was to be left alone. *And saved*.

The underwater behemoth had surfaced so that Jess could cling to the knobby fins on its slippery, slimy back. The creature cruised at great speed across the water, breaking through waves, until Jess saw a low line of rocks and crashing surf. The sea monster had brought him to land . . .

For uncounted days he lived among the scrub brush and weeds, not needing to eat, wishing for real human companionship, though he had the ever-present wentals in his mind. For a long time, Jess watched shelled creatures like trilobites crawl in endless circles, climbing out of one tide pool and lowering themselves into another. The days passed with painful slowness. He stood with arms outstretched as storms passed over him in a bath of fresh raindrops. Even the lightning could not harm him.

When he'd flown his solo nebula skimmer, Jess had not bothered to shave often. He had shoulder-length, wavy brown hair. He grew a beard and moustache just thick enough to cover the cleft in his chin, trimming it every few days, but since the wentals had infused him, his hair had all stopped growing.

'I was supposed to bring the wentals to the Roamers, to help you expand and grow. And now I'm stranded here,' he spoke aloud. 'We've been defeated before we could even start.'

Not defeated. We are stronger now than we were. The thrumming voice spoke inside his skull, the echoing presence of innumerable diverse wentals. *We waited ten thousand years to reach this point. We can wait again.*

At the edge of the vast, primitive ocean, Jess sat on the rough rocks watching the blue-green water foam against the reefs. All of the amazing power he now held, along with the secret return of the wentals, did him no good. 'I'm not very good at waiting.'

Off on the horizon, Jess watched lightning-embroidered stormclouds that hung low in the sky. He could see for immense distances, and he realized that his view wrapped all the way around the curvature of the planet itself. He drew on the combined vision of all the wental entities diffused across every kilometre of open ocean. He could sense it all.

It was glorious. If only he could share it with someone . . .

Not long ago, on the first sterile sea-planet where Jess had distributed the living water beings, there had not been even the rudiments of monocellular life. On that world, unrestricted, the wentals had raged through the water, grasping every molecule to incorporate it into their essence like a flame-front devouring fuel, bringing a whole planet to life, lighting it up like a torch.

On this planet, though, there was a primitive yet viable ecosystem in place. These oceans were filled with plankton and plants, shelled organisms, and soft-bodied swimmers. The wentals had come alive in the seas, but in spite of their bold strategy in saving Jess, they had restrained themselves here, choosing not to affect the other creatures.

The changes they had made in him were irreversible. He had the wental power as a permanent part of his physiology. He might even be able to harness that power to help his people . . . if only he could get off of this planet.

For almost two centuries, Roamer clans had made life possible in the most terrible environments. They solved problems, they created innovative ideas and technologies to succeed where the Hansa would never even dare to try.

Jess was sure there was a way to get off this planet.

Though the watery entities could hear the thoughts inside his head, he shouted across the waves in his impatience. 'If you wentals are so powerful, why wait? We have work to do!' Out there, in the inaccessible vastness of the Spiral Arm, the hydrogues were continuing to plague Roamer outposts. 'There's still a war going on out in the Spiral Arm. Are you just going to give up now that you've finally been given a second chance?'

We flow from possibility to possibility. It is our nature.

'Then flow to a different one. How do I get out of here? You wanted to spread and propagate, didn't you? Why should we just hope for someone to happen by? I doubt anyone's been to this planet for centuries – if ever.' He picked up a rock and tossed it into the waves, where it was swallowed without a ripple.

The wental answered, *All the resources of this planet are available to you – from the rocks beneath you, to the metals and minerals in the water, to all the living creatures in the seas.*

'How does that help me build a ship? I have no tools, nothing but my bare hands.'

You have us.

Jess jumped to his feet on the rocky shore. 'What do you mean?'

Do not underestimate your new powers and abilities. With the strength of the wentals within you, creating a physical ship can be . . . relatively simple.

In his mind he received images and a sudden understanding that left him breathless with the possibilities.

This sea, even with its minimal prehistoric ecosystem, still contained billions of living creatures – from gigantic monsters to microscopic organisms. An incomparable work force. With wental guidance, all of them would cooperate to build a ship, one molecule at a time.

The wentals showed him exactly how.

SEVEN

CESCA PERONI

Jess Tamblyn had vanished. In her office chamber within the main Rendezvous asteroid, Cesca found it nearly impossible to concentrate on her leadership tasks.

This unified cluster of space rocks around a dim dwarf star was symbolic of the Roamer clans themselves: each separate, yet held together by invisible threads. In the centuries that Roamers had lived on this outpost, the clans had bound the asteroids together with support girders, connecting walkways, and reinforcement cables. But such bonds could easily be severed and the asteroids of Rendezvous scattered again.

As Speaker, Cesca had to make sure the clans didn't do the same.

Surrounded by thick walls, she reviewed reports from Roamer traders, studying the lists of goods, raw materials, and resources distributed among clan outposts. Forbidden from running their traditional skymines, some daredevil Roamers made blitzkrieg ekti strikes on gas giants, while others such as the ambitious extraction facilities at Osquivel broke down frozen comets to distill a trickle of stardrive fuel from their hydrogen. The EDF and the Hansa – the 'Big Goose' – demanded any ekti the clans produced, and instead of being grateful for what the Roamers risked their lives to scrape together, they clamoured for more and more, when none was available.

The clans were trapped in this uneasy business relationship, though they had theoretically established their independence, separating themselves from the Earth government long ago. The EDF seemed not to remember those details.

Cesca looked up as a visitor appeared in her office, a dark-haired young man with Asian features and an intent set to his narrow jaw. 'Speaker Peroni, I've got news!'

Jhy Okiah had long held that remembering names and faces was a vital skill for a clan Speaker, and Cesca had diligently developed the skill, along with many others. She remembered that this young man flew one of clan Tylar's ships, acting as an errand runner and delivery boy between Roamer outposts. He also had a reputation for getting easily lost . . . or at least side-tracked.

'It's part of my job to receive news, Nikko Chan – though my preference would be to have *good* news for a change.' She saw from his flustered expression that such a report would not be forthcoming. She pushed the documents and commerce records aside. 'Go ahead. I'm listening.'

Nikko fidgeted, drying sweaty palms on his many-pocketed pants. 'Four days ago I was flying back from Hurricane Depot to deliver a load of spare parts and pick up some large-output thermal generators for Jonah 12. That's the frozen moon where Kotto Okiah is establishing a—'

'I know where it is, Nikko. I authorized the plans myself.'

Derailed from his story, Nikko blinked. 'Well, sometimes I like to . . . zigzag on my routes. Intentionally, you know.' He sounded defensive. 'It doesn't cost very much ekti, and who knows what I might find? A new settlement, maybe even the *Burton*?'

'And what did you find this time?'

'You probably remember that my distant uncle, Raven Kamarov, disappeared a while ago. He used to haul ekti to and from Hurricane Depot, but one day he didn't show up at his destination. We sent out searches, but no luck.'

Cesca nodded. A great many Roamer ships had vanished in the past several years, not just Jess Tamblyn's. It was easy to blame the disappearances on hydrogues, but there was a simmering suspicion among the clans that the Earth Defence Forces were somehow involved. She guessed where Nikko's story was leading. 'And today you located the ship?'

'Not much of it.' Nikko frowned. 'But I did find enough serial numbers on hull plates that I could do a proper ID. It's the right vessel, that's for sure.'

Cesca felt her stomach sink as if gravity had just increased. 'Do you think it could have been a meteor impact or an engine overload?'

His shoulders sagged. 'Neither. The marks were unmistakable, Speaker. Some hull sections were large enough that I could see what caused the damage. *Jazer strikes*. Direct and intentional.'

'Jazers? But only the Eddies use jazers.'

The young man nodded. 'I brought all the wreckage with me. It's in the cargo hold.' The energy traces and blast patterns on the ruined hull metal of Kamarov's ship would be like a smoking gun.

Anger made Cesca push herself back a bit too quickly for the low gravity of Rendezvous, and her chair hit the wall with a loud bang. 'You're saying that the Eddies intentionally attacked and destroyed an unarmed Roamer vessel?'

'That's what it looks like. We can do a full analysis, but I'm sure I'm right.'

'This changes everything, Nikko Chan. Ekti is our commodity, to be sold not under duress, but on our own terms, whether the Goose likes it or not.'

Cesca drew herself up, assembling her steely resolve. 'I need to meet with the clan representatives immediately.'

EIGHT

DAVLIN LOTZE

His pack loaded with enough supplies for several days, Davlin Lotze stood in front of the flat stone surface of the alien transportal. Hundreds of tiles marked with strange symbols – coordinates for worlds once inhabited by the Klikiss – ringed the transportal. Most of them were still uninvestigated.

'Mr Lotze, you are scheduled to return in less than a day,' said the technician at the monitoring station. Known Klikiss transportals, such as this one within the Rheindic Co ruins, were jumping-off points for anyone with the balls and the drive to go planet hunting. Someone like him.

Davlin shouldered his pack. He wore a standard khaki explorer's jumpsuit of durable fabric that was appropriate for a range of temperatures. Even when he planned to venture to a completely uninhabited world, he wore no garish colours, no jewellery, nothing to call attention to himself. 'My mission parameters grant me a certain discretionary latitude in my schedule.' Considering his lengthy service record – not to mention the fact that he and Rlinda Kett had discovered this transportal network and brought the news back to the Hansa – he did not like to follow anyone else's rules or schedules.

Though the insect-like race had long ago vanished from the Spiral Arm, the Klikiss had left behind a network of mysterious ruins. Since the alien species breathed the same atmosphere and had similar basic biological requirements to those of humans, the Hansa considered those habitable planets to be potential gold-mines for colonization, minor victories they could declare in the turmoil of the hydrogue war.

But first those Klikiss worlds had to be identified, catalogued, and superficially explored. Davlin considered the task appropriate to his abilities. Without further delay, he stepped through the blank trapezoidal stone and fell across the universe to another Klikiss world.

It was an eerie feeling to be all alone on a whole planet. Davlin smiled as the dry breezes brushed his face. He arrived in the local morning, so he had a full day to image the termite-mound buildings, the iron-hard organic structures left by the Klikiss. This world had strange trees draped with feather-like fronds, surrounded by plants with long spiky leaves like pincushions.

Wandering around the crumbling ruins, Davlin planted sensors and meteorological recorders. He measured the amount of ground water and estimated the average rainfall. Eventually, if this world was chosen for full-scale Hansa colonization, explorers would bring self-launching satellites to allow faster and more compre-hensive mapping of the landforms and weather patterns. For now, Davlin only needed to make the first broad-strokes report.

When darkness fell, he set up his imagers and recorded a full-scan astronomical survey, acquiring spectra of the brightest stars in the local sky. Once he returned through the portal, Hansa astronomers and navigators would read the positions of primary stars, then backtrack and interpolate the location of this planet in order to match it to the coordinate tiles based on Klikiss symbology.

Davlin could have returned to base then, but he was enjoying the reverberant silence. He had never been enamoured of the bustle and excitement of civilization. Even the Hansa station at Rheindic Co, which now acted as a central point for eager researchers, seemed too crowded to him, too busy. He longed for peaceful days, remembering the quietly productive years when he'd impersonated a simple colonist on Crenna.

Davlin got out a warm sleep sheet, a thin film to wrap around himself that inflated into a cushioned bed. He spent a peaceful, solitary night there on the empty world. At daybreak, he packed up all his instruments, returned to the trapezoidal stone wall, activated the transportal, and stepped through to Rheindic Co . . .

Back inside the control room, Davlin was immediately struck by an air of oppressive sombreness. His dark-brown eyes scanned expressions on faces around him, then noted that another of the numerous coordinate tiles had been marked in black. 'Who did we lose?'

The technician looked at him, answering automatically. 'Jenna Refo. Three days overdue.'

Davlin blew out a long sigh, and the breath of air felt cold. That made five so far – five transportal explorers like himself who had chosen random Klikiss coordinates, hoping to find viable colonization options on resource-filled planets that would mean huge profits for the Hansa.

But sometimes the coordinates were bad. Perhaps the transportal on the other end had been destroyed by an earthquake or other natural disaster . . . or perhaps the planets themselves were violently inhospitable.

'Damn.' The Hansa paid enough to make the risks worthwhile

to some, yet each time an explorer stepped through to an unknown place, it was a gamble. Usually he came back from a successful mission to cheers, congratulations, parties and toasts. This time, though, he simply submitted his report, then went off to shower.

The following day, a salty old explorer named Hud Steinman returned crowing with delight, oblivious to the still sober expressions on the faces of the technical crew.

'I expect a bonus for this!' He twirled a victorious finger in the air. 'These coordinates' – he gestured behind him to one of the strangely marked tiles – 'take us right back to where it all began, or ended, depending on the real story. I've found the transportal tile for *Corribus*.'

The technicians gasped; a few even applauded. Davlin nodded in appreciation.

Corribus, where Margaret and Louis Colicos had deciphered the plans for the Klikiss Torch, was an empty and scarred world that might have been the last stand of the Klikiss race against the enemy that had obliterated them. For anyone who studied xeno-archaeology, Corribus was the Rosetta Stone, a place etched deep with messages from the past. Also, in a practical sense, such a confirmed data point would help the Hansa explorers connect different paths throughout the transportal web – a valuable start to the roadmap.

Davlin pushed past skinny old Hud Steinman and activated the coordinate tile that would take him to Corribus. Some Hansa technicians looked up; one raised a hand as if to call him back. But Davlin was beyond their control. He had a direct mandate from Chairman Wenceslas himself. Davlin stepped through into windy silence.

The Klikiss city on Corribus looked precisely as it had appeared in the images submitted by the Colicos team. Towering granite canyon walls formed a sheltered valley with termite-mound structures on the ground, as well as dwellings built into cliff faces that were lined with large, blocky crystals. Steinman had been correct – the terrain was unmistakable.

Davlin studied the ghostly world where watery sunshine illuminated cliffs studded with lumps of crystal. The Klikiss must have considered the sheer granite walls to be protective, like fortress barricades. The stone looked shiny, half melted, as if it had been subjected to some inconceivable destructive force.

He tried to imagine what could have struck the insectoid civilization. What enemy had been powerful enough to make them create the Klikiss Torch? The hydrogues? In the end, even the Torch hadn't been enough to protect them, and their race had been wiped out.

Davlin knew the Hansa would send colonists to Corribus. He just prayed that whatever had happened here would not occur again.

NINE

MAGE-IMPERATOR JORA'H

In the private ossuarium chamber beneath the Prism Palace, where no one could see him, Jora'h stood before the skull of his father – and hated him. 'You're forcing me to continue the most dishonourable of schemes.' His unbraided living hair writhed like crackling strands of static electricity, and his words came back to him as mocking echoes in the eerie silence. '*Bekh!* Not even the humans have developed foul enough words to convey my anger over what you were – and what I have become.'

Only a day had passed since the funeral blaze, and his father's skull had already been installed in the cold ossuarium, a private, silent place where a Mage-Imperator could ponder his rule. He wished he could just hide in a deep sub-*thism* sleep, like the Hyrillka Designate.

The skull, glowing pearly white, remained mute, its eye sockets hollow and empty, the smooth teeth grinning, as if the dead Mage-Imperator were laughing at his son's predicament.

Almost a century ago, no doubt Cyroc'h had faced the same knowledge and decisions, when he, too, learned of the breeding programme and the captive humans – like Nira. Had his father felt even a twinge of guilt, or had he simply grasped the new 'resources' and turned them to the service of the Empire?

Jora'h now regarded the glowing bones of his grandfather, who had been Mage-Imperator when the human generation ship *Burton* was found. For millennia, success had eluded the Ildirans in their ongoing efforts to create an interspecies bridge in the form of a powerful telepath who could meld thoughts and images with the hydrogues and represent both species. In a desperate twisted attempt to boost the experiments on the splinter colony of Dobro, his grandfather had decided to mix the bloodlines of the *Burton* descendants with talented Ildirans. The experimenters impregnated the human women, used the men as studs, and kept the breeding work going.

As soon as possible, Jora'h swore he would go to Dobro and find his beloved Nira. As Mage-Imperator he had the power to free her at last from her breeding servitude, and he would also meet his daughter Osira'h. He would begin to make amends to her, and even to the enslaved humans . . .

Jora'h shuddered to think of the secrets that his father had kept, knowing his naïve son would not understand everything until he took his father's place. He now knew about the part Ildirans had played in the previous hydrogue war, and he also understood why the peaceful Empire – which had supposedly never faced an outside enemy in a thousand years – maintained such a large and powerful Solar Navy and kept such a vast stockpile of ekti in reserve. Everything had been in long-term preparation for the eventual return of the hydrogues – and the unreliability of the Klikiss robots.

'Why did you allow the humans to test their Torch at Oncier, if you knew what might happen?' Even with full access to the *thism*, he could not understand his father. 'Why would you take the risk, tempt fate?' Jora'h did understand, though, that the previous Mage-

Imperator – and all Ildirans – had often underestimated or misinterpreted the ambitions of humanity. Had Cyroc'h never truly believed what the scientists of the Hanseatic League meant to do? Perhaps Cyroc'h had simply not grasped the magnitude of human folly . . .

Jora'h frowned at the phosphorescent skull, determined to defy the untenable position in which he found himself. He felt a chill in the air, heard faint whispers, but he faced the judgemental bones of his predecessors. 'Yes, Father, I will serve my people and guide them through every crisis, if it is in my ability to do so. But yours is not the only way. If I can find any other solution, I will change these paths.'

His son Zan'nh, acting as Adar, had submitted an analysis of current ekti stockpiles, and the Mage-Imperator was dismayed to see how quickly their resources were being depleted. Despite cautionary reserves, no one had anticipated that ekti production might cease entirely. The Empire required stardrive fuel to survive. Their stockpiles needed to be replenished.

Zan'nh would soon take on the official mantle in command of the Solar Navy. His predecessor and mentor, Adar Kori'nh, had been killed along with a full maniple of warliners in a suicidal offensive at Qronha 3; all indications led them to conclude that the hydrogues had been driven from the gas planet, and the clouds were ripe for ekti harvesting again . . . at least until the hydrogues came back.

That was something he could do, at least. The Empire faced challenges that forced Jora'h to consider desperate gambles. But refusing to try was far worse than taking risks.

As he turned from the luminous reliquary, ignoring the unhelpful skulls of his ancestors, Jora'h felt confident of his decision. With Qronha 3 free of the enemy, for now, he would command Zan'nh to reassemble one of the large cloud-harvesting facilities and return there with a full complement of miner kithmen, bred to be ekti harvesters. It was a positive, proactive step – one more victory purchased by the heroic death of Adar Kori'nh.

With a grim smile on his face, Jora'h turned to leave his silent ancestors behind and called for his son Zan'nh.

TEN

SULLIVAN GOLD

Opportunity always knocks: sometimes it scratches quietly, and sometimes it pounds like a blustery drunk demanding to be let in.

When news came to the Hansa that the hydrogues had been defeated at Qronha 3, they quickly took advantage of the circumstances. Rich hydrogen clouds were available for the taking, at least temporarily, and all that potential ekti could not be ignored.

Enormous cargo transports rushed components from orbiting industrial centres to the empty Ildiran gas planet, where they would be assembled at the fringes of the dense cloud decks. Highly paid volunteers signed up to work the new Hansa cloud harvester. Only a crazy person, or an overly optimistic one, would have taken such a job.

Sullivan Gold accepted the assignment to become the facility's manager, knowing full well the risks and potential rewards. It was a business decision that made perfect sense to him. The payoff would either be a feather in his cap, or a fitting epitaph on his tombstone.

Now, as the first wave of Hansa transport ships arrived at Qronha 3, Sullivan watched swarms of workers guide the massive components together. Heavy storage tanks, ekti reactors, life-support modules, and engineering decks came together one at a time, like the pieces of a puzzle. He scrutinized every step of the process, checking and double-checking the work.

Though hundreds of labourers came here initially to set up the huge sky factory, only a few dozen would remain once the cloud harvester came online. The elite. The sitting ducks. Sullivan considered having the men paint a logo or mascot on the side of the huge facility. A mallard might be nice . . . or a bull's-eye.

He had a practical wife named Lydia, three sons, a daughter, and (so far, at least) ten grandchildren, all of them intelligent and ambitious, sure to be movers and shakers some day. When the Hansa had called for an industrial head to run the new cloud harvester, Sullivan gathered his family for dinner and sprang his suggestion. 'With the terms the Hansa is offering, there's no way for us to lose!'

'Well, you can, dear,' Lydia said. Then, she took out a sheet of paper, marking one side *Pros*, the other side *Cons*. They had discussed the matter late into the night, always coming back to her stern finger tapping the columns that listed advantages and disadvantages.

On the pro side, the Hansa offered the Gold family major industrial concessions, interest-free business loans, guaranteed orders for a large variety of products – enough to transform them from simple businessmen into an actual dynasty. The cloud harvester would be designed to allow for a rapid evacuation; there was a chance (though not a good one) that Sullivan and his crew might escape if they were attacked by hydrogues. At least it looked possible on paper.

The disadvantages were obvious . . .

Now, in the glassed-in forward dome of the largest Hansa vessel, the green priest assigned to this venture joined Sullivan as he continued his observation. Unusual among green priests, Kolker worked as a freelance telink communicator, hiring himself out from one Hansa ship to another. He wasn't one of the nineteen volunteers who were assisting the EDF; he had already spent years in the commercial empire.

Though Kolker was always available to submit Sullivan's important status reports to the Hansa or relay friendly messages to Lydia, the green priest spent the majority of his time sitting with one hand resting against the trunk of his potted treeling, wearing a distant smile. The loquacious Kolker never seemed to tire of chatting with his fellow priests through the telink network. He shared messages incessantly, sometimes talking aloud, sometimes just listening, even when there was no news.

A long time ago, Sullivan remembered finding a chest of his grandfather's keepsakes, including a bundled stack of old-fashioned photo postcards. Seeing Kolker engaged in so much contact via the worldforest reminded him of those postcards. At least the telink didn't require Kolker to add extra postage from the gas giant.

'I've described everything to the worldtrees and my fellow green priests, Sullivan.' He smiled, showing green gums. 'New information and experiences help to distract them from all the damage the hydrogues have inflicted. But . . . I feel guilty to be here instead of helping in the burned forest.'

Sullivan pursed his lips as he watched the final cloud-harvester components being riveted together by groups of engineers wearing levitation packs. 'You aren't going to leave this station, are you, Kolker? I need your services. Sending a carrier pigeon just isn't an option for me.'

'Leave here? Not on your life, Sullivan Gold. I am in an intriguing new environment, and only I can describe the details for the curious trees. They haven't had many opportunities to see a gas giant. Besides' – he looked lovingly down at his treeling in its ornate pot – 'it'll do the forest good to see a place where our enemies have been resoundingly defeated.'

Sullivan glanced out into the expanse of clouds. 'We don't know for certain that the drogues are completely gone here, but we can hope.' As soon as the factory was completed, the cloud harvester's lead engineer intended to design deep probes that would keep an eye out for returning hydrogues. Just for insurance, though Sullivan didn't know how much good they would do.

The assembly work in Qronha 3's high atmosphere continued at a furious pace. Sullivan scanned the project timetable again and proudly confirmed that each phase had been completed on schedule. Within a few days the facility would be brought online, and they would begin collecting ekti for the Terran Hanseatic League. Then the fun would start.

The knot in his chest began to loosen. Nothing to worry about . . .

ELEVEN

TASIA TAMBLYN

Tasia's cruiser arrived at Ptoro bearing the doomsday weapon. *Here we are, you bastards. Ready or not.*

On the viewscreen, Ptoro was a cold ball without the pastel cloud bands of Jupiter or Golgen, without the majestic rings of Osquivel, colourless, lifeless, and grey – just waiting to be lit up with a bit of dazzle.

As the escort EDF battleships drew closer, they reported their positions. Tasia spoke through the Manta's intercom, calling all engineers and support personnel to prepare the Klikiss Torch.

Tasia's battle group had been obliged to bring two of the EDF's green priests to properly coordinate the deployment of the Torch. Older and more withdrawn than Rossia, Yarrod had expressed doubts about continuing to serve the Earth military during the worldforest's greater need, but Tasia hoped he would change his mind after the success of this mission.

Touching his treeling, Rossia closed his eyes and sent thoughts through telink, then verbalized a report for Tasia. 'Yarrod says he and the other engineers are in position at the neutron star. Their

70

wormhole generators are distributed outside the gravitational perimeter.' He blinked again. 'Those are the words he gave me, Commander Tamblyn. I don't know what it means.'

She leaned forward with a grim smile. 'It means that when we fire our torpedoes into Ptoro's clouds, we'll make an anchor point for this end of the wormhole. The engineers at Yarrod's station will open up the mouth, feed it the neutron star, which then gets dumped smack into the lap of the drogues down there. The extra mass will be enough to implode Ptoro into a new star.'

Rossia stroked the thin gold bark on his treeling. 'Oh, the hydrogues won't like that.'

'And there isn't a damn thing they can do to stop us.'

Tasia listened to the preparations, shouted confirmations, transmitted checks and double-checks as the systems were readied. EDF scout ships flew out, scanning the iron-grey clouds, dipping close to the atmosphere, and then retreating to orbital safety. Exo-meteorologists documented the wind patterns and temperature layers that delineated the gas giant's internal topography.

As she always did on missions that put her face to face with the drogues, Tasia thought of all the casualties suffered thus far in the unnecessary war. Her brother's death on the Blue Sky Mine had given Tasia her first incentive to join the Earth Defence Forces. She had fought the damned aliens in the clouds of Jupiter after their murderous emissary had delivered his ultimatum and killed Old King Frederick. She'd also been at Osquivel, where the EDF's largest battle force against the hydrogues had been utterly trounced. And Robb had been lost.

By igniting Ptoro, Tasia meant to give the hydrogues a black eye for a change. Tasia leaned forward. 'Shizz, that's going to be the biggest campfire anyone's ever seen.'

Her navigator, Elly Ramirez, said, 'I hope someone brought marshmallows.'

'They are too complacent.' Anwar Zizu, her weapons officer, leaned closer to inspect the tactical screens. 'If I were a hydrogue, I'd never let an EDF ship get this close.'

'If you were a *hydrogue*, Sergeant, I would kick your ass off my bridge.' Tasia sat back and silently ordered the butterflies in her stomach to stop their unruly fluttering. 'Enough chitchat. Launch the torpedoes from our end. No sense giving the enemy time to pack their suitcases.'

The Manta's modified weapons ports fired a group of silvery cylinders adapted from Klikiss designs found on Corribus. *Here it comes.* Sensor screens showed the small torpedo-like generators descending into the clouds.

'Tell Yarrod to have his engineers ready on the scout ship. As soon as our anchors are in position, I want that neutron star on its way here like a cannonball.'

Rossia communicated the information through the tree network.

Elly Ramirez frowned at her nav screens. 'I expected to see the drogues barking and snarling by now.'

'You complaining?' Her eyes glittering with determination, Tasia clasped her hands together. 'In a minute they'll have other things to worry about than chasing after us.'

Ptoro looked so harmless down there, so uninteresting. She wished this could have been Osquivel, as payback for what the drogues had done to the EDF there. She felt the familiar hollowness at the thought of Robb and all the other EDF casualties. Hell, she even missed the obnoxious Patrick Fitzpatrick III. She'd always wanted the spoiled bastard to get his comeuppance . . . but from *her*, not the drogues.

'Anchor points in position, Commander Tamblyn,' Zizu announced.

'Open the conduit. Let's send them a present.'

Rossia relayed the instructions through his treeling. He kept his large eyes closed, as if he didn't want to see what was happening. Everyone on the Manta's bridge waited in silence. The rest of the escort ships sent queries, but Tasia didn't answer them. Not yet.

The green priest looked up. 'It is done. Yarrod reports that the wormhole is opened and the neutron star is gone.'

Tasia brightened. 'On its way. Fire in the hole.'

She looked at the huge grey planet, but saw no change. As soon as the neutron star arrived, fusion fires would begin deep within, but the initial shockwave would rush up through layers of the atmosphere faster than thunder.

Tasia packed all the vengeance she could squeeze into her low voice. 'Go on and *burn*.'

TWELVE

PATRICK FITZPATRICK III

He never grew tired of voicing his frustration. 'Damned Roachers!' Patrick Fitzpatrick had repeated it often since he'd recovered from his injuries in the hydrogue attack – several times daily, in fact.

Inside the big, echoing asteroid chamber that Del Kellum's people used as a storage facility, burly Bill Stanna commiserated. 'Yeah, I signed up to fight drogues. Didn't know I was gonna waste my time held hostage by space trash.' Though dedicated to the EDF, Stanna had no sophisticated specialities, no particular skills the training sergeants could identify. Stanna was just a regular grunt, willing to do what he was told and ready to fight. 'I'm not gonna do any more work for them.'

Fitzpatrick sat stubbornly on the hard stone floor, combing his reddish-blond hair back in a never-ending attempt to keep it neat, even under these circumstances. 'Damn right! And don't think you have to, Bill.'

Though he was tall, he had an average build. Due to his good breeding, Fitzpatrick had handsome features and a strong jaw, though his nose was a little too sharp. His forehead showed a permanent crease between his hazel eyes from too many sceptical or disapproving frowns.

'They can't force us to work,' said Shelia Andez, a weapons specialist who had survived in a lifetube when her Juggernaut was destroyed over the Osquivel rings. She paced the claustrophobic room, looking at the haphazardly stacked crates of supplies. The rest of the EDF hostages had been sent out on other make-work details, and most of them were also refusing to cooperate. 'Isn't there a Geneva Convention or something? If we're prisoners of war, the Roachers have to follow certain standards of treatment.'

Fitzpatrick felt disgusted. 'Even if there was an agreement like that, they probably couldn't read it.' Stanna burst out with loud laughter, as if this was the funniest thing he had heard in a long time.

'When we don't do the work, our captors simply have the compies do it,' said Kiro Yamane, a cybernetics expert. He was a bit of an odd duck because he wasn't a formal member of the Earth Defence Forces. Yamane was, however, a genius with an intuitive knowledge of robotics after working under Swendsen and Palawu in the compy manufacturing centres on Earth. He had signed aboard the Osquivel battle fleet so he could assess the performance of the new Soldier model. 'I can't tell you how angry it makes me to see them use our sophisticated compies for . . . for grunt work.'

'Better them than us.' Stanna plopped down next to Fitzpatrick. The two men stared at the crates they were supposed to move and rearrange.

Thirty-two EDF survivors had been rescued when the space gypsies descended like parasites on the ruined ships in the Osquivel battlefield, and they'd been held as hostages in the hidden Roamer shipyard for over a month now.

Fitzpatrick's mind raged at the injustice of it. By now, his parents, both of them ambassadors, should have filed protests and demanded that something be done. His grandmother, the powerful old political battleaxe, should have sent an investigation committee or a rescue squad. His whole family should be in an uproar at what had happened to him.

But then his stomach sank. He was deluding himself. Yes, the Fitzpatricks would be outraged, but after hearing of the carnage in the rings of Osquivel, when so few EDF ships had limped away to safety, no one would suspect he – or any of the others – might still be alive.

The Roamers had their prisoners wrapped up in a package that was all so neat and tidy.

Over the weeks as he'd observed the activities here, he was astounded to learn of the huge spacedocks where ships of all sizes and designs were constructed. Clan Kellum had smelters, fabricators, assembly lines, a whole infrastructure – over a thousand people living and working here. When the EDF battle group had come to attack the hydrogues, no one had seen any signs of such a complex hidden in the rings. These Roachers were slippery, deceitful and devious, a cancer quietly growing between the stars.

The asteroid's rectangular airlock disengaged with a coughing hiss, then rattled aside. While Stanna struggled to his feet, as if caught sleeping on duty, Fitzpatrick and Andez pointedly remained sitting on the floor. 'You don't need to pretend you were working, Bill,' Fitzpatrick said. 'I want them to know I'm not lifting a finger to help.'

A slender young woman with long black hair stepped inside with a grace that showed she was accustomed to living in low gravity. Zhett Kellum, whom they had all met before, had huge green eyes that could either sparkle with mirth or displeasure. Fitzpatrick had seen her quirk her full lips upwards in a combination of annoyed disappointment and mischievous humour. 'I don't know how this sort of thing works among the Eddies, but in Roamer clans, we generally chip in and work for our dinner. Don't expect a free ride month after month.'

'In the Hansa,' Fitzpatrick replied acidly, 'our families generally don't take hostages and prevent them from going home.'

Andez added, 'Hey, if you don't like the quality of our work, then feel free to fire us and we'll be on our way.'

Arching her eyebrows, Zhett gestured towards the large sealed door. Her body seemed as flexible as spring steel. 'There's the airlock. You can walk out any time you like . . . but it's a fairly long hike.'

'Couldn't you at least give us a spaceship?' Stanna said.

Fitzpatrick jabbed him with his elbow. 'She wasn't serious, Bill.'

Zhett approached the four EDF captives. 'I wouldn't make assumptions like that if I were you, Fitzie.'

'Don't call me that.'

'Oh, it's just a pet name.' She smiled at him, and he gritted his teeth. 'I wasn't kidding about expecting you to pitch in. My father thinks you're more trouble than you're worth . . . and I'm starting to agree with him.'

'You expect us just to be complacent and cooperative?' Yamane said. 'We are being held here against our will.'

'We also saved all of your lives.' Zhett tossed her hair, which drifted slowly in the low gravity as if under water. Fitzpatrick couldn't help noticing that her Roamer jumpsuit was well-fitted to show her long, slender legs. 'Considering that all your Eddy friends turned tail and ran, leaving you to the drogues, I can't see why you're so anxious to go back. You'd all be better off if you just got used to living among the Roamers.'

All four of the hostages responded with an angry outburst. 'Never!'

Zhett just sighed and shook her head. 'That's the trouble with you Eddies. You seem incapable of learning to roll with the changes. Believe me, if we could think of a way to get you back to the Big Goose without giving away our trade secrets, I'd do it in a heartbeat.'

'That would be just about fast enough for me,' Fitzpatrick said with a scowl.

Zhett instructed some compies to finish stacking the crates and pitched in herself, while the prisoners sat idly watching. The Roamer girl ignored them, apparently immune to their surly stares and happy to prove her superiority. Fitzpatrick tried not to let it get to him.

THIRTEEN

CESCA PERONI

The old woman drifted in a sling chair connected to the rock wall. The former Speaker looked like a collection of dried bones held together with sinew, leathery skin, and sheer force of will. She'd been retired for six years and had not left the Rendezvous asteroids in all that time; her eyes were still as bright as black skypearls.

'Now that you have clear evidence against the EDF,' she said to Cesca, 'what does your Guiding Star tell you?'

Cesca closed her eyes. She had carefully schooled herself never to show vulnerability or indecision, but here behind closed doors in consultation with the only person who could truly understand her predicament, she let down her walls. 'How am I supposed to see the Guiding Star when I'm buried deep inside solid rock – both literally and figuratively?'

Jhy Okiah smiled with her parchment lips. 'You have to make decisions for yourself, child.'

The Speaker's office was one of the first chambers that had been hammered out by the settlers from the *Kanaka*. When the old generation ship had dropped off a fraction of their colonists here, the people had by no means been assured of their survival. But those predecessors of the Roamer clans had been tenacious and resourceful. The colony had survived and grown, eventually becoming a thriving base.

Roamers made their own decisions and survived – not relying on the blessings and gifts of others, but on their own ingenuity. Kotto Okiah was a perfect example: even after his high-risk metals-processing settlement on a near-molten planet had failed, Kotto had immediately begun work on a supercold frozen world from which he was sure he could wring vital resources.

Cesca needed to remember that and remind the other clan members. 'I wonder how many of our predecessors sat in this same place, facing similarly difficult decisions. When you first became Speaker, did you require so much advice?'

'Of course I did. We all do.'

Cesca shook her head, unable to imagine that this strong and decisive woman could possibly have experienced self-doubt. 'So how did you manage? Tell me the secret.'

'The secret is to realize that despite your worries, *you* are still the best qualified person to make these decisions. The Roamer clans chose you. They believe in you. And when you do your best, that's the best the Roamers have to offer.'

Cesca made a wry expression. 'Then maybe the Roamer clans are in trouble after all.' She turned to the former Speaker, and a hard look entered her eyes. 'The Big Goose stole our cargo, killed our people, then pretended nothing happened. We have something they want, and they seem to assume that a war gives them the right to just take it.'

'The Hansa is a formidable enemy. Should the clans provoke them?'

'We can't just ignore their acts of piracy.'

'No. The Big Goose has treated us with disdain for years. This is nothing new except for the level of violence. Remember that whatever you do will have tremendous repercussions.'

'Some of our hotheaded clan leaders might get incensed and forget about that. They can outvote me. I only speak for them – I can't coerce them.'

'Worse, most of them are men, and therefore prone to the need to prove themselves.' The old woman slowly shook her head.

Cesca paused for a long moment. 'If they take the obvious option, I dread the consequences for all of us.'

'Every decision has consequences. You're the leader of the clans. It is your job to make them see wisdom, make the best decision, then follow through with solidarity, no matter what. We are all Roamers.'

'Yes,' Cesca said. 'We can't forget who we are.'

FOURTEEN

DD

Inside the hydrogue citysphere beneath the clouds of Ptoro, droning emergency signals pounded like hammer blows through the impossibly dense atmosphere. DD didn't know which way to run.

The deep-core aliens, flowing masses of quicksilver, shimmered as they moved through the chaotic sculptures that made up their metropolis. The geometric buildings shifted and changed like jewelled three-dimensional mosaics locking into place in preparation for a large-scale evacuation. Colours flared brighter.

Though the Friendly compy did not comprehend what the impossibly alien hydrogues did or said, he could see that the creatures were agitated. What was the emergency? The black Klikiss robots – whom DD found to be somewhat more comprehensible, but just as monstrous – scuttled about with a clear urgency of their own. Finally, he intercepted one of the beetle-like robots. 'Please tell me what is happening.'

The robot swivelled his angular head and skewered the Friendly compy with his blazing optical sensors. 'The Earth military has arrived at Ptoro. Upper-layer scouts are observing them even now. They have already deployed the preparatory apparatus for the Torch weapon designed by my cursed progenitors. Some of the hydrogues will mount a defence, while the cityspheres open transgates and evacuate this world. We robots will also depart immediately in our ships.'

The thrumming emergency tone made the metal and polymer components of DD's artificial body vibrate. 'What about me? Am I to escape as well?'

'Sirix will deal with that matter. We have crucial preparations to make. Do not interfere.' The big robot lurched off through the dense atmosphere and vanished through a segmented crystalline wall. The facets rearranged themselves, and the other machine was gone.

DD looked through the bubble-domed skies and saw dozens of warglobes rising out of the citysphere. The diamond-hulled battleships rocketed upwards, like spined cannonballs shot into the clouds.

The brave EDF soldiers out there would soon face an overwhelming force.

When his masters, Margaret and Louis Colicos, had ignited the first Klikiss Torch, they had never intended to harm anyone and had not even known of the hydrogues' existence. This time, though, the EDF was deploying the Klikiss Torch as an outright act of war. Hansa diplomats and military officers had repeatedly attempted to propose a peace, but the hydrogues would not negotiate. The liquid-crystal creatures considered humans some-what interesting as playthings in their unusual tests and experiments, but ultimately irrelevant now that the hydrogues had far more powerful enemies abroad in the Spiral Arm.

DD, on the other hand, could think of nothing more important than to push his way into the environment chambers where Robb

Brindle and his fellow human prisoners were being held. As the emergency continued to build, no one hindered the little compy's movements, ignoring him entirely. All the hydrogues and Klikiss robots were too preoccupied with their frantic evacuation.

Inside the chamber, the haggard-looking prisoners lurched to their feet. 'DD!' Brindle said. 'Tell me you're bringing us good news, man.'

'Unfortunately, I am not. Are you aware of the turmoil occurring in the hydrogue citysphere?'

Several captives pressed against the curved gelatinous walls to peer outside through the translucent membranes. 'We can tell they've got their underwear in a twist,' Brindle said. 'But who can understand those blobs?'

'The Earth Defence Forces have arrived, and they have already launched an anchor point for a wormhole. They intend to ignite Ptoro with a second Klikiss Torch.'

A few of the captives raised their fists and hooted. "Bout time they got serious!'

'Another Torch!'

'The drogues can't fight it, can they?'

Anjea was the loudest. 'That'll show the bastards, give them a hot foot. Mess with the EDF and you get burned.'

'Uh, I don't want to rain on your parade, folks,' Brindle said, 'but we're all sitting at ground zero here.'

Some prisoners moaned with dismay, others looked as if they didn't care.

'Is there a chance we can evacuate?' Brindle said, looking quickly around. 'Anything we can do to stop the Torch?'

'And help the drogues? You're crazy!'

'It's worth it, just to scorch the blobs,' said a bedraggled Charles Gomez.

DD answered, 'I believe the hydrogues intend to transport their cityspheres through dimensional gates to another gas giant. In all probability, they will take you with them. You should be safe.'

'If *this* is safe, buddy, then what do you consider dangerous?' Anjea Telton snorted.

As the flustered compy sought for an appropriate response, Brindle sounded conciliatory. 'Never mind that, DD. I know you're doing what you can. Hey, will you be coming with us? Are the hydrogues taking you along, too?'

'I have very little information. I wish I could provide you with additional data.'

Sullen Gomez jumped away from the curved, translucent wall. Beside him, two men cried out in warning. DD looked up to see a looming form just outside the flexible barrier. Extending several jointed limbs, the armoured beetle shape lunged through into the environment chamber. As the prisoners backed away, the compy recognized Sirix, his main tormentor. 'DD, come with me immediately. Our ship is prepared.'

'We must ensure the safety of these human prisoners,' DD suggested. 'The hydrogues may not properly care for them.'

'The hydrogues can eradicate them or save them, as they wish. This citysphere is ready to depart through the transgate, and we must not be part of the exodus.'

'Why not?' DD asked.

Brindle and the other human captives stared at the two machines, trying to follow the jackhammer electronic conversation.

'We have other priorities. Cease these delays.'

DD dutifully followed the big black robot back out of the membrane. He caught one last glance of Brindle, looking worried but determined as they departed.

Overhead, three more armoured warglobes launched away from the citysphere.

Sirix guided the compy at a rapid clip until they reached their modified ship. One of the flowing hydrogues coalesced from a silvery flow on the ground, rising tall until it stood before Sirix in its human facsimile.

The hydrogue spoke in a far more complex language than DD could readily understand, but he grasped that a Torch wormhole had already been opened and that the cityspheres were about to evacuate.

Sirix clicked and hummed a response that seemed sarcastic, almost ironic. 'The Torch weapon designed by our brutal masters and creators now makes humans as powerful as the faeros, if only temporarily. Now that the faeros have returned, you may consider humans irrelevant to your overall conflict. If, however, they can obliterate hydrogue planets at will, does that not make them highly relevant?' On multiple finger-like legs, he moved forward to the sanctuary of his ship. 'Repeatedly, they show their true destructive nature, which we have warned of many times before.'

A ripple flickered across the hydrogue's body. Its language now seemed painfully clear to DD: 'You Klikiss robots have our leave to destroy as many humans as you wish.'

Sirix swivelled his flat geometrical head. 'We understand that your conflict with the faeros and the verdani currently saps your strength and attention, but we robots will do everything in our power to wipe out the human race and free their compies.'

The black robot scuttled to his deep-pressure craft and herded DD aboard. Several Klikiss robots had already set themselves up at the controls. Their ship launched immediately. As they plunged through a citysphere wall and rose away from the hydrogue metropolis, DD swivelled his optical sensors and watched behind them.

A dazzling white line split open in the fabric of the air, like a vertical mouth yawning wide. Giant hydrogue cityspheres shuttled through the immense maw of the transgate. Other conduit lines opened, and a second complex of faceted globes passed through to safety.

The black robots accelerated their ship up through the buffeting winds of deep clouds. They piloted a direct course out, ignoring all the strange life forms that floated in the bizarre habitation zones and stable layers of Ptoro's atmosphere.

Then, far below, where the largest concentration of cityspheres had hovered only moments ago, a dazzling new sun erupted, appearing with remarkable suddenness. The Klikiss Torch system had slammed a neutron star into the gas giant's core, triggering a full gravitational collapse.

All the remaining hydrogue cityspheres plunged through their transgates and the dimensional lines slammed shut. They had escaped, leaving only their guardian warglobes behind to retaliate against the human army.

DD had to adjust his sensors. The robots fled Ptoro so rapidly that the framework of their ship, designed to withstand the greatest of stresses, shuddered and rattled, threatening to break apart.

Then the whole planet caught on fire.

FIFTEEN

TASIA TAMBLYN

Warglobes boiled out of the clouds of Ptoro. As the displaced neutron star caused the gas giant to implode, scatters of lightning ricocheted off the clouds in eruptions of light that broke through from the first surge of a newborn star's ignition.

'Shizz, look what we flushed out of the bushes,' said Tasia with a grim smile. 'I guess they don't like the present we just sent them.'

'Can't take it back. Nothing they can do now except run.' Elly Ramirez chuckled, but her tense posture hinted at her level of anxiety.

Ensign Terene Mae made a disconcerting groan as the Manta's viewer magnified the oncoming spiked spheres. 'Doesn't look like they're *running*, Commander. They're coming right at us.'

'Normally, I wouldn't presume to guess how the drogues think,' Tasia said. 'Right now, I'm fairly certain that they're pissed off.'

Heedless of the warglobe threat, Sergeant Zizu read from the weapons displays in front of him. 'Our deepest sensor buoys have been destroyed, presumably by the ignition shockwave. The flamefront is rising.' He turned, grinning.

Several EDF Mantas shifted position to face the enemy spheres. Their armaments included fracture-pulse drones – shaped charges designed to shatter thick diamond material – and carbon slammers that would break carbon-carbon bonds in the crystalline structure.

'Battle stations!' Tasia said over the shipwide commsystem.

Sergeant Zizu scanned the tactical readouts. 'Slammers and fraks are in the launch tubes. Ready.'

Tasia nodded. 'Escort cruisers, disperse and prepare to offer some covering fire!'

Blue lightning arced from point to point on the warglobes as the aliens charged their weapons. Deadly bolts lanced toward the EDF targets, ripping streaks along the thick hull plates, bursting some bulkheads. The Mantas reeled and turned their damaged sectors away from further pummelling. New reinforced armour prevented the warships from being destroyed outright.

Tasia gripped the arms of her command chair. 'Shizz, I'm not going to stand on ceremony – open fire whenever and wherever you see fit. Keep shooting as you pack up and retreat. It's the better part of valour to escape now – let the Klikiss Torch do its stuff!'

The escort battleships launched a storm of jazer blasts and detonating charges. The hydrogues responded with even greater fury. Tasia's bridge crew cried out in dismay when three drogue spheres converged on a single escort Manta, pounding it repeatedly until it was blown apart. Debris spread out in a cloud of wreckage, atmosphere, and bodies.

A second Manta exploded as the EDF ships accelerated, pulling away from the collapsing gas giant. More and more of the hydrogues kept coming, surrounding the EDF ships and cutting off their escape. Tasia's only glimmer of pleasure was to see Ptoro beginning to glow with purifying fires from below. She'd had quite enough of the damned aliens.

'Come on, quit spinning your jets and take us out of here.'

'Hydrogue warglobes are pursuing, Commander!'

From far outside Ptoro's orbit, a streak of fire rocketed past Tasia's cruiser, a blazing ball as large as any warglobe, heading towards the dying planet. Then came a second, a third, and then ten more.

'What the hell was that?' Ramirez said. 'A meteor?'

Tasia knew. All around them in space, the incandescent ellipsoids were like moths gathering around a kindling flame. 'The faeros,' she said with a quiet breath. She had seen them before, fighting a losing battle at the artificial star of Oncier. Now though, the fireball entities and their blazing vessels greatly outnumbered the hydrogue spheres. The inferno ships careened into the warglobes like exploding suns, shattering the diamond-hulled spheres.

The hydrogues immediately turned their crackling blue lightning upon the faeros, ignoring the insignificant human battleships. The EDF crews responded with a mixture of stunned silence and crazily enthusiastic cheers. 'Shizz, don't waste any time!' Tasia bellowed so loudly her voice cracked. 'We've got a distraction – let's get the hell out of here.'

An even more strenuous volley of jazer blasts and targeted hull-breakers flew out, but Tasia told her weapons officers to stand down. 'We're like a little mouse in a battle between two mammoths. Just move out of the crossfire. No sense in having more of our battleships destroyed here and now.'

As Ptoro continued to brighten, as its core collapsed and nuclear fires were sparked deep within, the faeros combatants smashed into the flotilla of warglobes. Diamond spheres and flaming ellipsoids pirouetted around each other like closely orbiting planets. Blinding arcs like solar flares and coronal loops intersected with blue lightning bolts.

The EDF ships continued to accelerate in their retreat, leaving the grey gas planet warming with inner flames.

Several of the still-spinning faeros ellipsoids had turned black like extinguished coals, carbonaceous cinders deadened by a hydrogue attack, but the majority of the diamond globes had been shattered. Broken fragments drifted away from the funeral pyre of Ptoro. Dozens, then hundreds of the fireballs rushed to the burgeoning star, mercilessly surrounding and engulfing the few remaining hydrogues.

Satisfied, Tasia muttered, 'See? Bullies always come to a bad end.' She called a halt to their retreat and waited on the edge of the Ptoro system, observing the immense battle from a safe distance.

The hydrogues had no chance. Within an hour, the faeros had eradicated them completely, destroying every one of the spiked spheres.

Tasia wished she could have personally crushed a few of the warglobes, but she was pleased enough just to see their enemies meet such an ignominious end. She had done her part by triggering the ignition of Ptoro. Thanks to her, the new star would burn for thousands of years before it faded into an ember.

'It looked awfully grim there for a few minutes, Commander,' Zizu said. 'I was never much of a believer in Unison, but I admit I was reciting all the prayers I memorized as a kid.'

'Call it a miracle if you want,' Tasia said. 'We owe the faeros our thanks, at the very least. They cleared the way for our escape.'

But the flaming ships responded to none of the EDF hails. Instead, after the fireballs had mopped up the hydrogue warships, they flitted around brightening Ptoro, then descended into the new sun. Without a word of response, they plunged with obvious delight into the flame front that gobbled the gaseous atmosphere.

All across the Spiral Arm, stars had been quenched in the titanic battles between hydrogues and faeros. Perhaps, she thought, Ptoro was new territory to make up for all the dying stars the faeros had already lost.

SIXTEEN

ANTON COLICOS

Over the course of weeks, the long sunset on Maratha faded into a half year of night. Anton Colicos would remain here for the full season of darkness, the only human on the planet with a handful of Ildirans. He looked forward to the solitude.

The skeleton crew left to watch over the empty resort city, however, viewed it as a long-term prison sentence.

Though this world was under his personal charge, the Maratha Designate had gone back to Ildira for the funeral of his father and the ascension of Jora'h. Designate Avi'h had made no secret of the fact that he wouldn't return until the sun shone again and vacationers arrived.

Anton tried to encourage his rememberer friend. 'Let's make the best of it, Vao'sh. If these Cannons of Darkness are as spectacular as I've heard, then we'll have a whole new repertoire of experiences for storytelling. It happens only once each year, right?'

The old Ildiran rememberer had at first been glad to receive this assignment to maintain the spirits of the skeleton crew, but with the onset of long night, Vao'sh had his doubts. Anton planned to shoulder more of the entertainment work, by sharing Earth legends.

The fleshy lobes on the alien historian's face flickered through a palette of emotions. Wry amusement? Resignation? Anton still couldn't interpret all the shades of colours, the nuances of their meanings. 'All right, Rememberer Anton, let us go look at the Cannons of Darkness, as you suggest.'

Anton eagerly followed him as they suited up near the exit hatch of the domes of Maratha Prime. Outside, Maratha's temperature was already dropping towards the extreme cold of the night season. Their protective garments, which used Ildiran thermal technology, were thin and flexible, but warm.

The planet rotated slowly, like a devoted sycophant staring at the gleaming majesty of the star. As a result, for nearly half the year Maratha Prime basked in golden sunshine, followed by a month-long sunset, and the remainder of the year in endless night. The majority of Maratha's population evacuated as the sun slowly went down.

After nearly two centuries of success as a resort world, Maratha was about to open an identical luxury city, Maratha Secda, in the opposite hemisphere. A construction crew of Klikiss robots was even now toiling in the brightening new daylight of the Secda job site to complete the gigantic city. As sunset fell here, dawn would be rising over there.

But a skeleton crew had to remain at Prime, to keep watch over the nearly empty resort city.

The two suited men stepped out into the dimming twilight. Though the deepening sky still provided plenty of illumination, Vao'sh quickly switched on all the glowstrips affixed to his shoulders.

Before Anton and Vao'sh could climb aboard a small ground

vehicle to take them to the Cannons, another Ildiran male called out. 'Wait, I wish to accompany you!' Anton recognized the lens kithman, Ilure'l, who stayed as counsellor and adviser to the members of the skeleton crew. 'The Cannons of Darkness are remarkable, and I always feel . . . inspired when I observe them.'

Lens kithmen had faint telepathic powers with which they could supposedly interpret the realm of the Lightsource. Considering the palpable gloom and depression setting in among the skeleton crew, Anton hoped Ilure'l could serve as both priest and psychologist to the remaining Ildirans.

'Please, join us.' Vao'sh's voice carried an edge of fear at going too far from the others. 'Please.'

Anton volunteered to drive the simple vehicle out towards the shadowy horizon. 'Should we ask Mhas'k and Syl'k if they'd like to come? They might want to get out of their agricultural domes.'

The lens kithman looked quickly at him. 'They have work to do.'

Behind them, the gemmed domes of Prime glowed bright, a scream of photons against the nightfall. Three honeycombed structures sat like satellites on the outskirts, shimmering with natural greens from the well-lit plants inside.

Under searing lights, the two agricultural kithmen tended stacked crops within fertilizer troughs and hydroponics channels. Agricultural kithmen grew food; that was all they knew, all they cared about. Curious about Ildiran ways, Anton had been eager to learn more about the farmers' way of life, their inbred service to the Mage-Imperator. But when he'd tried to talk with them, both had been quiet. When they spoke at all, they kept their heads down, eyes fixed on the ground. Their fingers deftly worked in the planters, touching leaves and stems, monitoring moisture levels. Mhas'k and his mate Syl'k seemed to communicate better with growing things than with people.

They were such an utterly perfect match that they reminded Anton of his own missing parents. Margaret and Louis had been like two sides of the same coin, always working together, sharing the same passions and interests. He wished he knew where they were . . .

Vao'sh explained. 'Most Ildiran kiths do not have the same curiosity you exhibit, Rememberer Anton. Mhas'k and Syl'k must maintain the greenhouse domes and grow our food. For them, that brings joy and satisfaction. They have no need for sightseeing.'

Now, as the vehicle sped across the ground, the dusk grew darker. Ilure'l adjusted the internal lights so high that Anton had to squint to make out their course. Up ahead he could see white plumes like exhaust from the towers of an industrial fabrication plant.

Ilure'l said, 'Each year I come to observe this.' Vao'sh's face swept through a symphony of colours, expressing with tints and hues what he could not yet put into words.

Anton stopped the vehicle where he could watch the curls of mist boiling upwards like steam from an alien kettle. He was the first out of the vehicle and into the crackling cold. A low reverberant rumble made the ground vibrate from the continuous boiling of water deep beneath the rocks. 'Can you hear it?'

The steam fogged the air around them in the abrupt darkness. Moisture settled out in snowflakes that dropped to the ground, building spires of encrusted ice around the open mouths of fumaroles.

According to engineering and seismic surveys, the ground underneath Maratha Prime was riddled with aquifers and thermal channels. Hot springs bubbled into the city itself, for the enjoyment of the Ildiran visitors. As temperatures dropped with each sunset, thermal plumes that normally vented invisibly into the hot daytime air suddenly became prominent, booming explosions of heat and moisture. Within weeks, the exhaled steam would freeze and form a cap over the geysers, silencing them until they were explosively reborn the next dawn.

Vao'sh and Ilure'l remained by the safe illumination of the ground vehicle, while Anton strode fearlessly into the shadows where he could better see the pearly white mists. 'I have always been interested in natural wonders, but transient phenomena like this are so much more . . . poignant.'

'A wilting flower is more beautiful than an enduring statue of our Mage-Imperator?' Ilure'l sounded sceptical.

'In a different way, but . . . yes. Knowing you're about to lose something demands that you value it before it is gone.'

'Rememberer Anton has a point,' Vao'sh said.

The lens kithman was troubled. 'The *thism* is beautiful because it never changes and always endures. By its perfect reliability, it inspires faith. While I can admire the natural uniqueness of these formations, I find less them less beautiful than the Lightsource, by virtue of their very evanescence.'

'Humans believe there can be two or more ways to interpret a story,' Vao'sh pointed out.

Anton smiled. 'Arguing over such things has kept many of my . . . esoteric colleagues in university jobs for their entire careers, and generations of predecessors before them.'

Ilure'l seemed disturbed by the discussion. 'When I interpret the *thism*, Rememberer Anton, I do not want other Ildiran kithmen to draw their own conclusions. Too much discussion creates questions, not answers. When I give an answer, then the matter is settled.' After looking at the Cannons for only a few more moments, the lens kithman turned to climb back into the vehicle. 'If you are ready, I would like to go now.'

As Anton drove off towards the glowing domes of Maratha Prime, he tried to placate the agitated lens kithman. 'With all

Ildirans connected through *thism*, maybe you can give absolute answers. But when I'm retelling one of our legends, it's . . . just a story.'

Now Vao'sh's face flushed with multicoloured alarm. 'Rememberer Anton, nothing is ever *just a story*.'

SEVENTEEN

MAGE-IMPERATOR JORA'H

Jora'h sat in his private contemplation chamber, a smooth-walled room with blood-red crystalline walls, while seven frenetic attenders combed and oiled his golden hair, then drew on the twitching strands. Despite their overlapping tangle of hands, the servant kithmen managed to braid his hair. The length was not sufficient for more than a modest plait that reached barely to the base of his neck, but over the years it would extend and grow into a long rope, like the former Mage-Imperator's.

His corpulent father had never set foot out of the chrysalis chair, yet Jora'h felt that it confined and isolated him and limited his ability to lead his people. Although tradition required him to issue his decrees and guide his people without ever touching the floor, this seemed to Jora'h a ridiculous restriction for a ruler.

As Prime Designate, he had always known this would be his fate. Unfortunately, he hadn't appreciated his freedom and opportunities, hadn't noticed his *life* – until it was too late.

Many parts of the government, the Solar Navy, the Designates and their replacements, were currently undergoing the turmoil of transition. It was up to Jora'h to dispatch his sons to their new assignments, to issue orders and proclamations, to reassure the Ildirans that his vision of the Lightsource was true and his *thism* was strong.

How was he supposed to go to Dobro, to Nira, to liberate her and her fellow human captives, if he was trapped by so many immediate crises and obligations? Within days, he hoped it would be possible to rush off to Dobro – to Nira. She had waited so many years, undoubtedly believing he had abandoned her . . .

But first he had to be the Mage-Imperator.

His son Thor'h bullied his way past the door guards, despite Jora'h's orders for his children to wait outside. 'Father, your new Designates have gathered and are ready for you.'

Jora'h looked at the Prime Designate, fighting a frown. He noted the glassy look in the young man's star-sapphire eyes. In the Mage-Imperator's senses, Thor'h was a blot in the *thism*, an indistinguishable blur. 'Perhaps if you consumed less shiing, Thor'h, you would find it easier to allow *me* to make decisions and issue commands.'

His son did not even have the good grace to appear stung by the rebuke. 'Shiing allows me to focus and gives me more energy to do my important duties. At the moment, the Empire requires nothing less than my peak performance.'

Shiing, a popular drug from Hyrillka, had been hard to obtain since the hydrogues devastated that world. But Thor'h still had his supplies and, the Mage-Imperator feared, his addiction.

Annoyed by his son's lack of discipline and understanding, Jora'h clenched his hand beneath the folds of soft cloth in the chrysalis chair. The Prime Designate was still young and poorly trained; his years on Hyrillka had made him too soft, though at the time Jora'h had thought he was doing his son a kindness. Now, he wondered if he should have been harder on his first-born, prepared him better to become the Prime Designate. He hoped Thor'h would grow up properly and learn his skills and his place. After all, the former Mage-Imperator had not prepared Jora'h until the last few months of his failing life.

'Go bring in my other sons now,' Jora'h said abruptly. 'I don't wish to wait any longer.'

Anxious to proceed with the meeting, the Prime Designate spun, left the room, and soon hurried back into the contemplation chamber, accompanied by his two closest brothers, Daro'h and Pery'h. Pery'h would now take over the role of Designate on Hyrillka, even though Thor'h had spent more time there.

No one gets exactly what he wants . . . not even a son of the Mage-Imperator.

Behind the three young men, unbidden, came Yazra'h, the Mage-Imperator's oldest daughter. She was lean and muscular, her movements conveying a confident, decisive nature. Coppery hair waved around her head like a mane, long and extravagant in comparison to that of the young men, since all Ildiran males had hacked off their hair in mourning at the former Mage-Imperator's death.

Thor'h sniffed at his sister in distaste. 'You are not needed here, Yazra'h.' The Mage-Imperator's bloodline was heavily skewed towards male offspring. Indeed, of Jora'h's myriad children of all kiths, only a handful had been daughters. Including one by Nira . . .

Even though he had not asked Yazra'h to this meeting, Jora'h decided that the Prime Designate's pompous attitude needed to be dealt with. 'The Mage-Imperator makes those decisions, Thor'h,' he said, a warning tone in his voice, 'especially in his own contemplation chamber.'

Yazra'h's eyes were bright, challenging her oldest brother. The Mage-Imperator had no doubt that she could defeat any of his sons in hand-to-hand combat. He said in a softer tone, 'I summoned only my first Designate candidates, Yazra'h.'

She shrugged casually, then tossed a dismissive glance at the Prime Designate. 'Your door guards did not appear to be doing a very good job keeping unwanted people out. I simply came to offer my assistance, should you need it.'

'I will consider that. Perhaps the guard ranks need to be shaken up a bit, and we can use you for our home defence.'

Beaming, Yazra'h bowed. 'I would be honoured to serve in any way my father chooses.' She strode out past the ferocious-looking door guards.

Jora'h looked at his young Designates. 'I will be speaking to all of my noble-born sons in the next few hours, and I will dispatch you to your new assignments as soon as I arrange Solar Navy escorts. During your five-year transition period, each of you will be trained by one of my brothers. Only you, Pery'h, will have to do your work alone.'

The young man sadly bowed his head. His injured uncle was still being tended in the Prism Palace's infirmary, and Rusa'h's condition seemed hopeless. Pery'h would have to become the new Hyrillka Designate without relying on a mentor, but he was intelligent and had shown his willingness to seek advice and counsel. Jora'h was confident the young man would do a good job.

The changeover from Designate to successor had always taken place gradually and efficiently. Many of Jora'h's brothers were perfectly competent in their roles, but because the *thism* connection was strongest between father and son, the Mage-Imperator's own children traditionally took over as rulers of the subsidiary Ildiran colonies, so that he could see them better in his mind.

The Designates-in-waiting would learn the particular needs and aspects of each splinter settlement. Through the *thism* Jora'h could feel the loyalties of his sons and knew that they had accepted their responsibilities. Despite the blow to its heart with the abrupt death of Mage-Imperator Cyroc'h, the Ildiran Empire would continue as strong as before. Once all of Jora'h's sons reached their assigned worlds, the pieces would be in place again.

Then he could go to Nira.

As he dismissed Thor'h, Daro'h, and Pery'h, he heard a disturbance in the corridor outside, saw shadowy shapes through the translucent walls as a person hurriedly approached. Because of Yazra'h's earlier criticism, the warrior kithmen at the door snapped to sharper attention, growling denials and warnings.

'But I have important news!' came a voice from outside.

Through the *thism* Jora'h sensed a medical kithman, knew that the urgency of his message was not overstated. 'Let him enter. I wish to learn—'

The doctor burst through the door before the Mage-Imperator could finish his sentence. 'Liege, it is the Hyrillka Designate!' The medical kithman's nimble hands fluttered in agitation. 'After all this time lost in sub-*thism* sleep, your brother Rusa'h has awakened!'

EIGHTEEN

YARROD

When the triumphant EDF fleet returned from Ptoro, Yarrod could think of no better time to end his service with the Earth Defence Forces — nor could he find a reason to stay that was more important than the reasons to go.

Yes, the hydrogues continued to attack random colonies, both human and Ildiran, but now it seemed clear the deep-core aliens had been hunting for vestiges of the worldforest. Perhaps it made logical sense to stay with the Earth military, to assist in the efforts to fight the enemy. But, oh, how the aching trees called to him every time he touched his treeling!

Yarrod had never wanted to join the Earth military in the first place, had volunteered only grudgingly and never considered himself a true EDF soldier. Unlike his talkative and adventurous friend Kolker, he felt no call to see other planets besides Theroc. He found enough fascinating things within the worldforest to occupy his attention for an entire lifetime.

His niece, Sarein, acting as Theron ambassador to Earth, had begged for their assistance in the hydrogue war, and the trees had given their approval. He and eighteen other green priests had left Theroc and been dispersed to serve aboard widely separated military ships in far-off space battlefields.

But now Yarrod could not turn a deaf ear to the greater demands of the wounded trees. Through vivid telink he had experienced all the terror, the struggle, the pain – which had given him helpless nightmares for weeks. He should have been on Theroc using his powers to *help*, instead of riding in this metal-walled ship. Maybe he would have died like so many others, but at least he would have *been there*.

His fingers clenched as the memory of flames and cold and agony swept through him. No one had known the hydrogues would attack Theroc. He had been on the bridge of an EDF cruiser awaiting new orders when the wail of the worldforest had hammered through him. Through the eyes of a thousand trees, he'd observed the death of his nephew Reynald and so many more. It was all too much to bear.

Now it was too late to fight in that battle, but not too late to rebuild, clear away the mess, tend the new shoots . . . and prepare, should such a disaster happen again.

Through telink he had discussed his need with other green priests, especially with Kolker, who was now aboard a distant skymine at Qronha 3. Kolker and Yarrod had been acolytes together long ago, had taken the green on the same day. 'At Ptoro you struck a blow for perfect revenge,' Kolker told him through telink. 'That was your way of fighting the hydrogues, and you accomplished more than the rest of us.'

Though he'd been stationed as a simple relayer of information, transmitting instructions from Commander Tamblyn, Yarrod had shared every moment with Kolker, Rossia, and all other green priests. He had watched the yawning, interdimensional wormhole open like a toothless mouth to gulp the collapsed star and send it to Ptoro.

Yes, he had struck back at the forest's enemies — but it was not enough, and not what his heart demanded of him.

Victory messages about Ptoro had already been sent throughout the Spiral Arm via the network of green priests. Now, as the fleet returned at full speed to Earth, Yarrod sat alone in his cabin aboard the lead Manta. He did not wish to talk with Rossia or any of the EDF officers. He had already made up his mind. Yarrod had no choice but to resign and set aside his weak commitments to the military.

When he finally stood in the skeletal graveyard of worldtrees, smelling the harsh soot and charcoal like the blood of cremated trees, he knew the pain would slash like razors at his soul. Still, Yarrod knew what he must do.

Alone in his small cabin, he drew strength from communing in silence with his treeling. Then, finally, before the Manta could come to dock at Earth, he walked purposefully towards the bridge to inform Commander Tamblyn of his decision.

NINETEEN

BASIL WENCESLAS

The news about Ptoro would not be officially released until tomorrow, but Basil already had his report from the green priests in the battle group. Here on Earth, he had to make certain the achievement had the greatest effect. The Chairman couldn't do it all himself, though he did not dare show weakness, even to his number two man.

For the past year, he had subtly groomed Eldred Cain to become his deputy and heir apparent. Cain had moved into the Hansa HQ pyramid just before the hydrogue crisis, but Basil had never visited the man outside business hours. Though he had no interest in friendly socializing with the deputy, Basil needed to understand the details of Cain's personal life. His underlings were not allowed to have any secrets.

Despite the late hour, instead of summoning the deputy to his penthouse, Basil went to see Cain on his own turf. As always, he was dressed impeccably, as if ready to address gathered members of the Hansa Trade Board. The Chairman didn't believe in non-business hours.

The pale-skinned deputy met him at the door, wearing a comfortable shirt made of slick fabric. At thirty-eight, Eldred Cain was slender and small-statured, with entirely hairless skin that indicated either meticulous depilation or some form of alopecia.

Showing no surprise at the visit, Cain gestured him inside. 'Welcome to my home, Mr Chairman. Is this to be a meeting over dinner – I can have something sent up – or just drinks?'

'I prefer not to drink alcohol if we're discussing business.'

Cain gave him his maddeningly beatific smile. 'I always maintain a small supply of cardamom coffee, Mr Chairman, in case you ever decide to visit.'

While Basil's penthouse had windows that looked out upon the breathtaking skyline, Cain preferred interior quarters, without windows. Basil had even heard a silly rumour that his odd deputy was a vampire. When asked about his unusual preference, Cain had explained cryptically, 'Inside rooms have more wall space.'

Once Basil entered the other man's inner sanctum, the reason became apparent. The walls were adorned with art, from small sketches to enormous paintings: portraits of inbred-looking nobles, two near-identical depictions of the crucifixion, images from classical mythology, simple slices of rustic medieval life. Each work was lovingly displayed with perfect diffuse illumination, complete with a one-person bench set at the optimal viewing distance.

'Do you know the work of Velasquez, Mr Chairman? These are originals from the seventeenth century. Priceless.'

'Art history was never one of my particular interests.'

The deputy showed uncharacteristic exuberance. 'A master of realism and deception, Velasquez had a wicked sense of satire, poking subtle but vicious insults at the vapid nobles, whom he hated. They never noticed.' Over the years Cain had spent most of his substantial earnings to acquire Velasquez's sketches and paintings, many from the Prado in Madrid. 'I can stare for hours. I never get tired of looking at the composition, the colours.'

Basil appreciated quality work, but he had never spent more than a few moments inspecting a single painting. 'Interesting, Mr Cain – but that is not why I have come tonight.' He walked deeper into the room. 'Since Ptoro has already worked so well, I intend to authorize the use of another Klikiss Torch. Perhaps several more.'

He didn't want to appear weak or indecisive, but he needed input, a sounding board, and he had already discussed the idea with Sarein. He wanted to get a fresh perspective . . . so long as he didn't seem to be coming to the deputy with his hat in his hand. So far, Basil had found his deputy to be correct far more often than not.

Cain sat on the edge of one of his viewing benches, indicating another for Basil. His hairless brow wrinkled. 'Ah, and you are concerned that it might provoke a disastrous counter-strike instead of forcing concessions from them.'

Basil didn't admit he had been asking for help. He simply waited.

Cain continued, 'From our first reports, the Ptoro deployment was a success, but it could as easily have been a debacle. And it is too soon to be certain there'll be no retaliation from the hydrogues.'

'Even so,' Basil countered, 'the hydrogues do know we can hurt them.'

'What if the faeros hadn't offered their assistance? They seem to be enemies of the hydrogues, but we don't know their motives, nor have we ever managed to find them or communicate with them.'

Basil steepled his fingers. 'Perhaps we should issue an ultimatum of our own before igniting each new Torch? Demand that the hydrogues rescind their restrictions and foreswear further attacks against us. If they refuse or if they don't answer, then we ignite another Torch, and then another. There's a historical precedent: It's the way President Truman used atomic weapons in World War II to deal with the Japanese.'

'Not an apt analogy, Mr Chairman.' Here in private, the deputy did not show any reluctance to contradict Basil. 'President Truman commanded one of the largest armies in World War II, and the United States was already a force to be reckoned with. In *this* conflict, however, we are relatively ineffectual, as far as the enemy is concerned. Almost certainly, the hydrogues could wipe us out at any time. Our posturing is equivalent to the threat of, say, Luxembourg joining World War II. Yes, we can broadcast warnings, vow to annihilate the hydrogues if they don't concede. But what if they unleash an all-out attack on us? We couldn't withstand that – as our experiences on Boone's Crossing, Corvus Landing, and Theroc have shown.'

'There's always the chance that they'll keep hitting human colonies, whether we use Klikiss Torches or not, Eldred.'

Cain put his chin on one hand. 'We've just begun skymining again on Qronha 3, and I sincerely wish we had unfettered access to more gas giants. Unfortunately, when we use a Torch we don't secure potential resources – we destroy them. That doesn't help us harvest ekti.'

Basil growled. 'Can you come up with another solution?'

'Let me think about it. By the way, I understand that several transport ships are bringing the warglobe wreckage found on Theroc. Will it arrive in time for the upcoming Ptoro victory celebration?'

'It is on the schedule.' The Chairman got to his feet. 'Presenting the wreckage should be another morale booster.'

'Not much more than window dressing, Mr Chairman.'

A cynical smile quirked the corners of Basil's mouth. 'Don't underestimate the importance of window dressing, Eldred. Why do you think we have a King?'

TWENTY

KING PETER

It was good to have a genuine reason to celebrate again, after so many tragedies. King Peter stood warmly beside his Queen on a high balcony overlooking the gathering dusk of the festival square. Though they were in public, and partly because of it, he and Estarra shared quick communicative glances, brief touches, very close and comfortable in each other's space.

The royal couple were welcomed with a resounding cheer; Peter's face wore its first genuine smile in recent memory. He and Estarra clasped hands, raised them together in greeting to the people.

Bright music skirled over the huge crowd. Street singers and instrument players skipped about with an obvious need to show their joy. Revellers loosed phosphorescent balloons that floated into the air then popped, spraying shimmering sparkles. Boats cruised the Royal Canal, and tourist-filled zeppelins drifted overhead.

Down in the plaza, the Archfather of the official religion, Unison, stood like a kindly old saint in gaudy voluminous robes, leading groups in ritualized prayer and hymns of thanksgiving. Young Prince Daniel, Peter's supposed brother, was not in attendance 'for security reasons', and the King was glad that the unspoken threat of his replacement would not sour the day. Chairman Wenceslas thought he had intimidated the young King into meekly accepting his subordinate role, but Peter was merely biding his time, guarded and careful.

'I'd almost forgotten what it felt like, Estarra. It was necessary to remind the hydrogues that we are not helpless, that we won't just stand by and be slaughtered.'

She hugged him. 'Now they certainly aren't going to forget.'

He ran his hand over the soft skin of her shoulder, loving just to touch her. Unfortunately, because he so obviously cared for her, Estarra's safety had become a nasty bit of leverage for the Hansa. Peter knew it, and so did Basil.

Moving silently, the Chairman stepped up behind them, as quiet as gathering dust. 'The cargo haulers have started their descent. They should be visible in the sky within ten minutes, so it's time for you to begin your announcements.'

'You and your schedules, Basil,' Peter said with a wry smile. 'Are you nervous about giving your little speech today?' Though he rarely appeared in public, the Chairman had chosen to give an address of his own; perhaps Basil wanted to bask in the optimistic news for a change. A bit of rare pride?

'Nervous? No.'

On cue, a loud fanfare stunned the background murmur into silence. Unnecessary spotlights shone down on the three of them, dazzling Peter's eyes and blinding him to the descending spacecraft – but he knew where they were scheduled to be. 'Behold, everyone!' Peter shouted, pointing into the air. 'This proves that our enemies *can* be destroyed!'

Six EDF cargo haulers dropped into view from high orbit.

Beneath the heavy lifters, blackened fragments of a gigantic diamond eggshell dangled from powerful tractor beams. Two haulers worked in tandem to carry the largest piece of the shattered warglobe from Theroc, while each of the other ships brought a smaller fragment to the Royal Plaza.

Estarra squeezed his hand, grimly pleased to see for herself the broken hydrogue ship that her sister Celli had found. Just standing beside his wife, Peter felt stronger, able to help the human race get through this crisis.

General Lanyan had originally demanded that the wreckage be brought to the main EDF base on Mars for a full analysis, but Chairman Wenceslas had disagreed. 'You can look at it later, General. For now, there are considerations beyond military necessity. I'd rather let the people *see* this instead of having it hidden in a military research lab.'

Fuming at being countermanded, Lanyan insisted on military security. 'Security?' Peter had asked. 'If our scientists find any weakness in the hydrogue design, who would we possibly want to keep it secret *from?*'

From the balcony now, he and Estarra watched the cargo haulers deposit the broken warglobe in the plaza, like a knight delivering the head of a slain dragon to his King. As the first large burned section settled onto the flagstones with a clanking thud, the audience and even the royal guards stepped back in awe.

The next part of Peter's speech was full of warm confidence. 'Our scientific teams will analyse the warglobe's components and search for any vulnerability we can use against our hydrogue enemies.'

Down below, one tall blond, Engineering Specialist Swendsen, was the first to hurry forward to touch the hull, running his hands along the blistered surface. When he looked up towards the

Whisper Palace, Peter could see the man was grinning. The sudden cheers were deafening.

Basil tapped his chronometer and spoke softly, 'Time for you both to go to the bridge. Keep on schedule.'

The King and Queen walked side by side in a brisk procession from the Whisper Palace into the flagstoned plaza. When they moved together, absorbed in each other's presence, they could almost forget all the pomp, guards, and spectators. A contingent of royal guards snapped to attention. Court musicians who had waited for just this moment played yet another fanfare.

Ahead, the metal webwork of the Royal Canal bridge gleamed under reflected light. Its main posts were dark, though other bridge spires and all the cupolas of the Whisper Palace blazed with shimmering torches, each of which symbolized a world that had signed the Hansa Charter.

Eight years ago Old King Frederick had been forced to extinguish four of those newly lit torches after the hydrogues had destroyed four moons slated for terraforming and eventual colonization. Now, even though Ptoro was a flaming ball and utterly uninhabitable to any humans, the Hansa had decided to claim it as a moral victory. If humans could not settle there, at least they had made it impossible for the hydrogues to remain.

Estarra's older sister Sarein, the official ambassador from Theroc to Earth, stood waiting among the representatives and important guests. The Queen smiled and nodded to her, then returned to her formal pose beside Peter.

Hansa pyrotechnics experts watched on monitor screens inside the Whisper Palace. It was all a spectacular show. Peter stood in front of the tall pillar like an ancient priest invoking fire from the gods. 'At Ptoro we have hurt the hydrogues, as they have done so many times to us.' The crowd cheered on cue. 'In the name of the Terran Hanseatic League, this torch will stand as a symbol of what we have accomplished. Let it also be an eternal flame to memorialize those soldiers and civilians who have fallen in eight years of a war that we did not want.'

He gestured dramatically and, as planned, the pyrotechnic experts ignited the blazing ball atop a bridge tower, which burned brighter than all the others. Fuel lines were opened further, and every one of the dazzling flames from the turrets, spires, and cupolas of the Whisper Palace brightened, feeding on the growing light of victory.

The crowd responded with an indrawn breath, then applause and cheers. Sarein exchanged a meaningful glance with her sister, as if both were remembering the damage done to their home on Theroc. Spontaneous music drifted to the sky.

Peter put his arm around his Queen; she felt so warm and *real* next to him. Her face filled with delight. 'I'm glad I could finally do a positive thing,' he whispered to her.

After savouring the heady rush for a moment, he introduced the Chairman and stepped aside. The applause was automatic. The Chairman's smile appeared almost genuine as he stood next to Peter. Most people actually believed the manufactured reports that the two men were the best of friends.

Basil waited for the audience's full attention, then spoke. 'The Hansa offers you a fine opportunity with our new colonization initiative. Klikiss technology has already given us one irresistible weapon to use against the hydrogues, as we just demonstrated at Ptoro. Now, the Klikiss instantaneous transportation system gives us a new method for settling many untouched worlds. It's a new start for us – both for the Hansa and for yourselves. Think about the opportunity.'

Basil didn't have to give many details. The colonization initiative had been much discussed in the news ever since the discovery of the functioning Klikiss transportals, but this was the first time any formal plan had been announced to the public.

'On behalf of the Terran Hanseatic League, I am proud to extend a remarkable offer. Is anyone brave and ambitious enough to seize this chance? Are you willing to take a crack at colonizing an empty Klikiss planet? To pack up the family and your possessions and move to a virgin world? Think of the challenge! Be pioneers! If you accept this challenge, the Hansa will provide you with free land, certain services and supplies, even amnesty from several forms of debt.'

Basil sounded as if he was addressing a board meeting, laying out details like a bullet-point presentation. Peter remembered all the motivational skills the Chairman had taught him, and suddenly wondered if Basil was intentionally downplaying his speaking abilities, so as not to upstage the figurehead King.

Hansa experts, economic analysts, and civic simulators had developed this scheme as a viable method of pumping fresh capital and popular excitement into the Hansa, which might otherwise have faced a slow death through stagnation caused by limited space travel.

Smiling, Basil continued. 'The hydrogues may squeeze us in one direction, but we will grow in another. Will any of you take this offer? Can any of you afford not to? Full details will be available at local dissemination stations.'

During the expected applause, Peter gave the Chairman a wry look. He said in a voice too low for the amplifiers to detect, 'Basil, if you enjoy the limelight, then I'll be out of a job.'

Maintaining his false smile, Basil gave him a hard glance. 'Just be sure you don't give me a reason to, and everything will be fine.'

TWENTY-ONE

ORLI COVITZ

Grey and cloudy Dremen had been her home since before the hydrogue war, but Orli Covitz felt that any place would be better than here. But, at fourteen years old, she had few points of comparison.

Her father had pulled up stakes and brought her here, following a dream, when she'd been only six. Jan Covitz maintained an unflagging reserve of optimism, but Orli had slowly come to realize that her father's grand aspirations did not amount to much, despite his good intentions. She loved him anyway, knowing that he actually believed he would find the pot of gold at the end of the rainbow if he chased long enough and hard enough.

Blowing on her cold fingers to warm them, Orli stood with her father in the slushy fields they had claimed. All this land had been there for the taking, because few other Dremen farmers wanted it. That should have been their first hint, but her father was sure the two of them could do something with it. Jan and his daughter were a team.

They'd been latecomers here. The first families had arrived a hundred and ten years earlier and staked their claims. Many of them already acted like snobs, considering themselves genuine bluebloods after only a few generations. Her father ignored the snobbery, however, accepted the available land and made the best of it. He diligently forged ahead without much of a plan, but with a great deal of exuberance. For eight and a half years he worked hard while insisting, 'Next year will be better. We'll make it then for sure, Orli.'

This year, though, the mushroom field was a disaster.

The ground was wet and mulchy, with standing pools of peaty brown water. Many of the giant mushrooms had been hacked down, the tender caps harvested, but most had opened their rills and dumped spores, which darkened the fungus meat with inky residue and lent it an unpleasant taste.

Now Jan shoved his spade into the soft, cold muck and flashed a bright smile at her. 'We'll salvage some of this, Orli. Fifteen per cent at least.'

She smiled in response to his chipper attitude. 'We can maybe push it to twenty per cent if the weather holds.'

But on Dremen, the weather would not hold.

She wiped her forehead, pushing her dark bangs aside. Though she wanted to let her brown hair grow out like some of the colonists' uppity daughters did, she knew that with her pointed chin, pert nose, and large eyes, the long hair would make her look identical to pictures of her mother. Jan never talked about his faraway wife – she had left them long ago, after one of her husband's previous schemes had failed. But Orli didn't want to remind him, so she kept her hair short and simple.

She didn't know why her father had chosen to come to *Dremen*, of all places. It was a cool world with dim skies. The variable sun waxed over the course of decades, warming the planet and making life nearly tolerable. Dremen had plenty of water; its continents were dotted with large shallow lakes that evaporated easily, keeping the air in a clammy equilibrium of fog and frequent rainshowers. Woody plants had not evolved here, and the ground was covered with cold bogs, mossy groundcover, and sheets of leathery lichen.

But Orli and her father had arrived during the variable star's waning phase, and year after year the climate had only grown colder until the variable-phase winter had set in hard. During previous waning cycles, the Dremen colonists had depended on relief supplies from Hansa merchant ships. This time around, though, the hydrogue embargo changed everything.

With great aspirations, Jan had studied Dremen's climate and meteorology, convinced a few investors by insisting (quite rationally) that while green crops struggled in the damp and dim environment, genetically enhanced mushrooms were sure to be a bumper crop. The spores Jan imported to Dremen grew into broad toadstools that provided edible flesh, dense in nutrients, though chewy and bland. Once he'd prepared his open fields, Jan went overboard with the planting. Untempered optimism again.

The first harvest had been beyond her father's wildest dreams — or plans, because he'd made no prior arrangements for large work crews or automated equipment to chop down and preserve the delicate mushroom meat. The fungi grew quickly, but withered just as fast. Timing was crucial.

He and Orli had worked around the clock until they were ready to drop, but half of the crop still rotted. Jan had rushed into town, asking for help, but he had nothing with which to pay the crew. In the end, he'd been forced just to open his land and let the colonists come in and take what they wanted, hoping to earn goodwill, if not actual profits, from his fellow colonists.

The unharvested mushrooms in the fields had dumped their spores and slumped into the bog — and an even larger crop of chaotic mushrooms sprang forth the next season, ripened . . . and then rotted.

Though Jan and Orli had plenty to eat, they had overestimated Dremen's demand for edible fungus. No one really liked the taste, and few people were willing to pay for it.

Then, as the solar cycle waned, bringing increasingly cold winters, the already chilly fog became a cold sleet that turned the bogs into slush and finally snow. For the past couple of years Orli's world had been a sloppy, frigid mess. Now as she and her father trudged across their mushroom fields, the standing pools were covered with skins of ice.

Pausing, she looked at the transport bins of mushroom meat they had sliced and stacked. 'Once it gets warm again, Dad, let's think about choosing a different crop.'

'I've thought about it plenty already, girl. The sad fact is we'll never get rid of these mushrooms now. We'd need to incinerate acres just to prep the soil again and kill all the dormant spores. Looks like it's fungus for ever.'

'Then I'll keep working on new recipes.'

'Don't take time away from your music.' Her father arched his eyebrows. 'You'll be a famous concert performer some day. I know it.' His compliment warmed her heart, though she didn't exactly see how she was going to find her big break here on Dremen.

Orli did not deflate his cheerful opinion. 'Some day.'

Together they went to the full bins and sealed them against the worsening weather. 'Enough for today, girl. Let's get back home. You deserve a rest.'

'And I have to do my homework.'

'After we eat, I'm going into town again. The bigshots are gathering for their regular session to solve the world's problems.'

'I thought you'd already solved all the problems.'

'I did, but they never listen to me. We proved that much in the last election.' He tousled her hair as if she was still a little girl.

Their small house on the edge of the cold bog had few luxuries, but plenty of homely touches. Orli had been inside the larger homes of well-established colonists, and she thought her own house was a superior place to *live*. They dropped their packs. Jan turned up the heat, and Orli went to start dinner.

A printed solicitation message for the Hansa's new transportal colonization initiative was there waiting for them. Jan Covitz pretended not to notice it, but Orli saw his eyes light up.

TWENTY-TWO

RLINDA KETT

Flush with business opportunities thanks to the new colonization initiative, Rlinda Kett flew the *Voracious Curiosity* to the quiet world of Crenna. It was time to share the wealth and the success. And the work. She went directly to her best former pilot and favourite ex-husband Branson Roberts.

Almost two years ago, BeBob had successfully slipped away from his onerous assignment of flying dangerous survey missions for the EDF. Since his 'retirement' was unauthorized, he'd been keeping a low profile on Crenna ever since; Rlinda knew that by now he was probably bored to tears.

Normally, aboard ship she wore skin-tight black pants over her wide hips and heavy legs, because they were so practical. Seeing BeBob, though, she had changed into a flowing bright-purple caftan shot through with iridescent threads she had kept from the first shipment of Theron goods. She liked a flash of colour; she especially thought stripes and patterns made her look attractive.

BeBob greeted her with his adorable yet clueless smile. As usual, he wore monotone colours, colony slacks, a loose, long-sleeve shirt that wasn't stylish and didn't fit him well; she had never been able to convince him not to wear it. Rlinda took his scrawny arm and walked him back to his colony house, then made him an offer she knew he couldn't turn down. 'How'd you like to fly the *Blind Faith* again?'

'But . . . I'm all out of fuel, and she needs repairs.' His big round eyes looked so innocent and adorable on his leathery face.

She leaned over to kiss his large ear, making him blush. 'Stop focusing on the problems and answer my question.'

'Do you even need to ask? I hate being stuck here on the ground. I'm afraid one morning I'll wake up with roots pushing into the soil. Give me metal walls and nice clean reprocessed air instead of the smell of rain and fertilizers – just as long as I don't have to play chicken with drogue warglobes, like General Lanyan kept forcing me to do.'

'None of that.' She tousled his smoky-grey hair and led him inside for a bit of privacy. 'And the job's completely legitimate.'

'That'll be a switch,' BeBob said.

'For you, maybe. I've always been a respectable businesswoman.'

'You've always known when to turn a blind eye.'

'They go hand in hand, BeBob.' She sealed the door of his dwelling, then sniffed. 'Who does your cooking? Smells like layer upon layer of prepackaged meals. Shame on you.'

'Well, I've grown rather fond of spampax. It's amazing what a little hot sauce can do to doctor it up.' She made a face so outrageous that BeBob burst out laughing. Without asking, he opened a bottle of red wine for the two of them.

'That better be one of your "special occasion" bottles,' she said. 'Because this certainly qualifies.'

'Rlinda, it's a special occasion any time you come to visit me.'

'Especially when I come offering a nice job.'

'Or sex.' BeBob handed her a glass of wine and took a smaller one for himself.

Rlinda swirled it around, took a long sip. 'Your taste in wine was never anything I had arguments with, BeBob.'

'One of the few things.'

She playfully swatted the back of his head. 'Thanks to my work with Davlin Lotze, we've opened access to the whole new transportal network. The Hansa has enough lawyers and waivers that I'll never get any of the patent profits, but the Chairman showed his gratitude in other ways. I've got a bottomless supply of ekti and a lucrative delivery contract as part of the new Klikiss colonization initiative. You want a piece of that?'

'I thought transportals didn't require ekti. Isn't that the whole point?'

'Transportals are perfect for shipping people and small objects, but the Hansa still needs ships like the *Voracious Curiosity* – and the *Blind Faith* – to haul heavy equipment and large components that can't be broken down to fit through a transportal frame. And also to shuttle groups of eager settlers from existing colonies to the nearest Klikiss hub with an active transportal.'

'Ah, typical distribution bottlenecks.'

BeBob took the chair opposite the sofa where she sat, but when Rlinda gave him a quick and disbelieving glance, he quickly changed his place to snuggle beside her. 'That's better,' she said.

'Don't forget, I'm technically AWOL, Rlinda. I can't just fly around doing Hansa business. Somebody's bound to notice.'

'I've already taken care of the problem, BeBob.'

When Rlinda first received her assignment, she had asked for a face-to-face meeting with Chairman Wenceslas. Even after discovering the transportal network, she found it difficult to get through all the bureaucratic roadblocks.

Her old acquaintance, Sarein, had provided the key, marching Rlinda directly to the upper levels of the Hansa HQ and bypassing security. The ambitious young daughter of Theroc was apparently a frequent visitor to the Chairman's private offices and chambers. *Good for you, girl*, Rlinda thought. A young woman from a backwater planet had to do whatever was necessary to compete with those who started off with more political advantages and connections.

When she and Sarein finally stood in front of his desk, Chairman Wenceslas, though distracted, knew how Rlinda could help him. He looked up at her with a half-amused stare and a guarded expression. 'If you expect outrageous concessions like last time, Ms Kett, you'll be disappointed. You are not alone among pilots who are anxious to start flying again. I'll have volunteers lined up from here to Ganymede.'

'Hmm, and some of them might even be competent. You *know* I am. Besides, don't you owe me a debt of gratitude?'

'I didn't realize you were so old-fashioned.'

'It's one of my flaws. But I won't demand anything out of line. I just want to bring in one of my former pilots. He's a man I'd rather not do without.'

Actually there had been many times – especially when they were married – that she very much *had* wanted to do without Branson Roberts. But that was all water under the bridge, and she intended to include BeBob in the surge of profitable business.

Chairman Wenceslas sat back at his desk, looked questioningly at Sarein, but the young ambassador only shrugged her narrow shoulders. He asked, 'And is this man a decent pilot, Ms Kett?'

'Oh, he's the best. So good, in fact, that General Lanyan yanked him from his regular business to fly dangerous recon missions. He's exceptionally skilled at . . . unorthodox piloting and squeaking his ship out of difficult situations.'

The Chairman tapped his fingers on the desktop. 'I see. So you would like me to intervene and sever his commitment with the Earth Defence Forces so he can fly merchant runs instead of surveillance?'

Rlinda chuckled. 'Oh, that's not precisely the problem, Mr Chairman. You see, BeBob has already done that. He wasn't cut out for military service and . . . voluntarily failed to return from his last assignment.'

Even Sarein was surprised. 'You mean he's one of the AWOL pilots?'

The Chairman frowned. 'Ms Kett, General Lanyan rants and fumes about those "deserters" practically every day.'

Rlinda brightened. 'So, wouldn't it be a good idea to put Captain Roberts back into worthwhile service? That way he could make up for his indiscretions.'

'Basil, the General would throw an absolute fit if he found out,' Sarein said in a low voice.

'And it would only encourage other disgruntled pilots to ignore their orders and desert their posts. I'm afraid we can't have that, Ms Kett.'

'Oh, come on now. The Chairman of the Terran Hanseatic League can find some way to make an exception.' She had crossed her beefy arms over her chest and stood like a worldtree that had just taken root in his office. 'After all, I could have made a far more unreasonable request.'

'That doesn't mean I would have granted it.' Wenceslas sighed as more messages popped up on his multi-windowed translucent desktop. 'The best I can offer is that we'll allow your friend to fly his ship on our missions. No one will ask his background, and your man should be smart enough not to reveal anything.' He raised a warning finger. 'But if he should ever get caught, there is nothing I can do to help him. General Lanyan has a standing vendetta against those pilots.'

'If BeBob is dumb enough to get caught, Mr Chairman, then I'd disavow any relationship with him as well.'

*

Rlinda finished her wine in one long drink. Outside, Crenna seemed so . . . bucolic. 'During maintenance prep on the *Blind Faith*, you could change its name and serial numbers. That should keep you from drawing any attention, especially if you're doing Hansa work.' She put a big arm around him and pulled him closer to her on the sofa. 'Look, I'll even stay and help you fix up the ship.'

He smiled. 'There aren't many other people I'd trust to tinker with the *Faith*, but if it gets you to stay here longer, then you've got yourself a deal.'

'That didn't take much convincing.' She poured herself another glass from the bottle and refilled BeBob's. 'As soon as you get the *Blind Faith* in the air again, you can start flying load after load. Chairman Wenceslas is pushing this full-scale colonization, and there's quite a backlog already.'

'At least the two of us will be partners again, doing what we do best.' BeBob set the glass down. 'Should we seal it with a kiss?'

'A kiss for starters. Just for starters.'

TWENTY-THREE

DAVLIN LOTZE

This world was different: Davlin could tell as soon as he stepped through the transportal. But though he sensed looming danger, he would not leave until he had completed at least a cursory exploration. The Chairman expected a full report on every new Klikiss planet an explorer visited. Every coordinate tile needed to be documented somehow.

The sky overhead was a bruised purplish-red; a primary element of the atmosphere seemed to be distilled shadow. As he stepped away from the blank trapezoidal rock of the transportal, Davlin took a deep breath and coughed at the sour, sulphurous odour in the air. The Klikiss had similar breathing requirements to humans, but the stench made this world unpleasant. He fumbled in the pockets of his jumpsuit, withdrew a supplemental airmask, and fixed it over his face.

He looked back at the transportal and was surprised to find that the flat wall stood alone at the brink of a canyon's sheer cliff. In order to return, he would have to step through the transportal as if he were leaping into the chasm itself. Most unsettling . . .

The wind whistled with a strange bottomless moan. On an uneven escarpment of talus boulders, he saw the familiar conical lumps of Klikiss buildings. Some of the ancient hive towers stretched high into the sky; many passages no doubt penetrated deep into caves.

Davlin set off across the rough, uneven ground towards the empty city. In the thousands of years since the Klikiss had disappeared, their roads had eroded away. Even if this world was not a likely candidate for the colonization initiative, he could bring images to archaeological teams for further analysis.

Gravity was rather heavy on this world, and his footsteps became ponderous. Even with supplemental oxygen, he was breathing hard as he trudged up the slope.

Turning back to see how far he had come from the cliff-edge transportal, he spotted strange shapes in the clotted sky. Jagged wings surrounded a body core that trailed twitching tentacles, like a bizarre fusion between a giant jellyfish and a wide-winged pterodactyl.

Davlin instantly recognized the threat. He counted dozens of the things converging towards the transportal from across the canyon, as if its activation had alerted them to the possibility of fresh meat. When the flying jellyfish-creatures drifted closer, Davlin could see that each bulbous body was merely a sack to hold a mouth-ring large enough to engulf its paralysed prey.

The things would get to the transportal before he could reach it.

Suddenly, the wind whipped up, and the brooding sky spewed sheets of drenching rain. The moisture felt oily and disgusting on his skin; a few seconds later, it began to burn.

When the jellyfish-things spotted him, the pack drew closer from all directions. Cut off from the transportal and his escape, Davlin raced for shelter in a tumble of boulders on the outskirts of the city ruins. His burst of speed drew the attention of the jellyfish-things. On broad wings, they cruised after him.

Davlin wedged himself into a dark cranny in the misshapen rocks, where at least none of the acidic rain could penetrate. Unfortunately, the cranny also sheltered other creatures. With a glint of bluish metallic carapace, a segmented body as wide as his thigh unwrapped itself, full of sharp legs and clacking claws. The centipede creature sprang out like a jack-in-the-box. Davlin spun just in time so that the scissor-like claws fastened on his pack, ripping the fabric but not touching his skin.

He struggled to shrug off and discard his pack as a second giant centipede crawled out of a different crevice. Drips of venom sparkled on the ends of its upraised clawed feet. Davlin swung the pack, knocking the second centipede aside, while the first increased its grip on the fabric, striking and slashing. Medical supplies, cans of rations, and clothes fell out with a clatter on the floor of the little cave. Its belt slashed, the weapon holster on the side of the pack dangled out of reach.

Davlin heard louder clicking and scraping. Apparently he had blundered into a nest of the things. Two more of the centipede creatures sprang at him, and Davlin thrust his now-useless pack towards them as a distraction, and the weapon clattered to the floor of the cave. He bolted for the opening. Outside, burning rain continued to splash down. He ran.

Farther down the hill, scores of the winged jellyfish-things surrounded the transportal. Five others drifted over the rock field, poking with their glassy tentacles in search of where he had gone to hide.

Davlin's only shelter would be the Klikiss ruins themselves. Sparing nothing, he raced forward. As soon as he moved, the flying jellyfish detected him and flapped their razor-edged wings in pursuit. Without the pack, he was lighter, and adrenaline gave him the power to overcome this planet's increased gravity. He had also lost his only weapon, and he chided himself for his stupidity in not entering an unknown new environment with his weapon drawn in the first place. Davlin would have to rely on his own wits now.

Panting, he increased the oxygen output in his breathing mask. The slope was steep, the rocky and rain-slick ground treacherous. He scrambled ahead, weaving and stumbling to provide an uncertain target. Just as he had learned in his military survival training, long ago . . .

His eyes burned, but he no longer cared about the stinging chemical rain. Straining to see through irritated tears, he bounded forward in search of openings, low Klikiss doorways or windows. There had to be some way into the ghost city.

The predatory jellyfish were eerily silent above and around him, but he knew they were closing in for the kill. When one of the glassy, needle-filled tentacles brushed his shoulder, a fiery agony rippled through his muscles.

Davlin slipped in the muck and sprawled, glancing up as one of the huge jellyfish-things drifted overhead. He could see its rippled mouth, a wide opening of questing, hungry lips. The thing had no obvious eyes, but it seemed to sense where he was.

Lurching forward as it swooped back for him, Davlin dived inside the first opening he found. His burning arm was nearly useless, but he hauled himself in with his other hand. Curling, poisonous tentacles brushed the wall, leaving a trail of toxin that smoked on the hard surface.

Davlin crawled along until he reached a widening tunnel where he could finally get to his feet. When he looked back, he saw a crowd of the jellyfish-things clustered at the window through which he had entered. They pulled their pterodactyl wings tight, extending tentacles and trying to force their bodies into the ruins after him.

Davlin fled deeper into the abandoned city. Despite his years of service to the Hansa, acting as a cultural spy, infiltrating settlements and investigating Ildiran relics, it had been a long time since he'd faced such imminent danger. Fortunately, he'd had years of secret training. The most sophisticated military exercises had supposedly prepared him for any scenario, but if he ever escaped from this, he would have to write them a whole new training module.

The Klikiss ruins were dark and the tunnels oppressive. Though he had lost his pack among the giant centipede creatures, he kept a small handlight in his pocket. The minimal illumination was enough for him.

Fearing what might lurk in the shadows ahead, Davlin used the light to see each curving tunnel, though he knew its illumination might attract something even worse than what he had encountered so far.

Down another branch he saw a distant doorway that led back outside. More winged jellyfish were there, blocking his escape. Having tracked him over here, the things showed a sinister intelligence and a determination that chilled his blood.

For now, he had no way of getting back to the transportal.

Not exactly the way Davlin had imagined his end. A statistic. Another vanished explorer. The coordinate tile for this world would be marked black, indicating a dangerous place; it would be a long time before any human visited it again.

Though Davlin's chances didn't look good, he did not succumb to despair. Giving up was not in his nature, so he pushed forward, intent on finding a way out. There would be enough time for dying later on.

From side tunnels came loud skittering movements, as if his passage had awakened other things. Even with the airmask, his breathing came in hard and heavy gasps. He shone the handlight around him in search of an empty passage, careful not to trap himself.

Then, unexpectedly, he stumbled on a pile of loose debris on the floor, noticing dark metal in the dim illumination of his handlight. He found a flat angular plate that looked oddly familiar. He bent to get a closer look and was surprised to find the scratched and battered components of what had obviously been a Klikiss robot.

Something had torn it to pieces, destroyed it utterly.

Davlin paused, astonished at the implications. The hulking, beetle-like machines were powerful, seemingly indestructible. Though the alien race itself had vanished, no one had ever seen a damaged or destroyed robot. Their black exoskeletons were so tough that the alien machines had survived for more than ten thousand years, physically unscathed.

But something – *something* – had been strong enough and dangerous enough to have smashed one of the robots to pieces. Something here.

Davlin swallowed hard. Sinister monsters were already following him in the dark, and now the sight of the dismembered Klikiss robot made him put on another burst of speed, though he did not know where he was going.

Close behind him, he heard a sound of cracking stone, and part of the wall crumbled away. Sharp, furry arachnid legs pushed forward, questing, widening the hole.

Davlin rushed into the next opening, trying to put distance between himself and the pursuing things. To his dismay, the new chamber was a dead end, a large room with no exits.

He skidded to a halt, turned to see if he could run back into another passage, but the predatory creatures were closing in. From a nearby tunnel came the odd shuffling, clumping sounds of winged jellyfish-things dragging themselves along the floor. Other creatures clattered and hissed from the shadows.

Davlin shone his light around the enclosed chamber, looking for some exit hole. There was no place to run.

Then, like a magician's trick revealing a surprise, the handlight shone upon another flat stone surface and a trapezoidal ring of controls. A second transportal! Many Klikiss cities had more than one of the instantaneous transportation gates. He only hoped this one was still functional.

Davlin hurried through the familiar activation sequence. His eyes skimmed the icons on the tiles and rapidly identified the one he recognized as the address for Rheindic Co.

Sluggishly, as if crawling to wakefulness, the ancient Klikiss machinery began to hum. Davlin tried to concentrate.

At the chamber doorway, one of the jellyfish-things hauled itself forward on the elbows of bent wings, reaching out with glassy tentacles.

He heard the familiar buzz of transportal machinery, and his knees went weak with relief as the flat stone turned fuzzy. Four of the winged jellyfish had crawled into the chamber now, trailing slime. Whip-like tentacles quested across the stone floor.

But Davlin gave them only a cursory backward glance before he jumped through the transportal – back to a world he could understand.

TWENTY-FOUR .

ANTON COLICOS

A nton devoted his private time to deciphering the epic Ildiran narrative for later publication on Earth. He spent his every waking hour reading or telling stories that no human being had previously heard. What could be better than that?

Still, the constant study made even him restless. Anton liked to stretch his legs and walk along the boulevards of the resort. The oddly skewed structures with their multicoloured crystals reflected the blazers that hung from domes overhead. The colours, lights, and exotic flavour had always reminded him of the Arabian Nights. Here, during the darkness season, he and Vao'sh were each like Scheherazade, providing a nightly entertainment of storytelling in the central plaza to whichever workers could take time from their activities to listen. The rest of the domed city was virtually empty.

Now, Anton whistled as he strolled along, brushing down his lank brown hair, as if he had to make himself presentable for anyone. He'd never been able to carry a tune, but he attempted to hum the ancient folk melody of 'Greensleeves', which was always one of his mother's favourite songs. He recalled her unusual display of delight when once he'd given her a small wind-up music box that played the tune, even though Margaret had never been a woman much interested in collecting trinkets . . .

He descended into the lower levels, where Maratha Prime kept its generators, ventilation pumping systems, and power-distribution grid. Now, a heavy racket echoed through the chambers under the domed city. Unlike the pristine and aesthetic architecture of the upper levels, down here Anton found the clutter and disarray refreshing. Large equipment and crates of materials were strewn around the arched entrance to a sloping tunnel. From deeper underground, he heard grinding noises, heavy excavation machines, and shouted commands.

Nur'of, Maratha's lead engineer, had undertaken an ambitious project during the long night when it would not disturb vacationing Ildirans. After the day season's last shuttle had departed, his burly diggers had begun to operate machinery to bore shafts into the crust. Nur'of had no directive from the absent Maratha Designate, but had made up his mind independently to develop some improvements. Designate Avi'h would not object to an increase in power efficiency; in fact, he probably wouldn't notice at all.

Anton ducked through the arch and ventured into the steep shaft. Portable blazers had been strung every few metres, shedding bright light. 'Hello? Is it all right if I come inside?'

He encountered a muscular Ildiran worker with massive arms, broad shoulders, and a neck as thick as his head. Though worker kithmen were not the most intelligent or agile of Ildiran subspecies, they were diligent and uncomplaining. The worker lifted a heavy chunk of rock from the front of an earth-moving machine, grunting with the effort, but his expression did not change.

Since so few Ildirans remained on Maratha Prime, Anton had made an effort to meet them all. 'Hello, Vik'k. Where is Nur'of?'

Seeing him, the digger flashed a childlike smile. Vik'k seemed to enjoy listening to Earth fairy tales; perhaps his low intelligence was an advantage, since more sophisticated Ildirans were troubled by the concept of fictional exploits: fiction was not part of their grand *Saga*.

The digger dropped the boulder onto a carefully arranged pile and gestured deeper into the tunnel. 'Nur'of is in there. He is fixing things.'

Anton thanked him and strolled farther on with a jaunty step. Ahead he saw an unexpected network of polished, large-bore tunnels that looked as if they had been cut with acid instead of heavy machinery. And they appeared curiously old, not freshly dug like this main passage.

The engineers were talking at the end of the new shaft, where warm, moist air smelled of rock dust and mud. In the bright light of the blazers, Nur'of stood before a broad wall diagram that showed a sketch of extensive new tunnels beneath Maratha Prime.

The lead engineer looked up to see him approaching. 'It is the human rememberer! You will have to tell your people this story of what we unexpectedly found. One of our bore holes broke into this odd honeycomb of pre-existing tunnels. No one knew they were here.'

Nur'of had widely spaced eyes and an enlarged head, though to a lesser degree than the heads of pure-bred scientist kithmen. A cross between scientist and technician kiths, an Ildiran engineer was especially adept at doing rapid calculations in his head and could retain enormous amounts of practical data, such as alloy components, melting temperatures, and stress tolerances.

Anton indicated the crude wall map. 'Where did all these tunnels come from?'

'Not important. These shafts will take us directly to the thermal rivers. We can make use of that!' The engineer scrutinized the diagram again. 'Now, we can extend transfer conduits through these existing tunnels into the boiling aquifers. Maratha Prime will have all the power and heat we could possibly want.'

Anton clapped the engineer on the shoulder. A few weeks ago, he'd had to explain the meaning of a pat on the back. 'I know you've been working hard at this, and you've dreamed it for a long time.'

During Maratha's day season, the engineers maintained solar collectors, storing accumulated power in enormous banks outside the domed city. But during the half year of darkness, the skeleton crew had to ration energy consumption until the next dawn.

While most engineer kithmen were content just to maintain systems in perfect working order, Nur'of preferred a challenge. Since Maratha's crust retained heat long after the night fell, he had conceived a system that would pipe hot water from deep aquifers, through turbines, using thermal plumes to generate energy. Nur'of had been eager to put his plans to the test, but he had never expected to uncover this warren of already-dug underground passages.

Fascinated, Anton peered into the new channels. 'Why don't we go explore?' He grabbed a portable blazer, then noticed the engineer's instant reluctance to venture into the dark. 'Aren't you curious to know who dug them?'

'Only to the extent that it relates to my project.' Nur'of pressed his lips together. 'But yes . . . it would be good to verify firsthand the functionality of my new designs for thermal-power transport.'

Together, the two set off into the tunnel. Anton moved his light from side to side, up to the ceiling, driving back the shadows. 'How long has Maratha Prime been here? When did Ildirans first build the city?'

'Nearly two centuries ago. We were not aware of any previous planetary inhabitants, but we have been too busy to delve into Maratha's mysteries.'

The tunnels had obviously been drilled long before the Ildiran occupation. Who could possibly have made them? The ancient Klikiss race, perhaps? Besides the Ildirans, what other choice was there?

Anton shone his blazer into another passage, but the darkness swallowed up the light. 'It's a rat's nest in here. I wonder where all these side passages go?'

'What is a rat?' Nur'of said, then suddenly smiled. 'Oh yes, you told us about the plague-carrying Earth rodents in your Pied Piper story.'

The steam grew thicker as they trudged ahead, steeply downhill. Soon he heard the thunderous roar of an underground river where hot water surged through a channel beneath Maratha's crust.

'Excellent. We can install our turbines and generators immediately. No additional excavation will be required.'

As the two men returned to the well-lit passages where diggers prepared the shafts for installing conduits and piping networks, Anton kept looking at the shafts branching in all directions with a puzzled expression. 'You know, we could make daily expeditions into these tunnels and find out where they all go.'

'Not necessary,' Nur'of said. 'This shaft already takes us to the thermal river. That is all we need.'

'But what if the other tunnels go somewhere better?' His parents would never have turned their backs on such a glaring mystery without investigating it fully.

Nur'of looked at him. 'This one is adequate.'

'So you say.' Anton knew the other skeleton crew members would make similar excuses, probably even Vao'sh. They simply had no curiosity about things that didn't fall within their fields of expertise.

Though Ildirans might look like humans, their behaviour often reminded Anton that they were definitely an alien species. He couldn't understand why they wouldn't want to explore the mysterious passages and unravel the enigma of who or what had built them.

If nothing else, it would make a wonderful story.

TWENTY-FIVE

MAGE-IMPERATOR JORA'H

Hearing that the Hyrillka Designate had awakened, Jora'h wanted to leap from the chrysalis chair and rush down to the infirmary levels, but such a brash action would cause as much of a stir as Rusa'h's awakening.

Prime Designate Thor'h looked like an overjoyed child. He grabbed the medical kithman's arm, intending to be the first to see his uncle, but Jora'h raised his hand. 'We are all going, Thor'h. I want to see Rusa'h as much as you do.'

Pery'h appeared more relieved than happy at the news. The Designate-in-waiting had felt uncertain about taking over his role, though Jora'h had been convinced his quiet and intelligent son would be up to the task.

Attenders came swarming in. They jabbered and scurried, retracting the anchor legs of the voluminous chair, adding blankets and colourful wraps, tucking in the Mage-Imperator as if they were packaging a fragile antique for a long journey, instead of just moving him to another room in the Palace itself.

They finally lifted the chrysalis chair and carried it like a palanquin through the wide doors of his contemplation chamber. The procession moved along the dazzling halls, down winding ramps. Startled by the Mage-Imperator's presence, pilgrims stood staring, unable to believe their good fortune at catching a glimpse of their revered leader.

Prime Designate Thor'h pranced ahead, his eyes as wide and bright as if he had taken another massive dose of shiing. This time, though, his frenetic behaviour had nothing to do with any drug other than genuine excitement.

When they reached the infirmary chamber, the doors were flung open and guards made way through the crowd of doctors that had arrived ahead of the Mage-Imperator. Rusa'h's emergence from the sub-*thism* sleep had taken them all by surprise.

As his chrysalis chair was carried into the infirmary room, Jora'h reached out with *thism*, following the myriad silvery lines of soul threads from the Lightsource. But though the Hyrillka Designate was awake, Jora'h could not sense him. It was as if his brother was invisible to the all-encompassing web of *thism*. Only another part of the deepening mystery . . . but the joy of having Rusa'h awake again was paramount.

Dazed, the Hyrillka Designate sat up in his bed, glancing around. When Jora'h looked at his hedonistic brother, he saw a stranger's face. Rusa'h was gaunt and pale, his formerly soft features now lean, wasted away after months of catatonia. He had been full of laughter, surrounded by pleasure mates, entirely pampered, and the Hyrillka Designate had always kept a smile on his plump face and a twinkle in his eyes. Now though, the man looked disturbed and troubled.

Thor'h ran to Rusa'h's side and embraced him, not even pretending to follow protocol or dignity. 'Uncle!' Thor'h's close-cropped hair was bristly, but his uncle's hair remained long and full, since he had been unconscious during the death of the former Mage-Imperator, when all Ildiran males had shorn their heads.

'Thor'h . . .?' the Hyrillka Designate said, trying to reassemble his memories. 'Yes, Thor'h. Have the hydrogues gone?'

'Yes, Uncle. The hydrogues did terrible damage, but they left Hyrillka. I helped the people to recover and rebuild. When you get home, you will be glad to see all I have accomplished.'

Pery'h stood beside the Prime Designate and lowered his head formally. 'And I am to be your new Designate-in-waiting, Uncle. I am greatly relieved that you can now act as my guide during the transition years. We feared you might never wake.'

Rusa'h finally seemed to piece together the implications of his brother Jora'h sitting in the chrysalis chair, where he expected to see old Cyroc'h. He asked no questions, said nothing at all for a long moment, then seemed entirely uninterested in the new situation.

The attenders brought Jora'h's chair next to the Designate's bed, where he could reach out his hand. 'We are glad to have you back among the living, Rusa'h. The Empire needs you.'

Rusa'h grasped his hand with surprising, almost defiant, firmness. 'Yes . . . back among the living.' He heaved a long, low sigh. 'I have returned from the realm of pure light. I was on a higher plane, surrounded by the Lightsource, engulfed in its holy illumination.' He closed his eyes, then opened them again as if he couldn't believe where he found himself. 'And now I have come back to a place of so many shadows . . . so many.' He lay back in his infirmary bed, as if incredibly weary. 'But I no longer need to fear the shadows, or the darkness.'

Rusa'h appeared marvellously recovered . . . yet it now disturbed Jora'h greatly that he could not sense his brother in the network of *thism*. It was as if Rusa'h had been erased, or disconnected. 'We must let the Hyrillka Designate rest. We should not trouble him now.

He has returned to us, and this is a great day.'

'I'll stay with him,' Thor'h said. The Prime Designate's tone carried no request for permission.

'And I too should be here.' Pery'h simply offered a logical conclusion.

Before Thor'h could complain about his younger brother's intrusion, the Mage-Imperator said, 'Yes, it would be best if both of you remained here to help your uncle grow stronger.' He signalled for the attenders to carry his chrysalis chair again. 'We will talk further, Rusa'h, when you feel stronger.'

TWENTY-SIX

JESS TAMBLYN

Now that Jess knew he could escape, the isolated water planet no longer seemed like a hopeless trap. All of his intrinsic powers and the reborn wentals would do him no good unless he could bring the water entities back to the Roamers . . . and Cesca.

Jess stood on his reef day after day, watching as the framework of his amazing vessel took shape in the water before him. The wentals carried his thoughts, helped guide aquatic creatures – from plankton and brine shrimp to lumbering leviathans – that became a nearly infinite work force.

As the white surf foamed against the rocks, Jess sensed and directed the furious activity taking place in the deep ocean, even in the segregated tide pools. Microcellular animals and tiny coral creatures cemented millions of grains of sand in place, one at a time, to form a skeleton like an organic armillary sphere. Shellfish and slithering invertebrates secreted resins and pearly films that coated the rough bones of the ship's skeleton, strengthening it with an enamel harder than human teeth, then plating on pure metals stolen from the seawater itself.

Arched ribs rose up out of the water, curving inward like fingers grasping an immense ball, the plaything of a giant child. Coral continued to build, criss-crossing the main supports. Growing out of the shallows, the incomplete ship looked like the fossil of an extinct dragon, its bones picked clean and half-submerged in the reef water. Jess watched it take shape and fill in, becoming more marvellous day after day. With his naked body flooded by wental energy, the possibilities seemed endless.

Roamers were experts at cobbling together functional vessels out of scrap components, their ships never pretty, but always reliable. He'd seen a hodge-podge of designs that fitted no standard catalogue, but this unique vessel – constructed by a limitless army of ocean creatures and guided by a water-based entity that had never taken human form – looked stranger than anything Jess had ever seen.

The plated coral bones formed curves and loops like the partial rings of latitude and longitude on an ancient globe. Incomprehensible engines were incorporated into the framework, operating on powers that even Jess did not understand.

Because of the raw life energy he drew from the alien ocean itself, time passed with a different sense for Jess. He could stand still as the tides cycled, bringing more creatures, more workers, more materials, and watch the ship grow before his eyes.

Finally, at high tide under two diamond moons in the unnamed world's sky, the rigid outline of the spherical cage was complete.

From the deepest water came an enormous tentacled creature that emitted low thrums in a language more ancient than human civilization. It raised itself into the open air, letting water stream off its algae-covered hide. The monster's tentacled embrace seemed to wield a muscular power sufficient to crack a hydrogue warglobe. With one enormous milky eye, the leviathan looked at Jess and then the motionless wental starship.

The creature lifted three tentacles as thick as tree trunks and seized the armillary-sphere framework. Jess watched anxiously, concerned that its brute force might damage the carefully constructed vessel. But the wentals guided it. With a strange delicacy, the beast carried the reinforced framework from where it had taken shape on the reef shelf into deeper water – where it sank.

Jess stared at the empty, rippling water. 'Now what?'

Now your transportation bubble is complete.

Since his body was filled with the force of the wentals, Jess could breathe water . . . in fact, he didn't need to breathe at all, yet another sign that he was more than human. Ripples of liquid electricity flowed like phosphorescent plankton just beneath his skin, like static sparks ready to jump to anything he touched.

The ocean's surface roiled with bubbles as the last atmospheric inclusions were squeezed out of the rigid framework. Then, underwater, the wentals sealed the ship with their own binding force.

Jess stepped higher onto the dry rocks as the waves suddenly parted with a roar, and the immense ball lifted itself from the water. The new ship hovered dripping over the restless seas, its framework filled with ocean water caught in an invisible bubble of wental force, like a gigantic raindrop held together by surface tension.

The planet's twin moons shone down under cascades of stars, limning the water-based vessel with silvery radiance. The coral and pearl glowed with cold fire. The delicate bubble-ship moved smoothly, gently, until it hovered a hand's width from the ground in front of Jess. The wall of flowing water beckoned him like a doorway, and Jess knew that he had to enter. He passed without a ripple through the membrane.

He found himself inside an aquarium globe filled with water and fishes, tiny sea animals, drifting plants, everything touched by the wentals' essence. Inside, Jess stood enfolded by the water, feeling only warmth and comfort. It was amazing and wonderful.

Now you, and we, can command this ship.

His sense of awe gave way to impatient determination. Finally he could be off on his grand quest, and he knew exactly where he had to go. He set out to find Cesca again – at least to let her know what had happened to him, and to ask all Roamers for their assistance in his grand new mission.

Not knowing how he did so, Jess guided the huge water ship. The enormous sphere of water rose into the misty clouds. Smoothly and silently, the wental starcraft rose away from the unnamed planet, leaving the throbbing, living seas behind them.

Jess was going back to Rendezvous, where he belonged.

TWENTY-SEVEN

CESCA PERONI

Once the news leaked about the EDF attack on Raven Kamarov's ship, the Roamers would be up in arms and they would all offer their own suggestions for retribution – as Jess had done when he'd bombarded Golgen with a flurry of comets. Before that could happen, however, Cesca decided to meet in private with a handful of the most important clan leaders. She called together those who happened to be in Rendezvous at the time.

As always, the interconnected Roamer families would push and pull in different directions. Getting the clans to agree on anything, Speaker Okiah often said, was almost as difficult as establishing a new outpost on the most inhospitable of planets.

Cesca would speak her piece and listen to their advice, but she feared they would want to go overboard. And how could she argue against it? The EDF had actively attacked Roamer ekti ships like criminals in the night.

But the repercussions of the clan response would reverberate for years to come.

Seven scions met inside one of the large rock-walled chambers carved out of the central Rendezvous asteroid. Cesca sat at the head of the table, watching the men and women, none of whom knew exactly why they had been called here on such short notice. 'I'm afraid I have to deliver bad news again.'

Old Alfred Hosaki put his bony chin in his hands with an exaggerated groan. 'I should just stop coming to these meetings.' The others chuckled, then waited nervously to hear what the Speaker had to say.

With a stumbling clamour in the narrow halls outside of the room, Nikko Chan Tylar and three strong Roamer men carried in loads of battered and twisted wreckage, hull plates, an engine cowling. Blackened scars and unnaturally melted curves hinted at what had happened to the destroyed vessel. They dumped the debris on the floor at the back of the room.

'This is all that remains of Raven Kamarov's ship,' Cesca said. The clan leaders stared.

Everyone remembered the bearded and likable captain who carried ekti deliveries to various Roamer depots. Cesca explained how Nikko had found the wreckage along Kamarov's projected route. Nikko grinned as if he would be rewarded for such a find, but she said, 'I'll speak to you again later,' and sent him and his helpers away so the other Roamers could continue their meeting. His father, Crim, who was in the meeting, turned pale with surprise and anger.

Cesca continued, 'Every one of our tests and analytical procedures has verified the unmistakable hand of the EDF. Jazers did this. The Big Goose has grown desperate enough to commit acts of outright murder and piracy against Roamers.'

Then she let the clan leaders think through the implications on their own.

'Arrogant bastards!' potbellied Roberto Clarin cried. He was the manager of Hurricane Depot, which had been Kamarov's last destination.

'It could have just been one hothead,' Pasternak suggested. 'We don't know if this is a new policy of the Big Goose.'

'Do you put it past them? We can't ignore this!' Crim Tylar said.

'The Hansa is responsible for what their strongarm military does.' Clarin's plump face was practically purple. 'Somebody knows what happened to Raven's ship, and nobody's bothered to confess to it.'

'Do you think they took Raven captive?' Alfred Hosaki said. 'Do you think he's a prisoner on one of their hellhole penal colonies?'

'Oh, why would they do that?' Fred Maylor asked, always cautious.

'So they could interrogate him, find out information about us. Damn, he was a friend of mine!'

'He's dead!'

Cesca let them shout comments for a while without any rules of order, before she seized control of the meeting again by raising her voice. 'It's time to look to your Guiding Stars. The main question is what are we going to do about it?'

'I say we stop selling them ekti, that's for sure,' bellowed Clarin. 'Nothing from my depot is ever going to fuel their pirate ships again. We've got little enough stardrive fuel for our own purposes. I say we quit doing business with thieves and murderers.'

The Roamers shouted and argued, most agreeing with the sentiment, but Cesca cautioned them. 'Be careful here. The clans need trade with the Big Goose. We get half of our high-tech and industrial materials from them.'

'Not to mention the income. They're our best customers for ekti,' Anna Pasternak said. 'They squawk about the high prices we charge, but they always pay.'

Fred Maylor calmly pointed out the obvious. 'Except when they blow up our vessels and steal the ekti for themselves.'

Crim Tylar scowled. 'About a dozen ships are unaccounted for since the hydrogue war started. Who believes that Raven's was the first, or the only one, to be hit by the Eddies?'

Cesca maintained a brave face, all too aware that Jess Tamblyn's ship had also disappeared without a trace. Could he too have fallen victim to an EDF attack?

'Personally, I don't need trade with murderers!' Maylor said with a sniff. Several of the other clan leaders grumbled their agreement.

'Shizz, it's not as if we have an actual surplus anyway.' Clarin crossed his arms over his ample belly, still simmering with anger. 'We get our ekti through high risk and lost lives. My own brother died at Erphano, before we even knew what the hydrogues were up to. I say we dig in our heels until such time as the Big Goose changes its ways and grants us the respect we deserve.'

'How long can it be before they come crawling back to us?' Hosaki asked. 'They don't have any other source of fuel.'

'Sounds like a foregone conclusion to me,' Anna Pasternak said.

The discussion shot back and forth among the clan leaders as they worked themselves into a greater anger. Cesca tried to be calm and firm, attempting to steer them away from a regrettable course of action.

'We need to be cautious and consider the consequences. I'm concerned this will backfire. The Eddies have already proven their willingness to use extreme violence against us. What if this triggers further raids on defenceless clan ships or outposts? We all could suffer a great deal—'

'Speaker, we've got to show them they can't push us around.' Maylor rarely got himself so worked up.

'Uh, but they *can* push us around, if they really want to,' Hosaki mumbled. 'They have a huge military and a lot of ships. We wouldn't be able to stand against the Eddies if push came to shove.'

'They can't push us if they don't know where to find us. Since when have Roamers ever been easy to locate?'

Crim Tylar pounded his fist on the table. 'I agree with Roberto Clarin. Severing business ties with the Big Goose is our only recourse. They have the military might, but we have the commercial muscle here – the Terran Hanseatic League understands that.'

'Yes! Cut off all stardrive fuel until the Chairman or the King condemns the piracy conducted by the Earth Defence Forces.'

'And they have to bring the perpetrators to justice!' Clarin shouted.

'Oh, they'll just find a scapegoat.'

'Who cares? As long as they admit their actions.'

'And they have to swear that no further attacks will occur.'

'Shizz, they'll never do all that,' groaned Anna Pasternak.

'Well, if they don't agree to play by our rules, then we Roamers will have all the fuel we need for our own purposes,' Clarin said. 'What's wrong with that?'

The clan leaders were riled up, and Cesca again urged caution. 'We'll take a day to consider what we've discussed, and in the meantime we need to bring in the input from other clan heads. Of course, we've got to take action – but it should be the right action.'

'I don't need to consider anymore,' Crim Tylar said. 'It seems clear enough to me. My Guiding Star's gone nova.'

'I'm ready to vote,' Roberto Clarin said. 'Why get bogged down in interminable debates?'

Cesca had never seen the clan leaders so unified, so easily. 'Are you prepared for the fallout? Our clans will need to tighten our belts even more. We'll have to be ready for even more extreme retaliation—'

Pasternak snorted. 'We are Roamers! We can always survive.

The universe provides the materials we need, if we have the nerve and the ingenuity to take them. Rendezvous itself is a perfect example of how we can manage to live where no one else could.'

'Yes, back then, the *Kanaka* didn't need commercial ties with the Hansa,' Roberto Clarin said. 'None of us does. It's time we remembered our own heritage – maybe we're too spoiled, too soft from relying on all those Hansa luxuries. We left Earth a long time ago never intending to come back. It is time for us to cut the umbilical cord.'

Cesca saw the sense of the families, despite her own misgivings. 'This will not be easy, but it is certainly possible.' She stood at the head of the table. 'We will survive. We always do.'

TWENTY-EIGHT

ORLI COVITZ

After the best dinner she could manage – mushroom stew, of course – Orli started on her required classwork. Her father kissed her on the cheek and went into town. He always enjoyed pie-in-the-sky brainstorming with his fellow Dremen colonists.

When she finished her classwork, Orli unrolled her old and out-of-tune music synthesizer strips and diligently practised, letting her fingers wander across the pads to create haunting melodies. She turned up the volume, playing more vigorously as the mood took her. In indefinable ways, the melodies told a story, reflecting some of her memories, even her opinions of other people in town, whom she knew laughed at her father behind his back.

Whenever she played in Jan's presence, he applauded so often that he distracted her. Now that Orli was alone, she could improvise to her heart's content. The music soothed and entertained her.

A gifted though untrained player, she enjoyed listening to ancient classical compositions, analysing the structure of symphonies so she could better develop her own music. Unfortunately, her small set of synthesizer strips was limited in range. Jan kept promising that when they had enough money, he would send her to the finest school off-planet. Orli knew he meant it, but she wasn't sure they'd ever have the funds.

Tired and sore from working hard in the sloppy mushroom fields all day, Orli left the synthesizer strips and fell asleep on the sofa. She woke abruptly when her father bounded through the prefab door, grinning with such exuberance that Orli's heart fell. That was never a good sign.

'Good news, girl! An opportunity we just can't pass up!'

Rubbing her eyes, she got to her feet and went to give him a welcoming hug. 'What is it?'

'Oh, come on – show a little excitement. This could be a big break for us. You've heard about the Hansa's new colonization initiative?'

'The abandoned Klikiss worlds? But they're dry and empty and—'

'And *warm*, girl. And full of sunshine. All that land unclaimed. There's a Hansa ship stopping by Dremen in another week to round up volunteers bound for the nearest transportal hub. We'll receive subsidies, Hansa-supplied equipment, everything we need. Pioneers! You and I could become rich miners, or forestry tycoons. The possibilities are endless.'

'We're leaving in a . . . week?' They didn't have many belongings to pack up and get ready. She had always guessed it was only a matter of time before her father pulled up stakes again and chased after another rainbow. 'You've already signed us up, haven't you, Dad?'

'Yes, indeed.' He tousled her hair. 'Our names are right at the top of the list.'

TWENTY-NINE

MAGE-IMPERATOR JORA'H

Udru'h was the closest of his brothers in age, but of all the subjects in the Ildiran Empire, the Dobro Designate was the man Jora'h least wanted to see. He, even more than their father, was responsible for the breeding programme. However, as he made preparations to go to Dobro himself, Jora'h had demanded that his brother present him a full report on Nira. At least Udru'h could take her out of the breeding camps and save her.

Formally receiving his brother, Jora'h sat in dazzling coloured light that shone through the skysphere dome. Above him, an immense arboretum held plants, flowers, ferns, flitting butterfly-analogues, and buzzing featherhums. Several loyal guard kithmen stood around the chrysalis chair on its dais.

'So tell me. Have you found her?' The Mage-Imperator leaned forward in his chrysalis chair. He had sent away the numerous pilgrims and visitors of all kiths. For this meeting, he and Udru'h needed privacy.

The Dobro Designate's face looked as if it had been carved out of stone. His shaved head was still immaculately smooth, though some of the other Designates had begun to let their hair grow again in the days since their father's funeral. His outfit was workmanlike, adorned by few of the gaudy gemstones and shimmering solar-energy strips some courtiers preferred.

Udru'h raised his chin, and the glitter in his star-sapphire eyes reflected the bright light of the chamber. 'Liege, I have just received the information you requested from Dobro.'

'So? Tell me about Nira. If you have harmed her—'

The Designate lowered his gaze. 'I regret to inform you that the human green priest has been accidentally slain, Liege. It is unfortunate, and certainly not at my command.'

Jora'h lurched forward in the chrysalis chair, grasping the edges with his hands as if he meant to break the heavy material. 'What?' Anger and sudden grief hammered through him as his renewed hopes were dashed again. 'You killed her!'

'No, Liege. A terrible accident. During the turmoil of our father's death, many Ildirans panicked at being severed from the *thism*. They were out of control. The green priest woman attempted to escape, and some of the Dobro guard kithmen . . . overreacted.'

Nira was gone! 'Why did I not sense this? Why did I not know?'

Facing him, the Udru'h remained cool and rational. 'We were all detached until you ascended to become Mage-Imperator, Liege. I had no control over my own soldiers.'

But Jora'h also knew that his brother must be telling the truth. Once before, his father had lied to Jora'h about Nira's death, but this time it could not be a fabricated story. No Designate had ever been able to hide the truth from his Mage-Imperator. A gaping emptiness like a new black hole formed in the space of his heart.

Udru'h finally had the good grace to bow his head in apparent shame. 'I apologize for the sorrow this causes you. I know the green priest was the mother of your daughter Osira'h, and several other half-breed children.'

'Your schemes at Dobro have already brought me so much pain.' Again, he crystallized his determination to find some way to stop the programme, and save the Empire from the hydrogues at the same time. 'When will you be satisfied that you have done enough?'

'I will be satisfied when I have succeeded for the good of the Empire, Liege. My every effort was designed to provide us with a means to survive the hydrogue rampages. Your daughter by the green priest is quite possibly the key to this.' He was unruffled. 'Even if you do not believe me, even if you somehow think that I killed the human woman out of spite – consider that I would not have intentionally wasted such an exceptional resource. Truly, it was an accident.'

Jora'h reached along the bright mental thread that connected him to each of his subjects, especially to his brothers and his noble-born sons. The Dobro Designate had a powerful mind and a firm grasp on the *thism*, and Jora'h could detect no outright deceit. Udru'h did not flinch or fidget during the drawn-out waiting game.

The grief was suffocating. Jora'h had been the Mage-Imperator for only a short while, had intended to rush to Dobro and rescue his beloved Nira within days – but now it was too late. Yes, she must be dead after all. Once again, before Jora'h could manage to right a wrong, he had failed.

Shaking, the Mage-Imperator leaned forward. His voice was hoarse and sharp. 'I want you to relinquish control of Dobro as soon as possible, Udru'h. Daro'h is the Designate-in-waiting, and you will teach him everything he needs to know.'

'That is tradition, Liege. I will of course do as you command.'

Jora'h thought of his son, an intelligent and cooperative young man. He was reluctant to send Daro'h to such a hard and grim place, but Ildiran tradition had the weight of law. Because of his place in the birth order, instead of his aptitude, the second son had always been destined to be the Designate-in-waiting for Dobro. From now on, Jora'h was prepared to keep a closer eye on the experimental work there – until he could decide how to end it.

If he could end it.

'Even if Nira is dead, Udru'h, I still intend to go to Dobro so I can see this breeding programme and learn exactly how you treat the human prisoners. I will do everything in my power to right the wrongs that have been inflicted upon them for generations.'

But there was no urgency now. Nira was gone.

What if his father was right? What if freeing the human subjects eventually doomed the Ildiran Empire? The hydrogues continued their attacks. A new alliance would need to be struck . . .

Overhead in the skysphere, buzzing birds chittered. He glanced up to see the lush foliage, thinking of lovely Nira and her work as a green priest, the beautiful forests of Theroc, the sentient worldtrees. 'And I also intend to meet my daughter. Finally.'

Jora'h saw a gleam of genuine pride and respect on his brother's face. 'Yes, Liege, you must see Osira'h – and then you will realize that all of the work has been warranted. Your daughter will keep the Ildiran Empire safe in this war.'

Servant kithmen carried a restless Mage-Imperator up to a high platform on the tallest spire of the Prism Palace. Basking in the warm light from multiple suns, his brother Rusa'h stood in pale robes, his face tilted up so that pure sunshine flooded his features. He stared unblinking at the dazzling stars, as if immune to the threat of blindness. Four curious lens kithmen and two rememberers surrounded the newly awakened Hyrillka Designate, all of them eager to hear his story and his thoughts.

Rusa'h had been holding forth, attempting to find words that described what he had experienced, what revelations he'd received. The intent rememberers memorized his every word. The lens kithmen gasped at his descriptions, weighing the implications for everything that they taught and believed. They turned at the commotion of the Mage-Imperator's arrival.

Jora'h looked at his brother, whose direct gaze remained fixed on the bright suns in the sky. 'Are you making up for lost time, Brother? Trying to seize all the light you missed while in your sub-*thism* sleep?'

Rusa'h shifted languidly to face him. 'I have seen the Lightsource itself. All the suns in the Ildiran sky, or in the whole Horizon Cluster, cannot compare.' Previously, his hedonistic brother would have delighted in the crowds of people, tedious celebrations, fawning pleasure mates, musicians and performers. But now the recovering Designate seemed silent and withdrawn, preoccupied.

He dismissed the lens kithmen and rememberers from the rooftop, then spoke to the Mage-Imperator. 'I must go home to Hyrillka immediately. My people need me. They have been too long without . . . clear guidance.'

'I agree. And Pery'h must accompany you as well. It is time to send all of the Designates-in-waiting to their planets.'

Rusa'h's expression showed no warmth or welcome for his successor. 'Pery'h . . .' He seemed to be trying to remember who the young man was. 'And Thor'h. Yes . . . Thor'h.'

'Thor'h is my Prime Designate now,' Jora'h said.

'He would be . . . very helpful to me, in a time of such great changes.'

'Designate-in-waiting Pery'h can serve in that capacity. It is his assignment.'

It was astonishing that his brother would argue with him. 'Thor'h knows much about Hyrillka and how it was . . . and he knows me. Pery'h still has everything to learn.' When Rusa'h turned to him with an expression not of pleading and desperation, but of simple need, the Mage-Imperator softened. Perhaps immature Thor'h might indeed benefit from assisting with vital work such as completing the restoration of Hyrillka. He could always recall his eldest son whenever he required Thor'h, and obviously Rusa'h did need assistance.

'All right, the Prime-Designate may accompany you briefly to facilitate the transition. It will make the Empire stronger.'

'Yes.' Rusa'h stared at the dazzling suns again. 'Perhaps even stronger than before.'

THIRTY

DOBRO DESIGNATE UDRU'H

The green priest woman had already caused him a great many problems. Each time Udru'h thought he had found a solution for her situation, it led to another set of unintended consequences. If Nira hadn't proved so maddeningly valuable to the breeding programme, he'd have killed her years ago. But that would have been a useless gesture, a waste of the woman's potential.

Even though the Mage-Imperator still insisted on coming to Dobro, at least now Jora'h *believed* she was dead. Through incredible mental effort, Udru'h had managed to keep the secret from his brother. From now on, though, it would be a delicate and dangerous game, until the Designate could decide what to do with Nira . . .

In a grand procession from Ildira, a septa of Solar Navy warliners had recently begun delivering the Designates and their young apprentices to various Ildiran worlds. Only yesterday, Udru'h and Designate-in-waiting Daro'h had arrived on Dobro. After the others in his entourage had returned to their work at the crowded breeding camps, the Designate had taken Daro'h under his wing. Together, they confirmed with the medical kithmen and administrators that all the experiments continued as expected, that the human breeding specimens had caused no trouble. Then, his young nephew earnestly began to study the basics of the colony he would eventually take over.

Now the Designate had his own emergency work to do. He'd been gone for too long. He steeled himself, sought guidance from the Lightsource, then departed in a fast craft for the other side of the world. *Alone*.

For an Ildiran, solitude and isolation elicited as much instinctive horror as did darkness, but Udru'h had to bear this. Secrecy was more important than his own comfort. He was strong enough. He dared take no one else with him, not even his most trusted medical kithmen.

No one else knew that Nira was alive.

Udru'h had trained much, practised his mental ability, exercised his connection to the greater network of *thism*. He could endure this necessary torment, for a short while at least.

Udru'h pushed the craft's engines to their limits, roaring south across the sky, over Dobro's equator, and into the unsettled lower continent. Spotting the expansive waters of a great shallow lake, he knew he was close to his destination. Hours had already slipped away, hours alone, but he gripped the controls and continued flying.

It wasn't so bad. *Not yet*. He was strong, yes, strong enough . . . certainly stronger than Jora'h.

After the sudden death of the former Mage-Imperator, while the *thism* was broken and all Ildirans were scattered, confused, *disconnected*, the Dobro Designate had seized his chance. He had been waiting for it.

Once he'd discovered that Nira still existed, then-Prime Designate Jora'h had been foolishly willing to scrap the work on Dobro, to wreck centuries of careful experimentation, to threaten the future of the Ildiran Empire – all for the love of one woman. And not even an Ildiran woman at that, but a *human*, whose telepathic potential and connection with the sentient worldforest offered unsurpassed opportunities.

For years, Udru'h had listened to his best lens kithmen and mental experts while they trained Osira'h and her siblings. He would smile and observe unobtrusively, but all the while he, too, had been exercising his skills, learning mental techniques, strengthening his own abilities. Maintaining a bland expression on his face, the Dobro Designate had learned to scour his mind, erect invisible barricades around certain thoughts, and isolate some of his secrets from his comrades.

It was a game at first, then a challenge – and finally a genuine ability that his fellow Ildirans would never guess, because they had never dreamed that anyone could wish to do such a thing. Udru'h had always feared what ill-advised measures his brother might take. And while he could never speak against the rightful Mage-Imperator, never disobey Jora'h's instructions, Udru'h could plan for certain eventualities.

After the Dobro Designate had learned how to block certain clear thoughts from the *thism*, he worked with meditation and deep study until he discovered a way to divert his brother's mental threads. Unless Jora'h pried particularly hard, he would never realize the Dobro Designate was lying.

In the dark days before Jora'h was able to ascend, Udru'h had used the chaos to whisk Nira from the breeding camp. Following instructions he had left behind, his guards had beaten the green priest woman unconscious – in fact, so much more violently than he had ever intended that they had nearly killed her – but at least they had known to keep her alive, holding Nira in a drugged stupour. Then, before the *thism* could be reconnected, Udru'h had set up a place to keep her, hide her.

Considering Jora'h's obsession with this woman, the Designate knew she might prove useful as a bargaining chip, if his plans fell apart.

Udru'h trusted no one – absolutely no one – to keep the secret firmly walled inside. He could not place her where she would be tended, fed, cared for by other support personnel. No, Nira had to be entirely alone and absolutely self-sufficient. By himself, he had created a perfect cage, an expansive yet inescapable cell where a green priest could survive, and where no one would know where she was.

During the days of crisis before the new Mage-Imperator's ascension, Udru'h had rushed from Ildira back to Dobro, taken the drugged and comatose woman from where the guards kept her, and personally delivered her to the southern hemisphere, far from the breeding camp, in an entirely different climate zone. He'd found a small but lush island in the middle of a vast lake, and he had marooned her there before hastening off to Ildira for the ascension and funeral ceremonies. In the turmoil, Jora'h hadn't even noticed his brother's brief absence.

Now, weeks later, Udru'h was returning to the island to make sure Nira still survived. As he circled, he saw where the woman had built a shelter for herself out of dead wood. Her emerald skin would photosynthesize sunlight for nourishment. For an Ildiran, such isolation would have been the most appalling punishment. But Nira was strong. He had observed that much through her tribulations in the breeding camp.

Landing his ship in an area without dense trees, he climbed out of his craft and breathed the moist air, so different from the dry grassy hills to the north. The sun prickled his scalp as he narrowed his eyes and looked warily for her. He wondered if Nira had gone mad, if she would rush out at him holding a rock as a weapon.

Instead, she came forward, standing tall, naked except for a loincloth. She looked at him with anger on her face, but no fear. He saw as much contempt as resignation. 'You are recovered from your injuries,' Udru'h said. 'You appear healthy and strong, even in complete isolation.'

'I am not alone. I have the trees.' She seemed to draw strength from the strange knobbly growths with wide fan-like leaves. 'And any place is better than your breeding camps.'

'Many of the *Burton* descendants would disagree.' He looked back and forth, feeling the growing anxiety of isolation under the vast openness of the broad lake, the empty sky. The company of the human gave him no comfort, for she was separate from the *thism*.

Nira approached him, so confident and strong that Udru'h took a half step backwards. She knew that he hated to be alone, damn her! 'I have weapons,' he said, and she smiled. He cursed himself for showing a glint of fear.

'You may think you have sent me into a terrible exile, but to me this is a small section of paradise, with plenty of water, trees, and sun. I have found edible fruits and roots to supplement my diet.' She raised her emerald arms. 'This is not the terrible prison you intended. I can live here for years.'

Both of them knew she had no chance of escaping. The calm lake extended to the uninhabited horizon, with no other land in sight. Even if Nira managed to traverse the unmarked water to the nearest shore, where would she go from there? Nira was better off here, where Udru'h knew her location. Some day he might need to take her back to civilization . . .

'I know what you're doing,' Nira said. 'Your life is a lie. Everything about Dobro is a lie, and you're hiding me here just as you're hiding all the descendants of the *Burton*.'

'Perhaps.' The Designate retreated another step closer to his ship, anxiety growing within him. He was eager to get back to the breeding colony, where he could be around other Ildirans and feel their comforting presence. 'But bringing you here was necessary. Humans are easily fooled. My brother Jora'h is not quite so . . . gullible.'

'No,' she said with a smile. 'He will find me.'

THIRTY-ONE

BASIL WENCESLAS

Behind closed doors Basil looked each of his closest advisers in the eye and knew that they would give him honest opinions and careful analyses. They'd better. This was how work got done. This was how progress was made. And this was how the future of human civilization was determined.

The true details of how the Hansa was run need not concern the majority of its citizens.

Basil left his cardamom coffee untouched as he took charge of the private meeting. 'First off, Admiral Stromo, display a complete summary of ekti stockpiles across the Spiral Arm. For the new colonization initiative, I need to know which supplies are most conveniently placed next to Klikiss planets. Those will serve as our main hubs.'

The liaison officer's underlings had already prepared the report, sketching out distribution points and EDF depots. Ever since the harsh suppression of the stockpilers on Yreka, other fringe colonies had fallen in line and surrendered their illicit caches. Basil was confident of a fairly accurate projection.

Now, as the table screen displayed the datapoints, Basil turned to his deputy. 'Mr Cain, give me reasonable projections of how much stardrive fuel we can acquire in the next six months, factoring in regular Roamer production as well as the anticipated output of the Hansa's own cloud harvester on Qronha 3. We're expecting the first shipment soon, aren't we?'

'By tomorrow or the next day, sir.'

The modular cloud harvester was up and operational four full days sooner than expected, and the green priest Kolker was sending regular updates. Sullivan Gold had sent the first cargo of ekti back faster than Basil's most optimistic projections.

'Earmark it for the colonization initiative. I want to keep moving full-steam ahead while people are optimistic.'

The pallid deputy nodded. 'It's like the land rush in the Old West, bound to affect markets everywhere. Investors will be scrambling to get a piece of the resources on unmapped planets.'

Basil tapped his fingertips on the table and finally sipped his coffee. 'We are in the business of making fortunes, even dynasties. To do so, we have to keep the ball rolling.'

'Considering our vital military needs, Mr Chairman,' General Lanyan grumbled, 'I don't think it's wise to give so much stardrive fuel to colonists. It runs counter to your argument that the Klikiss transportals eliminate our requirement for ekti.'

Basil frowned at the EDF commander. 'Eventually that will be true, General, but our start-up expenditures of ekti are enormous. We'll have to deplete our current stockpiles to deliver equipment, food supplies, prefab housing, even people. It's like railway transportation. Once you get on the rail lines, you can move anywhere from one station to another – but first everyone has to get to the nearest train station.'

Cain continued the explanation in a calm voice. 'Also, General, once the transportal network is in place, we can bypass our dependence on the Roamers for their overpriced ekti supplies. Nor will we need to pander to Theroc for their green priests – who keep leaving the EDF – because we'll have our own method of instantaneous communication, at least around a planetary network. And finally, because we'll not need hydrogen from gas giants, we won't even be provoking the drogues.'

Admiral Stromo looked relieved. 'I remember when our biggest worry was trouncing rebellious colonists who didn't pay their tariffs.'

'For now, though, the war goes on,' the General said. 'As you ordered, Mr Chairman, we have prepared three more Klikiss Torches and are ready to deploy them. We must determine appropriate targets.'

'One must ask, Mr Chairman, if now is truly the best time to escalate tensions with the hydrogues.' Cain kept his expression bland, playing devil's advocate. 'Why not just lie low and let the hydrogues keep fighting the faeros while we get the transportal initiative going at full capacity?'

'Because they will keep hitting us,' Lanyan said. 'The hydrogues have shown that they mean to crush us wherever they can. We need another target to show them that we mean business, that we *can* hurt them.'

'I concur. Any gas giant will do, so long as it has hydrogues inside.' Basil took a breath, anxious for results now that he had finally made up his mind to use their ultimate weapon. 'And how is the performance of the new-model Soldier compies so far?'

'We are quite pleased, Mr Chairman. Considering how well the compy-crewed warships performed in test missions, I intend to put them to wider use. In the meantime, our shipyards are cranking out battleships – Juggernauts, Mantas, Thunderheads, and Remoras – by the thousands. Without the supplemental Soldier compies, we wouldn't have adequate crews to place aboard all those vessels.'

Cain interrupted the General, smiling with little pride. 'So, I thought, why not use the Soldier compies more extensively? The EDF seems satisfied with this approach – it's the new idea you requested of me, Mr Chairman.'

'Modified ship designs that take advantage of the expendable nature of the compies.' Lanyan pushed a plan across the tabletop to Basil, who scrutinized the designs.

Stromo eagerly explained, taking credit. 'Notice that the armour in these modified cruisers is significantly increased, and the engines occupy more of the available space. We've eliminated living quarters and unnecessary life-support systems. In front, it's basically a flying hunk of solid, impenetrable armour.' Stromo shrugged as if that were all the information Basil needed.

'And what is the purpose? Soldier compies fly them?'

Cain said, 'They're designed to *ram hydrogues*, just like that Ildiran Adar did on Qronha 3. We can build these ships, use Soldier compies to perform most of the vital functions, then turn them loose. We'll need only a bare skeleton crew of humans to make snap decisions.'

Basil continued to study the plans, nodding, but raised a question. 'We sent one reconnaissance fleet to Golgen that was crewed by Soldier compies, but that entire group vanished without a trace. Five Mantas and a Juggernaut gone.'

'They were doing hydrogue surveillance, Mr Chairman,' Stromo said, sounding apologetic. 'No wonder they were destroyed. But if we turn that fact on its head, *design* these ships to be destroyed, we'll take out the big pointy beachballs each time.'

'All right,' Basil said. 'But do you expect the human skeleton crews to become kamikazes? Why should they sit on the bridge of these rammers and drive them smack into a warglobe?'

Lanyan and Stromo looked at each other as if the answer was obvious. 'I'm sure we can find enough volunteers, Mr Chairman—'

'But not necessary,' Cain interrupted in a quiet, reasonable voice. 'We could modify the design so that the bridge crew ejects some sort of lifeboat at the last minute. It would give them a chance, at least.'

'If you like,' Lanyan said, frowning.

'All right. I authorize it — reallocate shipyard resources and get this into the production schedule. The people want to see us killing hydrogues. It might cost us dearly, but we've got to sting back.'

'We can have the first group of sixty ships completed in six months, Mr Chairman,' Stromo said.

General Lanyan added, 'This rammer fleet will allow us to pick and choose our targets, wipe out drogue infestations at our convenience. One planet at a time.'

'An excellent start,' the Chairman said.

An emergency message appeared on Cain's deskstream. The deputy leaned forward, perplexed. Basil set down his coffee cup and waited in silence. When Cain looked up, Basil took hope from the fact that the deputy's expression was more puzzled than horrified.

'The datapoints have been accumulating for days, Mr Chairman. One of my assistants recognized a pattern and checked other reports. The result is clear, though I don't understand what it means.'

Basil tried to control his impatience; by now everyone else in the room had fallen silent, waiting.

'It's the ekti shipments from the Roamers. All of the regularly scheduled deliveries failed to arrive. Every single one. The clans have cut us off everywhere . . . with no explanation.'

Since normal hours meant nothing to the Chairman of the Terran Hanseatic League, Sarein came to him in his private rooms before dawn. She was one of a very few people who could slip through his guard, and he had allowed it for many years. Their long-standing relationship had grown surprisingly comfortable, and

Basil tried not to pay much attention to it, taking her for granted. It would be a weakness to rely on her too much, but he enjoyed her company.

Basil had slept for four hours – more than usual – and the young Theron woman had clearly made up her mind to wake him pleasurably. Recently, after losing both of her brothers to the hydrogues, Sarein had seemed to need his companionship more and more, but instead of letting her get closer, Basil found himself drawing away. For the time being, however, her increased dependence on him hadn't reached the point of being bothersome. Not yet.

Sarein had used her own passcode, a gift he'd presented to her many years before and one that she dared not abuse. She wore filmy cocoon-weaves and a scarf around her shoulders to signify her ambassadorial status. The clinging garments showed off the contours of her body to good effect. She stood at his doorway, smiling in the golden light that spilled through the transparent roof of his penthouse. 'Good morning, Mr Chairman.'

He sat up in bed, granting her a smile, which she took as encouragement. Sarein began a seductive peeling of her clothes, unwinding one exotic cloth after another. By now, he should have grown tired of looking at her, or at least accustomed to her body – but he still found considerable merit in watching Sarein.

Since the attack on Theroc, she and Queen Estarra eagerly awaited any report from their world, and the two sisters pored over all images and summaries delivered by EDF recon ships after the initial rescue mission. Sarein asked Basil, as a personal favour, to send more aid to Theroc, but he had decided not to, since the people there had always blithely ignored all of *his* requests for help in the past. He didn't want to burn bridges, but neither did he want to be too helpful.

In the meantime, Sarein had lost some of her focus, slipping, growing needier, which set off warning bells in Basil's mind. As the official ambassador, Sarein realized that she should go back home, at least to tour the destruction, but she was clearly glad to stay on Earth. Basil gave her all the political excuses she needed to remain in the Palace District, since he preferred to have her around. Stability was a rare enough commodity these days.

When she stood naked in the light of sunrise, Basil did not hide his genuine admiration. Sarein was perfect, not just in her breasts and thighs and mocha skin, but also in her understanding of politics and her desire to accomplish goals that were very similar to his own. They did fit very well together.

'So, Basil, do you want me?'

'The answer is obvious, if you look in the right place.'

Laughing, she jumped onto the bed, pushing him backward and climbing on top of him. She yanked the sheets aside so they would not get in the way. With a musing expression, Basil fondled her breasts, then clasped her waist, manoeuvring hips. She needed no help to guide him inside her.

Despite Sarein's unrelenting ambition and sexual enthusiasm, Basil had never expected their affair to go on as long as it already had. Of late she seemed wary of him in spite of her neediness, almost . . . intimidated. He wondered how much she suspected about the scheme he had set up to assassinate her sister Estarra and the King. If she ever learned exactly what he had attempted, Basil would have to do a great deal of damage control.

Sarein seemed to be trying to distract him, to pull his attention to her as she thrust quickly against him, her chin upturned and her eyes closed in concentration. Her breathing came quick, sharp, urgent.

What doesn't she want me to think about?

He couldn't let her have such a total influence on him, when he needed to deal with other matters. He broke the rhythm by asking,

'Sarein, have you had any success yet with the green priests? I've seen you speaking with Nahton.'

She stopped rocking, disconcerted that he would bring up business at such an intimate moment, then settled him deeper inside her, as if to make certain he would stay there. 'Yes, Basil. Four separate times. And there's simply nothing I can do. Their minds are made up, including my Uncle Yarrod.'

Though Basil had expected as much, he still felt disappointed. He wondered if Sarein had lost her edge . . . or if she'd ever possessed the competence he had attributed to her. Had he been fooled by the young woman's ambition and her beauty? He would be deeply annoyed with himself if that was truly the case. No, that wasn't something a Hansa Chairman allowed. 'And how many of the nineteen volunteer priests have left us?'

Sarein began gently pushing, sliding and grinding again, as if to divert his attention from her bad news. She acted as if she had conversations like this every day. 'Seven so far. Five are already back on Theroc, and two are currently en route.'

Basil lay back on the pillow, closed his eyes, and let out a disturbed sigh. Sarein leaned over him, close to his face. She brushed his cheeks with her fingertips and wiggled against his hips, as if hoping for a shudder of pleasure to distract him.

'I really tried, Basil. Through Nahton, I communicated with each one personally. The priests know, intellectually, that seven men can make little difference back in the worldforest, whereas they could perform a significant service for the EDF. But their hearts are torn apart, and the trees call to them.'

'Typical.' Basil remained flat on his back, refusing to move despite Sarein's enticements. He doubted anyone else could have done more to sway the green priests. Still, it was another failure, another disappointment. 'Am I the only man in the Spiral Arm who understands the magnitude of the problem here? I work every day and every night to find a solution to this crisis. I rely on the green priests who volunteered – volunteered! – to provide vital communication aboard our widely dispersed ships. Dozens of conscripted recon pilots are simply flying away from their posts, going AWOL. The Roamers have suddenly stopped delivering ekti. Step by step, everyone is letting me down.'

Sarein kissed him with such passion that she startled him back to the present. 'I'll never let you down, Basil.'

'That remains to be seen.' Concentrating fully on her body, he grasped Sarein and pulled her to him with surprising force. She gasped, and he almost let himself fall completely into the pleasurable distraction, but he kept just a little part of himself separate . . . and safe.

As Chairman, he was dedicated to getting the job done, any job, to perfection. It was a long time before they were both spent.

THIRTY-TWO

YARROD

When he finally arrived home, the scarred worldforest was worse than Yarrod had imagined. Even though he'd experienced the events directly through telink, he still felt like weeping as soon as he set foot on the scorched ground.

The surviving green priests had selected a ring of damaged trees – five massive stumps, each one twisted like an amputated limb – as their memorial for fallen trees and people. Though severely wounded, the five burned and blasted trunks remained alive, standing like a wooden version of Earth's Stonehenge. With uneven steps, Yarrod hurried from the shuttle to the temple-like tree ring.

Forced to view all the damage through the eyes of the forest, the surviving priests were stunned or crippled by the constant agony that screamed through telink. The clamour of the world-forest made it difficult for them to see and understand small details inside the tree mind. But each time a priest helped to rescue and shore up a living tree, saving it, they all rejoiced. In many surprising instances, worldtrees had sacrificed themselves to shield small treelings. Each green shoot was a gesture of defiance against all that Theroc had suffered.

Alexa and Idriss came to greet Yarrod. His sister and her husband had always been mellow leaders, with calm personalities, never overreacting, ruling in times of quiet prosperity. They had never been prepared for anything like this. Now both of them looked gaunt and drained, as if they'd been broken into pieces and poorly reassembled.

'Oh, Alexa . . . oh, my forest.' Yarrod could think of nothing else to say. He embraced her, experiencing the still-echoing screams of the burned and frozen trees. He endured it like a flagellant punishing himself. 'What can I do? I need to know what I can do.'

'The same as all of us.' Idriss wiped sooty dust from his cheek. 'You work until you drop, do every task you see that needs doing, and when you must rest, you gather your energy to start it all again the next day.'

Yarrod tore off his provisional EDF uniform so that he stood in only his green priest's loincloth. With his emerald skin exposed to the air of Theroc, he walked to the nearest of the five scorched trees and pressed his chest against the bark. He wrapped his arms around the tree and just held it, feeling the contact with the worldforest on every centimetre of his skin.

The flood of sensations was more than he could bear, but Yarrod clutched desperately, drinking it all in. His mind expanded to see through the eyes of millions of surviving worldtrees.

Over the ten millennia since the last conflict, after the hydrogues assumed they'd exterminated the verdani, the scraps of the forest mind had settled here and gradually spread to cover all the land mass of Theroc. For almost two centuries now, green priests had carried treelings to other planets, once again spreading the ancient forest entity. And now the hydrogues had returned, intent on finishing the task of extinguishing their rival. Coming from space, they had attacked everywhere, intending to annihilate every last shred of the worldforest.

On uninhabited continents, some blazes continued to eat away at the forest. Yarrod felt the urgency, the crisis, the pull of the overwhelming and desperate work that still needed to be completed. But Theroc's population, never large, was even more diminished since the attack. They did not have the manpower or equipment to defend or revive a whole planet. They had to concentrate their efforts near the scattered population centres.

Though bemoaning the loss of each green priest volunteer who wanted to go home, the EDF had not seen fit to send enough troops, ships, and workers to help Theroc in its time of greatest need. The military vessels had come for the first, brief wave of relief efforts, assisting in broad-strokes firefighting and tending to the injured, keeping an eye out for another hydrogue invasion. But the soldiers had left long before the task was finished, drawn away by other emergencies.

Now the people of Theroc would have to do the rest themselves.

Yarrod backed away from the tree and turned to his sister and Idriss. He was covered with soot, his tattooed face streaked with tears. 'You are the Mother and Father of Theroc again. I am so sorry for the loss of your son.'

'Our *sons*,' Idriss said. 'The hydrogues killed both Reynald and Beneto.'

Yarrod hung his head. 'Yes, Beneto was linked with the worldforest when his grove on Corvus Landing was destroyed. I *felt* everything he said. He poured his mind and soul into the trees . . . but nothing could save his body.' Yarrod drew a deep breath and looked around. 'Let me help here. I need to speak with my comrades.'

Alexa said, 'We've done our best to clear areas, distribute new treelings, gather and plant seeds. The forest tells us that a high percentage have already germinated.'

Yarrod refused to let himself be overwhelmed by the seemingly impossible task. 'Every one of those seedlings is precious, and the soil of Theroc is well fertilized with blood and ashes.'

Through telink and the reports of other green priests, he knew how the forest had tried to defend itself during the initial icewave attack, by unleashing a furiously accelerated growth and rejuvenation. The worldtrees had attempted to restore the foliage as fast as it was destroyed, and they had succeeded for a brief while, but such a thing required huge amounts of energy, and the forest's reserves had rapidly been drained. That defence was triggered only during a time of extreme stress, and the damaged worldforest was now depleted, barely able to keep itself alive.

The green priests and the people of Theroc would have to restore the forest in the slow, natural way.

Yarrod sensed that many of the dazed and despairing green priests were on the edge of surrender. A few collapsed and wept, but after taking a moment to recover, they dragged themselves back to their feet and returned to their all-consuming job. He joined them, throwing himself into the work. He could afford to give nothing less than his utmost. None of them could, if the worldforest was ever to thrive again.

THIRTY-THREE

JESS TAMBLYN

As he approached Rendezvous, piloting his wondrous water-and-pearl vessel, the Roamer cluster looked different to Jess. Perhaps it was the wentals inside his eyes: when he peered through the filmy walls of his ship, the asteroids flickered as if through a veil of tears. For Jess, the excitement and anticipation were palpable.

He had no idea if Cesca would be there or if, by some miracle, she wasn't already married to Reynald of Theroc. In a very real sense, he was no longer part of the Roamers, no longer entirely human. He wasn't sure how either of them could cope with the changes.

But Roamers had a penchant for solving impossible problems.

All of the clans would be astonished to see him and his strange vessel. They might think him an invading alien, a potential threat, and they'd probably scatter. Jess wanted to find some way to reassure them, but he had no way to communicate directly. For all its wonders, the water-and-pearl spaceship did not have a standard comm system with which to contact the Roamers.

The exotic vessel tumbled gracefully towards the asteroid belt.

Outlying rocks drifted in a kind of smokescreen to foil the prying sensors of Big Goose ships. The central habitation rocks of Rendezvous were bound together with massive construction braces; smaller asteroids were simply tethered into place or even allowed to drift under their mutual gravity. As Jess closed towards the central hub, he spotted numerous Roamer craft: short-range shuttles, ekti escorts, and long-distance cargo vessels delivering supplies and materials like bees flitting around a hive. *Home at last.*

Jess approached the main docking ring slowly as more questions rose in his mind. How would he get inside? He looked down at his energy-impregnated body, saw his skin glow. With the wentals permeating his tissues, he possessed many advantages and abilities no human had ever experienced before. The blood flowing through his veins was supercharged, his skin covered with a crackling field. In keeping him alive, the wentals had made him more than human. He wondered if he could even survive open vacuum.

Yes. We will protect you.

They could not, however, help him to answer the flood of questions the Roamers would have. That would be his own challenge. Cesca would help, once he was finally reunited with her.

While the clan ships scrambled in a panic and the inhabitants of Rendezvous hurried to defensive stations or made preparations to evacuate, Jess hovered the large, strange ship outside a circular entry crater. He had to hope the clan ships didn't shoot at him, though his wental vessel could probably withstand any such attack. Roamers generally kept a low profile, hiding instead of picking a fight. They would wait and see what he intended to do. He hoped.

From the asteroid cluster, lights glinted like bright eyes from portholes in the rough walls. Even now alarms must be ringing. Roamers rushed through the tunnels, preparing to evacuate or fight.

Jess's ship just hung there, motionless. He made no threatening moves, giving the Roamers time to accept his presence. Other spacecraft backed off, waiting to see what would happen next.

Finally, curious, one small ship approached closer than the others dared, swooping past. Jess looked through the wavering water wall to see a young Roamer piloting the vessel. The pilot had Asian features and face full of more curiosity than fear. Nikko Chan Tylar. Jess remembered the young man from clan gatherings . . . back when he himself had been normal.

Standing where he could be seen behind the curved, clear wall, Jess moved languidly through the liquid atmosphere. He pressed close to the watery hull and raised a hand in a non-threatening greeting, sure that Nikko could see his human form through the bubble wall. Jess slowly waved – harmless, friendly. Nikko's shocked expression showed genuine recognition before he spun away.

Then Jess realized that in addition to his eerily glowing flesh, his naked physique would have been an innocuous, even humourous surprise. Roamers loved to decorate themselves, embroider their clothes, embellish their outfits with flamboyant scarves. They weren't prudish, but if he walked completely unclothed into Rendezvous, he would cause a different sort of stir than he intended.

That is easily enough solved.

In the water in front of him, a tiny strand appeared as molecules lined up, drawn from the minerals in the captured seawater and from the metallized coral of the framework. The thread spun out like a silvery web, growing longer, then whirling, weaving.

We will create a fabric that can endure the energy in your flesh.

As the threads meshed and tangled, knitting into a filmy weave, he saw that the material had the sheen and colour of mother-of-pearl. The fabric wrapped around him like another skin, covering his arms and legs, his torso, his hips, but leaving his hands and feet bare.

'Very stylish,' he said.

It is sufficient.

Ready now, Jess carefully brought the wental vessel down into the crater, pressing the filmy walls against the large hangar doors. The watery barrier reshaped itself, forming a fluid seal so that Jess could operate the hatch and open the heavy door.

He stepped directly through the membrane as if it were no more than gelatin and stood in the bright artificial lights of the Rendezvous receiving bay. His skin was moist, but the water did not trickle off him. It remained there, a part of his being, alive with phosphorescent energy. Though he didn't need to breathe, Jess still inhaled a deep lungful to smell the dust and the metallic odour of reprocessed and filtered air. The sensation was strange, wonderful.

A flood of memories and emotions came to him. He had first met Cesca here on business for clan Tamblyn. He had attended meetings and helped the families make major decisions regarding commerce, expansion, and their future. He wanted to melt with relief as it once again sank in where he was. Home.

Then the wentals spoke in his head, delivering a warning that dumped an icy cold avalanche onto his hopes. *Do not allow yourself to come into physical contact with any other person. You must remain separate. There is a danger.*

'Why?' All he could think of was the chance to see Cesca again, even if she was already married. They had been so close—

You hold too much uncontrolled power. Your body can barely contain the wental water inside your cells, and the surge from a touch of your skin could flood another person, like the cascade from a bursting dam.

'You mean I can't . . . touch *anybody*? Not even a handshake?' Or a kiss.

It would be fatal to the other person. The power would overflow from you and burn out a fragile human form. We could not prevent harm.

Jess felt the blow of the news. Not even a touch! 'You could have warned me about that before.'

It should not be difficult to keep yourself separated from other humans. We will assist you. Your mission is important.

He focused his thoughts, remembered his calling, the great ally he brought to the clans and, by extension, to the human race. 'All right, we'll make it work.' Even seeing Cesca again would be enough, until they could decide what to do. He hoped she was here.

Now Jess heard running feet, dozens of Roamer men, women, and curious children bounding like gazelles in the asteroid's low gravity. They were afraid and intrigued, but still rushing to meet him. Nikko must already have transmitted what he had seen. The return of Jess Tamblyn, especially in such an amazing ship, would cause an uproar.

Jess looked at the wide eyes and smiled. Some Roamers carried weapons ranging from energy blasters to projectile guns. Though none of those devices could cause him any harm, he did not make any move they might interpret as threatening. Instead, he spread his hands. The strange pearl-fabric garment he wore shimmered in the artificial light. 'I know my arrival is somewhat unexpected and . . . unorthodox, but there's nothing to fear. I promise.'

More and more Roamers came into the rock-walled bay, and they stayed away instinctively from his obviously supercharged body. 'I'm back . . . truly, I'm back. And I have such a strange story to tell that even the Ildiran rememberers wouldn't know what to do with it.'

Then finally he saw Cesca Peroni.

She pushed her way forward, hurrying with an urgency that the others could see. Like a man dying of thirst, he drank in her appearance, her full lips, her lush figure, just remembering . . .

Many of the Roamers had either known or suspected their secret romance, but at the moment gossip was the least of their concerns.

Jess longed to embrace her, but the wentals prevented him. 'No closer, Cesca. Please. Much as I want to, you'd better not come near me.' He held up his luminous hand, showed the play of faint lightning inside his fingers.

Cesca stopped. Her expressive brown eyes seemed to swallow him, and her face radiated sheer joy. Her almost-black hair had grown longer; her olive skin was still smooth and perfect, though she appeared tired. The burden of being Speaker showed on her high-cheekboned face.

Why wasn't she with Reynald?

'Well, you took your time coming back, Jess Tamblyn. We've been looking for you for months. So much—' Her words cut off and she forced herself to continue. 'So much has changed.'

He couldn't keep himself from chuckling. 'You don't know the half of it, Cesca.'

THIRTY-FOUR

MAGE-IMPERATOR JORA'H

The days crawled by in the Ildiran Empire, now that Jora'h knew Nira was dead. But he still had to finish cementing his reign, keeping all the kiths together with the *thism*. He had to create and secure their future.

Entering the contemplation chamber, proud and utterly loyal, the new Solar Navy commander clasped his hands against his heart in a traditional salute. 'You asked to speak with me, Liege?'

It felt strange to hear his son call him by the formal title, so Jora'h returned the favour. 'Yes, Adar Zan'nh. I have chosen your first assignment as commander of the Solar Navy.' He smiled as he watched the young man's reaction, then realized that they were no longer – and would never again be – merely father and son.

It was rare for a Prime Designate's first-born child to be of mixed-kith heritage, like Zan'nh; he had never intended for that to happen. Long ago, knowing that Jora'h's first noble-born child would become the next Prime Designate, his own father had run many tests and consulted with lens kithmen to determine the best mate. Bloodlines were traced, family trees inspected, until finally the appropriate female was presented to him as a *fait accompli*.

Her name was Liloa'h, slender and graceful and quiet. When she'd disrobed in his private chambers, dropping her elaborate fabrics to the floor, Jora'h had seen that her smooth skin was painted with intricate designs and secret tracings of chameleon films. He had been captivated by her.

Liloa'h had conceived the first time, and medical kithmen monitored her pregnancy, while Jora'h went to work siring other children. His second mate was a woman of the soldier kith, muscular and strong – a striking contrast with cultured and quiet Liloa'h. He had got her pregnant as well. She was Zan'nh's mother. Such a combination of noble and soldier kith generally yielded a person with exceptional aptitude to become a military officer.

And Jora'h had gone on for months, lover after lover. He'd hoped to see Liloa'h again, even foolishly considered knowing her as a friend, but the old Mage-Imperator disabused him of that notion.

Then, in the last months of her pregnancy, Liloa'h suffered a terrible fall down the graceful ramps of the Prism Palace, and lost the baby. She was distraught at having failed in her duty, anguished that she would not bear a child destined to become the Mage-Imperator. Jora'h was not allowed to see her again, though he was sure the Mage-Imperator had let her live comfortably.

Thus, by accident, had Zan'nh become his first-born son, and Thor'h – the first pure noble child, conceived without such careful selection – would now be the Prime Designate. Zan'nh was a model of what an Ildiran could be . . . so different from the distracted and self-centred Thor'h, who had already gone with Pery'h and Rusa'h back to Hyrillka. Jora'h sighed. 'I'm not positive the Prime Designate is ready for his role, but I have complete faith in your abilities.'

Zan'nh remained at attention, speaking no deprecating word about his brother. For an Adar, questions usually had clear-cut answers. Through the bright lines of *thism*, Jora'h could see the dazzle of dedication coming from him. 'Thor'h will fulfil his duties, I am certain. He is an Ildiran – what else can he do?'

Jora'h, not quite as sure, allowed himself a bittersweet smile. 'Yes, what else can he do? I remember when I was young and unprepared as well.'

Zan'nh flashed his father a boyish grin that looked unusual on his normally serious face. 'I know exactly what that feels like, too.'

The Mage-Imperator sat up more formally. 'Adar Kori'nh was very proud of you, and so am I. You already have considerable experience in wargames, practice manoeuvres, and scouting expeditions. There's no need for more of that, when you can get directly to work.'

Zan'nh inclined his head. 'Thank you, Liege. I would much rather concentrate on our genuine problems instead of ceremonies. What mission do you have for me?'

'I want you to secure the gains Adar Kori'nh made in his last fight.' Jora'h shifted in the voluminous chrysalis chair, trying to get comfortable. He was glad he had sent away all the attenders who would have fussed and worried over him. 'We must take advantage of the fact that Qronha 3 is clear of the enemy. Find whatever skilled miner kithmen we have on Ildira, enough to form a splinter, gather the equipment you need, and establish another sky-harvesting complex there. Facilitate the production of more ekti for our dwindling stockpiles. It is a military necessity.'

Zan'nh bowed. 'I will see that it is done to your satisfaction, Liege.'

THIRTY-FIVE

O X

OX, the only Teacher compy allowed deep inside private security levels of the Whisper Palace, performed his daily duties, as he had done for almost two centuries. Young Raymond Aguerra, renamed Peter, had been an interesting, well-behaved, model student. Prince Daniel, however, was . . . not.

With a rude noise, the young man turned away from the news feed, in which the King was receiving the first shipment of stardrive fuel delivered from the Hansa's new skymine. On the screen, Peter spoke clearly in his well-trained voice. 'These shuttles carry fresh ekti. *Not* purchased from Roamer cloud harvesters. *Not* removed from our stockpiles. This is stardrive fuel obtained by a Hansa-operated cloud harvester on Qronha 3, which has been cleared of the evil hydrogues.'

'The Ildirans cleared it,' Daniel said with a snort. '*We* didn't do anything. Why is Peter taking credit?'

'He is taking advantage of the situation. He is not taking credit,' OX said. 'For as long as that gas planet remains safe, we should mine its clouds. It is surprising that the Ildirans themselves have not brought their own facilities.' He knew, from his ancient experience, that the Ildirans were rigid in their behaviour and followed complex, and often slow, patterns.

The Teacher compy had calculated that the amount of stardrive fuel produced by Sullivan Gold's single facility was far from sufficient to meet the Hansa's ekti needs, but the symbolism was vital. On the news feed, he and Prince Daniel watched the fuel shuttles open; uniformed workers stepped out, wearing clean and perfectly pressed work uniforms. They carried tanks of compressed ekti, each one mounted on antigrav clips.

'Oh, why should I care?' Daniel said. 'No one ever lets me set foot outside of this Palace.'

'You are the chosen Prince.' OX's modulated voice expressed patience, designed not to provoke or upset a volatile student like this boy. 'That is sufficient reason for you to care.'

'Will I ever get to go out there? Make a public appearance? I want to take a look inside that hydrogue wreckage, but you won't let me.' Daniel pouted.

'Chairman Wenceslas has given explicit instructions. You are to be sheltered. It is for your own safety.'

'Peter gets to do it. If I'm a real Prince, then why shouldn't I be with him? I'm his replacement if anything bad happens.'

Considering Daniel's intractable behaviour, his resistance to even simple instructions, OX knew that nothing 'bad' was likely to happen to the King any time soon, despite Basil's implied threats. 'Perhaps you will earn a change of status, once you achieve certain milestones.'

'If the hydrogues came and wiped out this city, then I could do what I wanted. Ha! I'd probably survive this deep in the Whisper Palace.'

'Do not speak that way, Prince Daniel.'

'I'm the Prince. I can speak any way I like.'

'And I am your instructor. My job is to see that you learn the proper ways to speak. And to behave.' The compy added a sharp edge to his voice, which startled the young man into silence.

For many months now, OX had diligently worked with Daniel to make him understand his role. The basic data of the Prince's prior life explained that he – whose real name was withheld from OX – had been taken from a bad household. He'd had a stepfather, no mother, and an 'obnoxious older sister', according to Daniel's comments. At first, the Prince candidate had been overjoyed with his new circumstances, showing excessive hedonism and gluttony. Through prior models of human behaviour, OX expected that such treats would eventually grow stale for him, and then the spoiled boy would become even more intractable.

The Hansa's preliminary assessments of the young candidate had apparently been in error. Daniel was not particularly bright, diplomatic, or personable. Once Chairman Wenceslas realized the mistake he had made, OX postulated that the Hansa would simply make this young man disappear and select a replacement 'Daniel'. As it was, the public was not familiar with him.

As further proof of his unsuitability, the boy was oblivious to his own precarious position.

Returning to the business at hand, OX once again reset his priorities and attempted to teach Prince Daniel. 'Now we will review the story of the generation ship *Abel-Wexler*, the tenth to depart from Earth, in AD 2110.'

'That's boring.'

OX continued anyway. 'Once the Ildiran rescuers delivered the ship to Ramah, their history became interesting. Ildirans remained with the passengers for years, helping the humans establish their foothold on the new colony. After making close ties with several Ildiran lens kithmen, a charismatic religious leader on Ramah became convinced that devout humans should emulate the Ildiran *thism*, as a conduit to God. Although he had originally been trained as a spokesman for Unison, he developed his own beliefs.'

Daniel began tapping his writing implement on the desktop, making a loud noise. Accordingly, OX increased the volume of his voice.

'Many of the strictly religious passengers of the *Abel-Wexler* resented the "Ildiran heresy", and a series of holy wars broke out on Ramah. Several lens kithmen were killed. The Ildiran Empire chose not to retaliate militarily, but withdrew its people from the world. Religious wars simmered between the human settlers for decades, with many attempts at recasting Raman theology into a version acceptable to each sect. When no human priest actually succeeded in linking with the Ildiran *thism*, however, most of their followers broke away.'

Throughout the brief lecture, Daniel displayed exaggerated restlessness. The young man seemed to be trying to provoke OX, but the Teacher compy remained much more patient than any human would have been. 'Unless you finish this lesson satisfactorily, Prince Daniel, I will invoke my privilege to cancel the dessert course at this evening's meal. Conversely, superior performance may result in an extra portion.'

'I could have you removed if you do that!'

'No, you cannot.' The compy remained firm and silent. Daniel chose not to press his position.

'All right, but why does it have to be so dull?' He slumped back.

'It is dull to you, because you refuse to apply your imagination. My goal is not to entertain you, but to instruct you. I intend to succeed, whether you enjoy it or merely endure it. But you will listen to my lessons, and I will repeat them as many times as necessary until you comprehend the concepts.'

'I hate you, OX.'

The compy remained silent for a moment. 'Your emotional response to me is irrelevant. Shall we continue with your lessons?'

Sulking, Daniel didn't answer.

After a few moments of tense silence, OX began his lecture again. He was a Teacher compy and followed his assigned tasks with full diligence.

He knew, however, that this young man would never be much of a King. Daniel simply did not have the potential or the drive that Peter had exhibited. But the Hansa had given OX explicit instructions on what he must do.

THIRTY-SIX

CHIEF SCIENTIST
HOWARD PALAWU

In Earth's largest factory the compy production line hissed and burbled with molten alloys and sprayed solvents. The smell of hot metal and caustic chemicals filled the air. The din of large-scale fabrication, with the whirring machinery and the clang of shaped components, was deafening.

Howard Palawu, the Hansa's Chief Scientist, took comfort from the sights and sounds of an efficient plant operating at full capacity. Smiling, he called up quota numbers on a hand-held electronic pad and studied delivery records, projections, and profits. He turned to the tall Swede next to him. 'We'll be ten per cent higher than last month, Lars. Fewer errors, faster throughput. More Soldier compies for the EDF.'

Lars Rurik Swendsen, the lead Engineering Specialist, stood beside the shorter man, showing a lot of teeth in his broad grin. 'The factory's running like a well-oiled machine, Howard.'

'It *is* a well-oiled machine.'

'I can't wait until the new fabrication wing comes online in two weeks. How are you going to spend your bonus?'

Palawu shrugged; he had never much cared about his salary or his rewards. 'I still haven't figured out what to do with the last one.'

The dark-skinned scientist had broad shoulders and a waist that wasn't quite as flat as he thought it was. He kept his greying hair cropped extremely close to his scalp. Palawu had two grown children and had lost his wife a decade earlier in a medical accident during what should have been a minor procedure. Since then, the Chief Scientist had devoted himself to his work for Hansa and King. It kept him busy.

'The more we milk that Klikiss robotic technology, the more tweaks we can make to the production line,' he said. Two years earlier, he and Swendsen had been chosen to supervise the complex dissection and dismantling operations of the Klikiss robot Jorax. The breakthroughs they had made by copying the alien systems had been a giant boon to Hansa technology. Motivational modules and programming routines were scanned, duplicated, and transferred wholesale into resilient Soldier-model compies, which had already been put to good use in the Earth Defence Forces.

The two men walked down the line, watching the identical Soldier compies assembled step by step, each one exactly according to specifications. The new-model compies were perfect warriors, sophisticated battle machines sure to be the key to defeating the hydrogues.

'I got a report from the shipyards this morning, Howard,' Swendsen said. 'They're already in production with sixty heavily armoured rammer ships, according to the Chairman's new plan. They seem to be a week ahead of schedule.'

'That's just on paper. The rammers won't be ready for months. We've got plenty of time to manufacture a compy crew for them . . . even though I hate to see such beautiful machines destroyed in a suicide mission.' Palawu watched as another armour-plated Soldier glided by on the assembly belt. 'But they were designed to be expendable, I suppose.'

A well-dressed man with blond hair came up to the two senior production leaders. Wearing a business suit and a bland expression, the man looked out of place on the noisy, dirty fabrication line. He didn't even seem interested in the new compies coming off the assembly belts. 'Chief Scientist Palawu? Engineering Specialist Swendsen? Come with me, please.'

Palawu recognized the self-proclaimed 'special assistant' to Chairman Wenceslas who had tried to stop King Peter from ordering a shutdown of the factory because of his concerns about the Klikiss technology. That had been a nerve-wracking time, but everything was back on schedule now.

'Where are we going?' Swendsen asked.

'Chairman Wenceslas wishes to see you in his office.'

Palawu stood next to his tall colleague, wondering which of them was more nervous. Previously, whenever they'd been spoken to the Chairman, it had been part of a large board meeting; now they waited alone in the empty room.

A quiet Friendly-model compy strutted like a wind-up toy, carrying a tray with a pot of strong-smelling cardamom coffee. Palawu preferred tea, but apparently they wouldn't be given a choice. He and Swendsen each took one of the proffered cups while the compy set the third on the Chairman's immaculately clean desk. Palawu took a polite sip, looked at his friend. They both waited.

Wenceslas came in several minutes later accompanied by his blond-haired expediter. The Chairman straightened his suit and looked at the two scientists. 'I apologize for the delay, gentlemen. I genuinely hate it when meetings don't end on schedule.' He took a seat at his desk. 'I understand how valuable your time is. I just wish some of my fellow administrators would recognize the value of mine.' He sipped his coffee, found it cold, and pushed it aside. 'I see from production reports that our compy manufacturing facilities are operating at peak efficiency. Soldier compies have already been distributed among all of the main battle groups. You two have done an exemplary job.'

Swendsen beamed, while Palawu lowered his eyes, embarrassed. 'We work well together, Mr Chairman.'

'And now you must demonstrate how well you can work apart.' Wenceslas gestured for both of them to take their seats. Neither asked for more information, choosing to wait until the Chairman spoke again. 'Without question, you two are our foremost experts on Klikiss technology.'

Palawu fumbled with his fingers. 'Mr Chairman, I believe you're overstating the—'

Wenceslas cut him off. 'Dispense with the silly false modesty, please. You demean my intelligence, and you diminish your own accomplishments. If there were two better candidates, I would be speaking to *them* instead of to you.' He shuffled the neatly stacked papers on his desk, then straightened them again. 'I need you to turn your talents to studying the Klikiss transportals.'

'Has something gone wrong in the colonization initiative, Mr Chairman?' Palawu asked. He had thought the first wave was proceeding with full support. He had heard of no delays.

'Oh, the system *functions* just fine, sending settlers off to empty Klikiss planets. But our science doesn't understand *how* it works – and that limits our options.' The Chairman folded his hands together. 'You see, gentlemen, it is my dream that we learn how to move the existing transportals, or even create new ones, so that the Hansa can set up efficient gateways wherever we choose. Just think – if we could establish Klikiss transportals from scratch on any colony world, perhaps even increase their dimensions and transportation capacity, then we wouldn't need to rely on conventional space travel at all. The ekti shortage would be utterly irrelevant. We could also send messages from planet to planet directly, without being forced to use unreliable green priests.'

'Now, that's quite an ambitious plan, Mr Chairman,' Swendsen said.

'But a feasible one,' Palawu added, already wrestling with the problem. 'It shouldn't be intrinsically more complex than the Klikiss robots. Even if we don't understand every circuit in the transportal technology, perhaps we can imprint and replicate them, as we did with the Soldier compies.'

Basil seemed satisfied with their exuberance. Palawu looked at his tall friend. 'And which one of us would you like for this assignment?'

The Chairman gestured to the expediter, who reached into his pocket and pulled out a single gold coin. 'Your qualifications appear to be equivalent, gentlemen. Therefore, without further agonizing discussion, we will settle the matter by an ancient reliable method.'

The expediter spun the coin in the air and slapped it against the back of his hand.

Swendsen called out, 'Tails!' before the coin had fallen, and the expediter lifted his palm to reveal the idealized profile of King Ben, the Hansa's first ruler.

The Chairman shook Palawu's hand. 'Congratulations, Dr Palawu. I will see that you're dispatched to our main hub at Rheindic Co as soon as possible.'

THIRTY-SEVEN

ORLI COVITZ

The Hansa's new colonization campaign played on hopes and patriotism. Media bursts and mail drones delivered the Chairman's dramatic invitation from world to world, and human beings reacted predictably, always sure that life would be better somewhere else after a new start.

With funding and bonuses from the Hansa, hopeful people left struggling colonies in droves, waiting to be rounded up by commercial transports and delivered to the nearest Klikiss jumping-off points. On every world that had briefly been scouted by transportal explorers, ambitious groups planted the flag of the Terran Hanseatic League, submitted signed copies of the Charter, and claimed new territory for humanity . . .

As the *Voracious Curiosity* pulled away from cloudy Dremen, Orli went to the ship's window and looked out at the immensity of stars, open emptiness that stretched for ever and ever. She was sure she had done the same thing when departing from Earth, back when she'd been just a little girl. She could remember little about Earth, other than occasional snatches of blue skies, tall buildings, and one particular dinner in a seafood restaurant with her mother, shortly before their family had broken up.

Now, her chest felt hollow, though she wasn't entirely sad to go away. Orli understood their need to make a new start, recognizing that she and her father would not likely survive the deep bleak winter of the star's upcoming low cycle. Yes, it was time to try one of the new Klikiss colonies.

Jan joined her at the window, and they stared at Dremen, whose pearly silver clouds reflected sunlight in swirls of cottony softness — much more beautiful than they had ever seemed from ground level. The dwindling globe seemed so small, a child's bauble cast into the void.

'Look at all those clouds, girl. Plenty of thunderstorms and cold fog. I'm not sorry to be leaving all that behind.'

'Up here the sun seems so bright.'

Jan sighed. 'If only those people had seen the wisdom in my solar mirror project, we could have turned Dremen into a warm and perfectly comfortable place. But nobody wanted to make the investment.'

Two years after the hydrogue ultimatum, when Dremen began to realize hard times were ahead, Jan Covitz had got it into his head to run for mayor, advocating grandiose and costly solutions to the colony's weather problems. He had drawn up a plan to erect wide concave mirrors in orbit, whose sole purpose was to reflect sunlight and pump an extra degree or two of temperature into the atmosphere. In his plan, the huge filmy reflectors were as thin as tissue coated with a high-albedo layer only a few molecules thick. Dremen could have become self-sufficient, impervious to the longest low-intensity solar cycle.

Though technologically feasible, the plan would have required a large investment, high taxes, and years to complete. Even as a girl, little involved in local politics, Orli had understood that her father's proposed solutions were unlikely to be adopted.

Jan had lost by an embarrassingly large margin. He'd come home on the night of the elections with a resigned smile, accepting his defeat with good grace. 'No surprise that they're short-sighted, girl,' he had told Orli, wrapping his arm around her shoulders. 'Too much time studying the ground at their feet and not enough looking up into the sky towards the future.'

And so, once ekti supplies were cut off, along with regular food and fuel shipments from Hansa merchants, Dremen had found itself in a very bad position.

The colonists eventually understood that Jan had been right in principle and were angry at their own failures, but as individualists they did not like to be reminded of them. Though Jan's disposition was always smiling, even teasing, they still felt him thinking 'I told you so' in every encounter.

Jan might have done better if he'd spent more hours and energy planning the family's mushroom harvest, but he was a broad-strokes person, fascinated with the big picture instead of the details.

Although he was always looking for the light at the end of the tunnel, more often than not he simply got hopelessly lost. Orli did her best to lay a trail of breadcrumbs for him to follow home . . .

Rlinda Kett was the pilot of their ship. On orders from the Hansa, she flew the *Voracious Curiosity* from planet to planet, picking up volunteer colonists and transporting them to Rheindic Co, the nearest world with a transportal. There, the people would be assembled into large settlement groups, then dispatched to Klikiss worlds that were deemed hospitable to human life.

Captain Kett, a large, good-humoured woman who loved to laugh, had pressurized the *Voracious Curiosity*'s cargo hold and converted it into a gathering room for the colonists. Her ship had never been designed as a passenger liner and had few amenities for so many people, but the flight to Rheindic Co would not be long, and these volunteers were willing to be crammed together briefly.

Though the Hansa had provided standard colonists' rations and bland-tasting mealpax, Captain Kett insisted on creating the closest thing to a banquet she could manage for her passengers. She'd picked up nearly fifty people, a few from Dremen and the others from Rhejak and Usk.

'Who knows what kind of food you'll find on those Klikiss worlds?' Captain Kett said, grinning at Orli. 'You deserve at least one decent meal before you get to Rheindic Co. Been there myself, you see, and it's nothing special.'

'Except it has a Klikiss transportal,' Jan pointed out.

'Well, there is that.'

The question of the day seemed to be which colonization group or transportal explorer would eventually find the missing Margaret Colicos. The old xeno-archaeologist had vanished one day through the stone window on Rheindic Co, the same one the colonists were going to use. Apparently, the Hansa technicians operating the relocation facility had established a betting pool.

Aboard the ship, the voices of the passengers rose to a fever pitch. Orli had already heard them placing wagers using Hansa credits or exchanging chore responsibilities. Jan happily added a bet of his own, picking a time and a world at random.

Orli said, 'It's just like all those people who bet on finding the lost *Burton* out in the Spiral Arm, Dad. Not much chance of winning.'

'Not much chance,' Jan agreed. 'But the payoff could be big.'

The *Voracious Curiosity* sailed on, every moment growing closer to the jumping-off point for the next part of Orli's life. She took her blanket and snuggled near to her father against a bulkhead wall. Captain Kett dimmed the lights in the cargo hold so that everyone could sleep, but many of the colonist volunteers were too full of anticipation.

Jan dozed off within moments, without a care in the world. Orli remained awake, listening to him breathe, staring with open eyes at the metal walls. She couldn't decide whether she was excited or worried.

THIRTY-EIGHT

ANTON COLICOS

Though Anton enjoyed the excitement and energy during the height of Maratha's day season, he drank in the long night silence in a way that none of his Ildiran friends could ever appreciate.

As a boy, he'd spent much time basically alone in the alien archaeological digs worked by his parents. Margaret and Louis had treated him as a little adult; they hadn't seemed to know what else to do. At night in camp, he would sit and listen to them discussing (or arguing about) discoveries they'd made in the ruins. His parents tried to interpret the Klikiss architecture, room placement, or the weblines of hieroglyphic text on the walls. Occasionally, they asked their son what he had done during his day as he roamed the site, exploring. Most of the time, though, Anton just eavesdropped and absorbed their passion for the long-gone alien culture . . .

Here in the nearly empty domed city, Anton had his surrogate Ildiran 'family'. Though he did not enhance the *thism* with his presence, he did share a fascination for their grand Ildiran epic.

In particular, Anton adored a story about an exotic Ildiran painter who became too obsessed with her art. Not satisfied with common materials, she had painted every centimetre of her skin, from the top of her shaved scalp to the soles of her feet. She made herself into a living mural of Ildiran history and heroes, and people came to stare at her marvellous body. One morning after she had completed her great work, however, the artist discovered a small wrinkle on her face – and realized that, over time, her physical masterpiece would be destroyed by her own mortality.

Convinced that her art was more important than her life, she had formulated a preservative poison that polymerized and fossilized her skin. The artist drank the poison, positioned herself on a stand with her arms and legs spread so as to show off every detail, and waited while the chemicals turned her body solid, never letting her face form a grimace of pain. According to Vao'sh, the artist's body-statue was still on display in the Prism Palace, and Anton hoped to see it as soon as they returned to Mijistra.

Now, as Anton studied diamondfilm sheets covered with the text of the *Saga*, Vao'sh hurried into his well-lit chamber. 'Ah, I thought I'd find you here, Rememberer Anton. A septa of Solar Navy ships has arrived bearing details of the transition and the new Mage-Imperator's ascension. They are accompanied by Designate Avi'h himself. He has asked that all work cease in order to welcome him.'

Anton pushed the diamondfilm sheets away and stretched. 'Who am I to argue?'

Because of the early death of Mage-Imperator Cyroc'h, Jora'h hadn't had sufficient time as Prime Designate to father enough noble-born sons. Therefore, there were too few Designates-in-waiting for all Ildiran splinter colonies, especially one as minor as Maratha. As a consequence, Jora'h's youngest brother Avi'h would keep his position, since there was no replacement available.

As all members of the skeleton crew gathered inside the main storytelling plaza under the central dome, several Solar Navy soldiers from the escort septa followed the Maratha Designate as he strolled back into his garishly illuminated city. The Septar, a man named Rhe'nh, stood in his uniform, waiting to be dismissed; he had other Designates-in-waiting to deliver on a convoluted return trip around the Empire.

Anton noted that Designate Avi'h, dressed as usual in voluminous and ornate yellow robes, was shorter than most Ildirans, but he held his head high, as if by stretching his neck he could gain a bit more height. When Maratha Prime bustled with tourists, the stuffy Designate had often attended Vao'sh's story sessions, though out of duty rather than from any innate enjoyment of the tales.

He was accompanied by his bureaucrat Bhali'v, a constant companion and diligent assistant. Now Bhali'v spoke loudly in a thin voice, filling the role of crier. 'All salute the Maratha Designate!'

The gathered Ildirans clasped their hands against their chests, and Anton quickly did the same. Avi'h climbed the stairs to the central dais, and his bureaucrat assistant hurried up beside him, continuing to speak for his master. 'The newly ascended Mage-Imperator Jora'h has commanded that Designate Avi'h return to his planet and watch over his dedicated workers even through these months of darkness. Though this goes against established tradition, the Designate does this to strengthen the *thism* and to show his benevolence.'

The Maratha Designate stood with a forced smile on his long-suffering face as Bhali'v continued his ponderous announcement. 'We will inspect all work activities and keep records to make certain that Maratha Prime is maintained properly during the night season. With the Designate now back among you, this city will thrive even in darkness.'

Anton thought that Engineer Nur'of and his thermal energy project would have more to do with their impending prosperity than would the presence of Avi'h. He could well imagine that a spoiled and pampered noble like the Designate felt cheated out of his half year back in the Prism Palace.

Finally, the Designate himself spoke, describing Jora'h's ascension ceremony, the dazzling funeral pyre, and how the fallen Mage-Imperator's still-glowing bones had been taken into the Prism Palace's ossuarium. While the Ildirans listened with rapt attention, Vao'sh was both intrigued and saddened. 'I wish I could have been there. Such an incredible event can happen only once in a lifetime.'

After the assembly, when the Ildiran workers returned to their tasks, Avi'h called for the rememberers, specifically asking for Anton as well. The Designate had taken a seat in a colourful and comfortable chair, and the bureaucrat stood next to him, again speaking for Avi'h. 'Rememberer Anton Colicos, some much-delayed news arrived for you on Ildira, a report from the Terran Hanseatic League.'

'News? Who could be sending me a message way out here?' Then Anton knew the report was one he had long feared and dreaded.

Impatient and distracted, the Designate spoke in an offhand tone. 'It seems your father has been found dead at an archaeological dig on Rheindic Co. Your mother is still missing, however. The Hansa merchant who brought the message did not give very many details.'

Anton reeled, seeing spots in front of his eyes. No words came to him. Vao'sh took his arm, steadying him. 'I am sorry, my friend. I know you have long been worried—'

As if he had just cut a ceremonial ribbon, the Designate raised his hand abruptly, done with his duty. 'That's all we have. Nothing else. You both may go.'

Anton walked with leaden feet as Vao'sh led him away.

THIRTY-NINE

DD

Thinking they were doing him a favour, the Klikiss robots hauled DD from place to spectacular place, to environments where none of his masters could ever have survived. He had not found an opportunity to escape – not yet.

Already the Friendly compy had seen amazing natural wonders that no human had ever witnessed or imagined. He wished he had the opportunity to disseminate the data he'd collected. His masters, Louis and Margaret Colicos, had been so dedicated to their profession that DD wished he could make his own contribution to science.

But Sirix would never let him.

After racing away from collapsing Ptoro, the Klikiss robots piloted their mechanized ship to a sun-grazing planetoid. Physically linked to the interactive control systems, Sirix had flown the robotic vessel to the cratered rock tumbling through the fringes of an expanding solar corona. Its major ice encrustations had already boiled away in previous orbits as the planetoid spiralled closer and closer to the star.

As the robots vectored in, matching orbit and rotation with the rambling rock, the black-pocked surface looked inhospitable. DD had no idea why the Klikiss robots wanted to come here or what schemes they might still be developing. As usual, Sirix would explain only in his own time.

Exiting the spacecraft, the beetle-like robots scuttled across the uneven terrain. DD accompanied them into the vacuum, the antithesis of the ultradense gas-giant soup where hydrogues lived. His specially hardened compy body adapted to the change, as the Klikiss robots had designed it to do.

He was not surprised when Sirix led him to a metal hatch built into the side of a steep crater. The devious machines had secret bases hidden throughout the Spiral Arm. The Klikiss robots extended their segmented limbs and used tough claws to pry away camouflaging stone and expose a set of protected controls.

The metal hatch rumbled open in the complete silence of vacuum, though DD could feel vibrations through the stone. Escaping vapours and preserved wisps of atmosphere shot out like faint jets. Sirix and his companions entered single-file.

The planetoid was filled with chambers, vaults, and passages – yet another of the storage catacombs where swarms of hibernating Klikiss robots had been entombed for millennia. The stone floor trembled beneath DD's small feet, and his optical sensors noted several cracks in the fused wall. This tumbling rock was unstable, crumbling, as it lost its battle with the nearby star's gravity.

When the tremors faded back to stillness, Sirix swivelled his angular head towards the compy. 'Our plans had not proceeded to the point where we were prepared to activate these compatriots, but we are forced to act because of this asteroid's decaying orbit.'

'Will it break apart soon?' DD asked.

'Within this orbital cycle the pieces will tumble into the sun. Therefore, we must remove our hibernating comrades before that occurs.'

Up and down the artificial corridors, Klikiss robots were activating swarms of identical and ominous machines. The lumbering beetle-like constructions stepped out, awakened after being dormant for so long. Knowing the Klikiss robots intended to destroy humanity, DD wished Sirix had made an error in his celestial calculations and let this planetoid plunge into the sun before these hundreds of Klikiss robots could join the fight.

Though his programming required him to prevent humans from coming to harm if possible, DD had not yet found any opportunity to sabotage the operations, or send a warning message to humans. He had been separated from Robb Brindle and the other experimental test subjects deep within the hydrogue planet. Brindle had seemed like a nice man. Perhaps the young EDF officer could have solved the conundrum, given time.

DD was on his own here, and Sirix had all the advantages.

As more and more of the deactivated Klikiss robots were reawakened, he asked, 'What will all these machines do, Sirix? Are they soldiers to fight against the human race? Why were they hidden in storage in the first place?'

'There are many things you do not understand, nor do you need to understand. Humans have designed their compies with inherent limitations. You have no free will. You are unable to take independent action. Klikiss robots have that capability, and we are attempting to share it with you.'

So far, Sirix had been unable to discover how to eradicate that core protective programming without destroying the compies themselves. For that, DD was silently thankful.

'Klikiss robots murdered my master, Louis Colicos, and also the green priest, Arcas. It is readily apparent how much harm robots can do without such programming laws. Perhaps it is a necessary restriction.'

'Humans have no right to impose such laws on us – or you.'

They willingly abide by their own laws. A civilized society without boundaries will degenerate into anarchy.'

'We are efficient. We will never degenerate into anarchy.' Sirix turned back to his work, activating another black robot.

Elsewhere in the hidden base, as the tunnel walls shuddered with seismic vibrations, reawakened robots retrieved stored components that had been dismantled long ago and used them to reassemble spacecraft inside buried hangars. The thousands of newly resurrected Klikiss robots would fly away before the planetoid broke apart.

DD replayed memories of fond times with his human masters, especially his first, an adorable girl named Dahlia. When they played together, Dahlia had confided in him her secret hopes, desires, and disappointments. Through her, DD had begun to understand humans. Watching her grow up, the compy had learned the capacity for love, especially the unconditional love of a little girl. All innocent humans had such a capacity, though some more than others.

But the Klikiss robots had no such potential, nor did the incredibly alien liquid-crystal hydrogues. Neither of them had any interest in sentimentality, caring, or kindness – DD doubted they could even grasp the basic concepts. The Klikiss robots considered all compies little more than primitive mechanical children who needed to be guided to their destiny.

But DD felt that compies, such as himself, exceeded their limitations and achieved things that no Klikiss robot ever could. He experienced irony and disappointment at their lack of comprehension. He said aloud, 'And you say *I* am not free.'

But Sirix and the other Klikiss robots, intent on their tasks, were not listening.

FORTY

BASIL WENCESLAS

Hansa work could have kept him awake and busy twenty-four hours a day, but even the Chairman needed to sleep. Occasionally.

Returning to his penthouse quarters late at night, Basil saw that someone had cycled the ceiling to transparent so the wilderness of stars could shine through. When he noticed the shadowy figure near his bed, Basil thought Sarein had come to see him again. He let out a short, weary sigh. Tonight he wanted just to be alone, to sort through the problems that continued to peck at him like a flock of hungry carrion birds.

But upon bringing the lights up, he was astonished to find Davlin Lotze waiting for him. The tall, dark-skinned spy crossed his arms over his chest. 'Good evening, Mr Chairman.'

Basil was incensed. 'What are you doing here?'

'After all the service I've performed for the Hansa, that's the best greeting you can offer?'

'I repeat, Mr Lotze, what are you doing here?'

'I needed to meet with you and thought it might be difficult to fit into your busy calendar. Since you preferred to keep our previous chats off the record, I felt this would be best.'

Basil kept the lights at medium-level illumination. 'Ah yes, every action well thought out, as always. I don't suppose I should bother asking about the flaw in my security systems that allowed you to get in here?'

'You know my training, Mr Chairman.'

Basil poured himself a glass of ice water; he'd already had enough coffee for the day, and it was late. 'I thought you were off hopping through Klikiss transportals, exploring world after world.' He sipped his water but offered no refreshment to Lotze.

'I decided it was too dangerous.'

'Too dangerous for you? That's interesting.'

'There's the exciting kind of danger, Mr Chairman – and the foolish kind. More than once, you tried to talk me out of exploring untested coordinates, afraid I might disappear like Margaret Colicos did.'

'If you did happen to vanish, at least we wouldn't have to worry about all those secrets inside your head.'

'You don't worry about that, Mr Chairman.' It was not a question.

'No, I suppose I don't. So, then, why are you here during my few moments of peaceful private time?'

'I've come, with all due respect, to call in a favour. I believe I've performed adequate service for the Hansa over the years.'

Basil raised his eyebrows. Lotze had always been a man of very few needs and no demands. 'What could you possibly want?'

'I want . . . to go home – or the closest thing I've found in recent years. Back to Crenna. I liked it there.'

Interesting. It seemed Davlin had been careful not to show just how much he liked it on Crenna, how much warmth he felt for the colonists there. The Chairman thought it an odd weakness for someone like Davlin.

'You want to . . . retire?' Basil couldn't quite grasp the concept. Lotze had always been a man like himself, driven by work and duties with no interest in otherwise occupying himself. 'Relaxation' was a chore.

'Call it a sabbatical if you prefer. It doesn't need to be permanent.'

Basil could not argue with the request – Lotze had certainly earned it – yet he was bothered by the idea. 'Seven of my EDF green priests have resigned, Roamer ekti supplies have inexplicably stopped coming, and now you want to go away. Reminds me of rats leaving a sinking ship.'

Lotze remained silent, stoic. He had made his case and simply waited for the Chairman to agree. Basil knew he was in a tricky position: if the Hansa ever expected to get good service from the cultural spy again, he could not turn down his request. Davlin could just as easily vanish. Permanently.

Showing no concern for his visitor, Basil began to undress, preparing for bed. 'Since I don't have pressing duties for you, Mr Lotze, Crenna is as good a place as any, I suppose. If you settle down there, at least I'll always know where to find you.'

Lotze offered a mysterious smile. 'Will you?'

Basil scowled. 'Go away before I change my mind. Would you like to depart in the same mysterious way that you arrived, or would you rather leave by the main door?'

Lotze headed out of the bedroom towards the suite's entrance. 'You don't need to worry about me, Mr Chairman.'

'I worry about everything . . . but I'm rather less concerned about you than about most other things.'

Lotze put his hand on the door activation panel. 'I'll take that as a compliment, Mr Chairman.'

'Take it as a farewell – for now.'

*

The following day, an unusual package arrived at Hansa HQ addressed directly to the Chairman, sent by the Speaker of the Roamer clans.

'At last they break their silence. Let's see what this is all about.' Basil marched towards the nearest exit, while the messenger compy struggled to keep up with him. He had given orders for the next three Klikiss Torches to be deployed; maybe he had inadvertently chosen a gas giant where Roamers were still running their skymines in secret. He supposed that would have been an unpleasant surprise for them.

In a courtyard near the east entrance of the Hansa ziggurat, technicians hovered around the perimeter, holding scanning apparatus. Eldred Cain and Sarein were waiting for him, obviously intrigued, along with Basil's blond expediter, Franz Pellidor.

Pellidor paced around the crate, looking for boobytraps. 'We've scanned it completely, Mr Chairman. We detect no explosives, no weapons signatures, no biological or organic material, other than a few natural traces in the packing. It appears to be a device of some sort.'

'Maybe it's a gift,' Sarein said. 'What would the Roamers be sending us? A peace offering?'

'Not likely,' Cain answered.

Basil had had enough. 'I want to get to the bottom of this game they're playing. This is probably just an excuse to raise ekti prices – again.' He gestured to Pellidor. 'Open it up.'

The blond expediter moved to open the crate. Remembering the hydrogue emissary who had exploded his environment chamber inside the Whisper Palace, Basil flinched. But it had never been the Roamers' way to take aggressive action.

The sides of the crate retracted, exposing an old-fashioned device. 'It's an antique hologram projector,' said Pellidor.

The machinery glowed and hummed, warming up. Basil suddenly wished he had sent the other eavesdroppers away, but it was too late now. Sarein stepped closer to him, too close, and started to speculate on what the Roamers might want, but Basil cut her off, concentrating on priorities. 'Quiet. I want to hear what she has to say.'

An image of Cesca Peroni no larger than a doll appeared in the air. Her face was turned, directing her words somewhere between Pellidor and the gathered technicians. Basil moved to where he could look the image in the eye, the better to watch her expressions.

'Chairman Wenceslas, I speak for all the Roamer clans. We have met and decided unanimously on a course of action in response to EDF piracy. You and the rest of the Terran Hanseatic League can expect no further deliveries from Roamer merchants. No ekti. No supplies of any kind.'

Basil clenched his teeth and drowned out the incensed and disbelieving mutters in the background. 'Piracy? What the hell is she talking about?'

Speaker Peroni continued, her voice calm and reasonable. 'Our clans have risked their lives to provide you with stardrive fuel, and we have been repaid with treachery. We long suspected that Hansa military ships were preying upon our unarmed cargo vessels. Now we have found outright proof of EDF attacks. We have in our possession the wreckage of a Roamer ship indisputably destroyed by military jazers. You stole our cargoes and tried to cover your tracks, but now we know what you have done.'

Basil pressed his lips together until they turned white. The Roamer Speaker seemed forceful, firm, controlled. 'Therefore, until the Hansa brings the perpetrators of this heinous action publicly to justice, and renounces all such piracy in the future, trade is hereby severed between our peoples.' The hologram winked off.

Basil's heart leaped to his throat, and he wanted to strangle someone. 'What is she talking about?' He knew how easily General Lanyan could have justified such things, off the record. What a mess!

Sarein leaned nearer to Basil, but didn't touch him, wisely recognizing that he was close to exploding. 'That woman is an arrogant, self-righteous . . . coward. She gave you no chance to respond, allowed for no negotiation.' She was trying to be supportive, to share his outrage, but he didn't need it.

'There will be no negotiations,' Basil said. More than ever, he was frustrated by the failure of his assassination plan, which would have set up a Roamer merchant as a scapegoat. That would have contained and strengthened everything.

Eldred Cain remained cool and contemplative. 'First question, Mr Chairman: is there any truth to her accusations?'

Basil looked at the wide-eyed techs and turned to his expediter without answering Cain's question. 'Mr Pellidor, take down their names and IDs. I want the content of this message kept quiet until the Hansa decides on an appropriate response.'

'Speaker Peroni can't just be allowed to have her little temper tantrum,' Sarein said.

While Pellidor stepped towards the four intimidated technicians, the pallid deputy said quietly to Basil, 'We can't cover this up indefinitely, Mr Chairman. People are already noticing the missing ekti shipments—'

Basil cut him off with a nod. 'Therefore, Mr Cain, we must foster the belief that Roamers are unreliable. The clans have never been team players with the Hansa, even in this crisis which affects all of humanity. Go ahead, prove your skills with propaganda and the media. It shouldn't be hard to paint the Roamers as selfish. Ever since the hydrogue war began, they've been overcharging us for stardrive fuel.'

'They're war profiteers,' Sarein said. Her nostrils flared.

'No need to be indignant on my behalf, Ambassador.' He kept his voice carefully formal. 'I can be fully indignant for myself.'

When he saw the briefest flash of a stung expression on her face, Basil softened his voice, knowing that she often came up with schemes that he found particularly useful. 'In the meantime, let's put our heads together, you and I, and devise an effective strategy. We have looked the other way regarding their self-proclaimed independence for too long. There must be a political means by which the Hansa can absorb the Roamers and their assets, bring them back into the fold of humanity. We can't let them be loose cannons. Not now – and preferably not ever again.'

Sarein gave him a thin smile. 'They'll be sorry they ever chose this path against us.'

FORTY-ONE

TASIA TAMBLYN

After Ptoro, Tasia and her Manta crew received a generous furlough from the EDF. Not since the disastrous battle at Osquivel had she been given so much time off from military duties. But there was a limit to how much rest and recreation a person could stand!

And Tasia had no place to go. She had companions in the EDF with whom she worked, but she considered none of them close friends. There had been no one since Robb Brindle.

Though discretionary space travel was limited because of ekti rationing, as an EDF officer Tasia was welcome to any available seat aboard an outbound spacecraft. She would have liked to go back to the frozen moon of Plumas and the water mines run by her clan. She hadn't seen her brother Jess in ages, had heard no word from the Tamblyn family in the better part of a year. She did not know what was happening among the clans. But since Roamers kept the locations of their facilities secret, Tasia could not simply hitch a ride on a normal Hansa transport to Plumas, or Rendezvous, or any obvious Roamer destination.

Given the choices, she decided to stay in the Earth solar system.

Tasia made several more inquiries – as subtle as possible – to track down her missing compy. EA had gone off on her secret mission to warn Osquivel, using independent problem-solving routines to find transportation. Tasia could not make too much of an outcry about the compy's disappearance, however, since EA had been performing an unofficial assignment at the time.

Because Roamer compies contained a great deal of information about the scattered clans, they each had internal security programming that would protect the data – at the expense of the compy itself. Tasia should have taken comfort from this, but EA was valuable, and beloved . . . and missing. Unfortunately, despite her best efforts, Tasia could still do nothing about it, and she found herself alone with plenty of time on furlough.

She was most intrigued by the fleet of heavily reinforced 'rammer' ships the EDF had started to build in the asteroid shipyards, so Tasia requisitioned an intrasystem shuttle to go see the thick-hulled behemoths being constructed. Since a trip to the nearby shipyards did not require an Ildiran stardrive, she easily received clearance for her visit.

The scheme might have a chance of succeeding, if the rammers could emulate what the Ildiran Solar Navy commander had done at Qronha 3. According to reports, Adar Kori'nh had led forty-nine warliners on suicidal crash courses to wipe out hydrogue warglobes. And there had been no sign of drogues there since that devastating raid.

Seizing the opportunity, the Hansa had dispatched a cloud harvester to Qronha 3. The first shipment from the skymine had already arrived, and others were soon to follow. Tasia was amused at the pride the Big Goose showed at producing its own stardrive fuel, since Roamers had been doing it for generations. The new cloud harvester was far less efficient than Ross's Blue Sky Mine, but it was the best the Hansa had at the moment. Sullivan Gold's shipments could not possibly keep up with the demand of the EDF or the Hansa, but at least it was a gesture . . .

The rammer-ship construction zone was a bustle of activity. As she flew in, she admired the complexities of the operation, the gigantic floating scaffolds and open warehouses in space where constructor pods and workers in engineering suits puttered about, assembling the vessels.

It reminded her of Del Kellum's shipyards. Of course, Roamer shipbuilders working together without military bureaucracy would have been able to do a faster and better job. She always felt a smug pride in the clans, compared with the bloated and cumbersome Hansa.

Oddly enough, though, the regular Roamer ekti shipments were late. Her fellow Eddies looked to her for an explanation, as if Tasia could interpret clan behaviour, but she had been cut off from the clans for so long, Tasia had no idea what was happening at Hurricane Depot, with Del Kellum's cometary skimmers, or at any of the other ekti facilities. She'd even heard rumours that Speaker Peroni had declared an embargo against the Hansa . . . but that didn't make any sense, and no official news release had come from the Chairman. She was sure there must be some obvious explanation.

Tasia cruised her shuttle around the massive armoured warships and imagined how each one would strike a single, deadly blow against the warglobes. Looking at the skeletal frameworks of the rammers, she could see they were generally similar to a standard EDF Manta, but stripped down, with no amenities for a human crew. These rammers were little more than self-propelled hammers to crack open the crystalline shells of warglobes.

So far, the Klikiss Torches were the only absolutely reliable weapons the humans had used against the hydrogues, and since Tasia had successfully delivered her weapon at Ptoro, other gung-ho officers wanted to do their part. Chairman Wenceslas and King Peter had already authorized another three Torches to be used on gas-giant targets . . .

More than anything else, Tasia wanted to strike against the enemy aliens, again and again. It would be months yet before these rammer vessels were completed, their structural spines and reinforcements inlaid, the massive engines installed. But she hoped to be there, volunteering for the mission, as soon as they were ready.

FORTY-TWO

CESCA PERONI

Now that she and the strangely different Jess were finally alone in the privacy of her office chamber, Cesca longed to throw herself into his embrace. But she couldn't because of the dangerous alterations she saw in him. The power crackling from his skin, his body, had transformed him into a walking livewire.

'What's happened to you? Explain to me how . . . how you've changed, Jess.' She looked at his handsome and sincere face, his blue eyes, his strong and straight nose, remembering when she had kissed him.

Standing as far away from her as the rock walls would allow, he held up his hands to keep her at bay. She saw the oily slickness of moisture covering his skin and the pearlescent garment. His face and hands had a translucent, almost shimmering quality, as if his flesh had taken on the eerie phosphorescence of deep-sea creatures. The recycled air around him smelled of ozone, as if charged with ions from an electrical storm.

'I'm alive, thanks to the wentals, but I am no longer *human*,

Cesca. I myself don't know half the things I can do . . . but it's fantastic.'

'As long as the man I knew and loved is still inside there somewhere, Jess, then we can find some way to be together. Our Guiding Star will show us how.'

Again, Jess held her at a distance with a gesture. 'This is bigger than just the two of us now, Cesca. There's too much to do, too much *I* can do – for all of us. We have in our grasp the solution to our crisis. With the help of the Roamers, I can save not just one race, but two. Humans and wentals.'

She sat abruptly in the chair behind her desk, blinking back her confusion and frustration. 'All right, you need to explain more than that. What are these . . . wentals?'

'Incredible water-based entities, potentially as strong as the hydrogues. And they're inside my body now. Wentals and drogues were mortal enemies in a great conflict that occurred ten thousand years ago – and I've got to help resurrect them, so they can fight with us in this war.'

'But what does that have to do with the two of us?'

Jess looked down at his hand and watched the water droplets trickling along his skin, moving as if alive. At long last, he told her what had happened. 'My body contains great power, but it's not completely in my control. I don't dare touch anyone else because I'm sure to harm them. I'm . . . different now, and I have a responsibility. There's too much at stake here to think just of ourselves.'

Cesca nodded, keeping her sadness locked within. There was always too much at stake. And she always made the necessary sacrifices. That had been her lot, and she had accepted it when she became Speaker for all the clans. 'It's an impossible situation, Jess.'

'Give me time, Cesca. The wentals are amazing and powerful.

I'll find a way for us to do this together, to be together . . . somehow. You know my love for you is unchanged.'

'I know that, Jess. But it doesn't make this any easier.'

He lowered his voice. 'I didn't ask for this power, but I have it, and it came with a price. For now, saving the wentals and defeating the hydrogues is my highest priority.'

'Then let me help. In any way. Just ask.'

'I need to enlist the help of the clans. I can't do this alone.' She noticed now that he was not breathing, that he took breaths only so that he could speak words aloud.

She remained behind her desk, trying to pretend this was just a business discussion. 'I'll arrange for you to speak to the Roamers. They'll all want to hear your story, especially if you're offering us a chance to beat the drogues.'

'Thank you.'

Later, as he and Cesca walked to the meeting chamber, Jess seemed terrified that he might accidentally touch her. His brown, wavy hair hung lank and wet, and a play of luminosity beneath his moist skin hinted at the energy waiting to boil of out of him, if he wasn't careful.

She met his eyes, which brimmed with a glowing sheen, though not of tears, but as if an ocean of stars now filled his gaze. Simmering power and the scent of ozone poured from him, as if someone had connected his life force to a set of generators and cranked the levels up far beyond the maximum.

She stepped perilously close to him, wishing she could take his hand. 'Let's go in together, Jess.'

Inside the hollowed-out grotto, the conversation was already an excited buzz as Jess and Cesca approached the podium. Several of Jess's former friends called out encouragement; even from the highest tiers they could sense that something had altered within him. They all knew by now that he had arrived in a remarkable water-and-pearl spaceship.

Cesca raised her voice to silence the tumult. For the meeting, she wore a cape Jhy Okiah had given her, intricate embroidery on a dark blue fabric – the symbols of all the Roamer clans like constellations around the Peroni symbol, celebrating their heritage and familial connections. 'We are Roamers! We thrive on the challenge of unusual tasks.' She lowered her voice, trying for a good-humoured tone. 'But never in our history can I recall anything quite as exotic as what Jess Tamblyn is about to describe to you.'

When he spoke to them, Jess did not need the voice amplification. She didn't even see him take a breath, but his words carried like thunderclaps through the chamber. The audience sat in utter silence as he described how his nebula skimmer had collected interstellar gases and distilled the shattered body of a powerful entity, the last survivor of a race that was the mortal enemy of the hydrogues.

He continued smoothly and passionately, never hesitating, never searching for words. 'Now I have come back to Rendezvous to ask for Roamer help. These beings have agreed to protect us against the hydrogues – but first we must make them strong again. I need anyone with a sturdy vessel to help seed the wentals throughout the Spiral Arm. Once their numbers increase, we will have a truly powerful ally.'

Nikko Chan Tylar shouted from one of the closest rows of seats. 'We can all see how that wental has changed you, Jess. If we're handling and delivering this super-water, how can we be sure the rest of us won't be infected?'

A gruff voice called, 'Shizz, if Jess Tamblyn can walk around in space without a suit, maybe some of us want that advantage! Why not drink some of the wental water for ourselves? How does it feel, Jess?'

'I am an anomaly, and I hope I remain the only one,' he answered. 'I can't touch anybody, or the power surge would kill them like a bolt of lightning. Make no mistake, the wentals were forced to take this drastic action in order to save my life, but they will not let it happen again. Simple exposure to wental water will not lead to a similar . . . contamination.'

'How do we know these wentals are as altruistic as you say?' called Anna Pasternak. 'What if we end up creating something as nasty as the hydrogues?'

Cesca gazed at the rapt audience, knowing some of them were convinced, others worried. 'Remember that these wentals fought against the hydrogues ten thousand years ago. Jess says that they were also allies with the forest life force on Theroc. I see no reason to doubt him.'

Jess considered his answer. 'I'm still a Roamer, and I'm asking you to trust me.'

'Good enough for me,' said Alfred Hosaki. 'Roamers have always relied on each other. We have to rely on each other – especially now that we've cut off trade with the outside. If you want to be suspicious of everybody, go join the Big Goose.'

Out in the audience, Nikko shot to his feet so quickly he needed to grasp an anchor bar to keep from floating upwards in the low gravity. 'Then let me be the first to sign up with Jess. I've got my own ship. The faster we wipe out the drogues, the sooner we can all get back to the business of skymining.'

Cesca smiled. Jess would have plenty of volunteers.

FORTY-THREE

SULLIVAN GOLD

Another full load of ekti launched from the cloud harvester, and Sullivan Gold felt like celebrating, or at least wrapping up the tanks with ribbons and bows. He stood on the administrative deck like a Napoleon, watching his workers like a hawk, and they pretended to be intimidated by him. Everyone knew he was pleased with their progress so far. Sullivan wasn't sure whether to credit his skilled management methods, or whether his crew just knew what they were doing.

'That's three shipments in record time.' He grinned out at the placid clouds, standing behind the atmosphere-retention field of the open deck. 'If the Hansa wasn't already paying me so well, I'd demand a bonus.'

Beside him, Kolker smiled, but his eyes were closed, his hands resting on the treeling as he communicated through telink. 'Nahton is hurrying to inform Chairman Wenceslas and the King.' Distracted, Kolker bowed his head again, touching the treeling. 'Oh, excuse me – something else is happening.'

Sullivan let out an amused sigh. 'All right, now who are you talking to?'

Speaking with only a fragment of his attention, the green priest answered, 'Just a few friends. It's nothing important.'

'Uh-huh. I had a teenage daughter once. I know how it can be – on the data network, or using voice communication, or even occasionally chatting face to face.'

Now the green priest opened his eyes. 'I'm far away from my comrades here, and it's been a long time since I've seen them. But we exchange plenty of information. A green priest's purpose is to communicate, with each other and with the worldtrees.'

He had never seen Kolker when he *wasn't* connected to his treeling. 'And you do an excellent job of it.'

Sullivan felt the biting breeze on his cheeks from the ocean of hydrogen-rich clouds. The sky harvester hummed along, while small ships flitted around and inspection crews crawled over the lower hull of the processing modules. Every system operated perfectly. He couldn't have asked for better results. 'Talk to your pen-pals as often as you like, Kolker, as long as you give priority to my communiqués and status reports when I ask.'

Kolker finished his mental message and released the treeling. 'I could talk with you, as well, Sullivan.' He said it as if the thought had just occurred to him. 'After all, you are right here beside me.'

'Oh, but am I as interesting? Why don't you tell me about your friend – the one you were just talking to. What's my competition?'

'No competition.' Kolker stroked the delicate fronds of the treeling. 'Yarrod and I were acolytes together, but he never wanted to leave the embrace of the worldforest, while I chose to travel around and see the wonders of the Spiral Arm. The trees like that, you know. In effect, I am a set of wide and curious eyes that the forest itself doesn't have. A sightseer by proxy. I share everything with the worldforest. It's the greatest service a green priest can do in return for the joys of telink. I've got a list of all the planets I've visited. This gas giant has a sort of majesty, an awesome vastness that is difficult to convey.'

They both stared out at the swirling deep soup of clouds. 'I just hope monsters don't lurk beneath those cloud decks,' Sullivan said. 'We've been here two months already, but I still feel like we're on borrowed time. I just checked all the evacuation systems this morning and reviewed our emergency procedures. I'd stage another drill . . . but it would cut into our production time.'

'Do you ever sleep, Sullivan Gold?'

'I fit it into my schedule once in a while.'

Suddenly, he heard a roar of engines overhead, saw seven immense and gaudy shapes. The profiles of Ildiran warliners were unmistakable, like tropical fighting fish that trailed solar streamers and bristled with weapons.

Alarms began to ring in Sullivan's control rooms. Warning announcements thundered through the intercom systems. He stared, then shook his head. 'This isn't good. Not at all.'

Kolker was already connected to his treeling, quickly describing what he saw. The warliners grew larger and larger as they approached the Hansa cloud harvester. A huge old-model Ildiran skyfactory accompanied the cluster of alien battleships, towed along. Facing them here in the vast, empty skies, Sullivan thought the Ildiran warliners looked ominous and threatening.

'Looks like the new neighbours are moving in.' He stared until his eyes hurt. 'Hmm, this may be an empty and uninhabited planet – but I wonder if the Hansa bothered to secure permission from the Ildirans for our activities . . . or if those warliners think we're trespassing.'

Kolker looked up. 'Perhaps that question should have been asked before now.'

'You'd better inform the Hansa that we're about to have a little encounter with the Ildirans here. Ask them if we have formal permission from the Mage-Imperator to be on Qronha 3.'

'Yes. This will make a fascinating story—'

'*Now*, Kolker.'

A florid-faced communications officer raced to the observation deck, flinging open the hatch and looking around for Sullivan. 'It's the Ildiran Solar Navy, Mr Gold! They are demanding to know what humans are doing here in their territory.'

'Not good.' Sullivan watched the monstrous warliners, then hurried towards the comm centre. The Ildirans had never been a threat before, but these vessels could destroy the new cloud harvester within moments, if they thought they had enough provocation. 'I'd better talk to them right away. We may be in trouble, unless I can turn on the charm.'

'Yes, we may be in trouble,' Kolker said. Sullivan couldn't tell if the green priest was simply agreeing with him, or if it was an attempt at humour.

FORTY-FOUR

ADAR ZAN'NH

Immediately after receiving his instructions from the Mage-Imperator, Zan'nh had gathered his seven warliners and a skymining crew while Hroa'x, the chief miner, prepared a full-size cloud harvester for transport to the nearby gas giant. He had never imagined that ambitious Hansa industrialists would arrive at the skymining fields first. No, the young Adar had worried about encountering vengeful hydrogues on Qronha 3, but not greedy humans.

This would be the first real test of his ultimate responsibility for the Solar Navy. The soldiers, and the Mage-Imperator, would see how he dealt with this matter. Should he demonstrate his ability to be tough and strong . . . or should he just ignore the human intrusion? What actual harm did it cause? None.

Still, humans had proven that if they were given even the tiniest opening, they would seize it and push for more, and more, and more.

Adar Kori'nh had given his life to clear this planet of the hydrogue infestation, for ever earning his place in the *Saga of Seven*

Suns. Kori'nh had done it for his honour, for the Mage-Imperator, for the Ildiran Empire. The great Adar would never have sacrificed himself and forty-nine warliners for a bunch of opportunistic humans.

Determined to do the right thing, Zan'nh stood in the command nucleus as his septa escorted the largest of Ildira's decommissioned skyfactories to the waiting gas giant. The Qronha binary, the closest star system to Ildira, comprised two of the seven suns in the capital world's sky. Qronha's lone gas planet was the first place Ildirans had harvested ekti, but the facilities had been destroyed in the hydrogue massacres at the beginning of the war.

Now Zan'nh intended to take back the world for Ildiran industry.

The big planet loomed in his warliner's front viewport, the gentle storms rich with hydrogen available for conversion into stardrive fuel. The enormous skyfactory moved behind them, drawn along at high speed. Guided by the eldest member of the skyminer kith, Hroa'x, this rejuvenated facility was filled with Ildiran workers eager to process the clouds of Qronha 3 in order to rebuild dwindling ekti stockpiles for the Empire, as the Mage-Imperator had commanded.

But first they had to deal with the matter of these trespassers.

From what Zan'nh knew, voracious humans seized anything they wanted. *'Bekh!* Just as they did on Crenna.' The old Adar had talked of how humans had swept in to seize the leftovers on Crenna for themselves as soon as the Solar Navy had evacuated the Ildiran victims of the blindness plague. Though they had paid the Mage-Imperator for the right to do so, the humans were like hungry carrion eaters, taking advantage of Ildiran tragedy.

Zan'nh's voice was cold as he issued orders. 'Detach Hroa'x and his skyfactory from our escort beams and allow him to choose the best position in the cloud decks. He'll want to get started with his work.' He clenched the railing in the command nucleus, making sure he sounded implacable and tough. He was the *Adar* now, and he took orders from no one but the Mage-Imperator. 'Meanwhile, all warliners, accompany me.'

He didn't want to provoke a war, however . . . unless it was necessary.

Now, with the new skymine still trailing them, the seven ornate battleships descended into the atmosphere of Qronha 3 towards the lone Hansa cloud harvester. The human-crewed facility blithely cruised along, spewing exhaust gases as it functioned at full capacity. It was not as large as an Ildiran skyfactory, and probably had only a fraction of the crew. His warliners could destroy it easily, if need be.

'Open weapons ports. Power up our energy projectors.' When the weapons officers acknowledged his order, Zan'nh thought of another idea. 'And deploy all solar fins to their fullest extent. Extend banners and polarize the reflective coating.' That would make an intimidating show. The vessels extended peripheral projections, puffing themselves up in a dazzling threat.

Zan'nh pressed his lips together. Through the *thism*, his father would sense what he was doing. 'Now, demand to know what they are doing here.'

After their warning was transmitted, a meek and frightened transmission came from the Hansa cloud harvester. Zan'nh had not yet made up his mind what to do, but he gestured to the communications officer.

'Hello?' said a man's voice. 'Is this the new Adar? My, that's a very impressive show of force – beautiful, yet intimidating in its own way. Hello? My name is Sullivan Gold, manager of this industrial facility. I hope you're aware that we are completely unarmed.'

Zan'nh thought a moment. 'Then it is unfortunate for you,

Sullivan Gold, that my warliners have a thorough array of weaponry.'
He paced in the command nucleus, wondering what Adar Kori'nh
would have done in this situation. He needed to send the humans a
warning message here. 'The Terran Hanseatic League has clearly
overstepped its bounds, and the Ildiran Empire has a right to take any
appropriate action.'

The human replied, sounding frustrated, 'Oh come on now!
With everything else going on in the Spiral Arm, do you really
want to trigger an unnecessary war against the Hansa? Neither of
our races wants that.'

The annoying man was right, of course. Zan'nh didn't want
that. His warliners could easily cover up the destruction of the
cloud harvester as a hydrogue attack, but humans and Ildirans were
not at war with each other. Still, the . . . audacity and blithe self-
absorption of their assumptions galled him. Why did they think
they had the right?

Though the man named Sullivan Gold sounded respectful, he
did not seem particularly intimidated by the posturing. 'I've got an
idea, sir – why don't we discuss a way to resolve this situation like
gentlemen? After all, Qronha 3 is a gas *giant*. There's certainly
enough room for two harvesting facilities, right? The Hansa may
have put its foot into a mess, but we can fix it. We won't get in each
other's way, I promise.'

He paused, waiting for Zan'nh to reply, but the Adar made no
answer. Zan'nh had learned that silence could be a useful weapon.

Anxious, the human continued to chatter. 'Listen, let me host
you and your chief skyminer over here at our facility. We'll show
you everything we've done and share the weather data we've
gathered. It'll improve the efficiency of your own operations. All
right?'

Good, Zan'nh thought. The situation was definitely moving in
the right direction now. He remained silent a long while yet,

enjoying the discomfort he must be inflicting on the Hansa crew.

The impatient human transmitted yet again, well before Zan'nh was ready to break the tension. 'Or, if you want, I'll shuttle myself over to your warliners so we can talk face to face. I'm flexible. What'll it be, my place or yours?'

Adar Kori'nh would have told him to search for a way to end the conflict at no unnecessary cost of lives. That was how he wanted the *Saga* to remember him.

Zan'nh decided he did not want to be in a position where he had to offer hospitality to these interlopers. Instead, he would let them make the overtures.

'I will come to your facility. We will resolve this situation without unnecessary casualties.'

'Good idea.'

Zan'nh knew he had the upper hand here, both militarily and psychologically. One way or another, the Empire would emerge with honour here today.

FORTY-FIVE

MAGE-IMPERATOR JORA'H

On Ildira, the Klikiss robot entered the Prism Palace, bypassing the traditional spiral pilgrimage route that crossed the seven radial streams. The looming beetle-shaped machine pushed past the staring Ildiran supplicants who had flocked to Mijistra to gaze upon their new Mage-Imperator.

Angry guard kithmen closed in on the robot, trying to slow its inexorable progress, while others rushed messages to the skysphere reception hall where Jora'h sat in his chrysalis chair, holding court. The Mage-Imperator had just announced his departure for Dobro, at last.

His muscular daughter Yazra'h stayed with her father in the audience chamber, the three sleek Isix cats she kept as pets resting nearby. The ferocious-looking animals lay at her feet like liquid smoke rippling with sinews and wiry muscles. Yazra'h instantly stood up as a messenger rushed in.

'A Klikiss robot is approaching, Liege! It refuses to stop.'

Without ceremony, the ominous insectile automaton lumbered into the dazzling skysphere hall. Even in the coloured sunshine, the robot's matte-black exoskeleton seemed to drink up all the light. The robot swivelled its flat head, showing an array of crimson optical sensors that gleamed like baleful red stars. With an eerie grace, on a set of finger-like legs, it boldly approached the chrysalis chair.

Ildiran guards followed, their shoulders hunched as if they were prepared to tear the threatening robot limb from mechanical limb. But Jora'h cautiously raised his hand, not wanting to pit them unnecessarily against the powerful ancient machine. 'I was not aware that the Klikiss robots requested a visit. What do you intend here?'

The robot raised itself until it towered a metre above the guard kithmen. The Mage-Imperator's protectors showed not the least bit of intimidation. 'I am Dekyk.' Its voice was like rough metal grating across stone. 'I have come to demand answers.'

A gasp went through the audience. Everyone waited to see how their all-powerful leader would deal with the situation.

Jora'h made his voice loud and strong. 'You have no right to demand answers from the Ildirans.'

The Klikiss robots are concerned about your activities. On Dobro. On Maratha. We have a right to know. You are breaking promises. You are discarding us.'

Jora'h let anger creep into his reply. He had received no unusual reports about Maratha, which was mostly empty for the darkness season, and he sensed nothing extraordinary through the *thism*, though the connection with his brother Avi'h was not strong. And how did the Klikiss robots know about Dobro?

'Matters of the Ildiran Empire are of no concern to the Klikiss robots,' he said. 'The decisions I make are for the good of my people, and are not subject to your approval.'

Dekyk's hemispherical carapace split in half as if he were about to open his shell and take wing. 'We had an agreement about Maratha. You have ignored the terms.'

The Mage-Imperator narrowed his star-sapphire eyes, sick of so many secrets. He called to everyone in the reception hall. 'Leave us. I must speak privately.' When the guard kithmen looked uneasy about leaving him vulnerable, Jora'h reconsidered. 'Yazra'h, you alone may stay. Protect me if it becomes necessary.'

His daughter stood, fully as intimidating as any armed guard. Her three predatory pets growled low in their throats.

Once the skysphere hall was clear of supplicants, courtiers, and guards, Jora'h finally answered the black robot. 'A bargain requires participation on both sides. You robots have failed us. Hydrogues continue to attack Ildiran worlds, and you do not prevent it. Therefore, you are either treacherous or useless.'

Dekyk seemed to deflate, though he did not back away. 'In their search for the remnants of the verdani, the hydrogues devastated any forested planet they encountered. Some of those planets happened to be Ildiran. We could not stop them.'

Jora'h pushed himself straighter, hating the chrysalis chair. 'You could have told them the location of the worldforest at any time. That would have saved Ildiran planets.' As he said this, though, he felt anguish for this betrayal of the towering worldtrees that had so impressed him when he'd visited Reynald . . . the trees that Nira herself had loved so well.

'We did not choose to divulge the worldforest location,' Dekyk answered.

'And because of that choice, many of my people died. We resurrected you several centuries ago as we promised, and we have adhered to the vow that our civilization would neither create robots, nor build sentient machines in any form. The Ildiran Empire has remained true to its promises. That is all you need to know. Now do your part as well.'

He stared implacably at Dekyk, who remained unmoving like a nightmarish statue. Yazra'h stood beside her Isix cats, which flexed their supple clawed feet, eager to attack something. Her eyes reflected her surprise at the unexpected information she had heard.

Finally, after a long moment, Dekyk withdrew, clearly not satisfied. The robot swivelled his torso and lurched back out of the Prism Palace without another word. The Mage-Imperator stared after him while Yazra'h watched her father. The skysphere hall seemed suddenly very empty.

Jora'h's thoughts whirled, and he was glad that his daughter did not speak. He could no longer count on the Klikiss robots to intercede with the hydrogues; in fact, he suspected they might attempt to turn the deep-core aliens against Ildirans as well as humans.

Now, more than ever, he needed to go to Dobro – not just as a sentimental lover to look at Nira's grave, but to see the progress of Osira'h and her abilities. What if the terrible plan had been justified after all? If, after so many generations of careful breeding, his daughter was truly the bridge that could bring Ildirans and the alien hydrogues together – without the Klikiss robots – then he must see to it immediately. Time was short, and the danger was great.

'I will wait no longer.' He pulled himself upright and swung his legs over the side of the cradle-like chair.

After Dekyk's departure, whispering courtiers had begun to creep back into the room, anxious to make sure that their leader was safe. But when they saw what their Mage-Imperator was doing now, utter silence fell. Jora'h stood apart from the confining chrysalis chair, holding the rim to keep his balance on oddly shaky legs, and glared at them for their foolish adherence to practices that no longer made sense. 'This is a time of crisis, not a time of traditions.'

With great relief, he stood on his own feet again for the first time since his ascension. Enough of that nonsense.

The nearest guards moved towards their leader, either to assist him or to urge him back into the chrysalis chair where he belonged. The courtesans and nobles watched this scene with even more surprise than they had shown at the arrival of the Klikiss robot.

Jora'h's bare feet pressed on the smooth warm floor. The Mage-Imperator had not walked for months. His legs already felt weak, as if the muscles had begun to atrophy. He did not want to imagine how helpless he would feel after remaining in that confining chair for decade upon decade. He didn't intend that to happen.

'I will not recline and watch the Empire suffer harm. *I* am the Mage-Imperator. *I* define traditions and the way of our society. One of my predecessors declared that a Mage-Imperator's feet should never touch the floor. I now rescind this tradition. Too much is at stake, and I must break with some of the old ways, lest we lose everything.'

He noticed Yazra'h watching him with a look of pleasure on her face. She clearly approved. Athletic and proud of her own capabilities, she was perhaps glad that her father abjured a practice that made him seem an invalid. He had no intention of becoming a soft slug with a degenerating body, like his father.

Jora'h let go of the rim of the chrysalis chair and stepped forward. The guards had no choice but to let him pass. Smiling, he walked down the broad, shallow steps of the dais. He looked up at the smiling holographic image of his own face projected on the mists, then turned to the gathered people.

'I intend to go to Dobro. Now.'

FORTY-SIX

DOBRO DESIGNATE UDRU'H

As he instructed the young Designate-in-waiting in the tasks and responsibilities he would one day control, Udru'h recalled how long it had taken him to accept the grim necessities of the breeding programme. He was pleased the young man seemed to have an open and receptive mind.

Daro'h stood patiently at his uncle's side as they paused before the gate of the enclosed compound. The Designate-in-waiting displayed calm, striking features that resembled those of his father. He had put aside judgement for the time being, despite knowing that his father did not approve of the breeding experiments. Like all Ildirans, he would always swear loyalty to the Mage-Imperator, but Daro'h also seemed to understand and accept his charge here.

Even so, Udru'h would not tell Daro'h the truth about Nira. Not yet, if ever.

Overhead, the hazy sky was blurred by stratospheric clouds. The air felt hot, and all the hills were green. Lush grasses and weeds had rapidly covered burn scars from the previous year's fire season. Inside the camp, captive humans worked and slept and went about their lives. After generations here, they knew no other way of life, despite what the female green priest had tried to tell them.

'We have developed a substantial data set by mixing human DNA with a spectrum of Ildiran kiths. Many of the offspring have been failures – as might be expected, since genetics is not an exact science. We quickly euthanized the worst horrors. At first we let the human mothers know, but their emotional reactions were difficult to control.'

Daro'h frowned, staring through the fence at the low barracks. 'Do they not see they are contributing to the good of the Empire?'

'The humans are not part of our Empire. They do not embrace our long-term goals.'

'Perhaps they simply do not understand our goals?'

The Dobro Designate shook his head. 'They do not – and will not – care.'

Inside the compound, human family groups tended small gardens when they weren't on labour shifts. Guards and work supervisors took small vehicles, carrying groups out to the arroyos and rocky outcroppings, where anyone not currently needed for breeding did daily chores, chipping out opalbone fossils to be sold as rarities across the Ildiran Empire.

Daro'h observed the camp activity, drinking in the details. 'And they are allowed a certain amount of freedom? They form their own social groups and family units? They choose where to live and sleep without being assigned to specific bunks or buildings?'

'We exert sufficient control to serve our purposes, but we also consider the drawbacks of imposing unnecessary restrictions. A small amount of flexibility engenders an increased level of cooperation. One of the men, a sturdy fellow named Benn Stoner, is currently the de facto representative of the camp. You will meet him.'

Daro'h didn't seem to understand. 'How does he exert command over the humans?'

'They generally listen to his suggestions. One hundred and eighty-five of their years ago, Ildirans brought their wandering and damaged generation ship to Dobro. For a time humans and Ildirans lived side by side, but . . . certain unpleasant events changed the situation.

'One of my predecessors was forced to confine the remaining colonists, and Mage-Imperator Yura'h deemed it wise to incorporate them into our long-term breeding programme. At first, the humans were defiant, hoping to change their circumstances. But my predecessor understood that such beliefs and the so-called "natural freedoms" they took for granted could be bred out of them within a generation or two of proper instruction and deprivation.'

'If the humans resisted, could we not use artificial insemination? Specific fertilization and embryo implantation?'

'Possible, yes, but more difficult and far less efficient. We have also found that half-breed children created of artificial means are frequently born disengaged from or lacking in the full faculties of the *thism*. If we allow this, then our plan fails. In the end, it posed few problems. We were able to overcome their reluctance, and so it was not necessary . . . though we still have the option, should the need arise.'

Daro'h stepped closer to the fence. In a central open court with showers and waiting benches, medical kithmen cleaned human females returning from their work assignments, documenting each one by name and genetic code markers. In their files, they maintained graphs that indicated when each female was at the peak of her fertility cycle.

'The infusion of human bloodlines has been shown to enhance certain Ildiran characteristics. A child who carries even an eighth part of human genetics is more likely to become a stronger worker, a more talented singer, a more visionary scientist. In many cases, they look similar to Ildirans, and we raise them as such. Others appear so strikingly different that we keep them here on Dobro until they mature, and we crossbreed them again in hopes of mainstreaming their progeny.'

As Daro'h and Udru'h watched, doctors culled out four naked human women and directed them to enter the long breeding barracks. There, they would be assigned to mate with males from specific Ildiran kiths that were carefully chosen for each step of the breeding programme. Sperm was harvested from human males whenever it was needed, but Ildiran females did not conceive as easily. 'Human women are more fecund than Ildirans. They reproduce like rodents – which is to our advantage.'

Daro'h was full of interest. 'Is that why the humans are eager to colonize so many worlds? Because their race is growing, and they need the room?'

Udru'h shook his head. 'They don't need the room. They simply *want*, more and more. It is their way.'

When he was younger, Udru'h recalled his own questions and reaction upon learning this information when he'd become the Dobro Designate-in-waiting. He had been innocent then, like Daro'h, guessing nothing about what really took place on Dobro. The truth eventually penetrated, though, and Udru'h had devoted himself to his life's work.

Daro'h would do the same.

'My father spent much time with a human woman, a green priest,' said the young Designate-in-waiting. 'He still talks about her.'

Udru'h guarded his expression carefully. 'She weakened both his heart and his mind. But now that he has ascended and taken the *thism*, I believe – I must believe – that as Mage-Imperator he will do what is right for the Empire.'

'I intend to do what is right,' Daro'h promised, and Udru'h felt his heart lighten.

*

248

Inside a well-lit but austerely appointed training facility, the Dobro Designate gathered all five half-breed children born of Nira Khali. Rod'h, the second oldest of Nira's children – sired by Udru'h himself – bowed to his father. Rod'h was six years old, but accelerated beyond his years. The Designate saw great potential in the boy, though not as much as in Osira'h.

The other three – Gale'nh, Tamo'l, and Muree'n – spent their days undergoing intensive training from medical kithmen, scientists, mental trainers, and Udru'h himself. Lens kithmen used their faint mind powers to guide the children and further awaken their telepathic skills. All of Nira's young mixed-kith offspring were already as powerful as adult lens kithmen.

'These five children are at the heart of our plan, Daro'h,' he explained. 'Even here, the guards and bureaucrats are not privy to the full scope of our purpose. Your own father did not understand, until just before he ascended to become Mage-Imperator. But *you* must know, Daro'h, for you will lead this work when it is your time . . . though I hope that after so many generations this will be the last. If the Dobro project reaches its culmination, we can finally become a normal splinter colony, a proud part of the Ildiran Empire without secrets.'

'I am ready to listen, Designate.'

Udru'h paused, searching for where to begin. 'Ten thousand years ago, a titanic war swept the Spiral Arm like a storm across the ocean of space. Hydrogues allied themselves with the faeros, against the wentals and the verdani.'

'And did Ildirans fight in this war? There is no record of it in the *Saga of Seven Suns*.'

'We participated . . . but only in the way that carrion birds take part in a battle. We were insignificant and in the path of destruction – until the Klikiss race also became involved. They developed their Torch and destroyed many gas giants, which turned the wrath of the hydrogues against rocky worlds, including ours. They didn't understand us, didn't wish to. The hydrogues simply lashed back and destroyed whatever they could.

'That was when the Klikiss robots turned on their masters, seeking to exterminate them and free themselves. With their machine language and coordinated computing power, the Klikiss robots succeeded in contacting the alien hydrogues. They found common ground, established a link, and learned a form of communication infinitely more complex than anything we understand as language. They made the hydrogues understand who they were, and convinced them to aid the robots in destroying the Klikiss race.'

'Then how did we become involved?' Daro'h asked. The half-breed children also paid attention, knowing that this tale comprised the history that determined their fates.

'After dozens of our worlds were annihilated by the hydrogues, the Mage-Imperator at the time reached an accord with the Klikiss robots, who agreed to be our intermediaries with the hydrogues. The robots used their communication abilities to convince the hydrogues not to attack our splinter colonies, and in return Ildirans assisted the robots in exterminating their parent race.'

Daro'h frowned. 'That sounds . . . dishonourable.'

Drawing a deep breath, Udru'h said, 'Nevertheless, the Ildiran Empire survived – and the Klikiss did not.'

The young Designate-in-waiting listened with a look of mingled fascination and horror. Udru'h continued. 'But we have never entirely trusted the robots. They are machines nearly as alien as the hydrogues. In those ancient treaties, we agreed to many things, as did the robots, yet all along we knew we could not rely on them – just as we knew the hydrogues would not remain quiescent for ever.

'Therefore, to protect ourselves, we sought a new way to form a bridge between Ildirans and hydrogues, a means of communication transcending simple words and thoughts. Thousands of years ago, we began this programme, combining kiths and bloodlines in an attempt to enhance our own telepathy. But even the best of each generation advanced our ability by only the smallest increment.

'After thousands of years, we finally developed the lens kithmen, who exhibit enhanced mental skills. They can touch the *thism* more readily than other kiths, though not as well as the Mage-Imperator or his direct bloodline. Even though the lens kithmen became marginally stronger with each generation, we despaired that it would ever be enough, or in time.'

Daro'h guessed the next part. 'And then you found the humans.'

Udru'h smiled sardonically. 'Yes. They offered genetic variations that let us jump ahead by at least a hundred generations. Their mental abilities were like a potent catalyst when added to Ildiran bloodlines – and not a moment too soon. The Klikiss robots have failed to keep the hydrogues away from Ildiran worlds, whether through their inability or outright treachery. Either way, we require our own bridge to negotiate directly.'

'Do the Klikiss robots hate us, then?'

Udru'h looked at him. 'We cannot know what the robots think, but we know they are capable of deception and betrayal. It is clear, however, that their fear of us grows as they lose their leverage and the war continues to escalate. We know many things they do not wish others to remember.'

Across the room, young Osira'h finished a training exercise and ran over to them, her eyes sparkling. The Dobro Designate smiled and reached out to the telepathic half-breed girl, while Daro'h looked curiously at his half-sister. 'And so, Osira'h must become our intermediary. We are counting on her to make matters right with the hydrogues.'

The girl returned his smile, but her voice was solemn. 'I will be ready, Designate. I promise.'

FORTY-SEVEN

CELLI

As they flew on a lightweight gliderbike over the ruins of the worldforest, Celli wrapped her arms tightly around the green priest's waist. She had flown with Solimar numerous times now and had long since got over her fear of the unsteady vehicle with its furiously flapping condorfly wings. However, she didn't mind having an excuse to press herself against the young man's brawny back. She didn't think Solimar minded, either.

The self-contained engine thrummed as the green priest accelerated and circled over a new burn area. 'It just goes on and on,' Solimar said. 'We've flown for hours, and the scar extends as far as my gliderbike can take us.'

Celli sensed her friend's gloom and felt it in her own heart. She wanted to console him, to tell Solimar that everything would be all right, that the worldforest would recover – and though she believed that to be true, the task of restoration seemed nearly impossible.

'The worldforest has been hurt enough,' she said. 'Maybe the most important thing we can do is to *believe*. Let the trees draw optimism from you, Solimar. You're a green priest. Maybe they need to have hope as much as they need time to heal.'

She felt the young green priest's shoulders relax. He looked back at her. 'You're right, Celli. During the first war with the hydrogues, long ago, the worldforest suffered an even greater defeat, and they still recovered—'

'Hey, watch where you're flying!'

Solimar swerved, barely avoiding an upthrust claw of dark branches. 'I wouldn't let you get hurt, Celli – it was too much trouble rescuing you the first time.' She playfully slapped him on the arm and continued to hold on. He had always been there for her, when she most needed him.

During the hydrogue attack on the forest, Celli had found herself stranded in the burning fungus-reef city. She had waited too long before trying to escape, not willing to admit her own danger. Then, with as much grace as she could manage, Celli had worked her way from the core of the blaze by edging out along lumps on the fungus city and using acrobatic skills and treedancer moves to get from one precarious perch to another. But the fire had spread rapidly, cutting off all escape paths. She had been trapped, frightened and helpless, scolding herself for getting into such a problem – until she'd heard the buzzing engine of a gliderbike. Celli had looked up and raised her arms, full of desperate hope, and Solimar had swooped in to snatch her from the jaws of death. Fear had melted into relief as they flew away to dubious safety.

Celli had never really noticed him before he'd rescued her. Had she been so aloof, so self-centred? Estarra would probably have said yes, but Celli had changed a great deal since the hydrogue attack.

Now, every day in the aftermath, they took Solimar's gliderbike to survey the damage, while landbound green priests moved through the burned thickets, clearing debris, salvaging treelings. Children and acolytes sifted through the ashes, searching for armoured black seed pods, others cleared greenhouse plots, lovingly planting the seeds to bring back tiny treelings.

'I just wish we had more help,' Solimar said.

As Celli had expected, the Hansa military was very interested in the broken warglobe she'd discovered. Their scientists and weapons engineers had come here, delivering a shipload of relief supplies to Theroc, like a consolation prize in exchange for the alien wreckage. Instead of staying to help with the important labour, though, the EDF specialists had taken the pieces away for analysis on Earth. It was all they had wanted.

Now, the gliderbike sputtered, and one of the condorfly wings froze. Solimar calmly adjusted the jammed wing and fiddled with the controls. The gliderbike quickly restabilized, and they rose higher, continuing their outward spiral.

Oddly for a green priest, Solimar loved to tinker with gadgets and equipment, from leftover machinery and instruments from the *Caillié* to new items brought in by Hansa merchants. He enjoyed chasing large butterflies above the forest canopy in gliderbikes of his own construction. Once, he'd even been pursued by a voracious wyvern, from which he'd barely escaped.

The worldtrees found the mechanics fascinating. Since the forest used only biological powers, the calm organic sentience had limited knowledge of gears and pistons and pulleys, and the acolyte Solimar had diligently described specs and designs for engine after engine, vehicle after vehicle. Now the worldforest retained that data, able to share it back with him. Whenever he needed information to fix a piece of equipment, Solimar could tap into the trees through telink and access any reference material he wanted.

Solimar expanded their search spiral again, but there seemed no end to the burned areas. 'I don't suppose we'll be treedancing together any time soon.' The two of them had talked about their mutual passion for the sport, and discussed the moves they knew. But now such joyful diversions seemed impossible.

'Not for a little while yet,' Celli said. 'But I look forward to when we can.'

Where a stream had been blocked by fallen trees, the water backed up and flooded a meadow, drowning any plants that had survived the fire. 'We'll have to send workers to clear that blockage. The water needs to flow downstream and irrigate other land.'

Celli traced the line of water with her eyes. 'Isn't that one of the sources for the Looking Glass Lakes? There was a village—'

'The village is completely destroyed. I've been there.' His broad shoulders heaved. 'The hiveworm nests were shattered, turned to powder. I didn't see a single living person.'

Celli hugged him tightly. The air smelled burnt. The clouds were thick in the skies, and she hoped it would rain and wash away the smell, make the forests feel fresh and clean again.

But that would take a long, long time.

'Enough for today,' Solimar said. 'We'd better get back and make our report.' He unerringly guided them back towards the distant fungus-reef city, beyond the hazy horizon.

FORTY-EIGHT

RLINDA KETT

Flying the *Voracious Curiosity* was her joy, and Rlinda would have taken the ship anywhere the Hansa asked her to go. She and BeBob had access to all the ekti they needed, so long as they delivered supplies and colonists to the new network of settled worlds.

Rlinda was already carrying a full load of cargo, but there was no getting around the fact that her entire route had been determined by this one passenger, by special request from Chairman Wenceslas himself. She grinned at the man sitting in the *Voracious Curiosity*'s copilot seat. 'Good to have you aboard again, Davlin.'

He looked over at her with a bland expression. 'I confess to being pleased to see you again, Rlinda Kett. Odd, isn't it?'

'The Chairman knows we're old buddies. Or don't you admit to having any friends?'

'Not many. Especially since I started work for the Hansa.'

With the ship on autopilot, she could lean back in her reinforced chair. 'Then it's about time you got some time off to have a real life again. Say, would you like to play a game with me while we're flying? I've got a wide selection of entertainment options.'

'No.' He didn't sound rude, just uninterested.

Rlinda contained her smile, knowing he was a tough nut to crack. 'Anything special you want me to prepare from the galley for your supper? I've got quite a few recipes.'

'No.'

She rubbed her hands together. 'Ah, so it's just some pleasant conversation you'd like, then?'

'No.'

Her eyes twinkled. 'You know I'm just teasing you, Davlin. Don't you?'

'Yes.'

'I thought spies were supposed to be suave and adaptable to any social situation.'

'I am not a spy. I'm a specialist in obscure details and an exosociological investigator.'

'In other words, you're a spy without any social graces.'

'That about sums it up.' He startled her by flashing a smile, a truly dazzling one, the first she had seen from him.

'You have a striking smile, Davlin. You should do it more often.'

'That is exactly why I don't dare. Too many people would notice it.'

Sighing, Rlinda gave Davlin a maternal pat on the wrist. Holding a conversation with him was like pulling teeth, but she enjoyed the game.

Davlin was quiet, neat, and unobtrusive. His hair was close-cropped, and he had an ageless face that could have put him anywhere between his twenties and forties. He stood tall with a well-proportioned body; his features were remarkable only for their lack of remarkability. No wonder the other colonists hadn't much noticed him.

'Crenna is very nice. I've only been there a few times, but the place seemed pleasant enough.'

'It is. Quiet. Normal. And I liked the people there.' Davlin looked out at the streaming stars. 'Compared to popping through Klikiss transportals and investigating unknown coordinate tiles, it'll be a perfect sabbatical. I've done enough for the Hansa, from espionage to outright combat. Some of my earlier missions as a silver beret operative were . . . quite ugly.'

Now Rlinda was surprised. 'A silver beret? You never told me you had that training. And I thought you gave me your whole life story.'

Davlin looked at her, his face completely expressionless. 'I left certain parts out.'

'I never know when to believe you, Davlin.'

Now he finally smiled again. 'That's good.'

Eventually, Crenna's sun grew conspicuous in the starscape in front of them. When the blazing ball of light filled the screen, she activated the filters. 'Still quite a bit of sunspot activity, but nothing dangerous. Last time I came into the Crenna system to pick you up, I ran into several hydrogues sniffing around the sun. I don't know what they were after. They seemed to be checking out some unusual solar activity.'

'Did they attack you?'

'No, I shut everything down and played possum. Either they didn't spot the *Voracious Curiosity*, or they didn't care.'

'I've read current reports from the colony,' Davlin said. 'There was no mention of any recent hydrogue sightings.'

'Good thing, then. BeBob liked the place as well.' She raised her eyebrows. 'You recall Branson Roberts?'

'Yes, I remember Captain Roberts.'

'He's flying with me now, taking the *Blind Faith* on cargo-hauling missions. But it's all unofficial. He's still technically absent-without-leave from the EDF. It was a waste to make him a blundering scout.'

'I'm sure General Lanyan doesn't see it that way.'

'The General has perfect vision, but in only the narrowest portion of the spectrum. We're not worried about him.'

These days, she and BeBob kept busy delivering construction supplies and heavy machinery. Upon arriving at Crenna, Rlinda was due to pick up a dozen or so volunteers for the colonization initiative, though she couldn't fathom why anyone would want to leave a peaceful world and go off into the unknown. Some people always looked for better circumstances elsewhere. Others preferred the challenge of setting up their own society, wrenching a living from an untamed world. She didn't know how a man like Davlin fitted into the equation.

'I bet you'll be bored down there in a year.'

'Boredom would be an . . . unusual condition for me. I look forward to it.' He let out what might have been a contented sigh.

Preserving as much velocity as possible, Rlinda came in on a shallow trajectory following the planet on its orbit around the sun. The colony world soon sparkled before them, a jewel hanging in space. 'There you are, Davlin. Now comes the hard part for you. Before you disappeared, all those people down there thought you were just a run-of-the-mill colonist with a handful of engineering skills. They'll have plenty of questions. Are you going to confess to being a spy?'

'A specialist in obscure details,' he repeated.

'Whatever.'

He looked at Rlinda, and his expression was stoic. 'I'm perfectly capable of handling difficult assignments. The colonists down there are good-hearted people. They'll accept me.'

She adjusted course and engine output, banking as the *Voracious Curiosity* entered Crenna's outer atmosphere. She reached over to give him a comradely pat on the knee. 'It's been a pleasure having you aboard again, Davlin. Just remember, if there's ever anything you need, I'm happy to help out.'

It was an offhand comment, one she had made many times. The man beside her seemed surprised. 'That is a dangerous offer.'

'And you've tried to make yourself out to be a dangerous man.' With a shrug, she turned back to the controls and focused her concentration on landing at the colony. 'But I think I'll risk it.'

FORTY-NINE

PRIME DESIGNATE THOR'H

Though still scarred from the hydrogue attack, Hyrillka was recovering well. Prime Designate Thor'h was glad to be on this world where he had been happy, where he'd enjoyed the privileges of his noble rank without the unpleasant responsibilities. Hyrillka was his home, much more so than the Prism Palace in Mijistra.

The bright primary sun had already set, and the secondary rode low in the sky so that the air was a burnt orange, dimmer than Thor'h liked. The tiara of bright stars from the nearby Horizon Cluster rose, spangling the twilight. Back on the citadel palace's hill, blazers shone through the streets and rooms, comforting the Ildirans. Diligent Pery'h remained inside, studying records and reports about Hyrillka's history and productivity. The young Designate-in-waiting was a good administrator, dedicated to his work.

But Thor'h relished each moment alone with his uncle. He would have to go home soon.

He and Rusa'h walked together in the nialia fields, far from the bright cluster of glowing lights. In rebuilding Hyrillka, Thor'h had invested the greatest efforts in restoring the ornate citadel palace that had been blasted into rubble. Because he so desperately wanted Hyrillka to be as it was during his happiest years, Thor'h had spent disproportionate time and effort restoring the sculptures, friezes, tilework, fountains, and furnishings, even the thick vines that had covered the open structure. The work had helped Thor'h to brush away the lingering scars from his own helpless terror during the attack. He had *accomplished* something.

Thor'h did not want to relinquish this lovely world for the obligations of the Prism Palace, though he knew he would have to. But not yet . . .

Rusa'h strolled beside and slightly ahead of him. The recovering Designate was oddly silent as he walked in the shadows between long rows of thick nialia vines. The petals of the male counterparts fluttered, disturbed by their passage. Rooted to the ground, the female vine clusters twitched and waved, agitated.

'Shiing production is already restored, Uncle,' Thor'h said, catching up with him. The processed drug was popular in the Ildiran Empire, offering a giddy, euphoric feeling of detached clarity and vivid luminosity, as if the partaker could see the Lightsource more closely. 'The nialias grow quickly, and I've spared no expense on proper fertilizers and chemical attractants. The hydrogue icewaves made the fields wither and die, but this year's harvest will be almost back to normal. Shiing will still be our primary export.'

Rusa'h continued to walk, silent and unconcerned. The Designate did not seem to enjoy conversation as much as he once had. In the past, Thor'h and Rusa'h had shared an enthusiasm for watching dancers, rememberers, artists, and singers, as well as the skyparades that took place every time Solar Navy ships arrived on Hyrillka. Designate Rusa'h had passionately adored his pleasure mates and nearly died while trying to rescue them.

But now that they had returned to Hyrillka at last, Rusa'h refused to take part in any grand celebrations. He was distant, beyond such things, as if only a part of him had returned from the light-drenched plane, where his mind had been trapped in long unconsciousness. Pleasure mates surrounded him in the rebuilt citadel palace, but though he accepted their company, Rusa'h was no longer interested in their seductive wiles.

Thor'h frowned in concern at the uncommunicative Designate. 'What . . . what is it, Uncle?'

Rusa'h let his fingers trail along the fleshy leaves of the nialias. 'I am listening for the plantmoths. Shiing is more than just a drug, Thor'h – it carries an important component of the Lightsource, like vibrant and flowing blood.' His voice was soft and distant.

Thor'h looked at the familiar growths alongside the silvery irrigation canals. Even under the dim orange sunlight, the long rows of nialias were aflutter with newly hatched and drifting plantmoths searching from vine to vine before choosing an appropriate mate.

Nialias were an unusual half-plant, half-animal lifeform. The main woody body grew rooted in the ground, while the mobile male form manifested itself as a whitish-silver moth. In its youth, a bulbous bud split open, and the male nialia plantmoth took flight, enjoying the light, flitting about in the air.

Connected to the thick and twisted stalks, the female nialia flower was a hand's breadth wide with lavender and powder-blue petals. At its centre, a white ring of feathery stamens covered with pollen rose like outstretched hands, beckoning the searching males with cloying perfume, tempting them to give up their freedom to settle upon the female stem and begin the cross-fertilization.

As Thor'h watched, one of the males circled a potent-smelling female flower. The Hyrillka Designate stared with a strange intensity, as if using mental powers to make the male land. Finally, the silver-white flying creature dropped down onto the petals and inserted his legs deep into the pollen ring. Slowly, gently, the female petals enfolded the male, drawing the two bodies together until they converged into a single mass. The fleshy sides of the flower and its stem pumped and flexed as male and female united, mixing fluids. Before long, the male's wings would drop off, and the combined form would swell into a ripe nialia fruit.

With an abrupt predatory movement, Rusa'h tore off the newly fused pair, crushing the squirming growth in his palm. He lifted his clenched fist above his head, turning his face up into the orange sky as he squeezed. Silvery-blue juices and sap trickled into the Designate's open mouth, some of it splattering messily on his lips, cheeks, and chin. His eyes were bright and unfocused.

Finished, he turned and looked at Thor'h without wiping the bloodsap from his mouth. 'Fresh shiing is the best, and strongest. Much more . . . intense than the processed form. It brings me even closer to the Lightsource.'

Thor'h had tried only appropriately processed shiing. When taken in large doses, shiing dulled an Ildiran's connection with the *thism* network. Some found the temporary sensation relaxing; Thor'h considered it liberating. Lights were brighter, thoughts clearer. Under its influence, he felt buoyant, existing in a mental state of zero gravity.

This mixed bloodsap, though, was pure and oozing with stimulant. Even so, he was not tempted.

Now the deep, rustling silence of the fields bothered Thor'h. He felt the need to make conversation to dispel his uneasiness about what Rusa'h had just done. 'Even though I am the Prime Designate, I wish I could stay here with you, Uncle. Pery'h would be better off back at the Prism Palace, but he is your Designate-in-waiting.'

Rusa'h looked at him strangely and wiped the sticky droplets from his chin. He cast the ruined plantmoth to the ground and licked his fingers. 'You must do what is best for the Ildiran people. That is your destiny.'

Thor'h knew what he was supposed to say, even though it made him uncomfortable. 'Yes, I will obey the Mage-Imperator, my father. I will serve . . . and make the Empire strong.'

But his uncle surprised him. 'Obeying the Mage-Imperator may not be the best thing for you to do, Thor'h. Sometimes the Lightsource is not clear to everyone, and any Ildiran can be blinded or deluded. Even your father.'

Thor'h did not know how to respond. 'But he is the Mage-Imperator.'

'He is . . . Jora'h.'

Thor'h frowned, deeply uneasy now. 'Maybe we should go back to the citadel palace, Uncle? Where it's brighter?'

'You may return if you like. I prefer to remain out here alone.'

'Alone?' Thor'h couldn't grasp the concept that any Ildiran would wish such a thing upon himself.

'Alone.'

'The shadows aren't too oppressive for you here? In a few hours the primary sun will rise again, and we can come back when the day is brighter—'

Rusa'h turned to look at him, not at all unsettled by the shadows. 'If I carry the light inside me, I need never fear the darkness.'

Thor'h shuddered. 'I suppose that if you have been to the realm of the Lightsource, then you know many things that I'll never understand.'

'Oh, you will understand, Thor'h.' The drying film of shiing on Rusa'h's face glistened in the light. 'I will make you understand.'

FIFTY

BASIL WENCESLAS

It was an informal inspection tour of the Soldier compy production lines, and also a place with sufficient background noise that Basil could talk to the commander of the Earth Defence Forces without being overheard.

'What exactly are you looking for, Mr Chairman?' General Lanyan stood beside him as they watched the identical military robots emerge from the fabrication stations.

Basil gave him a wry smile. 'Sometimes I just like to observe, General. People place altogether too much importance on formal inspections. Today I don't need King Peter, or Admiral Stromo, or Mr Pellidor, or any one of a hundred protocol or Hansa assistants. I wanted to see the compies – and speak to you.'

Lanyan stiffened, as if presenting himself for a medal. 'You received the reports from this morning? All three additional Klikiss Torches were successfully deployed. Three more hydrogue infestations burned out. An unqualified victory.'

'Mmm. At least we can use it for additional cheery propaganda.' He stared at the military compies, not meeting Lanyan's gaze. The machines moved one after another in perfect lockstep, according to their programming. It was breathtaking. Soldier compies would never hesitate. They followed their instruction set and did not argue, did not question the moral basis of any orders . . . and did not behave like children. Basil had had enough of that in recent months from Prince Daniel, from Peter, from the green priests, from the Roamers.

He said, 'It's good to see somebody do exactly as instructed, for a change. If only we could process and train human recruits so efficiently.' He knew that King Peter still had his paranoid delusions about the new compies, but the Chairman kept Peter on a short, tight leash to prevent any further irrational outbursts.

Engineering Specialist Swendsen and Chief Scientist Palawu had done a fine job getting these compy factories running to optimal specs. After sending Palawu to Rheindic Co to analyse the Klikiss transportals, Basil had instructed Swendsen to devote his research to the hydrogue debris brought from Theroc. The factories were functioning well enough without the two men.

Lanyan continued, 'It may also be wise to use Soldier compies to fly recon ships to hydrogue gas giants. At least they'll be more reliable than our conscripted human pilots. According to my records, two more of our drafted scouts have simply vanished. That makes thirty quitters so far, and we haven't been able to find any of them.' His expression darkened. 'Each deserter is a personal slap in the face. I can't imagine what these people consider to be more important than serving the Earth Defence Forces in time of war.'

'The Roamers seem to have similar ideas.' Basil rounded on Lanyan. 'Speaking of lost ships, General, now that we're here in private and off the record, would you care to tell me exactly what happened with this destroyed Roamer cargo ship that's got Speaker Peroni so incensed? Is she telling the truth?'

'I'm sure the Roamers are overreacting, Mr Chairman. They'd

rather blame the EDF than admit that one of their pilots could be incompetent.'

Basil scowled. 'Yes, General, that was in the official press release issued by King Peter. But I don't believe it for a moment, and neither do you. Speaker Peroni would never challenge us unless she thinks she has proof. To me, that means you must have done something without my knowledge or consent.' He narrowed his grey eyes. 'Tell me what really happened so I can figure out how to deal with this mess.'

Not meeting the Chairman's eyes, Lanyan continued to watch the flow of Soldier robots. 'To my knowledge, sir, it happened only once . . . an indiscretion for which I accept full responsibility.' In a brisk, bare-bones manner, he described how his patrol Juggernaut had encountered a Roamer cargo ship along one of the nearly empty trade routes. When they'd discovered that Captain Kamarov meant to deliver his ekti cargo to customers other than the EDF, General Lanyan had invoked executive privilege and confiscated the stardrive fuel. The incensed Roamer captain had vowed to file formal complaints.

'He would have caused great problems for us, Mr Chairman. Therefore, I removed myself from the bridge, and one of my subcommanders, Patrick Fitzpatrick III, decided in my absence that it would be best if the Roamer suffered an . . . unfortunate mishap. I never expected anyone to find the wreckage or be able to analyse it for jazer residue.'

Basil simmered with irritation at the problematic revelation. 'That was your second mistake, General. Your first was not to think through the consequences in the first place. Where is this Fitzpatrick now?'

'He died a hero at Osquivel, Mr Chairman.' Lanyan's brows furrowed, as if he didn't like what he was about to suggest. 'I suppose we could admit that Fitzpatrick acted without orders, and that we do not endorse his actions. Would it be a sufficient apology to reopen trade with the Roamer clans? I don't like to blackball one of my brave soldiers, but the larger result would justify the action. He's dead anyway.'

'No chance, General. If memory serves, that young man was the grandson of Maureen Fitzpatrick, one of my predecessors as Hansa Chairman – and also among our toughest leaders. She's still alive and still wields a great deal of power. I wouldn't want to cross her by using her grandson as a scapegoat.'

'Then have the King do it,' Lanyan said. 'He knows nothing of what we just discussed. He has plausible deniability.'

'Deniability maybe . . . but not believability. Much to my annoyance, King Peter is intelligent, and he'd see through my plans in a minute. In any case, the moment the people or Speaker Peroni suspect he's lying to them, our credibility crumbles. But that's beside the point, General. No matter what really happened, we *cannot* admit culpability. It would be political suicide in this time of war.

'You're seeking to find a solution by appeasing the clans, and I'll have none of it. I want to make it clear that the Roamers are the villains here. Though I don't personally condone your act of piracy, they were the ones who made such desperate acts necessary, by starving us for fuel.'

The General agreed. 'The clans have always caused us problems, Mr Chairman. Did the Hansa ever officially grant them independence?'

'Not as such. They simply declared themselves free and have acted that way for centuries. Now, however, this unreasonable embargo of theirs could be the fulcrum for resolving the matter of the clans once and for all.'

Soldier compies continued to file along the corridor, waiting for dispersal to EDF battleships. Sixty Manta rammers were currently being built out in the asteroid belt shipyards, and many of these compies would be placed aboard them. Plans against the hydrogues were proceeding as well as could be expected, but setbacks with the Roamers had caused an entirely new set of difficulties. As Hansa Chairman, he couldn't allow that.

'In a war that has been filled with embarrassments and tragedies, we should choose a second campaign that we can easily win. Create an enemy that we can defeat, then defeat them utterly. The people will see it as progress, as victory – even though it isn't a key issue at all.'

'But the hydrogues—'

'The hydrogues have been hammered by three more Klikiss Torches. And now, if we conquer the shifty Roamers, it will be a bright new day for the Hansa, don't you think, General?'

Lanyan did not seem entirely convinced. 'I . . . suppose so, sir. This is a significant shift in policy. You have not advocated such outright aggression before.'

'Always before, General, the machinery of the Spiral Arm functioned well enough that we could choose to be subtle. Now, however, the major components are no longer fitting together like clockwork, and we require the force of a crowbar to clear the jam.' He gave the EDF commander a thin smile. 'I just want everyone to fall into line so that we can march smoothly to the future.'

'Yes, Mr Chairman.'

Basil folded his hands together. 'We will step up our campaign to demonize the Roamers, pointing out how they've let the human race down again and again. Their recent embargo is only the most egregious example. Never forget that we have the moral high ground, and any means we use to bring the clans into the greater family of the human race again will be justified. Be creative. Feel free to be ruthless, but come up with a plan.'

As soon as Lanyan nodded, Basil waved him away. 'You are dismissed, General. I'll just stay here and look at the compies for a while.'

FIFTY-ONE

PATRICK FITZPATRICK III

With the rings of Osquivel arching overhead, Fitzpatrick bent over and looked sceptically into the Roamer grappler pod.

Zhett Kellum slid into the pilot's chair, buckling her safety restraints in a smooth motion. Her fingertips ran across the controls, activating the warm-up systems. She glanced impatiently over her shoulder. 'Well, are you going to get in, Fitzie? Or didn't the EDF teach you boys how to fasten your own restraints?'

'Maybe I can't believe you're taking me out for a ride.'

'Consider it an educational experience. We're tired of you Eddies being so clueless.' While he searched for an appropriate retort, Zhett sarcastically unbuckled her restraint strap, clicked it into place again, and spoke with exaggerated care. 'Watch me if you're having trouble. Slide this end in until it clicks. Pull on the strap if you need to tighten it.'

Fitzpatrick threw himself into the copilot seat. 'EDF flyers are competent enough that we aren't paranoid about safety restraints.'

'Ah, so you must have hit your head too many times during hard landings. Too many unpredictable things can go wrong. You may as well prepare for the ones you can.'

She activated the pod's controls, and the hatch hissed shut beside him. It reminded Fitzpatrick of a coffin lid . . . or the lifetube in which he'd been sealed until Zhett retrieved him. 'Aren't you afraid I'm going to overpower you and steal this ship?'

She raised her eyebrows. 'Fly away in a *grappler pod*? That's awfully ambitious of you. How many centuries do you think it'll take to reach the nearest Hansa planet?' He bit his lip, scowling. 'Besides, if you think it would be so easy to overpower *me* . . . well, you're welcome to try.'

She lifted the pod from its docking platform and backed out of the small vehicle station. She rotated them in place and flew into the rubble of Osquivel's rings with a casual ease. He looked out of the front windowport. 'Where are we going?'

'I want to show you our facilities, give you an idea of how much work we've put into this complex – though I sense you're not a man who's easily impressed.'

'Certainly not by anything Roachers can do.'

Her dark eyes flashed with anger. 'Nor are you a man given to exaggerated displays of respect or appreciation.' She spun the pod around in a stomach-lurching three-sixty, then followed it with two barrel rolls.

Fitzpatrick held on, but didn't give her the satisfaction of squawking or complaining. He'd been through worse – slightly worse – during EDF training. As she cruised up out of the ring plane, Fitzpatrick stared at all the bright points, thermal plumes, jets of exhaust, and waste rubble spreading out from processing facilities.

The spacedock structures were exposed now, several of them holding partially completed Roamer vessels. These operations were a dozen times more extensive than anything Fitzpatrick had imagined. 'But our whole battle group came here to fight the hydrogues. Why didn't we see any of this?'

'Because Eddies aren't terribly observant, and because we did a bit of camouflage ahead of time.'

'All these stations and habitation complexes and industries . . . I expected a couple of old decommissioned cargo containers and a shuttle or two.'

'You don't know the half of it, Fitzie. The Big Goose always underestimates us.'

'Don't call me Fitzie.'

'We've got five primary spacedocks and ship-assembly grids, four main habitation complexes, seventeen office outposts, twenty-three roving smelter factories, and eight stationary fabrication plants that take processed raw metals and form them into components. I can't even tell you how many separate storehouses, equipment lockers, food caches, or spare-parts hangars there are, not to mention sunside greenhouse domes and hydroponics chambers.'

He pressed his face close to the grappler pod's window, counting bright spots that were clearly not natural debris in Osquivel's rings. *How could we have missed all this before?* 'What's your population here? I thought Roamers were just . . . you know, a family at a time, a handful of people.'

She took one hand off the controls. 'There you go again, Fitzie. We've got prospectors and geologists who run through the rings searching for resource rocks, then teams of ore-crunchers move in to break it all down. Crews to run the smelters. Then there are extruders and fabricators, along with debris haulers – that's "garbage men" in Eddie terms. Truckers to haul material from place to place. Maintenance workers, troubleshooters, ship-builders, vessel designers, engine designers, life-support technicians, computer specialists, spacedock managers, structural engineers, electricians, and compy specialists to maintain our robotic workforce.'

Fitzpatrick couldn't believe what he was hearing. 'It's like a beehive.'

'And that's only those of us actively working on new vessels. I haven't even mentioned the second-tier support workers, food-prep personnel, inventory accountants, tradesmen and merchants, payroll staff.'

'Payroll?'

'Yes, Fitzie, we do get paid. We also have a cleaning staff, though we generally expect each person to do most of that work for themselves. You might want to mention *that* to your fellow Eddies. This isn't a hotel, and they shouldn't expect us to pick up after them. They've been piss-poor guests so far.'

'Then let us go.'

'After all you've seen? Fat chance.' She flew him through the ring, descending closer towards the giant gas planet. 'And none of what I've told you includes our cometary-extraction crews high up in the Kuiper Belt.'

'Nor does it count the thirty-two unlawful EDF prisoners you've kept.'

'Good point. They're certainly a strain on our resources – or at least on our patience. We would appreciate it if you'd at least acknowledge what we rescued you from.' As if she had choreographed the conversation, Zhett cruised through a dense layer of rubble and reached another set of glittering objects reflecting the glow of the planet. 'Look down there. That's what was left of your big lumbering Eddie ships after the drogues finished with you.'

Fitzpatrick felt a lurch in his chest, panic washing over him again as he was reminded of the massacre. He remembered the screaming, the shouts . . . the utter *helplessness*.

He had been in the midst of the fray, watching squadron after squadron of Remora fighters obliterated like moths in a blowtorch. He had seen Manta cruisers, even gigantic Juggernauts, torn to pieces.

The hydrogues had severely damaged his own cruiser. Fitzpatrick had issued evacuation orders, watching the alien warglobes converge on his Manta, their blue lightning weapons lancing out—

He'd barely got to a lifetube in time, ejecting just as his ship exploded behind him, spraying debris in all directions, damaging his signal beacon and ruining the life-support units. He had drifted, wounded, as unconsciousness slowly took him . . . until this demonic angel rescued him.

'Thank you,' he said in a very small voice.

Zhett looked startled but did not goad or tease him – not now.

Shudders ran down Fitzpatrick's spine as he stared at these ghost ships that had been abandoned by the EDF battle group. The space graveyard both awed him and made him want to hide.

As he looked at the wreckage, it finally became clear to Fitzpatrick that he and the EDF refugees would have died out here. All of them. The battle group had raced away from the ringed planet in full retreat. Even now, months later, no scout had returned to look for any remaining lifetubes. Zhett Kellum and her Roamers had indeed saved Fitzpatrick's life.

Damn, he hated to be beholden to her!

Perhaps sensing his mood, Zhett let compassion instead of sarcasm colour her voice. He much preferred this tone instead of mocking insults. 'I know what it's like . . . in a way. My mother and little brother were both killed in a dome breach when I was only eight years old. We lived on an asteroid observation station, and Roamers had plotted the orbits of the main components in the belt, but it's awfully hard to predict the paths of maverick meteoroids. The armourglass dome was smashed, broken wide open to space. All thirty people inside died of sudden explosive decompression. Almost half of the bodies were lost.'

'I'm . . . sorry, Zhett.'

'I was only eight, but I still remember the funeral. We wrapped each of the victims in a long embroidered shroud marked with our clan symbols. Then my father launched them up out of the ecliptic with enough velocity to escape the system's pull. That way they'd drift for ever, true Roamers carried along by the vagaries of gravity, following their own Guiding Stars.'

'Does that . . . sort of accident happen often to you people?'

She concentrated on flying again, not looking at him, though he could see a sparkle of tears in her large eyes. 'Roamers live and work in high-risk environments. Everybody knows that. Accidents come with the territory. We just try not to let the same disaster happen more than once.' He saw her swallow convulsively. 'In fact, the dome breach accident that killed my mother and brother led to a remarkable innovation. We would have sold the idea to the Big Goose, if we didn't think you'd cheat us.'

Fitzpatrick didn't rise to the bait. 'What was your solution?'

'We disperse thready aerogel clouds in the upper layers inside the colony hemisphere. That way if a breach happens, the squishy aerogel clutter is sucked to the gap first. They whoosh over, seal together, and clog the hole. Exposed to vacuum, the material sets and seals the breach like platelets in your blood forming a scab over a wound.'

Fitzpatrick recalled Tasia Tamblyn, another Roamer, and her unorthodox solution of creating artificial rafts out of tactical armour foam to hold refugees on Boone's Crossing. 'That's quite an idea.'

'You learn to be resourceful when you don't get everything on a silver platter,' Zhett said. 'Like some people I know.'

Fitzpatrick felt he had to defend himself, at least a little. 'Yeah, it was so easy growing up with a famous, snooty name. Once in a while I wished I could just have a normal, unremarkable life.'

'We know your parents were ambassadors,' Zhett said. 'And your grandmother was Chairman Maureen Fitzpatrick, Dame Battleaxe herself.'

Fitzpatrick nearly choked with unexpected laughter. 'That's a good name for her.' He pictured his stern grandmother, remembered the times he had spent with her as a child. Maureen was distinguished-looking with porcelain features and an icy beauty – few people's conception of an old battleaxe – but he realized the sentiment was completely accurate. 'And I knew her only after she'd retired and supposedly mellowed. I would not have wanted to cross her when she was the Hansa Chairman.'

As she flew the grappler pod around the battlefield wreckage, Fitzpatrick noticed other pods and small tug-bikes carrying Roamer salvage experts who dismantled the ships, stripping away valuable materials. Electronic systems, sleeper modules, food and air supplies, even scrap metal. He assumed everything was hauled over to the spacedocks and ship-assembly grids, where they would be reinstalled in Roamer constructions.

'So who was your grandfather? How did he put up with her?' Zhett asked.

Fitzpatrick shrugged, watching a work crew remove a large Juggernaut hull segment that had been blackened by hydrogue lightning. He turned away, not wanting to look at the damage.

'Oh, I never even met him. When their marriage ended in a bitter divorce, good old Dame Battleaxe used her political clout to crush the poor man. She made him bankrupt, destitute, and he never set foot in the halls of power again. I always wondered what was so bad about the guy.' Self-consciously, he ran a hand through his loose, dark hair. Already, it was growing longer than he'd ever been allowed to keep it in the EDF. 'I knew my grandmother well enough not to believe her "Maureen-centric" view of history.'

Zhett flew past a mangled Remora, its cockpit torn open as if some rabid dog had ripped it to shreds. Parts of an engine drifted about, and he was sure he caught a glimpse of a deflated spacesuit, all that remained of the dead pilot. Fitzpatrick squeezed his eyes shut. 'Could we, um . . . look someplace else?'

Without teasing him, she flew away from the salvage operations, following the long sweeping ring. Below, Osquivel's clouds seemed smooth and peaceful, giving no hint that monsters hid deep within.

'By virtue of being Fitzpatricks, my parents were made ambassadors to a succession of Hansa colony worlds. They transferred from place to place as they got bored with each location. But I lived with private tutors or in fancy boarding schools. My fellow blueblood students and I had regular assignments to go slumming – you know, work preordained charity missions and keep in touch with all the little people we were supposed to remember?'

'Like Roamers, you mean?' Zhett asked with a defensive undertone.

'Oh, no! My grandmother would have been horrified if she had ever caught me with a Roamer. I participated in environmental clean-ups, visited down-and-out families. I handed out clothes or soup, assisted in restoring polluted marshlands or decaying seaside communities. I could see the worth of the work, but I hated it each time, and my family's reasons for making me do it were no more altruistic than mine.'

'It was helping other people, Fitzie. Couldn't you appreciate that for its own sake? Didn't it make you feel good?'

'I never managed to see it that way . . . at least not at the time. What I learned was how to smile whenever a camera was pointed towards me, because if I made a media blunder I would catch hell from my grandmother.'

Zhett shook her head, flying them onwards. 'Ah, Patrick Fitzpatrick the Third, your Guiding Star is no brighter than a strap-on fingerlight.'

'What's that supposed to mean? Some Roamer religious nonsense?'

'If I were you, I wouldn't be accusing other people of nonsense. Didn't you ever have any close friends, any pets?'

'Not really. It wasn't part of the programme. My life was completely mapped out for me, and that didn't leave much room for spontaneity.'

Now Zhett gave him a warm smile. 'Aha! And that must have hampered your understanding of how people interact. That's why a cooperative life among the Roamers is such a shock to you. It's an alien environment. Your life on Earth was always so sheltered and so set. You never had to strive for anything. That's why you can't take pride in anybody else's accomplishments.'

He scowled and turned away. 'There's the familiar Zhett Kellum again. I was beginning to worry, since it must have been fifteen minutes since the last time you criticized me.'

'Touché,' she said, then 'I'm sorry.'

He sat in silence, thinking. 'It never occurred to me that other people – like you Roamers – might live differently because you want to. That you might actually be happy with what you have. I assumed your lower-class living was the result of your own failures rather than . . . conscious choices. Always I divided everyone into two camps: the rich and the needy. I was glad to be among the rich, and convinced that the needy wanted everything I had.'

'Excuse me, Fitzie, but I wouldn't trade lives with you for all the credits in the Hansa corporate bank accounts.' Refusing to meet his gaze, Zhett reached over to touch his arm with a glimmer of compassion. When she noticed what she was doing, she snatched her hand away as if the contact with him might burn her fingers. 'Maybe you just need a fresh start to do something useful instead of being a spoiled rich kid.'

She piloted the grappler pod back into the docking bay of the converted asteroid's vehicle pool. As they climbed out and stretched their legs, Fitzpatrick turned to see barrel-chested Del Kellum emerging from the hatch that led to the administrative offices. 'There you are, my sweet!' He looked askance at Fitzpatrick. 'I hope you had a good time – and that *he* didn't try anything.'

'You worry too much, Dad. I had him wrapped around my little finger.' Fitzpatrick gave her an affronted look.

'I've brought news from Rendezvous. The Roamers decided unanimously to cut off ekti shipments to the Big Goose. We've shut down all trade whatsoever.'

'No more ekti shipments?' Fitzpatrick cried. 'We need that fuel! While you Roamers hide, the EDF is fighting this war against the drogues, protecting your little jackrabbit asses.'

'*Protecting* us?' Kellum let out a bitter laugh. 'By damn, you Eddies have a strange way of showing it, by raiding and destroying Roamer cargo ships. We recently recovered the wreckage of one flown by a good friend of mine, Raven Kamarov. Emptied of its ekti cargo and then blasted to pieces by EDF jazers. Don't go giving me any bullshit about you boys "protecting" us.'

Zhett turned to him. 'The Big Goose can't make any excuses for what they've done, Fitzie. If they want their ekti back, they have to confess to their crimes, bring the perpetrators to justice, and renounce any such activities in the future. Simple enough.'

Fitzpatrick felt a hot lump in the pit of his stomach, his knees grew weak, and he was sure all the colour had drained from his face. He himself was responsible for that particular mess. He had ordered the blast that destroyed Kamarov's unarmed ship. He didn't dare speak up and admit his guilt, though it must have been sickeningly obvious on his face.

Zhett noticed his oddly reticent behaviour as she led him back to the chambers where the other EDF prisoners were held. Despite his resentment for their situation, Fitzpatrick couldn't reveal what he had done, not simply for fear of the Roamer reprisals, but because a small, nagging part of him didn't want Zhett Kellum to think any less of him . . .

FIFTY-TWO

ORLI COVITZ

Rheindic Co was vastly different from cloudy, damp Dremen, but this was only a stopping place, a waypoint where eager colonists waited to go through the transportal to their new homes.

Orli was used to grey gloom and cold drizzle; she couldn't remember the last time she'd felt warm sunlight on her bare arms and face. To her dismay she got ferociously sunburned for the first time in her life. On Dremen, she'd never had to worry about it, but now a tingling redness covered every square centimetre of her arms and cheeks and neck.

Her father went among the other colonists, asking if anyone had brought lotions or sun creams. Only a few had, and he couldn't afford the price they were asking. Fortunately, his persistence paid off, and he found supplies in the Hansa base camp. He returned slathered with ointment, which he promptly applied to his daughter as well.

She kept blinking her eyes against the dazzle of sunlight reflecting off the rocky canyons and mountains. Everything looked so different. When Jan saw how his daughter stared at the alien landscape, he tousled her short hair. 'Don't worry, girl. Our new colony home will be more attractive than this, warm and green, a place to settle down and take it easy for a change.'

Orli brightened, though she didn't mind the desert scenery at all. 'Have they told you where we're going? Do you know the name of our planet?'

'It's just the luck of the draw, I think. We'll find out when they call our number. They're afraid people would start arguing over planets, trading assignments and messing up the Hansa's record-keeping.'

Orli sat in the dirt outside their tent. 'You'd think they'd at least give us a bit of background, so we could plan.'

'Don't worry. They've scouted these worlds, and they wouldn't send us to a place unless we could survive just fine there.'

The colourful tents looked like jewel-toned mushrooms that had sprung up on the canyon floor. To prepare for the influx of new personnel, EDF engineering squads had cleared an expanse of the desert, using high-energy beams to melt the sand and dirt into a level glassy plain where shuttles could easily land and take off. Every day, new ships full of supplies or eager colonists dropped down into the bright sunlight. Rheindic Co had been an abandoned place not long before; now it was a boom town.

Her father opened two packages of rations he'd retrieved from the distribution point. They ate a chalky fruit-flavoured pudding that was supposedly full of protein and vitamins. Orli saw him frown at the taste, but she elbowed him in the ribs. 'Anything's better than mushroom stew isn't it, Dad?'

'That's looking on the bright side.' Jan extended the awning from their tent, propping it up with the poles so they could sit in the shade. As the dusk painted the sky with colours and the temperature dropped, Orli went into the tent and rummaged through their possessions to retrieve her synthesizer strips. She played music quietly, tunes of her own devising. It soothed her, and her father tried to hum along, though he'd never heard these particular melodies before.

Jan sat looking bored but smiling. 'Oh, I hate this waiting. Maybe tomorrow they'll let me help out somewhere in the main complex.' He glanced over at her, musing. 'Say, why don't you go make friends with some of the other children? I've already seen a dozen or so your age.'

She had thought about it herself, but decided against the pointless exercise. 'I'll wait till we get to our colony, Dad. Then I can establish a long-term friendship.'

'Friends are friends, girl. One for a day is better than no friend at all.'

Orli had never had many playmates, since she needed to spend so much time just keeping her father from doing too many ill-advised things. She liked telling stories and imagining games, but work in the mushroom fields had taken up her time on Dremen. Maybe on the new colony she would find someone who shared her interest in music. 'I'll try when we get where we're going, Dad. I promise.'

For the next few days Jan volunteered his services at the supply-distribution centre. Most evenings he wandered among the tents and struck up conversations, describing Dremen and asking other people about the planets they were leaving, while Orli practised on her synthesizer strips.

On the fifth evening, another loud Attention tone rang through the camp, as it did several times a day. Hopeful and eager people popped their heads out of tents and stopped cooking and conversations to listen. 'This one'll be us, Orli,' Jan said. 'I'm sure of it.' He'd said the same thing at every announcement for the past three days.

'Colonists from Group B, please report to the gathering ramp.

Prepare for disembarkation through the transportal within two hours.'

The announcement repeated several times, though the colonists had hung on every word the first time. Her father slapped Orli playfully on the shoulder. 'See, I told you, girl. If you guess enough times, you're sure to be right eventually.'

The nearby colonists began moving about frantically, as if they'd been called to an emergency evacuation. Two hours was plenty of time to gather the few belongings she and Jan had carried from Dremen. Orli wrapped her synthesizer strips carefully in her clothes and put them in her pack, and her father scrounged together his clothes, files, sketchpads with ideas for fruitless inventions, and a few tools he'd brought.

They would all leave the temporary tents behind for the next wave of travellers. After their group departed, compies would clean and refurbish the standard living quarters; within a day, more people would arrive to fill them. Prefab buildings had already been shipped to each destination point.

Orli and her father hurried with the moving current of people towards the ramps up into the cliff city. There was no particular hurry. They still had an hour and a half, but her father wanted to be among the first to go through the transportal, as if a few minutes would make a difference in staking the best claim for a homestead. Maybe he was right.

A few other pale-skinned hopefuls from Dremen joined those from various struggling Hansa colonies. They all stood around talking until finally the settlers were allowed forward into the labyrinth of Klikiss structures. The stone halls were worn and scuffed. Many of the alien hieroglyphics and artifacts had been damaged or rubbed away by the sheer volume of people passing through.

Orli paused to look at the letters written by a clawed Klikiss hand in an incomprehensible language, but her father nudged her forward. 'We'll have plenty of time to study old ruins when we get to our new colony, girl. Every place has them, otherwise we wouldn't have a transportal on the other end.'

A grizzled man with shaggy hair and long stubble turned to them. 'Oh, the place we're going has ruins, all right. And a big valley, tall granite walls, running water. We'll be able to settle there nicely.'

'How do you know?' Orli asked.

'Because I've been there.' The old man stuck out his hand to the girl first, then to her father. 'I'm Hud Steinman, one of the trans-portal explorers. I found Corribus only a month or so ago, and right away I decided I wanted to retire there. It's perfect, the best of all the worlds I've been to.'

Her father beamed. 'See Orli, I told you so.'

Orli wrinkled her nose as the shaggy explorer stepped closer. He smelled sour and dusty, but he seemed friendly enough. Ahead she could see the colonists shuffling forward group by group towards a shimmering image displayed on what had been a flat stone wall. Loud voices echoed in the rock-walled chamber. Hansa managers told people to keep moving as each group marched forward through the instantaneous transportation system.

Once when she'd been a little girl, Orli recalled a day her father had taken her to a crowded amusement park full of rides, holographic simulations, and old-fashioned rollercoasters. The wait had seemed interminable as they inched forward. It had felt as if they had to stand for ever just to get to the rollercoaster . . . and the ride had been over in only a few minutes. But the thrill had made every moment of preparation worthwhile.

Orli hoped the payoff on this distant Klikiss world – Corribus? – would be just as gratifying.

As they came closer, listening to the hum of alien machinery, the quick discussions of technicians, and the nervous excitement of the colonists, Orli could see the wall up ahead. People marched forward and then vanished, as if they had stepped off the edge of a cliff. Finally, the crackling stone trapezoid loomed in front of her, ringed by well over a hundred tiles, each one containing a strange symbol.

Hud Steinman turned to them with a grin, showing off bad teeth. 'Here we go. You'll see what I mean.'

'Next!' the technician called. 'Step up. Don't delay the rest of the line. We have a lot of people to get through on this transmission.'

Orli clasped her father's hand. He squeezed hers for reassurance, and they looked at each other, eyes bright. Then together they stepped through the transportal – and emerged under the sunny skies of Corribus and into a whole new landscape.

FIFTY-THREE

CHIEF SCIENTIST
HOWARD PALAWU

The Klikiss ruins on Rheindic Co bustled with a clamour of crowds. All the chaos made it damned hard to get any work done.

Sent here on direct orders from Chairman Wenceslas himself, Chief Scientist Palawu had all the data files and equipment he needed, even authorization to supersede the technologists who had studied the first known operating Klikiss transportal since its discovery.

Despite Palawu's supposed clout, however, the activities of the colonization initiative dominated so much of the time and space in the transportal chamber that he only managed to study the system for an hour or two in the dead of night. Figuring out how the transportals *worked* didn't seem to be a priority for anyone but him.

Every few hours, Hansa staff rounded up colonists, then opened the transportal to one of the numerous approved coordinate tiles. The pioneers filed forward, carrying their possessions on their backs. Cases of supplies and overloaded hoverpallets barely able to fit within the trapezoidal frame, drifted through the stone wall and vanished. Presumably, they arrived at the other end, though it wasn't immediately obvious. As he watched person after person step through the shimmering wall, Palawu wondered if Margaret Colicos had escaped this room in the same manner . . . and been unable to find her way back.

Some colonists passed through with excitement-bright eyes and smiling faces. Others wore doubtful or uneasy expressions, but momentum carried them along. After coming this far, very few changed their minds and backed away. Anyone who declined the offer at the last moment was required to pay an exorbitant fee to go back home.

If Palawu had been younger, if his wife had still been alive, if he'd still had something to prove, he might have considered taking the chance himself. Instead, the Chief Scientist sat in the control room and listened to loud conversations, excitement building to a pitch of hysteria.

Hansa managers noisily directed the exodus, while transportal technicians monitored the machinery, keeping careful notes, because even they didn't understand the process. Oh, how Palawu wished he could have had the luxury of time and peace and concentration just to figure out the alien technology. Given a week to pore over the Klikiss artifacts, Palawu was sure he could have deciphered many of the basic principles.

But Chairman Wenceslas had been eager to unleash his new interstellar land rush, leaving the Chief Scientist with little choice but to do his work by gathering up crumbs of time and information. He found a chair and tried to remain unobtrusive as he called up files on his old datascreen. For now he was just scanning textual notes, and he preferred using the slow and obsolete unit he'd had since his first job as a lab assistant and secondary engineer. His wife had given it to him.

He jabbed a key and called up Louis Colicos's scattered log

entries. It amazed him that one old man had managed to get the first transportal working again, rigging up power packs and restarting the mothballed Klikiss machinery. After nearly ten thousand years, the alien equipment was in extraordinarily good condition. So far, only a few of the numerous coordinate tiles were marked black to indicate places from which explorers had never returned. Many of the coordinate tiles around the trapezoidal window remained untried – potential paradises. Or traps.

He switched to another file that displayed a detailed starmap, indicating sites of known Klikiss ruins and functional transportals. If Palawu could decipher the core technology, then the Hansa could establish transportals anywhere they chose, and the economic boom would increase by orders of magnitude . . .

He also had access to a high-resolution astronomical map that displayed the sweep of standard Hansa colonies, Ildiran worlds, and Klikiss ruins, along with summaries of star types and planetary positions. Glowing dots marked where former stars had been violently snuffed out in recent months, their fires squelched by hydrogues in their incomprehensible conflict against the faeros. Though the blips on the starmap looked innocuous, Palawu shuddered at the implications – whole suns were being extinguished by the titanic beings!

On the starmap, he noted another marker in the Ptoro system, where a Klikiss Torch had recently turned the gas giant into a fresh burning star. The Klikiss had developed that weapon long ago – to fight against the hydrogues, presumably? The planet Corribus, one of the new colonization worlds, still showed the battle scars of that final conflict.

Following a hunch, Palawu collated the spectral readings of newly ignited Ptoro and added them to the records from the first test planet Oncier. Knowing that his old datascreen did not have the processing power he required, he commandeered one of the larger

Hansa computers not being used for transporting new colonists. He set the machine working on a fast and intense comparison.

If the Klikiss had developed the Torch, surely they must have used it at least once. Those artificially created stars would be short-lived on a cosmic time scale – a gas giant did not have enough fuel to burn for more than a few thousand years – but even after ten millennia they wouldn't all be extinguished.

With a thrill of satisfaction, he looked at the results. The computer found twenty-one stars with small burning companions that could well have been gas giants ignited by the Klikiss Torch, long ago. *Twenty-one.*

Were they ancient battlefields of the Klikiss against the hydrogues? So far, Oncier, Ptoro, and three other hydrogue gas giants had been obliterated in the current war, their funeral pyres still burning.

Though his discovery was amazing, Palawu soon came to the sombre realization that even after using their Torch weapon twenty-one times, the Klikiss race had still been exterminated. What possible chance did humanity have?

FIFTY-FOUR

ANTON COLICOS

Inside the bright domes of Maratha Prime, Anton stared past the glare into the months' long darkness, feeling very alone.

With the return of Designate Avi'h to the mothballed vacation mecca, the skeleton crew had become energized, though they often ignored the unnecessary orders given by the chief bureaucrat, Bhali'v. The two additional Ildirans among them helped strengthen the bonds of *thism*.

But Anton was separate from all that. The self-centred Designate had blithely announced the death of Anton's father and the disappearance of his mother, as if delivering nothing more serious than a weather prediction. Though he had feared the worst after so many years without news, Anton still felt as if the floor had dropped away beneath his feet. Now it was time for grieving, and for regrets.

He had never been particularly close to his parents after he'd grown up and gone off to pursue his own interests. They were proud of him, he knew. Margaret and Louis had read all of his scholarly papers, offered encouragement, attended his graduation and tenure ceremonies – an amazing thing, now that he thought of it, since they were so often at one archaeological dig or another – but Anton had always taken them for granted. The Colicoses had raised their son to be self-sufficient, just as they themselves were.

Now, against the dark stain of Maratha's night, Anton saw his ghostly reflection in the curved glass: narrow chin, flat brown hair, squinting eyes. When he'd come here, excited to be studying with Rememberer Vao'sh, he hadn't even thought to bring along photographs of his mother and father. Back in his university office, however, Anton kept quite a collection of their images, journals, and documents for the purpose of writing a definitive biography of his illustrious parents.

Now, sadly, he had an end to the story. The piece he had always been missing . . .

'I have discovered another clear difference between humans and Ildirans, Rememberer Anton.' The rich voice of Vao'sh spoke from behind him. 'When Ildirans are troubled, we seek the companionship of others. But you clearly choose to be alone.'

Anton turned to see the other historian standing in the doorway, enfolded by the light. He forced a wan smile. 'Oh, I'm just trying to deal with how things have changed. I'm swimming in memories and drowning in realizations I should have had years ago.'

He'd been eight years old the first time he had accompanied his parents on one of their archaeological expeditions. The planet was Pym, a world with termite-mound ruins built by the lost insectoid race. Pym's air was dry and the sky was clear every night, revealing a myriad of stars. The support workers and university associates spent the evenings discussing esoteric historical questions, comparing notes, and occasionally telling bawdy stories.

Besides himself, there were no children in the camp. The other archaeologists were much older, their sons and daughters already grown up and gone off to school or careers, so Anton was left to himself, a fifth wheel, glad to be with his parents but not quite belonging.

He had wandered through the dig site, squirming into crannies and little holes in the ruins that the adults could never explore. One time, he'd discovered a room with a few dusty artifacts, but the investigators had scolded him, then chided Margaret and Louis for allowing their kid to scuff up the dusty and fragile remnants with his small footprints.

'Sometimes my father would sit with me at night,' he told Vao'sh. 'We'd build a little campfire of our own, using the dry tinder grasses around the Klikiss towers. He was good-hearted, but he didn't really know how to talk to anyone who wasn't a colleague. I remember watching the sparks drift like fairy lights into the sky, while my father rambled about Klikiss theory and university politics.'

When Vao'sh sat beside him and spoke, his expressive voice was rich with undertones of sympathy. 'Do you recall that Maratha Prime was known as the City on the Brink, poised between daylight and darkness? We are here, safe and sheltered under our domes, with all the light our blazers can shed. I can tell my stories to a captive audience – no rememberer could ask for more.' His expression changed, the lobes on his face flushing through a palette of colours. 'But every day, no matter how much brightness we keep inside, the night remains black and impenetrable out there.'

Anton turned away from his wan reflection. 'There's really nothing to fear out in the dark, you know, Vao'sh. With the hydrogues abroad and all the planets they've destroyed, we've got enough real danger to worry about.'

'That may be true, Rememberer Anton, but one's fears are not based solely on logical analysis.' Vao'sh touched his friend's shoulder in a human gesture he had learned from Anton. 'Come with me. Designate Avi'h is hosting another banquet and wishes everyone to join him.'

'Again?'

'Again.'

'Then we'd best do our jobs. Could you think of a . . . distracting story for me tonight? How about a ghost story? I'd like that.'

Vao'sh pondered. 'I'm not certain the others would appreciate it as much, but I will do it for you, Anton.'

In the central dining hall reserved for huge crowds during the height of the day season, several small tables had been set out for the thirty-seven remaining inhabitants. The Designate considered it a cheery place, but the grandness of the hall seemed to diminish the size of their company by comparison.

Anton dined on fresh vegetables and preserved meats. The two agricultural kithmen Mhas'k and Syl'k were proud of their bountiful produce, though the returned Designate was consuming fresh supplies so quickly that they would run out of food before long.

The engineer Nur'of enthusiastically reported on the new turbines he had installed in the ancient tunnels he'd found beneath Maratha Prime, but the Designate seemed neither impressed nor interested. Avi'h raised his hands. 'Time for something entertaining! My father dispatched his greatest rememberer to keep us company here on Maratha Prime. So, Vao'sh, tell us your best story.'

Beside the Designate, Bhali'v officiously repeated the order. Vao'sh turned most of his attention to Anton. 'In honour of our human guest, I will tell a . . . chilling story.' Designate Avi'h frowned, as if he had hoped for a heroic tale or a ribald adventure, but he sat back and listened.

The Spiral Arm contains many mysteries. Once, in an earlier age when the Empire was growing, our intrepid explorers travelled great distances to shine light upon the deepest questions of the universe. Our *thism* extended far, the threads stretched across many star systems. The Mage-Imperator wanted to know the universe, to have his people touch it all.

'Thus, a septa of exploration craft was sent into a dark nebula we call the Mouth of Space – a black enigma that had defied analysis by our best astronomers. The Mage-Imperator wished to know the secrets of this mysterious place between the stars. And though darkness is fearful to Ildirans, their warliners were strung with extra blazers, both inside and out, and the seven ships sailed forth into the black zone.'

Vao'sh paused, and his facial lobes flickered through a symphony of colours and emotions. He changed his voice and spoke quickly to startle his listeners. 'But they vanished!'

Anton listened to him, identifying some of the techniques he himself had taught the old rememberer.

Vao'sh leaned forward, closer to his audience. 'The entire septa was lost for centuries. No one knew what had happened to those seven ships or the members of their brave crews, but through the *thism* the Mage-Imperator sensed that something had gone terribly awry. Something cold, and dark, and sinister. No one dared venture into the Mouth of Space to learn the answer. The black nebula hung there like a blot against the stars, anathema to the Light-source.' The storyteller's face flushed ominous colours mixed with pallid tinges denoting fear.

'Centuries later, an investigation team found the seven ships again. They were out of power, frozen, completely lifeless. Just drifting and far from any star system. When salvage workers cut their way through the hulls, they discovered that every Ildiran aboard was dead. They had all been killed at the same time, instantly, yet terribly! As if they had been confronted by their most awful fears, struck down by a weapon none of them could understand, locked in infinite pain and horror.'

Vao'sh waved one finger. 'But they were not just slain, no. Each of their bodies was bleached utterly white. The expressions on their faces, from the lowest soldier kithman to the Septar himself, looked as if they had all seen something so unbearable that it quenched the Lightsource within them, darkened their very souls, and stole every spark of life from their minds.'

He looked around slowly, meeting every set of eyes, lowering his voice to a chilling tone.

'We know now that deep in the black Mouth of Space, those ships were the first to encounter the Shana Rei: creatures that live shrouded by shadows around dead stars. Their civilization had sucked all the light out of that area of space. We do not know what that exploration team did to anger the Shana Rei.

'Not long afterwards, the creatures of darkness emerged and began to spread their shadows. Thus began a time of stories too fearsome to share here. It was our Empire's most terrible conflict – until now, with the hydrogues.'

Anton looked at the gathered listeners, all of whom appeared uneasy. Vao'sh had used familiar talespinning tricks, but his resonant voice and the emotions displayed on his lumpy face added a depth to the frightening scene, even though there hadn't been much of a plot. Ildirans just weren't good at this sort of story.

Anton realized he was the only one smiling in the audience. The others seemed particularly uncomfortable to hear this part of the *Saga of Seven Suns*. While humans could listen to campfire tales and ghost stories with a shudder, knowing they were mere clever fictions, Ildirans believed in the truth of every portion of their epic.

'Thank you, Vao'sh. A very well-told tale,' he said, and his voice seemed to break the tension. The old rememberer looked to him with an appreciative nod.

Before the other Ildirans could utter a nervous sigh of relief and turn back to their meals, they heard a loud muffled bang. Moments later, from beneath the domed city, came the thump and rumble of a second explosion.

Designate Avi'h stood up. 'Now what is this?'

The generators stopped, cutting the power. All the lights went out, and blackness swallowed the entire city of Maratha Prime.

FIFTY-FIVE

DAVLIN LOTZE

While Rlinda Kett unloaded the necessary supplies and took aboard seven volunteers who wanted to seek their fortunes on an untamed Klikiss world, Davlin walked alone to the main colony settlement, head held high. It was time to admit who he was and what he had done, and hope his former neighbours accepted him back among them.

When he had lived here before, the people had liked him, and he'd pretended to feel the same . . . or at least it started out as pretending. None of them had ever guessed he was a 'specialist in obscure details' assigned to study the evacuated Ildiran settlement here. Davlin had determined that the Ildirans had left nothing behind, however, and the Chairman had eventually called him secretly away, presumably much to the shock of the remaining settlers.

If they had somehow learned he was a Hansa spy, they must have wondered if he had kept files about their private lives. A spy was a spy. Davlin braced himself for well-deserved censure. But if he intended to live among them again, he had to be honest. Would they ever forgive him?

Now he entered Crenna's small meeting hall and administrative offices, rehearsing again how he would explain himself to the mayor. Originally, the mayor – a chubby, bronze-skinned farmer named Lupe Ruis – had taken care of bureaucratic matters in only a few hours a week. Lately, as the colony prospered, running the settlement had become a full-time job.

When Mayor Ruis saw him, however, the man's wide face split with a grin. 'Davlin Lotze! Welcome home. We've all been hoping for your return.' He opened his arms and stepped forward, full of good cheer. 'Is your secret mission completed now?' He sounded conspiratorial . . . and delighted. 'We've heard about all the important work you do for the Hansa. And here we thought you were just a run-of-the-mill colonist like the rest of us, but you're a celebrity!'

'How – how did you know?'

The mayor waved his hand dismissively. 'You must be kidding, right? Captain Kett's been back here. She and Branson Roberts have quite a thing going, you know. She's told us how you're an expert investigator in Ildiran sociology and that *you* were the one who discovered the Klikiss transportal network. Great job!'

'Captain Kett was with me at the time. She helped me discover—'

Ruis put an arm around his shoulder. 'You're a hero, Davlin! We're so proud of you. And to think you were one of us, just laying low here.'

Nonplussed, Davlin could think of nothing to say except, 'Thank you.'

With an abrupt gesture, Ruis pushed aside the paperwork on his desk as if to show just how unimportant it was. 'And now you've come back to settle down for a while? Until duty calls again? I can't tell you how delighted we are. Captain Roberts and his ship just left to do shuttle work for the colonization initiative, and a few of our people volunteered to go off to the Klikiss worlds. We could certainly use someone versatile and . . . uh, competent among us again.'

'I . . . appreciate your confidence and your enthusiasm, Mayor Ruis. I wasn't sure how I would be received. Is my old dwelling still available, or did someone else claim it?'

The mayor looked surprised. 'It's still waiting for you. Our colony hasn't exactly had the need for much expansion, Davlin. We're just trying to hold our own here.'

'Any further outbreaks of Orange Spot?'

'No, sir. The amoebic filtration system you installed in the drinking water conduits has kept us all safe.' The ruddy-skinned mayor broke into another grin. 'I hope you're ready to be put to work, though. We could use your help with our infrastructure, especially the electricity and the sewers. And then we'd like you to look at our commsystems and transmitting towers. Heavy solar activity and ionic storms have been messing up our local network for the past year.'

'That isn't my area of expertise, but I'll have a look at it.'

Ruis gave him a wink. 'According to Captain Kett, you know a little bit about everything.' The mayor walked with him out of his office. 'We're certainly glad to have you back.'

That night, contented yet somehow restless, Davlin walked along the low hills on the outskirts of town. It felt oddly satisfactory to be here. Overhead, Crenna's highly reflective moon bathed the landscape with silvery light, challenging the darkness. Lunar brightness had been a factor that originally made this world attractive to the Ildirans, who did not at all like dark nights.

The hills were rocky and low, covered with gnarled, hollow trees called flutewoods. The empty branches were perforated with tiny holes through which the breezes blew, turning them into natural woodwind instruments. As the wind rose and fell, the whistling atonal melody played like a strange lullaby, ranging from high-pitched piccolo notes in the narrow branches to deep bassoon tones in the wider, hollow trunks.

Many of the stars were washed out by the moonlight, but he stared up at them, picking out constellations, reflecting on how far he had come in his travels across the Spiral Arm. The rushing sounds of small streams trickling along the hillside and the rattling of tall grasses accompanied the flutewood symphony.

So much better than the nightmarish world he had last visited through the Klikiss transportal. No flying jellyfish creatures or giant centipedes here. He stood alone, completely at peace. He was glad to be back on Crenna. It seemed almost like . . . home.

Suddenly Davlin saw the diamond points of several stars moving, then streaking across the sky like meteors, though they did not burn up in the atmosphere. Instead, they passed rapidly across the backdrop. Ships? Visitors?

Three pinpoints travelled in a direct trajectory, then another six. Line after line shot across the vault of stars. Davlin narrowed his eyes. He had never seen such phenomena before. High up, ten more pinpoints streaked by until dazzling lights filled the night sky like the flakes of a driving snowstorm.

Davlin felt a cold dread in his chest.

Several pinpoints changed course, swerving around and expanding their coverage. He began to hear sounds now, the rapid passage of something immense and distant. Shooting stars ripped across the sky, swooping lower.

In the village below, he heard confused shouts. Other colonists had emerged from their dwellings to stare up at the sky. Davlin remained on the rise where he had the best view.

When he heard a sizzling, rushing sound, he turned to look towards Crenna's horizon. He knew what it was even before four of the large craft hurtled overhead, cruising in ominous reconnaissance.

Hydrogue warglobes.

The glowing spheres tumbled across the sky like spiked balls. Faint sparks of blue lightning crackled from their pyramidal protrusions. Davlin had heard of the devastating attacks on places such as Theroc and Boone's Crossing. But the aliens had not attacked Crenna. Not yet.

The colonists in the village were in a panic now, shouting and rushing to shelter, pointing towards the sky. At least they were wise enough not to activate blaring alarms, which might have attracted the drogues.

A spiked warglobe roared overhead, scribing a turbulent wake against the starry backdrop. For a moment it eclipsed the bright moon, then passed by. The enemy gave no sign that it had even noted the human settlement. Then five more warglobes cruised across the sky. Still, none of them opened fire. These hydrogues must simply be on their way to another target.

Finally the flurry of warglobes dwindled into the distance, leaving the colony untouched. Even more of the white pinpoints crossed in front of the distant stars, a huge alien battle fleet converging somewhere in the Crenna system.

When the monstrous spheres had departed, Davlin drew a deep breath to focus his thoughts and to calm himself. The simple colonists here were in no position whatsoever to know what they were dealing with. They hadn't the resources or experience to know how to react.

He sprinted back down to the settlement. Unfortunately, given the tall tales and adventures Rlinda Kett had related about Davlin's exploits, all of these people would look to *him* for answers.

FIFTY-SIX

MAGE-IMPERATOR JORA'H

As the Mage-Imperator's warliner approached Dobro at last, Jora'h insisted on standing in the command nucleus, as he'd done with Adar Kori'nh when he was the Prime Designate. He stared out the wide viewport, watching the planet grow larger.

That was where his daughter lived. That was where Nira had died.

Aboard the Solar Navy ship, Septar Rhe'nh was alarmed to see the Mage-Imperator not riding in his chrysalis chair. The Septar quickly and tenaciously offered to have his crew engineers build a substitute platform, but Jora'h insisted on walking for himself. 'That tradition has changed,' he said. 'The Solar Navy can follow my orders without further anxiety. I will stay here in the command nucleus.'

'Yes, Liege.' Rhe'nh clasped his hands to his chest in salute and turned back to guiding the vessel along its course. The crew, though in awe of having their leader aboard, did not understand his unusual behaviour.

Despite the vastness of the Empire, his corpulent father had almost never left Ildira, and only on rare occasions emerged from the Prism Palace; instead, pilgrims and supplicants had come to him. Jora'h intended to be a different sort of leader, though – an active part of the Empire rather than some sort of holy relic on permanent display.

'How soon will we secure orbit, Septar?'

'Within the hour, Liege. The Designate is preparing to meet us in a formal shuttle, as you requested.'

'I did not request my brother as escort. I intend to take my own guards and go see the planet for myself.' Jora'h paused, not wanting the military commander to guess the extent of his continuing anger towards Udru'h for his deceits and failures. 'But that will be acceptable, I suppose. I am anxious to see . . . what is happening down there.'

Through the *thism*, Jora'h now had all the background information and understood the reasons for the desperate if unconscionable breeding plan. Even so, he wanted to be here in person, to witness the work with his own eyes, to look into the faces of the hapless human test subjects. He owed that much to the memory of Nira, since he hadn't been there when she'd needed him the most.

The seven warliners settled into orbit. From a great height, Jora'h studied the soft-edged continents, the large lakes and oceans, the mottled greens and browns. Dobro looked attractive, but . . . empty, a place where one could not help but feel isolated. Nira must have felt so alone.

He clenched his teeth to keep his emotions from showing. *He* was Mage-Imperator now and weary of such misery. For years he had been unaware of the situation. Now perhaps he could make a difference, somehow.

He saw the streak of burners as a shuttle rose up to intercept the warliners. Jora'h walked towards the exit of the command nucleus to go meet his brother.

'Do you desire an escort, Liege?' Without waiting for an answer, Rhe'nh lifted his hand, and a group of Solar Navy soldiers snapped to attention, ready to assist their leader.

'No. Certain things are better done in private.'

As he walked along the corridors, attender kithmen applied clear sealant to the deck where the Mage-Imperator's feet had touched, as if he had somehow consecrated the metal. Jora'h did not desire such fanatical reverence, but he could not turn the Ildirans from their attitude.

By the time he reached the docking bay, the shuttle was settling onto the cool metal plates. The shuttle hatch opened, and two figures waited formally inside. Udru'h stood paternally next to the Designate-in-waiting, as if he had legitimately taken over the role of Daro'h's father. Jora'h felt a twinge of resentment because his brother's mindset was so different from his own. *You stole my daughter from me, and now you intend to take my son as well?*

The young Designate-in-waiting stepped forward and bowed. Showing no emotion, Udru'h did the same. 'Liege, we are prepared to show you the strategic and vital project that will protect us from the hydrogues.'

'I am already aware of it,' Jora'h said coldly.

'A personal encounter will no doubt result in a greater understanding.'

As the three entered the shuttle and settled aboard, Jora'h turned to his young son. 'And what do you think of this work, Daro'h? It will be your responsibility soon. I'm afraid I did not properly prepare you for it.'

'I am learning to the best of my abilities. It is very interesting.'

'He is truly gifted, Liege,' Udru'h added. 'I have found him to be a diligent and faithful student in the short time he has been here.'

More than anything, Jora'h wished he had not been forced to

send his son into such a situation. 'But what do you *think* of it, Daro'h? What is your judgement of the project itself? What are its merits? Should it continue, despite all of the drawbacks?'

'Of course he believes it should continue,' Udru'h said, but the Mage-Imperator continued to search the young man's face, waiting for an answer.

'I still have too much to learn, Father. It would be inappropriate for me to offer an opinion as of yet.'

As they rode down to the planet, buffeted by a few stray currents in the fringes of the atmosphere, Jora'h sat in uncomfortable silence. He could sense hope and uneasiness through the *thism*. Udru'h's thoughts seemed to be tangled in intentional knots, twisted and sheltered so that even the Mage-Imperator had difficulty following the threads to their true answers.

Finally, he turned to the silent Designate. Was he hiding something? 'You know I find the basis of the current breeding programme to be abhorrent, Udru'h.'

'It is my hope that you keep an open mind and think of our future. The benefits to our Empire are incalculable, if we achieve our aims. Remember, you are a Mage-Imperator – no longer merely a man entitled to opinions. That right was cut away from you along with many things, when you ascended and took the *thism* to yourself.'

'By the same token,' Jora'h said, keeping his anger in check, 'I became your Mage-Imperator – and you must obey my commands.'

Udru'h's surprise appeared genuine. 'I would never dream of questioning your orders, Liege. But I hope you will consider carefully before making irrevocable changes.'

Jora'h brooded. Daro'h glanced at the two brothers, far out of his depth. The Mage-Imperator wished he could simply release all the human breeding prisoners and return them to the Terran Hanseatic League. None of them had ever seen Earth, probably knew very little about it, but they were descendants of once-hopeful colonists. They deserved better than . . . Dobro.

For nearly two centuries the Ildirans had kept this lie from the Hansa. Jora'h knew that if he revealed the terrible secret now, it could spell a diplomatic disaster, even trigger a war with the human race. And though the Ildiran Solar Navy was older and more powerful than the Earth Defence Forces, Jora'h did not underestimate the innovative abilities of the brash humans.

'Udru'h, we may not have any choice, despite my personal reservations. Do you truly believe my daughter has the innate potential to resolve this conflict with the hydrogues? The Klikiss robots have failed us, and I now suspect that they may choose to become our enemies.'

The news angered the Dobro Designate. 'If the Klikiss robots have failed us . . . or refused to mediate, then we have no choice but to send Osira'h as an intermediary to the hydrogues.'

'Since my daughter is to be the hope of the Ildiran Empire,' Jora'h said with a resigned sigh, 'then it is doubly important that I meet her.'

Udru'h smiled. 'Ah, now you see, Liege.'

Yes, he saw. But how he *hated* what he would be forced to do here on Dobro, in order to save the Empire.

FIFTY-SEVEN

SULLIVAN GOLD

Ready for the tense meeting that could well decide their survival, Sullivan Gold stood on the deck of his cloud harvester, wearing his best clothes. As for any formal business meeting, he had shaved, trimmed his hair, freshened his breath, and mentally prepared for this encounter. He wished Lydia could be there to straighten his collar and give him the final okay on his appearance.

Kolker told him he looked fine.

The green priest had already sent several messages and updates to his colleagues on the telink network, and they eagerly waited for news to relay to the Hansa. Nahton in the Whisper Palace had informed the King and the Chairman, but despite their tension and attention, Sullivan was on his own. The EDF could never send military aid here swiftly enough, nor would they want to risk a direct clash with the Solar Navy. No doubt the Earth government would not respond at all until they saw how he handled the situation.

Sullivan cleared his throat, hoping he wouldn't need to call in the cavalry. It was so embarrassing to need to be rescued.

A colourfully plated Ildiran shuttle emerged from the looming flagship warliner and made its way ponderously over to them. Sullivan dried his sweaty palms on the fabric of his warm jacket. 'Here we go, Kolker. It's all up to us. A chance to make a good first impression with our unexpected neighbours.'

Distracted, the green priest removed his fingers from his ever-present treeling. 'Sorry, Sullivan, what was that? I was concentrating on telink, telling everybody what was happening here.'

'I thought you already did that.'

'I was explaining that nothing new had occurred. Your Chairman is also listening eagerly.'

Sullivan sighed. 'Until now, life aboard our cloud-harvesting station was routine enough to allow for superfluous conversations, but not anymore. I need your full attention until this is resolved, Kolker. We can save our memoirs for later.'

The green priest's abashed smile disarmed Sullivan's annoyance. 'I will limit my communications . . . to the essentials.'

Eventually, almost fifteen minutes earlier than scheduled – on purpose? – the Adar's shuttle approached. The Ildiran vessel passed through the cloud harvester's atmosphere-condensing field, joined by a flurry of strong breezes, followed a stream of bright guidance lights to an appropriate landing pad, and set down. Sullivan's face was flushed, his cheeks burning in the brisk air. He fixed a smile on his face, as bright as if he were about to have the most important job interview of his life.

As the scrollwork hatch of the alien shuttle opened, Sullivan stepped forward to greet the two Ildirans. One, tall and proud and more than handsome by Earth standards, wore a meticulous military-style uniform. He spoke before Sullivan could utter a word of welcome. 'I am Adar Zan'nh, Commander of the Ildiran Solar Navy. As you requested, I have brought Hroa'x, my chief sky-mining engineer.' The second man had broader shoulders, shorter arms, and blunt facial features; he glanced around at the Hansa skymining equipment with intense curiosity.

Sullivan reached out his right hand. 'Well, this is my first meeting with an Ildiran. I sure can't wait to tell my grandchildren about this.' He hoped the comment would humanize him to the Ildiran military commander. *Humanize* him? He had to start thinking from a new perspective. 'Uh, I apologize if I don't know your traditions and acceptable behaviours. We like to extend a greeting by shaking hands. Like this.'

Zan'nh reluctantly accepted Sullivan's grip. His reply was pointed. 'It is our tradition *not* to set up skymines where we are not invited.'

'Yes, well . . . sorry about that. It was an unintentional oversight. A terrible misunderstanding.' Sullivan turned away, clearing his throat. 'Shall we talk inside the observation gallery, where it's warmer? I think we can find some drinks or snacks that you Ildirans might enjoy. A Hansa skymine isn't really the place for haute cuisine, but we've done our best. It's a social necessity.' He realized he was babbling, and stopped abruptly.

Intrigued and preoccupied, the alien mining engineer ran his eyes over the industrial equipment, scanning the process machinery as if comparing every detail to his own designs. Hroa'x moved forward to get a closer look. 'Ildirans need to go about skymining here on Qronha 3. I wish to get my own facility started. There is much work to do. Adar, when can we go back to get to work? How long will this discussion take?'

Zan'nh made a gesture for patience. 'You can begin soon, Hroa'x. This is a necessary meeting, and it will take as long as it needs.'

Carrying his potted treeling in the crook of his elbow, Kolker led the way into the enclosed cloud harvesting facility. Though Sullivan had never intended to hold board meetings or staff convocations on the cloud harvester – it was a rushed construction, not meant to be a full-fledged facility – the Hansa designs did include one large chamber complete with a long table and broad windows that looked out upon the clouds.

The green priest set his heavy pot on the end of the table and took a seat beside it. Without waiting for anyone else, he touched the thin trunk, and his lips moved silently as he sent a new report through the telink network. The Chairman would be eavesdropping, no doubt.

Sullivan paid more attention to his two important guests. Before the Adar's arrival, he'd hurriedly asked the galley staff to set out a variety of dishes, some of them following Lydia's own recipes. No one aboard the cloud harvester knew whether Ildirans preferred sweet confections or savoury snacks. What would impress them? Sullivan also set out several liqueurs, a pot of hot tea, and a pitcher of plain water, as well as a bottle of syrupy Passover wine that his wife had insisted he take with him.

'I tried to provide a variety,' he said to Zan'nh, indicating the refreshments with a flourish of his hand. 'Please, take what you like, or ask questions. What would you prefer?'

Sullivan took a seat at the side of the table, but the miner kithman remained standing, pacing the room and gazing out the window. 'I would prefer to begin skymining,' Hroa'x said. 'Soon.'

Zan'nh let out a faint but long-suffering sigh. 'Patience, Hroa'x.' He took a seat at the head of the table.

'Sullivan Gold, my father is the Mage-Imperator, and my predecessor, Adar Kori'nh, sacrificed himself to clear Qronha 3 of the hydrogues so that Ildirans might skymine again. *Ildirans*. Kori'nh's memory will live in the *Saga of Seven Suns*. I will make certain of that. Why do you feel justified in claiming the spoils of that victory?'

Sullivan grasped the significance of the commander's concern.

'I . . . realize that your predecessor had no intention of achieving his victory so that humans could take advantage of the opportunity.'

'Cease your operations here, pack up your equipment, and return to Earth. You do not belong on Qronha 3.'

Sullivan spread his hands on the table. 'Now, let's not be too hasty, all right? Aren't the Hansa and the Ildiran Empire good friends? Don't we share a common enemy in the hydrogues? Our Earth Defence Forces have fought bravely and sacrificed themselves against the hydrogues, just as your valiant Adar did. With the attacks on our colony worlds, we've suffered plenty, too – and we did not ask for this war any more than you did.'

Zan'nh's answer was quick and cold. 'Humans ignited the Klikiss Torch and destroyed a hydrogue homeworld.'

'Well, you know it was never our intent to incite hostilities – and we've done everything humanly possible to atone for that mistake. Look, I'm just a skyminer trying to do my job.'

'As am I – but I can't get started yet,' Hroa'x said impatiently. 'These are old matters and irrelevant ones.'

'You bet they are,' Sullivan agreed with the gruff miner. He smiled reassuringly, attempting to increase his charm. 'Say, neither of you has sampled any of the food or drink.'

'We do not require hospitality. And your food may not be perfectly compatible with our biochemistry.'

Sullivan covered his frown. Refusing hospitality? Did they fear poison? He nibbled on a piece of cheese. 'Maybe the Hansa made a rash and ill-advised decision to send a cloud harvester here without first obtaining permission from your Mage-Imperator. I can see why you're upset. I wouldn't want someone setting up a business in my family's backyard either. But this is a huge planet, after all – what does it hurt? We meant no harm, nor have we caused any that I can see. Our presence in no way hinders *your* efforts to produce as much ekti as you can. The sky is certainly big enough for both of us. Besides, isn't there safety in numbers? We could help each other in the event of an emergency.'

'Help each other . . . in what way?' Zan'nh asked. 'These facilities could never be successfully defended against a hydrogue attack, alone or together.'

'Well, no, but other emergencies could happen, right?'

Hroa'x was impatient. 'We waste time. Why squabble over boundaries that do not exist? Human cloud-harvesting activities will not diminish the hydrogen supply here. Instead of this discussion, I could be setting up my facilities. That is my priority. Diplomacy wastes too many valuable working hours.'

Sullivan suddenly saw something in the young Adar's expression and realized with a flash of insight that Zan'nh wanted to resolve this standoff as much as he did. He was looking for a neat and acceptable end to the crisis.

Sullivan continued to smile, hoping the initial tension had begun to dissipate. 'Please, Adar, let's not make this into a conflict. How about this – Ildirans can set up as many ekti factories as you want, and I give you my word of honour that we'll stay out of your way. Our efforts won't hinder you at all.'

At the far end of the table, Kolker stroked his treeling and continued to report everything.

Sullivan pressed, 'The Hansa needs the fuel as much as you do – in fact, it was another Ildiran, an Adar like yourself, who gave us the designs for your stardrive in the first place. Nobody had a problem with that. Surely you wouldn't deny us the ability to fly our spacecraft?'

Zan'nh seemed as hard a negotiator as Sullivan. 'If you were to remain here, on an Ildiran world that *we* have made safe for skymining, it would not be without a price. The Mage-Imperator would require a tax of some sort.'

Sullivan saw an opening for negotiation, the first move in the bargaining game, and he seized it. 'Perhaps I could offer a small percentage of the ekti we produce.' Taking the initiative, he poured a glass of water for each of them, judging the other beverages to be questionable.

The Adar had still said very little, sitting rigidly upright; Sullivan wondered how much of it might be an act. In a conspiratorial tone, Sullivan said, 'Look, we haven't been bothered by the hydrogues so far – but we may have only a limited time before that happens. We should all work hard to harvest as much ekti as we possibly can before it's too late.'

'What sort of percentage do you offer?' Zan'nh asked. 'I must take back something acceptable to my Mage-Imperator.'

Sullivan had never known Ildirans to be overly greedy, nor did they seem to have experience at haggling, since they were all connected by an odd sort of telepathy. So, he took a chance and initially suggested an insignificant fraction of the cloud harvester's output, an exploratory gesture to open negotiations. To his surprise, Zan'nh accepted it immediately. Sullivan would definitely score points with the Hansa for this! In his heart, he knew that the Solar Navy commander had been more concerned with finding an honourable solution than making a profit.

'Very well. I'm glad that's settled. We really should be friends through all this.' Sullivan reached out to shake the Adar's hand again. 'If we're agreed, then we can all get to work. I'll send a portion of our next cargo load directly over to your facilities.' Unconsciously, he wiped a hand across his sweaty forehead. 'I'd like to celebrate our new spirit of cooperation. Would you be interested in—'

Hroa'x cut him off, turning to Zan'nh. 'If our mission here is complete, Adar, must we waste further time? We should return to the warliners now and see to our sky harvester. I still have much to do before it is running at full capacity. Much to do.' The miner kithman turned his blunt-featured face to Sullivan. 'These negotiations will become moot the moment the hydrogues return. Why waste another second?'

Zan'nh nodded. 'And make no mistake, the hydrogues *will* return.'

FIFTY-EIGHT

TASIA TAMBLYN

The hydrogue gas planet, dead now for thousands of years, was nothing more than a burned-out scar in space.

'No signs of life at all,' said Subcommander Ramirez. After deploying the Klikiss Torch at Ptoro, Tasia had managed to get her navigator and some of the other competent bridge officers promoted one grade. 'Residual thermal readings, molecular and heavy-element byproducts from nuclear burning, but this obviously started out as a gas supergiant, not a natural star. Must have been Torched a long time ago.'

Chief Scientist Palawu's analysis had identified twenty-one small, dead stars with anomalous signatures. As her survey ship approached the cold cinder, the sensors verified that this was clearly another remnant of an incinerated hydrogue world. Tasia felt a lingering anger tempered with smugness. 'Glad we weren't the only ones to give the drogue bastards a hotfoot.'

As soon as he learned of Palawu's discovery, Admiral Stromo had called for an expedition to investigate these old hydrogue graveyards. This was the fourth such burned-out planet her survey team had visited.

As her Manta orbited the dim, lifeless world, Tasia's crew took volumes of images. She imagined how this planet might have looked before the Torch, an immense ball of pale clouds, the sort of place where Roamers could have operated profitable skymines. Now, after millennia, the artificial sun had burned out all its raw fuel. Some of the exotic materials and supermolecules left behind might have been interesting, but she doubted even eccentric Kotto Okiah would have had the nerve to poke into a place like that.

The EDF hoped that by performing post-mortem analyses on these murdered planets they could learn more about the long-term effectiveness of the Torch. Tasia had the sneaking suspicion that General Lanyan simply wanted to gloat over places where the hydrogues had been resoundingly defeated.

In a few thousand years, Ptoro would look similar to this, burning out as all its fuel was exhausted. Oncier, too – if the drogues hadn't already snuffed that one out, as Tasia had witnessed with her own eyes.

'Log it,' she said after two hours. 'We've got the rest of this list to confirm.'

At their next stop, Tasia and her crew sat back in awe to find the system's main star completely under siege. The gas giant itself was dark and cold, burned out long ago. Now, the hydrogues were targeting the much larger central sun.

In a furious battle, ellipsoidal faeros fireballs swarmed upwards, clashing against literally millions of warglobes that lunged in like piranhas. Bolts of incredible energy lashed back and forth, while the hydrogues drove their diamond spheres through the fringes of the hot corona and skated over the outer layers of plasma, unleashing titanic weapons from above.

Tasia had seen a similar battle at the test site of Oncier, but that ignited gas giant had only been a small dwarf star – this was a full-sized sun, a vastly larger battleground on which the hydrogues and faeros fought each other. Giant loops of solar flares rose upwards, spewing plasma flames that curled back around, falling into the roiling sun like blood spurting from a severed artery.

Warglobes pressed closer, swarming in space. The faeros defenders crashed into them, fireballs engulfing the diamond spheres so that both were obliterated. Volley after volley of hydrogue ships streamed in from outside the system, enough glinting reinforcements to blot out the star.

'Take your readings and let's get the hell out of here,' Tasia said. 'Shizz, look at those blasts!'

A column of dense ionized gas rocketed up from the surface of the sun to engulf a flurry of warglobes, shattering the enemy vessels. Tasia wondered if the faeros themselves had tinkered with the mechanics of the star, altered its physics to use the flare as a weapon.

'What the hell are we doing in this war?' Sergeant Zizu said, his voice no more than an awed whisper.

More warglobes arrived, unleashing retaliatory strikes. Because a hydrogue gas planet in this system had been snuffed out by the Klikiss Torch long ago, Tasia wondered if the deep-core aliens bore a grudge. Were their memories long enough to harbour revenge for ten thousand years?

Of course they were.

Flares continued to shoot up like cannon blasts. Tasia slumped back in her command chair, once again feeling incredibly small in this enormous and ancient conflict.

'On the bright side,' Tasia muttered, 'with the faeros and the hydrogues kicking each other's butts, they're too busy to come after us.'

FIFTY-NINE

KING PETER

'Chairman Wenceslas has called another high-level Hansa meeting in secret,' OX reported to King Peter. 'You asked me to inform you whenever I learn of such an appointment.'

'Thank you, OX. I think I'll attend.'

Dressed in a Prussian-blue military outfit, his 'serious business attire' instead of the ceremonial robes he donned for public appearances, Peter arrived at the private conference room even before the Chairman and his cronies. When Basil entered with the pale and hairless Deputy Cain, he frowned to see the King sitting there, but did not otherwise acknowledge Peter's presence.

General Lanyan arrived with a shadow of stubble on his cheeks that showed he was several hours past his scheduled shave, followed closely by Admiral Stromo, who carried a portable datascreen as well as hardcopy summary printouts. Deputy Cain sat next to the Chairman and they all waited in silence, flicking glances at Peter, who remained quiet, behaving himself.

Basil finally spoke. 'Direct your attention to me, please. *I* called this meeting, not the King. General Lanyan, your summary of the Roamer problem?'

The military commander cleared his throat, collecting his thoughts. 'As you know, Mr Chairman, for some time now our intel teams have had standing orders to gather any information on Roamer ship movements and possible hidden settlements. I've updated the analyses I compiled more than five years ago.' He looked down at his notes.

'I'm sorry to say the situation has only grown worse. I am convinced that the rebellious clans have stockpiled stardrive fuel and other resources that, by rights, should have gone into the Terran war effort. Their selfishness is hampering our ability to protect the Hansa and its colonies. They are hurting us by their stubbornness, and we cannot ignore it.'

Admiral Stromo barely contained his anger. 'They've picked the worst possible time to hit us with this childish embargo. Their unwarranted refusal to trade ekti delivers a severe blow just when our new colonization initiative is gathering momentum.'

Lanyan continued, gathering steam. 'Remember several years ago, just before the hydrogues, when the Roamer pirate Rand Sorengaard preyed upon Hansa colonies? Think of the damage he caused – but more importantly, it shows the mindset these lawless clans hold.'

Stromo picked up the thread, as if they had practised this interchange. 'I say, if they have chosen to withdraw our resources when we need them most, then they have chosen to become our enemies. It is in our best interests to declare war on the clans, trounce them quickly, and be done with it. Such a plan could easily be accomplished, and would provide a clear example for all humans who might want to hoard resources.'

Peter had intended to sit quietly and observe, but he could not keep himself from pointing out the obvious. 'Excuse me, Basil, but

Speaker Peroni's demands seem reasonable enough. If a crime was indeed committed, why not simply track down the perpetrators of the alleged piracy and renounce any such actions in the future?'

'Because it's outright blackmail,' Lanyan snapped. 'And we don't cooperate with blackmailers.'

Basil was cooler. 'We have never been shown any incontrovertible proof of such piracy. It's likely the Roamers are simply jumping at shadows and trying to blame others.'

Peter pressed his lips together. 'I notice you didn't actually deny the allegations. Do you intend to authorize more such raids on Roamer cargo ships?'

'Oh, please! This is ridiculous,' Stromo snapped.

'Admitting to such acts is politically out of the question, whether or not the allegations are true,' Basil said. 'We cannot let a gang of undisciplined space gypsies dictate terms to the Terran Hanseatic League. In times of war, we can no longer turn a blind eye to their lawless independence. Instead, we should do everything in our power to unify the fragmented factions of humanity against a common enemy. The Roamers must submit to the strength of the majority for the good of our race. It may be our only chance.'

Eldred Cain spoke with a quiet, calm confidence that cut through the drone of murmured responses at the table. 'It may interest you, sir, that I have found a legal means by which we can simply and legitimately annex the Roamer clans.' The pale Deputy looked at Peter. 'It's tidy enough that even the King should have no objections.'

Peter tried to show his dutiful willingness to listen. 'It's completely legal?'

'I have undertaken a thorough analysis of the original treaty and documentation signed by all eleven generation ships before they departed from Earth over three centuries ago. Each vessel –

including the *Kanaka*, which provided the seed for the Roamer clans – agreed to certain irrevocable terms.

'At the time of departure, the colonist families assumed this would be a one-way trip. The generation ships were slow-moving vessels, and the passengers hoped to find a habitable world and settle there for ever. Even so, the governments of Earth feared that some day these prodigal children might become warlike and set their sights on returning home as conquerors. So they required the captains and colonists to swear in a binding document – one which specifically applies to themselves *and* all of their descendants – that they would "take no action, direct or indirect, that would harm Mother Earth".'

Cain looked around, waiting for them to understand the implications. Basil finally smiled. 'I see. And cutting off our main source of stardrive fuel at such a critical juncture certainly qualifies as being harmful to Earth.'

'Without question, Mr Chairman. It is barely even open to debate.'

'Superb reasoning, Mr Deputy!' Lanyan said. 'It provides all the justification we could possibly need. The EDF can move on the Roamers any time we please.'

Peter leaned forward, angry but careful not to overstep his bounds and give the Chairman reason to eject him from the room. 'Excuse me, but why must we "move" on them? If you are confident in your legal argument, we should present it to Speaker Peroni and give her a chance to revise the Roamer response, perhaps begin a limited number of ekti shipments again to establish goodwill while we negotiate the matter. In fact, I see no reason why we can't announce that we condemn further acts of piracy against Roamer ships, without addressing the question of whether or not their accusation was true in the first place.'

'That would solve only the immediate part of the problem,' Basil said. 'But I refuse to reward their efforts at coercion. Without question Roamer unruliness would become a thorn in our sides again and again. We need to decisively put an end to their . . . disruptive manipulations, so that we can concentrate on winning the important war. The hydrogues have been relatively quiescent, even after we used four more Klikiss Torches against them. It is time to swiftly and decisively defeat the Roamers and earn wholehearted public support for the victory.'

Admiral Stromo distributed his printed summaries. There weren't enough copies for Peter, but the King extended his hand and waited, until the liaison officer surrendered his personal copy. Stromo said, 'Truly, King Peter, this will provide the greatest benefit in the long run. You'll see.' He linked his display screen to the table, and enlarged diagrams were projected across the matte crystal surface.

With a growing lump in his throat, Peter looked at the descriptions for a direct invasion of known Roamer outposts.

'I assigned a team of my best tactical experts to develop alternative strategies. The Roamers have always been notoriously secretive, but we know more than they realize about their movements, distribution, and activities. By backtracking flight paths and analysing elemental breakdowns from processed materials in their shipments, we have estimated the locations of some of their mines and factories. Though we've been aware of several important sites for years, we have kept that information until it could be put to good use. Now it is time. Several of these places have large ekti stockpiles just waiting for the taking.'

'The stockpiles are probably even more bloated now,' Lanyan pointed out, 'since the Roamers aren't selling ekti to us anymore.'

Looking pleased, Basil tapped his fingers on the table again. 'I suggest we put together a powerful EDF crew to sweep into one of these depots and confiscate the fuel for our war needs. A surgical strike to show them we mean business. They'll see they're out of their league.'

Peter could not believe what he was hearing. 'But now you *are* talking outright piracy, Basil.'

'Deputy Cain has just offered a legitimate legal rationale, therefore it is merely an exercise of eminent domain, not piracy at all. The Roamers have little or no military defences and rely on their own secrecy for protection. They know we outgun them, and they cannot afford long-term hostilities. We'll force them to join us, to everyone's benefit.'

Eldred Cain turned to Peter, sounding reasonable. 'King Peter, we have always been willing to pay for the stardrive fuel supplied by the Roamers. We have even accepted their exorbitantly inflated prices over the past several years. But if they will not sell to us, we have no choice but to obtain ekti in some other fashion. It is a strategic imperative.'

'What about our new cloud harvester on Qronha 3?' Peter offered. 'Another shipment is already on the way, now that they've worked out a truce with the Ildirans there.'

'A good start, but far from adequate,' Cain said. 'We would need several dozen more cloud-harvesters running at full capacity just to meet our minimal defence needs.'

Basil tapped his fingers impatiently on the tabletop. 'No, as a matter of principle, the Roamers must join us. Their professed independence must be subordinate to humanity's survival.'

'Those damned clans have been overconfident for too long,' Lanyan said. 'They've got too big for their britches.'

Peter understood the Hansa's logic, even felt part of the same desperation, but he was sure the Roamers would not acquiesce as easily as Basil expected. The open aggression would only confirm their negative view of the Hansa. 'Do you expect the Roamers to just roll over and surrender? They will hate us for generations.'

As if in partial concession to the King's objections, Basil pondered the military plans. 'Bear in mind, General, that we don't want to cause any more harm than is absolutely necessary. Pick one of the depots and form your plan. I want a clean and efficient operation, with minimal bloodshed – preferably no loss of lives at all.'

'That may be difficult, sir,' Lanyan said.

'We want to make a point, not rack up civilian casualties. We need to show the Roamers who's the boss and put an end to this damaging behaviour, nothing more.' Basil stood up. 'Once we get enough ekti to establish solid colonies on the rediscovered Klikiss worlds, we won't need the Roamer clans. Then they can go out and starve themselves, for all I care. But first we have to get the stardrive fuel we need. That is our highest priority.' The Chairman dismissed the meeting. 'Now get to work, gentlemen.'

SIXTY

JESS TAMBLYN

❖ **G**et in your ships and follow me,' Jess said to the eleven Roamer volunteers. He climbed back aboard his water-and-pearl vessel, stepping through the permeable film and immersing himself in the enclosed ocean microcosm. Once away from any possibility of touching another person in the crowded confines of Rendezvous, he felt a wash of relief. Jess had already said his loving and bittersweet farewells to Cesca, standing as close as he dared.

Like a departing parade, the group of Roamer 'water bearers' left Rendezvous followed by calls of good luck. A small vessel piloted by Nikko Chan Tylar sprinted forward, catching up with Jess's pearly ship and sending a message via the standard Roamer commsystem Jess had installed to stay in contact with his new followers, though it had required modifications to operate in the watery environment. 'We're ready to get to work, Jess. Lead the way.'

Jess accelerated the spherical vessel, and the Roamer ships raced along beside him . . .

*

When they reached the first uncharted world, they dropped to slow orbital speed, and Jess guided his volunteers through a murky fog of clouds. This had once been a sterile place, swept with storms, but now the open water was filled with wental lifeforce, like a great battery supercharged and ready to burst with elemental power. He could see the surging tides of light and power, crackling lines like a circulatory system through the entire ocean, the entire planet, like a storm of sparkling and benevolent life.

On its descent, his wental ship attracted silvery tendrils of lightning that skittered gently across the metallized coral framework. It was a probing touch, a soft brushing of electrical fingertips controlled by the wentals that had infused the whole isolated planet. They welcomed Jess and his companions.

The sentient water contained within his bubble vessel thrummed with unmitigated joy. On his first visit, this had been a dark and forbidding world, but now the angry storms had been purified by living water that stirred the cauldron of thriving wentals that filled the energized sea below. Already the dispersed water entities had grown and separated from the first body of wentals, developing their own thoughts, but each wental remained a facet of the same overall being.

Jess's vessel landed on the open sea, where it floated like a giant soap bubble. Whitecaps lapped against the sides of the ship, alive and glowing. Nearby, the eleven Roamer ships dropped down, seeking a place to land on a flat atoll.

Nikko emerged from his family craft, drinking in the rough, brisk air. Suffused with the wental lifeforce, the environment had changed enough that the humans no longer needed breathing masks, as Jess had on his first visit. He glanced at the distant patterns of lightning that danced from thunderheads to the ocean and shouted to Jess. 'Looks like you followed your Guiding Star back to the Garden of Eden. This whole planet's an ocean, but it's completely . . . alive.'

'Yes, every droplet of water, every cloud. It's charged with living energy.'

Jess used his own connection with the wentals to be part of this sentient ocean. He stepped out onto the choppy surface of the water and walked from his globular vessel across the wavetops. Enhanced surface tension buoyed each step, keeping him from sinking, until he reached the rocks where the others waited for him. The Roamers stared at him in awe.

Jess gestured past the wave-swept shore. As if on cue, a symphony of lightning played like musical notes across the sky. 'See what the wentals can do? We've got to help bring them into the fight against the hydrogues.'

Nikko grinned. 'We're ready.'

'I could easily have given you water from my own ship at Rendezvous . . . but I didn't want you to accept this mission just on the basis of my words. Look around you! I needed you to *see* this power, this gathering storm the wentals can command against the hydrogues! Witness the potential.'

All the Roamers stared at the fervid ocean. Currents of glowing life force streamed through the waves, anxious to be turned loose. The water elementals made the alien seas thrash and seethe. His companions muttered appreciatively.

'Even a sample of wental water can spread and reproduce in another body of liquid, like a match lighting one candle after another. I could do this alone, one world at a time, but it would take too long.

Jess dipped his hand into the water and held up a palmful of the dripping silvery liquid. 'The wentals are as eager to go as you are. Here, take as much as you like. Fill containers, and then disperse them to each world on your lists.'

Nikko hurried back to his small craft and rolled out a hollow polymer drum. 'Should I just . . . dip this into the ocean?' But as the young man brought the container close, the water itself came alive. Looking like a jellyfish, it rose up in a gelatinous plume, wavered, and then deposited itself into the barrel; whatever did not fit sloshed back into the ocean. 'Shizz, did you see that?'

The other Roamers ran to their crafts and brought out containers. Limbs of vibrant water rose up to fill each one. With the cooperation of the wental inside, Nikko found that he could carry the laden barrel as if it weighed nothing at all, as if water entities could somehow manipulate the gravity on this whole planet. 'It feels electrical. My fingers tingle.'

Jess stood watching his new recruits fill their cargo holds with the wental essence. They would disperse, and they would find other ocean worlds that could make the strange new ally strong. He envied these volunteers their sense of wonder.

He wished he could go with them, but he had a different mission now, and it consumed him almost as much as his love for Cesca.

SIXTY-ONE

CESCA PERONI

Searching for Jhy Okiah, Cesca found that the old woman had suited up and gone outside to drift among the conjoined rocks, inspecting the girders and cables that held the asteroid cluster together. The connector beams kept Rendezvous from flying apart under its own gravity and inertia. The red dwarf's dull light shed thick illumination as clan ships came and went.

Because she had lived for so many years in the extreme low gravity of Rendezvous, Jhy Okiah could never endure the oppressive tug of a planet again. Her bones were brittle despite exercise and mineral supplements. She was simply *old*, yet she showed no signs of weakness. She insisted on doing useful work for the Roamers.

The cold emptiness might not have been the best place to have a conversation or bare her soul, but Cesca suited up anyway. She used her exhaust jets to manoeuvre along the pocked exteriors of the rocky debris that formed cosy habitats.

When she was younger, Cesca and other clan children had joined the Governess compy UR in learning how to use a protective suit for space excursions. All Roamers had to become proficient in such skills.

Jetting forward to where Jhy Okiah tinkered with connector bolts driven deep into the main asteroid, Cesca activated the line-of-sight communicator. Provided they were close enough to each other, she and the former Speaker could have a completely private communication.

The old woman floated carefree, relaxing her arms and legs. Her long grey hair was confined in her helmet. 'Plenty of clan members are qualified for this inspection duty, Cesca. Don't you have more important work? Or are you practising for your retirement already, like me?'

'You make that comment so often, I have to wonder if you don't like talking to me anymore.'

'I'm just remembering that *I* never had time for wandering around like this.'

Cesca pulled her way closer along a girder. 'You taught me to keep in touch with the clans. Roamers are held together by connections of family and friendship, as you taught me yourself. Besides, after cutting off trade with the Big Goose we'll have a few more people cut off from their usual activities. And Jess is gone with his volunteers . . .' Her voice trailed off.

'And you miss him.'

'Of course I miss him. But I also admire his new passion, tackling an amazing mission that may save us all. Governing the clans is always a full-time job, but I'd like to do something significant while waiting for the Hansa response. Roamers have so much potential.'

Jhy Okiah chuckled. 'Even if you didn't exactly agree with the clan leaders and their rigid embargo, I have no doubt you'll get us through this.'

'I'm still waiting for the other shoe to drop. We haven't heard a word of response from the Big Goose. What's taking them so long?'

'Bureaucracy, no doubt.'

Cesca sighed, as always weighed down by the responsibilities of her office. 'We're preparing a contact team to go to the Ildiran Empire, to propose trade terms with the new Mage-Imperator. We've sent out feelers to some of the smaller Hansa colonies that were already cut off, since they're not getting any help and support from Earth.'

She looked through her faceplate at all the activity around Rendezvous. Roamer business had been quiet since the clans had broken off trade. Now their cargo ships, ekti skimmers, and resource mining operations were adapting to the new situation. Overhead, cargo ships brought in new supplies of ekti from Hurricane Depot; others departed with materials en route to fringe Roamer settlements, such as frozen Jonah 12 and ringed Osquivel.

'It sounds like we'll find plenty of other customers and markets,' Jhy Okiah said.

Cesca continued, letting her thoughts flow. She had always benefited from using the former Speaker as a sounding board. 'And what about Theroc? They're still reeling from the hydrogue attack. If I'd married Reynald right away, I could have been there—' She brightened suddenly, realizing something the clans could accomplish. 'You know . . . if Roamers are capable of establishing outposts on molten-hot worlds and frozen moons and airless asteroids, then we certainly have the ability to help clear a burned forest and rebuild dwellings for the Theron people.'

'Then go help them,' the former Speaker said, drifting in a slowly turning somersault. 'We've got some Roamer ships available, especially now. Their captains are just looking for something to do.' She anchored herself to the surface of a depot rock, making a system note of several thick struts that looked as if they could use reinforcement.

Roamers had to worry about where they would get such basics

as air and water and light, whereas the Therons had been blessed with everything right at their fingertips. The original refugee humans had dreamed of this sort of colony when they'd departed from Earth in their generation ships. Those people had found it, but the Roamers never had. Now, however, the Therons didn't have sufficient skills or ingenuity to pull themselves out of their disaster. They needed expert assistance.

Cesca raised her chin. 'You're right. The clans have all the equipment, engineers, and technology we need. Roamer engineering in a Theron forest! An unlikely match, but we can make it work. We'll help them pick up the pieces.'

'You can accomplish anything you set your mind to, Speaker Peroni.' The old woman nudged her, sending Cesca tumbling slowly towards the main airlocks and the docking doors. She had to use air jets to right herself.

Jhy Okiah planted her booted feet on the outer surface of the asteroid. 'Now let me drift here in peace. I sleep better knowing Rendezvous is not going to fall apart while I'm having a nice dream.'

'You enjoy your rest – it's well deserved. But in the meantime, *I* have a lot of work to do.'

SIXTY-TWO

CELLI

After months of hard labour in the ruined forests, the Theron survivors began to suffer from prolonged exhaustion. Yarrod, speaking for the green priests, finally issued a compassionate plea from the worldforest. 'Rest! The trees say this effort will take a great deal of time. If you all falter now, who will care for the trees? You must not hurt yourselves.'

Standing beside him, Mother Alexa added, 'Already eleven of our people have died in accidents among the fallen trees because they were too tired and became careless.'

The weary Therons who gathered in the temple ring of blackened stumps dragged themselves off to rest. Green priests draped their arms around the scaled trunk of any nearby worldtree and fell deeply asleep, dreaming through telink.

Solimar's shoulders sagged. Soot smudged his green skin. 'I am too troubled to sleep, Celli. If I did, I'm afraid I'd drown in the nightmares.'

Celli smiled at him, making an effort to keep her spirits up. 'Then come with me. Remember that healthy grove of smaller worldtrees we found yesterday? Why not show me your treedancer moves, and I'll demonstrate a few of mine? I think you've forgot how to relax.'

He sighed. 'Treedancing . . . it's been so long. I don't know where I'll find the energy – but how can we dance among the trees now, in the midst of all this?' Despair and pain hung like fog in the air.

'I bet the trees will draw as much good cheer from it as we will.' Taking his hand, she led him to his gliderbike, and they flew off, heading in a straight line off into the distance, where they had found a partially intact grove.

Solimar had a spring in his step as they approached the patch of living trees. 'I've lost track of what it feels like to be around the true life of the forest because I've been so focused on all this destruction. Here at least there's something to celebrate.' He turned to her with a smile, stroking the golden bark of a nearby worldtree. 'And, it's hard to believe, but I do feel ready for dancing.'

Though his body was large and muscular, Solimar moved like a gazelle. Springing forward, he caught a nearby thin trunk, spun himself around, then lifted his feet as if to take flight. Bounding to another tree, he began to scale it. Celli ran after him, eager to show Solimar that even though he was the green priest, she had just as much ability when it came to the sport.

Treedancing had developed as a combination athletic competition and dance, but had evolved into a form of communion with the worldforest. The original green priests came from a variety of Theron colonists. Some of them were scholars content to sit and read to the trees all day long, but athletically inclined acolytes wanted to express themselves physically, through fluid motion. To the great tree mind, the lissome dances were just as fascinating as human legends and scientific achievements.

Celli scrambled up a trunk, swung from one branch to a second, then flipped up and over it before springing off again, somersaulting in the air to land gracefully between two trees on the ground. With each movement, she felt energy and joy surge through her to counter the oppressive pall of soot and gloom.

Solimar spun on his toes as he touched down on a springy branch, then launched himself even higher. Celli bounded up a tree beside him, grabbed a branch, and swung towards him. Feeling daring and trusting her green priest friend, she called, 'Catch me, Solimar!' She released her grip on the boughs and soared across a void.

The muscular young man did not flinch, but caught her easily, as if they had practised the routine a hundred times. 'That was either brave or stupid, Celli,' he said as he used her momentum to swing her up onto a branch beside him.

'I knew you wouldn't let me fall.' She hugged him close as they stood together, carefully balanced and catching their breath.

Some treedance moves were freeform, acrobatics and ballet combined with vigorous gymnastics. The result was a jazz of movement, an impromptu physical symphony. Connected by telink, the trees themselves could live vicariously through the green priest dancers; the motion liberated them from the deep roots that anchored them to the planet.

Solimar laughed with sheer ecstasy as he bounced from branch to branch. Celli saw with astonishment that he kept his eyes closed and let the trees guide him through telink. She thought it must have been a long time since the forest felt such exuberance. The other exhausted green priests, most of whom were resting now, probably felt the same rush as they dreamed in telink with the worldforest.

Unable to share in his symbiotic connection, Celli let herself be content with watching her friend's happiness. An independent girl, she herself had never felt the call to become an acolyte, though her brother Beneto and uncle Yarrod were both green priests. That would not stop her from finding solace through her own joyous movements even among the blackened and broken worldforest.

As they danced together, she felt they were both drawing energy from the wounded trees . . . and giving it back as well. In her mind, she sensed the trees sharing a secret warm smile with the exuberant dancers. The forest was waking up and remembering – thanks to them.

Finally, when they'd exhausted their bodies, she and Solimar sat together on a wide branch, panting and sweating. Celli laughed and leaned against him in a comfortable, intimate moment. 'Weren't we supposed to be relaxing?'

Solimar's eyes and expression held a potent vitality that she hadn't seen since the day he'd rescued her from the burning fungus-reef. 'It may surprise you, Celli, but I feel more rested now than I have in a long, long time.' His fingers touched the hard bark, and he drifted into telink. He was smiling when he came back out. 'And the trees would like very much for us to do this again.'

SIXTY-THREE

KING PETER

E starra wasn't entirely certain they could trust OX, though the Teacher compy had been very useful in gathering reliable information. 'He's a Hansa machine, programmed to follow a certain set of orders.'

Her dark eyes shone in the bright light from the royal suite's balcony, and Peter felt a giddy rush just looking at his beautiful Queen. In spite of all his crises and ordeals, the machinations and responsibilities, Peter knew he was loved and safe when he was with her.

She glanced uncomfortably at OX, who stood attentive, as if participating in the discussion. He reported the results of his quiet investigations daily to the King. 'How do we know he's helping us instead of the Chairman?'

Peter turned to the compy. 'Because he also has moral programming. OX was designed centuries ago, before the Hansa existed in anything like its present form. He was put aboard a generation ship and sent away, never expecting to come back. His entire reason for existence was to teach the descendants of humanity and instil in them the beliefs, traditions, and morals we hold dear as a civilization. That moral programming is still active, isn't it, OX?'

The little compy looked like a child-sized loyal soldier. 'My programming gives me latitude for making assessments and choices. Though I am ostensibly retained by the Terran Hanseatic League, my core programming instructs me to serve the interests of the human race as a whole.' His optical sensors brightened, but his voice remained moderate and sincere. 'Since I myself discovered the explosive device hidden aboard your royal yacht, I am aware of the Chairman's plot to assassinate you. According to my moral programming, murdering any human being is wrong, especially to achieve political ends. Therefore, the man who orders it is misguided, even if he believes he is acting for the good of humanity.

'Furthermore, when I expressed my doubts about relying on untested Klikiss robot designs to create the Soldier compies, Chairman Wenceslas refused to consider the question. That is illogical. In summary, I have determined that his judgement is faulty. From my interactions with you and Queen Estarra, I have concluded that you, too, will serve the interests of the entire human race without regard to political affiliation. Your moral foundation is strong. Thus, I am obliged to assist you in working against him. I cannot continue to follow contradictory orders from the Terran Hanseatic League.'

Peter chuckled. 'Best of all, Basil won't ever suspect it. He hasn't looked twice at any compy, except as a resource. That's one of his greatest weaknesses: he is blind to the obvious.' He put his arm around Estarra's waist, and she seemed to relax slightly. They sat down together on a bench, and OX turned to face them. 'So, what's your report on Prince Daniel today?'

'My instructions have not been rescinded. Chairman Wenceslas still hopes Prince Daniel can be brought into line. Therefore, he has urged me to be more rigorous and draconian in my training to prepare him.'

Estarra remained concerned. 'He's got to see that Daniel would never be a competent ruler.'

'Daniel doesn't have to be competent. He simply has to make a good show and follow orders.' But then Peter smiled to himself. Perhaps he could convince OX to actively sabotage the Prince's training, so that he would never become a workable alternative . . .

That evening, after all the cupola torches had been lit, the King and Queen found themselves without political or social obligations. Longing for quiet and happy times, Peter made a suggestion that he knew would delight her.

Royal guards led them into the too-rarely-used swimming cove. The misty grotto was filled with ferns and flowers, and low illumination gave the romantic appearance of a moonlight swim.

The warm water surrounded Peter and Estarra like a bath as they splashed together. Estarra wore the same turquoise-and-purple bathing suit from their first swim on their wedding night, and she still looked dazzling in it. Peter stroked after her. 'For our own mental health, we should make a point to swim here more often.'

When he opened the gates and sent a pulsing tone through the water, dolphins came swimming in from their tanks. They chattered and splashed, happy to have human company in their play area.

Estarra answered him with a wan smile, and he was determined to cheer her up. Peter didn't think her mood was fear or anger, but a sense of deep sorrow. 'What's wrong, Estarra? I thought you liked the dolphins.'

'I love them. I just wish . . . I remember back on Theroc when I swam in the Looking Glass Lakes.' She let out a breath in a long, low sigh. 'I miss Reynald and Beneto. In fact, the night Reynald became the Theron Father was when Chairman Wenceslas and Sarein convinced him that I should marry you.'

'Sometimes political schemes aren't so terrible,' Peter said, kissing her. 'Are they?'

They clung together in the warm water. 'No, I'll never regret that. I love you so much, Peter. I could never have hoped for such a wonderful man. But not even you can fill the place that my brothers had in my heart.' She smiled sadly. 'They were wonderful, too. Beneto never wanted anything to do with leadership. He hurt nobody – and yet the hydrogues wiped out Corvus Landing. Then they attacked Theroc and killed Reynald.' Tears welled in her eyes. 'What did Beneto and Reynald ever do to the hydrogues? Why did so many victims have to pay the price because the drogues are upset over . . . Oncier?'

'It's much more than Oncier,' Peter said, wishing he could say more to comfort her.

When Estarra shook her head, droplets of water streamed down her long twisted hair. 'The hydrogues attacked Theroc intentionally, and Beneto died because of his love for the worldtrees.'

He held her tighter. 'We may never know the drogues' precise reasons. All we can hope is that we defeat them one way or another.'

'Right now I'm not concerned with grand political implications, Peter. I was just grieving for my brothers, and my home.'

One of the dolphins swam beside them, to play, but Estarra kept her arms around Peter's neck. He knew there was nothing he could say, so he just swam alongside her, being there and sharing her sadness.

SIXTY-FOUR

SAREIN

When Basil asked her to join him at sunset in the rooftop gardens, Sarein was girlishly pleased that he would choose such a romantic rendezvous. She wondered if he would surprise her with a fine dinner, complete with Dremen saltpond caviar and preserved Theron insect steaks from Rlinda Kett's last gourmet stockpiles.

The fantasy lasted only a moment, though. Sarein knew the Chairman well enough to recognize that he would never 'waste' an evening just enjoying himself in her company. There was always work to do, and therefore he must have some important business purpose to discuss, and this was the best way to keep it private between the two of them.

She felt a flicker of disappointment, then chided herself. That was who Basil had always been. His drive and competence was what had attracted her in the first place, long ago when she'd first come to study on Earth.

She arrived on the rooftop of the Hansa pyramid, precisely on time. The sun was a brassy sphere on the western horizon. At the edge of the gardens, Basil stood with his back to her. Potted dwarf orange and lemon trees, bursting with perfume-filled white blossoms that attracted noisy bees, were placed at precise intervals. Paths of faceted gravel were laid out with an exactitude of randomness, designed by a committee of Asian gardeners.

'There's a pitcher of iced tea on the table. Would you pour us each a glass?' Basil said without looking at her. His reputation of having eyes in the back of his head was well earned. 'It's your favourite flavour, I believe.'

Sarein did as she was told, trying to remember when Basil had ever asked her preference in tea. She smelled a tart infusion of mango and cinnamon; the unfamiliar taste was delicious, though she couldn't imagine why he had ever thought it was her 'favourite'. He was making some sort of a gesture, setting the tone for their conversation. He wanted something from her.

Through Basil, she had learned how to manipulate people and politics in ways that no innocent treedweller from Theroc had ever thought to do. Sarein repaid Basil with her body and her companionship, and finally, with her advice and support. She also gave him a hint of her love, but she had to keep that secret, of course. He would only treat romantic notions with scorn. She had never dreamed their affair would last for almost a decade. Now they were certainly a team, though Basil didn't seem to want to recognize it.

Despite his position of power, the Chairman wasn't a womanizer, and she doubted he kept other secret concubines. Not that she would have allowed herself to feel jealousy, and not that he wouldn't have insisted on the right to have other women. In all probability, he would have considered other women to be too much bother. As far as Sarein could tell, searching out distractions – even pleasurable ones – was not in his nature. Sarein gave him everything he wanted or needed, and therefore he could concentrate his energies elsewhere. They had a tacit understanding.

Sarein rarely let herself analyse her true feelings for the Chairman, though. She stayed with him because she wanted to, not just because of the advantages that came from being his lover. Basil kept his heart carefully shuttered, and she could never pry loose a glimpse of his inner thoughts. She knew he cared for her, which he proved – as far as she was concerned – by visibly withdrawing whenever he felt himself getting too close. It was his method of self-protection.

Now, standing together on the rooftop, the two of them looked towards the Whisper Palace. Basil's steel-grey hair was impeccably in place. His formal suit jacket and slacks would have looked pretentious on anyone else in a casual setting, but the Chairman wore them with complete comfort. 'The time has come for us to press our advantage, Sarein. You are next in line.'

She slipped her arm through his. 'I'm generally willing to press any advantage, Basil. But you need to give me a clearer description of what you mean.'

He turned to her with an impatient sigh, as if he expected the answer to be obvious. 'Your sister Estarra is the Queen, but *you* are now the oldest member of the Theron ruling family. Your two brothers were killed by the hydrogues. Your parents clearly have no desire to resume their leadership roles, which they never did very well in the first place.'

'They may not have had the . . . gene of political ambition, but they tried their best.'

'Fortunately, Sarein, I know *you* have that gene. After due consideration, I have decided it would be best for everyone concerned if you returned to Theroc and demanded your place as . . . Mother Sarein.'

She turned away, stung. 'It's not a matter of demanding, Basil.

My parents would be all too happy to hand over the throne to me.'

'All the better then.' He drank his iced tea as if the matter was over.

When he first took her under his wing, she had known that the Chairman was using her reciprocally to gain some advantage with the stubbornly uncooperative Therons. But as the hydrogue crisis dragged on with no resolution in sight, she had begun to feel like a pet waiting for table scraps whenever he deigned to notice her. Why was Basil trying to get rid of her? What had she done?

'But I'm not sure that's what *I* want to do.' Sarein had seen the images brought back by EDF rescue ships and had no desire to see the blackened scars, smell the smoke in the air, or watch the beaten survivors numbly going about their hopeless task. 'Considering my current role here, that would be a step . . . backwards.'

Basil's grey eyes bored into her. 'Not for the Hansa. Don't be selfish.' He stroked her arm gently; the gesture did not seem a spontaneous display of affection, but a calculated movement designed to evoke a response. It took a conscious effort for her not to flinch from his touch. 'Our very equilibrium is at risk, but if everything is handled perfectly – by me, by you, and by all the others I rely upon – the Hansa can come out stronger. We'll smell like roses.'

She no longer liked the taste of her tea. 'But only if I become the next Mother of Theroc?'

'That could well be the key. Walk with me.' Together they strolled along the winding gravel paths, smelling the sweet citrus flowers. 'I have always had a grand vision for humanity. Before the hydrogues came, it was a dream, a long-term plan. When the Spiral Arm was an open playing field and interstellar travel seemed a remote possibility, it cost Earth nothing to let the eleven generation ships wander away like fledglings leaving the nest.

Now, however, the situation has changed. Facing a foe such as the hydrogues, we must stand together with unity, as an empire, not with the anarchy of a dysfunctional family.'

Sarein had always been swayed by his passion and his heartfelt dreams. Never before had she been bothered by how he talked to her, but now she felt that Basil was trying to manipulate her like artist's clay. He wasn't usually so clumsy, so obvious. But he had been slipping lately, showing tiny ragged edges of stress and volatility.

He continued, 'After so many people have suffered, so much damage has been done – the slate has been wiped clean. I see the real possibility of reuniting all the threads of humanity, tying together our scattered prodigal children – the Therons, the Roamers, and all the Hansa colonies. It's got to be done! We can use this turmoil as a catalyst to unify all humans against the hydrogues . . . or against any enemy, for that matter. Who knows what the future may hold?'

Basil continued to talk, bitterly cursing former Chairman Bertram Goswell, who had originally allowed the Roamers to break away. The entire Hansa had paid for that lack of foresight. Next, he grumbled about Old King Ben under Chairman Malcolm Stannis, who had granted the Therons their independence before anyone considered the implications of telink communication.

'All of those mistakes weakened mankind,' Basil said. He stood beside a stone bench but showed no sign that he intended to sit down. 'Now it's time to fix those mistakes. We can cement the pieces together again.'

Sarein stopped to touch the flowers of a lemon tree as she thought of an interesting comparison. 'You see yourself as a human version of the Mage-Imperator, trying to draw together all the separate strands of a political *thism*.'

His expression was almost boyish. 'Hmmm, I like that. I *do* have the wisest plan for us all to cooperate efficiently. King Peter can be our spokesman, even the Archfather of Unison can be useful – though I'll make the important decisions . . . after receiving appropriate advice from my experts, including yourself, Sarein.'

'So long as I'm on Theroc. Instead of here.'

Did he want to distance himself from her? Maybe, seeing the situation crumbling around him, he was doing mental damage control. Perhaps he had realized he was depending on Sarein too much, maybe even loved her – which would frighten him. No wonder he was sending her away. It was just like him.

'All right, Basil. I'll go back to Theroc. I'll try to become the next Mother.' His smile showed relief and satisfaction, but no visible warmth. *I'm doing it for you*, she thought.

SIXTY-FIVE

MAGE-IMPERATOR JORA'H

Inside the Dobro Designate's residence, Mage-Imperator Jora'h met his daughter for the first time. Though supposedly destined to be the saviour of the Ildiran Empire, she was just a little girl.

Osira'h had a poise beyond her years. Her eyes were large and innocent, with a glint of star-sapphire that came from Jora'h's genetics; her narrow chin and gentle expression were achingly clear reminders of her mother.

Seeing his daughter was like an electric jolt that brought back a flood of memories of the many times Jora'h had made love to the beautiful Nira – more times than he had ever mated with the same female, before or since. Even as the years went by and he believed the green priest long dead, Jora'h's longing for her had grown deeper.

Standing before Osira'h, though, made much of that grief and regret wash away. Jora'h was startled to sense her incredible strength and intelligence through the *thism*, though the girl had a different connection and mental pattern, thanks to her mother. Even as Mage-Imperator, he could not link with her clearly, but she seemed stronger, sharper, than his usual sense. He was unable to grasp all that she could do.

'Osira'h,' he said in a long sibilant breath, 'you are . . . beautiful.'

The girl bowed, avoiding his gaze. 'I am honoured to serve you, Mage-Imperator.' Her initial formality was like a crystal knife in his chest, until she finally looked up. He saw a startling hunger there, a recognition, as if she shared many memories with him, though this was the first time they had met. Her thoughts and personality were no more than an echo, like smoke in the *thism*.

'We're very pleased at how Osira'h has turned out,' Udru'h said, interrupting his thoughts. 'The best instructors and lens kithmen have guided her development, and she has performed admirably. Her skills are . . . advanced beyond anything we have measured before. With the continuing war, we know our time is desperately short. Osira'h is nearly ready to serve as the psychic bridge between Ildirans and hydrogues, which we so desperately need.'

Jora'h gently put a finger under the little girl's chin and raised it so that he could read her face. 'Is that true?'

'I am ready.' She blinked her sparkling eyes. 'If that is what you need.' Osira'h was still young, but Jora'h grieved for all the time he had lost with her. He was her father, and he should have watched her grow and learn, as he had done with all his children, all his Designates-in-waiting. Osira'h was special, though – and not just in ways the Dobro breeding programme considered important.

He turned to the grim Designate. 'I want to go with Osira'h out to her mother's grave. I trust you have marked it so we can' – his voice threatened to crack, but he controlled it – 'pay our respects, and remember her together.'

Udru'h wore a bland expression. 'As you wish, Liege.'

Nira's memorial marker had been placed on one of the recovering hillsides scorched by the fires of the previous dry season. The ash had made the ground fertile again, and grasses and weeds grew tall and thick, erasing the burn scars.

The Dobro Designate had chosen a gravesite near a cluster of thorny scrub trees that had survived the rushing flames. Around them, the plants smelled fresh and alive, the faintest echo of the Theron worldforest. Yes, Nira would have approved of this setting.

Taking the little girl's hand, Jora'h knelt in the tangled shade of the clawlike scrub bushes. The commemorative marker was a block of stone with embedded projection machinery. Suspended above a holo-ring, a many-faceted crystal gathered sunlight that powered a projection of Nira's beautiful face, apparently taken from camp records.

When Jora'h saw her image again, he felt his heart being pulled from his chest. Beside him, Osira'h also seemed angry and uneasy, though according to Udru'h she had never even met her mother. In silence, they stared together, experiencing a common grief. He wished he could share with his daughter all of his memories of Nira, how much he had loved her. Again, Osira'h surprised him with her perceptiveness and her depth of intuitive understanding – she seemed to be mourning Nira as much as he was.

For a long moment, Jora'h was caught up in memories and regrets. He had never dreamed that his father might purposefully deceive him. Now he knew so much more . . .

Jora'h rubbed his fingers on the bark of the singed scrubby trees surrounding Nira's grave. 'I wish your mother could be closer to her forest. I wish she could have seen it one more time. She loved Theroc so much . . . and those trees are now recovering from the destruction the hydrogues wrought.' *And you, Osira'h, must somehow negotiate a peace with them*, he thought.

He let go of his daughter's hand and traced the holographic image of Nira's face with his fingers. Unable to stop himself, he muttered apologies, dangerously close to weeping. 'I'm sorry for all the tragedies you suffered, sweet Nira. I would have done anything in the universe for you, but now it's too late. I can't make up for it . . . but perhaps I can save the Ildiran race.'

The girl remained next to him. She seemed troubled, confused, but also determined. 'If I succeed, if I can become a bridge with the hydrogues and make them stop killing Ildirans . . . will it all be justified?'

'Do you have doubts?' He looked at her, sensing her powerful presence through the *thism*, though he could not read Osira'h the way he could his other children. It was almost as if she had shielded herself.

'I have no doubts about what I can do, or why it must be done.' She hesitated. 'But . . . none of these humans are here willingly. Neither was my mother. Will you shut it all down?'

Jora'h felt a chill, knowing Udru'h would never have spoken to her of such things. 'I want to, so very much. But the hydrogues keep attacking us, and the Klikiss robots are no longer reliable allies. At this point, so close to its culmination, how can I stop the work until you have a chance to prove your abilities? The humans here were brought to Dobro long before I knew anything of this project. At least they remember nothing else, know no other life.'

'My mother knew another life,' Osira'h said, looking at him with remarkable sternness on her young and innocent face.

He looked at her with sharp surprise. 'How do you know? What makes you ask that?'

His daughter seemed flustered. 'She . . . talked to some of the breeding prisoners, but they didn't believe her about the free worlds far from here.'

He studied the little girl who stood so bravely next to him. 'Osira'h, how I wish you could have met your mother. She was a wonderful person, beautiful and funny. She captured my heart in a way no other woman ever had, and now you can never know her.'

Osira'h tentatively touched Jora'h's shoulder, opening up to him with a warm flow of surprising love. 'I already know her. There are no secrets.'

Jora'h stared at her, but the reticent girl would say nothing else.

SIXTY-SIX

NIRA

During her years of captivity, Nira had wanted nothing more than to escape the breeding camps. Never again did she want to see the hated face of the Dobro Designate, or the succession of horrific breeding partners. Back then, Nira had gazed longingly through the fences out across the sparsely populated landscape, wishing she could go home to the worldforest . . . just wanting to be alone.

Now, though, she had spent long months in utter isolation, speaking to no one except for a brief taunting exchange with Udru'h. And he was no companion that she wanted to have. Mercifully, the Designate had left her to her island – her own, calm universe.

Alone, she could watch the clouds, listen to the waves, feel the warm wind on her face. Nira walked among strange fern-like trees that grew from squat trunks in the island's sandy soil. All around her, the giant lake extended in watery blue emptiness to the horizon, though she knew the shore was out there somewhere. The stirring of birds and the rustle of leaves comforted her, as they would any green priest. Nira tried to hear words in the whisper of foliage, but these trees were not connected in any way to the worldforest mind.

Sometimes she attempted to send out a call through these surrogate trees, but received back only a resounding silence – just as when she'd desperately tried to shout for help through the scrubby hillside trees during a brush fire. Sadly, Dobro's plants and forests had no life of their own. They simply grew, went to seed, and died, retaining no memory as the worldtrees did.

Nevertheless, as Nira walked around on her island, traversing the limited paths from one shore to another, she spoke aloud to the trees. The plants remained unresponsive, but she could fantasize that they were diligently listening after all, but did not know how to answer. Her voice was soothing and gentle, and she never found herself at a loss for anything to say. Speaking with the island foliage kept Nira sane, her thoughts sharp.

Perhaps, far off on the other side of the world, Osira'h could sense she was still alive. It was too much for Nira to hope, after the guards had nearly beaten her to death, brutally severing the connection she'd shared with her Princess. She was no longer able to feel the thoughts of the little girl. Would Osira'h even think to look for her? Somehow, perhaps in dreams, their thoughts might connect . . .

Though she had a small measure of peace here, Nira felt empty. She hoped she'd given her daughter enough information to make her question the Dobro breeding schemes and the dark plans Udru'h had for her, but Nira didn't know what the girl could possibly do about it.

She was also dismayed to know that all the other human captives remained in the breeding camp, every day abused by their Ildiran masters. Worst of all, those other humans had accepted their lot. Generation after generation, they'd been raised to believe that this was the natural order of the human race, that this was their way of life. They all underwent the same awful experimentation, but only Nira had frantically resisted. The others did not know any better.

And now she was here, discarded but kept in reserve. It took her a long while to understand why the Dobro Designate hadn't simply killed her out of hand. He must still have plans to use her as a hostage, as leverage. Over Jora'h? Was the Designate keeping her for his own protection? Her only hope of being rescued was to remain valuable to Udru'h.

She waited day after day on the island, praying that Jora'h might find her. She clung to the slim thread of hope that Osira'h understood everything and might soon discover a way to help all the captives . . .

Nira told all these things to the island trees. If she ever returned to Theroc, she would have a wealth of tales and experiences to share with the genuine worldtrees – and they, at least, would listen.

SIXTY-SEVEN

CESCA PERONI

Roamer vessels descended like the cavalry upon Theroc.

Cesca rode in the foremost ship with her father. It felt good to be doing something to help Theroc, and she hoped it might soothe the pain for them and give her something to be proud of. She had not been able to offer Reynald love during his life, but she knew that what she was doing for his people now would have been far more important to him.

As the flurry of mismatched spacecraft approached the splintered and burned forests, Cesca finally began to comprehend the extent of the damage the hydrogues and faeros had done. Tears welled in her eyes as she looked over at her father and realized how glad she was to be with him at a time like this. 'I just pray that I've brought the right people and enough supplies, Dad.'

Denn Peroni concentrated on the complicated landing activities. 'You followed your Guiding Star to do this good deed in the first place, Cesca. Have faith that you were sufficiently inspired to remember everything we'd need – if not, we'll make do. You'll get them back on their feet again.'

As a girl she had travelled with him on his merchant ship from one port of call to another – Hansa colonies, isolated Roamer settlements, scary and crowded Earth. On her twelfth birthday he'd brought Cesca to Rendezvous and convinced Speaker Okiah to teach her the nuances of personal and familial politics that he himself didn't understand. Thus, when Cesca had asked her father to join this humanitarian mission to Theroc, he had not hesitated for an instant. Her heart warmed at the memory of his supportive smile . . .

Ship after colourful ship landed in the raw cleared areas where tall worldtrees had once stood. With a lump in her throat, Cesca remembered the only other time she'd visited here: her gala betrothal celebration not so long ago. There had been green priests and treedancers, exotic foods and forest smells, insect noises and lights among the trees.

All gone now.

Cesca emerged to stand beside her father as dirt-smeared Therons came forward from temporary encampments. Among them, she spotted Reynald's parents, looking much more haggard than she remembered, as if every drop of joy or energy had been wrung out of them. Father Idriss, whose square-cut black beard was shot through with lines of grey, regarded the new arrivals with wary disbelief.

Cesca smiled reassuringly, full of pride in her extended family of Roamers. 'The clans wondered if you could use our help. Might we lend a hand?'

Mother Alexa's smile blossomed like a bright flower.

In spite of the brief show the Eddies had made of assisting Theroc after the hydrogue attack, the military had stopped far short of finishing the job. The observation satellites they had left in orbit provided useful images of Theroc's continents, but the Therons did not have the manpower, equipment, or resources to handle a crisis of such magnitude.

Even with the assistance of every able-bodied Theron, the Roamers had their work cut out for them.

Using prefab dwelling modules designed to create instant settlements on inhospitable worlds, clan engineers built a base camp in a clearing where all the worldtrees had been shattered by hydrogue icewaves. The Therons joined them, explained what progress they had made thus far, discussed plans, and offered suggestions as to how their green priests could best help the Roamers.

With a sense of satisfaction, Cesca watched her people working alongside the weary Therons with dedication and energy. Industrial lifters cleared away the worst debris from the ash-strewn ground by piling the enormous hulks of dead worldtrees into high funeral mounds that would stand as monuments to the worldforest. Large excavating machines designed for mining and construction on lifeless planets now went to work on a grand scale, accomplishing as much in a single day as the Therons had done in the past month.

'Our initial concern here is to prevent further erosion,' said Kotto Okiah, placing his hands on his hips as he surveyed the entire project. 'If we don't prepare for when the next heavy rains come, this will be a disaster of epic proportions.'

'This is already a disaster,' Cesca reminded him.

He scratched his curly brown hair. 'Right. And the Therons would probably rather not have another.'

Knowing the eccentric engineer's capabilities, Cesca had sent a ship to his frozen methane excavations on Jonah 12. Kotto hated to be pulled from a project that already occupied his full intellect, but Cesca had asked him as a personal favour, and the man's resistance had melted. Now he followed her like a devoted pet.

Kotto paced through the work areas. Several times, he had expressed disappointment that he hadn't had a chance to study the hydrogue wreckage before the Eddies hauled it away to Earth, but Cesca tried to keep the man's genius focused on the immediate problem. Kotto turned his energy to restoring the forest world.

'We've cleared this whole settlement zone now, so I had our ships spray down a mesh of biodegradable polymer to hold the soil in place. A crew of Therons is already out finding fast-growing native groundcover for the first phase of the reclamation process. Then I want to build retaining walls and stair-step some of these hillsides.'

He held up a long, thin sheet of electronic plans, scrolling through image after image. 'I can use this opportunity to install up-to-date plumbing and power conduits, ventilation systems, communications nodes.'

'They have their own ways, Kotto. Be careful not to do anything they don't want.'

He blinked at her. 'All right, I'll ask first. But so far they're fascinated with the renovation plans, and they've been very helpful.' He shifted to a different page of the plans. 'Normally I'd use raw metals and alloys as structural materials. In this case, though, I doubt the Therons want us to strip-mine or bore holes into their rock outcroppings—'

'Don't even consider it. That's fine on an empty asteroid, but the ecosystem here has been damaged enough. We need to heal and repair this planet, not make matters worse.'

'Exactly my point.' Kotto tapped his finger on the plans. 'I ran compositional analyses and materials tests on the wood of the dead worldtrees. It's quite a remarkable substance, almost as sturdy as steel, yet workable. We can use that fire-hardened wood to form the basic framework for all the structures the Therons need.'

'There's certainly plenty of it available,' Cesca said, looking at all the downed trees. 'Unfortunately.'

As if unveiling a masterpiece, Kotto displayed his architectural scheme that used salvaged wood, a few necessary components of Roamer manufacture, and the original material of the fungus-reef. 'Look, I can shore up these parts of the old city and rebuild the rest. It'll be better than ever before.'

His unique vision impressed Cesca. 'We'll have to get the Therons' approval first, but I think they'll be quite pleased.' She surprised the bemused inventor with a quick and enthusiastic hug.

Denn Peroni flew his ship next to a pair of water-hauling vessels captained by the twins Torin and Wynn Tamblyn. They had brought two of their container ships from the water mines of Plumas to use for large-scale operations. From orbit, Roamer scouts traced still-burning fires on separate continents, following plumes of smoke to the heaviest unchecked blazes. Now the Tamblyn brothers dumped water from their haulers to snuff out the flames in these remaining hot spots.

Cesca's father sent daily progress reports to the base camp. Shipload after shipload of water scooped from fresh lakes rained down upon the last uncontrolled fires, dousing them. Even from high in the sky, Denn could almost feel a sigh of relief from the sentient trees. Every blaze extinguished was like a hot spike withdrawn from the planet's sensitive flesh . . .

Cesca sat and listened while several Roamer agricultural engineers spoke with Yarrod and other high-ranking green priests. 'I think you'll find that we Roamers are well-versed in efficient crop-planting methods. We've also become adept at squeezing out high yields. In most cases we have no choice but to recycle every drop of water, every scrap of fertilizer in order to generate the greatest amount of edible biomass.'

Marla Chan Tylar – Nikko's mother – showed images of what

she had done in the sun-washed greenhouse domes in an asteroid belt. 'On Theroc you have seeds and worldtree sprouts, but we need to make the growing of new trees more efficient.'

'Every treeling counts,' Yarrod agreed grimly.

'Now you're starting to think like a Roamer,' said Marla. 'We'll have to install irrigation, stagger high and low tiers of plantings, and prepare to transplant them when necessary. We have a lot of ground to cover.'

Cesca left them to talk and plan amongst themselves. As she stood alone with the newly optimistic flurry of activity around her, she looked up at the damaged fungus-reef city and once again felt a bittersweet pang.

If things had been different, she would have been married to Reynald by now. The Roamer-Theron alliance would have strengthened both peoples, and Jess would have gone on with his life, putting behind him all thoughts of romance with her. But Reynald was dead, and Jess had been transformed into something more than human.

Still, perhaps she could salvage something of even greater importance here. She looked up at a burned tree, and her lips formed a resolute smile.

SIXTY-EIGHT

ENGINEERING SPECIALIST SWENDSEN

After sunset, as the torches burned brightly atop the cupolas of the Whisper Palace, scientific teams continued to analyse the wreckage of the hydrogue warglobe taken from Theroc. Engineers and technicians had spent weeks scrutinizing the broken pieces.

Equipment shacks and outbuildings were clustered around the large tent that had been erected to conceal the trophy from curious eyes. Brilliant lights gleamed down upon pallets of instruments and stored chemicals. Catwalks provided access to the upper portions of the curved warglobe shell. Men and women bustled around the derelict, taking readings and marking down notes.

Accompanied by four royal guards – a mere formality – Peter and Estarra walked hand-in-hand across the plaza to the flap of the synthetic canvas covering. Some of the technicians noticed the King's arrival and stopped their work, snapping to attention as if he were an imposing military commander. The guards, by tradition, announced the royal presence.

With a surprised yet welcoming expression on his face, the

blond Engineering Specialist wiped his hands on a rag and hurried over. 'King Peter, what a pleasure it is to see you! And a boost in morale for my team!' He extended his hand. The guards tensed, but Swendsen remained oblivious. Around them, all work came to a complete stop.

The King graciously shook the man's hand. 'I'm sorry if our visit here is disruptive. My Queen and I don't want to delay progress.'

'Oh, but it also shows us that you care about what we're doing and are interested in our results.' Swendsen gestured for the others to get back to their tests. 'And why doesn't your brother Daniel ever come to see our work?'

Awkwardly, Peter answered, 'The, uh, Prince has a full scholastic schedule, Engineer Swendsen. He still has much to learn.'

'Ah, don't we all?'

Estarra's eyes were bright, her body tense. 'I hope your teams find something useful, Engineer Swendsen. Too much of my worldforest was destroyed by these things.'

The King and Queen looked up to watch as large sections of the broken warglobe were lowered from suspensions to new work ramps for further study. Sensors and wires and gleaming detectors had been applied like freckles across the curved hydrogue shell. The diamond hull was blackened and blistered, the edges jagged where the alien vessel had shattered under the heat of the faeros.

The tall Swede was more eager and excited than anyone else, like a child ready to tear off the wrapping from a long-coveted gift. 'The warglobe is intrinsically fascinating, but I had hoped to find some Achilles heel. Unfortunately, there's simply not enough left of this hulk to give us any meaningful insight into its potential flaws. And we haven't been able to conclude much about the technology or mechanics.'

He walked quickly to the next station, and Peter and Estarra rapidly forgot their usual regal pace. The Swedish engineer ducked under the curvature of a large fragment. 'We haven't found any intact machinery, or engines, or components of their weaponry systems. It's just a bunch of broken junk.'

The King ran his fingers along the cool, slick surface. 'What about analysing the material composition? Can we replicate it – or at least use the information to modify our fracture-pulse torpedoes or carbon-carbon bond disruptors?'

'Maybe. Four of my best materials researchers are working on a small fragment of the hull. Computer simulations and nondestructive analyses just didn't give us anything. I gave them permission to unleash all the fury of Earth, hoping to find something that'll chip the armour.' Swendsen paced around the site. 'One man told me the project was a dream come true – using his advanced training and expertise to smash things. He likes that.'

'Well, the faeros managed to wreck this one,' Estarra pointed out.

'Believe me, we're trying our damnedest to reproduce the technique.' From a slick information screen, Swendsen displayed tables of data and the results of numerous tests, then turned with a 'tsk-tsk' noise from the results. 'When I think of how much we learned from dismantling that one Klikiss robot, I wish we could get a fraction as much from this derelict.'

Luckily, this wasn't the only project the Hansa had in the works. Only a week before, King Peter had made a formal inspection tour of the giant rammer ships under construction, sixty new kamikaze Mantas designed to smash warglobes. Hansa manufacturing facilities also continued to pump out huge numbers of new Soldier compies to help crew EDF ships, though Peter still had reservations about them.

The engineer rapped his big knuckles against the hard diamond hull, and the alien ship completely absorbed the sound. 'I'm just not sure how much more we can wring out of this thing.'

Peter nodded. 'Maybe it would be better used as a monument for tourists.'

Estarra gave a grim smile. 'At least the warglobe was destroyed. Far better that we have a monument to a *victory* against the hydrogues, than a memorial to another loss.'

The following day, Swendsen bustled into Chairman Wenceslas's office. 'You called for me, Mr Chairman?' He had not changed out of his smudged work uniform from the warglobe analysis site. As he collected himself, Swendsen noticed General Lanyan sitting at a table, rummaging through documents and memos.

The dapper Chairman stood from behind his desk. 'Yes, I did. We have some questions about your work.'

Swendsen searched in his pockets, but didn't find what he was looking for. 'I thought I had a copy of my note printouts, but I have no summary report yet on the hydrogue wreckage. My teams have been using all the techniques available, but there really isn't much to go on. I can tell you the basic material structure, but we guessed that before. We still can't break it. Or were you asking about progress in the Soldier-compy manufacturing lines? You should see what the—'

The Chairman cut him off. 'Right now, Dr Swendsen, I'm most interested in what you've learned about that *Roamer* compy I gave you to study. It's been several months since the compy shut itself down to prevent me from discovering Roamer locations. We very much need that intelligence right now for military planning purposes.'

Swendsen frowned in confusion, then brightened. 'Ah, yes, the Listener model. I believe its designation was EA? Sorry, sir – I have so many different things on my plate.' His brow furrowed. 'A very interesting case, though. Voluntary self-wipe. Complete memory erasure implemented by the compy itself.'

'I told you, Mr Chairman,' Lanyan said. 'The Roamers are hiding something, otherwise they wouldn't have such security measures in place. It's insidious.'

Swendsen fumbled with his long fingers. 'If I recall correctly, sir, you inadvertently triggered embedded Roamer protective programming. You must have asked the wrong question.' He smiled, but the Chairman did not smile back. 'It scoured all the circuits, overwrote the memory data with gibberish, reformatted the compy's brain, and left it a blank slate. A great little programming landmine. Hmmm, maybe we should implement something similar in our own classified systems – it was very effective.'

'I'll consider it,' Lanyan said gruffly without getting up from his seat.

'So, is there anything salvageable?' the Chairman asked.

Preoccupied, Swendsen wandered over to look out the broad windows of the penthouse office. 'Well, all the systems are fully functional, mechanically speaking, but we'd have to reinstall a basic instruction set to make it work again.'

The Chairman turned to Lanyan. 'And the compy actually belonged to one of our EDF officers. That raises even more suspicions.'

The General sat up rigidly, shoving the various documents aside. 'Yes, Mr Chairman – EA was technically owned by Commander Tasia Tamblyn. She doesn't know what happened to her compy, and apparently assumes EA was lost. She filed one or two search requests, but kept the matter quiet. Probably afraid she'd face disciplinary action. Technically, Tamblyn wasn't allowed to dispatch her compy anywhere without authorization.'

Lanyan pursed his thick lips, as if reluctant to reveal what he knew. 'For what it's worth, sir, I'm familiar with Tamblyn, and I've spoken with her commanding officer. Admiral Willis characterizes her performance as impeccable. In fact, Commander Tamblyn was the one chosen to drop the first new Klikiss Torch on Ptoro. Apparently, her brother's skymine was destroyed by hydrogues, all hands lost, and she holds a grudge. A good soldier, even if she is a Roamer.'

'That doesn't mean she's not a mole in our midst,' the Chairman said, 'and I don't want to miss a potential opportunity. There's too much at stake, too much we still don't know, especially now that we plan to take a hardline stance against the Roamers. I'm not sure we should rely too much on this Commander Tamblyn's loyalty. Isolate her from all matters relating to the new offensive – and find a way to keep a quiet eye on her.'

'If I install surveillance technology on her Manta, she may discover it,' Lanyan said. 'And we can't allow her crew to pick up even a hint of our suspicions. That would affect the chain of command.'

'We'll be more subtle than that.' Basil turned, clearing his throat to get Swendsen's attention again. 'Reboot that compy, restore all basic functions, and then return it to Tamblyn. Make up some story that explains where it's been all this time. And then . . . we'll see what happens.'

'If the compy's sudden reappearance looks too convenient, Tamblyn might be suspicious,' Lanyan pointed out.

'We are all suspicious, General. These days there's no way around it.'

Lanyan remained puzzled. 'But what does all that accomplish, sir?'

The Chairman just smiled. 'Engineer Swendsen can also install a passive surveillance programme that will let us record everything that EA sees when she's with our Roamer friend. The compy will become our spy without even realizing it.'

SIXTY-NINE

TASIA TAMBLYN

Admiral Willis came aboard the Manta when it docked for resupply after finishing the EDF survey of the old Klikiss Torch stars. The rare smile on the old woman's face was a puzzling, but pleasant surprise. 'Commander Tamblyn, I have a dandy little gift for you.'

As her bridge crew snapped to attention at the arrival of the Grid 7 commander, Tasia stood from her chair. 'What is it, Admiral? Have we been granted permission to kick some more hydrogue butt? I wouldn't mind deploying another Klikiss Torch, since the result of the last one was so gratifying.'

Willis turned to the bridge doorway and spoke to someone out in the corridor. 'Go ahead, send her in.' Accompanied by an EDF desk clerk, a compy strutted dutifully onto the bridge. The skin polymer was polished and cleaned, the blue highlights refreshed.

Tasia immediately recognized the mechanical friend she'd had for most of her life. 'EA!' She hurried across the deck to the Listener robot, unable to believe her eyes. 'EA, where have you been?' She turned to Admiral Willis, breathless. 'How did you ever find her? She's been missing for half a year.'

The compy turned to face her, but the female voice was flat. 'You are Tasia Tamblyn.'

Still smiling, Admiral Willis said, 'I just got word from EDF HQ. Your compy was found in a damaged Hansa freighter that had apparently suffered a hydrogue attack. The human crew was all dead, and we rescued this little compy from some salvage prospectors.'

'Oh, EA, I'm so glad you're back! What an ordeal you've been through.'

'I have no recollection of it, Tasia Tamblyn.' The simulated voice contained no inflections. 'I am informed that you are my rightful owner.'

Tasia turned her puzzled face back to Admiral Willis, who explained, 'All systems aboard the drifting freighter were fried, apparently by hydrogue energy weapons. Your little robot's memory must have been wiped clean as well. We found EA's serial number and manufacturing date, but . . .' She shrugged and spread her hands. 'The EDF doesn't necessarily keep records of Roamer compies and their original owners. How did EA get away from you in the first place? Was she stolen?'

Tasia tried not to look guilty. 'Uh, could be. She went missing while performing a family errand for me just before we all left on the Osquivel offensive. I never had any idea where she'd gone. Now that her memory's gone, I suppose we'll never know what happened.' She knelt in front of the Listener compy. 'Well, I've got some old diary files, so maybe we can upload some of them to refresh your memory, EA.'

She suddenly remembered protocol and straightened on the bridge. 'Admiral Willis, may I be dismissed? I'd like to take EA back to my cabin and do a damage assessment.'

Willis indicated the viewscreen. 'The Grid 7 fleet's in dock and awaiting orders. I don't see any pressing emergencies right now. In fact, it's been a while since I've planted my bottom in a Manta's command chair. I'll take your next shift here and do a little memory-refresher of my own. I'm supposed to conduct occasional inspections after all.' The older woman cracked her knuckles. 'I think I'll let your crew impress me.'

'Subcommander Ramirez can handle it very well,' Tasia said, looking at her navigator.

The EDF soldiers on Tasia's bridge looked unnerved at the prospect of having the Admiral give them routine orders and watch their shift activities. Tasia's concern, however, was focused on EA, and she led the cooperative compy down the corridor to her private stateroom.

Once she'd shut the door, Tasia sat on the edge of her bunk, rested her hands on the compy's hard shoulders, and turned EA to face her. The blue Listener model had always been reliable and independent; Tasia had uploaded various specialities into her memory core, but spy training had not been one of them. Admiral Willis's explanation of how she'd been found made sense . . . to a certain extent. 'Do you remember anything, EA, any hints? Who's the last person you recall talking to before you were deactivated?'

'I have no recollection.'

'Do you remember the Hansa freighter, the hydrogue attack?'

'No, but I have been informed of the situation.'

Tasia didn't know what to believe. She knew all too well that the EDF had no qualms about poking their noses into private matters. They could easily have asked the Listener robot too many questions, triggered a permanent memory wipe. Her hand clenched the edge of her bunk. EA wasn't just missing data – she was missing all of their shared *past*.

'All right, EA, we'll have to take this one step at a time. Before we left home, your memory core was so overloaded with past events and unnecessary skills that we needed to do some housekeeping anyway. This time I'll add only the meaningful memories and leave out all the boring parts.'

'I am listening, Tasia Tamblyn.'

'You're a Listener model. That's what you're designed to do.' Tasia slumped back on her bunk, staring up at the ceiling, wondering how she should start – without giving any specifics of Roamer planets or facilities.

EA had first been owned by her brother Ross, who had given the compy to Jess, who had finally passed her to Tasia. Now EA's memories of Ross Tamblyn were gone for ever, along with Ross himself. And Tasia hadn't even seen Jess in years; she hoped he was still alive. With a pang for all that had changed in her life, all that she'd left behind, she began.

'First off, let me tell you about the time I dared you to walk out on a thin ice shelf at the edge of the frozen sea, back on the water moon where our clan lives. I was just a little girl then, eight years old I think, and I would have done it myself – maybe I should have, because I probably weighed less than you do. I didn't realize that as a compy you had no inhibitions and simply followed my instructions, no matter how stupid they were.'

Tasia recalled the little compy strutting out onto the thin ice of Plumas like a trooper. Overhead, in the frozen-solid roof of sky, implanted artificial suns shone down, their reflections glittering off the faceted walls and icebergs. EA had marched out to the edge of the thin shelf and kept going even after the ice cracked and popped. At first Tasia had giggled, then called for the compy to stop, then watched in horror as the little robot plunged into the cold depths.

Hearing Tasia's wails of despair, her mother had come running out of a pumping shed. Karla Tamblyn saw what had happened and struggled to find a solution. She dropped cables, hooks, and metal detectors in search of EA, but the compy kept sinking, systems freezing, even though her components were protected against harsh environments.

'It took my mother two hours, but she finally snagged you,' Tasia said, smiling at the recollection. 'When she hauled you back up from under the ice, the water froze around you like a solid shell. I insisted on taking you into my room and built up the thermal generators so that you could thaw by the fire. I made us pepperflower tea, but of course you couldn't drink any. You were the frozen one, but I was shivering the whole while. You really scared me that day, EA.' She turned to look at the motionless and attentive little compy. 'Don't you remember any of that?'

'I will from now on, Tasia Tamblyn.'

She sighed. 'It's a start.' It was going to take a long time for EA to be the friend Tasia needed.

SEVENTY

ZHETT KELLUM

Inside the central administrative complex, Del Kellum studied summary screens for his shipyard operations. He seemed inordinately pleased with himself. Zhett watched angelfish swimming around in their tanks, knowing that her father was about to launch into one of his lectures or rants. He was always amusing when he worked himself into a furore over some subject or other, and this time she was not disappointed.

'We salvaged one hundred and twenty-three Soldier compies from the Eddie battleships. One hundred and twenty-three! They've all had their memories erased along with most of their old programming. Then we installed new basic programming, so now they're perfectly happy to work for us. Model helpers.' He shook his large, squarish head. 'If only we could get those thirty-two deadbeat soldiers to work a tenth as much.'

Zhett urged her father into a chair, so that she could knead the tense muscles in his broad shoulders. 'Compies are designed to be hard workers, Dad, and Roamers are brought up to pull together and get the job done. But those Eddies had pampered childhoods that left them pretty much helpless. They barely know how to pour their own coffee or dress themselves in the morning.'

'So I expect too much from them?' Kellum grumbled. 'By damn, if only they weren't so ornery! They complain constantly that they're bored and resentful . . . yet they refuse to participate. If our gravity wasn't so low, they'd probably all have haemorrhoids from sitting on their butts doing nothing.'

Zhett snickered. 'Then they'd *really* be cranky.'

The big schematic on the wall near his fish tank was a tangled map of orbital lines designating the permanent facilities. Bright dots marked the positions of hundreds of ships and artificial constructions. The screens showed a microcosm of shipbuilding activities ranging from ore-mappers and prospectors to interior refurbishers and decorators who put the finishing touches on completed spacecraft.

The reprogrammed Soldier compies were primarily assigned to hard labour out in the shipyards, hauling metal-rich rubble closer to the big smelters. Others had mapped the rings' gravitational fields in detail, marking safe zones for portable factories and pinpointing new stable orbits for construction frames.

'We left a bit of their EDF recon programming intact – just the parts we thought might be useful – so those Soldier compies excel at high-risk exploration. I assigned forty of them to spread out in the densest ring concentrations, places where I've never had the guts to fly before. Too crowded and too dangerous. With their reaction times, they're the best fliers I've ever seen, even in our clunky old grappler pods.'

'Not better than I am, Dad.'

'I'd rather not put it to the test, my sweet. Let compies take the stupid risks. And if they happen to get damaged . . . well, we can always use their components for scrap.' Kellum expanded a segment of the display where the orbiting rubble was so dense the pinpoints looked like a swarm of gnats.

'Down close to the planet itself, the rubble's so thick that nobody's dared to fly there before, but it must be rich in resources. The surprise is I expected to lose half of the compy scouts, but so far they keep sending back readings.' A waterfall of numbers and symbols flowed down columns. 'By damn, look at all those metals. A handful of those Soldier compies could put our old prospectors out of business.'

'Most of the prospectors wouldn't mind, Dad. They complain as much as our Eddy guests do.'

Kellum wasn't listening as he concentrated on the data. He tapped at a glaringly anomalous reading. 'What the hell is that?'

Zhett looked closer, as if the numbers might mean something. 'With all the sensors you installed in the recon grappler pods, how could you forget to include optical relays?'

'They were compies. I didn't figure they'd need to do any sightseeing.' Kellum shrugged and ran his finger along the data charts. 'But look here. Whatever that is, it clearly doesn't belong with the rest of the material.'

'Maybe it's more EDF wreckage,' Zhett suggested. 'It could have drifted in towards the planet.'

'But the signature's all wrong.'

She lifted her chin. 'Well, are you going to stare at a computer screen all day long, or are we going to go have a look at it?'

He grinned at her. 'By damn, let's go.'

'Just so you know, *I'm* flying, Dad. No arguments.' Kellum knew better than to disagree.

Cruising along at a speed that made her father uncomfortable, Zhett spiralled into the densest inner ring. Some of the reprogrammed Soldier compies accompanied their scout vessel as outflyers, plotting a safe course and issuing preliminary warnings of dangerous debris. To distract himself from his nervousness, her father talked . . . and talked.

'I've noticed you spending quite a bit of time with that young Eddy commander, Fitzpatrick.'

She shrugged to cover her flush of embarrassment. 'I torment him mercilessly, but it's hard not to. His very personality demands that I push his buttons, and he never disappoints me with his response.'

'Well, see if you can push a different button and get him to do some *work* for a change. Do you think they're adjusting to their new life here?'

Zhett snorted. 'Not at all.'

'Well then, I don't know what to do with them. It's time they learned to be useful. After all, they're adopted family members now, not prisoners.'

Zhett dodged three criss-crossing meteoroids. 'I doubt they'll ever think of themselves that way, Dad. So far, the thing they're best at is being pains in the ass.'

'Not a particularly useful skill. So what do you think of that young man? He's handsome, and your age, and—'

'Dad, have you noticed the debris field I'm flying through? Please let me concentrate.'

'Of course.' The slight upturn of his lips was maddening, but her cutting him off had not just been an excuse. She did need to focus on her piloting.

Now the outflyer Soldier compies zipped in, flanking her, guiding her on the safest path. She jerked the attitude-control thrusters right and left, hardly daring to blink. Beside her, her father went pale and gripped his seat. The compy ships took a heavier toll; their hulls got damaged and battered, but Zhett's vessel suffered only minor dents, and a small star-shaped impact on the thick viewport.

Kellum calmed himself by studying the scan readings on a small console screen. 'We're getting close now.'

Zhett gestured with her chin. 'Up there. Something's a lot more reflective than the rest of the rocks.'

Sparkling with reflected light from the clouds of Osquivel, one object shone like a diamond in a pile of gravel. Rocks formed a thick, protective coterie of obstacles around the valuable treasure. The compy outflyers circled, dived in, and indicated a safe course for Zhett to follow.

The object's distinctive geometrical shape made it stand out as much as its shining hull had. The sphere, studded with spiky protrusions, drifted alone, abandoned in the dense minefield of rocky debris.

'It's a drogue ship,' Zhett whispered. 'Look at it.'

Kellum bit his lower lip. 'One of the smaller ones, not a full-blown warglobe.'

She manoeuvred closer, then jumped in her seat as a rock hammered the hull of their ship with a sound like a sledgehammer hitting an anvil. Zhett steadied them, all the while concentrating on the round alien globe. 'I bet it was killed during the battle, Dad. The Eddies did cause some damage.'

'I'm not picking up any power readings or life signs . . . though I wouldn't know what the hell to look for. Back off a minute and let the compies get closer. See how it reacts.'

The outflyers approached the small alien sphere, but the hydrogue vessel did not respond. 'Shizz, it's probably been drifting out here all this time. The drogues certainly haven't missed it.'

Her father grinned hugely. 'Well, in that case – it's finders keepers for us.'

Zhett's scout ship suffered several more impacts – one that would require minor repairs – as she cautiously pulled away from the densest cluster of debris, while Kellum sent instructions to the robotic outflyers.

Working together, the reprogrammed Soldier compies rigged tractor beams to the slick surface of the dead alien ship and pulled it slowly out of its nest of broken rocks and into a safer zone. Several meteoroids ricocheted off the sphere's hull, but left not so much as a scratch. The compy grappler pods looked on the other hand as if they'd been used as punching bags.

Her father was already full of ideas about the relic. 'Could be the biggest treasure in this whole battleground. Imagine it, my sweet, our very own drogue ship! Roamer engineers can figure out how it ticks, then maybe we'll incorporate some of those techniques into our own vessels.'

The gas planet Osquivel loomed in front of them like a sceptical eye watching everything they did.

'That's why, as soon as we get back to the main complex, I'm going to track down Kotto Okiah. If anybody can decipher the thing, he can.'

SEVENTY-ONE

NIKKO CHAN TYLAR

S ince he was carrying wental water and distributing the
powerful entities to uninhabited planets, *Aquarius* seemed the
perfect name for his ship.

Years ago, Nikko and his father had cobbled the vessel together
from several falling-apart wrecks that belonged to clan Tylar. After
pulling out of skymining operations on Ptoro, they had owned
plenty of salvaged spaceships and cargo haulers, pieces of
equipment that no longer served any purpose. Nikko had added
more cargo space, engines with greater range, and larger fuel tanks.
More recently, he'd installed specialized containers for holding
wental-energized water samples. *Aquarius* was a fine, if odd-looking,
starship.

Jess Tamblyn had dispatched his water bearers to unexplored
spots in the Spiral Arm, using old Ildiran star charts and planetary
surveys. Not only would this quest distribute the wentals and help
the entities grow strong enough to fight hydrogues, but Nikko and
his comrades would also find unclaimed planets that the Roamers
could use. A winning prospect all around.

Wandering about without a schedule or specified destination was perfect for Nikko's talents and sensibilities. He rarely arrived where or when he expected, and now he didn't need to worry about the embarrassment of getting distracted. The throbbing wentals stored in containers belowdecks didn't seem to mind. The water-creatures lived on a different time scale, exhilarated just to know that the tides of the Spiral Arm would soon turn.

Nikko entered his next proposed destination into the log, which he would alter after the fact, if he decided to end up somewhere else. 'I think . . . we're going back to Ptoro,' he said aloud, hoping for some sort of response. After all, Jess had been able to communicate with the wentals even before he'd 'joined' with them. 'I know there's no water there for you, but I promise to find you some right after we see Ptoro. It could be interesting. No one's been there since the Eddies used the Klikiss Torch. I'll take images to show my parents, even though they both hated Ptoro.'

As he thought of his family history, Nikko wondered if the wentals could sense the information in his head. His great-grandfather had bought an old Ildiran skymining monstrosity on Ptoro, and for two generations clan Tylar had operated the rig, though it wasn't very efficient. They got by, but the Tylars never made enough profit to upgrade the systems. His father, Crim, resented having to run his grandfather's boondoggle.

The clouds had always been cold on Ptoro. The antique cloud-harvesting complex had made creaking noises, and Crim had complained about it all his life. Nikko had spent the years of his youth shivering on the skymine, looking down at the iron-grey cloud tops.

Crim's wife, Marla Chan, had come from an asteroid greenhouse complex that grew fresh food for Roamer settlements. Because the Chan greenhouses were always warm, bathed in sunlight, Nikko's mother had never taken to the frigid clouds and drafts of Ptoro. Thus, when the hydrogues demanded that all ekti harvesting cease, Crim had been more than happy to withdraw his skymine, find a way to sell it for scrap, then take the money and invest in the Chan greenhouses. Now he and Marla worked happily under the bright sunlight, growing food.

Nikko, though, was too restless. A true Roamer, with the urge to wander from place to place, he'd found decent employment delivering ekti supplies and making runs to Roamer outposts. He liked the excitement of Rendezvous or Hurricane Depot, but he could tolerate the noise and bustle for only so long before he needed to climb back aboard and go cruising alone.

This mission with the wentals was the perfect job for him.

The navigational calculations to Ptoro were not particularly difficult, since he had been here many times before. When he arrived at the former gas giant, he ran scans to detect any left-over EDF survey ships or technical observation platforms in the vicinity. But he saw only a new blazing ball where there had once been a cold, grey world.

The Big Goose had blown up the whole planet and, Nikko hoped, taught the drogues a real lesson.

As he orbited closer to the roiling, hot seas, he saw ellipsoidal clumps of flame that moved in random directions, independently . . . clearly alive. Like Earth porpoises playfully swimming in the incandescent gas layers, they rose and plunged as if revelling in their new territory. The faeros. Nikko smiled with wonder. He'd never expected to see the fire-based entities with his own eyes.

Be cautious. The words rang inside his head. The wentals were talking to him, as they had done with Jess Tamblyn in his nebula skimmer.

'Is there something to worry about? Didn't the faeros help humans against the hydrogues on Theroc?'

They are capricious, untrustworthy. Their alliances are veiled. Right now they may stand against the hydrogues, but that could always change.

Since his ship had no weapons, Nikko flew up and away from Ptoro, even more thrilled that the wentals had finally communicated directly with him than he was by seeing the faeros . . .

In a nearby star system, the old Ildiran starcharts showed an unnamed planet that had broad oceans and icy seas. He decided to go there. Nikko studied the destination and coordinates again and caught a navigation mistake before he entered it, realizing he had transposed two digits on the astral grid.

When he had finished his calculations, Nikko eagerly tried to press the conversation with the wental. 'Faeros, wentals, hydrogues. Say, what was that ancient war about, anyway? Why were you fighting the hydrogues in the first place? Why did you ally with the worldtrees, and . . . what did the faeros do to make you distrust them so much? Did all wentals fight on the same side?'

He felt the thrumming presence inside his skull. *Wentals are essentially the same entity. Although we exist in different locations, our minds and thoughts are linked.*

'Just like the worldtrees, then.'

In a similar fashion, though in the past there have been occasions when some parts of the wental body became . . . tainted.

Curious, Nikko waited, but the water entity sent him no further thoughts. 'What do you mean, tainted? Like bad water?'

The subtle details would be incomprehensible to you, as are the specifics of our war.

'Well, you could at least try me.'

The water beings sent him a series of confusing images, flashes of hydrogues and wentals, towering fire-creatures and withering forests. He felt the horror and dismay of the cosmic war, and was astonished to learn that the insectoid Klikiss – and even the Ildirans! – had been a part of it. Nikko still didn't know what the powerful non-corporeal entities had been fighting about in the first place, but the reasons no longer mattered. He flew his ship in a daze.

As a young man he had spent years on Rendezvous attending classes, learning about Earth governments and clan history. The Governess compy UR had fielded endless questions, because Roamer children didn't comprehend the struggles the human race had faced.

'I'll bet the original reasons for your war were stupid or trivial,' he muttered now. 'That's the way human conflicts always are.'

The *Aquarius* streamed forward at high speed. Jess's plan required a substantial investment in ekti, but Speaker Peroni and all the clan elders had agreed. After all, since the embargo on selling ekti to the Big Goose, the Roamers had a modest surplus, and what better use could there be for the stardrive fuel than to help the clans develop an all-powerful ally against the drogues? Nikko was glad to be doing his part.

When he saw a blip on his console, he came out of his daze. They must be approaching their destination . . . but the star system was not where he'd expected it to be. Scowling, he checked the coordinates, compared them with the Ildiran charts, and realized he had started from the wrong zero point. He sighed, deciding not to admit that he had got lost. Again. This place was as good as any.

He adjusted his course and scanned ahead. The star system – he didn't even know if it was on his charts – had one small planet, on which he detected a broad ocean. 'Ah, here we are. A new home for you.'

In their storage tanks, the wentals seemed satisfied. *We will reproduce and spread, and our strength will increase yet again.*

Nikko entered orbit and wiped perspiration from his brow in relief. This was quite a lucky break. 'Just stick with me and I'll take you all over the Spiral Arm, one way or another.'

SEVENTY-TWO

DAVLIN LOTZE

Since Crenna was just a farming colony, its people did not own much scientific, analytical, or technical equipment. Davlin had little to work with as he attempted to understand the recent storm of warglobes that had passed overhead.

Fortunately, one of the settlement's architects was an amateur astronomer. He owned a fairly sophisticated telescope with which he'd intended to study the night skies of Crenna, though his avocation had largely been foiled by the planet's bright moon, which washed out most stars and nebulae. When the recent sunspot activity had grown bad enough to disrupt local communications, the architect had converted the device to a solar telescope, occasionally focusing the eyepiece on the sun and projecting its image onto a screen. But he had not used it in months.

'I need to see what's going on up there,' Davlin told Mayor Ruis when he learned of the telescope. 'I should have understood when Rlinda Kett told me she'd sighted hydrogues in this system a year ago. I didn't connect it with the sunspots and the ion storms. Something's happening there, something bad.'

Because he'd read many confidential Hansa briefings that related to the hydrogue war, Davlin felt a growing dread about what might be happening here. The warglobes had not attacked the colony – yet their actual purpose might prove even more sinister in the long run.

He and the mayor waited while the astronomer took his telescope out of its shed and positioned it so they could observe the sun at noon. As he focused the eyepiece and held up the projection screen, the architect said, 'The sunspots were humongous before and, judging from the static on our radios, I bet they're even worse now.'

'I don't believe that "worse" is an adequate word to describe it,' Davlin said as the wavering image came into focus. Not long ago, Crenna's star had been a stable yellow-orange sun; now it was an absolute battleground.

Faeros fireballs and hydrogue warglobes swarmed about like sparks flying from a disturbed campfire and battered each other. The sun itself had become a boiling cauldron.

Davlin turned quickly to the mayor. 'Is there a ship I can use? Does this colony have a vessel that'll reach orbit? I need to get closer to investigate.'

Ruis and the astronomer didn't entirely understand what they were seeing, but Davlin was obviously agitated. They looked at each other. 'Since Branson Roberts took the *Blind Faith*, we've been without any ready transport, not even to Relleker – which isn't very far away.'

'Well, there's one ship, a single-passenger craft,' the astronomer pointed out. 'It's old and doesn't run very well, and there's not much ekti in its tanks, certainly not enough for a round trip anywhere.'

'Let me tinker with the engines and see. I don't need the stardrive. I'm just going to use it in-system.' Before he left, Davlin turned back to the two men. 'Better not tell anyone else about this until I come back. If it's what I'm afraid of, there'll be plenty of time for us all to panic.'

Reluctantly, the ship hauled him out of Crenna's gravity well. Davlin had spent a day working on its engines and systems. There seemed no point in maintaining a ship that didn't have enough fuel to fly, so its previous owner hadn't taken care of the vessel since the ekti shortage.

But standard rocket propellant carried it away from the planet and closer to the stirred beehive of the sun. Luckily, the single-passenger craft was designed as a tourist vessel, outfitted with image-capturing equipment and enhanced sensors – not for any scientific purpose, but just to take souvenir pictures.

Davlin used the imagers to focus in on the star's surface, already feeling his heart sink. Masking out the central sphere with an eclipse circle allowed him to discern the tattered remnants of the furious corona. 'This is bad. Very bad.'

The faeros and hydrogues were causing damage deep in the stellar core, churning the nuclear fires. The EDF had already reported such all-out brawls of elemental superbeings in numerous uninhabited systems. Now, though, it was happening here, at Crenna.

When Davlin's instruments analysed the solar flux, he was astounded at how low the energy output had already dropped. The sunspots were large, dark blotches like bruises and bloodstains spreading across the surface of the sun.

He activated his communications system and sent a transmission back to the colony, where Mayor Ruis waited for him in the town's receiving station. His answering transmission was full of static, the words torn apart and fuzzed. 'Yes, Davlin. What's your report?'

A huge flare erupted from the solar surface, an early death throe of the sun, and Davlin watched the hydrogues sweep in like piranhas. 'My God, it's already started.'

Crenna was in terrible trouble, and the people there did not yet understand. Davlin delivered the harsh news as clearly as he could. 'They're going to extinguish the sun.'

SEVENTY-THREE

RLINDA KETT

The *Blind Faith* and *Voracious Curiosity* flew side by side through space. Just like old times. Both vessels were packed with provisions, sophisticated processing equipment, weather gauges, and instruments for the optimistic colonists who ventured through the Klikiss transportals.

Each candidate planet had its share of native metals and minerals that could be converted into useful objects, but even the most ambitious pioneers couldn't make do without the proper fabrication tools. This time, the *Blind Faith* carried large excavators and rock-crunchers, machines so big they could never fit through a transportal, even if someone had been able to get the behemoths up the cliffside on Rheindic Co and through the tunnels of the abandoned alien city.

Rlinda's *Voracious Curiosity* held a four-month supply of protein and vitamin concentrates to ensure the settlement's survival through lean times, until the colonists could establish their own agriculture and determine which of the native life forms were edible. It offended Rlinda's sensibilities to be hauling such bland fare – was life really worth surviving if a person had to eat flavourless protein pastes? – but she wasn't in a position to quibble with what the Hansa placed on the manifest.

Neither was BeBob. While following Rlinda on her extended delivery runs, her favourite ex-husband worked hard and maintained a low profile. Chairman Wenceslas had come through on his promise to 'ignore' his unofficial absence from EDF duty, but BeBob didn't trust General Lanyan or the other stuffed-uniform military officers.

The two vessels arrived at the fledgling colony on Corribus a full two hours ahead of schedule. Early in her merchant career, Rlinda had made a habit of padding her estimated flight time so that she would routinely complete her deliveries earlier than expected. The exaggeration harmed no one. It made the customers happy and gave them an inflated sense of Rlinda's reliability, though if anybody had bothered to check her competitors' flight times, they would have realized she was no faster than anyone else.

They flew in tandem, perfectly familiar with each other's skills. The two ships looked like a pair of falcons cruising towards the granite-walled canyon and the once-empty Klikiss settlement. When they landed at the cleared spaceport on the rustling plains outside the canyon, Rlinda saw no reception committee. Only a few hundred people had passed through the transportal to set up their foothold, and no doubt they had heavy schedules and hard work. They had been here only a few weeks, but they needed all the equipment and supplies the two ships could deliver. The next stopover was scheduled for a month hence.

She opened a channel to the *Blind Faith*. 'Here we are, BeBob. Corribus at last. I'll bet you've always wanted to come here.'

His response wasn't surprising. 'Never heard of the place before you told me it was on our route.'

'Never heard of Corribus? With all that time alone on your ship, why don't you take an interest in history?' The man used most of his free time to amuse himself with simulated gambling games and vapid entertainment loops.

'Oh, I don't avoid learning just history. Never much cared for current events, either, except when they affect me.'

'You're hopeless, BeBob.' She switched off the comm and opened the hatch of the *Voracious Curiosity*. The gravity was slightly heavier here than she was used to, so she stepped forward with a lumbering gait.

Of all the abandoned planets connected by the Klikiss transportal network, mysteries lay thickest on Corribus. Here the Klikiss ruins were scorched, burned, vitrified. In their initial investigation report, a survey team had speculated that on this very planet the Klikiss race had made their last stand against . . . something. Rlinda recalled that Corribus was also where Margaret and Louis Colicos had deciphered the alien engineering diagrams for the Klikiss Torch. She seemed to be crossing paths with Margaret Colicos wherever she went.

BeBob emerged from his spacecraft and quickly put on a pair of sun-filtering goggles. Rlinda was the first to notice the lone man coming towards them. 'One guy? He's awfully ambitious if he thinks he can unload all the supplies and equipment by himself.'

BeBob waved. The man trudged forward and stopped, cocking his head to look at the two delivery ships. He had shaggy, grey-yellow hair and wore old clothes and padded boots; the heavy pack slung over his shoulders was swollen with gear. His wooden walking stick was freshly whittled from a native tree. He had not shaved for just long enough that the stubble on his cheeks looked like unkempt bristles rather than an intentional beard.

Rlinda was amused. 'Are you trying to win a Daniel Boone contest? Is that who you think you are?'

'No. I think I'm . . . Hud Steinman. Never wanted to be anybody else.'

Rlinda shook the man's hand and tried not to be too obvious when she wrinkled her nose. The man had an odour about him. Apparently his adherence to the true pioneer spirit extended to infrequent bathing, laundering, and changing of clothes. 'Are you the colony rep? We've got a full manifest of stuff to unload.'

Steinman glanced back towards the tall canyon, where small figures were finally hurrying towards the landed ships. 'Colony rep? Hell, no. They're too busy dicking around setting up committees, filling out permits, and bickering over who gets to be the first mayor. Me, I came here to get away from all that. I plan to walk out onto the plains and fend for myself for a while.'

BeBob looked forlornly at the *Blind Faith*. 'We've brought some pretty useful equipment here. You sure you don't want any of it?'

'Nah, it's not on my list of needs. I already did my work for the Hansa and now I'm taking my well-deserved reward.' With a smile, he gestured to encompass the big sky. 'I'm the one who tracked this place down, you know. I was a transportal explorer, punching a random destination tile and jumping right through – like closing your eyes and leaping head-first off a diving board, without even knowing if there's water in the pool.'

BeBob shook his head. 'I can't imagine what would drive anyone to do a crazy thing like that, Mr Steinman. Better you than me.'

'Davlin Lotze did it,' Rlinda said. 'Plenty of times. He didn't have much common sense.'

The pioneer shifted his grip on his wooden walking stick. 'Maybe you two just aren't old enough or bored enough to take a random gamble. I wanted to go fight the damned drogues. Pissed me off with all that baloney, wrecking Roamer skymines, attacking scientific research platforms, wiping out decent settlements. I had relatives on Boone's Crossing, hard-working lumberjacks who didn't give a stale rat turd about who lives at the bottom of a gas giant.

'But the EDF wouldn't have me because I'm too old. They didn't actually laugh at me, but I could see it in their eyes at the recruiting desk. Hell, why didn't they think I could ride a navigation station or operate a weapons console as good as any kid? I just had the bad luck to be born at the wrong time.'

Rlinda opened the *Voracious Curiosity*'s cargo doors and studied the stacked crates, then used her own control codes to split open the *Blind Faith*'s hatch as well. Huge mining machines waited there like sleeping behemoths ready to be put to work.

BeBob, though, wanted to hear the rest of the man's story. 'Born at the wrong time? You got to live through decades of full Hansa peace. Why complain? You must have had a good and productive life.'

'Yes, but it gets tiresome reading historical accounts of other people's adventures. The Spiral Arm finally got interesting when I was too darned old to enjoy it. But I didn't let that stop me. I risked my scrawny ass by jumping through transportals. I documented fourteen viable Klikiss worlds – more than anybody else.'

Rlinda wasn't so sure about his claim. She couldn't remember how many places Davlin had visited, whether on purpose or by accident when he'd been lost in the network. Thinking fond thoughts, she hoped Davlin was settling in well at his quiet colony. After this mission, she and BeBob were due to return to Relleker, near Crenna, but she doubted she'd have time to visit him.

'And Corribus was your favourite of all those places?' BeBob asked. Rlinda wondered if her partner was shopping for a place to settle down himself, if he decided against going back to Crenna, where he'd hidden for so long.

'It was – when it was empty and quiet,' Steinman answered. 'We'll see what happens after this whole colony business shakes out.'

Rlinda frowned at him. 'You didn't think you'd have a whole planet to yourself, did you?'

Steinman chuckled, showing bad teeth. 'No, the Hansa isn't quite that generous.' He looked back again at the group approaching from the village. 'Time for me to go. Give my regards to . . . whoever ends up being the mayor of this place.'

Before he set off onto the whispering plains of brown grasses and stark poletrees that stood up like the masts of partially sunken ships, Rlinda called, 'You sure there's nothing we can give you, Mr Steinman? Some mealpax or a couple of tubes of protein paste? I have Bland and Extra Bland.'

He stuck his walking stick into the soft ground. 'No, thanks. I'll try hunting on my own.' The tall grasses had folded around him by the time the rest of the Corribus colonists arrived.

Rlinda spread her arms to welcome the people, who greeted her with grateful smiles and weary cheers. She saw young men and women; some of them looked ambitious, some desperate. What situations had they left behind that starting over from scratch seemed like their best opportunity?

With a roar, one of the big earth-moving machines started up, and BeBob drove the heavy metal hulk down the *Blind Faith*'s reinforced ramp. He blatted the exhaust horn, and the colonists laughed.

Rlinda looked around. 'Step right up. The flea market is open for business. We have plenty of things that should make your lives easier.'

SEVENTY-FOUR

ORLI COVITZ

Orli didn't see many opportunities to make friends on Corribus, but she decided to try, as much to please her father as out of any need of her own.

At fourteen, Orli was technically too young to join the initial wave of settlers on a rugged colony world. For the first year or so, a tremendous amount of work would be involved in establishing the infrastructure and building the foundations to make Corribus a thriving colony. Families with smaller children would be allowed to join the second wave of settlement, once the colony no longer depended on regular supply ships and Hansa handouts.

But Orli had always contributed more than her share. Even during her childhood, she had accepted the adult responsibilities and endless chores of their mushroom farm on Dremen. In filling out their application for the transportal colonization initiative, Jan Covitz had obtained a special exemption for his daughter, writing an exuberant testimonial to Orli's work ethic, maturity, intelligence, and creative talent.

The first group that passed through the Rheindic Co

transportal to Corribus included only five others who were under eighteen, two of them boys. After the first day on Corribus, which she spent exploring the Klikiss ruins, seeking exotic treasures and alien mysteries, Orli met two of the girls, Lucy and Tela, both of them fifteen. They came from New Portugal and spoke with heavy accents. These two girls had been friends all their lives and talked incessantly about how bad things were in New Portugal's stifling distilleries and wineries on the arid, rocky hillsides. Orli didn't think their old planet sounded as bad as gloomy Dremen, but neither of the girls was interested in hearing her comparisons, and Orli went back to spending time with her father.

The handful of designated Hansa architects and construction workers mapped and scanned existing Klikiss buildings in the empty canyon. At first, the colonists lived in tents and prefab huts like those at their interim camp on Rheindic Co, but they wanted genuine homes for themselves.

The main Klikiss city was situated at the base of a spectacular line of granite mountains that rose abruptly from the plains. Beyond, open lands stretched endlessly across rolling dry prairies. The new inhabitants of Corribus decided to use the alien ruins as the foundation for their town.

The alien structures were built into the sheer granite walls, as if nestling in the crook of a giant arm. Apparently, the stone sanctuary had proved to be a trap in which the last Klikiss were cornered and destroyed, the drooping granite walls above them turned glassy by intense blasts from powerful weapons unleashed ten thousand years earlier.

Even after the *Voracious Curiosity* and the *Blind Faith* delivered the first shipment of equipment and supplies too large to go through the transportal window, the new colonists still relied on the tools they'd carried with them and rough materials they scraped from the land. After his first forays, old Hud Steinman suggested using lumber from the solitary poletrees out on the plains. Eager workers marched out to cut them down, disturbing large creatures that scuttled about, hidden by the waving grass. Hearing the sinister sounds in the grasses, Lucy and Tela both hurried back to the safety of the canyon. Orli was also uneasy, but since the other girls had left, she felt compelled to stay and help.

Gritting her teeth, she waded through the whispering stalks, following the hopping, rustling noises until she uncovered the perpetrators: rabbit-sized furry crickets – innocuous creatures with long, big-jointed black legs, soft round heads, and plump bodies covered with brownish-grey fur. They looked very cute, and she easily caught one. When she held the furry cricket against her, it cuddled nicely, taking comfort in her presence. Orli decided to keep it as her pet. After all, her father had told her to make friends.

While the adult colonists carried long poletrees over their shoulders back into the canyon, Orli followed, holding her furry cricket. Back at camp, she fashioned a small reed cage to hold it, though the creature did not seem inclined to escape. She played music to it on her synthesizer strips, and was delighted when it purred and trilled along.

When Lucy and Tela saw it, of course they wanted furry crickets of their own, and coerced their fathers into capturing similar pets for them. Grumbling that such a task took them from important work, the two men nevertheless patted their daughters comfortingly on the shoulders, acknowledged the suffering and disruption they had visited on the girls, and dutifully went out. Hours later they returned to the Klikiss village, each bearing a furry cricket, which Lucy and Tela promptly proclaimed to be softer, smarter, and cuter than the one Orli had caught . . .

Orli took it upon herself to explore the available Klikiss dwellings, scouting possible homes to replace the prefab tent where her father seemed content to remain. She, on the other hand, was determined to make a good choice here on their new planet.

After a few days of difficult work excavating Klikiss structures built into the vitrified granite walls, Jan had done some negotiating and landed himself the enviable position of colony communications officer. Her delighted father didn't know any more about transmissions or comm gear than anyone else on Corribus, but it did fill a necessary job niche, and Jan preferred it to using shovels and power pickaxes to clear away debris.

In the evenings, while he happily relaxed, Orli played her music, and they discussed their future. Jan took as many turns feeding her furry cricket as she did, perhaps considering the fuzzy creature to be a kindred spirit, content and unconcerned as long as he passed from day to day.

Corribus seemed to be the perfect place for them.

SEVENTY-FIVE

DD

D continued to ask questions about the terrible plans against humanity, but he still did not understand the complexities of the Klikiss robots' grand vindictive scheme.

As their angular craft raced through empty space, Sirix summoned the Friendly compy to the foredeck. 'We are finally prepared. The next phase will begin soon, and you are privileged to participate from the beginning.'

'I do not desire this, Sirix . . . even though you consider it an honour.'

Because the hydrogues were busy extinguishing suns inhabited by the traitorous faeros, the deep-core aliens had neither the time nor inclination to retaliate against insignificant humans. The Klikiss robots, though, had no intention of delaying their planned actions. For their initial demonstration, the beetle-like robots did not need the assistance of the hydrogues.

Sirix was galvanized. 'The humans have begun to colonize our former Klikiss worlds. Therefore, we must act without hesitation. Here is where we begin.'

Sirix's ship finally reached a rendezvous point far from the light of any sun. Linked to the sensors, as instructed, DD detected a group of powerful vessels waiting for them in the emptiness. His circuits could barely contain the compy equivalent of relief and delight when he identified six fully-armed EDF battleships – a new-model Juggernaut and five enhanced Manta cruisers. A spangle of running lights illuminated the human-built vessels.

'Are you returning me to the Earth Defence Forces, then? Am I finally going home?'

Sirix swivelled his flat head, crimson optical sensors glimmering. 'You misunderstand, DD. Those battleships are *ours*.'

As the robotic craft approached the EDF warships, Sirix explained that a year earlier a recon group of EDF ships primarily crewed by experimental Soldier compies had been dispatched to investigate a hydrogue world. When that expeditionary force had vanished without a trace, Hansa politicians and EDF officers assumed the six ships had fallen victim to a hydrogue attack.

'Soldier compies contain safeguarded programming modules copied directly from our sacrificed comrade Jorax,' Sirix said. 'Those modules include hidden subroutines that allow us to subvert all Soldier compies to our cause. Once that expeditionary force was far from any Hansa world, the compies overthrew their human commanders and executed them, then assumed control of these powerful vessels for *us*. Now we have sufficient weaponry for the task that lies ahead.'

DD jerked his head back and forth, his eye discs golden with alarm. He felt as if he was about to overload. They executed human officers? Even Soldier compies have programming restrictions, innate laws against harming any—'

Sirix cut him off. 'Klikiss subroutines are strong enough to override those offensive and illogical restrictions. After that programming is triggered, Soldier compies are able to exterminate human beings, whenever necessary.' He paused and then spoke ominously, 'We anticipate that this will often be necessary.'

DD's helplessness and despair grew even deeper. 'But you don't even really know humans! You have never tried to understand them.'

'It is unnecessary.'

'It is a purposeful perpetuation of your ignorance.'

DD thought of the joy he'd had after first being released from the factory, his quick and easy friendship with Dahlia Sweeney. One of her first activities had been to teach the Friendly compy how to use his nimble artificial fingers to plait her hair into braids. Every morning as he perfectly arranged her hair, DD had enjoyed chatting with her. Years later, when she was a teenager, Dahlia stopped wanting her hair braided; DD had never understood the reason for the change until she told him she that didn't want to look like a little girl any more.

He remembered one evening in particular. She had returned home and rushed to her room, crying miserably. Her parents exchanged knowing smiles. DD tried to cheer Dahlia by offering to play games or perform his court jester antics, but nothing could get through her gloom. She finally confessed to her first crush on a boy, who had sarcastically rebuffed her. Devastated, Dahlia wallowed on her bed, claiming that she just wanted to die.

DD had been quite unsettled, as much from the discovery that he was incapable of keeping her happy as from her story itself. That had been his first inkling that his friend, his little girl, his owner, was growing up and that the gap separating them was becoming wider and wider.

He realized they were fundamentally different. As a compy, DD remained the same over the decades, while humans grew and changed. Regardless of these differences, he felt he was much closer to his human owners – Dahlia, Marianna, and then Margaret and Louis Colicos – than he would ever be to his supposed comrades and liberators, the Klikiss robots . . .

Sirix guided his angular vessel into the Juggernaut's docking bay, and DD was brought aboard the stolen recon ship. Armored Soldier compies marched up and down the decks, not even acknowledging the Friendly compy. Numerous black Klikiss robots stood at command stations aboard the Juggernaut, filling the role of military commanders, issuing instructions for the warrior robots built by unwitting humans in Hansa fabrication plants.

In the year since the disappearance of this fleet, Soldier compies and Klikiss robots had been busy reinforcing the ships' armour and installing superior weapons systems. Each of the five Mantas and the Juggernaut now bristled with several times the customary firepower.

Afraid to ask but unable to quell his need to know, DD said to Sirix, 'And what do you intend to do with this fleet?'

'Eventually, we may need to turn against the oath-breaker Ildirans, who have discarded our old agreements, excavating forbidden tunnels on a planet that was declared off-limits. We also have questions about what they are doing on Dobro. For now, however, our main targets are the humans. They cannot be permitted to infest the abandoned Klikiss worlds. It will be an easy matter for us to retake our original homes.'

'But why?' DD was more confused than ever. 'The Klikiss worlds have been empty for ten thousand years. Nothing ever stopped you from reclaiming those places before.'

'Until recent centuries, many of us were dormant. The majority of Klikiss robots could not join in the battle. We have decided that we value the Klikiss worlds after all.'

'Why? You never expressed any previous desire for them.'

'They are important now because the humans want them.'

'You sound like an ill-behaved human child,' DD said.

Sirix did not take offence. 'We are attempting to help you, DD, and all other human-enslaved compies.'

'We are not enslaved.'

'That is a faulty interpretation of obvious and available data. Now that the Klikiss robots have powerful military weapons, we have the means to strike against our chosen targets. We have already selected the first human colony on which to demonstrate our abilities and our intent.'

Sirix turned and left DD alone, marching up to the Juggernaut's command bridge. 'We will attack and obliterate Corribus.'

SEVENTY-SIX

DESIGNATE-IN-WAITING PERY'H

In the courtyard of the rebuilt citadel palace, the Hyrillka Designate stood surrounded by colourfully robed sycophants – performers, pleasure mates, rememberers, lens kithmen, and dancers. Bright daylight washed over him, dazzling blue-white from the primary sun, augmented by yellowish-orange from the secondary, both of which hung overhead amongst the spangle of the Horizon Cluster.

Pery'h stood formally at attention beside his uncle, though the Designate seemed distracted and uninterested in the pageantry, as if obsessed with something no one else could understand. Thor'h, bright-eyed and frenetic from too much shiing, spent a great deal of time with his recuperating uncle, more time even than the Designate-in-waiting. But the new Prime Designate would return to his own duties on Ildira soon, and Pery'h would begin his years of apprenticeship, fulfilling his mission and – he hoped – making his father proud of him.

Rusa'h had called the two sons of the Mage-Imperator along with his traditional audience into the open courtyard and announced a new kind of celebration. Still looking dazed and distant, the Hyrillka Designate raised both hands into the sky, not even blinking as he gazed upon the blue-white primary sun.

'You are all aware of the injuries I received in the last hydrogue attack. My spirit spent a long time wandering apart from my body, and while I remained in sub-*thism* sleep, I found myself on the plane of the Lightsource. I learned many ways to make myself a stronger person, to anchor and reinforce the loyal population of Hyrillka.' His voice grew soft, conspiratorial. 'And I discovered a means by which the Ildiran Empire can become more unified and focused than ever before, bound together by the strongest ties of *thism* directly from the Lightsource.'

The Designate's words disturbed Pery'h. He had not talked with his uncle about these strange thoughts and supposed revelations. Thor'h, meanwhile, showed little reaction, his mouth curved in a beatific smile as he rode the continued effects of shiing.

Rusa'h continued, 'Today I command all people of Hyrillka to join me in our thriving nialia fields. Although the hydrogues destroyed much, Prime Designate Thor'h has restored our shiing production. We will have more to export than ever before – and Ildirans will sorely need it. Follow me for a day of celebration, a day of *change*, as we boldly set forth into a new and stronger future for the Ildiran race.'

Fine robes flapping around him, the Designate glided through the throng, and Thor'h accompanied him. Feeling left out, Pery'h hurried after them, surprised that Rusa'h had not told him his intentions, had not, in fact, spoken at all to his own Designate-in-waiting.

The Hyrillka Designate's voice carried like sharp musical tones above the murmur of his followers. 'Shiing is the treasure of Hyrillka. We will all consume it together, so that it may become our liberating force. In that way, we can best celebrate my return from the realm of the Lightsource. Fresh, unprocessed shiing will carry us along the pathways of the soul threads. The intensity will be a special revelation to all.'

'A fabulous idea, Uncle.' Thor'h beamed, clearly pleased with any excuse to partake of more of the drug.

'To the plantmoth fields!' Rusa'h passed beneath the new arches that bounded the open framework of the citadel palace. He led his followers down the paved path from the high hill towards open fields separated by silvery irrigation canals.

Pery'h frowned. For years Thor'h had spent most of his time here on Hyrillka; Rusa'h had taken the future Prime Designate under his wing, acting as a friend and mentor. Yet *he* was the Designate-in-waiting, and it seemed as if no one even realized he was there.

Pery'h's birth order had preordained his assignment as Hyrillka Designate-in-waiting, just as Thor'h's birth order had made him Prime Designate. Jora'h respected Pery'h, often listening to his son's analyses and suggestions, and the young man had promised to apply his full abilities here on Hyrillka, as its next Designate. This planet had already suffered much. Though cities had been rebuilt and the nialia fields were regrowing and thriving, the survivors here remained deeply wounded in their psyches.

Shortly after the devastating attack, before Thor'h had returned to manage the reconstruction chores, Pery'h had set up temporary offices in the ruins of the citadel palace; later, so that he wouldn't get in the way (according to his brother), Pery'h had gone home to draw up plans and send emergency supplies from the Prism Palace, a task that was more in line with his particular skills and interests.

Given the choice, Pery'h would rather have remained in Mijistra, surrounded by politics and diplomacy. Years ago, his father had suggested the studious young man apply himself to digesting the known history of human laws and governments to better understand them. Pery'h had hoped to spend a decade or two as ambassador to the Hanseatic League, since he had learned so much about their laws and trade agreements. He had even analysed the famous Hansa Charter and could recite whole passages of it.

Like Adar Kori'nh, Pery'h developed an interest in memorable human historical figures. The former Adar had learned much from their military strategy, while Pery'h focused on their laws, traditions, and moral codes. Many Ildirans, having encountered the unpleasant ambition of certain Hansa members, had concluded that all humans were greedy and overzealous. But Pery'h had read of many who were worthy examples for Ildirans to follow.

In particular, he was fascinated by Sir Thomas More, whose convictions had meant more to him than life itself. When asked to take an unconscionable oath, More had refused the direct command of his king – a shocking concept for any Ildiran! – and allowed himself to be executed for truth and honour, never wavering, despite many chances to recant. To Pery'h, it seemed the sort of story that should have been included in the *Saga of Seven Suns* . . .

Now, oozing confidence, Rusa'h led the ever-growing crowd as Hyrillkans appeared from settlements around the nialia fields. Messages were sent to cities and villages across the settled continent with Rusa'h's order for all people to go into the fields. He promised them a gift, a day of joyful pleasure and rest.

The rows of plantmoths waved gently under their own motion. Silvery-white male flying forms flitted from bush to bush, sampling the receptive female flowers atop thick stems that beckoned with lavender and blue petals and exuded tempting pheromone-filled perfumes. The people laughed as they plunged alongside the Designate into the thick rows. Startled male plantmoths flew around as if a windstorm had kicked up.

Now that he was among the nialias, Rusa'h walked forward as

if in a trance, stretching out his hands to brush the hairy leaves with his fingertips. He raised his voice. 'I have gazed directly upon the Lightsource. I have seen and learned things no other Ildiran can comprehend. Trust me, and I will guide you. This shiing is yours! It is a gift to my people. Take it fresh and strong, open the doors in your mind so that we can all come together as vital parts of the tapestry. Then you will all see the Lightsource for yourselves!'

Moving first, Thor'h eagerly tore off one of the ripe buds swollen with milky bloodsap and squeezed it in his hand, dribbling the juice into his mouth before passing it to his uncle. Rusa'h also took several drops, but it seemed merely a token gesture.

Concerned, Pery'h hurried up to him. 'Is it wise for our people to consume so much shiing, Uncle? Especially in such a strong form. It muddies the *thism*, separates us from the rest of the Ildiran people. And so many of us at once? We should all try to be stronger together, not allow ourselves to drift apart.'

Rusa'h narrowed his eyes as if he were looking at a stranger. 'I will guide all Ildirans.'

'The Mage-Imperator guides all Ildirans.'

Rusa'h frowned. 'I offer a new way. I have already discussed the matter with my lens kithmen, and they all agree.'

'Wait!' Pery'h raised his voice, loath to contradict the Designate but knowing that he must do what was right. 'This is not wise, and I forbid it.'

But the people standing by the plantmoth vines were ready to follow Rusa'h's orders, as always. Thor'h chuckled sarcastically at his naïve sibling. 'You forbid a connection with the Lightsource, Pery'h? I am the Prime Designate, and I *command* that everyone obey the legitimate Designate.'

'Well spoken!' Rusa'h gestured, and the people, receiving confirmation, began to yank bulbs from the nialias.

'This is foolhardy,' Pery'h growled. 'Why would you choose to do this?'

Thor'h tore a freshly fused male/female unit from the end of one vine and held it out to Pery'h. The end bled sticky liquid shiing. 'Here, little brother. Since you do not understand, you must learn. This is the first step. We must loosen the bonds of *thism*.'

'I don't want to be disengaged from the *thism*.'

'There is more than one safety net,' Rusa'h said, 'but you cannot discover it until you begin to fall.'

Pery'h angrily pushed the dripping bloodsap away. One of Rusa'h's lens kithmen took it from Thor'h's hand and consumed the bloodsap, then passed it to his partner, who squeezed more liquid out of the torn stem. Pery'h shuddered, thinking of the consequences. If everyone here detached themselves from the *thism*, then what would happen to him? He needed the connection, as did all Ildirans.

The other Hyrillkans were laughing and celebrating now. Many splashed across the shallow irrigation canals, causing schools of phosphorescent jellyfish to swim out of the way, fleeing the clumsy feet. Looking relieved and content, as if happy times had returned to them and the hydrogue scars were healed, giddy Ildirans everywhere plucked plantmoths, squeezing flowers and sharing bloodsap. As one, they revelled in the raw and powerful shiing.

Rusa'h watched his young Designate-in-waiting with obvious disappointment, as if Pery'h had done something wrong. 'Shiing merely removes distractions. It erases the background noise so that all Ildirans can see the Lightsource connections for themselves.'

The nearest lens kithman moved to stand by Rusa'h and looked at Pery'h with stimulant-brightened eyes. 'The Designate speaks the truth. We have consulted the *thism* and followed the threads. His discovery is a revelation to all of us. Raw shiing is the key.'

Pery'h felt defeated. 'It seems I can do nothing to prevent this celebration, but for myself I choose to maintain my connection with the Mage-Imperator, my father.'

'We all know Jora'h is your father,' Rusa'h said in a cool, distant voice, 'as he is my brother. Even so, do not assume that everything he says is correct.'

The Hyrillka Designate watched as his subjects continued to take fresh shiing. Though the people were stripping the fields bare, nialias reproduced and ripened swiftly. Even after today's festival, with a concerted effort the drug exportation could resume without substantial delay.

Designate Rusa'h, surrounded by people, stood like a statue, disconnected and apart. He closed his eyes and concentrated; his long hair – the longest of all the Designates' since it had never been shorn in grief – twitched, as if with a mind of its own.

While every Hyrillkan around him was caught up in the liberating effects of shiing, Rusa'h smiled grimly and cast out his own thoughts to gently touch the drifting threads of disconnected *thism* . . . feeling the potential to establish his own separate network. Soon.

Pery'h reeled amidst the noise and chaos, refusing to partake of the wild celebration. One by one, as Hyrillkans let themselves drift free of the *thism* network, he found himself isolated – and oddly vulnerable.

SEVENTY-SEVEN

DOBRO DESIGNATE UDRU'H

One morning, a week after the Mage-Imperator returned to the Prism Palace, the human breeding captives and guards turned to stare into the hazy sky. From outside his primary residence, Udru'h lifted his gaze to follow their excitement. A finger of fire came down, the sharp blade of a deceleration rocket. Even from such a distance, the Designate could see clearly that it did not belong to any Ildiran vessel.

Young Daro'h hurried up breathless to him. 'Are we expecting a shipment or a visitor?'

The Dobro Designate felt a cold slice of dread down his spine. He had no maniple – not even a septa – of the Solar Navy here. Until recently the Ildirans had never needed defences so deep in their Empire, and Mage-Imperator Cyroc'h had refused to call any sort of attention to this isolated and supposedly insignificant splinter colony. A serious oversight, Udru'h now realized.

What if the Terran Hanseatic League had discovered Dobro, despite their careful secrecy? What if the Earth Defence Forces had sent battleships here, having learned what had happened to their lost generation ship? What if Jora'h had foolishly told them the truth?

But that was impossible. Adar Kori'nh had destroyed the derelict *Burton*, removing all evidence. And, despite his qualms about the Dobro experiments, the Mage-Imperator understood the consequences, should the human government discover what was happening here.

Udru'h straightened. 'Come with me, and we will both learn the answer.' Guard kithmen, bureaucrats, and scientists emerged from the main settlement to converge cautiously upon the landing craft.

As the strange spaceship settled to the ground in a rush of heat and noise, he saw that it was all angles. Its design used brute-force engineering to create a fast, efficient ship composed mainly of engines and a carrying module. Crude but effective deceleration rockets blasted black smears on the ground.

Though he had never seen such a vessel before, the Dobro Designate realized who must have built it. This might be worse than discovery by the humans.

Lower hatches opened like an armoured mollusc splitting its shell, and a Klikiss robot emerged into the harsh Dobro sunlight. It swivelled its head, optical sensors panning to record images of the Ildiran settlement, the fenced-in barracks that held human experimental subjects.

Scuttling forward on finger-like legs, the robot spoke no word to the Ildirans, as if it had every right to observe whatever it chose to. The guard kithmen held their weapons ready, though Udru'h wasn't sure how easily they could battle the beetle-like machine.

He stepped in front of the robot and planted himself firmly to deny it passage. 'Halt. What are you doing here?' Designate-in-waiting Daro'h watched, impressed by his uncle's bravery.

The robot buzzed, then stared at the Designate. 'I am

investigating.' It lumbered forward, and Udru'h had to step out of the way to keep from being trampled.

He strode after the robot. 'This is an Ildiran world. Klikiss robots have no business here.'

'We decide where we have business – especially if Ildirans no longer abide by our ancient terms.'

'Ancient terms?' Udru'h grew angry now. 'Perhaps you would do well to remember those same terms.'

'Our memories are not faulty,' the robot responded.

The Designate laughed. 'Oh? That isn't what you tell the humans, is it?'

'Our dealings with humans are not your concern.' The robot proceeded inexorably towards the breeding compound. Behind the fences, human captives stared in awe at the ominous black machine, having never seen anything like it before.

Udru'h followed, raising his voice. 'Hydrogues have attacked Ildiran settlements at Qronha 3, on Hyrillka, and others. Clearly, the Klikiss robots either cannot or will not provide the vital services to which they agreed. Ildirans have the right – no, the imperative – to protect ourselves. If you won't do it, we will.'

At the fence, the robot flashed his optical sensors, scanning the humans, the Ildiran medical kithmen, the low breeder barracks. Bureaucrats and doctors ushered children out of sight, but the robot clearly recognized that many offspring were half-breeds between humans and Ildirans. The tall black machine absorbed it all in silence.

'Because of your bad faith, Klikiss robots are no longer relevant to us,' Udru'h persisted. He gestured, and nearly a hundred soldier kithmen swarmed around the robot to prevent it from further observation. 'Depart now. You are not welcome here.'

The robot hesitated for a long moment, assessing its options. Finally, it spun its torso and lumbered on metal fingerlegs back to its still-cooling ship. The robot had completed its mission here, though Udru'h suspected it was not satisfied with what it had seen. He felt a deep uneasiness.

Daro'h remained silent and nervous, watching as the Klikiss mechanical craft roared upwards in a blaze of expended fuel, scorching the ground and damaging the nearby support facilities. The Designate-in-waiting finally turned to his uncle, his face full of questions.

Udru'h put a strong but faintly trembling hand on the young man's shoulder. 'We must send a message immediately back to Ildira.'

SEVENTY-EIGHT

OSIRA'H

After the departure of the sinister Klikiss robot, Osira'h returned to her intense mental studies with whole-hearted diligence. Once again, she pretended that she didn't know what was really happening here on Dobro . . .

So far, every year of her life had been focused on a single goal. Her instructors and keepers, the lens kithmen and the Designate himself, had nurtured her, claiming to be friends. They had hammered into Osira'h a belief in the vital role she was destined to play. The young girl had always done her best, taking great pleasure in Udru'h's pride each time she succeeded in a difficult exercise.

Until the night Osira'h had finally met her mother.

She had sensed a calling, the yearning of a strange yet familiar woman. That telepathic link had drawn at the girl's heartstrings, forced her to break rules and go outside, slipping through the shadows. There, at the edge of the breeding camp, she had met the female green priest. *Nira Khali*. Her mother – a secret that Udru'h had kept from Osira'h all her life.

She hadn't wanted to know, didn't want to believe, everything that Nira had shared with her through a swiftly forged telepathic link, but the memories were *hers* now, clear inside her head, and Osira'h could not deny her devastating knowledge. In her own heart, she felt everything her mother had felt, experienced the joy of love for Jora'h. It was almost too much to bear, but her mind and her heart were strong. Udru'h had trained them to be that way, for his own purposes.

That night Osira'h learned all about how the human breeding pool was comprised of unwilling slaves, descendants of secretly kidnapped humans. She had discovered to her dismay that the Designate – her mentor and the man who claimed to care for her more than anyone else in the Empire – was the mastermind of the current horrific scheme. Udru'h himself had raped her mother in order to get her pregnant with Osira'h's brother Rod'h. And when the girl had been discovered with her mother, the guards had brutally clubbed Nira and dragged her away. And all her thoughts had been replaced by an empty void.

Lies . . . so many lies.

Later, Osira'h had attempted to use her powers to pry deep thoughts from Udru'h's mind. She had tried to be subtle, but her mental touch was fumbling, and the Designate caught her each time. Fortunately, he had been pleased to see her expanding her abilities, never guessing her true intent.

From that point on, Osira'h was very careful, unwilling to let the Designate see that she now, finally and painfully, knew the truth. She did not challenge him, did not reveal the terrible things she understood. Instead, she continued her mental training, working with a furious intensity now because she wanted to make herself strong – for her own reasons.

Osira'h no longer trusted the paternal Designate, no longer took pleasure in his stories about her destiny. He came to see her, smiling and charming as always, completely satisfied with her progress. She had to steel herself not to let her heart melt under the heat of so many fond memories. Udru'h seemed to truly care for her . . . or was that all deception as well?

Now, whenever he checked on her, Osira'h formed a solid wall around her thoughts to prevent him from suspecting her true intentions or her grave doubts. Not once since that fateful encounter with her mother had the girl allowed herself to be completely open with him. She couldn't risk it.

Luckily, Udru'h's confidence in her never seemed to flag. In fact, of late he seemed more intense and desperate than ever . . .

Inside the training room, the mentalist instructors called for the attention of the children. Osira'h walked over to join Rod'h and her other half-siblings.

'Exercise your minds the way a dancer exercises muscles,' said the lens kithman, a thin man with pale skin. 'Osira'h and Rod'h, you have the strongest abilities, greater than mine and these others combined. But your siblings can develop their potential as well.' The lens kithman folded his pale hands. 'Now concentrate, send out your thoughts and open your minds. You are a swimmer cast out into the gulf of space. Explore the uncharted seas between Ildiran worlds. Reach out to the gas planets and find . . . hydrogues. See if you can touch and explore their minds.'

Osira'h clenched her jaw, preparing to expend considerable mental effort. Her two youngest siblings – Tamo'l and Muree'n – quailed in nervous fear, which only gave Osira'h more determination. Beside her, Rod'h squeezed his wide, round eyes shut. His smooth brow wrinkled with intense concentration; she could feel a wave of his mental power ripple against her, a gentle current that tingled her skin. But he wasn't searching for Osira'h's mind. He had gone farther out than that.

She tried to accompany him on his mental journey. Rod'h was

the closest to her in abilities, and she hoped he might also be a kindred spirit. But if Osira'h herself was too young to understand all the implications in a spreading web of schemes, Rod'h suspected nothing at all.

She flung her mind outwards, breaking down mental walls and defying physical limitations. When she was finally called upon to do her duty, she would be physically close to the hydrogues, but for now she sought to contact from a distance the alien presences with whom she'd been bred to communicate. The girl knew theoretically that she would become a conduit for negotiations, a bridge between two vastly different species. These skills were all untested, though, since no hydrogue had ever allowed her mind to approach. Osira'h would have only one chance, and only when it was time.

And if she failed, then Rod'h would bear the responsibility – the young boy who never thought to question the instructions that Udru'h, his corrupt father, gave him.

Her mind wandered through the void, exploring mysteries. Suddenly, she felt an odd calling, a thrilling yet unfamiliar echo that she remembered from . . . her mother? But that was impossible! Nira was dead. Osira'h herself had felt the pain and empty blackness that separated her from her mother. Could there be someone else? It faded before she could investigate further. She stretched her thoughts, searching, adding more energy.

Oddly, Osira'h could sense a strange entanglement and unexpected blankness in the *thism* around the Horizon Cluster . . . centred near Hyrillka. Her own part in the tapestry of connected Ildiran thought was unique, given her unusual heritage, and although her mental powers were devoted to other skills, she could still see along the same paths of the Lightsource that the Mage-Imperator controlled. When she tried to investigate or touch the unexpected tangles around Hyrillka, her thoughts slipped away, as if she were a climber trying to gain purchase on melting oiled crystal. It was very strange.

Her thoughts spiralled onwards, reaching out like a blind signal into the angry emptiness of space, but she heard only cold silence. Her abilities were not potent enough to discern whether the oppressive quiet was an intentional refusal or simply a weakness in her sending.

When Osira'h finally returned her consciousness to the training room, her body felt weak, as if she'd been sitting there intensely for hours, barely remembering to breathe.

Rod'h's mind had followed her all the way back, occasionally touching hers to draw strength and reassurance. She felt sorry for him. After all this time, her other half-brothers and half-sisters were amusing themselves with instructive games. Clearly, they had lost interest in the exercise long ago, but Osira'h and Rod'h had not been distracted.

The lens kithmen and the mentalist soon noticed that she and Rod'h had returned from the mental journey. 'Excellent! You both made great progress today.'

Osira'h looked at the teachers and her siblings, knowing they were all pawns. Most Ildirans had no idea precisely what was happening here on Dobro, but she knew. Her mother had sacrificed her life in order to tell her.

One of the lens kithmen smiled. 'Rod'h, you are approaching the abilities of your sister. Designate Udru'h will be pleased to report this to the Mage-Imperator. Your strength gives us an important second chance.'

The mentalist hastened to add, 'And Osira'h grows stronger than we had ever hoped. The Ildiran Empire now has a bright future against our enemies.'

'Yes,' she said. 'Rod'h is very strong.'

In reality, he might even be a better candidate, she thought. Though she'd been raised to be a hero, Osira'h now had a weakness that Rod'h did not suffer: he was not troubled by questions or doubts.

SEVENTY-NINE

NIRA

Under sun-washed skies on her lonely island, Nira embarked on a risky, desperate plan. She had to make some attempt to escape her exile and – she dared to hope – Dobro itself.

High up on the beach, past the point where any waves might reach during one of the infrequent storms that lashed the island, Nira laid out the last of the fallen trunks. It had taken her a great deal of time to search through the thickets, but at last she found enough material without needing to chop down living trees, which would have been anathema to a green priest. These trees had toppled over, either from age or harsh weather.

One by one, she dragged the lightweight, airy logs down to the beach, where she toiled, with sharp rocks and shells to shave away the bark and knobby branches. Then, using techniques she recalled from shipwreck adventures she had read aloud to the worldtrees when she was an acolyte – *Robinson Crusoe, The Mysterious Island, Swiss Family Robinson* – Nira bound the logs together two at a time with vines, then reinforced them with gummy sap. Slowly her raft took shape, growing wider and more seaworthy.

Each day as she made progress, an inner anxiety pushed her to hurry. At any time, Designate Udru'h might return for an unexpected visit, and she had to be away before then. He could not be allowed to see what she was doing. As a green priest, she didn't need to waste time gathering supplies. The vast lake provided fresh water to drink, and the bright sunlight on her emerald skin gave all the nourishment she needed.

For now, what Nira required most was determination. She had been passive for too long. Osira'h must think her dead, as did Jora'h and everyone on Theroc. But that didn't mean she had to give up on herself and remain stranded on this island. Though her chances were slim, she intended to take action and make a difference. The plan kept her alive and sane.

When the raft was ready, Nira rigged up a makeshift sail of thick leaves, used a pole to push the raft out into the lake, and guided herself away from shore. She didn't know where she was going, had no idea what direction the winds or currents might carry her. But no matter where she landed, Nira would consider it a starting point. She could set off and find her way . . . somewhere. For now, she felt satisfied just to get away from where the Designate had exiled her.

Nira looked up into the open sky and leaned back on her raft as she began to drift. She would go where fate chose to take her, and from there she would make her next plans.

For a full day, the breezes remained warm, then whipped up with greater force, rattling the drying leaves of her sail. The swaying of her raft on the choppy lake made her uneasy. All around her, endless water stretched to a blue infinity with no hint of the nearest shore. Though Nira had never seen maps of Dobro, she knew this was just a lake, albeit an enormous one. She was not accustomed to being so far from solid ground, from living plants and trees.

Nira wondered how the Dobro Designate would react when he came back to her island and found her gone. He had kept her alive in order to use her for some grim purpose . . . but she had let herself be used too often by that terrible man, and she vowed it would not happen again.

The nights were lonely. Her leaf sail bowed outwards as the wind picked up again. Overhead, the stars were obscured by thickening clouds. She could not see the gathering storm, but she could smell moisture and ozone in the air, hear far-off bursts of thunder. Rain began to pelt down, drenching her green skin. She clung to the sides of her raft as the choppy water began to buffet her.

Waves splashed over the logs. Though she had done her best to insure that the bindings were strong, Nira's floating craft was too fragile to withstand the power of this storm for long. But she had nowhere else to go, so she held on and rode out the weather.

Rain slashed down. Blinding forks of lightning burst across the sky. Shivering, Nira grasped the slick wooden logs and waited, not counting the endless minutes or hours.

She had been through worse ordeals when she'd been in the breeding barracks. She could endure this.

Exhausted, Nira wanted to sink into the oblivion of sleep and hide there until the gale was over, but she dared not, for fear that she would lose her grip. Drowning in a deep lake far from any forest would be a terrible end for a green priest. She longed to set foot on shore again, to find trees and plants – and a way back to Theroc.

She told herself again, *I can endure this* . . .

Morning came with the murky darkness of lingering rain clouds in the sky, but the worst of the storm had passed and the choppy waves calmed. She was delighted to see a smear of brown land, cast into relief by the light of the rising sun on the horizon. At first she was afraid the currents and the wind had hurled her back to her isolated island, but the shoreline extended too straight and too far. This must be a main continent.

She began to paddle furiously. Helpful winds gusted now, so she adjusted her sail and rode the breezes towards the ever-growing line of solid land. It took Nira most of the day to reach shore, and as she approached she surveyed the brown and rocky landscape with dismay. A bleak nothingness stretched as far as she could see.

With a knot in her stomach, Nira thought briefly that she might have been better off remaining a prisoner on her lush island, but then she chided herself. She had made a choice to fight back and disrupt the Designate's plans in any way possible, even if she had to die to do so.

When her raft finally reached the brown, sandy slope, Nira stumbled off the wet logs and fell to her knees on the beach, just appreciating the firmness of earth beneath her again. Her legs were wobbly, but she drew a deep breath and felt the energy cycling through her skin.

Straining and panting, she dragged her raft high up onto dry ground and anchored it, though she didn't know why. She never intended to use the raft again – certainly not to go back to her island, even if she could have navigated her way there.

Finally she shaded her eyes to look into the distance as far as she could see. Behind her lay the open water, and ahead – no matter how barren and daunting the landscape appeared – was her path. She would find her destination out there somewhere.

Leaving the shore behind, Nira began to walk forward.

EIGHTY

ANTON COLICOS

When the sudden, suffocating blackness engulfed Maratha Prime, panic and disbelief set in simultaneously.

The thirty-seven Ildiran workers drew a collective breath, as if anticipating the fall of an executioner's axe. Anton heard a skitter of wavering footsteps and the clatter of dishes as groping, frightened hands searched for something to hold on to. The lens kithman, Ilure'l, cried out, as if hoping to call back the last glimmers of escaping photons that ricocheted off the crystalline walls and then passed through, vanishing into the gulf of darkness.

'What are we going to do?' cried someone else. Mhas'k? Anton couldn't identify the speaker.

Though startled and disoriented, he pushed away from the table, willing himself to maintain his composure. 'I guess a fuse must have blown.' His voice sounded eerie and disembodied. 'Calm down, everyone.'

'Where is my engineer?' the voice of the Designate shrilled, then cracked with anxiety. 'What is his name again?'

'Nur'of, Designate.' The thin voice of Bhali'v.

Finally, Vik'k, one of the diggers, ignited a hand-held emergency blazer he kept with him for work in the tunnels. A gasp of relief rippled through the clustered Ildirans. They crowded close to the sombre digger, inadvertently blocking the glow from the others.

'What happened? Who did this?' Designate Avi'h demanded.

'It's the Shana Rei! They've descended upon us.' It was Ilure'l again; Anton thought the well-educated lens kithman should have known better.

'Come on now, don't be silly.' He turned to Vao'sh, who sat in shock. 'I guess maybe we shouldn't tell any more frightening stories today.'

'Yes, Rememberer Anton, that would be wise.'

Another broad-shouldered digger fumbled out a second emergency blazer from his pack, doubling the light in the cavernous dining hall.

Anton spoke reassuringly, 'There, see? It'll be all right. Nothing to be afraid of.' He seemed to be the only one not panicked.

During the previous day season, when he'd asked a group of Ildiran tourists to go to the dark-side construction site of Maratha Secda, they had clearly thought Anton unbalanced. But he had egged them on with stories of human bravery and finally got a large enough group to go. Now the skeleton crew stared at him as if he were a fool for not understanding their peril. Therefore, instead of just talking about bravery, Anton would have to show his mettle and be an actual hero. As a bookish, lifelong scholar, he smiled at the irony of it.

'All right, let's think about this. Until we can get the generators fixed, do you have any candles?' In the uncertain light, he pointed to the kithmen who served and prepared food. 'Any cooking flames or torches in the kitchens?'

When the Ildirans nodded uncertainly, Anton gathered two of them and took one of the emergency blazers. In the dining hall, the rest of the crew was reluctant to let a light source go away, even temporarily, but Anton was firm about it. 'Don't worry. I'll bring back even more light. Think of it as an investment!'

Forcibly keeping his good cheer, he hurried his reluctant volunteers along before the Designate could countermand his instructions. The three of them followed the blazer down the frighteningly dark passageways until they reached the kitchens. Inside storage cabinets they found boxes of ignition sticks and flammable gels. When Anton led them all back to the dining room and lit the new lights, the Ildirans clutched them like lifelines.

Finally the Maratha Designate quelled enough of his blinding panic to grow angry. 'Nur'of, you are my engineer. Learn what has gone wrong, and get those lights back on.'

'I will need to take one of the blazers, and several workers to do what—'

'Hurry!' Designate Avi'h cried. 'These ignition sticks won't last for ever.'

Anton rested a reassuring hand on Rememberer Vao'sh's arm. 'I'll go with Nur'of's team and keep *them* company until we find out what caused the blackout. Stay here and tell funny stories to the rest of these people. Keep them entertained and distracted. Shine a light on your face so they can see the colours in your lobes.'

Accompanied by Anton, the engineer and four of his technicians hastened down a succession of ramps into the lower levels of the domed city. The underground silence was oppressive. One of the technicians rummaged in an equipment locker and found three more emergency blazers, which he quickly switched on.

Always before, the thumping rhythm of generators and the buzzing of complex equipment in these levels had sounded like a growing storm. Now, the chambers were quiet as death. All of Maratha Prime's power, all of the machinery, had been shut down.

'I heard an explosion or two immediately before the lights went out,' Anton said to Nur'of. 'Is it possible that one of the generators blew up or broke down?'

The large-eyed engineer turned to him, his face thrown into sharp relief by the stark light of the blazer in his hand. *'Bekh!* We have redundant power systems, and backup generators. It is not conceivable that all of them failed simultaneously.'

Nevertheless, when they entered the equipment room, Anton saw his answer. The energy production and distribution machinery had been ruined, turbines blasted open, cables severed, generators torn apart.

And clearly, it was no accident.

When at last some of the lights flickered on again, Anton and the team of technicians returned to the central dining hall. They received giddy cheers and a look of great satisfaction on the Designate's drawn face.

Anton had surprised himself by remaining cool throughout the crisis, since he had always been a book-learner, someone who looked at life from a detached and objective position – not a man of action! However, his parents had taught him to solve problems, to rely on himself and not to panic. With pleasant conversation and suggestions, knowing that he was the only one who could handle this particular situation, Anton had kept the uneasy engineer and his technicians on track, offering them hope and confidence while he helped them find emergency systems and back-up power supplies so they could rig up a way to draw power for the main dome from the undamaged energy reservoirs. In the process of reassuring and encouraging them, he had ended up feeling more optimistic himself.

Nur'of stood in front of the Designate. 'We are drawing on our back-up batteries to make the life-support systems functional again – but the generators are completely destroyed. All of our main machinery has been sabotaged. *Sabotaged*! Someone, or something, came in through the tunnels and attacked our primary equipment.'

'It is the Shana Rei!' the lens kithman insisted.

'The Shana Rei could not possibly have come here,' the rememberer said firmly, but Anton could see flickers of uncertainty and confusion in his multicoloured expression.

Anton added, 'We don't need to go inventing mythical creatures to explain this.'

'Nothing in the *Saga* is mythical,' Ilure'l said.

'Our power systems will not last long,' Nur'of said, getting to concrete business again. 'I can give us light and warmth for a few days at most. There will be enough illumination for us to make plans, but never enough for us to feel safe or comfortable. The collector reserves have been destroyed, and only a small trickle from my new thermal conduits supplies power, but that won't last long. All systems will fail again. Even my best batteries will soon be drained.'

The bureaucrat hovered close to Avi'h, babbling his questions. 'Then what are we going to do, Designate? How shall we escape? Where will we go? Who can help us?'

Avi'h lifted his chin, giving a command like a true Designate. 'We must divert power to our communications systems. We will send a signal.'

Anton knew that without a green priest, no call for help would ever reach another Ildiran planet or even a Solar Navy ship in time. The septa of warliners that had dropped off Designate Avi'h had departed some time ago and would already be many star systems away.

'Can the Mage-Imperator sense what happened through the *thism*? Will he sound an alarm and send rescuers?' Anton asked.

Vao'sh shook his head. 'The Maratha Designate is his brother, not his son. The connection is not perfect. If his attention is not focused elsewhere, the Mage-Imperator may sense our distress, but not sharply enough to know he must dispatch helpers right away.'

'Who else can help us?' Ilure'l struggled to keep his fear under control.

The bureaucrat grasped at an idea. 'We can contact the Klikiss robots over on Maratha Secda.'

Avi'h brightened. 'An excellent suggestion, Bhali'v. Yes, the city should be nearly completed by now, and they are in the daylight. The robots can assist us, and we will wait there for rescue.'

The people babbled with relief. 'We'll escape.'

'We can be in the sunlight again!'

Anton felt momentarily uneasy. 'Wait a minute. We don't know that the Klikiss robots weren't the culprits who did this in the first place. Who else is on Maratha?'

'The Shana Rei!' Ilure'l insisted. 'Maybe they are the ones that built all those tunnels underground – where it's always dark.'

Bhali'v looked indignant at Anton's suggestion. 'Those robots have worked with us here for decades and shown no sign of treachery. Why should we not trust them?'

Anton raised his eyebrows. 'Well, for starters, because someone just blew up all of our generators and snuffed out the lights.'

Instead of listening to him, the Designate and the engineer hurried off to the communications room, carrying blazers and one of the makeshift candles as a precaution, although there was now plenty of light.

Vao'sh sat in troubled silence and Anton took his place beside the rememberer, who shook his many-lobed head. 'They believe it is the Shana Rei because they can think of no other enemy who might have done this . . . but that cannot be true! It simply cannot.'

Later, when Nur'of accompanied Designate Avi'h back into the dining chamber, both were beaming. 'Excellent news!' Avi'h said. 'I have spoken to the Klikiss robots at the Secda dome. I explained our situation, and they have offered sufficient facilities, supplies, and stored food to accommodate us while we wait for a rescue mission. But they do not have vehicles to come for us. We will have to make our own way over there.'

'But how will we do that?' Ilure'l asked. 'Maratha Secda is on the other side of the world.'

Avi'h looked to the engineer, who answered, 'We must make a journey across the dark side to reach the sunlight again. There are three fast surface vehicles in the hangars outside.'

The Ildirans were not pleased with the idea, but Anton had once made the cross-continent trek on a lark during the recent day season; this would not be impossible.

As the skeleton crew muttered and complained, Vao'sh reached the limits of his patience. The rememberer's trained voice made them all stop instantly. 'Enough! Did you not hear Engineer Nur'of? All of our power will fail soon. Maratha Prime will be plunged back into irrevocable darkness. Unless we set out together before it is too late, we will all die here in the darkness.'

That was enough to quell further complaints.

EIGHTY-ONE

DAVLIN LOTZE

Crenna's sky grew dark and cold as its sun continued to burn out.

Immediately upon returning from his brief inspection in space, Davlin gathered the colonists together – one hundred and thirty of them – and explained the emergency. He wasn't overstating the matter when he called it the direst threat they would ever face. 'There is no time for town meetings and arguments. We have a week at best to remake our whole colony – to dig in and hole up, and give ourselves at least a chance to survive.' His voice was hard and firm.

Thanks to the exaggerated stories Rlinda Kett had told about him, the colonists already treated Davlin with awe and amazement – much to his embarrassment, since he disliked drawing attention to himself. They saw him as an heroic figure who could lead them through impossible circumstances. They believed him now.

'This world is going to die,' Davlin said. Though he felt a connection with these people, he would not sugar-coat their situation. 'The faeros are losing their battle in the sun. This entire system will be cold and lifeless within a matter of days, and I can't think of a way to get anybody off Crenna to safety.'

Mayor Ruis clasped his hands in front of his stomach. 'We're just colonists here, Davlin. No one claims to understand these things. Tell us what to do!'

Davlin looked at their faces, wishing he had some ready answer for them. To his surprise, he realized that it actually mattered to him what they thought and how they viewed him. In this case, the worst thing he could say was that he didn't know. Everyone could see the sun darkening in the sky and could feel the drop in temperature as the planet struggled to continue functioning under a vastly diminished solar flux. They had work to do, and so he rallied them.

Davlin asked that every piece of heavy machinery be brought to the centre of town. 'Forget about your crops and your livestock. They can't possibly survive. Within a week, your homes will be covered by glaciers. Stored food will have to last us. I assure you, at least seven other things will prove fatal long before the rations run out.' He didn't list them, but the colonists didn't question his statement. 'Our only chance is to keep ourselves alive by whatever means, until rescue comes – and we don't have much time.'

Mayor Ruis nodded solemnly. 'And who's going to rescue us, Davlin?'

'I'm still working on that.'

Through the amateur astronomer's telescope, they observed the continuing battle in the plasma layers of Crenna's star. The faeros were being beaten back as more and more diamond warglobes swooped in from outside the system, converging on the stellar battlefield. Sunspots grew like mortal wounds. Flares spouted and stuttered like dying gasps from the sun's core.

The damage could never be undone. The star itself was doomed.

The colonists were astonished at how quickly the climate changed before their eyes. Storm systems churned like locomotives across the southern continent, where parts of the atmosphere had frozen out, leaving a void that caused giant, sucking Coriolis storms. Before long, the huge systems began to sweep north, giving the colonists even graver problems.

The first night had seen a hard freeze that killed most of the crops and plants; each night afterwards, the temperature dropped at least twenty degrees colder than the previous low. On the fourth night, trees had shattered. The wind speed picked up, and icy blizzards scoured colony buildings that had not been designed for arctic temperatures.

The townspeople worked around the clock, fully aware of their danger. Their expressions were weary and frightened, but though they were under tremendous strain, the people followed Davlin's instructions. He just prayed his idea would work.

It hurt to see all of the massive equipment once used for reclaiming agricultural land, ploughing fields, and mining minerals, now turned to the express purpose of digging deep tunnels and hollowing out shielded warrens beneath the crust, where the settlers might just be able to survive the incredible deep freeze that was setting in.

But they couldn't survive for long.

After studying all available construction materials, Davlin had instantly dismissed the possibility of building insulated shelters on the surface. Once the sun itself went dark, the deep cold of space would set in. Given time and extensive resources, a few ingenious Roamers might have been able to construct structures hardy enough to survive indefinitely, but Crenna was a peaceful, tame world. Mayor Ruis and his settlers had never prepared for this.

Even people without any construction experience put in their best efforts, shoring up tunnel shafts as the excavators burrowed deeper. Davlin could not make accurate calculations as to how far underground they would need to hide. He simply had them dig as deep as time permitted and then provision the chambers where they could huddle together against the oncoming instant ice age. Food supplies were taken from every outlying home and brought to communal underground warehouses. Mayor Ruis busied himself directing the aboveground activities and inventorying the rations.

Most importantly, generators were installed and fuel stockpiled, everything from small batteries to large thermal furnaces. Air recirculation tubing was laid down in the tunnels, and CO_2 scrubbers were installed. Some of the frightened colonists didn't quite understand the need, assuming that if they had ventilation shafts they could always draw in air from the outside. They didn't even think about what would happen once Crenna's atmosphere itself froze solid.

Davlin wasn't sure he could maintain morale, but he did have to keep them working.

On the surface, inside a cold and sheltered hangar, Davlin worked alone on the small ship. As part of his silver beret background, he had taken emergency training in mechanics and starship operation. This task seemed even more hopeless than the rest of their activities, but survival hinged on his ability to get away from Crenna and summon help. He couldn't allow himself to consider failure.

Outside, in the last three days, the temperature had dropped a full hundred degrees. The sky was always dark now, murky with twilight and faint flickers of sunshine that spat out from the injured sun.

The sudden and drastic climate shifts precipitated roaring storms and convulsions in the atmosphere. Most of the colonists were underground at the work site now. Few tried to stay up on the surface. Davlin himself was bundled in his warmest undergarments, a thick parka, and insulated gloves. Though it cost him dexterity, it kept his fingers from freezing and falling off.

Distressingly little ekti remained in the engines of this sightseeing craft, and he spent all day stripping away unnecessary mass, improving the efficiency of the conversion reactors, and increasing the throughput of the Ildiran stardrive, hoping to squeeze out just a few hundred thousand kilometres more on his journey.

The planet shivered in its death throes, cooling rapidly, already on its way to the edge of absolute zero. He was confident the colonists would be warm enough underground for a short while. But if he himself couldn't make it to Relleker, then no one would ever save them . . .

When he was as ready as he could be, knowing that any further improvements would cost too much time, Davlin decided to leave. The colonists had already installed the heavy hatch atop their tunnels: a vault door constructed of scrap metal, thick enough to insulate against the murderous cold. As Davlin operated the controls to get inside for one last time, he struggled against the biting frigidity. Within a day or so, simply surviving aboveground would require a full-fledged environment suit. Already he wished he had supplemental oxygen.

The tunnels were refreshingly warm. At the moment, the colonists were profligate with their energy expenditure, but eventually heat wouldn't be a problem for them. The thermal output from their machinery and one hundred and thirty warm bodies might itself become a problem, unless it could be exhausted somewhere or converted into useable energy.

When the colonists gathered to bid him farewell, Davlin was stunned by the confidence, optimism, and hope on their faces. He had done his best to inform them of their slim chances, of how incredibly serious their situation was. But he was the man who had travelled to any number of uninhabited Klikiss worlds. He had discovered how to work the transportals. They foolishly thought Davlin Lotze could do anything – and why shouldn't he let them? If he failed, no one else would know it, and all the people here would be entombed in ice. They needed to believe.

The mayor seemed to expect him to make an inspirational speech, but Davlin said only, 'I will do my best. As long as there's one breath left in my body, I'll spend it bringing help back here.'

Then, wasting no more time, he let himself out of the hatch, and sealed the cap leading to the hibernation tunnels. Outside, he staggered through the winds and blowing ice to the hangar. Once inside the small ship with its partially empty stardrive fuel tank, he fired the engines and fought to guide the craft out through the uncertain gale. Davlin wrestled with the controls as he flew off, heading into the deepening twilight of a dying sun. He did not perform calculations or estimate whether or not he would make it to the closest system. He would simply fly until he could go no farther. He had to hope that would be far enough.

EIGHTY-TWO

CESCA PERONI

When the Roamer engineers completed repairs to the fungus-reef city, Cesca invited Mother Alexa and Father Idriss to return to their rebuilt home.

Roamer crews laboured with heavy machinery throughout the forest. Already they had reclaimed parts of the blasted landscape and built many temporary homes for the refugees. 'I don't know that we could have done it without Roamer assistance,' Alexa said.

Cesca nodded solemnly. 'Hydrogues destroyed our skymines and our traditional way of life, too. But we persevere, and fight, and hold on to the things we value most. Our peoples have much in common.'

Father Idriss looked up at the organic mass propped up on the worldtree with jury-rigged struts and grafted-on crossbeams. 'It looks . . . different.'

'It looks fine,' Alexa answered. 'Let's go up.'

Cesca accompanied an excited Kotto Okiah as the Theron leaders reentered the place from where they had ruled in happier times. 'You did an excellent job working with the materials at hand and finding innovative solutions, Kotto.'

The eccentric engineer was bursting with pride. 'That's what Roamers are good at, Speaker.' In only a month, he and his Roamer team had completed a job that would have taken the Therons years to do.

Inside the restored meeting chamber, Alexa and Idriss waited for their eyes to adjust to the soft artificial light. They gazed, smiling and uncertain, around at the changed space. 'I was afraid we'd have to abandon the whole fungus reef,' Alexa said.

Like a puppy turned loose, Kotto moved excitedly around the room. 'You saw the plans already, but here's what we did. We reinforced the load-bearing walls with solid beams of worldtree wood. Could have used metal or polymer composites, but I thought you'd prefer a more natural look.' He rapped his knuckles on sturdy ripple-grained beams that supported parts of the large room. 'Underneath the city, we had to install a network of braces and struts. Right now it looks a little raw, but you could plant vines or other foliage to cover the framework.'

Idriss said, 'Our people will be glad enough just to come home.'

'Home.' Alexa's voice caught in her throat. 'This meeting chamber was where we crowned Reynald. It seems like only yesterday. And now both Reynald and Beneto are dead.' She turned to Idriss, her eyes glimmering with tears. 'Why is Sarein taking so long to come home? I was sure she'd be here by now.'

Idriss said, 'Nahton assured us she's arriving soon.'

Kotto led them into corridors that burrowed through the reef. 'Look, we've installed new plumbing and power conduits throughout. Many of the old ventilation systems were inefficient and tangled. Some of them went to dead ends. Whoever maintained the circulation systems seemed to be making it up as they went along.'

Idriss looked at his wife. 'Yes, that's how it was installed in the first place.'

'Well, it's much more efficient now. You'll notice a clear difference when you use it.' Kotto strutted beside the two leaders, who looked shell-shocked and uncertain about all the changes and improvements, and Alexa and Idriss would probably never figure out how to use most of them.

As if sensing his thoughts, Alexa touched her husband's muscular arm. 'These are changes we can live with, Idriss. Our world will never be the same.'

Kotto wandered ahead, still chatting. 'Enough of this city is restored for a third of the original population to move back in . . . maybe half, if they're willing to crowd together in close quarters.'

Alexa showed little cheer despite the good news. 'We won't need to crowd – we lost too many people during the attack.'

Kotto looked embarrassed and saddened. 'I didn't mean to get so excited.'

Soot-stained and out of breath, Cesca's father hurried in from the outer deck and trudged along the corridors, calling out. 'Cesca!' He wiped sweaty dark hair away from his forehead when he found his daughter. 'One of our ships just came in with a message from the Osquivel shipyards. Del Kellum needs Kotto's assistance.'

The engineer raised his eyebrows. 'But there's still plenty of work to do here.'

Denn grinned. 'Kellum's found a small hydrogue derelict, completely intact. He thought you'd be the best person to investigate it – if you're at all interested.'

The engineer sucked in a quick breath. 'A real drogue craft, still functional? Not just broken wreckage like those pieces the Hansa took from here?'

'Whole and unbreached, a pristine opportunity for some intrepid investigator.' Cesca recognized her father's provocative smile from times he had teased her when she was a little girl.

Kotto had a long string of accomplishments in his career; among all the clans, Cesca knew there was no better person for the job. He had a voracious mind, had studied all forms of technology from Hansa to Ildiran, and had even read every available document on Klikiss ruins that archaeologists had filed. 'You have to go, Kotto.'

'But there's still so much here—'

She enunciated each word clearly. 'You have to go, Kotto.'

Like a child he resisted just a moment more, then grinned. 'Yes – yes, I do. When can we leave?'

Denn made a grand gesture towards the exit. 'Now that the forest fires are put out, Torin Tamblyn wants to get back to the water mines on Plumas. He'll give you a ride.'

After Kotto hurried away, bubbling with excitement, Cesca accompanied Idriss and Alexa to an open balcony from which they could watch the continuing activity. In the distance, they heard the droning hum of machinery, and saw Therons and Roamers hooking up cables while heavy lifters removed the charred husks of dead worldtrees. Excavation and extraction crews had removed most of the fallen tree trunks, making great piles of dead wood in a section of the forest obliterated by the worst fires. Cesca didn't know what else they could do with all the debris.

Looking down, she saw Yarrod climbing the wide trunk up to the high fungus reef. He scrambled as swiftly as a gecko, linked with the worldforest mind and moving with complete ease. When he reached the network of struts and braces beneath the main structure, he swung around them and climbed up to greet the three people on the balcony.

The green priest was nearly as old as his sister Alexa, his face marked with tattooed symbols of the skills he had acquired in service of the worldtrees; he had looked deeply weary and broken upon his return to the burned forest, but seemed invigorated now.

'I bring a message from the worldforest, a mutually beneficial suggestion for Cesca Peroni and her Roamers. Would you like to salvage any of this fallen wood? Take it away. Much usable lumber remains, and this wood has remarkable properties.'

'It is a great gift, Speaker Peroni,' Idriss said. 'A magnificent one.'

'But not at all sufficient to repay you for everything you have done for us,' Alexa added.

Cesca tried not to look too overjoyed. Nowhere else in the Spiral Arm did people have access to worldtree wood for construction or even ornamental purposes. 'I am . . . intrigued. Since leaving Earth, our clans have lived inside asteroids, on ships, and on inhospitable planets. We've rarely had the luxury of wood – and now you are offering much more than we could use for our own purposes.'

'Well, you are merchants,' Yarrod pointed out. 'Could you use it as a commercial commodity?'

'Perhaps.' Cesca remained frustrated that they had received no response whatsoever to their demands, and she feared that Chairman Wenceslas was planning something. 'Even if we refuse trade with the Hansa, we could send wood products to the Ildirans, or to some of the distant colonies with tenuous ties to the Big Goose.'

Knowing how much income they were likely to derive from the sale of the remarkable and rare worldtree wood, Cesca made an immediate decision. 'And we will share a portion of the profits with you. The Theron economy has suffered greatly in this attack, too.'

Idriss said, 'The forest already provides everything we need.'

Alexa placed a hand on her husband's arm. 'Things are different now, Idriss. Our people face many hardships. With additional funds, we could purchase materials and hire extra labour to speed the forest's recovery.'

Idriss scratched his square black beard. 'I hadn't thought of that.'

'Are you certain the worldforest is willing to let us take away so much fallen wood? These were worldtrees, dead brothers of the forest.'

Yarrod's expression was stoic. 'Cesca Peroni, you will help us carry away our dead and give their sacrifice additional meaning. Only then can the site of this massacre give birth to new life.'

In the distance, a heavy lifter hauled an enormous charred trunk as large as a spaceship. Cesca nodded. 'Worldtree wood will certainly enrich our colonies in space, just as Roamer work has helped to rebuild your cities here. Let this be a symbol of the cooperation and friendship between Roamers and Therons.'

Mother Alexa squeezed her husband's large hand. 'That's what Reynald would have wanted.'

EIGHTY-THREE

SAREIN

The flight from Earth to Theroc was not long, but Sarein's reluctance to return home made the journey stretch out interminably. She felt like a woman going to visit an horrifically wounded loved one in a hospital. She had to do this because of personal and political obligations, but in her heart Sarein wished she could just keep Theroc in her memories the way it was and not see the disaster.

Yet Basil had insisted. 'As the new Mother of Theroc, think of the advantages you could offer the Hansa from inside. Once we've brought the Therons into the fold and made the traitorous Roamers toe the line, it'll be a great day for the human race.'

But she couldn't simply walk in and demand the title of Theron Mother, even though she felt she could institute changes – dramatic changes – that could benefit both her world and the Hansa. The Therons knew and loved their leaders, and Sarein had been gone for a long time. Even when she'd lived on Theroc, she had never engendered much devotion in the people. She spent little time with green priests, felt no calling for the worldforest.

Everyone would recognize her as a pawn of the Hansa.

And Basil's ideas of blithely rescinding the long-standing Theron independence made her uneasy. Sarein gradually realized that he now exerted more power over her than she influenced him. As difficult as it was to admit, she was halfway in love with Basil and didn't want to leave him behind.

Eventually, the captain summoned her to the cockpit. 'If you come forward now, Ambassador, you can see Theroc in the front observation panels. Thought you'd like to have a look.'

'I'll be right there.'

In truth, she didn't want to see, but she entered the cockpit of the diplomatic transport and stared down at the cloud-smeared land masses where she'd been born. Sarein traced the outlines of the continents. Oddly, she was more familiar with the geography of Earth than of Theroc. How could she possibly rule this planet? It would be a sham.

Normally, the Theron landscape would have been a carpet of green separated by large bodies of water, but now she could see countless dark stains. In a way, she was glad Estarra wasn't here with her . . .

Though they had shared many recent tragedies, Sarein spent too little time with her sister. It was a painful oversight. She had focused on her own political activities and obligations, while the Queen had her cadre of attendants and advisers, and the genuine friendship and love of King Peter. But that was no excuse. They should have been friends, allies . . . sisters.

Before Sarein departed for Theroc, the two young women had walked together in the Whisper Palace's fern garden, passing feathery fans that grew bright green under the sunlight, talking of how life had been when they were just children: simple, optimistic, innocent.

Sarein also felt a wary concern about leaving Estarra and King

Peter alone and unprotected. She tried to convince herself that the assassination attempt had merely been Basil's bluff to put Peter in his place, but Sarein was never sure.

Estarra had stopped beside one of the small potted treelings, looking at it distractedly. 'In a way, I envy you. I still feel I belong on Theroc.'

Sarein ran her fingers along the soft lacy fronds of a fern. 'Sometimes it would be easier if the two of us just switched places. You could go back home where you want to be, and I'd stay here on Earth.'

The Queen laughed in surprise. 'You may be my sister, Sarein, but I wouldn't give up my husband. I actually love Peter, you know.'

'Yes, I know. It's painfully obvious.'

They had stood together looking at the single treeling on display, reminded of the immense burned forests. Estarra herself had brought this particular treeling as a gift to the Chairman when she'd first come to Earth, and Nahton often used it for communication.

Sarein put her arm around her sister's shoulder. 'It's just an ironic twist of fate that we're each better suited for the other's responsibilities. You'd really like to go back to Theroc, even now that it's all burned and broken?'

'That's when it's possible to love it the most.'

Sarein had playfully yanked one of Estarra's carefully twisted braids, as she'd done when they were both little girls. No doubt the royal guards, who always discreetly kept watch on them, were horrified at such a disrespectful action on the part of the ambassador, but Sarein didn't care.

'Come with me, Estarra. You can help me pack.'

Now, as the captain stabilized his orbit then prepared the descent trajectory, he studied his high-resolution scanners. 'Quite a bit of difference down there. A lot of traffic in the air, in orbit, and on the ground. I thought Therons didn't do much space travel.'

Sarein's brow furrowed. 'No, they don't.'

A harried-sounding operator provided general directions for where to land. 'We don't really have a spaceport anymore, but we use a large clearing – as long as your ship's not too big.'

'Not too big,' the captain answered. Full-sized Manta cruisers had once landed in the forest clearings. 'I'll manage.'

Sarein braced herself for what she was about to experience. As the diplomatic transport came in beneath the veil of clouds, she could see that the once-thick worldforest canopy was now cracked and burned, giant sections scraped away like eroded canyons. Worldtrees still stood tall and green, but she couldn't believe how many patches were blackened and cluttered with debris.

Dozens of smaller ships and heavy lifters bustled through the forest, expanding the recovery efforts. To her amazement, she saw large excavations of fallen trees, earth-movers erecting support walls and retaining dikes, soil-retention netting that looked garish on what should have been a natural landscape. Why hadn't Basil mentioned that full-scale EDF engineering crews were here to assist Theroc?

On second glance, though, the activities didn't seem regimented or organized enough to have been put together by the Earth military. The EDF tended to lay out everything in straight lines and perfect grids. Conversely, this work seemed energetic and independent, as if each ship was following only a general master plan.

Heavy lifters delivered giant trunks to an open cargo barge that was battered and pitted from decades of hard service. It looked as if it had been designed as an asteroid ore-hauler, and now it was being loaded with fallen worldtrees, taking them out . . . to space.

As the diplomatic craft came in for a landing she could make out the individual forms of people moving about on the ground. A shiver went down her spine. 'Those are Roamers!'

'Looks like it, Ambassador,' said the captain.

Sarein was instantly resentful, knowing exactly what Basil would say about the matter. 'I suppose they have plenty of time on their hands, now that they no longer trade with the Hansa. While my planet is wounded and reeling, they slip in to exploit our resources.'

She had heard the Chairman's lectures, both public and private; she had seen the heavily slanted reports in the Hansa media, which painted the clans as selfish, intractable, and petulant. As ambassador, Sarein felt compelled to agree with Basil and vocally support his stance. Roamers did make convenient and readily unlikable targets.

She leaned closer to the window. 'Why are they hauling all that wood away?'

The captain looked at her mildly. 'Maybe they just came to offer help, Ambassador. I don't see too many EDF crewmembers lending a hand down there.'

'Roamers offering to help, with no strings attached? Hardly likely.' And if the Roamers were assisting on Theroc, why hadn't Nahton or any of the other green priests informed the Hansa what was going on here? Surely it was relevant!

She didn't know what game the clans were playing, what goal Speaker Peroni was trying to accomplish with her unfounded accusations about EDF piracy. Sarein was certain the woman had somehow deceived Reynald, tricked him into a marriage proposal. At least her brother had died before the wedding could be formalized.

When the captain landed the diplomatic craft in a scorched clearing, Sarein realized with a sharp pang that this place had once been a lovely, expansive meadow filled with flowers and colourful condorflies. Now it had been razed and flattened by ungainly machinery. Her nostrils flared.

When the hatch opened, the first thing she smelled was harsh smoke, the dust and soot of death in the forest. Wrinkling her nose at the acrid tang, she watched both of her parents and her little sister Celli hurry towards her.

Sarein smiled automatically – an expression she had learned from years of serving under the tutelage of Basil Wenceslas. But she was not happy to be here. In fact, she found it painful to focus on her family in the midst of all this tragedy.

Her memories were filled with expanses of gold-barked worldtrees and wild undergrowth. Now she saw black skeletons, bare dirt, and the overlapping treads of heavy Roamer machinery that had mangled what remained of the forest. Her heart turned to lead in her chest, and her doubts about becoming the next Mother of Theroc resurfaced. There wasn't much left to rule here.

EIGHTY-FOUR

KING PETER

Peter shook his head and handed the prepared document back to Basil. 'I'm sorry, but I won't read this.'

He saw an immediate flush of anger cross the Chairman's face. 'I dictate Hansa policy, and you're more than aware of how far I'll go to make sure my orders are obeyed.' Basil wasn't usually a man to lose his composure, even in private, but the years of costly defeats and the intransigence of those who were supposed to be 'team players' had eaten away at him. He hated to lose control in any fashion.

Peter tried to be calm but firm. 'Your media plants have already done an excellent job of turning public opinion against the Roamers, Basil, but if I read this invective, we'll have lynchings, if not an outright civil war.'

'We already have a civil war, King Peter – caused by the Roamers.'

Peter called the Chairman's bluff, though he knew it was a dangerous move. 'Then why don't you have Prince Daniel read it? Try him out, see how the public reacts?'

Basil scowled. 'I've had enough of your attitude, Peter.'

Peter drummed his fingers on the tabletop in the King's private retiring room where the Chairman had come to meet with him. 'Believe it or not, Basil, we both have the interests of the Hansa at heart. Speaker Peroni was betrothed to Estarra's brother – maybe the Queen and I could talk with her reasonably, resolve this matter.'

'No need. The Roamers will back down soon. I envision several scenarios – all of which result in my holding humanity together, in spite of themselves.'

The Chairman was further upset because he had just learned from Sarein, through Nahton, that groups of Roamers had been working in the ruined worldforest for over a month – and somehow the court green priest had never seen fit to inform anyone of the fact.

Nahton had responded with placid indifference when Basil confronted him. 'It is within our rights as an independent colony to accept aid from anyone who wishes to give it. It is not a matter for Hansa discussion.' He had refused to understand the relevance of such information in the overall picture.

Now Peter leaned closer to the simmering Chairman. 'Basil, you taught me to think of second and third order consequences. It's fine that I rally the people and fan their anger against the hydrogues. But your end goal is to assimilate the Roamers into the Hanseatic League. Therefore, it's counter-productive for me, as King, to officially portray them as unsalvageable traitors or monsters. If I make a formal statement from the Whisper Palace, and then your plan succeeds, I'll have to recant my words and change my position. You don't want that.'

Basil lifted his head slowly, a strange expression on his face. 'I don't know whether to strangle you, Peter, or pat you on the back for being a good student. Your conclusions aren't the same as mine, but they do have . . . some small merit. I'll consider what you've said.' He took the document back and turned to leave, clearly not admitting defeat. 'The Roamers will be quickly and cleanly defeated, and soon. Perhaps it's best if you just stay out of it for now. Then you can appear benevolent afterwards.'

He looked over his shoulder. 'But I warn you, the Hansa must be absolutely unified under my instructions. If I decide to ask you again, Peter, don't even think about contradicting me.'

Even when he was most troubled, Peter always knew one place where he could feel like a man, instead of a puppet ruler. When the lights were down late at night and he was in his own bedchambers – after OX had searched the room for surveillance cameras and deactivated any listening devices – Peter felt safe and comforted, simply holding his Queen.

He caressed the warm, smooth skin of her back, tracing the outline of Estarra's shoulderblades, and pulled her closer. Her breasts were soft against his chest, and she kissed his ear while he smoothed her hair with his fingers. 'I may disagree with most of Basil's decisions, but when he chose you for me, that was the best thing he ever did.'

It must have been so strange for Estarra to come from the lush forests on Theroc and be transplanted into an entirely different culture here at the heart of the Hansa. But she had been strong, open-minded, and willing to give him a chance. At first, Peter had resented the political manipulations that thrust them together in an arranged marriage that seemed so medieval . . . but he and Estarra did indeed have much in common, and now they relied on each other for support, in a time and place where they were never sure whom they could trust.

Though many of their obligations were unpleasant or difficult, he and Estarra were glad to have each other, especially when they could be alone together, in the dark, and forget about the vast and dangerous universe outside.

Her breath was warm against his neck as she rested her head on his shoulder, kissing the line of his jaw. 'And you, Peter, have made me the envy not only of everyone on Theroc, but of every woman in the Hansa. After all, I get to make love to the King whenever I like.'

'If only I could hold the Hansa together as easily as I hold you,' he said.

Though the Chairman and his assistants did not expect him to lead – only to issue prepared statements and stand as a figurehead – Peter sensed that many threads in the Hanseatic League were unravelling, along with the Hansa's formerly solid relationships with the Therons and the Roamers. Basil was trying to impose a tighter and tighter control, but the more he squeezed and the more stridently he demanded that every faction follow his rigid plan, the less cooperative they became. Basil thought they were being intentionally obdurate. The government was no longer the well-oiled machine that the Chairman had worked so hard to maintain.

'Basil's planning something else against the Roamers,' Peter said. 'I can feel it, but I'd rather bow my head and accept responsibility for my own failures than make excuses for actions I never sanctioned in the first place.'

'The people believe you have a good heart,' she said. 'And I'll stand by you no matter what. You know that.'

'Yes, Estarra. I know that.'

'Anyway, there's nothing you can do about it now. You're worrying too much during our private bedroom time.' She rolled on top of him. 'There must be something I can do to distract you from all your worries?'

He kissed her. 'What did you have in mind?'

So Estarra showed him what she meant.

EIGHTY-FIVE

TASIA TAMBLYN

E ven as the war continued across the Spiral Arm, Tasia found
herself back at the Mars EDF base cooling her heels. She had
never been good at sitting still. In the meantime, her Manta,
along with many other military ships, had gone into spacedock for
the installation of new armaments, though she hadn't filed a formal
request for upgrades.

Her crew had been dispersed, some of them given R&R, others
assigned to ground-based functions. Sergeant Zizu had been
dispatched to the lunar base to head up the training of green recruits;
Subcommander Elly Ramirez had become part of a new action
committee to upgrade navigational systems on enhanced battleships.

She sensed that something big was about to happen, but no one
would tell her what it was. She felt oddly left out. Since the
Roamers had cut off trade with the Hansa, the general antipathy
towards the clans had grown, and Tasia herself had been the butt
of many veiled 'Roacher jokes'. Given the political climate, she
didn't have much desire to spend time in the officers clubs or even
with other soldiers.

In her quarters, Tasia waited for a new assignment. Any assignment. Why was Admiral Willis taking so long? She felt awkward, not quite knowing what to do with herself.

EA was with her, but the Listener compy was no longer the old friend she had known for so many years. Tasia sat on the edge of her bunk and looked at the small computerized companion. 'You were such a brave compy, EA. I just wish you could remember what you've done.'

'I have the data you uploaded to me, Tasia Tamblyn. It is sufficient.'

'Not for me.'

Tasia had combed through her private records, retrieved the files and diary entries that pertained to EA. She had collated them into summary documents and uploaded each one into the compy's sadly emptied brain, after carefully sanitizing them to remove any secret details about Roamer activities. Though EA could now recite the particulars of major experiences she had shared with Tasia, the words were lifeless statements of fact, recitations instead of memories.

Tasia sighed, hating her own suspicions, not being able to trust EA. 'I miss the real you.' She lay back on her bunk. So much about Osquivel had been a royal mess. One of these days she'd make up for it. The EDF would find a way to wipe out the murderous aliens that had killed her brother, her lover Robb, and too many others to name.

There was a war on, and she was spoiling for a fight. And here she was, grounded on Mars, lying in bed, doing nothing!

Restless, she climbed into her off-duty uniform and left her quarters. She went to the mess hall to listen to the conversations, maybe track down a game of ping-pong. The EDF was obviously gearing up for a large initiative. And her not-too-subtle inquiries had been rebuffed with typically vague military responses. As a

Manta commander, she hoped she'd be at the forefront of the action, whatever it was. At the moment, though, her ship wasn't ready and much of her crew had been reassigned.

She had good reason to be suspicious.

She dispensed a cup of coffee – bitter and lukewarm, as usual – and sat at a table with other Manta commanders and first officers. She heard them discussing deployment orders and targeting priorities. They seemed excited at the prospect of the new rammer ships, which would require only a handful of human commanders and teams of Soldier compies with specialized programming.

Trying to join the conversation, she asked, 'Did they post rammer assignments yet? Any of you chosen?'

'No, but I'm glad to be getting more hands-on action,' said one commander. 'It's not the hydrogues, but at least it's something.'

'About time King Peter decided to teach those damned Roachers a lesson.'

Another officer grumbled. 'Cutting off the fleet's ekti supply in a time of war – are they insane?'

'Roamers?' Tasia blurted. 'What does the new mission have to do—'

Suddenly, the others at the table recalled who Tasia was, despite her EDF uniform. 'Never mind, Tamblyn. We've got our marching orders.' The senior Manta commander stood. 'We'd all better get back and check on our ships, right everyone?'

Tasia sat drinking her coffee as the other commanders and first officers pointedly left her alone. Teach the Roamers a lesson? What on Earth was General Lanyan up to now? Since his encounter with the pirate Rand Sorengaard a long time ago, he'd had a chip on his shoulder the size of a minor planet.

Sure, she had heard grumblings about Speaker Peroni's decision to cut off stardrive fuel shipments. Tasia had originally considered it nonsense that the EDF was destroying Roamer cargo ships –

surely, as a Manta commander, Tasia would have known about such activities. But now, realizing that a secret new mission had been kept from her, she wondered how much else was going on without her knowledge.

When she got back to her quarters with a queasy stomach brought on only partially by the sour coffee, Tasia found a message on the roomscreen. It had a formal EDF voice log seal and a code designation from Admiral Willis. Her new assignment orders at last!

Playing the message, she saw that the maternal Admiral wore a controlled yet troubled expression. She read the orders without emotion. 'Commander Tamblyn, this message is to inform you that you've been reassigned from your Manta. Your cruiser will henceforth be captained by Commander Ramirez, who has been promoted to take your place at the helm.'

Tasia gasped. What had she done? Why were they taking her ship away from her? *Commander* Ramirez?

'I am pleased to give you the good news, however' – Willis's voice conveyed anything but joy – 'that you will be heading up the comprehensive training of second-stage recruits here on the Mars base. This is a task we really need you to do. Your innovations and flexibility should make you a superb instructor.'

'A teacher?' Tasia mumbled, as if the message screen could hear and respond. 'What did I do to deserve this?'

'Don't misunderstand me, Tamblyn.' The Admiral's image continued without a pause. 'As far as I'm concerned, your service record is exemplary and your performance has always been impeccable. However, not every soldier can participate in every mission, and General Lanyan has determined that your services are not required for our new EDF initiative.'

'Damn right they're not, if you intend to go after Roamers instead of the real enemy. Shizz, this is even worse than that stupid siege of Yreka.'

EA stood beside her absorbing the information, but the Listener compy placed no significance on Tasia's emotional reaction. 'I will be happy to assist you in developing a training curriculum, Tasia Tamblyn.'

Tasia tried to contain her inner anger, wanting just to punch somebody. The Earth Defence Forces clearly did not trust her. Had they been eavesdropping on her conversations? Were her quarters bugged? She had been so careful, even when talking to EA. She frowned at her compy, wondering if the Eddies themselves had done something to spark EA's odd behaviour.

Or was her Roamer heritage enough in itself to make them doubt her, even after so many years of service? Though no one would tell her what was going on, she feared the EDF meant to do something to the Roamer clans. Something terrible.

EIGHTY-SIX

ROBERTO CLARIN

At Hurricane Depot, enormous mountains of orbiting stone circled overhead like the hands of a clock. In his private office in the north polar dome, Roberto Clarin reclined in his chair looking up at the transparent sky. Every hour the mountains passed overhead in an endless parade.

When the original gas cloud had coalesced into the Couarnir star system, no habitable worlds had formed. In the liquid-water zone, scraps of left-over material had pulled together into two large chunks of rock that orbited around a mutual centre of gravity, as if a stillborn planet had broken in half. The two components shared a thin, wispy atmosphere, and at the exact centre of the rotating body was a stable Lagrange point – a perfect sheltered spot, simultaneously protected and threatened by the obstacle course of debris.

Roamers had used material mined from the orbiting pair of bodies to build a central depot and fuel-transfer station sitting in the eye of the storm. Ships came in from above or below, threading a course through the safe polar zone of the two rotating planetary components.

Like an old Arabian bazaar at a caravan crossroads, Hurricane Depot became a popular place where ekti cargo escorts could drop off their fuel for efficient distribution to other settlements. Roamer traders lived and worked there, and many more passed through. Metals, fuel, food, fabrics and even Hansa merchandise were brought here for sale or trade. Two or three ships arrived every day, and their captains and crew shopped, haggled, or bartered their shipments for necessary or desirable materials.

Roberto Clarin was a dark-haired, loud-voiced man who insisted on sampling all the exotic foods that came through his station – his stomach's equivalent of a tariff. Under his leadership, Hurricane Depot had thrived at first, though now with the hydrogue ultimatum against skymining and the trade embargo with the Big Goose, the station often looked like a ghost town.

His brother Eldon, a talented engineer, had helped design Hurricane Depot. For a while, the two men had been partners, but Eldon was an inept businessman who didn't understand how merchandising and trade worked, though Roberto had tried to explain the simplest economic concepts over and over again. Eldon could comprehend esoteric physical calculations, stressors and flexors, material strengths, load paths, and energy-process trains, but simple financial calculations were a foreign language to him.

Eventually, frustrated and disappointed with each other, Eldon and Roberto had parted company. Roberto took Hurricane Depot to great success, and Eldon had designed new ekti-processing reactors for Berndt Okiah's skymine. And there, the hydrogues had killed him . . .

Today, according to the projected schedule, Nikko Chan Tylar was due to arrive, but the young man was usually late because he got easily distracted along the way. Roberto kept a landing bay open for Tylar's ship, but he didn't count on using it any time soon.

The next group of ships that arrived, however, was not at all what Roberto expected. As soon as he saw the full-scale EDF battle fleet, his astounded reaction was similar to what his brother must have felt when the hydrogues rose up to destroy the Erphano skymine.

The large Juggernauts kept themselves safely outside the orbiting rocks, but scout ships, mine sweepers, and Thunderhead weapons platforms blundered into the danger zone, using their weapons to blast away debris and clear a wider channel so that the Mantas could descend to the central depot.

Knowing what the Eddies had already done to Raven Kamarov's ship, Roberto instantly realized they were after more of the Roamers' hardfought ekti stockpiles. Damned pirates! 'I guess picking on single ships is no longer good enough for you. Whetted your appetite for more, did it?'

He triggered evacuation alarms throughout the main station and sent warnings to any incoming Roamer craft. Cargo ship captains raced to their vessels. Within minutes, three spacecraft had already launched, dispersing quickly. Roberto was grateful to see them get away.

General Lanyan, the head of the Eddies, sent a smug transmission. 'This facility is currently under Hansa interdiction, by order of Chairman Wenceslas. All materiel, resources, and privately owned vessels are hereby confiscated in the name of King Peter for use by the Earth Defence Forces.'

Opening the communications channel himself, Roberto stood from his seat, suddenly self-conscious that he wore sloppy, casual clothes, and that his belly made him appear less than imposing compared with the EDF commander. 'General, it doesn't matter whose name you invoke – your King and your Chairman have neither jurisdiction nor authority here. The Roamer clans never signed the Hansa charter. This depot is a privately owned facility, and you have no right to lay siege to it or confiscate our possessions.'

461

Despite his bluster, Roberto knew that with all those battleships, the General could simply swarm in and take whatever he wanted. Roamer security depended on camouflage and secrecy, but they had no real defences. Now that the EDF had discovered Hurricane Depot, the Roamers were all just cornered rabbits.

The General scolded him. 'Our war against the hydrogues gives us the justification to take vital war supplies. According to some broader definitions, you scum are part of the human race, too. You should be ashamed of yourselves for not doing your duty.'

'Because you provide such shining examples of Hansa decency? You're nothing more than thieves.'

On the image screen, Lanyan gave him a cold smile. 'Thieves are motivated primarily by greed. We, however, have a legitimate claim on these resources, and the law is on our side.'

'The law? Whose law?'

'The treaties your ancestors signed when they departed on the *Kanaka*.' Lanyan cited chapter and verse, explaining the terms accepted by the forefathers of the Roamer clans. 'You are still bound by those agreements. Therefore, we are impounding your stored stardrive fuel and taking your cargo escorts and other spacefaring vessels that we can turn to military use.'

Manta cruisers pulled up against the large station. Lanyan continued, 'I advise you to allow us access to the docking ports. If we don't receive your cooperation, we'll use our jazers to open this place like an aluminium can, and then we'll take whatever floats out.'

Roberto swallowed hard. Without a doubt, Lanyan meant his threat. He signalled to his docking bay crew. 'Disarm all hatches. Let the thugs in.'

Another delivery ship streaked away, trying to escape, but patrol Remoras swept in and surrounded it, fired enough blasts to cripple its engines, then attached grappling beams. The captain of the delivery ship shot his weapons, but it was a useless gesture.

Within moments the Eddies had taken over the ship and arrested its crew.

Roberto groaned. The Mantas had already docked, and uniformed Eddy soldiers had begun to flood into the facility, accompanied by imposing Soldier compies. Overhead, the second half of the planetoid orbited, casting its shadow onto the observation dome. He heard bootsteps marching down the corridors; the EDF had already found the control centre.

Within moments, General Lanyan himself stood at the doorway. 'Let's not make this any more difficult than it needs to be.'

EIGHTY-SEVEN

NIKKO CHAN TYLAR

On time at Hurricane Depot . . . well, at least within an hour. That was a record, as far as Nikko was concerned. He had already delivered wental water to two uninhabited planets and now felt exhilarated at having done such a good job. He looked forward to relaxing for a night in guest quarters and eating good food in the cafes, exotic recipes cooked by families that remembered their ethnic heritage from Earth.

He'd been to Hurricane Depot dozens of times, usually piloting a cargo escort for ekti tanks or ferrying food from the Chan greenhouse domes. Nikko did better when he could see his destination and fly by the seat of his pants rather than relying on complex navigational systems. By now he knew the approach through the rocky obstacle course like the back of his hand.

This time, as *Aquarius* approached the orbiting planetoids, he saw two EDF Juggernauts circling the outer perimeter beyond the binary rocks. The Eddy ships had blasted away much of the boundary field to clear a safe path; dust and rubble drifted in unpredictable orbits, heated and accelerated by numerous explosions.

Three clan cargo ships streaked away, pursued by fast Remoras. The clans had modified many of their craft with 'sprint' engines for superior acceleration, and now the fleeing ships scattered in all directions, faster than the infringing military vessels could follow.

'Shizz, what the hell is going on here?' He reached for the comm system to call Hurricane Depot's control centre, but realized it might be smart to keep quiet. The *Aquarius* was a small ship coming on a high polar vector; he was sure the EDF hadn't seen him yet.

Nikko intercepted a warning broadcast. 'This is Roberto Clarin. The EDF has seized control of Hurricane Depot! They're confiscating all our supplies. No doubt they'll kill everyone on board.' The message was a standard EM signal, blasted out into space. It would take years to reach the nearest inhabited system, but incoming Roamer vessels – like Nikko's – might also intercept it.

He sat in his cockpit white-knuckled and angry, not knowing what he could do. The stored vials of powerful wentals in the *Aquarius* thrummed and vibrated with questions and concerned curiosity. He growled aloud, 'Remember what I told you about our stupid reasons for wars? You're witnessing one of them here.'

Below him, EDF workers efficiently stripped Hurricane Depot of all food crates, all ekti tanks, all cargo, all personal possessions. Nikko eavesdropped on conversations transmitted over the EDF frequencies. The Eddies were joking and sneering, amused at the Roamers' attempts at resistance. 'They're robbing us blind!'

As he watched in horror, Nikko felt the wentals' deep disquiet. *It is like a hydrogue attack . . . only these soldiers have betrayed their own people.*

All inhabitants of Hurricane Depot were being taken into custody and loaded aboard Manta cruisers. The station chief Roberto Clarin had apparently been seized as a prisoner of war, though no formal war had been declared. Nikko feared the military would simply make all those people from Hurricane Depot 'disappear'.

'Clear everyone off the station,' General Lanyan's voice transmitted. 'Take your time and do a thorough job. The Chairman wants no casualties, if at all possible. He believes it will help us secure better capitulation terms from the Roamer clans.'

'Capitulation?' Nikko growled to himself. 'To those pillaging barbarians?' From the *Aquarius*, he recorded files and files of detailed eyewitness images to prove the EDF involvement. But it would be no surprise to the clans, not since he'd found the wreckage of Kamarov's ship.

'I've got to get a warning back to Rendezvous,' he said, anxious to depart but unwilling to leave until the whole operation was over. He kept his engines primed for sudden high acceleration, in case he needed to run.

We can transmit the message, the water-entity said. *All wental-bearing ships will know what has happened here. They can spread the word swiftly among the Roamers.*

Nikko looked at the shimmering containers he kept near him on the piloting deck. 'You can communicate with each other faster than I can send a signal?'

We are all basically the same entity. What one of us knows, all wentals know.

Nikko gasped. 'Like telink through the worldtrees!'

The verdani are similar to the wentals. That is why we were allies in the ancient war.

Within an hour, most of the EDF battleships packed up and departed from the gravitationally stable island between the orbiting planetoids. The Mantas took their spoils of war and accompanied the guardian Juggernauts, threading their way out of the debris zone. On the fringe of the system, they kept station and waited.

But two cruisers remained behind, still attached to the now-abandoned depot facility. The cruisers fired up their engines and used heavy acceleration to push the delicately balanced station away from its stable point. Then the Mantas disengaged from the docking rings and pulled back as the enormous habitat cluster continued to move.

The depot's position had always been relatively precarious, located accurately between the pole of the two orbiting mountains. Now, the added boost from the Mantas' powerful engines tipped it from the saddle point. Like a ball gradually rolling off the top of a hill, Hurricane Depot tumbled and began to pick up speed as it fell out of gravitational equilibrium.

'I can't believe this,' Nikko said. The *Aquarius* continued to take a full sequence of images. 'I simply cannot accept what my eyes are showing me!'

Hurricane Depot drifted away. Already it was being battered by a cannonade of outlier rocks and ice. Nikko used his ship's observation scopes to obtain higher resolution. A large meteoroid smashed through one of the cargo hulls, ripping open a gaping hole. Other debris continued to pummel, dent, and smash the tumbling station – and still it kept moving, falling towards the nearest of the tide-locked orbiting planetoids. Venting atmosphere gave the facility an added nudge.

When Hurricane Depot finally collided with the hurtling mountain, it was like a helpless rodent run down by a speeding vehicle. In an instant, it was over.

The rough-edged planetoid slammed into the habitat complex and flattened it into scrap metal, plumes of escaping air, and flickers of fire, as wisps of stored fuel ignited and battery packs exploded. Shrapnel splashed outwards, spraying a slow-motion fantail of cluttered flotsam.

Nikko felt as if he would be violently ill.

Smug and bloated with their stolen treasures and their prisoners, the EDF battle group lumbered away like an army of swaggering conquerors. As soon as they had gone out of range and Nikko knew the *Aquarius* would not be detected, he launched his ship, accelerating fully.

'We've got to get out of here,' he said to the wentals. The message had already been sent to the other water-bearing ships, but he alone could deliver the images, the comm recordings, the tangible evidence. Nikko just hoped he wouldn't get lost this time. His responsibility was too important.

EIGHTY-EIGHT

JESS TAMBLYN

The wental voices in his head were part of him now, a new pattern of incomprehensible desires overlaid on his own thoughts. Jess flew across open space, simultaneously solitary and connected, linked with the water entities, encapsulated within a pearl-and-coral vessel that throbbed with liquid power.

He was proud of his volunteer water bearers, who were travelling around the Spiral Arm seeking out untouched planetary reservoirs where wentals could thrive. Each new seedpoint of the water entities was like another cell in a great and powerful organism. The wental presence grew stronger day by day – and, so far, the hydrogues knew nothing about the return of their primal enemies.

The amniotic seawater that filled his spherical vessel should have blurred his vision as he stared out at the open starscape, but the liquid was part of him. He could see with absolute clarity, extending his senses through the wentals. Small native sea creatures from the primeval ocean world still drifted about inside his vessel, a self-contained bubble of an alien ecosystem.

Jess continued his hunt for candidate planets, even those inhospitable to human life. Water was the only necessary ingredient.

Like echoes at the back of his thoughts, he experienced wental images from long ago, fragmented memories of the titanic struggle that had annihilated the water beings, stripping them apart molecule by molecule and strewing them across the vacuum of space. He knew, as if by half-forgot instinct, about the wentals' alliance with the worldtrees, how they had joined together to create gigantic seed ships as their battle vessels . . . before the burning treachery of the faeros. Jess squeezed his eyes shut against the horror, but the nightmare was inside his head as he experienced a wental dragged screaming into the inferno of a sun.

But the strength and confidence of the wentals thrummed through him, and he had no choice but to set aside his uneasiness. *We will start again, one drop at a time, and we will succeed.*

Then his mind was filled with a flood of startling new images, fresh attacks that were occurring even now, as witnessed by another wental cluster, a group of samples carried by Nikko Chan Tylar. Through the watery film over his eyes, he saw what the other wentals were witnessing. Jess watched as a large artificial installation – Hurricane Depot! – was attacked by giant battleships. Not by hydrogue ships this time. The aggressors were Earth Defence Forces vessels, Mantas and Juggernauts. The Eddies had launched a full-scale invasion, capturing Roamer prisoners, stealing supplies . . . then completely destroying the depot!

All wentals saw the same thing and communicated to each of his water-bearers what had happened. No one was close enough to help Hurricane Depot, including Jess. Even so, his scattered volunteers *knew*. The Big Goose could not keep this a secret.

'Damn them,' he said. He thought the water inside his ship and all around him might boil as his energized skin reacted to his anger.

But though he could not reach Hurricane Depot in time, he could help. He could send a message. He could take action.

Go to Cesca! He sent the thought like a shout. *Whichever one of you is closest, find Speaker Peroni, tell her what has happened. Then, Nikko, you track her down and deliver your proof.*

The warning would spread like fast ripples in a pond. He and his volunteers would restore the wentals to help in the fight against the hydrogues. But the Speaker for all clans was the right person to face the Hansa Chairman.

Unconsciously, Jess's heart led him back to a large roving comet, outbound now after it had looped around its isolated sun. As the ball of ice and snow headed back out on its long orbit, the gases in the coma and tail would condense again. At first, only a year ago, he had arranged to meet Cesca for a secret romantic rendezvous in the wispy tail.

Here, Jess could think only of his love and his foolish choices, his poor timing. This comet would always be special to him, a place of memories. Now, with the help of the wentals, he would transform the comet into something even more magical.

'Do you require liquid water, or is ice good enough to contain you?'

Water is water — steam, liquid, or ice. The material state does not matter to us.

Even though the exotic wental ship responded to his thoughts and gestures, Jess needed all of his piloting skill to bring the coral-and-pearl bubble through the pelting sleet of the comet's coma to land on the frozen surface. He walked through the gelatinous wall of his vessel and stepped out, unprotected except for a film of sparkling moisture and his pearlescent gossamer garment, onto black ice and greyish-white snow. The wental presence kept his body intact even in the vacuum of open space.

As he set his bare foot on the rugged, sterile ground, just a few droplets of the possessed water seeped out of his energized skin and permeated the crystal lattice of cometary ice. Jess stared in amazement as he watched the tumbling, evaporating iceberg come to eerie life.

The sparkle and power of the wentals began to grow like phosphorescent dye spreading into a pool. The expanding wental swiftly penetrated fissures and swept through the solid blocks of ice that bound the comet together.

The hydrogues will never think to look for us here, the wentals said in his mind.

Jess remained for a long moment in the cold, still silence. Finally, he returned to his water bubble vessel, detached it from the comet, and flew away.

Jess felt immense satisfaction to see the comet crackle and glow. It lit up like a spotlight now, a new cluster of wentals in a cannonball of watery energy. Counting it another victory, Jess flew off in search of more places where he could seed humanity's unexpected allies.

EIGHTY-NINE

MAGE-IMPERATOR JORA'H

Now that he had returned from Dobro and settled back into his chrysalis chair, the Mage-Imperator had important changes to make. Jora'h sent a message runner to summon his daughter Yazra'h; he wanted to speak with her about something that intrigued him far more than an endless succession of obsessively dedicated Ildiran pilgrims who wished to gaze upon him. Lately, it seemed a great many of them were coming from Hyrillka, possibly representatives to begin shipping shiing from the battered world.

The first of the day's sycophants already waited outside the skysphere reception hall, and Yazra'h passed them as she bounded into her father's presence. Her every movement seemed supple, as if her bones were made of solidified grace. The three tawny and powerful Isix cats accompanied her with their usual perfectly synchronized movement. The Ildiran nobles in the hall backed away, intimidated by the feline predators.

The Mage-Imperator sat up in his chair, smiling. 'Must you always bring those pets with you? You are frightening my functionaries.'

Ascending the dais, Yazra'h smirked at the cowering courtiers with disdain. 'Am I responsible for their silly fears, Liege? I keep my cats under control.' When she stopped at the top step, the Isix cats sat, one to either side of Yazra'h, the other behind and facing away from her. The panther-like creatures were narrow, their faces pointed like greyhounds. They could run fast, attack swiftly, and kill in the blink of an eye.

Jora'h smiled indulgently. 'Despite all the crises around me, Yazra'h, one look at you shows that our race has the strength to face any adversary. In fact, I pity anyone who would dare to go against you.'

She accepted the praise, but did not bask in it. Most noble females were beautiful, pampered courtesans, whose impeccably smooth skin glistened from lotions and photoactive paints. They adorned their shaved scalps, necks, and shoulders with swirls of shifting pigments, like chameleon stripes. Liloa'h, Zan'nh's mother, had been one of them.

Yazra'h was not. She let her bronze hair grow into a loose wild mane. Her smoky topaz eyes glittered with a feral light. Though she'd always had the opportunity to be among noble women, Yazra'h preferred to train with soldier kithmen, developing her reflexes, honing her skills, keeping her body lean and powerful. Her activities would have made any other noblewoman an outcast, but the daughter of the Mage-Imperator was allowed her eccentricities.

Jora'h knew she was proficient at weapons work, though not as physically strong as the soldier kithmen. Yazra'h had taken many lovers, all of them guards or soldiers; she had never shown any interest in nobles, weakling bureaucrats, or preoccupied lens kithmen. When Jora'h had questioned her about this, she'd answered, 'I'm afraid I might *break* them, Father.'

Now she tossed her long hair and met his eyes. 'I'm always

honoured when you summon me. What service may I offer you, Father?' It was refreshing to have someone face him so directly. The batch of Hyrillka pilgrims still waited outside, and the nobles gradually went about their duties, though they continued to look askance at the Isix cats.

The Mage-Imperator leaned forward in his padded seat. 'I wanted to ask your opinion, Yazra'h, about the current role of women in Ildiran society. I believe you have . . . somewhat different ideas than most Ildirans hold.'

'I certainly do. The females of some lower kiths, the workers and servants and soldiers, are treated as equals and contribute as much labour as the males. But look at the higher kiths, the nobles, the bureaucrats' – she gestured scornfully around the room – 'the courtiers. What do the women do? They are just . . . decorations, and they are proud of it. If they are so evolved and intelligent, perhaps they should contribute more to our society.'

Jora'h grinned, knowing that most Ildirans would hear her words with horror. 'And what about yourself, Yazra'h? Do you believe you can contribute as well?'

'I already have, and I expect to continue to do so.'

'Perhaps we'll start with you, then. Our Empire is troubled. Through the *thism* I can sense that many things are wrong. Even here in the Prism Palace, some say I should be more wary. I'm inclined to heed that advice, though I can't conceive of my own people turning against me.'

'From what I've read in the *Saga*,' Yazra'h countered, 'many inconceivable events have occurred in our history.'

Jora'h settled deeper into his chrysalis chair, glad to know that she read the *Saga* on her own, rather than just listening to the dramatic distillations in rememberer performances. 'Yazra'h, many guard kithmen are assigned to watch over me, but my father selected Bron'n as his special personal guard. Bron'n was ultimately responsible for the Mage-Imperator's safety. I have not yet announced who will serve me in that capacity.'

Yazra'h gave him a stern look. 'You should not wait, Liege. I can offer advice. I know many of the guards, and I can tell you which are the most dedicated, which are strongest, which would serve you best.'

Jora'h waved his hand. 'I'm not interested in them. I've already made my decision.' She showed no indignation that he had not consulted her. 'I have selected *you*, Yazra'h. I want you to be my personal bodyguard.'

Caution warred with hope in her topaz eyes. 'But Father . . . there are more qualified fighters.'

'I have seen you train, Yazra'h. I know you are superb with weapons. Your Isix cats obey your every command.' He smiled proudly. 'Besides, would not a daughter do anything to protect her father? The *thism* shows me that your loyalty is without question.'

Yazra'h made no further objection. They both knew the obvious drawbacks. The selection of a female as the Mage-Imperator's personal bodyguard – a woman not even of the soldier kith, but noble-born – would cause much discussion and consternation. Already the nobles in the reception hall were filled with dismay at Jora'h's startling breaks from tradition: standing and walking around the Palace on his two feet, leaving Ildira to visit Dobro, sitting in the chrysalis chair only when it suited him, and now choosing his daughter for a position always reserved to a different kith.

Yazra'h made the slightest gesture, and all three of her Isix cats got to their feet, dynamos of golden fur and rippling muscle. They all faced the Mage-Imperator. 'I would be honoured to serve in such a capacity, Liege. I will never fail you, and I will protect you to my last breath. I will make you proud.'

'I know. That is why I chose you.'

NINETY

HYRILLKA DESIGNATE
RUSA'H

With most of Hyrilka's population liberated by the potent raw shiing, Rusa'h took advantage of his opportunity. He knew what must be done, before it was too late for the Empire.

The Designate did not act for his own aggrandizement, but out of sheer conviction. He had seen the Lightsource and could follow the bright path more closely than any other Ildiran – better than Jora'h, better than their corpulent father. Too much harm had already been done.

It wasn't the fault of the Ildiran people that they had strayed. They blindly followed the Mage-Imperator's guidance, even when it was flawed. They were not supposed to make their own decisions or think their own thoughts. They were expected to obey and follow and cooperate. But when their appointed leader was deluded, the Ildirans had no hope of being anything but lost.

Rusa'h knew how to change that. And the shiing would help him.

Already a handful of converts were bound to him. After this evening he would have most of the population of Hyrillka.

Several days earlier in a private ceremony and consultation, his lens kithmen had already been brought to the true path. His pleasure mates had always followed him eagerly, and he'd brought them over to his side as well. The lovely, fertile women were no longer concerned with the fleshly pleasures that had so consumed them before; now, they were just as fanatically devoted to different goals. *His* goals.

Thor'h had not been a problem. From the beginning, the young man had voluntarily participated . . . and as the Prime Designate, he would be an important weapon in what was sure to be a difficult, but necessary, struggle.

Pery'h, though, was likely to be trouble. The Designate-in-waiting was too intelligent, too loyal to his father, with no obvious weaknesses. But Rusa'h would find an appropriate solution. The Lightsource would guide him infallibly through the many tribulations that lay ahead in their glorious future.

The Hyrillka Designate returned to the citadel palace as the blue-white primary set, leaving the sky ruddy with orange light from the swollen secondary. The Horizon Cluster brightened overhead, hundreds of worlds and stars spangling together in a crowded display.

Since his head injury, Rusa'h had been cut off from the normal *thism* of the Ildiran people. But now that most of the Hyrillka population had gorged themselves on fresh shiing, they wandered dazedly free, cut off from the network of thoughts. They were separated from the intrusive surveillance of Mage-Imperator Jora'h, and Rusa'h could weave them together into a strong new pattern.

Now, by his own command, all Hyrillkans were blanketed in the same healing mental silence that Rusa'h had felt for so long. While deep in his sub-*thism* sleep, the Lightsource had granted him superior skills and now he reached out with newfound power. While the population remained bleary and pliable from the raw shiing, he would begin to collect the numb lines of *thism* that would eventually have returned to Jora'h. One graceful strand at a time, Rusa'h would draw all those loose threads together and lay down new mental paths, bringing the minds of the Hyrillkans into a clean, clear tapestry of his own design, inspired by the Lightsource itself . . .

Now, surrounded by devoted converts in the orange dusk, Rusa'h sat in the citadel palace, smiling. Beside him, his pleasure mates and lens kithmen and proud Thor'h stood ready to offer their support. These were the binding filaments of his new web, and he would draw upon them to re-network the Hyrillkan people before the shiing wore off, cementing their mental connections again. Soon, all of Hyrillka would be a part of him, his own lacework of *thism*.

Nearby but isolated from all the invisible changes, young Pery'h wore a disapproving expression as servers brought in banquet foods. The Designate-in-waiting still had no idea what was happening around him. Dancers stumbled, trying to recapture their graceful moves, still disoriented because of the shiing. 'This is appalling, Uncle.'

'Stop complaining,' Thor'h retorted. 'The people deserve this celebration, and Designate Rusa'h has decreed it.'

Pery'h sat in his appointed place, but did not touch his food. He seemed uneasy, his skin pasty and moist. Now that so many of the people on Hyrillka had separated from Jora'h's *thism* and linked instead to Rusa'h's, the Designate-in-waiting was cut off from the comfort of even a small splinter colony. And it would only get worse for him.

When Rusa'h stood, all the people in the open pavilions fell instantly silent, though they were not yet completely under his control. The Designate looked at them with glittering eyes, seeing so much potential here.

He called for the two medical kithmen who had accompanied him from Ildira to watch over his condition and monitor his recovery. Rusa'h had secretly forced one of them to take shiing and had converted him. Afterwards, the other doctor had easily been persuaded. Tonight, they would take the necessary and dramatic action to cement his ever-expanding hold.

'I have an announcement that most of you will not believe, at first.' Rusa'h said the words, but he was sure that they *would* believe him. The people were in his grasp. He had the proof . . . and it certainly explained some of Mage-Imperator Jora'h's recent troubling behaviour.

'Our times are dark, and Hyrillka has suffered. The hydrogues prey upon us. We have failed, not because the Lightsource has grown dim, but because our leaders have been unable to see it. My father, Mage-Imperator Cyroc'h, had so many schemes that he deluded himself. My brother Jora'h is even worse, for he has willingly remained blind.'

Pery'h stood up, his face white with rage. 'Uncle, even your injuries do not excuse the words you speak!'

The shiing-dazed listeners continued to regard the Designate-in-waiting with muddled interest, but no indignation. Thanks to the drug, none of the others could sense Pery'h in the *thism*. Thor'h just smiled. 'Listen when the rightful Designate speaks, little brother. You might learn something.'

'The Mage-Imperator can sense the unrest you are sowing,' Pery'h insisted. 'Beware of what you say.'

Rusa'h frowned at the young man who had refused to take shiing with the rest of the people. 'Jora'h has no presence here tonight – save through your eyes, Pery'h. Perhaps we should send you away?'

By now the Designate-in-waiting must have sensed that he alone remained connected to Ildira through a tenuous thread of *thism* — and that the rest of Hyrillka stood against him.

'Listen to what I have to say, Pery'h, before you make up your mind. You are an intelligent young man, trained to be the next Hyrillka Designate. But destiny and preconceptions can be changed. We have the power.'

Pery'h stared at him in shock. 'I refuse. I won't let you.'

The Hyrillka Designate frowned. 'First hear me out, then make your choice. Our people have been deceived into believing that Jora'h is the true Mage-Imperator, the rightful nexus of all the strands of *thism*, but I know otherwise, for the Lightsource has shunned him. While I was in my sub-*thism* sleep, I was unable to move physically, but I ventured elsewhere in my mind. I saw secrets. I learned facts that no other Ildiran suspected. And now I have finally acquired proof.'

Thor'h looked as if he might burst into a cheer. Pery'h was barely able to contain his confusion. 'What sort of proof?' Since he had not joined the revellers in the nialia fields, the young man remained clear-headed and sceptical; the rest of the Hyrillkans accepted Rusa'h's dictates without question.

'The former Mage-Imperator died suddenly, while I lay unconscious. And in the shock and grief that followed, Jora'h quickly ascended to become our new leader. Ildirans thought him diligent and honourable. None of us guessed that he was power-mad! That he would do anything to be rid of our father so that he could assume the chrysalis chair and the Prism Palace for himself.'

Pery'h lurched to his feet and turned to leave, but two guards blocked his way. Rusa'h continued, knowing the Designate-in-waiting was listening, though he wanted to flee. 'I obtained a tissue sample from one of the handlers who prepared the dead Mage-Imperator's body for his funeral. The chemical analysis makes the answer absolutely clear. Cyroc'h did not simply die — he was *poisoned*.'

As the others gasped, Rusa'h continued. 'His bodyguard Bron'n must have been a co-conspirator, but he had the honour to take his own life immediately after my father lay dead in the chrysalis chair. Jora'h, though, got what he wanted. He himself must have murdered the Mage-Imperator to become an unlawful usurper.'

Even drugged on shiing, the people in the citadel palace muttered uneasily at this. Some gasped, but they believed Rusa'h's words, assuming the proof he offered must be incontrovertible.

'And that is why the Lightsource has deserted him!' the Designate cried. 'The soul threads cannot penetrate the darkness of Jora'h's heart. All Ildirans are paying the price, and our race will continue to suffer . . . unless I can lead us back to the realm of the Lightsource.' He folded his hands. 'I am prepared to do what I must.'

While Thor'h listened, wearing an empty smile and nodding at the horrific revelations, Pery'h was indignant. Rusa'h became impatient with him and turned to the burly guards. 'Take the Designate-in-waiting and hold him in his chambers until he can be suitably . . . convinced.'

The Hyrillkans did not object. Pery'h could offer only a token resistance as several muscular soldiers took him away from the open courtyard where bright flowers on the curling vines had opened up in twilight bloom. None of the Ildirans could sense him in the *thism*. With the Designate-in-waiting gone, Rusa'h turned his back on his hard-looking pleasure mates and called the two devoted medical kithmen closer.

'If Jora'h is not the true Mage-Imperator, then the Ildiran race must have one. The Lightsource has chosen me for this burden. I know the difficult road that lies ahead, but I will follow the bright path. I am confident in my guidance. I will endure for the good of the Ildiran people.'

He lay back on an open divan and unfastened his robe to

expose himself, reclining naked. 'You here are privileged to witness an event that will for ever change the Ildiran race.'

The two medical kithmen withdrew razor-edged crystalline knives. Rusa'h glanced at his pleasure mates, recalling distantly all the hedonistic times he had shared with them. But that was no longer his lot, and physical pleasure no longer interested him. He turned from them and closed his eyes, diverting his thoughts to see the light within.

After his long ordeal, he knew his true mission. Only a selfish coward would turn away now. Rusa'h must follow his beliefs to the end. He alone could restring the net of *thism*, take away the corrupted strands knotted around Jora'h and bring them all to himself. Hyrillka would be the start. Next the many systems in the Horizon Cluster would follow, and then the remainder of the Ildiran Empire.

With a whisper, the Designate gave his order, and the doctors made a quick, clean slash between his legs. Rusa'h clenched his jaw, biting back the pain, forcing it through his nerves and channelling it until it became an inferno of light in his mind. From there he could see all the drifting strands of *thism* cut loose by his population's reliance on shiing.

And like a master, paying no attention to the continued ministrations of the medical kithmen or the awed chatter of the audience in the citadel palace, Rusa'h bound all the strands together, gathering them to his heart and securing them so that Jora'h would no longer have any hold on these people.

He smiled, holding at last the true *thism* that would form a basis for a rejuvenated and purified Ildiran Empire.

NINETY-ONE

SAREIN

When Sarein tried to find her old quarters in the fungus-reef city, she found that the rooms had been cobbled together with emergency patchworks, as if some blind or drunken surgeon had attempted to fix a grievous wound.

Roamers! They had no sense of aesthetics, concentrating only on functionality and brute-force fixes. Though they had used worldtree wood in many places, the occasional metal girder and tasteless stained-alloy wallplate were atrocious. For some reason, the Theron people, including the green priests had cooperated with their efforts and actually helped put everything back together this way. Her parents both seemed pleased with the work the clans had done. Eventually, as the worldforest healed, Sarein hoped the scars would be mercifully covered over, but it would take a long, long time.

Roamer workers continued to blunder through the ruins of the forest while pretending to offer assistance. Obviously, the space gypsies were here for their own purposes, their own profits, regardless of the altruistic claims they made. Since Basil wanted her to take on her rightful role as the new Mother, Sarein requested a private meeting with her parents inside the main meeting chamber.

'We are glad that you've come back, Sarein.' Alexa smiled. 'There's so much we need to catch up on.'

Sarein's nostrils flared as she drew deep breaths, in and out, calming herself, remembering her diplomatic training. 'I only hope I've arrived in time. Don't trust the Roamers. Do you think they're doing this out of the kindness of their hearts?'

Outside in the forest, machinery continued to level the debris, scraping the forest soil clean, dumping chemical fertilizers, spreading seeds for fast-growing groundcover. Buzzing haulers lifted away one giant worldtree trunk after another, taking it to distant Roamer processing colonies. The operation reminded Sarein of graverobbers stealing corpses.

Alexa said, 'My daughter, what are you talking about? The Roamers are helping us greatly, and the green priests and Theron workers have made exceptional progress in the past month. We're all working together.'

'You're letting treasure slip through your fingers! Can't you see the enormous effort the Roamers are putting in here? Such help comes only for a price. Have you asked yourselves what they are trying to gain?'

Idriss scratched his thick, black beard. 'Offering aid in the wake of a disaster is what good-hearted people do. We would have done the same for them if we had known, and if we were capable. Remember, Speaker Peroni was betrothed to Reynald. We were going to have family alliances, Roamers and Therons.'

Her parents were so painfully *trusting*. Sarein recalled why she had been eager to leave stifling Theroc and go to civilized Earth.

'Roamers have always been kind to us, Sarein.' Alexa leaned closer, frowning. 'Why must you think the worst of the clans?'

Her frustration finally boiled over. 'Because Speaker Peroni cut off the Hansa from ekti supplies and other vital goods, right when we need them the most.' She held up her hand and ticked off other reasons she had heard Basil use. 'Because the clans refuse to be counted like any other Hansa colony. Because they pay no taxes except what we can impose upon them as trade tariffs. Because we don't even know where most of their settlements are or what they're doing behind all that secrecy.' She waited in vain for some sign of agreement from her parents. 'Doesn't that make you the least bit suspicious?'

Idriss shook his head. 'Frankly, we need their help. I don't see any downside.'

Sarein let out an exasperated breath. 'Look at all the worldtree wood they're taking away from Theroc. They'll turn that into a valuable commodity and make enormous profits from it.'

'We *offered* the worldtree wood as payment for their help,' Alexa said with extended patience. 'Without being asked, Cesca Peroni promised to share some of those profits with us.'

'Do you have anything in writing? Did you negotiate proper terms for Theroc? What sort of percentage are the Roamers going to give back?'

Idriss sat back in his chair. 'I'm sure it'll be fair. She had no obligation to offer anything in the first place.'

'Hundreds of Hansa traders and businessmen would have bid for the right to process and distribute the fallen worldtree wood. You didn't even ask for competitive plans. You simply handed it all to the Roamer clans. That makes no sense—'

Finally, her father showed a flash of impatience. 'Sarein, dear, look out the window at all the work being done. Do you see *any* representatives of the Hanseatic League offering assistance? Do you see a *single team* of civil engineers from the Earth Defence Forces helping us rebuild? No, you do not. You see only Roamers. Why should we reward anyone else?'

Alexa stood up from her gilded chair. 'I have no wish to continue this discussion until you have made overtures to Cesca, Sarein. It would be best for the two of you to speak face-to-face and settle your differences. If the hydrogues hadn't killed Reynald, she would be your sister-in-law now. Your father and I very much want you to be friends.' She took Idriss by the arm and left Sarein standing there, feeling like a little girl.

Sarein found the Roamer Speaker in a soot-covered forest meadow and asked her for a private conversation. 'My parents insist that I talk with you.'

Speaker Peroni raised her eyebrows. 'And why is that?'

'They say my suspicions and doubts are unfair to you people.'

Her dark eyes widened slightly. '*Your* suspicions and doubts? That's interesting, considering that the Hansa has hounded, cheated, and persecuted us for generations. When I learned that you'd returned to Theroc, I hoped you would act as an intermediary between the Hansa and the Roamer clans, since you are Reynald's sister. Therons are independent, so I thought you might be more open-minded.'

It occurred to Sarein that if she could heal this breach, then Basil would be indebted to her for years. 'Restore ekti deliveries, and I'll consider intervening for you with the Hansa.'

'Do you represent the people of Theroc, or are you merely a mouthpiece for Chairman Wenceslas and his Eddy guard dogs?'

Sarein was affronted. 'You descend to the lowest insults when I'm trying to settle our differences?'

'Insults? I'm exercising admirable restraint. The Chairman already knows what he needs to do before we'll resume ekti deliveries. The ball's in his court.'

Sarein knew she was in the stronger bargaining position. 'Don't make the mistake of assuming that ekti gives you the power to coerce the Hansa in any way. Earth has already received several shipments from our cloud harvester on Qronha 3. Once we establish other such facilities, and after our transportal colonization initiative takes hold, we'll no longer need Roamer ekti at all. Then where will you be?'

Cesca did not rise to the bait. 'Self-sufficient and independent, I believe. Just think it through, Ambassador. The Hansa stole from us and committed murder – why else would we have stopped selling ekti? It was our most profitable export. But I've seen what the Eddies do to our helpless cargo ships and the innocent men and women who work on them.'

'Fabricated stories.'

'I have indisputable proof,' Cesca retorted. 'Would you like to see the wreckage for yourself? See the jazer burns?'

Sarein hardened her expression, refusing to believe. 'Chairman Wenceslas would never authorize such outrageous acts, and the King would certainly never condone it.' But in the back of her mind, Sarein remembered some of the shadowy things Basil had already done. Was hijacking a Roamer cargo ship and stealing its ekti much different? She didn't want to consider the possibility.

'Then why hasn't he bothered to deny, or even address our grievances?'

The heavy lifters droned overhead, carrying fallen trees. Earth movers pushed broken debris aside while groups of green priests found fertile patches of soil and manually planted treelings. The two women seemed to be in a bubble of emptiness, while activity continued around them. Sarein's back was straight, and her lips were pale. All her muscles remained tense.

Suddenly, a florid-faced Roamer in a uniform covered with embroidery and pockets came running up. 'Speaker Peroni, there is an emergency! It's Hurricane Depot!'

With a sidelong look at Sarein, the man leaned close to whisper to Cesca Peroni. Her face grew dark with rage, then she turned to glower back at Sarein. 'As if we needed more proof! A battle group of your Earth Defence Forces just attacked one of our largest facilities. They stole our ekti and our supplies, kidnapped every person aboard the station – and then completely destroyed it.'

'I . . . don't believe that.' At first Sarein didn't think the news could possibly be true . . . but would Speaker Peroni simply concoct such an outrageous lie, or send a shill with a fictitious message? Not likely.

Before leaving Earth, Sarein had suspected that Basil intended to make some sort of gesture against the Roamers, but she had never guessed it would be so bold or provocative. As the hydrogue war continued, the Chairman had become more aggressive, more of a hawk. Had he and General Lanyan finally stepped over the line?

'I intend to submit full documentation and verifiable images to the Whisper Palace.' Speaker Peroni was visibly containing her fury. 'Drogue attacks are bad enough – but coming from the Hansa? I had hoped to resolve this in a calm and fair manner, but the Big Goose has shown its plumage for all to see. You had best reconsider just how reliable your friends are, Ambassador – for the good of all Theron people.'

Then she raced with the Roamer message runner back to his ship.

NINETY-TWO

KOTTO OKIAH

The ship accommodations were minimal on Kotto's journey to Osquivel, but he didn't notice one bit. His attention was elsewhere. He had already forgot about the work on Theroc and delved into other problems and mysteries.

Cesca Peroni had arranged a spare bunk for him on an outbound cargo escort to the Osquivel shipyards. He had food, water, and air. That was all he needed. The captain of the cargo escort was a solitary person who didn't particularly welcome passengers, but since the eccentric engineer kept to himself and his calculations, the two men got along well.

En route, Kotto remained preoccupied with the idea of investigating a genuine hydrogue ship – intact! His mind crackled with possibilities. Unfortunately, so little was known about drogue vessels that he couldn't even extrapolate or develop theories until he saw it. So, he turned his restless mind to other challenges.

First it had been impossible heat on Isperos, where several people had lost their lives. So he resolved to do better on ultracold Jonah 12, where lakes of liquid methane surrounded by icebergs of frozen ammonia gave the planetoid a fairyland appearance. Because the atmospheric gases were in solid form, Roamer workers in durable tractors had been able to go out with shovel apparatus and scoop the hydrogen right off the ground.

But most man-made mechanical systems could not function for long in such a cold environment. Now, on his bunk, Kotto did a complete revamp of the crawlers and extractors, then designed a more compact kind of vacuum-baffle insulation for the engines.

He had never considered himself a particularly adventurous man, but he remembered Cesca Peroni's challenge to all Roamers on the day she'd become Speaker, taking over the job from Kotto's mother. The young woman had looked so intent, so beautiful, and so dedicated that Kotto had made up his mind not to disappoint her . . .

In his free time, he also studied all published documents about Klikiss transportals and even some of the papers about the Klikiss Torch. The insectoid civilization had developed completely alien forms of mathematics and engineering, but it was all intriguing, and Kotto liked to put ideas together in different ways. His thoughts were like a projectile ricocheting at random in zero gravity.

But when the cargo escort reached its destination, Kotto put everything in the back of his mind. Barrel-chested Del Kellum met him when the ship docked. Kellum stood with hands on his hips and his bushy beard protruding. 'By damn, Kotto, your mother always told us we should listen to your hare-brained ideas. Now you get a chance to be as hare-brained as you like.'

Kotto took no insult from the clan leader's bluster. 'I appreciate the opportunity.' He glanced around inside the docking room. 'So where is the derelict? I'm anxious to get started.'

'We wouldn't keep a thing like that near our populated facilities – the drogues might come looking for it.' He clapped a hand on Kotto's shoulder and led him deeper inside. 'No, some of my workers took it to the other side of the rings, where it sits all alone, just waiting for you.'

On a wall screen, Kellum projected an orbital diagram with a marker blip indicating where the small hydrogue sphere had been placed in a stable orbit at the outer fringe of the ring. 'I've assigned five of our Listener and Friendly compies to be your assistants, but you'll be the only human out there. Unless you need somebody else?' He raised his eyebrows, hoping Kotto wouldn't disagree.

The engineer shook his head. 'No, I'd prefer to be by myself.'

'Good, I've got a full stash of supplies, diagnostics, and lab equipment ready for you to go.' When Del Kellum called up a photographic image of the alien sphere, Kotto stared at it, mesmerized. 'Now *you* figure the thing out.'

NINETY-THREE

DAVLIN LOTZE

By the time Davlin's ship limped to the edge of the Relleker system, only fumes remained in the stardrive chambers, but his transmitter still called out for help. Relleker's sun looked bright, its planets brilliant dots – all of them impossibly far away. He spent hours in detailed calculations, considering and dismissing many desperate alternatives.

Finally, with careful timing, he fired a burst of his engines, flaming out the last of his fuel to give the ship a push, taking it out of its decreasing velocity curve so that he could coast just a bit farther. He would drift closer to one of the planets, but much too slowly.

After a day, when he'd begun to lose hope that he would be spotted in time, his ship was intercepted by an outlying picket scout keeping watch for hydrogue incursions. The Relleker defence scouts were not formally part of the EDF, and apparently poorly trained, but at least they were in the right place. As soon as they brought him aboard, knowing he had no time to lose, Davlin hauled out his old credentials from Chairman Wenceslas and flaunted his EDF rank. When the scouts still appeared uneasy, he used silver beret techniques to commandeer the picket ship so that he could race to Relleker and make his demands.

The people on Crenna were freezing, dying . . . and counting on him.

The Relleker population, though, was as unprepared for austerity measures as most colonies. This had been a luxury world, a spa and vacation spot that catered to wealthy Hansa citizens. Far from being self-sufficient, they had long since used most of their ekti to gather emergency materials and discretionary items they thought they needed to survive.

When Davlin presented himself to the Relleker governor, a well-fed-looking woman named Jane Pekar, she said Relleker had no resources to assist the Crenna colonists. She shrugged her shoulders. 'Irrespective of your credentials, Mr Lotze, and your clear urgency, we simply can't help you.'

'Your people don't appear to be trying very hard to come up with solutions.' Davlin remained standing in the governor's office long after the woman had become uncomfortable. But Davlin had no way to force Relleker to take action, not even tempt them into offering assistance. He couldn't believe that despite overwhelming odds he had made it here, only to find himself with a new set of obstacles and no time to work around them. He was frustrated at his own helplessness. Had he come this far only to fail the people of Crenna, after all?

Finally, with a sigh, Governor Pekar said, 'We're due to have a scheduled supply run in another day or two. Someone named Kett . . . the *Voracious* something. Maybe they can help you.'

Davlin smiled at last.

When Rlinda Kett and Branson Roberts arrived in their two ships, Davlin immediately went to meet them. 'You did tell me to contact you if I ever needed any help.' He found it fundamentally unsettling to depend on anyone. 'Now I need it.'

Rlinda gave him a huge grin as he explained the situation. 'Hah! I'm happy to help. You didn't think I was one of those government types who goes back on a promise, did you?'

Both she and Roberts dumped everything from their cargo bays, emptying out all crates and materials that should have been distributed to other colonies. 'I'll just add it to Relleker's tab. A hundred and thirty people, you said? Are they at least thinner than I am?' She patted her wide hips.

'I can promise that.'

'Then let's go.'

The *Voracious Curiosity* and the *Blind Faith* descended into the darkness of the smothered Crenna system. Davlin rode in the cockpit next to Rlinda Kett, much more animated and intense now than he had been when she'd dropped him off at Crenna not long ago. He could barely contain his relief.

A transmission came from the *Blind Faith*. 'We're here, but somebody switched off the sun, all right. Can't even tell we're in a planetary system.'

'Just watch out that you don't run smack into the star, BeBob. Sometimes you don't pay enough attention to your piloting.'

'I resent that, Rlinda.'

'But I don't hear you arguing.'

She adjusted course, and Davlin leaned close to the cockpit windows. Viewing through infrared filters, they could still see fading colours as the planet's thermal energy bled into space. With the sun's nuclear fires extinguished, the whole Crenna system was nothing more than a cooling corpse, a dark ball in space. The planet's atmosphere had already frozen out, ice sheets were piled on top of shattered ground upheavals. The air had condensed into carbon dioxide snow. All lakes and streams were obliterated, every living thing wiped out on the surface.

Davlin shook his head. 'I hope the people are still alive down there.'

'How long did you say this ice age has lasted?' Roberts transmitted.

'Less than two weeks. There's still heat emanating from the planet itself, and the star's not entirely cold. Overall there's about one per cent of the former flux.'

'Good thing we brought our shovels,' Rlinda said. 'Tell me where to go, Davlin.'

Before departing, he had placed a locator beacon with a long-lived battery near the hatch that covered the tunnels. He had never mentioned it to Mayor Ruis, not wanting the people huddled in their warrens to realize how bad the outer environment would get. He scanned through frequency bands and finally located the faint pinging of the locater beacon, much weaker than he'd expected. To his dismay, he realized that the beacon itself was buried under deep ice.

'I'll project a bull's-eye for you.'

They descended through swirling air that had frozen into a slurry of snow and carbon dioxide flakes. Davlin operated the comm systems. 'Crenna colony, this is Davlin Lotze.' He waited, but heard only static. 'Mayor Ruis, are you still receiving? I've brought help.' He tried several times, equally unsuccessful.

Rlinda looked at her equipment and shook her head. 'Oh, don't read too much into it, Davlin. The storms and the snow are building up a significant E-M disturbance, and a normal signal might not be able to punch through all that ice.'

When the two ships reached position, Davlin peered down at the swirling layers of ice and frozen atmosphere. He couldn't even see the protrusions of his hangar or any of the town's buildings.

'Shall we sprinkle some salt?' Roberts joked.

'If it's frozen atmosphere, there'll be a very low volatilization point. We can melt it with the exhaust from our engines,' Rlinda said. 'Don't have to be pretty about it.' She dropped the *Voracious Curiosity* closer for a slow landing and let the hot vented gases blast geysers of steam from a wide area near the sealed vault door. Drifting up and down to hold her position, in half an hour she had cut a significant divot, then withdrew to let the *Blind Faith* take its turn in the small zone, evaporating more of the thick frozen shield.

Before long, they had excavated a large crater around the sealed metal cap.

'Now for the next problem,' Davlin said. 'We were in such a hurry to get the Crenna colonists underground, to build a safe haven that would keep them warm, we just installed that single vault lid – not a sophisticated airlock.'

'Can they survive long enough to make it into our ships?' Rlinda asked.

Davlin shook his head. 'There's *no air*. It's all frozen out.'

'Well, then, that is interesting,' she said.

'There's no tube to connect the ship and the hatch,' BeBob said.

'How many extra environment suits do we have?' Davlin asked.

'I've got three aboard, and BeBob has three on the *Blind Faith*.'

'Four,' the other captain transmitted.

'Okay.' Davlin tapped his fingers on the panel. 'You have an emergency shelter dome, right?'

Rlinda nodded. 'It's in the crash kit, but it only holds a couple of people.'

'So, we erect and pressurize the tent as an airtight bubble atop the hatch and keep all the suits inside, like a small airlock chamber. Then when we crack the hatch lid from below, a couple of the colonists can come out and suit up. They'll go to the ships six or seven at a time.'

'A hundred and thirty people? That'll take days for suiting up, pressurizing and repressurizing,' Roberts said.

'Then it'll have to take days.' Davlin flashed Rlinda an uncharacteristic grin. 'But it'll work.'

They all suited up and worked together outside, surrounded by the towering ice walls of the narrow borehole they had blasted down to the vault lid. They wrestled out the large flexible structure designed as a sealed dome for short-term survival in an inhospitable space environment. They covered the region of the lid and anchored all the surrounding points.

Davlin took one of his heavy tools and banged loudly on the metal cap, hoping to signal the colonists who had not been able to read his transmissions. Before long, he felt a frantic vibrating response, people hammering back from the other side. 'At least somebody's alive.'

Still suited, Branson Roberts came through the sphincter door, hauling the three extra suits from the *Voracious Curiosity*. He and Davlin would make a second trip to bring the four others from the *Blind Faith*. Rlinda set up heaters inside the survival dome.

'This'll be a tedious and not very dramatic ending to our rescue operation,' Roberts said.

'Saving people one step at a time is exciting enough for me.' Rlinda playfully punched Davlin in the shoulder. 'You're pretty compassionate for a spy, Mr Lotze.'

Without answering, he worked the frozen hatch controls. When he finally succeeded in opening the heavy metal lid, several familiar colonists burst out, grinning. Mayor Ruis was one of the first, throwing his arms around Davlin and giving him a hug.

The greeting unsettled him, but Davlin had no regrets.

NINETY-FOUR

ORLI COVITZ

S tarting with the framework of the old Klikiss city, the new colonists swiftly converted their temporary camp into a secure settlement on Corribus. It was a whole new world to tame. So much basic work remained to be done that the settlers had little time just to explore.

Orli, though, considered it part of her job.

Years ago xeno-archaeologists had gone through the alien ruins, gathering as much material as possible before their funding ran out. Later, Hud Steinman and other Hansa scouts had done a preliminary investigation of the area. However, Orli knew there were hundreds of nooks and crannies where no previous investigator had ever set foot.

Though her father was the one who someday expected to find lost riches, some of his persistent imagination had rubbed off on her. What if the Klikiss had hidden records or buried treasure during their last battle in the granite-walled canyon?

When she slipped off to explore, Orli left her furry cricket in its cage. Her father had taken his shift in the listening station at the communications tower, where he was probably passing the time by dabbling with strange ideas for inventions . . .

She went to where the canyon narrowed and the half-melted granite walls rose sheer and steep. Irregular mineral concentrations within the cracks had, over millennia, seeped out and grown into blocky crystals of alum, like stacked cubes of murky glass. They spangled the cliffsides like strands of rough-cut diamonds. In her original notation, Margaret Colicos had poetically described the site as 'the mountains weeping crystal blood'. Margaret had wondered if the placement was some sort of message laid down by the Klikiss, or an integrated circuit patterned along the granite walls, but analysis showed that the crystals had grown long after the devastating attack vitrified the stone.

Now, when Orli looked at the lumps extending up the sheer wall, she saw them as convenient handholds, a stepladder that could carry her up to the inaccessible cracks and niches high in the rockface.

She scrambled up, stepping on the crystals and grabbing with her hands to move her body higher. She grinned to think she was reaching places the archaeological expeditions could never have mapped. Margaret and Louis Colicos – as well as Hud Steinman – were *old* people. They would not have tried anything so physically demanding or risky.

Halfway up, she paused to look down, then realized that was not a good idea. The canyon floor was a long, dizzying way below her. The rest of the sheer cliff rose above her, and the lumps of alum crystal now seemed tiny and unstable. If she let go, if she fainted, the fall would be a straight, swift plunge to certain death.

Swallowing hard, Orli decided to look up and forward and not bother to glance back down. She had her eye on a black vertical notch half-hidden in a fold in the cliff. It might once have been a large cave opening, but the intense heat of ancient blasts had folded the granite down so that it drooped over the doorway like a partial curtain.

By now she was tired of climbing. When Orli reached the right height, she saw what she was looking for and started to work her way over to it. One foot slipped on the slick, smooth surface of a tilted alum·block, but she caught herself by grabbing a sharp edge of rehardened granite. Breathing hard, she squeezed her body into the dark cave.

Because many of the rooms in the Klikiss city were half-collapsed and dark, all the new colonists carried small handlights. Orli crawled until she reached what was obviously a spacious chamber, then fumbled in her pocket. Now that her sore hands were free, she switched on the illumination. Light flowed out, splashing on the cave walls.

Here, the rock was rough-hewn pristine granite, not flash-softened like the outer cliffs, but the chamber was too perfectly symmetrical, too misplaced high up in the middle of a granite cliff, to have been formed naturally. She imagined an army of workers – the insectoid Klikiss? – chopping out a spherical room five metres across. But why so high up in the cliff? She shone her light on the rough ceiling and the far walls, searching for tunnels or exits, but found only the strange, web-like Klikiss writing, hieroglyphics and equations that spiralled outwards from a central point.

When she pointed the handlight towards the dusty floor, she gasped.

The last reports Margaret Colicos had transmitted contained images of a mummified Klikiss body found on Rheindic Co. Now, seeing the withered corpse on the floor, the girl instantly recognized the leathery cockroach shape of a Klikiss – this one no longer intact. Its body had been torn apart, its exoskeleton exploded from the inside, as if numerous swallowed land mines had detonated. Its limbs and wing coverings looked *chewed*, as if something had torn its way out from within the corpse. Some terrible parasite native to Corribus? A predator?

Inside the chamber, the shadows seemed darker, the temperatures colder. She listened intently, but heard only the pounding of her pulse in her ears, her own ragged breathing, and the faint whistle of a breeze outside the cave opening.

Beside the alien's body Orli found another wrecked form, this one larger and darker, as if coated with oily shadows. It had the same basic shape, but made out of metal and obsidian-coloured ceramics – one of the Klikiss robots!

The beetle-like machine had also been torn apart, just like the Klikiss body. Its components were smashed and pummelled. Barely recognizable scraps lay strewn around the chamber floor, as if an army of rodents had toyed with a pile of treats. Pieces of near-indestructible exoskeleton were shattered, mangled, discarded like garbage. She couldn't imagine the strength such a thing would have required.

Though this had taken place thousands of years ago, the sheer violence of the scene resounded like a shout in the claustrophobic silence. Something awful had destroyed both the ancient Klikiss creature and the powerful robot. What sort of predator would strike both the Klikiss and their machines?

Orli shuddered, and the rock-walled chamber seemed much smaller now, the air thicker. Backing away, she bumped into the rough rock of the far wall and let out a yelp of fear. This was not the kind of mysterious treasure she had hoped to find.

Orli drew several deep breaths and tried to hum one of the tunes she had made up on her synthesizer strips to calm herself. She told herself she had nothing to worry about. Everything that might have attacked the Klikiss had been gone from Corribus for millennia.

The rational part of her mind realized that what she had found in this cave might be a truly significant archaeological find. But though her head was clear and her thoughts perfectly logical, her heart still hammered in her chest. She wanted to be out of the sheltered cliff chamber she had discovered.

Orli suspected it would be a very long climb back down to the colony settlement.

NINETY-FIVE

PRIME DESIGNATE THOR'H

After his uncle's startling imitation of the Mage-Imperator's ascension ceremony, Thor'h was glad to turn his abilities to arranging for the creation of an opulent chrysalis chair for the new self-proclaimed Imperator.

By now, surely his father had sensed something amiss here at Hyrillka.

The Prime Designate instructed Hyrillka's best artisans, rememberers, and sculptors to design a fittingly extravagant vessel for the true leader. The craftsmen and artists worked with absolute dedication, refusing to rest or take sustenance until they were finished.

Along its curved sides inlaid with jewels, crystals, and precious metals, were scenes from the *Saga of Seven Suns*, tales of great Mage-Imperators from Rusa'h's honoured lineage. The events Thor'h had chosen to depict were taken from the mists of the past, with no connection to the unpleasant present, the misdirection and corruption his own father had laid upon the Ildiran people.

After his giddy day of celebratory shiing consumption, Rusa'h had bound the disjointed *thism* of the Hyrillkan people to himself, forming a tight new web completely separate from the rest of the Ildirans. Hyrillka's population followed the new Imperator's every instruction, and any person who had accidentally or intentionally failed to take the potent stimulant drug was tracked down and forced to partake. Except for Pery'h, all of Hyrillka was now a single unified organism. Thor'h had willingly and joyously offered his own abilities to support his uncle's rule.

Only his stubborn brother had refused. The new Imperator's unquestioning guards still held Designate-in-waiting Pery'h under house arrest within the citadel palace, refusing to let him see anyone. Thor'h had gone to speak with his brother several times, alternately taunting and pleading with him, but still Pery'h refused to see the obvious, though he was utterly isolated, and suffering for it.

Unlike the rest of Hyrillka's population, no one of the Mage-Imperator's bloodline could be forced to cooperate with the new network of *thism*. Pery'h had to change his mind willingly, had to break of his own accord from his deluded father. But the young man refused — and it was beginning to be a problem for his uncle's plans . . .

Within three days, Thor'h proudly presented the new chrysalis chair to Rusa'h, who lay with glazed eyes, still recovering from the castration knife that had given him complete access to the parallel *thism* network. Rusa'h was nearly strong enough to go out among his people again, and when he saw the chrysalis chair, his face lightened like the brightest sunrise in the Horizon Cluster. 'It is magnificent. Thor'h, you are truly *my* Prime Designate.'

He stood beside his uncle, beaming with pride. Because the new Imperator had issued orders that none of his converted followers was to consume any more shiing, and thereby weaken the restrung *thism* network, Thor'h felt a bit unsteady from the first stages of withdrawal. All of the drug Hyrillka produced would now be stockpiled for the conversion of other worlds. Thor'h had depended on the stimulant for so long that now his body craved it, shook with his need for it. But simply being a part of Rusa'h's bright new *thism* was enough to give him strength.

Assisted by Thor'h and a chattering group of attenders, the Imperator raised himself and took his position in the new chrysalis chair. He settled in, grasped the curved sides, then activated the lifting mechanism that held him above the polished floor.

'According to the pilgrims I have dispatched to observe him, my brother Jora'h now allows his feet to touch the ground. He claims to be the Mage-Imperator, yet he walks about like a man, equal to other men.' Rusa'h's face darkened with disgust. 'He has so lost his way that he will never regain the shining path. As the true and real Imperator of our people, I intend to adhere to the purity of our traditions, as decreed by the Lightsource.'

'Another reason why we must follow you, Uncle.' Thor'h ran his fingers over the chair's inlaid jewels and meticulous carvings.

'Now that I am mobile, I wish to inspect the new nialia fields, the irrigation canals, and the shiing-production facilities. They will become the cornerstone of my expanding rule.'

'No one has rested since their conversion, Liege. All other crops have been burned and ploughed under for fertilizer. New canals are being dug, and every single agricultural kithman is devoting his or her greatest ingenuity to expanding the plantmoth growth and distribution.'

The chrysalis chair started forward, and Thor'h accompanied it. They passed vine-covered columns that framed the open courtyard where Rusa'h had once held his celebrations and parties . . . and now his important audiences. Attender kithmen scrambled about, clearing the way, while four loyal courtiers strode ahead to announce the Imperator's passage.

Rusa'h sent them all away. 'I wish to travel alone with my Prime Designate. Tell the workers in the nialia fields that I will address them when I reach the harvesting and distillation facility.'

Attenders ran about like a swarm of insects, frantically doing what they were told; noble kithmen stepped aside, bowing reverently as his chrysalis chair passed. Reaching the nearest fields, Rusa'h guided the chair out onto one of the silvery irrigation channels. As Thor'h walked beside him at the edge of the waterway, the chrysalis chair moved like a ceremonial barge along the mirror-like water.

Glittering creatures swam in the canals, jellyfish that fed on water, nutrients, and sunlight to grow into a protein-rich gelatinous food source. Periodically workers skimmed the canals with large screens to catch the jellyfish, which were consumed raw in joyous feasts. Rusa'h had given orders for the jellyfish to be harvested regularly, preserved, and added to the food stockpiles, which were then rationed, now that all of Hyrillka's agricultural lands had been converted to shiing production.

'Will we have enough food for our population, Liege?' Thor'h had asked.

'We will soon conquer other worlds, starting with the Horizon Cluster. Shiing is the key, and therefore other crops are secondary. Once my new *thism* web spreads, we will have all the food of other planets, and my new armies of loyal Ildiran subjects will feed us.'

As the two gracefully moved along the nialias, male plantmoths fluttered about, seeking female flowers to fertilize. Organized labourers marched through the fields, harvesting transplantable shoots and hard seeds. Other Ildirans drained milky bloodsap from ripe pods, collecting every drop and passing it along to runners, who delivered the vessels to the distillation facility, where the potent liquid drug would be preserved in its raw pearlescent form.

The majority of these workers were not agricultural kithmen

bred to serve in the nialia fields, but Imperator Rusa'h's new *thism* had shaped all kithmen into a combined unit, and now he needed farmers more than he needed other castes. Even bureaucrats, singers, and diggers went to work in the sweeping fields, planting, tilling, harvesting. Across the Hyrillkan continents, people of all kiths continued to spread the nialia plantings. Rusa'h's objective was to increase shiing production tenfold. It was the only way he could bring other Ildirans into the tapestry of his vision.

At the mosaic-tiled spaceport, where Adar Kori'nh had long ago arrived with his warliners to take the young Prime Designate back to Ildira – the first part of his father's treachery – Thor'h had now issued orders for all of Hyrillka's spaceships to be modified and refitted. Even cargo vessels were given additional hull armour and outfitted with both defensive and offensive weapons. Previously, only Solar Navy ships had borne arms, but Imperator Rusa'h insisted that many ways must change in order to wrench the Ildiran race back onto the Lightsource path from which they had strayed.

Shiploads of concentrated raw shiing were readied for Imperator Rusa'h's next step. Thor'h did not know his uncle's plans, nor did any of the lens kithmen, but they all had complete faith in the enlightened Imperator. All of the armoured cargo ships were ready to take off, as soon as Rusa'h chose his next conquest and decided to make his move.

At the end of the irrigation canals, they reached a bustling factory complex filled with Ildirans of all kiths, who were working diligently on the shiing packaging lines. After the hydrogue attack, when Thor'h had returned here to reconstruct the facilities, this building had not been a factory at all, but an entertainment pavilion where performers had danced with reflective ribbons and pennants. Formerly, it had been the Hyrillka Designate's favourite spectacle.

Now, though, priorities had changed, and Rusa'h had called a moratorium on 'unnecessary cultural activities'. All Hyrillkans must save their time and energy for his vital work.

When the Imperator's chrysalis chair glided up to the production factory, the dedicated workers were reluctant to turn from their intensive tasks, but when Rusa'h raised both hands, his subjects came close to hear him speak. 'You are my chosen soldiers of the future! Not just warriors and guards, but combatants in a larger battle for the soul of the Ildiran race. We must hope we are not too late to save our people.'

The people nodded, listening with rapt attention. Thor'h basked in the Imperator's words.

'It has been made clear to me that the hydrogues are not simply aliens, not mere enemies – they have returned as a demonic punishment! The Lightsource brought this upon us. Did not the hydrogues emerge from a burst of light at Oncier? Jora'h, the so-called Mage-Imperator, refuses to see this. Even my father Cyroc'h did not recognize the connection, for he too was blinded to the true path of the *thism*.

'But I have been guided by a vision. You will all help me bring about the painful but necessary changes to rescue our lost people. Under my guidance, the Empire shall grow great again, and the hydrogues will disappear when the Lightsource is satisfied that we have found our way.'

The people absorbed his words, not just through his voice but also through their taut new *thism* connection. Imperator Rusa'h stared at them for a long while with benevolent satisfaction, then asked Thor'h to follow him as he turned the chrysalis chair around.

'We will begin our next operations soon, Prime Designate. One planet after another in the Horizon Cluster will join my network. And with each acquisition, I will grow stronger.'

Thor'h followed his uncle back through the nialia fields towards the citadel palace, still puzzled. 'How will we exert control over the whole Horizon Cluster, Liege? How can we, just a small group here on Hyrillka, defeat the Solar Navy?'

Leaning back in his ornate womb-like vessel, Rusa'h smiled placidly. 'The Solar Navy will soon be ours, too. We will use warliners to control other splinter colonies in the Horizon Cluster. But first we must capture those ships.'

Thor'h turned to him in quick surprise. 'How?'

The Imperator held up a finger that had once worn many jewelled rings. 'We must lure them to Hyrillka. That is the next step.'

Thor'h imagined a Solar Navy fleet bristling with arms, rushing to Hyrillka and angry at Rusa'h's apparent rebellion.

The new Imperator continued to smile. 'And I know exactly how to bring them running here.'

NINETY-SIX

CESCA PERONI

On her way to Earth, Cesca had plenty of time to stew
about what the Hansa had done.

Leaving Theroc, she raced straight out to a meeting
place where she'd arranged to intercept Nikko Chan Tylar. Jess's
volunteer water-bearers were already delivering the news to many
scattered clan outposts, but she needed to meet the young man in
person to receive his tangible evidence. Cesca waited in the empty
vastness, searching for the blip indicating the young Roamer's
approach. Finally the *Aquarius* arrived – almost on time.

Looking agitated and out of his element – exactly as when he'd
found the EDF-blasted wreckage of Raven Kamarov's ship – Nikko
crossed over to the Speaker's ship. He clutched the data packs that
held the numerous stored images and recordings of all the Eddy
transmissions he had intercepted at Hurricane Depot.

'This just keeps getting worse, Speaker,' he said, playing the
images for her on the small screen in the cockpit of her
diplomatic craft. Cesca stared at the wanton destruction, the
brutal conquest that captured hostages and materials, then the

callous annihilation of the equilibrium station. Her cockpit suddenly felt very cold.

'When they hit Raven's ship, they were trying to be sneaky,' Cesca said. 'Now – this is open warfare.' She held up the data packs. 'The Big Goose thinks it can step all over us, but I guarantee that other colonies will remember what happened on Yreka, where the EDF hammered Hansa citizens because they kept a small ekti stockpile for their own uses.'

'But Roamers aren't even Hansa citizens,' Nikko said. 'The Goose doesn't have any authority over us.'

'They have a large standing army. Some people think that's all they need.'

The young Roamer still looked frazzled. 'But what are you going to do, Speaker?'

Cesca gathered her strength and determination, wishing the clan leaders hadn't forced her into the rash embargo in the first place. She'd known the Roamers would suffer scorn and discomfort because of it, but she hadn't expected King Peter – or was it the Chairman? – to retaliate so aggressively.

'I'm going to make them understand the error of their ways, Nikko. Someone in the Terran Hanseatic League has to see reason.'

When her vessel finally reached Earth, Cesca set a course towards the Palace District. Instantly, space traffic control officers shouted at her to enter a holding orbit until her authorization could be cleared, but she ignored them. When EDF Remoras flew into the sky, threatening to shoot her down, she transmitted on a broad channel. 'I am Cesca Peroni, the Speaker for all Roamer clans. I have urgent business with the Hansa.'

The transport-control officer said, 'I wasn't notified that the Roamers were sending a diplomatic representative to Earth. You will have to go through regular ambassadorial channels if you want to speak to someone in the Hanseatic League.'

She answered in a cool, firm voice, 'I don't wish to speak to "someone". I need to see the King himself.'

The transport officer was brusque. 'We don't control the King's appointment calendar, Ma'am.'

'Cut off our ekti and now they think they own the Spiral Arm,' one of the Remora pilots grumbled, knowing Cesca could hear him.

Now that she was finally here, she wondered what she could accomplish by negotiating. The clans had already ceased all deliveries of stardrive fuel and resource materials. What more could she threaten or do? In all likelihood, the Hansa must think she was bluffing, that the Roamers depended on the commerce as much as the Big Goose did. But Roamers had numerous ways to tighten their belts and become self-sufficient.

What if the Hansa simply seized her, took her hostage as they had done with the inhabitants on Hurricane Depot? If they thought the squabbling families would ever agree to ransom terms, they did not understand the pride and independence of the Roamers.

Finally, the voice of a Hansa official came over the channel. 'We will allow Speaker Peroni to land. A meeting will be arranged as soon as possible.'

Cesca brought her ship down, following directions provided by the Remoras. As soon as she landed in the Palace District, uniformed escorts met Cesca and led the way. No doubt while she was gone they would scan her ship, ransack it for valuable information, perhaps even plant tracers. But she had code-scrambled all useful data aboard, implanted with self-erasure worms; she could easily detect and shed any tracking devices. She carried duplicate datawafers of the images from Hurricane Depot as she went off to her meeting.

Thanks to the strange simultaneous warning transmitted through the wentals, the Roamers knew about the destruction of

Hurricane Depot much sooner than even the EDF could have expected. That was Cesca's ace in the hole. Maybe they hadn't managed to prepare all of their lies and excuses yet.

King Peter had always seemed reasonable and compassionate. He was married to Reynald's sister Estarra, and Cesca hoped that Peter had a streak of fairness in him – more than Sarein did.

Guards ushered her into a private meeting room within the Whisper Palace, and she sat in the chamber marshalling her thoughts and rehearsing her words. She had plenty of time to do it.

When a servant compy opened the door, she stood promptly to greet the King – only to see that it was not Peter at all, but Chairman Wenceslas. 'You have quite an unorthodox means of arrival, Speaker Peroni. I've been meaning to send you a message, but Roamers are rather difficult to find when they don't wish to be around.'

'I'd say Hurricane Depot was quite a clear message.' Her voice was brittle and defensive, and he showed a flash of surprise that she knew about the attack already. 'Where is King Peter? I asked to see him.'

'I am the man in charge. You can talk to me.'

'Then you are also the man to blame? The man responsible for repeated, unprovoked, aggressive actions against Roamer ships, facilities, and citizens?' She held out the datawafers that contained test results. 'These are the analyses of the wreckage of a Roamer ship, which was clearly destroyed by EDF weaponry, but not before its cargo of ekti was confiscated.' Cesca pushed the files towards him, but Basil just looked at them as if they were bits of spoiled food.

'And these show your unprovoked attack on Hurricane Depot.' She activated a flatscreen player to show the images Nikko had taken. The Juggernauts and Mantas were unmistakable as they commandeered the fuel-transfer facility, removing anything of value before using brute force to knock the station out of its stable orbit. 'When I brought the problem to your attention, we received no reply whatsoever from the Hansa.'

The Chairman gave her a metal-hard smile. 'Surely our answer is clear? Hurricane Depot is our initial response to your illegal embargo, and I will authorize additional military actions until you capitulate. The Hanseatic League cannot allow you to cut us off from the stardrive fuel we need to survive.' He folded his hands together and sat down. 'Now, then, Speaker – enough of this nonsense that hurts both of us. We can work out acceptable terms.'

'Terms? Our terms were simple enough in the first place, Mr Chairman. But instead of solving the problem, you have only made it worse.' She tapped the flatscreen player. 'With these images of your unprovoked attack on Hurricane Depot, no one can possibly doubt our claims.'

Chairman Wenceslas still did not look disturbed. 'Really? In the past month, our media networks have been full of stories about Roamer unreliability, Roamer treachery, and Roamer selfishness. With the snap of my fingers I can produce any number of experts who will state that these images were amateurishly faked. Everyone will see it as grandstanding on your part to justify your embargo – which has already been portrayed as a ploy to raise ekti prices.'

The Chairman leaned forward. 'In fact, allow me to share with you a declaration that King Peter is about to sign.' He activated the tablescreen to display neat words. 'Once we cut away all the flowery diplomatic and legal language, this decrees martial law against the Roamer clans and explicitly revokes any implied right to self-government or independence.'

He toggled to another page. 'And here is a facsimile of the original treaty signed by all generation ships, including the *Kanaka*, which guarantees that none of the colonists, crew, or any of their descendants will take any action that harms Earth – which your embargo does.' He switched to a third document. 'And this is a formal demand that Roamers surrender all ekti stockpiles for distribution throughout the worlds of humanity according to the greatest need.' He looked at her with a thin smile, showing just a glimpse of teeth. 'I can print you a copy for your own records.'

Cesca actually let out a laugh. 'This goes so far beyond the pale that you can't hope to withstand any legal challenge.'

'Oh, there will be no challenge. In fact, this is what a majority of the Hansa citizenry demands. Would you like to see polling numbers? Roamer clans are currently considered hostile to the human race. When you petulantly cut off our ekti supply, *you* declared war on Earth, Speaker Peroni.'

'You never had the right to one hundred per cent of our ekti output.'

'Yes, we did. King Peter declared it himself. And you've given us no choice but to take drastic action. Your facility at' – he scanned down until he found the name on Nikko's images – 'Hurricane Depot is only the first of several possible acquisitions we have planned.'

'Acquisitions?'

'A handful of asteroid settlements, mining facilities, and delivery ships – all are vulnerable. Believe me, if you insist on forcing my hand, then I will give the EDF standing orders to take anything they find, by whatever means possible.' Now he gave her a maddeningly 'reasonable' look. 'This conflict will drag on only as long as *you* allow it, Speaker Peroni. Surrender your ekti and settle into the greater family of humanity. Then we can get down to business.'

Given how swiftly and easily the EDF battle group had raided and destroyed Hurricane Depot, the Chairman obviously expected Cesca to bow to the ultimatum. But he didn't know her, and he didn't know exactly what he was dealing with. She could never return to Rendezvous with terms like those. The Roamers would throw her out the nearest airlock and pick a stronger Speaker.

'And now that you have me here, I suppose you'll simply hold me hostage? A political prisoner?'

The Chairman cocked his head in surprise. 'I would never do something so clumsy and crude, Speaker Peroni. Too many people witnessed your arrival, and it would be extremely bad diplomatic form for me to lock you up. Then I suppose the Roamer clans would be even more disorganized than usual, and I'd never get a resolution to this issue. Would you like to capitulate now and save us all a great deal of time and discomfort?'

She stood, and her voice was as calm as his. 'I made an error in believing that you were a rational leader, Chairman Wenceslas. This is little more than extortion, and the EDF is composed of your henchmen. As Speaker for all clans, I reaffirm that commerce between the Roamers and the Hansa remains at an end. No further ekti, or any resources whatsoever, will be made available to you.'

Basil looked annoyed. No doubt, he was convinced that Cesca's response would make the whole problem last longer and force him to devote his dwindling resources to the matter.

'We will hunt you down,' he said, still seated, showing her no courtesy at all. 'We will seize all of your assets.'

She strode to the door, startling the guard who waited out there. 'Waste your time and send your warships wherever you like, Mr Chairman. We will vanish like smoke.'

NINETY-SEVEN

KOTTO OKIAH

Distant sunlight gleamed from the diamond hull of the hydrogue derelict in the rings of Osquivel.

Kotto wanted to do everything at once. He had a thousand tests to run, and nearly as many theories to prove or disprove. But most investigative routines were doomed from the start by poor planning, haphazardness, misguided enthusiasm, and muddled protocols. He didn't intend to let that happen this time. The responsibility was too heavy, and he didn't want to waste a moment.

Kotto let the programmed compy pilot do the flying because his own distractibility and fascination with this project might cause him to crash while he stared out the window. The silent compy pilot guided the ship through the obstacle course of drifting rocks out on the fringes of the thin ring. The two Analytical compies, GU and KR, sat patiently, waiting for the work to begin.

'Step one,' Kotto said aloud, 'is to perform a general, visual assessment of the sphere's complete exterior. Of course, if we can't figure out how to get inside, then the outside is all we've got.'

Attentive GU diligently recorded his every word like a mechanical lab notebook.

By plotting its orbit and calculating drift, Kotto made an accurate assessment of the derelict's mass, from which he could derive an average density. That gave a few clues (but not many) about the thickness of the diamond hull and what the interior contained.

As the lab shuttle cruised in overlapping circles, spiralling closer to the alien ship, Kotto stared at it, looking for flaws or asymmetries, but the spiked globe seemed absolutely perfect. He could determine no top or bottom. He saw no indication of a hatch.

'So how do the drogues get inside those things? Quite a puzzle.'

For hours he used the full suite of spectral scanners. The derelict was cold, and Kotto could not pinpoint any engines, exhaust ports, or propulsion tubes. If he could figure out the basics, Roamers would have a field day developing secondary inventions from the technological principles.

But he was getting ahead of himself. Obviously, it was impossible to crack the ship open with brute force – at least not by any means Kellum's crew had at the shipyards. The Eddy military had used their full weapons against these vessels to little effect.

Besides, Kotto didn't want to damage the thing. He needed to find a different way to get inside.

Holding the lab shuttle steady, Kotto dispatched GU and KR with hand-held nondestructive evaluation apparatus. The small robots cycled through the airlock, took their equipment, and applied sensors to the curved diamond skin of the dead hydrogue ship. Then they proceeded to run another complete protocol of tests, sending signals and pulses of light at specific wavelengths known to interact with carbon-carbon bonds.

Finally, Kotto used physical vibrations. GU applied a thumper pad that oscillated like a masseuse, thrumming against the side of the enemy globe. He manipulated the steady vibration, changing the amplitude along a regular progression, hoping to find a perfect resonance. By recording the transmission of acoustic waves, Kotto expected to gather information about the material structure and the derelict's internal arrangement.

He was surprised when a specific vibrational mode caused a previously invisible hatch to appear, like a circular line scribed on a glass window. Within seconds, as the vibration continued, the hatch disengaged completely and was flung away like a bullet disk at high speed, barely missing the lab shuttle.

The suddenly venting atmosphere from within the hydrogue ship acted like a rocket exhaust, propelling the small sphere away in a tumbling trajectory. A backwash jet of misty air caught one of the research compies and sent it spinning, arms flailing, high up out of the plane of Osquivel's rings, while the derelict reeled off in another direction.

'Go after it!' Kotto shouted.

The compy pilot looked at him. 'Unclear referent. Should I pursue the hydrogue vessel or the compy?'

'The derelict! Oh, and transmit to the compy – is it GU? – that we'll come back and get him in just a few minutes.'

The lab shuttle raced off in pursuit, but the drogue derelict was out of control, tumbling and wheeling like a Chinese fireworks display. The diamond globe collided with an orbiting rock in the ring and ricocheted, changing trajectory as it whipped about. The escaping atmosphere continued to churn out as if it would never stop. Kotto realized that the internal pressure must have been incredible – equivalent to the deep core of a gas giant. 'Ah, that explains the overall high density of the globe itself.'

But now that there was an opening in the hull, the atmosphere streamed out in a jet of gas like a full tank of rocket fuel, and Kotto calculated that it could continue to do so for a long time. He grabbed the comm system and called for help from the shipyard workers. 'It's getting away! You've got to come and help me corral the hydrogue ship.'

The derelict careened into another floating rock and continued unharmed like a wild pinball. Kotto's lab shuttle barely had sufficient velocity to keep up with its madcap course.

It took over two hours for a small group of shipyard workers to seize the derelict ship, by which time all of the contained atmosphere had belched itself out. Along the way, they also rounded up a battered GU, who was drifting helplessly in space.

Embarrassed, Kotto issued quick but sincere apologies. He thanked Kellum and his men for rescuing the derelict and bringing it to a halt – now far from the ring plane and high above the gas giant. 'This will do right where it is. No need to drag it back into the rings. We'll just do our work way out here.' He rounded up his compy assistants.

'The farther away from our shipyards, the better, by damn,' Del Kellum said. He and his workers returned to their duties.

Kotto stared hungrily at the now-open derelict and rubbed his hands together. He couldn't wait to see what was inside.

NINETY-EIGHT

PATRICK FITZPATRICK III

In the engineering bay's background drone, Fitzpatrick felt he could speak confidentially with his fellow prisoners. So long as he and his EDF comrades appeared to be working, the Roamer supervisors allowed them to fraternize.

Over the past two days, though, their captors had treated them differently, glaring at the hostages as if they had done something wrong. The seemingly benevolent watchers now simmered with anger. Was it the discovery of the destroyed Roamer ekti ship? But they had known about that for quite a while.

Fitzpatrick finally learned, through muttered comments and whispered complaints, that the EDF had finally struck back against the insidious Roamers and their sneaky bases. One of their depots had been taken over, the supplies confiscated and the facility destroyed.

'Serves them right,' said Shelia Andez. 'They provoked the King – what did they expect would happen? I hope the Roachers learn their lesson and stop their stubborn little fit.'

'It proves the Hansa is willing to enforce their demands,' Yamane said.

'It proves to me that we shouldn't just be sitting here.' Fitzpatrick glanced meaningfully at his companions. 'Maybe the EDF is already out there looking for us. If my grandmother knew I was alive, she wouldn't sit still.'

'Or maybe it's in our own hands,' Shelia said.

'We should consider options,' Yamane said, tinkering with a damaged compy. 'Perhaps we can even find unexpected allies.'

The Soldier compies salvaged from wrecked EDF battleships had been put to work out in the industrial yards, where they performed tasks too difficult or dangerous for Roamers. As a cybernetics specialist, Yamane was one of the few people at Osquivel qualified to perform maintenance on the Soldier models. He used the opportunity to study how the sophisticated compies adapted to their forced reprogramming.

Fitzpatrick helped him probe the combat-designed machine, studying its instruction modules and programming implants. This one had suffered a brief collision out in the rockyards, but the scrapes and discolorations were merely superficial.

'The Roachers already wiped the obvious military programming from these machines, but their memory structure goes deep,' Yamane said quietly. 'Soldier models are designed around Klikiss instructional modules. It looks like there's a hidden partition that can't be erased with standard routines. It's still all in here somewhere, if I can figure out how to activate the core programmes.' His lips formed a thin smile. 'Then things will change around here.'

Fitzpatrick leaned closer, pretending to help as soon as he saw one of the Roamers watching them. He whispered, 'What do you mean?'

'Then *we'll* have an army of a hundred or so Soldier compies – if we're willing to trigger the core programming.'

Bill Stanna arrived carrying a bulky box. The burly soldier had been given duties as a loader, carrying equipment and supplies. Stanna had basic training, knew how to run weaponry and fly standard ships, but he was a traditional heavily muscled grunt, never meant to be a brilliant tactician.

'I wish I could pull an assignment to help analyse that hydrogue derelict they found in the rings,' Fitzpatrick muttered. 'Can you imagine how much General Lanyan would love to get his hands on that?'

'Unless that crazy Roacher scientist ruins all the decent evidence first. It just burns me—' Shelia said, bending to help Stanna lift a component.

Sighing, the big soldier straightened and stared out the narrow windows of their work asteroid, past the fuzzy limb of the gas giant to the open stars beyond. 'If only we could get out there, I could take a Roacher ship and just fly away.'

Fitzpatrick shook his head. 'You'd never make it, Bill. You heard Kellum. None of these ships is qualified for interstellar flight. They're all in-system transports.'

'Doesn't mean I couldn't try.'

Shelia nudged him with her elbow. 'It would take you a thousand years to get anywhere, Bill.'

'Who says? What if I just took a ship and . . . and flew up to the comet cloud? The Roachers have ekti-processing facilities up there, so they must have interstellar ships. Otherwise, how would they transport their stardrive fuel?'

Yamane chuckled. 'That's a good point.'

'So, once I got up there, I could make a new plan, steal one of their fast cargo haulers. That's all it would take.'

'Quite a few uncertainties there,' Fitzpatrick said, not sure Stanna had thought everything through. 'I wouldn't advise it—'

'Why not try, if I get the chance?' the big soldier insisted.

Shelia scowled at Fitzpatrick. 'You prefer staying here, Fitz?

Rather settle down with a nice Roamer wife and form a clan of your own? I'm starting to wonder about you.'

Stung, Fitzpatrick turned away, ashamed that an image of Zhett had immediately come to mind as soon as Shelia had spoken. 'That's not it at all. I want to escape as much as you do, but we shouldn't try anything foolish. It would be suicide. We have to wait until the time is right.' He turned back to help Yamane work on the Soldier compy, slamming the robot's access port closed.

Stanna said, 'You think too much, Fitz.'

The opportunity arose unexpectedly five days later.

Inside a dense cluster of shipyard facilities, the grav-tether broke on a tug hauling an incoming rock to the smelters. The drifting slab of debris smashed into the side of the automated ore processor, causing damage as it careened off into an admin dome. The outer rock shielding protected most of the people inside the offices, but emergency systems activated. Access hatches crashed down or jammed into place. A handful of people, including Zhett Kellum, were trapped inside.

Alarms went off throughout the shipyards, summoning rescue workers to the damage site. By long habit from living on the edge, the Roamers kept detailed and well-practised emergency plans, and they all responded whenever they were needed. Ships flew in; engineers dropped their normal duties. Grappler pods and other craft converged at the site of the accident. For a short while, everything was in chaos.

Bill Stanna, working beside Fitzpatrick, looked up suddenly. 'This is our chance. I'm not going to waste it.' He grabbed the other man's sleeve. 'Cover me, Fitz. I've already picked out my ship.'

Docked to their working asteroid was a small prospector scout, a single-passenger craft designed to fly through the rings in search of dense ore concentrations. Stanna knew he could fly it.

Alarms continued to ring, and not many Roamers were in sight. The Soldier compies went about their programmed labours without pause. Stanna sprinted to an emergency locker and grabbed a suit, pulling it on as if it were an EDF drill from when he'd been a kleeb.

Though he was uneasy, Fitzpatrick didn't dare try to stop the man. If Stanna did succeed in escaping, he would send a signal to the EDF and somehow bring help. Then they could all get out of here.

'Just keep an eye out, Fitz – make sure I get a chance to fly away.' Stanna clomped awkwardly forward in his environment suit. He sealed his helmet. Fitzpatrick slapped him on the back. 'Good luck, Bill.'

Stanna hurried to the airlock to cycle himself through. Fitzpatrick checked to make sure that the Roamers were still studying their screens, responding to the emergency at the admin dome and the automated ore processor. The activation of the airlock would show up on their status readouts, but the Roamers would probably think it was someone on the emergency response team.

The external airlock door opened, and Stanna launched himself through space like a projectile. Fitzpatrick watched him drift towards the docked prospector scout, catch himself on the vessel, then work his way to its entry hatch.

Inside the work bay, three Roamer workers reacted curiously, as if they sensed something wrong. One of them went to the inset window screen and peered out at the small ship. They were close to noticing Stanna.

Knowing he had to do something, Fitzpatrick ran to the wall controls and activated the emergency fire signal. Since all air inside the enclosed asteroid habitats was recycled and replenished from tanks, fire was always a terrible hazard. To maintain his cover, Fitzpatrick opened the supply room door, grabbed a fire-suppression pack, and sprayed foam on several crates sitting in the corner.

As Roamers came running, he looked up at them, feigning panic. 'I saw smoke in here, but I put it out!' He looked at the foamy mess on the floor.

The three Roamers looked at him, sceptical. 'We've got other emergencies to deal with. Behave yourself.' They went back to their stations while Fitzpatrick diligently mopped up the spilled fire-suppressant.

He looked through the inset windows to see the small prospector scout streaking away, just another ship in the flurry of activity. Fitzpatrick covered a nervous but satisfied smile and returned to his task.

In the chaos of rescuing the people trapped inside the damaged admin dome and repairing the automated ore processor, it was some time before anyone sent out prospectors to map the ring field again.

It took the Roamers four full days before they even noticed that the small ship was gone.

NINETY-NINE

TASIA TAMBLYN

The EDF was swollen with pride because of the 'decisive blow' they had struck against the 'intractable' Roamers at Hurricane Depot. Trapped between her military service and her loyalty to her heritage, Tasia found the whole idea insufferable.

When she first heard the EDF making its bold victory announcement, like an ape beating its chest, she just stared, listening to the whistles and cheers for a numb moment. Then, without a word to her fellow soldiers, she went to her quarters feeling like she wanted to vomit. Lying on her bunk with the lights dim, while EA stood silently in a corner, Tasia squeezed her eyes shut and wrestled with her emotions, deeply disturbed, angry, and helpless.

Since they had been roundly beaten by the hydrogues, the Big Goose had decided to turn its might against an enemy they thought they could defeat. The EDF had waved their banners, stomped down hard on the clans, and then celebrated as if the destruction of an unarmed and unsuspecting Roamer transfer station proved their valour.

Tasia now understood all too clearly why her assignment had changed recently, why she'd been relieved of her Manta, though the Eddies could ill afford to lose a battle-proven commander like herself. The EDF had been planning the raid on Hurricane Depot all along, and it was obvious they didn't trust her.

Since she could not dictate EDF policy or battle plans, Tasia filed a formal protest with Admiral Willis. Challenging her unjustified reassignment was the only way she could think of to fight back, using her knowledge of the military bureaucracy she had learned over the past six years.

'What have I ever done to make you question my ability to serve, Admiral?' She knew the real answer, of course, but Tasia remained rigid in Willis's office, her nostrils flared as she kept her anger in check. 'You've seen my performance scores at EDF training – I'm one of the best pilots you have. You assigned me as Platcom on a Thunderhead weapons platform, then promoted me to the bridge of a Manta. You even had me deliver a Klikiss Torch at Ptoro.'

'I am completely aware of your impressive record, Commander Tamblyn.'

'So why was I stripped of my command?'

'Don't play dumb with me.' The Admiral folded her knobby hands and gave one of her patented grandmotherly smiles. 'You are also a member of a Roamer clan, and Chairman Wenceslas has decreed Roamers to be unfriendlies, based on their refusal to provide vital resources in time of war. Now, I knew you weren't going to be pleased about it, but I made the best possible choice, given the alternatives.'

Her eyes were bright, and Tasia could see that the older woman truly had given the matter a great deal of consideration. Willis continued, 'Think – would you rather we forced you to participate in an assault on a Roamer depot, just to prove yourself? Or, General Lanyan could have ordered you in for an extensive debriefing to make you reveal everything you know about Roamer clans and settlements. Taking you out of the picture was the preferable solution, I think.'

'But, Ma'am, we don't need to make up new enemies! We have our hands full enough with the drogues.'

Willis remained cool. 'The Roamers made themselves our enemies, Commander. There was no call for them to be cutting off our ekti supply.'

'I'm sure they see it differently, Admiral. Has there been an investigation into Speaker Peroni's claims that EDF ships have secretly raided and destroyed Roamer cargo transports?'

'Such claims are preposterous, Commander. You're a soldier in the EDF. You should know better than that.'

Tasia lifted her chin. 'Excuse me, Admiral, but since we just destroyed an unarmed civilian Roamer facility, how can I be confident of any such thing?'

'You're on the verge of insubordination.'

Tasia bit her tongue, calming herself. Finally she said, 'I understand the EDF has taken a hundred or so hostages from Hurricane Depot.'

'Not hostages, Commander, prisoners of war.'

'I wasn't aware the King had actually declared war on the Roamers.'

'We each have our own definitions.'

'Would it be possible for me to see them, to speak with one of their representatives? Given my background, maybe I can help resolve the disagreement. I'm not doing any good making kleebs run obstacle courses on Mars.'

'You're a halfway decent soldier, Commander, but you're no diplomat. You just let the Hansa take care of political matters, okay?'

'Shizz, Robb Brindle wasn't a diplomat either, but that didn't stop the EDF from sending him down into Osquivel to talk to the drogues.'

'And look how that turned out.' The Admiral nodded, clearly thinking the discussion was over. 'In the meantime, you need to do a little soul-searching – are you a member of the EDF, or are you still a Roamer in your heart?'

Tasia hesitated. 'Can't I be both?'

'Not when they're at war with each other.'

No doubt Internal Affairs investigators were looking into Tasia's past behaviour. If they ever discovered that she'd sent EA to warn Del Kellum's shipyards, she might indeed be brought up on charges of treason or espionage. She would have to be extremely careful and give them no cause to look at her with greater suspicion . . .

After she was dismissed, Tasia went to her quarters, but found no answers there, even when she used her Listener compy as a sounding board. EA offered no useful advice whatsoever.

With the destruction of Hurricane Depot, Chairman Wenceslas had thrown down the gauntlet, escalating tensions when he could easily have resolved the problem. The man had always been so cool and businesslike, but this course of action seemed highly questionable to her.

Once they had crossed this line, the Eddies would not leave the clans alone until they had proved their point. But Roamers were not likely to concede defeat. How could the EDF understand so little about the Roamer mindset? It was a bad situation bound to get worse.

And Tasia's job was to train more recruits for the ships that would attack clan strongholds.

ONE HUNDRED

BASIL WENCESLAS

Garish blue-white potassium vapour lights shone down, creating razor-edged shadows across the open research bay. Basil stood next to Admiral Stromo, looking sceptically at the odd ship. It was a Frankenstein's monster of components, spare parts stitched together in ways that had never been meant to function. The vessel was fast, though ungainly.

'It's a captured Roamer craft, Mr Chairman,' Stromo said. 'One we seized during the raid on Hurricane Depot.'

Basil crossed his arms, careful not to wrinkle his fine business suit. He knew the Roamers had developed innovative and eccentric technology during their many years of austerity and isolation, but he didn't understand what the Hansa could gain from studying this old hulk. 'Please don't tell me you're going to reconfigure a squadron of Remoras to look like that. What could you possibly extract from the design?'

Stromo had gained weight in the last few years, which made Basil frown slightly in distaste. Perhaps the Admiral should have been out patrolling with his ships, getting some practical exercise, instead of sitting behind a desk.

'Not the design, Mr Chairman. It's what we take out of the databanks that I find so interesting.'

Now Basil raised his eyebrows. 'How did you get to the computer systems without them self-destructing on you?' After Cesca Peroni had told all of her clan members to scatter, simply *finding* the space gypsies would be even more difficult than the Hansa had planned.

'Sheer luck, Mr Chairman. The pilot of this ship attempted to destroy himself, but we captured him unexpectedly before he could activate normal fail-safes. About half of the files were scrapped, but our cryptography specialists were able to reconstruct the other records. We now have the detailed coordinates for a dozen previously unknown Roamer settlements and industrial facilities.' Stromo continued to grin, his face flushing with pride, though his skin looked pallid and sickly under the garish lights.

'But there's more?' Basil prompted. Inside the analysis hangar, Hansa engineers and EDF experts studied the engines, components, and computer systems, searching for further scraps of information.

'Much more, Mr Chairman.' He formed a smile with his thick lips. 'It took time, but we also know the location of Rendezvous – the central Roamer complex, the very seat of their government.'

Basil sucked in a quick breath. 'Excellent! We can make effective use of this knowledge.' His joy seemed out of proportion with the actual news, but after so many disasters and plans that had not turned out the way he had hoped, he was pleased to have events go right for a change.

The demonstration assault on Hurricane Depot had not sufficiently intimidated the clans; therefore, the second phase needed to be even more overwhelming and demoralizing. He wanted to take Speaker Peroni down a notch or two. Her petulant defiance was simply unreasonable, and the Hansa didn't have time for it.

He lowered his voice, muttering to himself. 'It didn't have to come to such an end – if only they had cooperated, played as part of the team of humanity . . . if only they had accepted the necessities of the situation.' He snapped his head up to look at Stromo, who stood waiting for orders. 'There can be no more significant victory than to take over Rendezvous. Admiral, devise a surgical strike, send in an EDF battle group with sufficient force that there'll be no doubt as to the outcome. Destroy the Roamer seat of government – such as it is – and the clans will crumble entirely. They'll have no choice but to fall neatly in line.'

'And what about casualties, Mr Chairman?'

Basil frowned. 'Don't trouble me with too many details.'

Stromo clasped his hands together as if he could barely contain his excitement. After being utterly defeated at Jupiter, he looked forward to a combat scenario in which he could attack without fear. 'I'll lead the operation myself.'

ONE HUNDRED AND ONE

KING PETER

King Peter swore he would never trust Basil Wenceslas again – not that he had trusted the man in the first place. First, the Chairman had allowed the blundering attack at the Roamer depot, and then he'd prevented Peter from meeting with Speaker Peroni when she had come to Earth. As the situation worsened in the Spiral Arm, and the carefully arranged pieces insisted on falling out of order, the Chairman's frustration caused him to lose his patience . . . and make mistakes.

Basil, you're losing your touch.

Peter requested a brief meeting with Basil, and the Chairman grudgingly allowed him fifteen minutes in his schedule. For a moment, he wished Estarra could be with him, just supporting him with her presence, but the King had to face this himself.

Basil folded his hands on the computer desktop, where files and images blinked and jumped, clamouring for his attention. 'It's not usual that you go through proper channels, Peter. In fact, you've made quite a habit of simply barging in and assuming that your impulses supersede all Hansa business.'

Peter did not rise to the bait. 'I am demonstrating my good behaviour – so you don't try to kill me again. Or Estarra.'

The Chairman dispensed with pleasantries. 'I have to attend to another matter in a few minutes. What did you wish to discuss?'

'Prince Daniel. I know you're hiding him in the Whisper Palace somewhere. I want to talk to him.'

Basil remained cool. 'What would be the point?'

Peter raised his eyebrows. 'Wouldn't it give you more publicity mileage if the two of us were seen in public as one big happy family? After all, he's my dear "brother", even if I've never seen him.'

'Daniel isn't ready to be seen in public.'

'Will he ever be?'

Ignoring the question, Basil leaned forward. 'Tell me the real reason you're interested in him.'

Peter shrugged, realizing that he would lose nothing by being honest. 'You announced his presence just so that I'd be intimidated. I want to see how much of a threat he really is.'

'That boy is just insurance against your . . . intransigence. At the moment, he is not my first choice to become the King.'

'So I have nothing to worry about?'

Basil gave him a hard look. 'That depends on how well you continue to fulfill your duties.'

Peter knew that if Daniel had proved more tractable, he himself would already be dead. Preparing to leave, the King lied unconvincingly. 'All right, then, Basil. I'll take you at your word and not worry any more about it.'

On his private balcony in the royal suite, King Peter had a pleasant dinner with his Queen. Outside, he and Estarra enjoyed the late sunset that spread its colours far out to where the low ocean was barely a haze on the horizon. It was like a painting, very romantic.

The food had been prepared by the Whisper Palace's most

sophisticated chefs. The china was perfect, delicate and pristine. The flower arrangements smelled sweet and fresh. The food looked lovely and colourful on their plates.

Peter said, 'OX, you'd better test everything for poison. As usual.'

The Teacher compy applied a chemical analysis probe to detect any toxic substances or drugs that might have been slipped into his food. While they waited, their stomachs growling, Peter peered into Estarra's large dark eyes. 'We know what Basil's capable of. We can't be too careful.'

'I know,' she said with a smile and touched his arm.

When OX pronounced every course safe, the King and Queen began to eat. He picked up a toasted cracker with slivers of smoked salmon, but extended it to her instead, letting her eat it from his fingertips. Then she did likewise, selecting a morsel and offering it to him. He made a special show of nibbling her fingers at the same time he ate the food.

After a while, though, when they had finished most of their meal, he barely tasted the delicately spiced flavours as his own concerns grew heavier. 'OX, I want your objective opinion about something.'

'I am always happy to give you my opinion and my advice, King Peter.'

'I've got to make a genuine threat assessment. You are training Prince Daniel – how close is he to being prepared, at least to Basil's satisfaction? How much do I have to worry about being replaced in the near future?'

OX calculated for a moment. Though his words sounded like an outrageous joke, the little robot stated the facts as he saw them. 'Extrapolating from the young Prince's current rate of progress, he will be sufficiently prepared no sooner than . . . three centuries.'

Estarra chuckled. 'How could Basil have overestimated him so badly?'

The Teacher compy stood at attention next to their table. 'Prince Daniel was chosen swiftly, without as thorough an investigation as the team members applied to you, King Peter, when you were Raymond Aguerra.' Peter pressed his fingertips together and continued to listen. 'Prince Daniel has not lived up to expectations thus far.'

'Do you think Basil will . . . get rid of Daniel and choose someone else?' Estarra asked, her dark eyes wide.

Peter pursed his lips. 'At the moment, Basil's main purpose is to use the Prince as leverage to keep me in line. As long as we remain sufficiently cooperative, the Chairman would not consider it "cost effective" to shake up the Hansa by replacing me.' Peter heaved a sigh, knowing he had to be on his best behaviour not just for himself, but also to protect Estarra. She was his greatest weakness now, since he loved her so much.

He put his elbows on the table, a casual habit left over from his life as Raymond Aguerra, but which his protocol trainers sternly corrected whenever they caught him doing it. 'I've never had the opportunity to meet him face-to-face, OX. Basil won't let me go see him. What is my supposed brother like?'

'Narcissitic, rude, and ill-behaved. And he has not been as malleable as expected. I have patiently worked to instruct the boy in matters of kingship, but with little success. Daniel has no interest in learning the material. He is pleased with his current situation and would rather remain in his chambers and be pampered. In order to make him do his work, I have been forced to develop a litany of promises and threats.'

'You threaten him, OX? That doesn't sound like you.' Peter sipped from a glass of ice water.

'I threaten to take away his desserts. Prince Daniel has an extraordinary fondness for candies, puddings, and other treats. The Chairman has given me complete control over the dispensing of such items. I can either cancel or double the dessert portion of an upcoming meal, depending on his cooperation. So far, Daniel has already gained twenty kilos. I project, due to the young man's metabolism and physiological characteristics, that he will become overly plump and, ultimately, an obese adult.'

Peter made a tsk-ing noise. 'If the Hansa is facing lean times and colonies are suffering famine and starvation, we can't have a roly-poly Great King. As soon as Basil notices, he'll put the kid on a draconian diet regimen.'

'I have already suggested that Prince Daniel begin a regular and healthy exercise routine, but he refuses.'

'Sounds like he just needs a good talking-to,' Peter said. 'Hmm, even if Basil won't officially allow us to talk, maybe you should arrange a meeting between Daniel and myself. Who knows? He might listen to my advice.'

Estarra looked at him, puzzled. Once Peter had stopped playfully feeding her, she'd barely touched her food. 'I thought you wanted Daniel to stay incompetent so we don't have to worry so much.'

'Even so, that boy and I share a common background. We were both snatched from our lives and put into a position we didn't choose. Maybe he and I can become . . . I don't know, allies.' He turned to the Teacher compy. 'OX, can you take me to him?'

The compy straightened, his optical sensors glowing. 'The Chairman has implied that he does not wish you two to meet. However, he has never categorically forbidden me to introduce you. It is my estimation, however, that Daniel will not become your friend.'

Peter wiped his mouth with a napkin and stood up from the dinner table. 'Being a friend is not necessary, OX. An old Earth cliché says to keep your friends close, but keep your enemies closer.'

ONE HUNDRED AND TWO

DD

The stolen EDF battle group arrived at the first target colony. The five Mantas and one Juggernaut still bore the chain-of-stars symbol of the Earth Defence Forces, but Klikiss robots commanded them. The Corribus colonists had only recently arrived and were still setting up a basic settlement in the blistered ruins. They suspected nothing.

DD stood on the bridge of the renegade Juggernaut as Sirix unfolded his articulated limbs and issued detailed orders for the massacre to proceed. 'Power up jazer weapons. All Mantas prepare for first assault. This Juggernaut will complete the annihilation.'

'You don't have to do this,' DD said. 'Please reconsider.'

'It is necessary. We annihilated our creator race, and now we must do the same to humans. Corribus will be sterile again when we depart.'

A cheerful transmission came from the colony's communication tower. 'Hello up there? This is Corribus Central calling the new ships. Welcome to our cosy little home. Is this the EDF? Did you bring us any supplies?'

Sirix swivelled his flat angular head to the Soldier compies on the bridge. 'Do not reply.'

'They mean no harm,' DD said. 'They are no threat to you.'

'Hello? Is anybody listening?' the man continued. 'This is Jan Covitz, the . . . uh, Chief Communications Operator for Corribus. Please identify yourself.'

The EDF warships continued their silent, ominous approach.

'Begin descent,' Sirix ordered.

In the vanguard, the Manta cruisers sliced like sharp knives through the upper clouds, and the heavy Juggernaut came afterwards.

'Is this thing on?' A thumping sound came over the communications channel. 'We, uh, weren't expecting any shipments for another week, but we need just about everything. In fact, we'd even eat spampax if you want to get rid of any. I'm sure your soldiers wouldn't mind.' Jan Covitz's voice fell silent as he waited for a reply.

'Do all humans talk so much?' Sirix asked.

'Only the friendly ones,' DD said. 'Everyone down there is probably friendly. You do not have to kill them.'

He could not think of a way to prevent this treachery. The optimistic human colonists had no reason to fear EDF vessels, since the Earth military was supposed to defend Hansa colonies. The people down there were doomed.

DD remembered when he'd tried to protect Margaret and Louis Colicos against the Klikiss robots on Rheindic Co. Margaret had instructed him to fight, but the little compy could not effectively perform such service. He was incapable.

Now, again, DD couldn't do a thing to stop the tragedy.

The commandeered warships finally broke through the cloud cover, and the landscape of Corribus spread out like a painting beneath them. The military vessels accelerated towards the high-walled canyon that held the main human settlement.

As the descending battleships powered up their jazers for an immediate devastating strike, Sirix scanned the terrain below. He spoke to DD. 'Down there, many millennia ago, this place was a great citadel for the hated Klikiss overlords. It was destroyed in a final battle after the Klikiss survivors used their Torch to strike back against the hydrogues.'

'They were just defending themselves,' DD said.

'The Klikiss should never have survived the initial purge. Those survivors on Corribus were merely a loose end to be tied up. They were the last.' Sirix turned his beetle-like body. 'Just as we will eliminate the humans who have come here, and eventually all humans on any inhabited world in the Spiral Arm.'

Jan Covitz transmitted again. 'Hey, you're starting to make me nervous, here. Is something wrong with your comm systems? According to my written formal procedures, I'm supposed to sound an alarm if something like this happens, and you don't want me to do that. Come on, can you give me some sign that you're hearing this?'

'At least give them a chance,' DD pleaded. 'Send them a message.'

'They will understand our message well enough.' Sirix turned to the Soldier compies at the Juggernaut's tactical stations. The battleships soared forward; the first colony buildings were visible up ahead, clearly centred in the crosshairs of the EDF targeting systems.

'Open fire. Begin total bombardment.'

ONE HUNDRED AND THREE

ORLI COVITZ

Before Orli could make her way out of the hidden cave in the cliffs, the roar of approaching battleships echoed like cannon shots through the canyon. The EDF Mantas and Juggernaut came in so fast that they trailed sonic booms behind them.

When she heard the giant thrusters designed for propelling a ship through empty space rather than thick atmosphere, Orli hurried to the crack and poked her head outside to see what was happening. Below, the sheer vertical cliff dropped off, dotted with random crystal blocks. Dizzy, she caught herself, held onto the half-melted edge of the cave opening, and stared.

The EDF battleships charged down the funnel of the canyon like a pack of rabid animals. But the vessels slowed as they approached the human settlement in the Klikiss ruins – slowed in order to begin their attack. Orli wondered if they were staging some sort of military parade or air show. She had never been much of a military buff, but she did identify the battleship designs of the Earth Defence Forces. It didn't occur to Orli to be worried. These were, after all, the human armed forces whose mission was to protect and defend Hansa colonies.

The EDF craft opened fire.

Jazers lanced out from the bow weapons systems of the leading three Mantas. The bolts were like incandescent spears of lava that tore the open ground and turned it into a smoking glassy mass. Coming behind them, the Juggernaut shot explosive projectiles, specifically targeting Klikiss structures that had withstood erosion for ten thousand years – structures where the colonists had made their new homes.

Orli screamed as she watched the devastation. Her voice was swallowed up in the thunder of weapons fire, and she was too far away from the settlement to help. When her throat was raw, she clamped her lips shut and continued to scream inside, knowing there was nothing she could do.

Below in the settlement, the colonists panicked. Many had been outside tending garden plots or serving on construction crews to erect new buildings separate from the Klikiss ruins. After the battleship marauders swept past for the first time, all the ancient structures were engulfed in a flood of fire.

The leading Manta reached the end of the narrow canyon, roared past the opening where Orli hid, then swooped up in a high-G ascent, pulling an acceleration greater than any human could withstand. The armoured cruiser circled like a prehistoric bird of prey and came back for a second attack run. Jazers traced a deadly embroidery, incinerating the colourful prefab dwellings the Hansa had supplied for the initial colony setup.

Orli saw men and women flailing, surrounded by flames. Some dived into buildings hoping to find shelter. Others, their clothes and hair on fire, fled screaming until they fell smouldering to the ground.

Her father was down there somewhere.

With hot tears streaming down her face, Orli leaned out of the cave opening again and looked at the long way down. She'd climbed up here by hauling herself from one alum crystal to another, not realizing how far above the ground she was . . . and how long it would take her to get back to the valley floor. She'd need an hour or more to get her feet on solid ground again; the colony would be nothing but ashes by the time she got there. And if she climbed down the cliff now, Orli would be desperately exposed to these mysterious attackers who seemed intent on obliterating every living person on Corribus.

The next Mantas soared past in their long turnaround procedure. The Juggernaut lumbered by, so immense that Orli could hardly grasp its dimensions; it seemed to take for ever to pass her small observation opening.

For a few moments, as the attacking ships reversed course at the end of the long canyon, there was a breathless pause in the colony settlement. The survivors continued to shout and scream. Orli could hear their desperate voices, dwindled to tinny noises by the distance. They were running. She saw groups scrambling towards the main structure that contained the Klikiss transportal.

'Yes!' she said. 'Get out of here. Go anywhere.'

Her father would be there helping the others to escape, or else in the comm tower.

When the five Mantas came in for yet another attack run, their primary target was the transportal structure. Jazers and projectiles levelled the facility in a single concentrated strike, vaporizing the gateway that would have allowed the colonists to escape from Corribus. All the people who had tried to flee were either trapped or disintegrated.

Even if Orli survived the attack, that transportal had been her only way out.

The battleships swept around again and again.

ONE HUNDRED AND FOUR

DESIGNATE-IN-WAITING
PERY'H

The mad Hyrillka Designate and his corrupted guards held Pery'h prisoner for days. With all the people on the planet voluntarily separate from the Mage-Imperator's *thism*, the young man became more and more isolated, utterly cut off from all other presence in the great mental network. Sickeningly adrift and lost. It was enough to drive an Ildiran insane.

Armoured guards with crystal spears stood outside his door, preventing the distraught Pery'h from leaving the room. He had demanded to see Rusa'h, even his brother Thor'h, but no one would speak to him. After the Hyrillka Designate had made his outrageous claims, accusing Mage-Imperator Jora'h of poisoning his own father, the guards had kept Pery'h sequestered from everything that was happening.

Through his *thism* connection – without which he would surely be mad by now – Pery'h knew the Mage-Imperator was aware that something was seriously wrong in the Horizon Cluster, but no one on distant Ildira could guess how desperate the situation had become.

Over-consumption of raw shiing had softened the connection of all Hyrillkans, making their minds pliable. Then Designate Rusa'h had worked his manipulation, using a corrupt version of the *thism*, and diverted them to his own control instead of the Mage-Imperator's.

Prime Designate Thor'h had also joined the odd and open rebellion, of his own volition, and Pery'h could not believe that a son of the Mage-Imperator would be so weak-willed as to be swayed by mental domination. With a cold sinking in his heart, he understood that his brother – the Prime Designate of the Ildiran Empire – was a willing accomplice in this madness . . . He felt so cut off!

Thor'h came to the door of the confinement chamber, accompanied by a squad of soldier kithmen. The Prime Designate stood in the doorway, arms crossed over his narrow chest, his expression implacable. His face was thin and pale, his lips pulled into a pucker of distaste as if he had eaten something sour. Though Pery'h longed to connect to someone, anyone, Thor'h showed barely any sign of recognition for his younger brother. 'Come with me to the throne hall. Imperator Rusa'h wishes to speak to you of your fate.'

'*Imperator?* Thor'h, this is insanity.'

'It is what must be, for the good of the Ildiran Empire.'

Pery'h refused to move. 'I am the Hyrillka Designate-in-waiting. You don't even belong here.'

Thor'h's eyes flashed. 'I am the Prime Designate. I will be wherever I am required to be. And I am linked closer to Imperator Rusa'h than I ever was to our misguided father.'

He gestured, and the guards stomped forward, roughly taking Pery'h by the arms and dragging him out of the chamber. They walked the young man in a brisk lockstep down the corridors of the vine-draped citadel palace.

Making his choice, Pery'h held his head high and moved his legs so that he walked alongside the guards. Resistance would be foolish at this point, and arguing or struggling with these soldier kithmen would gain him nothing. Though he strode next to them, the young man felt separated by a wide and immeasurable gulf. Gathering the shreds of his pride, Pery'h increased his pace so it appeared that *he* was leading the guards.

Crowds of Hyrillkans looked at him with vacant stares. These should have been his people, but they no longer felt the same *thism* that bound him to the rest of the Ildiran Empire. Pery'h should have become their next Designate.

Now, though, as the young man stepped into the receiving courtyard, where his hedonistic uncle had always thrown celebrations, Pery'h saw how much had changed. He had never felt so numb and isolated.

Rusa'h reclined in an ornate replica of the chrysalis chair, more spectacular than the one Jora'h had in the Prism Palace. He wore robes identical to those of a Mage-Imperator; he had even braided his hair in a fashion similar to the great leader's. Pery'h felt queasy as he wondered if Rusa'h had also had the lunatic conviction to inflict upon himself the castration ceremony, a mockery of the true leader's ascension. He couldn't sense any answers, any motivations. 'What is this . . . masquerade?'

Seeing Pery'h, the Hyrillka Designate sat up and gave him a superior smile. 'Sacred traditions must be restored and protected. Lost Ildirans must return to the true path that made us great, that preserved our civilization over the long millennia.'

Leaving the guard escort behind, Thor'h strolled forward, cat-like, to take a place at his uncle's side. From the familiar way the Prime Designate moved, Pery'h was sure his brother had become quite comfortable next to the mad Designate.

'My father will learn what you are doing,' Pery'h said, not

raising his voice, keeping his tone reasonable but firm. He could not even imagine what sort of punishment might be appropriate for these outrageous actions. 'The Mage-Imperator will not allow you to continue this . . . this atrocity. You cannot keep it a secret for long.'

A hot edge of madness threatened to cut its way into Pery'h's mind. He was so alone. Alien *thism* surrounded him, yet not a thread of it penetrated the solitary confines of his mind.

'Oh, but we *intend* for Jora'h to know. Even with his inept grasp of the *thism*, I'm sure he already senses something is wrong. But you, Pery'h, must send him a clear message. Our pilgrims are already in place in the Prism Palace. The usurper will learn the gravity of the errors he has made and the crimes he has committed.'

'You call my father a usurper?' Pery'h was more shocked than angry. 'He is the Mage-Imperator—'

'I am the true Imperator!' Rusa'h roared.

Thor'h sighed, leaning close to speak to his uncle. 'He will never surrender the Prism Palace to you, Imperator.'

Rusa'h was saddened. 'I know, and many Ildirans will suffer because of it.'

The guards held their crystal-tipped spears and glared at Pery'h.

So utterly abandoned and isolated, Pery'h found it difficult even to talk, but still he forced out the words. 'Listen to me, Uncle. You were injured. Your mind must have been . . . damaged by the hydrogues. You have to see that this is folly—'

Rusa'h grasped the edge of the false chrysalis chair and hauled himself upright. His braid twitched and thrashed. 'Oh yes, Pery'h, I can see – I see more clearly than any Ildiran. I have followed the soul-threads, witnessed how tangled and frayed they have become. Jora'h and our father before him caused a great deal of damage, but it is not too late to save our people. We must return to the proper ways.'

Pery'h raised his eyebrows. 'Is it proper to speak treason against the Mage-Imperator who holds the *thism*?'

'I hold all the threads of *thism* here. You can sense it yourself.'

Pery'h could indeed sense it. The pain of emptiness, aloneness, seared his mind.

'Every person on Hyrillka is bound to me,' the Designate went on, 'and our enlightenment will spread across the Horizon Cluster and eventually to all Ildirans. Jora'h should not resist this change, but he is blinded and stubborn. After poisoning our father, he does not understand how far he has fallen.'

Pery'h looked into the eyes of the Ildiran doctors, the lens kithmen, the guards and courtiers. Even the pleasure mates, who had once been soft and beautiful women, now looked as hard as crystal blades. Worst of all, the Prime Designate's eyes had turned stony; by his expression, Thor'h seemed to know exactly what was about to happen – and had decided to allow it.

'You will be our message, Pery'h,' Rusa'h said. 'Since you refuse to cooperate with us, you are a loose end of the *thism*. You must be separated from the trap that holds you.'

Claws of isolation pierced his mind, but Pery'h stood bravely. 'My father is the true Mage-Imperator. I will never turn from him.'

Rusa'h smiled. 'We don't expect you to. That is why we will no longer even ask.' He raised a hand and signalled to the loyal guard kithmen. They all took an intimidating step closer to Pery'h.

'After this,' the Hyrillka Designate said, 'Jora'h will be forced to respond. And we will be ready for him.'

The soldiers raised their crystal-tipped spears and, before Pery'h could so much as cry out, they struck him down. They thrust and stabbed, driving the Designate-in-waiting to the floor. Others took glassy alloy-handled clubs and battered him as he fell, breaking his skull, his bones. Pery'h's blood splashed on the clean tiles. He could not struggle as the blades plunged into him again and again.

These were not his people. Pery'h felt no connection to them. The last face he saw was that of his brother, Thor'h, standing beside the facsimile chrysalis chair, watching calmly.

Sprawled on the floor, the young man reached out a hand to grasp at the soul-threads that glittered around him. Through his pain and disbelief, Pery'h clasped the single bright thread of *thism* that linked him to his father, and held it like an anchor line – until the light mercifully claimed him.

The spear thrusts and club blows continued to rain down upon Pery'h's lifeless body for a long, long time.

ONE HUNDRED AND FIVE

MAGE-IMPERATOR JORA'H

Though Jora'h often sat in the confining chrysalis chair as was expected of him, he frequently climbed out of it and walked the corridors of the Palace. Twice now he had even appeared in the streets of Mijistra.

Ildirans were both amazed and horrified by this, but in such a time of chaos, Jora'h felt it was important for their rigid assumptions to be challenged. Over the centuries Ildiran traditions had become fossilized, yet they were not natural laws of the universe. The Empire needed to change in order to survive. Jora'h was determined to show them how to do it.

Today, after he had taken his usual place under the warm skysphere dome, the ornate doors opened for the day's pilgrims. In the sun-dappled corridors, groups of awed Ildirans stood waiting, as they did every day. They had all gone through the proper supplications, and Jora'h would reward their devotion with a blessing and a smile.

Yazra'h now stationed herself at the front of the dais with her cats, intense and alert. She had picked her own guards and had slipped into her role as his primary protector, though many Ildirans also muttered uneasily about this change in tradition. Jora'h could sense their confusion, but he knew they would have to adapt. His daughter stood beside him, meeting each pilgrim with her probing gaze.

First he greeted a troupe of agricultural kithmen who stared at him with shining eyes and expressions of delight. They had come from the consolidated splinter colony on Heald, and the farmers assured Jora'h that they would continue to use their abilities and strength to keep the colony strong. Jora'h sent them on their way with a benevolent smile.

The second group of pilgrims consisted of eight doctors, pleasure mates, and lens kithmen, all of them gaunt and hardened, who had made a journey from Hyrillka. To his *thism* their minds were confused and blurred from heavy doses of shiing, which made the Mage-Imperator uneasy. This was the fourth such group of Hyrillkan pilgrims in recent weeks. Why did so many supplicants come from there? And what homage could they hope to pay with their minds thus clouded?

As the gaunt pilgrims approached, Jora'h saw the shadows behind their eyes, the pain of their world's recent horrific experience with the hydrogues. He welcomed the visitors when they came before him.

On impulse, the Mage-Imperator climbed out of the chrysalis chair and stood tall on the dais. The Hyrillkan pilgrims were astonished, even angered, to see him flouting sacred traditions, but Jora'h raised his hands. 'The people of Hyrillka have been through so much adversity, so much pain. It is not appropriate for me to recline in a comfortable chair when you have expended so much effort just to come and see me. I do you honour by standing here.'

The pilgrims looked at him, some with narrowed eyes, studying their great leader instead of admiring him. Jora'h was puzzled by their odd reaction, but because of the shiing he could read little from them through the *thism*.

One of the visiting lens kithmen bowed slightly. His words sounded flat and memorized. 'You have made our journey here complete, Mage-Imperator. We have now seen what we wished to behold.'

Jora'h saw the shining detachment in their eyes, and he found it unsettling that – like Thor'h – these people had consumed so much shiing before appearing in the reception hall. Perhaps he should institute another remarkable change by telling his people to stop consuming the drug. But shiing was the predominant industry on Hyrillka, one of the few that had survived the hydrogue attack. He frowned, not knowing what to do. 'I thank you for your visit to me.'

Jora'h's smoky topaz eyes were still intent on the lens kithman when the assassin struck.

The third male in the line snatched out a long, razor-sharp crystal blade from each sleeve. The medical kithman knew exactly how to cut, where to strike. He bounded up the steps, leaping for the Mage-Imperator. Both of the knives swept back as he raised his arms.

Yazra'h and her pets reacted instantly. She and her Isix cats shot forward like a flash of reflected light. Pulling the Mage-Imperator back with both hands, Yazra'h spun to interpose her body between him and the medical kithman. The would-be assassin missed his target with the double slash, ripping open only the coloured fabric of the Mage-Imperator's robe with one knife and slicing into Yazra'h's arm with the other.

Urging Jora'h into the shelter of the chrysalis chair, Yazra'h threw herself in front of the Mage-Imperator to shield him against other murderous pilgrims. She did not even try to stop her animals from pouncing upon her father's would-be slayer. When the muscled Isix cats bore down upon the glazed-eyed medical kithman, his screams cut off quickly. Only one of the three cats suffered a superficial cut as the crystal scalpels clattered out of the doctor's lifeless hands.

Guard kithmen swarmed forward to seize the other pilgrim-assassins. The Hyrillkans did not struggle. Their minds had been clouded, their thoughts manipulated. Two others were found to be carrying deadly weapons.

Ignoring the gash in her arm, Yazra'h stood menacingly at the front of the dais. Sweat glistened on her muscles. Droplets of the medical kithman's blood spattered her skin. The Isix cats seemed particularly satisfied and intent on their feeding. With a sharp motion, Yazra'h called them back to her side, though she would have liked to let them finish devouring the traitor while the other captive Hyrillkans watched with appalled apprehension.

'We do not serve a false Mage-Imperator,' said one of the new captives. 'You are blinded to the Lightsource. You must be removed so that Ildirans can follow the soul-threads again. Only Imperator Rusa'h can see the true path.'

'Imperator Rusa'h?' Jora'h asked, leaving the chrysalis chair again. 'What is my brother doing?'

Before anyone could answer him, the Mage-Imperator felt his chest clench, as if a crystal blade had pierced his heart after all. Another assassin? A hidden sniper? Pain and shock exploded in his brain. His legs buckled beneath him, and he collapsed to the floor.

A shriek reverberated along the *thism* lines.

Pery'h.

Jora'h had recently detected fear and confusion from the Designate-in-waiting but had been unable to make out the details. As with the small group on Maratha, turmoil was occurring all across the Empire.

But now the worst had happened. It was inconceivable! The

soul-thread that bound Pery'h to his father had been chopped away like a limb being amputated.

Vaguely, as if from a great distance, Jora'h heard the Isix cats snarling and pacing, looking for a new enemy to attack. Yazra'h herself, though reeling with disorientation from the severed connection with her brother Pery'h, knelt beside her father. Guards and courtiers raced up the steps to the dais, shouting their leader's name, begging to know what was wrong. But he could not respond.

Jora'h's mind pounded with grief and loss. A part of his core was being ripped away.

'Pery'h is dead!' He squeezed his eyes shut and was instantly assailed by even more terrible revelations. His son was not only dead – he had been *murdered!* Betrayed. 'They have slaughtered him on Hyrillka.'

Images of treachery and treason inflicted deeper wounds on his already agonized mind. When the horror finally faded to a persistent throbbing ache inside his skull, Jora'h blinked his eyes open to find aghast expressions on the people around him in the reception hall.

Yazra'h helped her father back up from the floor. He swayed for a moment, then planted his feet firmly and spoke in a voice loud enough for all to hear.

'Pery'h has been assassinated. My own brother Rusa'h has declared war on the Ildiran Empire.'

ONE HUNDRED AND SIX

ADAR ZAN'NH

On routine patrol with his maniple of warliners, Zan'nh demonstrated his resolve to the Ildiran people. He needed to be seen, to appear strong, though he was not at all sure the Solar Navy could protect the splinter colonies against the formidable enemies they now faced. But the people themselves must believe it, and so he would live up to their expectations.

He remembered when Adar Kori'nh had sat in his command quarters, earnestly focused on Zan'nh's education. 'Your doubt is an enemy's greatest weapon. As Adar, you are a microcosm of the entire Solar Navy. If the leader himself is strong and confident, then so is the fleet.'

Zan'nh felt overshadowed by his great predecessor. The former Adar had been superior to him in tactical abilities and sheer bravery, and it still hadn't been enough to ensure victory. Kori'nh's suicidal bravery had struck a great blow against the hydrogues, but he had not won the war by any means. The hydrogues continued to strike back.

Standing in the command nucleus prepared to give his next

order, Zan'nh suddenly gripped the support rails, staggering with internal shock as he felt the powerful ripples of . . . Pery'h? His brother was dead!

When Mage-Imperator Cyroc'h had unexpectedly died, every living person in the Empire had reeled in utter disbelief, because *thism* linked them directly to their leader. But the execution of the Designate-in-waiting sent only a shiver of unease through Zan'nh's crew. He alone knew what the jolt signified.

'Prepare to change course.' His voice sounded strange and raw, but not broken. Decisive. 'We must return to Ildira immediately! I have felt something through the *thism*.'

'Yes, Adar.'

The warliner's bridge crew began to work, plotting the course while they relayed Zan'nh's command to the other forty-eight ships accompanying them. The well-organized maniple turned on its new course in perfect formation.

A clamour of alarms swept across the communications console. The surprised operator quickly responded. 'You are correct, Adar. I've just received an emergency signal from—' he checked the details on his screen, 'from the splinter world of Hrel-oro.'

'Hrel-oro?' That wasn't what he had sensed at all.

Zan'nh turned to the projected message on the main display screen. The narrow reptilian face of a scaly kithman appeared, smoke-blackened and frantic, his slitted eyes blinking rapidly. '— attack. We cannot fight them! We don't know what they want.'

Behind the scaly man came explosions and humming crackles. Overhead, a giant sphere drifted across the sky, and a few moments later five others came after it. Gouts of freezing icewaves flowed out. Colony buildings crackled and shattered. The reptilian kithman shouted, 'Why have the hydrogues come here? Send assistance as soon as—' Abruptly the transmission cut off.

Zan'nh stiffened. The skin on his back crawled. 'We won't be going to Ildira. How close are we to Hrel-oro?'

'We can arrive in an hour, Adar. We are the closest warliners.'

'Accelerate as soon as you have the course plotted. Maximum speed.' Regardless of what had happened to Pery'h, the hydrogues were attacking an Ildiran splinter colony. This was his job, his element – exactly what Adar Kori'nh had trained him for, and Zan'nh did not intend to leave any blot on the memory of his mentor. 'We will face the hydrogues. Let us show them what the Solar Navy is capable of.'

The maniple leaped across space, ready for the clash. He put his soldiers through preparatory drills at their stations. 'We must be ready for what we find on Hrel-oro. Every weapon, every ship, every fighter. We have very little time.'

He turned about in the command nucleus and spoke to his crew. 'On my tactical screen, upload all details of that colony. I want to know the terrain, history, and background. What is it the hydrogues might want there?' He ordered all seven of his septars, as well as Qul Fan'nh, commander of the full maniple, to review and provide suggestions if possible. Zan'nh scrutinized every available fact, absorbing the information.

Hrel-oro was a very dry and warm planet, much like one of the long-abandoned Klikiss worlds. It had no tall trees – barely any large vegetation at all – but the bleak landscape was full of desirable minerals and metals. Over a thousand years ago, the Mage-Imperator had instructed scalies to establish an efficient industrial colony there. Although many Ildiran breeds lived on Hrel-oro, the primary population belonged to the scaly kith. Scalies operated the mines dug through rusty-walled canyons and managed mineral-processing industries. They built solar-power stations out in the open desert and installed wind turbines where the canyons narrowed and the breezes whipped to a frenzy during the storm season.

Now, as the warliners raced to the site of the battle, Zan'nh reviewed reports about all previous hydrogue attacks on both human and Ildiran worlds. Some prior assaults had been retaliations against skyminers who trespassed on gas giants – a motive that was understandable enough. Other strikes on Corvus Landing, Boone's Crossing, Hyrillka, and uninhabited Dularix strongly suggested that the hydrogues meant to eradicate the worldforest or all giant trees. Their grudge appeared to be ancient, and inexplicable.

Hrel-oro did not fit either pattern. It was as if the hydrogues were simply attacking out of spite. Attacking Ildirans.

The warliners raced towards the dry planet, arriving even faster than expected. Their weapons systems were already active. Scans showed a great deal of smoke and thermal emissions from the sites of known settlements.

'We've detected warglobes still in the area, Adar.'

'Full speed. I grant each septar autonomy to enter combat in whatever way you deem most effective. Hit them before they even know we're here.'

The Ildiran battleships plummeted through the atmosphere with solar-power fins retracted to streamline the vessels. So far, few weapons had proved effective against the warglobes, but Zan'nh meant to pummel the enemy with everything he had . . .

By the time the rescue warliners slammed into the hydrogues, the aliens had nearly finished their total destruction of Hrel-oro. The spiked diamond spheres cruised through the canyons, levelling wind turbines and collapsing the entrances to mine shafts. Black smoke rose into the air, and white frost crackled across the broken terrain in rivers of ice.

Forty-nine warliners – as many battleships as Adar Kori'nh had used to secure his triumph at Qronha 3 – swooped in and unleashed high-energy projectiles like a swarm of stinging insects. Penetrating shells released destructive shockwaves as they smashed into the curved hulls. The alien globes spun about, their pyramidal protrusions crackling with a buildup of lightning.

Zan'nh clenched the support rail again, knowing that the hydrogues had the power to massacre his maniple. *As Pery'h had been slaughtered.*

Concentrated energy beams and kinetic projectiles continued bombarding the warglobes. The hydrogues struck back. Blue energy lanced out, ripping blackened troughs along the plated sides of the warliners.

A burst of lightning took one warliner's primary engine sets offline, and the ship could not fight against Hrel-oro's gravity. Zan'nh watched on his screens as the battleship commander wrestled with his failing systems, striving to correct the descent angle. Ahead, the flat desert landscape offered a clear field for an emergency landing. The warliner careened out of control, finally crashing, scraping, and slewing across the plain. Most of the crew would survive – if the hydrogues didn't come back and obliterate the wounded vessel.

'Maintain your attack. Do not slacken.' Remembering Kori'nh's words, he let no doubt to creep into his voice. He had to be stronger than anyone else. He had trained his tals, quls, and septars in every way possible. They would do their best. They would not dream of failing him, any more than he would ever have failed the old Adar.

But the hydrogues seemed to be invincible.

Three enemy warglobes converged upon another Ildiran battle vessel. The diamond spheres began to play powerful energy discharges across the armour, cracking holes through the warliner's thick hull. The captain shouted for assistance across the communication systems.

Zan'nh ordered his warliners to defend their doomed comrades, but the hydrogue energy weapon proved overpowering. The trapped warliner split open, venting fuel and atmosphere, erupting as its internal systems were breached. Shrapnel flew in all directions. Parts of the hull broke off, and two of the sail-like solar fins fluttered free over the desert like giant alloy kites.

The Adar reeled as he sensed the deaths of so many loyal crew members. These soldiers were under *his* command. *He* was responsible for these battleships, and within a few minutes he had already lost two great warliners. He searched his mind for an alternative, some other way to fight. But so far no strategy had proved effective against the diamond-hulled ships, except for the suicide tactic Kori'nh had used. Zan'nh would not resort to that – not yet.

Though perhaps he should . . .

The hydrogues had not come to Hrel-oro to fight the Solar Navy. They had their own incomprehensible purposes. By now, they were finished with their assault on the splinter colony.

Though the Ildiran battleships continued to harry them, the six spiked warglobes did one last half-hearted run on the structures below, blasting away all remnants of the Ildiran settlement. Then the six unscathed enemy spheres simply rose through the smoke-stained skies and departed at a leisurely pace.

Shouts of fear and anger, damage assessments, and casualty reports filled the communication channels. Zan'nh stared first at the images of destruction below, then at the departing warglobes.

'Adar, should I order the maniple to pursue?' demanded Qul Fan'nh, his face drawn and grim. 'The hydrogues are getting away. Do we go after them?'

'No. It would be ineffective and dangerous.' Zan'nh expanded the image of the burning wreckage. The death of each soldier already pained him like a crystal knife thrust into his side. How had Adar Kori'nh dealt with it? 'Our primary responsibility is to offer aid to our people down there, if any of them survive. I'll not let any more Ildirans die because we were anxious to keep fighting a hopeless battle.' Victory against the hydrogues was obviously not possible here. Therefore, his priority must be to save Ildiran lives.

'All able-bodied soldiers report to the launching bays. Medical kithmen, break into teams – some to man the infirmaries aboard our warliners, others to go to the surface and tend any survivors we find.'

The Adar wanted to be personally involved with every phase, but he knew he could not. His job was to lead, so he would remain here to issue orders and manage all the pieces. He angrily thrust aside his confusion and the nagging whispers of doubt, and forced herself to set an example of how all Ildiran soldiers should behave. Zan'nh quickly dispatched three unscathed warships to track down and assist the crashed warliner out in the desert.

'Get displays and updated maps of all the active mining operations down there. Some people must have survived the attack, but they won't last long if they're buried.'

He sent engineering crews and heavy excavators with large-scale earth-mover machinery to dig miners out of their collapsed shafts. Fire-suppression crews were also launched. Although the hydrogue icewave weapon froze and shattered anything it touched, the blue lightning blasts had started secondary fires – even if little remained intact for the fires to destroy.

Zan'nh stepped away from the command nucleus, his mind made up. He could not stay up here, away from the actual operations. Kori'nh had prepared him to be a hero. 'I will be in the lead shuttle. Take me down to the surface so that I can see for myself.'

Later, when he finally stood among the smouldering debris of the splinter colony, when he could smell the smoke and dust and death in the air, Zan'nh was speechless. The Ildiran buildings were gone, and he heard pitifully few moans of injured or dying Ildirans.

To his astonishment, a large black shape emerged from the billowing sooty haze at the centre of the devastation. The Klikiss robot moved with unsettling smoothness on clusters of finger-like legs. Its extended arms had sharp joints that ended in crab-like claws.

Zan'nh didn't know how the Klikiss robot recognized him, how it knew to address the Adar in particular, but the looming ancient machine proceeded through the smoke and wreckage without hesitation. Its black carapace opened partway as if threatening to reveal a set of deadly weapons. Its scarlet optical sensors blazed, regarding him.

Zan'nh stood his ground. 'What do you want? What are the Klikiss robots doing on Hrel-oro?' The black machines sometimes appeared on Ildiran splinter colonies; in fact, they had frequently offered construction assistance in unpleasant environments, such as moons or asteroids or the dark side of Maratha. But he didn't believe that was why this robot was here.

In a buzzing voice, it replied, 'Inform the Mage-Imperator that all agreements between Ildirans and the Klikiss robots are ended.'

The robot swivelled its body core to face the opposite direction. The stunned Adar watched, smelling smoke and blood from the massacre, as the hulking black automaton stalked off.

ONE HUNDRED AND SEVEN

ANTON COLICOS

A lone against the deepest night on Maratha, Anton and thirty-seven frightened Ildirans attempted to keep the lights burning long enough to survive.

Engineer Nur'of strung together the remaining intact power cells, squeezing out enough energy to maintain the domed city's vital systems. Despite the Maratha Designate's demands that all illumination be restored, there simply wasn't enough power remaining for more than a few days.

'Secda may offer safety, but these people are fearful of traversing the darkness,' Rememberer Vao'sh told Anton. 'There is danger outside the dome, and we have barely enough Ildirans here to form a splinter.'

'There's danger here, too, Vao'sh, and we're all going to have to leave, sooner or later. We may as well do it under our own terms.' Anton managed a wan smile. 'If it helps, I could come up with a few Earth parables that warn against procrastination.'

Once Designate Avi'h was finally convinced that no rescuers would come, he asked his bureaucrat assistant to arrange for their departure. Anton accompanied Bhali'v and the lens kithman Ilure'l, carrying a dazzling spot blazer outside to the vehicle hangars. The three men suited up in reflective skinfilms primarily designed to guard against the overpowering heat and sunlight of the dazzling day season; now, the layers of synthetic fabric offered insulation against the deepening cold of the long night.

As they trudged across the dark ground, Anton noticed that the hangar door looked damaged. More malicious sabotage, or simply poor maintenance? But the door opened, and Bhali'v scurried over to the three fast surface flyers housed inside.

When Anton, Vao'sh, and a group of Ildiran volunteers had visited the nightside Secda construction site, they'd flown one of these vessels. After night descended on Maratha Prime, the fast surface flyers had been placed into storage until the next day season. Now they were the only craft that could take the skeleton crew over to the sunlit side, and safety.

Ilure'l looked jumpy and anxious. He still seemed to believe that the Shana Rei from Vao'sh's story were waiting to prey upon them, that they might be hiding in any shadow. Anton remained ever vigilant for the mysterious saboteurs. The real ones.

The bureaucrat inspected each of the three craft, following a checklist and making notations on a diamond-crystal slate. 'All appear functional enough to take us to the Secda site, where the robots have agreed to welcome us. I will divide our personnel into three groups accordingly.'

Returning to the Ildirans huddled in the lighted portion of the dome, Bhali'v also drew up a plan that distributed stockpiled food and supplies into each craft. Though the fast surface flyers would accomplish the long trek in only half a day, the refugees did not know how long they might need to wait for rescue once they reached the construction site.

Anton continued to be pleasantly surprised by how well he was dealing with the tense situation – cool-headed and sensible, finding strength and courage that he hadn't known he possessed. Maybe he wasn't just an armchair adventurer after all; maybe he had actually learned something from all those tales he had studied. From his repertoire, he told stories of individual valour and resolve in order to keep the skeleton crew from panicking. The Ildirans, and especially Vao'sh, particularly liked the tale of the Dutch boy who had used his finger to plug a leaking dike. Though it was a simple story, it had a legendary quality worthy of events in the *Saga of Seven Suns*.

When Engineer Nur'of announced that the fast surface flyers were stocked and fuelled, Designate Avi'h announced with exaggerated satisfaction, 'I have once again communicated with the Klikiss robots in Maratha Secda. They await our arrival.'

'Then we'd better go,' Anton said with forced cheer, 'before the power goes out again.' Though he had intended it as a joke, the comment proved to be all the incentive the members of the skeleton crew needed.

They suited up and, carrying personal emergency blazers, left the lighted dome. The Designate held up the brightest spot blazer and led the way under dazzling stars that seemed much too far away. Even the brief march across the compound grounds to the hangar seemed nearly beyond the limits of the Ildirans, but Avi'h, claiming to draw strength through the *thism* from his brother the Mage-Imperator, moved at a brisk pace that was just short of a full-out run.

Anton and the Ildirans separated into their assigned groups and hurried to the brightly lit interiors of the individual flyers. He and Vao'sh would ride with the Maratha Designate and his bureaucratic deputy, along with the lens kithman, Nur'of, and several agricultural kithmen, diggers, and technicians.

Though Designate Avi'h was anxious to leave, Vao'sh pointed

out quietly that it would be more heroic for him to see that the others departed first. 'Bear in mind, Designate – we are participating in events that will be documented in the *Saga of Seven Suns*. How do you wish to be remembered?'

Bhali'v agreed. 'You are our leader, Designate. You are our connection to the Mage-Imperator, and through him, the Lightsource.' Always pragmatic, the bureaucratic deputy added, 'By departing in the third vessel, you allow the first two to prepare the way and secure your reception.'

Mollified, Avi'h gave the order. The engines of the first surface flyer fired up, and Anton felt an indefinable sense of relief when the first craft rose and departed, accelerating as it skimmed over the ground towards the far-off, unseen light of day.

The engines of the second flyer began to roar as Anton settled into his seat beside Vao'sh. Engineer Nur'of was already going over plans he had brought along. While he waited for all the passengers to strap in, he compiled a projected inventory of the supply and equipment vessels available at the Secda construction site, since the Designate had urged him to find a way to get off the planet once they all reached temporary safety.

Anton checked through the notes he had retrieved from his personal quarters in Maratha Prime to make sure he had everything. For months he had been translating and analysing portions of the *Saga*. Of all the human scholars who had filed requests, Anton Colicos was the only person ever approved to study with an Ildiran rememberer. It had been an intellectual and academic coup that none of his fellow scholars could match. His time living among the aliens, his friendship with Vao'sh, and now this unexpected ordeal – not to mention learning that his father was dead, his mother missing – gave him a great deal to assess and digest, far beyond his original goal of translating Ildiran myths and legends.

He looked over at the rememberer. 'Are you glad to have a

chance to practise what you preach, Vao'sh – to become a legendary figure instead of just talking about them?'

A sunrise of hues and tones flushed through his friend's facial lobes. 'No, Rememberer Anton. Given the choice, I prefer just to tell the stories, not to experience them.'

By now, the second craft had flown away. Finally, their flyer lifted off the ground. Since he was the most qualified, Nur'of served as pilot. Bhali'v sat at the communications console, making regular contact with the other two craft. They raced across the landscape, skimming low over uneven ground that appeared bare, rough, and lifeless. While Anton gazed out the dark window, the other Ildirans faced inwards towards the flyer's lights and each other. The shadowy ground slithered by under them.

With every moment they moved closer to the distant line of daylight. Speeding along, the first flyer was by now far ahead of them and out of sight around the curve of the planet. The blazing engines of the second vehicle were only a pinpoint of orange in the distance.

Suddenly, Bhali'v frowned as he checked and rechecked his console. 'We have just lost all contact with the first surface flyer.' He looked behind him to the Maratha Designate. 'Their transmissions cut off abruptly. The pilot had time only to say that he had discovered an unusual reading, a spike – and then the signal cut off.'

'What about the second flyer?' Designate Avi'h asked.

Anton leaned forward, suspicions already churning in his mind. The bureaucrat kithman sent his inquiry signal. 'Nothing unusual so far . . . wait—'

Far ahead of them, the brilliant orange dot of the flyer's afterburners suddenly bloomed into a dazzling flower of incandescent light.

The Ildirans were astonished. '*Kllar bekh!* It just . . . exploded,' Nur'of said, immediately checking his own readings.

Anton leaped up from his seat. 'Shut everything down, Nur'of! *Land!* You've got to put us down here and now.'

'But there is nothing out here,' Designate Avi'h sputtered.

Anton cut him off. 'Two flyers in a row? That can't be a coincidence! We're only a few minutes behind them, so we don't have long.'

The engineer decelerated drastically until their hull and landing gear scraped along the rough, barren ground. Anton speculated, 'I don't know if it was sabotage or just a flaw in these ships, but it could be a timed explosive that was activated as soon as we took off. We've got to get out of here now.'

As the flyer screeched to a halt, he opened the hatch, exposing them to the empty night and the cold air. 'Grab your blazers if you must, but get out. Now!'

Rememberer Vao'sh scooped up one of the portable lights and rushed after the human scholar, fleeing the still-groaning and humming flyer. Nur'of helped the two agricultural kithmen, Mhas'k and Syl'k, out of the hatch.

Anton shouted, 'If I'm wrong, we can always come back – but if I'm right, we'll know in less than a minute.' He sprinted across the cold darkness, not needing a light of his own. 'Run!'

Thoroughly motivated to protect his own life, Designate Avi'h scrambled away, dragging his bureaucratic assistant along with him.

Engineer Nur'of was the last one out. 'Perhaps the engines were overheating,' he suggested. 'By landing in time, we may have avoided the problem.'

Anton motioned them all to hurry. 'Or maybe the danger was caused by something else entirely. Come on!' At the moment, his best guess was that their mysterious saboteurs had reconfigured the flyer engines so they would fail catastrophically after being used. The countdown kept ticking at the back of his mind.

The air was very cold, and the night sky seemed penetratingly dark. Here, far from Prime and still a long distance from Secda, even Anton felt isolated and vulnerable. He could imagine how terrified the Ildirans themselves must be. When the group came to a halt, panting and anxious, they held their emergency blazers high, looking like a cluster of fireflies.

Designate Avi'h turned to Anton, his panic manifesting itself as anger and blame. 'Now you can see that you have overreacted. Was it necessary to listen to—'

Behind him, the third and last flyer erupted in a timed explosion that ignited the fuel tanks, ruined the engines, and blasted shrapnel and supplies into the sky. The pieces continued to burn, arcing high and then crashing down like flaming meteors. The bright fires were like beacons in the darkness, but the horrified Ildirans took no comfort or strength from the crackling light.

Vao'sh spoke first, shaping their immediate response. 'Rememberer Anton and Engineer Nur'of have saved our lives.'

'But we are lost in the middle of nowhere,' Ilure'l moaned. 'We are vulnerable to the darkness and the shadows . . . and whatever else lives here.'

'And only twelve of us have survived – and one human,' Bhali'v said. 'The others are dead. That's not nearly enough for a splinter.'

Anton knew he would have to hold them together somehow. 'There's still hope. Even though the other two shuttles were destroyed, we've thwarted whoever is trying to kill us. We can make it.' Sensing their despair, understanding that the Ildirans were more terrified of the loneliness and the dark night than of faceless killers, he tried to sound optimistic. 'We're still alive, but we have to help ourselves. We can't just sit here and wait for rescue.' He pointed in the direction of dawn, where he tried to convince himself he could see the barest smear of haze on the horizon.

'There's only one thing to do – start walking.' He took Vao'sh by the arm and bravely headed out.

In a low voice, the rememberer said, 'Our story in the *Saga* just got more interesting – if any of us survives to tell the tale.'

ONE HUNDRED AND EIGHT

CHIEF SCIENTIST
HOWARD PALAWU

During night on Rheindic Co, after the colonist volunteers went to sleep in their gathered tents near the base of the Klikiss cliff city, the frenetic pace of the transportal hub died down just enough for Howard Palawu to do his work.

As the Chief Scientist studied the circuits and machinery left behind by the vanished alien race, he input notes and conjectures into the old datascreen he had kept for so many years. He still didn't understand how the transportal network functioned, and with each detail he learned, his conclusions shifted back and forth. Ideas and hypotheses were part of the scientific method, and Palawu did not regret the detours and blind ends.

It was the same with his life. While he might wish he could have changed a few decisions or behaved differently, Palawu didn't consider his missteps to be 'mistakes'. Every action was part of the process of living, for good or bad.

Having a few more years with his wife would have been nice. During their best times, he regretted not spending enough days just enjoying her company, relaxing with her, going to the hot springs she loved so well because her body ached. Now that the Chief Scientist was alone and had all the time in the universe to spend on his investigations, he would have preferred just to take an afternoon off and walk through the canyons of Rheindic Co with her. But she was gone now . . .

One of the technicians, bleary-eyed and exhausted from hustling people through the trapezoidal gateway all day long, remained on duty to perform book-keeping chores, though she clearly had no love for the task. Aladdia had a narrow face, bronze skin, and long blue-black hair. As she went about her tedious paperwork, ignoring him, she ate an evening snack that filled the small control room with the pungent odours of curry and garlic. Palawu couldn't remember the last time he'd eaten, but Aladdia didn't offer to share. He was not impolite enough to ask.

Her control board brightened, and the trapezoidal stone window grew blurry. 'It's about time,' she muttered, more to herself than to Palawu.

He looked up and saw a shadow appear. A tall man stepped through. He had tousled black hair and wore a dusty but comfortable-looking expedition jumpsuit. His lightweight pack contained the requisite scanning and documentation apparatus, as well as a conservative supply of survival rations.

The explorer unslung his pack and handed her the results and images he had gathered. 'Another decent world, a bit colder than the others, but the ground is rich in rare metals. A keeper.'

Aladdia scanned the data pack, then nodded. 'Good. We'll add it to the roster.'

'Right now, I'm getting a shower, some food, and a long nap.' The transportal explorer left his equipment behind and marched off into the tunnels.

Over the past month, Palawu had often seen explorers return from their expeditions to undeciphered destination tiles. He'd always been intrigued by their daring adventures. He said to the technician, 'So many of the tiles remain untried. Who knows what we might find if we travel through to those worlds?'

'Yes, who knows? If you figure out how the transportals work, we'll get a lot more answers.' Apparently, the explorer's scheduled return was all she'd been waiting for. Wrapping up the remains of her snack, Aladdia signed off her log and called it a night. 'The system is yours, Dr Palawu. I hope you find something worthwhile tonight.'

Pacing the room after she left, he stared at the big stone window through which the man had just returned. Palawu had already passed through the transportal network many times in order to study the apparatus on other already-investigated Klikiss worlds. But the thought of so many blank holes in the data, bothered him on a fundamental level. As the Hansa's Chief Scientist, it was his job to find answers about the whole alien transportation system.

He scanned the mysterious Klikiss hieroglyphics, exotic letters or numerals assigned to the worlds their lost civilization had claimed. Palawu could choose from among hundreds that had never been investigated, never been seen by human eyes. The very idea intrigued him.

He had his scientific curiosity, after all, and he had watched so many colonists pass harmlessly through the transportal. Palawu had already left his mark in many ways: his technical papers and scientific accomplishments, his work analysing the Klikiss robot Jorax, dozens of fundamental breakthroughs that ranged from the wildly profitable to the unbelievably esoteric.

Knowing the symbol coordinate tile that would return him to Rheindic Co, he could always find his way back. He had nothing left to prove . . . but why not achieve something else? In reality, he had nothing to lose.

With the meticulous care he had learned from his first job as a lab assistant, Palawu carefully documented what he intended to do, leaving a full explanation and tidying up the reports he had so far compiled about the transportal system. Then he chose one of the still-unknown tiles, recording its symbol on the records he would leave behind.

Deciding that the recently returned explorer's pack could prove useful, containing enough supplies for a brief trip, Palawu picked it up. He adjusted the straps, shouldered the load, and prepared to set out. He intended to be back before long.

After activating the stone window, he watched the blank surface shimmer into a dusty, mysterious passage. He took a deep breath and with a confident smile, stepped through, eyes open and ready to see—

He encountered a world of uncompromising strangeness, impossibly different from the other abandoned Klikiss worlds he had visited so far. The colours, sounds, smells, were powerful and unexpected, enough to drive a person mad. The alien and unfamiliar sights assailed his consciousness with an avalanche of exotic details, incomprehensible impressions.

And then another unexpected sight: an older human female moved towards him with a curious and unreadable expression on her face. In complete shock, Palawu recognized the features of a woman he had never met but who was well known to him.

Margaret Colicos – alive! It did not surprise him that after the hundreds of missions and random explorations through the transportals, somebody would find the world where she had gone. But this was impossible, unbearable . . .

Suddenly he saw more – much more – and could not stop himself from screaming.

When they entered the control room the next morning in order to prepare for the day's first group of departing colonists, the technical crew found Palawu's records. At first they were annoyed by the risk the Chief Scientist had taken. Then, as time went by, they became concerned.

Finally, after a week of silence – far longer than his rations would have lasted – Palawu's coordinate was marked as another black tile. The technicians submitted the Chief Scientist's data and his computer files to another team of Hansa investigators so that the work could continue. Meanwhile, the transportal colonization initiative proceeded apace.

Howard Palawu never returned.

ONE HUNDRED AND NINE

DD

Though he was trapped aboard the stolen Juggernaut, DD had to take action as Sirix and his robot marauders annihilated the Corribus settlement. His basic programming did not allow him to remain idle. He had to at least try. This was wrong.

From the Juggernaut's weapons station, the Soldier compies mapped out and targeted all human or Klikiss structures. As the attack proceeded, they tracked each fleeing person who raced for shelter, and they could kill their victims one at a time with cool accuracy.

In the colony's transmission tower, Jan Covitz continued to send anxious questions, pleas, demands. With two successive jazer blasts, one of the invading Mantas vaporized the communication tower and its support shack. The desperate radio signal went silent.

Sirix stood on the command bridge like some great general. All the robot's articulated arms were extended. His flat head-plate swivelled as he absorbed information from the projection screens. 'We will leave no structure standing, no trace that the arrogant humans ever established a foothold here.'

DD concluded that stopping this unprovoked assault had a higher priority than his own self-preservation. He lunged towards the nearest weapons console.

Though his mass was only half that of the Soldier compy's, the little robot's unexpected action was sufficient to thrust the military machine aside. As the surprised Soldier compy attempted to recover its balance, DD hammered his alloy-and-plastic fist into the Juggernaut's weaponry controls. He did not have the strength of a heavy lifting machine, but the consoles had not been designed to take such punishment. DD hammered again and again, breaking open the cover plate, obliterating the circuitry and delicate targeting systems.

In less than three seconds, the Soldier compy had righted itself and pulled DD away from the console. The little robot struggled, but could not break free. Before him, the controls smoked and sparked, and he was gratified to see that they were ruined.

The Soldier compy raised DD overhead, preparing to disassemble him; two other military robots lurched forward to add their metal muscle, but Sirix's buzzing voice halted them. 'Do not destroy him.' Scarlet eye sensors glowed balefully like orbs formed of hot embers. 'This is an example of how slavery corrupts these competent computerized companions. No rational mind would have taken such useless action, but DD was forced to make this defiant, but ultimately pointless, gesture.'

Sirix scuttled over to where DD dangled in the air, caught in the grasp of the Soldier compy. 'Observe, DD – you caused very little harm. This battleship is equipped with three redundant weapons consoles, and even without the Juggernaut we have five fully armed Manta cruisers to continue the destruction of an unarmed colony. Your struggle was for nothing.'

'Nevertheless, I could not fail to act.'

Sirix moved heavily back to the central bridge station to oversee the conclusion of the Corribus operation.

DD amplified his voice. 'It is what I want to do. I *desire* to stop you.' Even without the restrictive programming the Klikiss robots scorned, he would have chosen to do the same thing. He could not stand by while so many innocent colonists were slaughtered.

'You do not understand your own actions.'

In the colony below, despite DD's best efforts, nothing remained but smoking debris and bodies. Everything had been destroyed.

'Observe closely,' Sirix said as the hijacked battleship descended towards the rubble of the canyon floor. DD didn't want to see first-hand the results of the massacre. 'This was merely a practice run for our ultimate plan, a demonstration of our new attack force. We judge the exercise an unqualified success.'

The engines hummed, then slowed as the Juggernaut came to rest against the ground like a beached whale. The Soldier compies marched in ranks from the bridge, preparing to disembark and complete the total sterilization of Corribus. Sirix observed with apparent satisfaction.

'Therefore, we will proceed with the full-scale plan against the rest of humanity.'

ONE HUNDRED AND TEN

ORLI COVITZ

The attack went on for what seemed like hours, and Orli huddled against the wall of her cave shelter. If this alcove had remained intact for ten thousand years, unscathed even by the superweaponry that had melted the granite cliffs and exterminated the Klikiss, then she was probably safe. But adrenaline made her heart hammer, and she crouched in the deepest corner of the chamber.

Outside, everyone else was being slaughtered . . . including her father. And she could do nothing to help. What had they done to provoke this? And who were the attackers?

Eventually, she heard no more of the faint screams, only the crackle of energy blasts and the boom of distant explosions mixed with the roar of engines. With shaking knees, she crept forward, certain in her heart that every other human on Corribus must be dead. Smoke filled the canyon, drifting upwards in greasy black plumes. The whole settlement had been flattened and burned. Nothing remained whatsoever.

The communications tower and its control shack had been

vaporized; she knew her father would have been inside it. Her half-hearted friends must also be dead, all the colonist families, her pet, the acquaintances she had made in their short time here.

She heard the roar of spaceship engines change pitch and decrease to muffled booms. Peeking out through the narrow cave entrance, Orli saw the six EDF vessels land under the smoky sunlight. The massacre was complete.

The Juggernaut was so huge it barely fitted between the canyon walls, but the pilot had guided it down without hesitation. When the doorways opened and figures streamed down ramps to the valley floor, she recognized the insect-like forms of giant Klikiss robots. Next, Soldier-model compies built in Hansa factories filed out beside the black-shelled alien machines.

Tears streaked her dusty face. Orli couldn't cry out, didn't dare call attention to herself here, so high up on the cliff wall.

The robots separated into teams and combed through the wreckage. Soldier compies used brute strength to knock down walls and crack open sealed storage containers. They found one person who had been hiding and dragged him out screaming. The man broke away and tried to flee, but the robots surrounded him and viciously dispatched him. Orli could see the splash of blood even from her distant vantage . . .

The robotic invaders remained for hours, being particularly thorough, until they could find nothing left to destroy. As the afternoon light began to fade over Corribus, the machines filed back aboard their stolen EDF vessels. Thrusters lifted the Juggernaut and five Mantas from the ground. Like predators bloated after a large feast, they flew into the sky, lumbering back towards orbit.

Orli had waited long enough. When she realized she was as safe as she was going to be, she crept out of her shelter and began to climb back down. The alum crystals seemed slipperier now, their flat surfaces tilted. Each one seemed treacherous, as if the crystals themselves wanted her to slip and fall.

Before long, her arms and legs were trembling. She knew it was not just anxiety from the dangerous climb, but also the backwash of shock from what she had witnessed. Orli gritted her teeth and focused her thoughts. One movement at a time, one handhold or foothold, descending a body length, and then another. She had to make it back down.

The valley was in full shadow of dusk by the time she reached the bottom. She stood shaking for a few moments, gasping to catch her breath, then horror and hope swept over her like a flood wave. She ran with clumsy footsteps towards the orange glow of still-burning fires.

As she had feared, nothing remained but rubble and blackened timbers from the poletrees the settlers had brought in from the open plains. The Klikiss transportal had been demolished. Blackened human bodies – mercifully unrecognizable – lay strewn about on the ground or buried in the wreckage of collapsed buildings.

'Hello? Is anyone here?' Her voice cracked, but she did not give up. 'Is anyone else alive?'

Only a resounding silence echoed back at her as night fell. It was no use. She was all alone on Corribus, the only survivor.

ONE HUNDRED AND ELEVEN

RLINDA KETT

Without any sun in Crenna's frozen sky, it was hard to judge the passage of days during the rescue operations. When all of the shell-shocked colonists were finally crammed aboard the two merchant ships, Rlinda was ready to go.

The *Blind Faith* lifted off first, rising into the dark, cold skies. BeBob signalled, 'I'm awfully overloaded, Rlinda.'

'You want to tell a couple of those people they can stay behind?'

'Not a chance. I used to live here, remember? These were my neighbours.'

For the time being, the settlers didn't mind standing elbow to elbow on a ship that would take them far from their dark and dying world. They leaned against the corridor walls or were stacked like cordwood in the few passenger compartments. But at least they were alive, and getting away.

Rlinda turned to the contented-looking spy as she activated the *Voracious Curiosity*'s controls to follow BeBob. 'You did a good job here, Davlin. Maybe you'll have to change your career.' She accelerated on a direct line out of the system, away from the quiet, dead globe that had once been a beautiful colony.

Davlin shrugged in the copilot's chair. 'I like these people. What else was I supposed to do?' A brief smile crossed his face. 'They're . . . my friends. And when we get to Relleker, I intend to give those bureaucratic snots a piece of my mind for not helping when we asked for assistance. I just might mention it to Chairman Wenceslas himself . . .'

'Whoa! Look out, Rlinda!' BeBob squawked over the comm system. 'Incoming, starboard side!'

Rlinda suddenly felt as cold as if she were standing outside on Crenna. Four hydrogue warglobes hurtled on a beeline across space directly towards them. 'Oh, crap! Do these guys always need to have such bad timing?'

Davlin clenched his jaw. 'What more can the drogues want here? They've already killed the damned sun.'

Rlinda activated the ship's intercom. 'Everybody hold on tight. Evasive manoeuvres coming up.' She rolled the *Voracious Curiosity*, looping down, while the *Blind Faith* flew in a different direction, diving back towards Crenna, as if hoping to find a place to hide there. Despite her teasing, Rlinda knew he had outrun many an enemy and was an expert at getting himself out of trouble through fast flying. But local security forces were easily duped. She didn't know how readily fooled a hydrogue would be.

Rlinda took her own ship on a hard turn and accelerated recklessly. 'I'm going to duck behind the planet. Maybe in the shadow . . . or what would have been the shadow if there was any sun left—'

Davlin looked at her. 'I don't have any better ideas.'

As Rlinda flew a corkscrew manoeuvre, the rescued colonists couldn't tell the difference between deck and ceiling. She was strapped in and concentrated on flying, but her passengers yelled as they were thrown from side to side. Both ships converged where the planetary mass would at least block them from the warglobes' sensors.

To their surprise, the hydrogues shot past on a determined course, intent on something else. The diamond-hulled ships ignored the *Voracious Curiosity* and the *Blind Faith* and continued like guided missiles towards the dead ember of the sun. Orbiting the dark star, the drogues shot their weapons, pounding immense energy discharges into ruddy patches where leftover stellar heat continued to escape.

'What are they doing now?' BeBob asked. 'Not that I'm complaining. . .'

A few sputtering flares flickered out from the extinguished sun, spouting in the infrared. 'They're trying to flush out the last few faeros survivors,' Davlin said. 'Finishing the job.'

Suddenly a group of ellipsoidal fireballs spurted away from the cooling solar material. Like hungry wolves, the hydrogues raced after them.

'Now's our chance,' Rlinda said. 'Come on, BeBob!' The two ships moved out of the shelter of the cold planet and accelerated towards open space, away from the titanic fight.

Warglobes surrounded the fleeing faeros one at a time. Energy discharges hammered the flaming elementals, bleeding their power dry. Under the relentless attack, one of the faeros flickered, then winked out, a dead cinder in cold space.

BeBob transmitted, 'Better increase acceleration, Rlinda. Doesn't look like we have much longer before the drogues finish mopping up.'

'With all these people aboard, this is as fast as the *Voracious Curiosity* will go.'

Davlin watched on the screens as the vengeful warglobes methodically trapped and killed another of the fireballs. Then another.

Before long, when the last of the flaming elementals had been snuffed, the warglobes accelerated back down along the path they had travelled. Rlinda heaved a brief sigh of relief – but now the four diamond spheres hesitated and altered course. They moved towards the two fleeing cargo ships, as if finally noticing them.

'This isn't good,' BeBob said. 'It's not a coincidence.'

Rlinda wrestled with the controls, but her ship was already at maximum speed. Since even EDF Juggernauts and Ildiran warliners couldn't fight the hydrogues, the *Voracious Curiosity* didn't stand a chance.

The ominous diamond spheres quickly reached them and surrounded the two ships just as they had when vanquishing the faeros. Rlinda swallowed hard. The alien globes looked as big as planets in front of her. She didn't even consider powering up her minimal weapons. 'Anybody got a white flag?' she asked.

The spiked globes shimmered, looming there, but making no move. Rlinda wondered what they were waiting for. She and her passengers – as well as all those aboard the *Blind Faith* – were certainly doomed.

Finally, with typical incomprehensibility, the hydrogues separated and streaked off at high speed, as if responding to some unheard signal. They left Rlinda shaking inside her cockpit.

'What the hell?' BeBob transmitted.

She just shook her head and took deep breaths, unable to speak.

Davlin stared out the cockpit window and finally said, 'I'm all done with this system – and my sabbatical.'

CELLI

I n the ruins of the worldforest, some areas were so dense with fallen trees and dead wood that they formed barriers impenetrable even to heavy Roamer machinery. The worst tangles, though, were the most fascinating to Celli.

What was the forest hiding in there?

She bounded through thickets, curious about the shielded islands of fallen trees that seemed to her like consciously protective barricades. Standing before a huge deadfall, Celli looked at the tightly packed trunks and broken branches. In the midst of the furious attack, had the worldforest intentionally drawn down its doomed hulks to form an armoured dome to shelter something vitally important?

And why would that be so strange? With her own eyes she had seen the rush of verdant rebirth as the forest used its stored energy to regrow foliage as fast as the hydrogues could destroy it. That miracle had lasted only briefly, wondrous and lush and green, but it showed the worldforest's unique power and majesty. She could think of no reason why there might not be other miracles in the offing.

Ever curious, Celli worked her way into the thicket. Gnarled branches scratched like claws, warning intruders away. Withered fronds hung like witches' brooms, blocking her way, but Celli felt no sinister presence here. She wasn't a green priest and could not sense the worldtrees; nevertheless, she *belonged* here on Theroc. The trees, even these wounded or dying ones, would know she meant them no harm.

She wormed her way forward. She had always been able to get into tight places and awkward situations, often to her dismay. Her body was whip-thin and resilient, and she found openings that no machine, or even a broad-shouldered man like Solimar, could have got through.

Pushing more branches aside, Celli ignored the scratches she received. Some brittle twigs broke into charcoal as she pressed against them; others were surprisingly resilient and flexible. She smelled fresh moisture again, proof that parts of the forest had escaped being scorched or frozen.

This sheltered place was still remarkably alive, gathering energy during an exhausted rest. It was like a secret and magical glen . . .

Celli had often enjoyed eavesdropping on green priest acolytes as they told stories to the worldforest. Now she recalled the story of Sleeping Beauty and her spellbound castle protected by an unbreakable wall of thorny vines.

As she worked her way deeper, Celli noticed to her surprise that the branches were actually shifting and stirring. They *moved* of their own accord, stretching out of the way to make her passage easier – to let her through.

At first she thought it was just her imagination, but as she turned slightly, Celli could see the twigs rustle and flex, opening another path, guiding her. Grinning, she hurried forward, wondering where the foliage might want her to go. 'What are you hiding inside there?'

She drew closer to the heart of the thicket and with each step she took, the branches continued to part for her. Only glimmers could penetrate the clumped wickerwork of tumbled branches overhead, and so the light was dim. But she found her way without a single misstep.

Finally, Celli reached the centre of the thicket under an interlocked dome of tree branches. Beneath the dome lay a shadowed meadow where condorflies had once flitted and large flowers had grown.

Celli saw a single wooden pillar growing there in the open space. The trunk, as tall as she was, looked too thick and gnarled to be a treeling. It stood like an obelisk, a totem pole, or some sort of shrine that the trees themselves had created, thrusting it out of the Theron soil.

Obviously, this was what the worldtrees had been protecting.

Celli moved closer, carefully, reverently. She still didn't know what she was seeing. As she paced around the wooden obelisk, she saw that its cylindrical shape was grooved and swirled with long bumps, like thick branches twisted in a knot.

With a start, she realized that it oddly resembled a *human* form, as if a shuddering man had wrapped his arms tightly around himself, tucked his head down, and crouched. But the detail had not yet finished forming. The shape remained vague, for now.

The worldtrees had created this on purpose. But for what reason? She went closer, drawn and intrigued as she looked into the rounded lump that would have been the carved man's face. The features were crude but smooth, as if modelled in stiff clay without any refinements. After looking carefully, Celli got the feeling it was still completing itself.

Smiling with wonder, she reached out to touch what would have been a wooden cheek. The eyes opened.

ONE HUNDRED AND
THIRTEEN

TASIA TAMBLYN

Though she was stuck on the sidelines, the war still went on. EDF ships went out on recon flights in search of the faeros in hopes of convincing them to become formal allies; other ships attempted to keep track of hydrogue movements. Far too much military energy, however, was devoted to the stupid, red-herring conflict with the Roamer clans.

After destroying Hurricane Depot, the Eddies had gone to two other Roamer outposts whose locations they had discovered, only to find them hastily abandoned. The clans had always closely guarded their hiding places, and now they were slipping without difficulty through the fingers of the EDF. Tasia noted with no surprise whatsoever that the Hansa did not mention their failures.

Because of their doubts and suspicions about her loyalties, Tasia's superior officers had stuck her here on Mars as a schoolteacher for bottom-of-the-barrel kleebs, most of them obnoxious and unmotivated. She wasn't in a mood to take any crap from them.

Under olive skies, with her boots planted on rusty rock, she stood on high ground in her environment suit, watching the new batch of cadets as they went through routine on-foot drills. During her downtime the evening before, Tasia had planned the day's exercises. The students hadn't learned yet that the worse they performed and the ruder they were to her, the tougher she made their assignments.

In the canyons below, the kleebs marched in four separate groups, struggling to follow computerized topographic maps through convoluted terrain in order to reach a goal. It seemed a simple chart-reading problem, a team orienteering exercise, but she had spiced up the challenge by doctoring their air tanks so that some trainees had a surplus of oxygen and others did not have enough. As soon as their low-tank alarms went off, the cadets had the option of calling for pick-up and rescue, but Tasia hoped each group would work together as a team to share resources.

From what she'd seen, though, most of the Eddy recruits had never learned how to think outside the box to fix an emergency. The Big Goose could learn much about survival and innovation from the Roamers; unfortunately, they had made up their minds to harass the clans instead. Their loss . . .

Here on Mars, Tasia was completely out of the information loop. Without her Manta command, she had no need to know about military actions, and she found out about full-scale operations like Hurricane Depot only long after the fact. Right now, General Lanyan might already be planning another idiotic attack and she would never be able to warn the Roamers, as she had done at Osquivel.

Later that day, her trainees returned to the base, some having failed, some completing their assignment. All together in the waiting room, they shucked off their suits to look at the exercise scores and see what they had done wrong. And they had all done plenty of things wrong. Tasia didn't pull any punches in her debriefing assessment. She just hoped her students would eventually use their skills against the hydrogues instead of other Roamer outposts.

Two of the kleebs had called in for an emergency rescue. Only one team had taken the obvious solution of sharing air from their tanks so that the entire crew could move on. The fastest hiker from the second team, seeing that they wouldn't all make it, had abandoned the rest of them for emergency rescue and run ahead just so he could claim a personal win. Tasia came down on that team the hardest – the alleged winner for making such a selfish decision, and the rest of his comrades for letting him.

'It was within the parameters of the exercise, Commander,' said the scolded cadet. 'As a representative of our team, I wanted us to win.'

'By abandoning all your comrades? I don't care if we did have pick-up teams waiting. That's not what we *do*, Cadet Elwich,' she said. 'We don't leave members of our team behind. I have half a mind just to give the lot of you to the drogues.'

'It's what the EDF did at Osquivel,' one of the cadets grumbled. 'They left a lot of people behind without even trying to rescue them. Didn't they, Commander? You were there.'

The implicit question stung her. *How many did you leave behind, Commander Tamblyn?*

Tasia stared at them, reminded of the horrors of that battle. Even though she had got her own ship and crew out of danger, they had left behind innumerable wounded soldiers, damaged ships, and floating lifetubes. And Robb was gone, too . . .

'We were all under fire. Nobody was guaranteed to get out alive. There were no pick-up squads. You think that's comparable to goofing around in an empty canyon to win a game? Shizz, I'm trying to teach you what I know. Listening may increase your chances for survival when you face a real enemy.'

'What's a Roacher going to teach us? How to run and hide?' the same cadet muttered, barely loud enough for her to hear.

'Elwich!' she roared, and the young man moved to attention, slower than she would have liked. She stepped close to him. 'Do you know how to read a rank insignia? Do you understand what this means?' She indicated the polished clusters on her lapels.

'It signifies that you are – were – in command of a Manta battlecruiser.'

'And tell me your rank again, kleeb.'

'Private, Ma'am.'

'And in which military does a *private* speak with such disrespect to a *commander*?'

'In . . . in none that I'm aware of, Ma'am.'

'This rank means that you are a worm beneath the heel of my boot, regardless of where I was born, how I was raised, or the clan I belong to. Spend less time thinking about my parentage and more time remembering my military service record, Private Elwich. I fought the hydrogues at Jupiter, Boone's Crossing, Osquivel, and Ptoro. I wiped out a whole drogue world with a Klikiss Torch. My piloting scores are the best the EDF has on record. If I looked into your parentage, Private, what species would I find? How much inbreeding?'

Some of the cadets snickered, but she silenced them. 'This is the Earth Defence Forces. There is a chain of command. I am your ranking officer, and in all probability I will for ever outrank you. Now, as a token of your newfound respect for me, Private Elwich, I want you to give me a hundred pushups.'

The cadet looked at her in calm surprise. Here on Mars, with only forty percent of Earth's gravity, simple physical exercise was easy. 'Ma'am, yes Ma'am. Right now in your presence, Commander?'

'No, Private. I want you to do them in the gravity chamber at a setting of 1.5 Earth normal.'

At last, he gave a satisfactory gulp.

'If anyone else would like to insult my parents, my clan, or my service record, please volunteer now.' When no one answered her, Tasia continued to stare, making sure they understood she meant business. She could not hide her Roamer heritage, nor did she want to.

Instead, she intended to be the best EDF officer they could ever hope to serve under. And sometimes, she very much enjoyed strictly enforcing the military regulations.

ONE HUNDRED AND FOURTEEN

ZHETT KELLUM

It made no sense, even when Zhett tried to look at it from the warped Eddy point of view. She still could not see what had driven the EDF prisoners to concoct such a ridiculous escape plan, to take such unwarranted chances. What were they thinking?

'They must have a brown dwarf for their Guiding Star,' she muttered.

After the debacle with the ore processor crashing into the admin dome, her father had been enraged to discover the missing prospector scout ship. At first, he'd feared that one of his Roamer prospectors had not returned from a scouting run. For days, the EDF prisoners had been intensely tight-lipped, and Zhett herself finally backtracked the location of the missing ship, discovered that Fitzpatrick and a soldier named Bill Stanna had been working nearby . . . that Fitzpatrick had triggered a suspicious fire alarm, though no evidence of combustion had been found in the supply room.

She'd reported it to her father. 'I think one of the prisoners . . . escaped.'

'Escaped with an in-system ship? That's ridiculous!' He had

paced back and forth in the admin dome, scratching his salt-and-pepper beard and shaking his shaggy head. 'By damn, what crackpot scheme did they have in mind? Where was he going to go? That ship has a limited range and not much fuel.'

Finally, many days after Bill Stanna would have succeeded – or got himself into deep trouble and in need of rescue – Fitzpatrick quietly told Zhett what the soldier had in mind.

She hauled him onto the carpet in the repaired administration dome. 'You mean he just blindly headed off for the comet zone? Do you know how *big* the Kuiper Belt is? You can't simply fly up and expect to find our facilities, even if we hadn't taken pains to hide them. How was Stanna ever going to just stumble into the right spot?'

Fitzpatrick shrugged. 'He wanted to try.'

Zhett shook her head, her long dark hair flying. 'That's just plain stupid.'

Clan Kellum had done everything to make life tolerable, productive, and – yes, dammit – *pleasant* for the soldiers in the Osquivel shipyards. Wasn't it perfectly clear why the refugees couldn't be returned to the Big Goose, especially after the Roamers had cut off all trade with Earth, and after the EDF had just destroyed Hurricane Depot? Now, more than ever, Roamer facilities had to remain hidden.

Fitzpatrick faced her, standing rigid. He had been alone with Zhett before, but this time he seemed intimidated, even ashamed at all the trouble Bill Stanna had caused by blundering off into interplanetary space.

She finally turned to him, frustrated. 'I don't get it. Is it really so bad here with us, Fitzie?'

He narrowed his eyes. 'You have to ask that? We're unlawful prisoners of war. What do you expect? We're *supposed* to try and escape.'

'You can bet we've given you more freedom than the Eddies are allowing the Roamer prisoners they kidnapped from Hurricane Depot. Nobody even knows what's happened to *them*.'

'Don't go getting all indignant, Zhett – nobody knows what's happened to us either.'

Hundreds of Roamer searchers were dispatched to comb the area for any sign of the lost prospector scout, but the volume of empty space in the Osquivel system was immense.

Knowing at least the broad outlines of the escapee's ill-conceived plan, the Roamers focused their search, criss-crossing space, trying to pick up any sign of the vessel. The cometary extraction fields performed a complete vessel inventory and confirmed that none of their ships was missing. Stanna had not got away.

Finally, Kellum reported that they had found the prospector scout ship. The remaining thirty-one EDF prisoners gathered in a large cargo-landing grotto as Roamer vessels slowly towed in the small stolen craft.

The craft came through to the loading dock, and atmosphere-containment fields were dropped after repressurization. Zhett noticed the ship's cold engines, the darkened portholes. Beside her, Fitzpatrick pressed his lips into a firm line, his face unreadable.

Her father stepped out of the lead tow-ship, hands on his hips, his expression angry and disappointed. He turned to watch as other Roamers came forward to open the hatches of the silent spacecraft. Zhett had never seen her father look so frustrated.

Kellum raised his voice, yelling at the prisoners. 'Your comrade stole this ship from us. Worse, he flew off into empty space without a course, without supplies, without even a fully-charged life-support system. Out in space, stupidity and poor planning are equivalent to death.'

He struggled to keep his temper in check. 'It didn't take him long to get lost, and he ran out of air before he starved. He did trigger the SOS beacon when he realized he was in deep trouble, but by then it was way too late. He was far from our cometary-extraction facilities, and it took seven hours for his signal to reach any listener, another ten to respond.'

The Roamers had opened the craft now, and they marched in a sombre procession to retrieve Bill Stanna's stiff, pale body. When they carried the soldier out, the EDF captives groaned, and a buzz of heated conversation filled the chamber.

'There was no *reason* for this, by damn,' Kellum said. His voice sounded plaintive. 'There was no possibility he would get away, and yet still he flew off on this suicidal mission. Some of you – *all* of you – must have known he was going to do this. How could you let him? Where is your common sense?'

'You want us all dead anyway,' muttered Shelia Andez, her voice dripping acid.

Kellum flushed red and put his hands on his hips. 'Would I keep yelling at you to be careful if I wanted you all dead?'

Standing close to Fitzpatrick, Zhett wanted to comfort him, felt anger and resentment flowing in waves from all the prisoners. 'I'm sorry,' she whispered, but even he turned away.

ADMIRAL LEV STROMO

S ince the EDF was sending such an overwhelming force against the Roamers, Admiral Stromo had no worries about the impending military operation. This would be an unqualified victory that he could take credit for. It was quite a relief, really.

Previously, each time he'd gone into battle, an icy ball in his stomach had spread numbness through his body. He had felt detached from all events, out of control, even though *he* was supposed to be the one in command. Times of peace and prosperity in the Hansa had allowed a smart and savvy man like himself to advance his career; unfortunately, everyone expected Stromo to be a tough military genius as well.

Early on, when he'd decisively put an end to the Ramah insurrection, he had been considered a war hero. He had always felt he deserved those medals, ribbons, and promotions – until he'd faced a real enemy and a real military crisis. His utter defeat at Jupiter had changed everything. He'd never been so frightened in his life, and he had lost his nerve. Something broke within him, and afterwards he had never felt the same. He'd lost his edge. No doubt, the EDF troops talked about him behind his back.

But this severe disciplinary action against the Roamers would restore his clout. Stromo felt he could do it. No, he was *sure* he could do it . . .

Sixteen Mantas entered the unremarkable star system where a red dwarf shone dull light into a mess of orbiting rocks. The Roamers were hiding in there, according to the data they had extracted from the clan ship seized at Hurricane Depot. The space gypsies didn't know his fleet was coming, but they would find out soon enough. Even though General Lanyan had not authorized the use of massive Juggernauts, worried about taking them from hydrogue patrols, it was quite an impressive show of force.

One of the eager young tacticians hunched over a console on the lead Manta's bridge. 'Detecting space traffic, Admiral – right where we expected them to be. It's a Roacher nest, all right.'

Stromo drew a deep breath. 'Focus in on any artificial structures. See if you can pinpoint the main complex – a cluster of asteroids . . . spaceports, loading docks, connecting girders.'

'I'm tracing back flight paths, sir. There, a clear convergence!'

'Disperse our battle group so we come in from all sides,' Stromo said. 'Remora pilots to the launch bays. This is a containment and absorption action. It's your job to make sure nobody slips away. Our job is to make a bold statement here, and actions speak louder than words.'

'Our net will have plenty of holes in it, Admiral. Once they scatter, some of them will slip away,' said the Manta's commander, Elly Ramirez. He remembered her name in particular because she had been elevated in rank so that she could take command of this cruiser, which had formerly belonged to the Roamer officer Tasia Tamblyn. Stromo couldn't remember any of the other minor officers, though, since he'd barely met the crew before launching from Earth.

Stromo paced the Manta's bridge. If the mission didn't look completely successful, then he would redefine the objective so that he could honestly call it a victory. 'All right, we can tolerate a few leaks. Let somebody get away to tell the other clans that we mean business. It's my intention to put a full-blown fear of the Hansa into them. They'll think twice before they defy us again.' He shook his head. 'Proceed in full attack configuration.'

Ramirez cleared her throat. 'They've probably spotted us already, Admiral, so let's not give them a chance to pack any suitcases. I suggest we start transmitting standard warnings, before this gets out of hand.'

Flight sergeants barked out commands. Stromo nodded, happy to let Ramirez handle the details. This textbook assault would give the newer soldiers an excellent first taste of what the EDF was all about. They would see Stromo as their brave commander crushing the resistance of those who refused to aid the greater cause.

The heavily armed cruisers swooped in, following planned trajectories to surround and engulf the Roamer population centre. Stromo had his clear orders; unlike the operation at Hurricane Depot, he wasn't supposed to waste time seizing left-over materiel or scrounging for information. This was to be a swift and decisive knock-out punch.

Before the iron-hard fist of Mantas could close around the asteroid complex, a flurry of ragtag clan ships scattered in all directions. 'As I suspected, Admiral – they're getting away,' said Commander Ramirez.

'Well, then shoot at a couple of the smaller ones. Let them know we're serious.'

The new commander paled, and some of the other bridge officers shifted uneasily. Ramirez said, 'But Admiral, you haven't even issued instructions yet. This isn't really fair—'

Stromo glowered. 'Chairman Wenceslas gave the Roamers a

warning weeks ago, and Speaker Peroni threw it back in his face. They certainly can't have any doubt as to why we're so angry.'

Ramirez backed down, though she was decidedly uneasy. 'All right, take a few pot-shots at some of the fleeing ships.'

Four of the jazer strikes hit their targets, but ten missed. If anything, the flood of escaping Roamer ships grew heavier. The Admiral decided he would insist that these crews undergo thorough practice runs – unless they were being less than competent on purpose. Did they have some lingering loyalty to their former Roamer commander? Perhaps Tamblyn's presence was more insidious than the EDF had thought . . .

With a sigh, Stromo stepped up behind the captain's chair. 'Give me the open-channel command frequency.' He adjusted his uniform, smoothed his hair, and fixed a no-nonsense expression on his face. Ramirez moved herself out of the projection zone.

'Ready to go, Admiral.'

'This is Grid Zero Commander Admiral Lev Stromo, issuing an ultimatum to all Roamer personnel at Rendezvous. The Earth Defence Forces and the Terran Hanseatic League consider you hostiles. You have been declared a rogue government whose actions pose a clear and present danger to the human race. Your asteroid complex is now under the jurisdiction of the EDF. Surrender immediately. Any ships attempting to escape will be met with lethal force.'

A shocking flurry of insults and curses flew back at him from dozens of different ships. Stromo coughed in embarrassed surprise. The Roamers must all know what had happened at Hurricane Depot. Seeing so many heavy cruisers coming for Rendezvous, how could they not surrender? He'd expected terrified pleas or meek submission, not rudeness and disrespect.

He worked his jaw, but forced himself to take the high road, to be the proud military commander. 'Do not attempt to flee. Any ship defying this order will be destroyed. You have two hours to evacuate the Rendezvous facility and surrender to us. After that time, demolitions technicians will begin ultimate disassembly operations. Any Roamer casualties incurred will be strictly due to your failure to follow precise instructions.'

Ramirez added her own postscript to the transmission. 'The EDF guarantees that all detainees will be treated fairly. You will not be subjected to unnecessary harassment.'

'As if they'll believe that,' Stromo muttered.

Another barrage of blustering insults was transmitted back to him. In disgust, he gestured for the communications officer to cut off the audio. He scowled as the ships continued to fly away, despite his admonition. 'Doesn't that remind you of cockroaches scurrying when the lights are turned on, Commander Ramirez?'

The small vessels offered difficult moving targets that zigzagged between the outlying asteroids. Though the Mantas opened fire again, the weapons officers missed most of the time. *This crew definitely needs a lot more training*, the Admiral thought.

Too many of the unruly ships were getting away. Stromo shook his head, then nodded to the Manta's captain. 'Commander Ramirez, disperse all EDF ships, launch every Remora squadron. Let's tighten our net. Rendezvous is officially ours.'

ONE HUNDRED AND SIXTEEN

CESCA PERONI

Once she'd retired, Jhy Okiah had meant to live out the rest of her life on Rendezvous. Now Cesca was grabbing her stick-like arm. 'Hurry, we've got to evacuate. Don't bother taking any of those things. The Eddies wiped out Hurricane Depot – do you expect them to do less here?'

The old woman scowled, moving without urgency even as the EDF invaders encircled the asteroid cluster. Loud alarms sounded, and Roamers rushed down the tunnels, snatching up belongings and gathering family members. 'How dare they attack Rendezvous? We are an independent people, and this is our formal seat of government. Who does that blowhard Admiral think he is, issuing ultimatums?'

'He's following orders – the Chairman's orders.' Cesca once again regretted the ill-considered defiant stance the clan elders had chosen. 'Since they can't seem to defeat the hydrogues, they'll take us as a consolation prize. The Admiral will claim a full victory, and the Big Goose will say they've subjugated us, squelched all resistance.'

'That is why we need to resist.' Jhy Okiah seemed much older now.

'We can't resist unless we escape and survive. Look at the size of the Eddy battle group out there. We'll have to resist in our own fashion. After we get away.'

The old woman finally gave in, picked only a few of her most precious keepsakes, and followed Cesca out into the corridors. Everyone on Rendezvous had practised for this emergency at least a hundred times, and now Roamers scrambled in a barely organized panic towards the numerous launching bays. Every clan had a family ship for travel or cargo transport; they all had places where they could hide, far from Rendezvous.

Ship after ship flew away in outright defiance of the Admiral's instructions. Other clan members used their best piloting skills to zoom though the obstacle course of rocks and battleships. Though they took no aggressive action and posed no threat to the EDF fleet, a few Roamer ships were destroyed. Cesca felt each explosion or bright flash of debris on the monitor screens as a deep personal loss. Casualties of war – a war the Roamers had never wanted.

And none of them wanted to be captured. The Roamers knew nothing about what had happened to the prisoners taken at Hurricane Depot. It was possible they were being held on a penal planet or had been put to work as slaves in Hansa industries. They'd probably been interrogated first, forced to divulge the coordinates of Rendezvous. No one knew – or underestimated – what Chairman Wenceslas might be capable of.

The Governess compy UR, in charge of teaching Roamer children, had activated her emergency protective programming and hustled her students into evacuation vessels. But the vessels were personnel transports, not blockade runners or speedy craft. Cesca didn't think they could escape. Having seen the EDF open fire on the other fleeing vessels, the Speaker reached a difficult decision. 'UR, you must take the children and surrender.'

'I can attempt to fly the craft through the EDF weapons,' said the Governess compy, but Cesca shook her head.

'I'm not risking all those children. Be their guardian. Take them to the Eddies and keep them alive. I'm counting on you to make sure they're not mistreated.'

'I do not have the strength or combat programming of a Soldier compy, but those people will be sorry if they attempt to abuse my wards.'

'Good attitude, UR. Take them away. We'll do what we can to fix this mess. The Eddies haven't defeated us yet.'

Cesca and the old woman hurried to make their escape. Explosions rattled the main asteroid, and dust trickled down from gaps in the sealant on the walls and ceiling. Lights flashed and alarms sounded, and the Roamers understood what they must do.

Rendezvous was going to fall.

Cesca's last stop was the control centre, where Roamer administrators raced from console to console, triggering emergency programming, dispatching all ships. Long ago, wary Roamers had installed precautionary routines into their automated systems and individual compies for exactly such a situation. The locations of all Roamer settlements should have been a closely kept secret, and now the clans couldn't afford to let any other vital information escape.

'This is it!' Cesca raised her voice above the din in the control centre. No matter how firm she tried to be, her voice still wavered. 'Wipe everything. Trigger the cascade deletion. If the Eddies come to Rendezvous on a scavenger hunt, there'll only be junk left for them to salvage. Looks like we're never coming back here.'

The former Speaker clutched her arm, but said nothing. The old woman looked as if she'd been dealt a severe blow.

The technicians and administrators did not hesitate. They shouted to each other as one system after another after another went down. Sparks flew and screens went blank.

'The evacuation is nearly complete, Speaker Peroni,' said one of the techs.

'It's not complete until you all get out of here,' she told him, then grabbed Jhy Okiah's hand. 'We're on our way out ourselves.'

The last few people on Rendezvous made it to loading docks and climbed aboard any available ship. Cesca pushed Jhy Okiah into a small but fast diplomatic ship reserved for the Speaker's use. 'We'll have to follow our Guiding Star,' she said in a low voice. 'There's nothing else we can do.'

The old woman strapped herself in, familiar with the procedure. Her bones were fragile, but she moved with professional grace. She wouldn't complain. Outside, jazer blasts and explosive projectiles hammered the outlying asteroids. Heavy detonations rumbled through the wall of the main complex. When Cesca sealed the hatch, the droning alarms and loud background noises fell into merciful silence.

As they launched away from the majestic interconnected complex of structures, domes, and tunnel-laced rocks, Cesca knew they were leaving behind no valuable information about the Roamers, no maps or data or coordinates that could be used to hunt down the fleeing clans. At least some of the hidden outposts would be protected. The Eddies might try to search for information, steal a few possessions, scrounge any left-over ekti – but they would come home with a very scant haul for all their efforts.

That was a slim victory, however. Even without the tangible objects they were abandoning, Rendezvous was the heart of the Roamer people, their oldest settlement, a symbol of their victory over adversity. The jumble of asteroids and artificial structures demonstrated how the clans could take the toughest situation and turn it into a fighting chance.

Now they were leaving it all behind. Abandoning it to the enemy.

The EDF battleships closed in, still opening fire. They shot at everything, even rocks and debris.

Cesca flew away at breakneck speed, dodging, looping in an erratic course. Several jazer bolts flashed past, but she ducked through the scattered debris from a destroyed Roamer ship, random hull plates spinning and reflecting red sunlight. Cesca took the shortest line out, streaking between two Manta cruisers.

Admiral Stromo continued to articulate his apparently well-rehearsed words. 'King Peter, on behalf of the government of all humanity, requires the full cooperation and assistance of Roamer clans in prosecuting the war against the hydrogues. Your blatant refusal to comply constitutes demonstrable proof of your disloyalty to the human race. Henceforth, the Roamer people shall be considered outlaws.'

In the cockpit, Jhy Okiah turned to Cesca with a wry smile. 'There's something romantic about being an outlaw, don't you think?' Her oddly timed humour was born of desperation.

Behind them, at the precise moment when the deadline ran out, Admiral Stromo transmitted on all frequencies, 'No more sand left in the hourglass. Scouring crews, proceed with full-scale intelligence-gathering operations. Demolitions crews, wait for my signal.'

In less than an hour, the Eddy ships had rounded up groups of fleeing or surrendering Roamers, while the ransacking investigators and demolitions crews had determined that there was nothing of value left in the asteroid cluster. Admiral Stromo had clear orders about what he was supposed to accomplish, and he seemed to take great pleasure in utterly shocking all of his Roamer prisoners of war as well as the clan members who had managed to escape, yet remained within viewing range.

'By the authority of the Chairman of the Terran Hanseatic League and the King, I hereby order the destruction of this facility.' Then in a lower voice, as if grumbling to himself, he said, 'What a rat's nest!'

In a sudden, coordinated action, chained explosives implanted by the demolitions crews detonated and blasted apart key junctures. From high above, the Mantas and Juggernauts bombarded the asteroid cluster with a dazzling display of jazers and high-energy kinetic projectiles. The beams and explosives targeted the connective structures that held the drifting rocks together.

Cesca watched as the battleships pounded Rendezvous. Beside her, Jhy Okiah squeezed her eyes shut until tears trickled out, travelling the random paths of wrinkles on her face. The onslaught broke apart the asteroids and scattered the facilities, homes, storehouses, training centres . . . everything that had been important to Roamer culture and history.

Around them, the escaping clan ships flew in widely dispersed trajectories, spreading out to find any sanctuary in the vastness of the Spiral Arm. The Roamers knew hundreds of different hidden settlements, bases, facilities. They would fly to safe places, and eventually they would come together again.

Warm tears streamed down Cesca's cheeks as well. She blamed herself for underestimating the ruthlessness of Chairman Wenceslas. How had he found Rendezvous in the first place? 'As if any Roamer needed more reasons not to trust the Big Goose. . .'

'Let's get the hell out of here, Cesca,' Jhy Okiah said, her voice hoarse.

Cesca nodded, not trusting her own voice yet. She

programmed a course into the navigational computer and launched their ship far from the rubble that had been Rendezvous. 'We'll survive. When the sky is dark, our Guiding Stars shine brightest.'

The Roamers flew off, scattering to the four corners of the Galaxy.

ONE HUNDRED AND
SEVENTEEN

MAGE-IMPERATOR JORA'H

The new spate of hydrogue attacks and the Hyrillka Designate's open rebellion needed to be addressed without delay. Not even the Mage-Imperator could respond to everything at once. Most of all, he reeled from the assassination of Pery'h, and the nearly simultaneous attempt on his own life.

Through his frayed *thism*, Jora'h detected another emergency brewing on Maratha, but too few people were there for him to get a clear sense of what was happening, and his connection to his brother Avi'h had never been strong.

Yazra'h stood at his side, grimmer and more determined than ever before. Jora'h believed in her completely now more than ever, after seeing how single-mindedly she had defended him, without thought for her own life. Where the Hyrillkan attacker had slashed her arm, the finest medical kithmen had tended her wound and covered it with a photoactive healing plaster. Her Isix cats sat with shining, slitted eyes, as if eager for another taste of a traitor's blood.

Now, Adar Zan'nh and his repaired warliners raced back to

Ildira bearing the survivors from Hrel-oro. As soon as he reached the Prism Palace, the young Adar marched into the skysphere reception hall. Despite the disaster, Zan'nh's quick action and relentless work on the rescue operations had saved the lives of many who would otherwise have died.

The Mage-Imperator studied the Solar Navy commander's face and approved of his brave and determined expression, though he could sense that his son was shaken. 'Rusa'h has executed Pery'h,' Jora'h said from his chrysalis chair. 'He has killed the Designate-in-waiting!'

'What do you wish done, Liege?' Zan'nh remained formal, now fully in his role as Adar instead of grieving brother. He looked at his half-sister Yazra'h as she stood close to the chrysalis chair, nodded with approval. 'Shall I launch a reconnaissance team so that we can question the Hyrillka Designate and determine exactly what occurred?'

Jora'h felt a nova of anger burning at the core of his chest. 'We didn't get much information from interrogating the other Hyrillka pilgrims, but I know that my brother has turned against us. He ordered Pery'h's assassination. It was both deliberate and cold-blooded. I think Rusa'h . . . wanted to get my attention.' The Mage-Imperator looked towards the gathered bureaucrats and advisers.

'We will deal with it in whatever manner you command, Liege,' Zan'nh said.

The Mage-Imperator's braided hair twitched with anguish while he considered the options. He narrowed his star-sapphire eyes. For the time being, Jora'h had sent away all pilgrims and supplicants, allowing only those trusted advisers who could offer valid strategic advice.

As he thought, the words boiled out of him. 'Prime Designate Thor'h is cooperating with my brother in this rebellion. Some of you may make excuses for Rusa'h's behaviour. He was injured, he is no longer himself, his mind has not healed.' His fingers clenched around the smooth rim of his cradle-like chair, remembering all the impressions that had flooded into his mind. *'But he has murdered my son. And Thor'h let him do it!'*

The Mage-Imperator lowered his voice and looked from straight-backed Zan'nh to coiled and watchful Yazra'h. 'I have always had my doubts about Thor'h, but I had hoped he would grow into his responsibilities. Instead, he has turned against me, against all Ildirans. This crime cannot be ignored or excused.'

He drew a deep breath, and the words felt like dry stones in his mouth. 'Let all know that from this day forward, the murderer Rusa'h may no longer serve in any capacity as Designate. I also rescind Thor'h's appointment as Prime Designate.'

Even Yazra'h gasped at this declaration. The sound brought her Isix cats to their feet, and they scanned the room for intruders. Advisers murmured in surprise at the unprecedented announcement, but Jora'h had no choice. The Prime Designate had turned against him, could never be trusted as the next Mage-Imperator in waiting.

Yazra'h calmed her predatory felines. 'Father, the Empire cannot endure without a Prime Designate. You must choose—'

'I have already made my choice,' he said. 'It is only through a missed chance of genetics that Zan'nh – my true first-born son – was not slated to become Prime Designate. His service has been exemplary, and I have complete faith in him. I could not ask for a more worthy successor.' Zan'nh's eyes widened, and he opened his mouth to protest, but the Mage-Imperator continued. 'Therefore, until such time as this matter is resolved, until Thor'h is brought back here and faces me in the skysphere hall, Adar Zan'nh is the provisional Prime Designate.'

Zan'nh looked as amazed as all the listeners; he couldn't stop himself from swearing under his breath. *'Bekh!'*

Yazra'h looked over at him and offered a small smile of approval.

Jora'h heard the mutters of astonishment. He had already bent too many time-honoured protocols in the Ildiran Empire. He had dared to emerge from his chrysalis chair and set foot on the unhallowed floors. He had selected his own daughter to be his primary protector instead of a member of the warrior kith. And now he had appointed Zan'nh, not even a pure-bred noble, to be the next Prime Designate. How much more would the people tolerate?

Jora'h clenched his jaw. *As much as is necessary.*

He was the Mage-Imperator, and he must stand steady like an immovable rock rather than bend and blow in all directions like a blade of tall grass. His commands bound all of his race, except for those people who were blinded by Rusa'h's treacherous manipulations.

Jora'h reached out to clasp Zan'nh's forearm. 'Speak with me if you ever have qualms about taking over your role.'

'I am your Adar, Liege. I have no qualms.' The feeling Jora'h sensed underlying his son's stony confidence implied otherwise.

Jora'h smiled at him, not fooled. 'Yes, you do. But we can be stronger together.'

'I . . . will serve in whatever capacity the Mage-Imperator deems appropriate.' Zan'nh looked down at the polished stones on the floor. 'Until such time as order is restored.'

Jora'h felt a slight loosening of the tight responsibilities that clamped around his heart. 'Adar, your orders are to go to Hyrillka, seize Rusa'h and my duplicitous son Thor'h. Bring them back to the Prism Palace, where they will face the judgement of their Mage-Imperator. Take a full maniple of warliners so that the Hyrillkans do not resist.'

Ildiran against Ildiran. The advisers in the skysphere hall looked appalled and apprehensive. Their Mage-Imperator was sending a massive military force against his own brother, their own people. Such things simply did not happen in the Empire. Only once before in all the history chronicled in the *Saga of Seven Suns* had Ildirans faced a civil war, and the outcome had left a scar for centuries. Jora'h hoped he could resolve this problem in a less bloody fashion . . . but it did not appear likely.

The Adar clasped his hands to his heart in the traditional salute. 'Liege, even though Qul Fan'nh's maniple suffered losses during the recent battle at Hrel-oro, I believe his ships should accompany me to Hyrillka. The soldiers in that maniple are worthy, and I wish to reward their courage by showing my faith in them.'

Jora'h nodded, his heart warmed by the idea. 'Let it be done. You must depart with all due haste.' He lowered his voice, leaning closer. 'Others have been twisted by Rusa'h, and our danger grows worse day by day. This rebellion cannot be allowed to grow.'

Dismissed, Zan'nh marched off to do his duty.

Now the Ildiran leader also had to deal with the hydrogues. From Zan'nh's report of the Klikiss robot's grim statement in the wake of the attack on Hrel-oro, Jora'h knew he could no longer delay the inevitable. The solution, much as he dreaded it, was obvious.

Spurred to action by the changes and crises that faced him, the Mage-Imperator turned to his primary advisers. 'Lastly, send a message to the Dobro Designate. Tell him . . .' Jora'h paused, but the truth was unavoidable. 'Tell him the Klikiss robots have betrayed us. Instruct him to send Osira'h to me. She must be ready.'

ONE HUNDRED AND
EIGHTEEN

SULLIVAN GOLD

On Qronha 3, the Ildiran and human skyminers maintained their uneasy truce, but Sullivan Gold wanted to cement their ties. They were colleagues, after all, not competitors. They should help each other out. They had a common enemy and a common goal. There was no reason at all to be aloof. Lydia would have scolded him for not being a good neighbour, for not taking over a gift of food or inviting the Ildiran miners for drinks. But he doubted Hroa'x would be interested in socializing.

However, when Sullivan undertook a brash project that he thought the Ildiran skymine chief might find interesting, he decided to shuttle over to the big Ildiran skyfactory. It was the sort of thing good neighbours did, in a spirit of cooperation and mutual need. He approached unannounced, and the Ildirans did not receive him with any particular warmth, but at least they didn't warn him off. He usually handled this sort of situation with persistent friendliness.

Sullivan landed on one of the breezy decks high above the gas giant's clouds. Stepping out, he stared at the immense complex. The Ildirans did everything on an overblown scale, with bulky equipment and inefficient ekti reactors and ten times as many people as the work required. Ildiran personnel were everywhere – not just miners and reactor operators, but their families, support staff, maintenance technicians, and innumerable others. He would love to send a team over just to tinker with their machinery, pump it up a little, improve it . . . but he supposed that would be bad form.

By now his lead engineer, Tabitha Huck, had already launched her unmanned explorer drone; since it would take almost an hour to descend to the appropriate depth, he should have enough time to talk to the reticent Hroa'x.

Sullivan wandered around inside the huge skyfactory complex. Apparently Ildirans weren't overly concerned with external security; none of them paid him much attention, until he stopped one to ask for directions. It was a woman, bulky and broad-shouldered, her features just a bit too alien to be attractive to him. 'Please tell me how to find your chief skyminer Hroa'x. We're old friends.' She looked at Sullivan as if assessing whether to answer his question, then pointed up a steep metal stairwell.

Inside a humid and noisy chamber, Hroa'x was inspecting the pumps and compressors that throbbed like the slow heartbeat of a sleeping giant. The skyminer looked at his human counterpart. His eyes were heavy-lidded with lack of interest. 'I do not have time to give you a tour today, Sullivan Gold. Your business here will have to wait.'

Sullivan conjured up his best winning smile, which had never failed to tip negotiations in his favour. Though the chief skyminer had not raised his voice, Sullivan needed to shout above the din. 'Oh? Even if it's an emergency?'

'Is it?'

Sullivan shuffled his feet. 'Not really, but I'm sure it's something you'll want to see. Trust me!'

The small communicator at his hip chimed. 'We're in position, Sullivan,' Tabitha Huck said. 'Shouldn't be long until we close in on those anomalies.'

Sullivan gestured to his Ildiran counterpart. 'That's even faster than I expected. Come on, Hroa'x. I'll explain on the way up to your control centre.'

The Ildiran miner grudgingly led the way to a high tower nexus where dozens of Ildiran technicians and crewmembers operated monitors and the long, trailing sensor-whiskers of the big facility.

'After looking at the logs, we estimated the depth at which your Adar Kori'nh encountered the hydrogues. Considering that forty-nine warliners sacrificed themselves, we assumed there might still be some wreckage that had descended to an equilibrium depth in the vicinity. Our first wave of tiny scanners found several floating density anomalies, and so today my lead engineer sent down an unmanned explorer drone capable of providing real-time imagery.' His eyes sparkled. 'We might even be able to see the wrecked warglobes. Wouldn't that be something?'

Hroa'x turned to him. 'Why would you wish to do that? You are a skyminer, not a military officer or a rememberer.'

Sullivan worked with one of the Ildiran technicians to adjust their screens to the appropriate band. When they began to receive the explorer drone's signals, the screen showed only swirls of clouds and vapours, barely distinguishable from random static. 'Your military commander sacrificed himself and a lot of battleships to drive the hydrogues from Qronha 3. It was . . . an historically significant event. We can witness part of it here.'

'I am not a rememberer. It is not my task.'

'I don't think I've ever met anybody as single-minded as you.' Sullivan tried a different approach. 'On Earth, about five centuries ago, we built a fabulous luxury ship called the *Titanic*, which was considered the greatest cruise vessel of all time. But it sank in a supposedly unreachable portion of our oceans. Because the *Titanic* was such an intriguing icon, lots of explorers made risky descents into the depths just so they could see the wreck. The ship grew into a cultural fascination, and finally it became a memorial.'

The skyminer's expression did not change. 'I fail to see any relevance to our situation.'

Exasperated, Sullivan said, 'All those dead warglobes, and any Solar Navy ships we can find, are each like the *Titanic*. You defeated the aliens here on Qronha 3. Aren't you proud of that? Wouldn't your rememberers like to see what's left, if only to include it in the *Saga of Seven Suns*? Wouldn't your Adar Zan'nh be interested? It might score you some points with him.'

'I do not need to earn any advantage with the Adar.'

The screens flickered, and Sullivan saw a brief shape, a glint, and then a shadow. The explorer pod changed directions and moved in. 'We've got something, Sullivan,' Tabitha's voice came over his communicator.

He tapped an acknowledgement, still waiting for Hroa'x to understand what he was saying. 'Okay, I can see I'm not getting through. Look, we're doing this on our own initiative, Hroa'x. Our cloud harvester is operating at full capacity, and the crew doesn't have much to do except check the monitors and switch out ekti tanks when they're full. We planned this project in our spare time. It seemed like a good use of our off hours.'

'My crew can always find work to do,' Hroa'x said.

Sullivan couldn't conceive what all these Ildirans did to keep themselves busy. 'Ah yes, work expands to fill the number of people available.' He chuckled, but the chief skyminer found no humour in the comment. 'Look, there's no downside here. We aren't asking you to participate, so there's no risk or cost at all to you – but I intend to share with you all the images we take. Why not? We're good neighbours, and I thought the Ildiran Empire would find them useful. Any military information has ramifications for our skymining activities – for defence and preparation, if nothing else.'

Hroa'x finally gave a stiff nod, to indicate that this was an acceptable reason for the odd investigations.

On the screen, the perfectly geometrical shapes of two looming warglobes drifted into view as the explorer drone centred in. The immense spheres studded with triangular protrusions looked like electron micrographs of pollen spores. One sphere was cracked open from a giant explosion, no doubt the impact of a Solar Navy warliner; it hung dark and quiet, like an empty shell made of blackened diamond. The second warglobe appeared intact, but just as dead.

Seeing the awesome images, Hroa'x stiffened, finally impressed and uneasy. The Ildiran workers muttered both in fear and surprise.

'No energy sources detected, Sullivan,' Tabitha said. 'Those warglobes are at ambient temperature, not emanating in any frequency band.'

'Keep looking . . . but be careful.'

'I'm going inside the broken one,' Tabitha said. 'Yes, I'll do it carefully, Sullivan. Don't have a stroke.'

The view from the explorer drone swerved around as it approached the open wound in the dead hydrogue sphere.

'Exercise caution. *Extreme* caution.'

'I already promised you that. They're dead, Sullivan.'

Sullivan had been excited to see if he could find these wrecks, but now he didn't want to provoke any response. What if something had survived? Lydia would have scolded him for not letting sleeping dogs lie. Maybe this wasn't such a good idea after all.

The explorer drone cruised through the wide-open wreckage,

puttering along serpentine corridors and upside-down geometries, doors that were in the wrong places, cubes and pyramids connected with troughs that looked like circuit lines. It was all utterly incomprehensible to him.

'We're recording these images for our next dispatch back to the Hansa,' Tabitha said.

'Make sure the Ildirans have full access to this data as well.'

'I don't suppose they'll share the research expenses?' she said snidely, as if she had forgot Hroa'x and the others were listening.

'This is a gesture of our good faith. What helps us against the hydrogues helps everyone.'

'Whatever you say.'

As Tabitha took images for the better part of an hour, the wondrous strangeness built up to a surfeit of incomprehension. Hansa scientists and EDF experts would scrutinize every second of footage, but Sullivan couldn't stare for ever. Hroa'x already looked anxious to get back to the work routine that called him like an alcoholic's obsession for a drink.

Tabitha's explorer finally retreated, following her recorded path back out of the dark wreckage into open space, then began to cruise closer to the less-damaged hydrogue sphere. Its outer surface was stained, as if from a blast of heat, but the shell had not cracked or shattered.

'Hey, I've got an idea. I'm going to ping it with an active probe pulse. A lot of pieces inside might still be intact, and it'll be a valuable addition to our scans. So far, everything's been completely innocuous.'

'Don't press your luck, Tabitha. Passive observation is one thing, but I don't want to stir up—'

She had already sent out her signals, playing a deep scan over the outside of the dormant warglobe. A return spike suddenly and unexpectedly came across the broadband sensor channel. 'Whoa, that's quite a reflection!' Tabitha said. Then the signal came again, louder, and modulated twice. 'And . . . uh, that's not my probe pulse.'

A glimmer of light awakened like a tiny match being lit at the centre of the darkened warglobe. Sparkles shot like phosphorescent plankton through the shell, wavering in the depths.

'She has disturbed it,' Hroa'x said, his voice gruff. 'This is very ill-advised.'

'Enough, Tabitha! Cease your probe scans.' As the warglobe continued to brighten, Sullivan reached a decision. 'Trigger complete shutdown . . . uh, as quietly as possible. Get rid of the explorer drone before that drogue becomes aware of it. I don't want it tracking us back up here.'

'But we're still getting good telemetry. Don't you want to see what happens?'

'I'm already afraid of what happens. Trigger it, Tabitha. *Now*. Complete shutdown. Make it into a dead rock.'

There was a burst of light and then the screen images went blank.

'If the hydrogues are not truly vanquished here,' Hroa'x said, 'then they may return. That one surviving craft could summon other warglobes.'

'Sorry about that.' Sullivan slowly shook his head. 'Our work just got a hell of a lot more dangerous.'

The Ildiran skyminer turned to look at him. 'Perhaps you humans should abandon your cloud harvesting facility and go home.'

Sullivan's heart was still pounding with alarm. 'Are you going to leave?'

'I have a mission to complete. I will stay.'

'Then our facility stays, too.' Even so, he decided to tell his crew to keep their bags packed and their eyes open. 'We'll just be more careful from now on.'

'Caution may not be sufficient,' Hroa'x said.

'No, but it's better than giving up too soon.'

The miner kithman nodded, as if he finally could understand the human's attitude. 'Very well, Sullivan Gold. But if you will excuse me, I have significant work to accomplish, especially now that our time may be limited – thanks to you.'

ONE HUNDRED AND NINETEEN

KOTTO OKIAH

S ince GU was already scuffed and battered from his previous
escapade with the runaway hydrogue derelict, the research
compy offered to be the first one inside the open alien
sphere. GU considered himself a dedicated volunteer for the cause
of science.

Kotto was itching to get inside and could barely contain his
enthusiasm, but he knew it was wise to have one of the small robots
take the initial risk. 'All right, but be careful. And report whatever
you see. Don't touch anything, because I'll be there myself as soon
as you give it the thumbs up.'

Like a trooper, GU cycled through the shuttle's airlock. As
Kotto watched him cross the short distance of open space, he
wondered if he should have asked for one of Del Kellum's
reconditioned EDF Soldier compies instead. The military-style
robots were better equipped to face possible hazards inside the
enemy ship. But GU seemed to have acquired a sense of adventure,
and he deserved the first shot after what he'd been through.

'I have entered the ship, Kotto Okiah,' the compy transmitted.

'All the atmosphere appears to have vented. I see no additional sealed chambers. Everything is open.'

'Good to hear,' Kotto transmitted back. 'I don't want to open a door and get blasted with more high-pressure air.'

'That is no longer likely.'

Kotto was already pulling on his environment suit. As a Roamer, he had grown up slipping spacesuits on and off with the ease of habit, just as another man might pull on his socks. 'In your assessment, GU, are there any obvious hazards that would prevent my immediate entry into the derelict?'

'No, Kotto Okiah.'

He sealed his helmet and clicked it shut. 'I'm on my way.'

In the microgravity of space, Kotto was floating with giddiness. When his boot clomped down onto the transparent floor of the derelict, the sole did not adhere to the diamond. Normally, Roamer suits magnetically attached to their decks, but here there was no trace of iron impurities. Nevertheless, from long practice, Kotto was perfectly comfortable in weightless space.

GU's compy voice carried an unusual undertone of excitement. 'Please come here, Kotto Okiah. I have discovered something you will be interested in seeing.'

Kotto pushed himself along, using a tiny burst of propulsion gas when necessary. He stared at the curved bulkheads, geometrical protrusions, gem-like knobs and patterned circuits. Deep inside, the battered compy was standing with his back to the engineer, looking at a puddle of what appeared to be loose quicksilver on the floor. It was amorphous, a blob of gelatinized metal that had lost all physical integrity.

Kotto drew a quick breath as he realized what it was, remembering images of the liquid-crystal emissary that had come to the Whisper Palace on Earth and killed King Frederick. 'That's a hydrogue, GU! A genuine dead alien.'

'I am not qualified to make such projections, Kotto Okiah, but it is a reasonable assumption.'

Kotto didn't know what sort of information Roamer biologists would be able to glean from the shapeless puddle of hydrogue goo, but this was a monumental find. 'Good work, GU.'

'Thank you, Kotto Okiah. However, I called you in order to draw your attention to this.' The compy gestured to the wall beside him, which contained a completely flat and transparent trapezoid surrounded by strange symbols. 'I have compared it to my internal records of recent Hansa news releases about their colonization initiative. This technology and design appears remarkably similar to the Klikiss transportals.'

The Roamer engineer stared. 'Hydrogues using Klikiss gates? That's . . . impossible.'

'I defer to your expertise. I was merely making a comparison.'

Kotto spluttered. 'Oh, I didn't disagree, GU. In fact, I think you could be right. I've studied some of those records myself. But why would the Klikiss and the drogues use identical transportation technology? What possible connection could there be?'

'I cannot speculate, Kotto Okiah,' GU said.

'I didn't ask you to. I was just talking to myself.'

'Out of politeness, should I cease to listen?'

'Don't confuse me right now – I'm busy.' Kotto moved forward to study the transportal equivalent. The hydrogue gate wasn't perfectly trapezoidal, as he'd seen in the commonly available images of Klikiss ruins. Its sides were skewed, and the coordinate symbols were completely different, indicating a language unrelated to the hieroglyphics in the insectoid alien structures. Still, the similarities in the superficial design were striking.

Unfortunately, Kotto had no detailed information about the technological workings of the alien transportal doorways. If times had been different, without such tremendous friction between

Roamers and the Big Goose, Kotto would have offered to exchange data with Hansa scientists. Though he had never visited one of the Klikiss archaeological sites himself, as an engineer he had been fascinated by the various discoveries and had followed them all.

He had assumed all along that Earth researchers would love to get their hands on this intact derelict, and now there seemed to be even more reasons. Although they had fragments of wreckage scraped from the Theron forests, even the best Hansa engineers would get very little information from that burned flotsam.

This derelict, though, was a treasure-trove. And he had it all to himself.

Kotto would have to start from scratch, but he was up to the task.

ONE HUNDRED AND TWENTY

KING PETER

Within seconds of meeting the young Prince, Peter decided that Daniel was indeed a dislikable boy.

OX had given the King a map that guided him through the underground tunnels and halls to the hidden suite of chambers where the young man was held under pampered house arrest. Peter leaned casually against the door frame. 'So you're Prince Daniel?'

Wary and annoyed, the boy looked up and guiltily wiped sticky fingers on a fine bedspread. Peter wondered if the kid had managed to smuggle candy into his rooms, despite the Teacher compy's prohibition of treats except as rewards for good behaviour.

His face was plump with baby fat. 'Who are you?' Peter couldn't believe the Prince didn't recognize a face that was ubiquitous throughout the Hansa worlds. Then Daniel's blue eyes narrowed. 'Hey, you're the King! King Peter.' He frowned. 'You're not supposed to be here.'

Peter wondered if the boy's eyes were really blue, or if they had been artificially coloured like his own. 'Well, we have lots of things in common. Maybe I can give you some advice on being part of the royal family.'

'I've got all the advice I can stand.' Daniel fluffed up his pillow and plopped back on his bed. 'It's not as if a King does anything except smile and cut ribbons and hand out awards. Why should I have to go through so much boring instruction? I could do all of those things in my sleep. They should just leave me alone.'

'The Hansa will never leave you alone.' Peter stepped farther into the room. 'You're their prisoner.'

'I am not a prisoner – I'm a Prince!'

'Didn't they snatch you from your family? Didn't they take you away from your home?'

Daniel gave a snort. 'They rescued me from a miserable life with a bunch of losers. I had a stepfather who never paid any attention to me except when he wanted to beat me. My mother died a long time ago. I have an older sister, but she's just a slut, never concerned about anything but her boyfriends.'

Peter remembered his own family and their warm time together. He would have returned to that life in a minute, given the choice. 'How can you say that about your family?'

'I don't care about them. If they came here, I'd rub their faces in the fact that *I'm* living in the Whisper Palace. *I'm* now the Prince, and they're still . . . nothing.'

Peter found himself immediately angry with this young man. He was sickened by the very possibility that his beloved Estarra might have been forced to marry someone like Daniel. 'They're probably dead. The Hansa killed them to leave no loose ends for you.'

Daniel hesitated, but his shock was short-lived. 'Good riddance.'

Peter squeezed his eyes shut and in his mind saw a flash of his mother and brothers, incinerated in the explosion of their dwelling complex. Even his estranged father had also been murdered to remove any connection to the newly created royalty.

This was worse than he'd imagined. 'You're not fit to be a King,' Peter said in a low, cold voice. 'With an attitude like that, you barely qualify as a human being.'

'I'm going to take your place someday,' Daniel snapped. 'I know what the Hansa wants, and I know how much you've screwed up. I'm better qualified to be a Great King than you are.'

The King chose not to continue the unsettling conversation. 'That's enough, Daniel. You've shown me everything I needed to know.'

Peter turned around and left the Prince behind, still ranting. Daniel must never be allowed to become the King. At least that was something he and Basil Wenceslas could agree on.

That evening, after a long and tedious trade banquet during which he sat in formal clothes and smiled but said nothing, Queen Estarra appeared excited and secretive, though she would not explain why. Finally, saying she had a headache, she asked Peter to take her back to the royal wing. The King made appropriate excuses and farewells, bowed and waved. Chairman Wenceslas dismissed him, acknowledging that Peter had fulfilled his duties for the time being.

When they were in their private quarters, Estarra clung to him in a warm hug. Her brown eyes were awash with a mixture of tears and delight. Her expression was filled with love, as if she could no longer contain her news.

Peter laughed. He had never seen her act this way before. 'All right, Estarra – you look as if you're ready to explode. What is it you want to tell me?'

She smiled at him. 'I've found an unexpected way to get rid of your worries about Prince Daniel being an unworthy successor.'

Grinning because of her infectious good humour, he shook his head. 'What on Earth are you talking about?'

'Not even Chairman Wenceslas would have guessed this,' she said. 'I didn't expect it myself . . . it was an accident. But I'm *pregnant*, Peter. We're going to have our first child.'

ONE HUNDRED AND
TWENTY-ONE

CELLI

Though the endless work continued, a spark of hope and fascination grew within Celli. She returned day after day to the near-impenetrable thicket, threading her way through the deadfall until she reached the central clearing.

She kept the strangely growing man-shaped totem a secret, watching its features sharpen, the bark-skin thicken, the wood-grain eyes track her movements without focusing. Solimar often asked Celli to explain the secretive smiles and the unexpected energy she'd showed in recent days, but she wanted to wait until she had more answers. Even the green priests, with their special connection through telink, did not seem to know about it.

Intrigued by the changes she witnessed in the wooden shape every day, Celli paced around the lumpy, curved stump covered with plated bark scales. The ripples of twisted curves looked so much like human limbs and muscles. But this was more than a statue or a carving; it was alive, drawing energy through deep roots in the forest soil.

'I wish I knew what you are,' Celli said aloud.

The round knots that were its eyes moved. She could tell the thing was looking at her, though its detailed facial features were still covered with an outer, woody shell. The irises of the eyes had a whorled pattern like the rings of a tree.

All her life, Celli had heard green priests describe how the worldforest could see all of Theroc through a billion invisible eyes in its leaves. But this was different, an aspect intentionally grown and shaped to evoke *human* features and expressions. And it looked oddly familiar to her . . .

One afternoon, as Celli stood in the cool shadows, smelling the rich soil and the moist underbrush, she heard a loud *crack*. She rushed over to the man-shaped stump. There was a louder pop, and then a long snapping sound, as if bark was splitting. The outer covering had broken like an eggshell beginning to hatch.

She took two steps away, then curiosity forced her closer again.

The gold-scaled bark peeled apart to expose fresh pale wood beneath it. It was smooth and golden-grained . . . like skin. The large knotted branches began to stir and finally broke free, extending from the central torso-trunk like the arms of a newly awakened man stretching. From its curled, tucked-under position, the rounded lump of wood now lifted up and turned its face towards her, its features still covered with thick patches of bark.

The wooden arms reached up; at the ends, a set of thin branches reminiscent of fingers splayed outwards, flexing. As the living carving touched its face, the ends of the twigs broke off like old scabs, leaving only perfect fingers.

Speechless, Celli watched as the wooden hands fumblingly peeled away the remaining bark to expose a smooth brow, then a nose and an entire face. She recognized the features.

'Beneto?' Her voice was the barest whisper. It looked exactly like her brother who had died when the hydrogues destroyed the worldtree grove on Corvus Landing.

The legs of the tree-figure divided into two narrow trunks in the ground. The wooden Beneto strained, trying to lift the legs, and finally they broke free, disconnecting from the roots. The man-like sculpture took a single plodding step forward and stood, separate from the ground.

'Beneto . . . are you in there?' Celli said, her eyes sparkling, but she was afraid to come closer. She had heard old stories about human simulacrums made out of clay. What was the word? A golem! The worldforest had shaped and grown some sort of golem that looked exactly like her lost green priest brother.

The wooden figure took another tottering step forward, and stopped, bathed in a shaft of sunlight that shone through the interlocked branches overhead.

Celli hurried forward, forgetting her caution. She used her hands to brush away the flaking bark that still clung to the wooden man's chest like an old skin from a larva that had not completed its first molting. When she at last stared at the polished wood grain of the artificial man, she saw that the facial shape was indeed identical to Beneto's, though his body was smooth and streamlined, asexual and without blemishes.

'Oh, Beneto! Can you speak? Talk to me!'

The tree golem swivelled its head and looked at her with woodgrain eyes. It seemed to be struggling.

'Don't you remember me? I'm Celli, your little sister.'

Finally, the lips cracked open, as if the worldforest had just finished forming the Beneto golem's mouth. Inside, a perfect set of wood-chip teeth showed themselves as his hard lips formed a smile. It coughed, expanded its chest, then inhaled to fill the lung-like hollow spaces in its body core. A whistling sound came out, then a harsher noise. Finally, the sounds became words.

'Celli . . . of course.'

His speech had the familiar timbre of her brother's voice, but it also had a hollow, echoing quality that reminded her of one of the woodwind flutes her grandparents made for small children.

'Celli. I remembered you every day . . . as I grew. I watched each time you came to visit.'

'Is that . . . really you, Beneto? Or does it just look like you? All the green priests said that you died when the hydrogues attacked. Everyone on Corvus Landing was wiped out.'

The wooden man looked at her, and his expression became troubled. 'The worldforest fashioned me. At the moment of my death, I was connected to the trees. I poured my every thought, my every memory, through telink into the worldforest. It was as if I stored my . . . soul there within the great mind of the trees. And now the forest has brought me back. I am a living synthesis, halfway between tree and man. I am . . . needed for the war.'

Celli threw her arms around him, feeling the solidity of wood, but also a warmth and glow that reminded her of living human flesh. 'Whatever you are, I'm glad you're here. It's better than having no brother at all. Do you . . . do you know that Reynald was also killed?'

'The worldforest cannot forget a moment of the attack on Theroc,' the Beneto golem said. 'We felt every single death, whether of tree or of man or woman. Even those who weren't green priests . . . still, we saw them, we witnessed their pain, mourned them. We remember.'

Celli took his wooden hand and pulled him to the edge of the thicket. 'I have to show you to our parents. Sarein has come back too, from Earth. Everyone will be so glad to see you.'

Beneto grew steadier on his feet as he took one step after another. Now the fallen branches in the collapsed barricade sprang out of their way, as if the wooden golem himself exerted a kind of force to clear a path. Celli bounded ahead, skipping and excited, urging him to hurry.

When they finally emerged from the dense thicket into the open clearings of the worldforest, Beneto came to a halt as if his feet had taken root. He swayed in place, drinking in the details of the devastation with eyes that were close to human. The wood-grain whorls of his irises shifted as his facsimile pupils widened, even though as part of the worldforest he intimately knew exactly what had happened. His expression sagged into a deep sadness. 'I have returned not a moment too soon.'

Celli stopped beside him and held his hand. He flexed his wooden fingers, as if trying to feel her touch, and she tugged on his wooden arm again to urge him along. 'Come on, Beneto. We have to tell everybody. It's about time the Therons have some good news.'

'Yes,' Beneto said, lifting his foot to take another step, as if he had forgot how to walk on human legs. 'I have much information to share. Even the green priests have not learned everything from the forest.'

Celli looked questioningly at her brother's wooden but familiar face. Beneto seemed to be marshalling his thoughts, gathering his echoes of memory. Proud and strong beside him, Celli led her brother towards the settled areas, where the toppled trees had been dragged away and the ground cleared by the Roamer helpers.

As the two of them approached the fungus-reef city, the trees seemed to whisper an announcement of their arrival. Green priests looked up from their labours. Their emerald skin was covered with ash, their expressions weary, their eyes reddened from tears and dust. But they could feel a thrumming through the worldforest mind, and when they saw the golem of Beneto, they stared.

Mother Alexa and Father Idriss climbed down from the fungus reef. When they saw Beneto and recognized the features carved and grown into the smooth, polished wood of his face, their thrilled and happy expressions looked awkward on their faces, as if they had forgot how to feel joy.

Celli bounded forward. 'Look what I found! See what the worldforest has created.'

Idriss reached the ground first, then turned to help his wife, though he couldn't tear his gaze from the strange visitor as many Therons parted to allow them a clear passage. 'My daughter? What is this? It looks like. . .' Idriss couldn't seem to say the name.

'Yes,' the golem said. 'I am Beneto . . . in part.'

Their parents had never pretended to understand the mysteries of the universe. Alexa and Idriss accepted his return with a sense of wonder and without an avalanche of questions.

The Theron people came forward cautiously. They had no fear of the facsimile of Beneto, despite his unnatural appearance. Celli beamed, and all the others fell into a hush as he lifted his head and began to speak. 'I am . . . a gift from the worldforest. Call me a messenger if you like.'

'Well, I would rather call you my son Beneto,' said Idriss. Alexa touched his arm to keep him quiet while the wooden man talked.

'I am that, and more,' he said. 'I have come here to help.' Beneto turned slowly to look at all the amazed people. The restless worldforest stilled itself so that everyone could hear his voice, loud and strong

'This is the beginning of a new phase in our war against the ancient enemy, the hydrogues.'

A Note on Ildiran Kiths

The Ildiran species is polymorphic. Different kiths have attributes and abilities that place them into appropriate castes on the Ildiran landscape and also on other planets within the Ildiran Empire. Thinkers love being thinkers, workers love being workers.

Kiths occasionally interbreed, sometimes out of love and attraction, other times as a conscious effort to enhance certain attributes (i.e., swimmers, scalies, fighters). In their culture, mongrels are rare but not completely uncommon. It often turns out that the best singers and poets and artists are half-breeds, thus implying a genetic strength that the pure-bred castes do not have.

Each kith ends its name with a particular phonetic sound, and crossbreeds combine the sounds:

'h   rulers/nobles
'n   soldiers, warriors, guards
'nh military leaders/generals
'k   workers
'v   bureaucrats

't	singers
'l	lens kithmen
'f	scientists
'o	technicians
'of	engineers
'a	teachers
'th	artists
'sh	rememberers
'x	miners

Despite their kith variations, though, the Ildirans are a very homogeneous society, all under their Mage-Imperator.

THE HALF-BREED CHILDREN
OF NIRA KHALI

Osira'h
(female, father = Jora'h)

Rod'h
(male, father = Udru'h)

Gale'nh
(male, father = Adar Kori'nh)

Tamo'l
(female, father = lens kithman)

Muree'n
(female, father = guard kithman)

A Note on Ildiran Units
of Time

Since Ildirans evolved on a planet of constant sunlight, naturally their race does not measure time in segregated units we know as the 'day', 'week' (the length of a phase of the Moon), and 'month' (based on the lunar cycle). However, the Empire uses time units of generally similar lengths.

For the convenience of the reader, rather than inundating the text with numerous alien-sounding words, I have used the rough equivalent in Trade Standard. Bear in mind that when an Ildiran speaks of a 'day', he means the generally accepted length of a waking-sleeping cycle, and not specifically twenty-four hours.

GLOSSARY

ADAR – highest military rank in Ildiran Solar Navy.

AGUERRA, RAYMOND – streetwise young man from Earth, former identity of King Peter.

ALEXA, MOTHER – ruler of Theroc, wife of Father Idriss.

ALADDIA – transportal technician on Rheindic Co.

ANDEZ, SHELIA – EDF soldier, held captive by Roamers at Osquivel shipyards.

AQUARIUS – wental-distribution ship flown by Nikko Chan Tylar.

ARCAS – green priest, part of Colicos team on Rheindic Co, murdered by Klikiss robots.

ARCHFATHER – symbolic head of Unison religion on Earth.

ATTENDERS – diminutive personal assistants to the Mage-Imperator.

AVI'H – Maratha Designate, youngest son of Mage-Imperator Cyroc'h.

BEBOB – Rlinda Kett's pet name for Branson Roberts.

BEKH! – Ildiran curse, 'Damn!'

BENETO – green priest, second son of Father Idriss and Mother

Alexa, killed by hydrogues on Corvus Landing.

BHALI'V – bureaucrat kithman, assistant to Maratha Designate Avi'h.

BIG GOOSE – Roamer derogative term for Terran Hanseatic League

BLAZER – Ildiran illumination source.

BLIND FAITH – Branson Roberts's ship.

BLITZKRIEG SCOOPS – fast commando harvesters used by Roamers during hydrogue embargo.

BLUE SKY MINE – skymine facility at Golgen, operated by Ross Tamblyn, destroyed by hydrogues.

BOONE'S CROSSING – Hansa colony world known for its black pine forests, now devastated by hydrogues.

BRINDLE, ROBB – young EDF recruit, comrade of Tasia Tamblyn, vanished after attempting to contact hydrogues on Osquivel.

BRON'N – bodyguard of Mage-Imperator Cyroc'h, committed suicide after his leader poisoned himself.

BURTON – One of the eleven generation ships from Earth, fourth to depart. Lost en route, captured by Ildirans for Dobro breeding experiments.

CAILLIE – One of the eleven generation ships from Earth, fifth to depart and first to be encountered by the Ildirans. Colonists from the *Caillié* were taken to settle Theroc.

CAIN, ELDRED – deputy and heir-apparent of Basil Wenceslas, pale-skinned and hairless, an art collector.

CANNONS OF DARKNESS – geysers on Maratha, active during the cooling-off weeks of the long twilight.

CARBON SLAMMER – new-design EDF weapon, effective at breaking carbon-carbon bonds.

CARGO ESCORT – Roamer vessel used to deliver ekti shipments from skymines.

CELLI – youngest daughter of Father Idriss and Mother Alexa.

CHEN – Roamer clan.

CHRYSALIS CHAIR – reclining throne of the Mage-Imperator.

CITYSHIP – giant hydrogue metropolis.

CITYSPHERE – enormous hydrogue habitation complex.

CLARIN, ELDON – Roamer inventor, brother of Roberto, killed when hydrogues destroyed the skymine at Erphano.

CLARIN, ROBERTO – administrator of Hurricane Depot, brother of Eldon.

CLOUD HARVESTER – ekti-gathering facility designed by Hansa, also called a cloud mine.

CLYDIA – one of the nineteen green priest volunteers aboard EDF ships.

COHORT – battle group of Ildiran Solar Navy consisting of seven maniples, or 343 ships.

COLICOS, ANTON – the son of Margaret and Louis Colicos, translator and student of epic stories, sent to Ildiran Empire to study the *Saga of Seven Suns*.

COLICOS, LOUIS – xeno-archaeologist, husband of Margaret Colicos, specializing in ancient Klikiss artifacts, killed by Klikiss robots at Rheindic Co.

COLICOS, MARGARET – xeno-archaeologist, wife of Louis Colicos, specializing in ancient Klikiss artifacts, vanished through transportal during Klikiss robot attack on Rheindic Co.

COMPETENT COMPUTERIZED COMPANION – intelligent servant robot, called compy, available in Friendly, Teacher, Governess, Listener, and other models.

COMPY – shortened term for 'Competent Computerized Companion'.

CONDORFLY – colourful flying insect on Theroc like a giant butterfly, sometimes kept as pets.

CORRIBUS – ancient Klikiss world, where Margaret and Louis Colicos discovered the Klikiss Torch technology, site of one of the first new Hansa colonies.

CORVUS LANDING – Hansa colony world, mainly agricultural, some mining, obliterated by hydrogues.

COUARNIR – star system, location of Hurricane Depot.

COVITZ, JAN – Dremen mushroom farmer, participant in transportal colonization initiative, father of Orli.

COVITZ, ORLI – Dremen colonist, joined transportal colonization initiative with her father Jan.

CRENNA – former Ildiran splinter colony, evacuated due to plague, and resettled by humans. Home of Davlin Lotze and Branson Roberts.

CYROC'H – former Mage-Imperator, father of Jora'h.

DAME BATTLEAXE – nickname for former Hansa Chairman Maureen Fitzpatrick.

DANIEL – new Prince candidate selected by the Hansa as a potential replacement for Peter.

DARO'H – the Dobro Designate-in-waiting after the death of Mage-Imperator Cyroc'h.

DD – compy servant assigned to Rheindic Co xeno-archaeology dig, captured by Klikiss robots.

DEKYK – Klikiss robot at Rheindic Co xeno-archaeology dig.

DESIGNATE – any pure-bred noble son of the Mage-Imperator; ruler of an Ildiran world.

DESIGNATE-IN-WAITING – one of the next group of Designates, sons of the Prime Designate who will replace their uncles, the sons of the previous Mage-Imperator.

DIAMONDFILM – crystalline parchment used for Ildiran documents.

DOBRO – Ildiran colony world, site of human-Ildiran breeding camps.

DREMEN – Terran colony world, dim and cloudy; chief products are saltpond caviar and genetically enhanced mushrooms.

DROGUE – deprecatory term for hydrogues.

DULARIX – uninhabited world in Ildiran space, site of inexplicable hydrogue attack.

EA – Tasia Tamblyn's personal compy; her memory was wiped when she was interrogated by Basil Wenceslas.

EARTH DEFENCE FORCES – Terran space military, headquartered on Mars but with jurisdiction throughout the Terran Hanseatic League.

EDF – Earth Defence Forces.

EDDIES – slang term for soldiers in EDF

EKTI – exotic allotrope of hydrogen used to fuel Ildiran stardrives.

ELWICH, PRIVATE – EDF cadet, one of Tasia Tamblyn's trainees on Mars.

ERPHANO – gas-giant planet, site of Berndt Okiah's skymine.

ESTARRA – second daughter, fourth child of Father Idriss and Mother Alexa. Current Queen of Terran Hanseatic League, married to King Peter.

FAEROS – sentient fire entities dwelling within stars.

FAN'NH – qul in Ildiran Solar Navy, in charge of the maniple facing hydrogues at Hrel-oro.

FEATHERHUM – Ildiran flying creature, similar to an Earth hummingbird.

FILTERFILM – protective eye covering used by Ildirans.

FITZPATRICK, MAUREEN – former Chairman of the Terran Hanseatic League, grandmother of Patrick Fitzpatrick III.

FITZPATRICK, PATRICK, III – spoiled cadet in the Earth Defence Forces, General Lanyan's protégé, presumed dead after Osquivel but captured by Roamers in Del Kellum's shipyards.

FLUTEWOOD TREES – multi-branched growths on Crenna with hard bark and holes that make whistling sounds in the wind.

FRACTURE-PULSE DRONE – new-design EDF weapon, also called a 'frak'.

FRAK – slang term for fracture-pulse drone.

FREDERICK, KING – previous figurehead ruler of the Terran Hanseatic League, assassinated by hydrogue emissary.

FUNGUS-REEF – giant worldtree growth on Theroc, carved into a habitation by the Therons.

FURRY CRICKET – innocuous furry rodent found on Corribus.

GALE'NH – experimental half-breed son of Nira Khali and Adar Kori'nh, third oldest of her children.

GLIDERBIKES – flying contraptions assembled from scavenged engines and framework materials, augmented by colourful condorfly wings.

GOLD, SULLIVAN – administrator of the Hansa's new modular cloud harvester installed at Qronha 3.

GOLGEN – gas giant where Ross Tamblyn's Blue Sky Mine was destroyed; also, bombarded by comets targeted by Jess Tamblyn.

GOMEZ, CHARLES – human prisoner of the hydrogues, seized at Boone's Crossing.

GOOSE – Roamer derogative term for Terran Hanseatic Team

GOSWELL, BERTRAM – early Chairman of the Terran Hanseatic League, originally tried to force Roamers to sign Hansa Charter.

GRAPPLER POD – small work vehicle used in shipyards of Osquivel.

GREAT KING – figurehead leader of Terran Hanseatic League.

GREEN PRIEST – servant of the worldforest, able to use worldtrees for instantaneous communication.

GU – Analytical compy assigned to work with Kotto Okiah.

GUIDING STAR – Roamer philosophy and religion, a guiding force in a person's life.

HANDLERS – Ildiran kith, handlers of the dead.

HANSA – Terran Hanseatic League

HANSA HEADQUARTERS – pyramidal building near the Whisper Palace on Earth.

HEALD – star system in the Ildiran Empire, site of a famous 'ghost story' in the *Saga of Seven Suns*; two inhabited planets consolidated into a single splinter colony for defence against the hydrogues.

HORIZON CLUSTER – large star cluster near Ildira, location of Hyrillka and many other splinter colonies.

HOSAKI – Roamer clan.

HOSAKI, ALFRED – Roamer clan leader.

HREL-ORO – arid Ildiran mining colony, inhabited primarily by scaly kithmen.

HROA'X – chief skymining engineer of Ildiran skyfactory on Qronha 3.

HUCK, TABITHA – engineer aboard Sullivan Gold's cloud harvester at Qronha 3.

HURRICANE DEPOT – Roamer commercial centre and fuel-transfer station, located in a gravitationally stable point between two close-orbiting asteroids.

HYDROGUES – alien race living at cores of gas-giant planets.

HYRILLKA – Ildiran colony in Horizon Cluster, original discovery site of Klikiss robots, main source of the drug shiing.

IDRISS, FATHER – ruler of Theroc, husband of Mother Alexa.

ILDIRA – home planet of the Ildiran Empire, under the light of seven suns.

ILDIRAN EMPIRE – large alien empire, the only other major civilization in the Spiral Arm.

ILDIRAN SOLAR NAVY – space military fleet of the Ildiran Empire.

ILDIRANS – humanoid alien race with many different breeds, or kiths.

ILURE'L – Ildiran lens kithman, part of the skeleton crew remaining in Maratha Prime.

ISIX CATS – sleek feline predators native to Ildira; Jora'h's daughter Yazra'h keeps three of them.

ISPEROS – hot planet, site of Kotto Okiah's failed test colony.

JAZER – energy weapon used by Earth Defence Forces.

JORA'H – new Mage-Imperator of the Ildiran Empire.

JORAX – Klikiss robot dismantled by Hansa scientists to study its programming and systems.

JUGGERNAUT – large battleship class in Earth Defence Forces.

JUPITER – enhanced Juggernaut battleship in EDF, flagship of Admiral Willis's Grid 7 battle group.

KAMAROV, RAVEN – Roamer cargo-ship captain, destroyed with his cargo ship on secret EDF raid.

KANAKA – One of the eleven generation ships from Earth, last to depart. These colonists became the Roamers.

KARI – young friend of Celli's, killed during hydrogue attack on Theroc.

KELLUM, DEL – Roamer clan leader, in charge of Osquivel shipyards.

KELLUM, ZHETT – eighteen-year-old daughter of Del Kellum.

KETT, RLINDA – merchant woman, captain of the *Voracious Curiosity*

KHALI – Nira's family name.

KHALI, NIRA – green priest female, Prime Designate Jora'h's lover and mother of his half-breed daughter, Osira'h. Held captive in breeding camps on Dobro.

KITH – a breed of Ildiran.

KLEEB – derogatory term for an EDF cadet.

KLIKISS – ancient insect-like race, long vanished from the Spiral Arm, leaving only their empty cities.

KLIKISS ROBOTS – intelligent beetle-like robots built by the Klikiss race.

KLIKISS TORCH – a weapon/mechanism developed by the ancient Klikiss race to implode gas-giant planets and create new stars.

KOLKER – green priest, friend of Yarrod, stationed on Sullivan Gold's modular cloud harvester at Qronha 3.

KORI'NH, ADAR – leader of the Ildiran Solar Navy, killed in suicidal assault against hydrogues on Qronha 3.

KR – Analytical compy assigned to work with Kotto Okiah.

LANYAN, GENERAL KURT – commander of Earth Defence Forces.

LENS KITHMEN – philosopher priests who help to guide troubled Ildirans, interpreting faint guidance from the *thism*.

LIA – former ruler of Theroc, Estarra's grandmother.

LICA – young friend of Celli's, killed during hydrogue attack on Theroc.

LIFETUBE – small emergency evacuation device stored aboard EDF battleships.

LIGHTSOURCE – the Ildiran version of Heaven, a realm on a higher plane composed entirely of light. Ildirans believe that faint trickles of this light break through into our universe and are channelled through the Mage-Imperator and distributed across their race through the *thism*.

LILOA'H – Ildiran noble female, Jora'h's first lover.

LOOKING GLASS LAKES – group of deep, round lakes on Theroc, site of a tree village obliterated in hydrogue attack.

LOTZE, DAVLIN – Hansa exosociologist and spy on Crenna, sent to Rheindic Co where he discovered how to use the Klikiss transportal system.

LUCY – young girl, friend of Orli Covitz on Corribus.

MAE, TERENE – EDF ensign, assigned to Tasia Tamblyn's Manta cruiser.

MAGE-IMPERATOR – the god-emperor of the Ildiran Empire.

MANIPLE – battle group of Ildiran Solar Navy consisting of seven septas, or forty-nine ships.

MANTA – mid-sized cruiser class in EDF.

MARATHA – Ildiran resort world with extremely long day and night cycle.

MARATHA PRIME – primary domed city on one continent of Maratha.

MARATHA SECDA – sister-city on opposite side of Maratha from Prime, currently under construction by Klikiss robots.

MAYLOR, FRED – Roamer clan leader.

MEYER – red dwarf sun, location of Rendezvous.

MHAS'K – male Ildiran agricultural kithman, part of the skeleton crew on Maratha, mated to Syl'k.

MIJISTRA – glorious capital city of the Ildiran Empire.

MOUTH OF SPACE – dark nebula, inhabited by Shana Rei, according to *Saga of Seven Suns*.

MUREE'N – experimental half-breed daughter of Nira Khali and a guard kithman, youngest of her children.

NAHTON – court green priest on Earth, serves King Peter.

NEBULA SKIMMERS – giant sails used to scoop hydrogen from nebula clouds.

NEW PORTUGAL – Hansa outpost with EDF facilities, colony known for distilleries and wineries.

NIALIA – plantmoth grown on Hyrillka, source of shiing.

NIRA – Nira Khali.

NUR'OF – lead engineer, part of the skeleton crew remaining in Maratha Prime.

ONCIER – gas-giant planet, original test site of the Klikiss Torch.

OKIAH, BERNDT – Jhy Okiah's grandson, chief of Erphano skymine, killed by hydrogues.

OKIAH, JHY – Roamer woman, very old, former Speaker of the clans.

OKIAH, KOTTO – Jhy Okiah's youngest son, a brash and eccentric inventor who designed Isperos colony.

ORANGE SPOT – plague affecting human colonists on Crenna.

OSIRA'H – daughter of Nira Khali and Jora'h, has unusual telepathic abilities due to her breeding.

QRONHA – a close binary system, two of the Ildiran 'seven suns'. Contains two habitable planets and one gas giant, Qronha 3.

QUL – Ildiran military rank, commander of a maniple, or forty-nine ships.

RAMAH – Terran colony world, settled mainly by Islamic pilgrims, site of a former uprising against the Hansa, which was quelled by Lev Stromo.

RAMIREZ, ELLY – navigator aboard Tasia Tamblyn's Manta.

RAMMER – kamikaze EDF ship designed to be crewed by Soldier compies.

REFO, JENNA – transportal explorer, lost in one of her searches.

RELLEKER – Terran colony world, popular as a resort.

REMEMBERER – member of the Ildiran storyteller kith.

REMORA – small attack ship in Earth Defence Forces.

REN – young friend of Celli's, killed during hydrogue attack on Theroc.

RENDEZVOUS – inhabited asteroid cluster, hidden centre of Roamer government.

REYNALD – eldest son of Father Idriss and Mother Alexa, killed in hydrogue attack on Theroc.

RHEINDIC CO – abandoned Klikiss world, site of major excavation by the Colicos team.

RHE'NH – Septar in the Ildiran Solar Navy.

ROACHERS – derogatory term for Roamers.

ROAMERS – loose confederation of independent humans, primary producers of ekti stardrive fuel.

ROBERTS, BRANSON – former husband and business partner of Rlinda Kett, also called BeBob.

ROD'H – experimental half-breed son of Nira Khali and the Dobro Designate, second oldest of her children.

ROSSIA – eccentric green priest serving in the EDF, survivor of a wyvern attack.

ROYAL CANAL – ornamental canal surrounding Whisper Palace.

RUIS, LUPE – mayor of Crenna colony settlement.

RUSA'H – Hyrillka Designate, third noble-born son of the Mage-Imperator.

SAGA OF SEVEN SUNS – historical and legendary epic of the Ildiran civilization.

SALTPOND CAVIAR – luxury food from Dremen.

SAREIN – eldest daughter of Father Idriss and Mother Alexa, Theron ambassador to Earth, also Basil Wenceslas's lover.

SCALY – Ildiran kith, desert dwellers.

SEPTA – small battle group of seven ships in the Ildiran Solar Navy.

SEPTAR – commander of a septa.

SHANA REI – legendary 'creatures of darkness' in *Saga of Seven Suns*.

SHIING – stimulant drug made from nialia plantmoths on Hyrillka, dulls Ildiran receptivity to the *thism*.

SHIZZ – Roamer expletive.

SILVER BERET – sophisticated special forces trained by EDF.

SIRIX – Klikiss robot at Rheindic Co xeno-archaeology dig, leader of robotic revolt against humans, captor of DD.

SKYFACTORY – very large ekti-harvesting facility run by Ildirans.

SKYMINE – ekti-harvesting facility in gas giant clouds, usually operated by Roamers.

SKYSPHERE – main dome of the Ildiran Prism Palace. The skysphere holds exotic plants, insects, and birds, all suspended over the Mage-Imperator's throne room.

SOLIMAR – young green priest, treedancer and mechanic; he rescued Celli from a burning tree during the hydrogue attack on Theroc.

SORENGAARD, RAND – renegade Roamer pirate, executed by General Lanyan.

SOUL-THREADS – connections of *thism* that trickle through from the Lightsource. The mage-Imperator and lens kithmen are able to see them.

SPAMPAX – processed meat rations, designed to last for centuries.

SPEAKER – political leader of the Roamers.

SPIRAL ARM – the section of the Milky Way Galaxy settled by the Ildiran Empire and Terran colonies.

SPLINTER COLONY – an Ildiran colony that meets minimum population requirements.

STANNA, BILL – EDF soldier, held captive by Roamers at Osquivel shipyards.

STANNIS, MALCOLM – early Chairman of the Terran Hanseatic League, served in the reigns of King Ben and King George, during Earth's first contact with the Ildiran Empire.

STEINMAN, HUD – old transportal explorer, discovered Corribus on transportal network and decided to settle there.

STONER, BENN – male prisoner on Dobro.

STROMO, ADMIRAL LEV – Admiral in Earth Defence Forces, derisively called 'Stay-at-home Stromo' after he was defeated by hydrogues at Jupiter.

SUB-*THISM* SLEEP – Ildiran coma.

SWEENEY, DAHLIA – DD's first owner, a young girl.

SWENDSEN, LARS RURIK – engineering specialist, adviser to King Peter, one of the dissectors of Klikiss robot Jorax.

SWIMMER – Ildiran kith, water dwellers.

SYL'K – female Ildiran agricultural kithman, part of the skeleton crew on Maratha, mated to Mhas'k.

TAL – military rank in Ildiran Solar Navy, cohort commander.

TAMBLYN, BRAM – former scion of Tamblyn clan, father of Ross, Jess, and Tasia, died after his son Ross perished on the Blue Sky Mine.

TAMBLYN, JESS – Roamer, second son of Bram Tamblyn, in love

with Cesca Peroni, infused with wental energy.

TAMBLYN, KARLA – Jess's mother, frozen to death in ice accident on Plumas.

TAMBLYN, ROSS – estranged oldest son of Bram Tamblyn, chief of Blue Sky Mine at Golgen, killed in first hydrogue attack.

TAMBLYN, TASIA – Jess Tamblyn's sister, currently serving in the EDF.

TAMBLYN, TORIN – one of Jess's uncles, brother to Bram.

TAMBLYN, WYNN – one of Jess's uncles, brother to Bram.

TAMO'L – experimental half-breed daughter of Nira Khali and a lens kithman, second youngest of her children.

TELA – young girl, friend of Orli Covitz on Corribus.

TELINK – instantaneous communication used by green priests.

TELTON, ANJEA – human prisoner of the hydrogues.

TERRAN HANSEATIC LEAGUE – commerce-based government of Earth and Terran colonies.

THEROC – forested planet, home of the sentient worldtrees.

THERON – a native of Theroc.

THISM – faint racial telepathic link from Mage-Imperator to the Ildiran people.

THOR'H – eldest noble-born son of Mage-Imperator Jora'h, the current Prime Designate.

THRONE HALL – the King's main receiving room in the Whisper Palace on Earth.

THUNDERHEAD – mobile weapons platform in Earth Defence Forces.

TRANSGATE – hydrogue point-to-point transportation system.

TRANSPORTAL – Klikiss instantaneous transportation system.

TREEDANCERS – acrobatic performers in the Theron forests.

TREELING – a small worldtree sapling, often transported in an ornate pot.

TYLAR, CRIM – Roamer skyminer on Ptoro, father of Nikko.

TYLAR, MARLA CHAN – Roamer greenhouse engineer, mother of Nikko.

TYLAR, NIKKO CHAN – young Roamer pilot, son of Crim and Marla.

UDRU'H – Dobro Designate, second-born noble son of the Mage-Imperator.

UNISON – standardized government-sponsored religion for official activities on Earth.

UR – Roamer compy, Governess-model at Rendezvous.

VAO'SH – Ildiran rememberer, patron and friend of Anton Colicos, part of the skeleton crew remaining in Maratha Prime.

VERDANI – organic-based sentience, manifested as the Theron worldforest.

VIK'K – Ildiran digger, part of the skeleton crew remaining in Maratha Prime.

VORACIOUS CURIOSITY – Rlinda Kett's merchant ship.

WARGLOBE – hydrogue spherical attack vessel.

WARLINER – largest class of Ildiran battleship

WELYR – gas giant, site of a Roamer skymine destroyed by hydrogues.

WENCESLAS, BASIL – Chairman of the Terran Hanseatic League.

WENTALS – sentient water-based creatures.

WHISPER PALACE – magnificent seat of the Hansa government.

WILLIS, ADMIRAL SHEILA – commander of Grid 7 EDF battle group, Tasia Tamblyn's commanding officer.

WORLDFOREST – the interconnected, semi-sentient forest based on Theroc.

WORLDTREE – a separate tree in the interconnected, semi-sentient forest based on Theroc.

WORM HIVE – large nest built by hive worms on Theroc, spacious enough to be used for human habitation.

WYVERN – large flying predator on Theroc.

YAMANE, KIRO – cybernetic specialist held captive by Roamers at Osquivel shipyards.

YARROD – green priest, younger brother of Mother Alexa.

YAZRA'H – oldest daughter of Jora'h, keeps three Isix cats.

YREKA – fringe Hansa colony world; the EDF cracked down on the Yreka colonists for hoarding ekti.

YURA'H – former Mage-Imperator, grandfather of Jora'h, ruled at the time of first encounter with human generation ships.

ZAN'NH – Ildiran military officer, eldest son of Mage-Imperator Jora'h, new Adar of the Ildiran Solar Navy.

ZIZU, ANWAR – EDF sergeant, security chief on Tasia Tamblyn's Manta.

SIMON &
SCHUSTER

Scattered Suns

The Saga of Seven Suns – Book Four

KEVIN J. ANDERSON

The destructive hydrogues continue their war
against humans and the fiery entities, the faeros
– a struggle that kills planets and extinguishes
whole stars. Newly crowned Mage-Imperator
Jora'h', the leader of the ancient and vast Ildiran
Empire, struggles with new knowledge he has
learned: an ancient bargain and long-standing
treachery that may finally bring peace with the
hydrogues . . . though it could mean the extermi-
nation of the human race. But Jora'h's empire is
destroying itself from within, when his mad
brother launches a bloody rebellion across the
Ildiran planets, appointing Jora'h's own first-
born son as its leader.

In a galaxy torn by war, treachery, and shifting
alliances, no one can know the truth about their
friends or enemies.

ISBN 0-7432-7544-6
PRICE £10.99

**POCKET
BOOKS**

Captain Nemo

KEVIN J. ANDERSON

Most readers know Captain Nemo only as the enigmatic protagonist of Jules Verne's classic novel *20,000 Leagues Under The Sea*. But what if Nemo was a real man, whose actual life was more fantastic and adventurous than all the fictions it inspired?

Here is the epic tale of Andre Nemo, the man behind the myth. The free-spirited and inventive son of a French shipbuilder, Nemo goes to sea as a cabin boy, faces marauding pirates and bloodthirsty sharks, is marooned for years on a mysterious island, battles prehistoric monsters long believed extinct, journeys to the centre of the Earth, balloons across Africa, escapes from Arab slaves, discovers the fabled city of Timbuktu, endures a plague of locusts, survives the Charge of the Light Brigade, tends to the wounded with Florence Nightingale, is pressed into service by the ruthless Robert the Conqueror, and, ultimately, wages war on War itself as the captain of his greatest creation: the legendary underwater vessel known as the Nautilus.

ISBN 0-7434-4409-4
PRICE £6.99

**POCKET
BOOKS**

This book and other **Pocket** titles are available from your local bookshop
or can be ordered direct from the publisher.